Indiana Cousins
TRILOGY

WANDA & BRUNSTETTER

THREE AMISH ROMANCES FROM A
NEW YORK TIMES BESTSELLING AUTHOR

Indiana Cousins
TRILOGY

BARBOUR
PUBLISHING

For more information about Wanda E. Brunstetter, please access the author's Web site at the following Internet address: www.wandabrunstetter.com

Published by Barbour Publishing, Inc., P.O. Box 719, Uhrichsville, Ohio 44683, www.barbourbooks.com

Our mission is to publish and distribute inspirational products offering exceptional value and biblical encouragement to the masses.

 Member of the
Evangelical Christian
Publishers Association

Printed in the United States of America.

A Cousin's
PROMISE

INDIANA COUSINS | BOOK 1

DEDICATION/ACKNOWLEDGMENTS

To my dear friends Arlene and Wayne Randolph. Thank you for introducing me to so many wonderful Amish people who live in northern Indiana. To my new friend Dale Burnet. Thank you for your willingness to share the experience of losing a leg with me.

Delight thyself also in the LORD:
and he shall give thee the desires of thine heart.
PSALM 37:4

CHAPTER 1

*A*ch, there's a bee in the van! Somebody, get it out of here before I get stung!"

Loraine Miller looked over her shoulder. Her cousin Katie's face was as pale as goat's milk, and her eyes were wide with fear. Ever since they'd been children and Katie had been trapped in the schoolhouse with a swarm of angry bees, she had panicked whenever a bee got too close. Poor Katie had been pelted with so many stings that day, much of her body had looked swollen. The doctor had said it was a good thing Katie wasn't allergic to bee stings or she would have probably gone into shock.

"Get it! Get it!" Katie screamed. She sucked in a deep breath and ducked her head.

The bee flew past Loraine's shoulder, buzzing noisily.

"Open your window, *schnell*!" Loraine said to her fiancé, Wayne Lambright. "We need to get that bee out before Katie hyperventilates."

Wayne quickly opened the window and shooed the bee with his hand.

"Did. . .did it go out?" Katie's chin trembled as she lifted her head. Her vivid green eyes glistened with unshed tears. Loraine found it hard to believe anyone could be so afraid of a bee, even though she knew the source of her cousin's fear.

"*Jah*, I'm sure it's out. At least, I don't see it anymore," Loraine said, hoping to reassure her cousin.

"It's gone, Katie, so you can relax." Wayne closed the window and nudged Loraine's arm. "You know what I'm thinking?"

"What's that?"

"I'm thinking I can hardly wait to get you on the Side Winder I've heard so much about!"

She grimaced. "It would be just like you to try and talk me into going on the scariest ride at Hershey Park."

Wayne's eyes twinkled. "Do you really think I'd twist your arm and make you do that?"

"She doesn't think it; she knows it," Loraine's cousin Ella spoke up from the back of the van.

Jolene, Loraine's other cousin, giggled behind her hand, while Katie's boyfriend, Timothy, snorted like one of his father's pigs.

"Remember, Loraine, you're the one who suggested we take this trip to Hershey Park," Jolene's brother Andrew said. "So I would think you'd be looking forward to going on all the scary rides."

"That's right," Ella's brother Raymond chimed in. "Getting scared out of your wits is the whole reason for going to an amusement park."

Wayne nudged Loraine's arm again. "Don't you remember how much fun we had when we went to the Fun Spot last Labor Day weekend?"

Loraine nodded. It had been fun to visit their local amusement park, but those rides weren't nearly as frightening as the ones she'd heard about at Hershey Park. Even so, she was excited to take this trip. Ever since she was a little girl, she'd wanted to visit Hershey Park and Hershey's Chocolate World. She loved chocolate and had heard there was a ride inside Chocolate World that showed visitors how the various kinds of Hershey candy were made. Their plans were to travel through the night, arrive in Hershey around 2:00 a.m., and check into the hotel their driver, Paul Crawford, had reserved for them. Then they would sleep a few hours and spend all day Saturday at the park. They planned to rest awhile on Sunday, and then maybe take a drive around the surrounding area. Early Monday morning, they would head for home. Loraine figured this trip could turn out to be more fun than if her parents had taken her when she was a girl.

Even though the Amish didn't celebrate Labor Day, Timothy, Raymond, and Andrew worked at the trailer factory in Middlebury and had Monday off, as did Loraine, who worked at the hardware store in Shipshewana. Since neither Katie nor Ella had full-time jobs, being gone for three days wasn't a problem. The same held true for Wayne, who farmed with his father. Only Jolene, a teacher at the local Amish schoolhouse, was scheduled to work, but she'd been able to get a substitute for Monday.

"I don't know about anyone else, but I'm more anxious to eat some of that *wunderbaar* chocolate than go on any of the rides at Hershey Park." Katie smiled and relaxed against the seat, obviously feeling better now that the bee was gone.

"Listen to you. . .talking about food already, and we're not even to Ashley yet." Timothy bumped Katie's arm. "Can't you at least wait until we leave the state of Indiana to talk about food?"

Katie muffled her snicker.

Loraine smiled. It was good to see everyone in such good spirits. Paul had been laughing and telling jokes since he'd picked them up at Jolene and Andrew's house in Topeka.

"Hey, Paul," Timothy called, "Katie's hungry, so we may have to stop soon and see that she's fed."

"I'll be stopping before we get to Highway 69," Paul said over his shoulder. "Will that be soon enough?"

Timothy needled Katie in the ribs. "What do you say? Can you hold out till then?"

She wrinkled her nose. "If you don't stop teasing, I won't go on any of the rides at Hershey Park with you."

"Is that a threat?"

"It's a promise."

Loraine looked over at Wayne and rolled her eyes. Katie was her youngest cousin, and she'd recently turned nineteen. Sometimes,

11

like now, Katie still acted like an immature adolescent. Timothy, who was twenty, wasn't much better, always goofing around, mimicking others, and making all sorts of weird sounds. But the two of them seemed happy together and planned to be married in the fall of next year. Maybe by then, they'd both have grown up some.

"I wish people would quit cutting me off and tailgating," Paul complained as he merged the van into heavier traffic. "Seems like everyone and his brother is headed somewhere for Labor Day weekend. If it's this bad now, I can only imagine how it will be on the trip home."

"Hershey Park will probably be crowded, too," Andrew put in.

Wayne gave Loraine's fingers a gentle squeeze. "This will be our last chance for an outing with our single friends before we become an old married couple, so we'd better enjoy every moment," he whispered in her ear.

He looked at her so sweetly she wanted to tousle his thick auburn curls, the way she sometimes did when they were alone. In just a little over a month, she and Wayne would get married, and then she could tousle his hair to her heart's content. By this time next year, they might even have a baby, and their lives would take a new direction—one that wouldn't include weekend trips to amusement parks. A baby would mean changing dirty diapers, getting up in the middle of the night for feedings, and so many new, exciting things. Loraine could hardly wait to make a home and raise a family with Wayne. It would be a dream come true.

She leaned her head against Wayne's shoulder and let her eyelids close. She felt safe and secure when she was with Wayne—enjoying his company and happy to know she'd soon be his wife. *I wonder what our kinner will look like. Will they have my brown hair and brown eyes, or will they resemble Wayne with his curly auburn hair and hazel eyes? Will they be easygoing and even-tempered like Wayne? Will they have a servant's heart—generous in spirit and sensitive to others in need?*

In her mind's eye, Loraine could see a sweet baby with curly auburn hair, gurgling and reaching chubby hands out to his father.

The van lurched suddenly, and Loraine's eyes snapped open. "Wh–what happened?"

"We're stopping for those snacks I promised you could get," Paul said as he pulled off the road and into a gas station. "If anyone wants anything, you'd better get it now, because I won't be stopping again until I need more gas."

Loraine climbed out of the van ahead of her cousins and turned to smile at Katie. "Since you're the one who said you were hungry, I guess you'd better make sure you stock up on plenty of snacks."

Katie snickered. "I plan to do just that."

~≈ ≈~

With a sack full of snack foods, Loraine crawled back into the van and released a noisy yawn. "Someone wake me when we get there, would you?" She leaned her head on Wayne's broad shoulder again. "I hope you don't mind me using you for a pillow."

He nuzzled the top of her stiff, white head covering with his nose. "I don't mind at all."

Loraine's eyelids fluttered closed once more. She was almost asleep when Katie let out an ear-piercing yelp. "Ach! Another bee's in the van!"

Loraine sat up straight. Sure enough, a bee buzzed irritatingly overhead.

Timothy and Raymond swatted at the troublesome bee with their hats.

"Ella, roll down your window!" Timothy shouted. "Maybe the critter will fly out like the last one did."

Ella quickly did as he requested, but the bee kept buzzing and zipping all around.

Katie screamed when it buzzed past her face. "Get it! Get it! Get it!"

"What's going on back there?" Paul called over his shoulder. "What's all the ruckus about?"

"There's a bee on the loose, and—"
"Paul, look out!"
At the sound of Ella's shrill scream, Loraine's gaze darted to the front window. A semi-truck headed straight for them!
Paul jerked the wheel, and the van lurched to the right. As the semi roared past, it slammed into the side of their vehicle. The van skidded off the road and smacked a telephone pole. It flipped onto its side and spun around. Metal crunching! Breaking glass! Screaming voices! Deafening silence. Loraine was sure everyone was dead.

CHAPTER 2

Rivulets of sweat trickled down Loraine's bodice as she stood in front of the window inside one of the waiting rooms at the hospital in Fort Wayne, watching the last orange strand of sky fade into darkness. Her family and the families of those who'd been riding in the van with her should be arriving soon. Oh, how she wished she had better news for the parents of those who had died.

Loraine pressed her forehead against the window and closed her eyes, trying to shut out the memory of the accident.

She took a few short breaths and tried to relax, but it was no use. This terrible nightmare was real and would not go away. If she could only wake up tomorrow morning and find that everything was all right—the way it had been before they'd gotten into the van. If Paul hadn't turned around to see what the commotion was about. If she and her friends had only stayed home today. But all the *ifs* wouldn't change a thing. The accident *had* happened, and Loraine, along with the others who survived, would have to deal with it.

Loraine turned away from the window and glanced at her cousin Katie, slouched in a chair across the room. Wearing a blank stare, Katie looked at the floor as though she were in a daze. As far as Loraine knew, she and Katie were the only ones who'd escaped serious injury, although they did have several bumps and bruises.

What can I say to her? How can I offer comfort to her hurting soul? Loraine drew in a deep breath and made her way across the room.

"There's a vending machine in the hall. Can I get you something? Maybe a cup of coffee or a bottle of water?" she asked, taking a seat beside her cousin.

Katie lifted her head but stared straight ahead, knuckles white as she gripped the edge of the chair as though she might fall off if she let go.

Loraine shifted in her seat, unsure of what to say or do. Finally, she went down on her knees in front of Katie. Gently, she pried Katie's fingers loose and held them in her hands. "Please, talk to me, Katie. Tell me what's on your heart."

Katie blinked a couple of times. "T–Timothy's dead." Her chin trembled, and her voice came out in a squeak.

Loraine nodded as tears pricked her eyes. "I'm so sorry for your loss, Katie. I'm sorry for everyone's loss."

Katie pulled her hands away and folded her arms. "I wish we'd never gotten in that van. I wish we'd stayed home where we were safe. I wish Timothy wasn't—" Her voice trailed off, and her mouth snapped shut with an audible click.

"We need each other right now, Katie. We need to talk about our feelings."

No response.

"Katie, please say something. It's all right to cry. Don't hold your feelings in. Don't shut me out."

Katie didn't utter a word. It was as though an invisible wall had been erected between them, and Loraine's cousin had withdrawn to her own little world.

Loraine rose from the floor and began to pace, sending up to heaven a silent prayer. *Dear Lord, please comfort Katie and be with the doctors who are working on the others. Please help me know what to say when their families arrive, and please keep my Wayne alive.*

A middle-aged man with thinning brown hair entered the

room. He smiled and held out his hand to Loraine. "I'm Robert Taylor, the hospital chaplain."

She shook his hand. "I'm Loraine Miller, and that's my cousin Katie Miller." She motioned to Katie, but Katie gave no response—just sat with her lips compressed and her eyes tightly shut.

"I heard about the accident you and your friends were in," he said. "I wanted you to know that I'm here to help in any way I can."

"I—I appreciate that."

"Are you waiting for family members to arrive?"

She nodded.

"I'd like to wait with you and offer my support."

"I'm sure everyone will need it as much as I do." Loraine looked at Katie again. "Katie's boyfriend was killed in the accident, and I think she's in shock. She's only said a few words to me since we left the emergency room and came in here. She seems to have shut me out."

"I'll try talking to her." The chaplain moved away from Loraine and took a seat beside Katie. "I'm the chaplain here, Katie. I'd like to pray with you," he said in a gentle, comforting tone.

No response.

"If you'd like to talk about what happened or how you feel, I'm here to listen."

Several minutes passed, and then Katie's lips started to move. She spoke so quietly Loraine couldn't make out the words. She moved back to the window, praying that the chaplain would be able to get through to Katie—help her deal with the pain.

Someone touched Loraine's shoulder, and she whirled around. Uncle Alvin and Aunt Leah, Jolene and Andrew's parents, stood behind her with worried expressions.

"We came as soon as we heard about the accident," Uncle Alvin said. "They wouldn't give us much information in the emergency room. Just said the doctors are still working on our son and daughter and that we should wait in here." His forehead wrinkled as he shot Loraine a pleading look. "Do you know anything?"

"Not a lot. The last thing I was told was that Andrew had suffered cuts, bruises, and a broken arm."

"And Jolene?" Aunt Leah asked with a catch in her voice.

"One of the nurses said something about possible damage to Jolene's auditory nerves, but that's all I know."

Aunt Leah glanced anxiously at the door. "I wish they'd let me go in. I need to see how my kinner are doing. I'm so worried about them."

"I understand. I'm worried, too." Loraine placed a hand on her aunt's arm, hoping to offer a little reassurance. Reassurance she really needed herself.

"What about the others? Was anyone seriously injured?" Uncle Alvin wanted to know.

Loraine nodded. "Our driver, Paul Crawford, was killed, and so were Katie's boyfriend, Timothy, and Ella's brother, Raymond."

"Ach! That's *baremlich*." Aunt Leah's eyes widened as shock registered on her face. "What about the others?"

"Ella has a concussion, and I was told that Wayne has some serious injuries, but I don't what or how bad they are." Loraine swallowed a couple of times. The not knowing clawed at her heart and made her body feel numb. If Wayne died, she'd probably go into shock the way Katie had.

For lack of anything better to do, Loraine motioned to the chairs across the room. "Should we have a seat while we wait to hear how Jolene, Andrew, and the others are doing?"

Aunt Leah and Uncle Alvin nodded and followed Loraine.

She introduced them to Chaplain Taylor, and they all took seats. Aunt Leah clasped Katie's hand. "I'm sorry about Timothy."

No response.

"Have Timothy's folks been notified?" Aunt Leah's question was directed at Loraine.

"Timothy's parents do know about the accident," Loraine replied, "but they haven't arrived yet and don't know he died soon after we got here."

18

Uncle Alvin grunted. "I hope we find out about Jolene and Andrew soon. I can't stand the waiting."

"I know it's hard to wait, but I'm sure you'll be told something soon," Chaplain Taylor said.

With a childlike cry, Wayne's mother, Ada, rushed into the room. Her husband, Crist, followed.

Ada clasped Loraine's shoulder so tightly she winced. "Have you heard any news about our son?"

Loraine rose from her chair and gave Ada a hug. "He's still being examined, but I was told earlier that he suffered some serious injuries."

"What kind of injuries?" Crist asked.

"I—I don't know. I'm hoping we'll hear something soon. I've been hoping and praying that he's not—"

"We're waiting to hear how our son and daughter are, too," Aunt Leah spoke up.

Ada's lips compressed into a thin, tight line. "So we don't know how anyone is?"

Loraine swallowed around the lump in her throat. "We do know that three people died in the crash."

"Who?"

"Timothy, Raymond, and our driver, Paul."

Ada groaned as she slowly shook her head. "I knew going to Hershey Park on a holiday weekend was a bad idea. I told Wayne that, too, but, no, he wouldn't listen to my advice. He wanted to please *you,* so he agreed to go." She lifted a shaky hand and pushed a wayward strand of grayish-brown hair under her stiff white head covering. "If Wayne's seriously hurt, then I'm sure you realize there won't be a wedding for the two of you in October."

Loraine cringed. She didn't need that reminder. She wished she could change the subject—say something to lighten the mood. Only she didn't know what to say, especially when she felt so discouraged and frightened.

Crist patted his wife's arm. "Let's not put the buggy before the horse. Our son's injuries might not be as bad as we think. Wayne and Loraine might still be able to get married as planned."

Ada shook her head, saying nothing.

"Would either of you like a cup of coffee or something to eat?" Loraine asked Wayne's folks.

"Nothing for me," Ada mumbled.

"No, I couldn't eat or drink a single thing." Crist shook his head.

A few minutes later, a young man entered the room and announced, "My name is Dr. Mayhew. I'm looking for members of Wayne Lambright's family." He glanced around the room. "Are any of you related to him?"

"I'm his father." Crist motioned to Ada. "This is his mother." He nodded at Loraine. "This is Wayne's fiancée. Do you have information about our son's condition? We need to know—is he going to live?"

Dr. Mayhew took the empty seat on the other side of Crist. When he cleared his throat, his forehead wrinkled into deep furrows, making him look older than he was. "Your son has several broken ribs, cuts, and contusions. His worst injury, however, is to his left leg. I'm afraid it's going to have to be amputated above the knee."

Loraine drew in a sharp breath and grabbed the edge of the chair to keep from toppling over. Wayne was a farmer. He needed two good legs. How would he deal with this tragic news? How would it affect their plans to be married?

"You—you want to cut off my son's leg?" Ada's voice trembled, and her eyes widened like those of a panicked horse. "Wayne's our only child! It would break my heart and his, too, if—"

"I'm sorry, but there's no other way." The doctor shook his head. "We can't save his leg. If we don't amputate, he could die."

Crist offered his wife a weak smile and slipped his arm around her shoulders. "We should be thankful our son's still alive. It could have been worse, you know. He might have died instantly like some of the others who'd been riding in the van. If the doctor can save Wayne's life by taking his leg, then we'll give our permission."

Ada glared at Loraine. "This is all *your* fault! If you hadn't insisted on him going to Hershey Park with you—"

"Now, Ada," Crist said in a calming voice, "don't cast any blame; it won't undo what's been done. Everyone in that van went of their own free will. Loraine didn't force Wayne or anyone else to go."

"That may be true, but you know our son—he'd do anything she asked him to do. He's never been able to say no to her." Ada's voice lowered to a whisper, as her gaze dropped to the floor. "I—I wish he'd chosen to marry Fern Bontrager."

A tremor shot through Loraine's body as hot tears pushed against her eyelids. She hadn't realized until now that Ada Lambright didn't want her as a daughter-in-law.

CHAPTER 3

Whispered voices. Strange smells. A heaviness in his body he couldn't explain. Where was he? What was going on?

Wayne groaned and struggled to open his eyes.

"It's okay, son. We're here."

"Mom, is—is that you?"

"Jah, Wayne." He felt the warmth of his mother's fingers on his hand. He heard the sadness in her voice. Something was terribly wrong.

"I'm here, too, son."

"Pop?"

"Jah."

Wayne's eyes finally opened, and two blurry faces came into view. "Wh–where am I?"

Mom squeezed his fingers. "You're in the hospital."

"Wh–what am I doing here?"

"You were in an accident," Pop said. "The van you were riding in hit a telephone pole, and—"

Pop's voice faded as Wayne's memories took over. There was a bee in the van. Katie was screaming. Paul turned around. A semi-truck came at them. Paul swerved. They hit a pole. Someone screamed. Then everything went black.

"Loraine! Is—is she hurt? Is she—"

"Loraine's all right. She and Katie suffered some bumps and bruises, but neither of them was seriously injured," Mom said.

A sense of relief washed over Wayne. He wouldn't know what to do if anything happened to Loraine. She was the love of his life—soon to be his bride. "Wh–what about the others? Were any of them hurt?"

Mom nodded, and her pinched expression let him know the news wasn't good.

"Who got hurt?"

"Jolene and Ella suffered head injuries, but from what we heard, Ella's was only a mild concussion." Mom pursed her lips. "Jolene suffered damage to her auditory nerves and lost her hearing."

Wayne drew in a sharp breath. "That's baremlich!"

Pop nodded. "You're right, it's terrible. Now she'll have to learn to read lips and speak with her hands."

"What about the others? Are they okay?"

"Andrew has a broken arm and a few other minor injuries, but he'll be all right once he heals." Pop slowly shook his head. "The other fellows weren't so lucky, though."

"Wh–what do you mean?"

"They didn't make it, son. Raymond, Timothy, and your driver are dead."

Wayne gulped on the sob rising in his throat. His friends couldn't be dead. There had to be a mistake. "Wh–where's Loraine? I need to see her!"

"She's in the waiting room." Mom glanced over at Pop. "We thought it would be best if we spoke to you first. There's something you need to know."

"What?"

"It–it's about your injuries."

"My brain feels kind of foggy right now, but I—I think I'm okay." Wayne managed a weak smile. "I'm alive, anyway."

"You have lots of bumps, bruises, and a few broken ribs, but the worst injury was to your left leg. It—" Mom covered her mouth with the palm of her hand as her voice broke on a sob.

"What's wrong with my leg?" Wayne struggled to keep his eyes open. He needed some answers. He needed them now.

Pop laid a hand on Wayne's shoulder. "I'm sorry to be tellin' you this, son, but you lost it."

"Wh–what are you talking about, Pop? What'd I lose?"

Mom sniffled. "Your leg was badly injured. It had to be amputated."

Wayne lifted his head off the pillow. "Wh–what'd you say?"

Mom patted his arm as if she were soothing a fussy baby. "The doctor took your leg from just above the knee."

Wayne's head fell back on the pillow as the stark realization of what she'd said settled over him like a dark cloud. He had only one leg. He was a farmer. He needed two good legs. He was getting married soon. His world had been turned upside down!

Sweat trickled from Wayne's forehead and dripped into his eyes. Mom wiped it away with a tissue. "We feel your loss, too," she murmured, "but we'll get through this tragedy together."

Wayne blinked a couple of times. "Does—does Loraine know about my leg?"

Mom nodded. "She was with us when the doctor gave us the news."

"What'd she say? How'd she take it?"

"I think you should ask her those questions." Pop turned to Mom and motioned to the door. "Why don't you go to the waiting room and get Loraine now?"

She hesitated a moment, released a deep sigh, and finally left the room.

Wayne's hand shook as he massaged his throbbing head. After the series of shocks he'd suffered today, he needed something to settle his nerves and block out the pain.

~ ❧ ~

"My son wants to see you."

At the sound of Ada's voice, Loraine jumped out of her seat. "Did—did you tell him about his leg?"

Ada nodded as tears welled in her eyes.

"How'd he take it?"

"Not well. I think he's more upset about losing two of his friends than his leg, though."

"Maybe the reality hasn't set in."

"Jah." Ada glanced around. "I don't see your folks anywhere. Haven't they arrived yet?"

"No, but I'm sure they'll be here soon." Loraine moved toward the doorway. "I'm ready to see Wayne."

As Loraine and Ada walked toward the elevator, the echo of their footsteps resounded in the hall. It reminded Loraine of her horse pulling her buggy up a hill. *Clip. . .clop. . .clip. . .clop.*

"I hope you won't say anything to upset Wayne," Ada said as they stepped up to the elevator.

Loraine bristled. "Of course not. What are you worried I might say?"

Ada pursed her lips. "I don't think you should mention anything about marrying him. At least not right now."

"What are you saying?"

"Wayne's lost a leg. He'll need lots of care, and—"

"We may not be able to get married on the day we planned, but we'll be married as soon as he's sufficiently healed."

A look of shock registered on Ada's face. "Then you're not going to back out on the marriage?"

"Of course not. I love Wayne, and I can't wait to be his wife."

"I—I just thought. . . ." Ada sighed. "I assumed you wouldn't want to marry a man with a handicap such as Wayne's."

Hoping, isn't that what you mean? "Wayne's handicap doesn't affect the way I feel about him," Loraine said without voicing her thoughts.

"You say that now, but you don't know how hard things are going to be for Wayne in the days ahead. He won't be able to farm anymore, and he'll need lots of care."

"I realize things will be difficult. Wayne will have many adjustments to make, but we'll get through it together." The elevator door zipped open, and Loraine stepped in behind Ada. She couldn't believe the woman thought she wouldn't want to marry her son because he'd lost his leg. But then, after Ada's earlier remarks, Loraine was sure Ada wanted Wayne to marry Fern instead of her.

The elevator opened, and as Loraine followed Ada down the hospital corridor, she sent up a silent prayer. *Lord, please give me the right words to say to Wayne. Help me not to break down in tears when I see him, and show me a way to let Ada know how much I care for her son.*

"Here we are." Ada halted in front of a door, drew in a sharp breath, and pushed it open.

Loraine stepped into the room. Her heart pounded against her rib cage, and the scene that greeted her blurred her vision. Wayne looked so pale and helpless lying in his bed. He looked like a sick little boy.

I can give in to my tears some other time, Loraine told herself. *Right now I need to be strong and positive for Wayne.*

"Let's leave these two alone so they can talk," Crist said to Ada. He moved toward the door.

She hesitated but finally followed.

At the door, Crist turned and gave Loraine a reassuring smile. "We'll be in the waiting room."

Loraine waited until Wayne's parents left the room before she moved to the side of his bed. "H–how are you feeling?"

"How do you think I feel? I lost my leg."

She nodded, barely able to speak around the lump in her throat. Wayne had never spoken to her so harshly. But then, he'd never lost a leg before.

He stared at the ceiling. "I guess you know what this means."

She seated herself in the chair beside his bed. "It means there will be some adjustments to make, and—"

"It means there will be no wedding for us at the end of October."

"Maybe not October, but when you're better we can—"

"I'm never going to be any better, Loraine. I'll always be without my leg."

"In time you'll be fitted with a prosthesis, and then—"

"I want my own leg, not an artificial one; it would slow me down. I'm a farmer. Farmers need two good legs." A deep groan escaped his lips. "If I can't farm, I can't support a wife and family. If I can't offer financial support, then I won't get married."

"Maybe you can find a different job—one that doesn't require you to be on your feet so much."

"I don't want another job. I've never wanted to do anything but farm." Wayne shook his head. "We can't be married, Loraine. I won't ask you to make that sacrifice."

"It wouldn't be a sacrifice."

"Jah, it would." His head lolled to one side, and his eyelids fluttered as though it took all his strength to keep them open.

Loraine was tempted to argue about whether they could get married or not but knew it was best not to say too much. Wayne was weak and needed time to heal from his surgery. They could speak of this again when he felt a bit stronger.

"Did—your folks tell you about the others?" she asked hesitantly.

He nodded. "If I'd known we were gonna be in an accident, I wouldn't have agreed to go to Hershey Park. I wish now that I'd said no."

Loraine's spine went rigid. Did Wayne blame her for the accident, too? "I–I'm so sorry. I wish I hadn't suggested the trip. I wish there hadn't been a bee in the van. I wish Paul—" She gulped on a sob, unable to finish her sentence.

"Does Paul's wife know he's dead?"

She nodded. "She took it pretty hard. So did Timothy's and Raymond's parents."

Wayne heaved a labored breath and closed his eyes. "I'm tired."

"Would you like me to leave so you can get some sleep?"

"Jah."

She leaned over and kissed his forehead. "I love you, Wayne."

No reply.

"Wayne?"

No response.

With an ache in her soul such as she'd never felt before, Loraine tiptoed out of the room, wondering what the future held for her and Wayne.

CHAPTER 4

The next few days went by in a blur as Loraine and her family comforted those who'd lost loved ones and those who were dealing with injuries. The day when they would attend Timothy's and Raymond's funerals arrived. Not everyone, however, would be in attendance. Wayne and Jolene were still in the hospital.

"Are you doing all right?" Mom asked when Loraine entered the kitchen that morning. "I see dark circles under your eyes, and your face looks awfully pale."

Loraine pushed a wisp of hair off her forehead and sighed. "I haven't slept well since the night of the accident, but I'm sure there are others in much worse shape than me this morning."

Mom nodded. "I feel terrible for my sister Verna. It's not natural for a parent to lose a child. It doesn't seem possible that Raymond is dead."

The ache in Loraine's heart struck swiftly, and she nearly doubled over from the pain. She felt so guilty for suggesting they make the trip to Pennsylvania. "If I hadn't asked Paul to drive us to Hershey Park, everyone would still be alive and well."

Mom left the stove where she'd been frying bacon and gave Loraine a hug. "I want you to stop blaming yourself. There was no way you could have known when you planned the trip that it would end in a tragic accident."

Loraine sniffed as a film of tears obscured her vision. "In my head I know that, but my heart says something different."

"It's hard not to blame ourselves when things go wrong, but you need to remember that the accident wouldn't have happened if Paul had kept his eyes on the road."

"Are you're saying it was his fault?"

"He made a mistake, but I'm sure he didn't do it on purpose." Mom's shoulders lifted in a brief shrug. "Rather than casting blame, we need to concentrate on helping our family and friends get through the funerals. It's going to be a difficult day."

Loraine nodded. "I've hired a driver to take me to the hospital later this afternoon. I'm sure Wayne and Jolene would like to know how everything goes at the funerals, since they're unable to be with us today. Besides, I need to see how they're both doing."

"Speaking of Wayne," Mom said, "I've been wanting to talk to you about something."

"Something about Wayne?"

"Jah." Mom cleared her throat a couple of times. "I talked with Ada at church yesterday, and she said because of Wayne's injuries, there won't be a wedding for the two of you after all."

Irritation welled in Loraine's soul. "He won't be well enough for us to get married in October as we'd planned, but as soon as he's feeling strong enough, we'll set a new wedding date." She saw no point in mentioning that Wayne had said they couldn't be married at all because of his handicap. She also chose not to mention that she'd overheard Ada say she wished her son had picked Fern Bontrager to marry. It hurt too much to talk about it. Besides, once Wayne felt better, he would change his mind. By then, she hoped to be on better terms with his mother. Things had to work out; she couldn't allow herself to think otherwise.

Mom drummed her fingers along the edge of the table. "I have some concerns about your marrying Wayne."

"What concerns?"

"I'm sure you must realize that his disability will probably keep him from farming."

"He can find another job—something that won't require two good legs. Something he can do from a wheelchair, if necessary."

"Loraine's right," Dad said as he entered the kitchen. "Wayne may have lost a leg, but he's a hard worker with a determined spirit. I'm sure he'll find a job that will allow him to provide adequately for our daughter."

Loraine swiped at the tears dribbling down her cheeks. She knew from what Wayne had said to her at the hospital the other day that he, too, was worried he couldn't provide for her.

The things he said were only the shock of learning he's lost a leg, she told herself. *Once he's had a chance to think more about it, he'll realize we can work through this together. That's what people who love each other do.*

~❧ ❧~

As Ella Yoder stood in front of her brother's plain wooden coffin, a sense of determination welled in her soul. In a short time, family and friends would arrive for Raymond's funeral. Later this afternoon, they would go to the Lehmans' for Timothy's funeral. Ella would need to remain strong. She'd have to look out for her younger siblings and take care of her mother's needs. Mama had taken the news of Raymond's death hard. She'd barely been able to cope since then.

Ella was glad the injuries she had sustained weren't serious. Her concussion had been mild, and the cuts and bruises on her legs and arms would heal quickly. She wasn't sure how quickly Mama would heal, however. Truth be told, Mama might never get over losing her firstborn son.

Ella heard someone approaching, and she whirled around.

"People are beginning to arrive," Papa said. "Loraine's here with her family. She wants to speak with you."

"Oh, okay." Ella stepped into the living room where Loraine stood with her parents, Amos and Priscilla.

"How's Wayne doing?" Ella asked, giving Loraine a hug.

"As well as can be expected."

"How long will he be in the hospital?"

"I don't know. I've hired a driver to take me to see him later today. I should know more then."

"I'm sure it's hard for Wayne not to be at his friends' funerals today."

"Jah."

"Losing a leg must be hard for him, too."

Tears pooled in Loraine's eyes. "He doesn't want to get married. He thinks he'll be a burden on me." Her voice lowered to a whisper. "Mom doesn't want me to marry Wayne, either. She as much as said so this morning." Her chin trembled. "Wayne's *mamm* is against us getting married, too. I think she's been against it from the very beginning. I just didn't realize it until the night of the accident."

"What are you going to do? I mean, if Wayne wants to call off the wedding, and your mamm and Wayne's mamm think you shouldn't get married—"

"I don't care what they think. I love Wayne, and I promised to marry him." Loraine lifted her chin a notch. "I'm going to keep that promise, no matter what anyone says."

"But if he won't marry you. . ."

"He will. He's just confused and hurting right now." Loraine slipped her arm around Ella's shoulder. "Enough about me. How are you feeling this morning? Does your head still hurt?"

Ella touched her forehead. "It feels better than it did a few days ago. I'm worried about Mama, though. She's having a hard time dealing with Raymond's death."

"I'm sure it's hard for all of you."

"Jah." Ella glanced toward the door. "Oh, there's Katie and her family. I wonder how she's holding up."

Loraine could tell Ella was doing her best to put on a brave front. Worrying about others seemed to be how she'd chosen to deal with her pain. Ella had always been a nurturing person, even when they were young girls. Loraine thought about the time her kitten had drowned in the creek. Ella had been so sympathetic that she'd given up her own kitten so Loraine wouldn't cry.

"Let's go talk to Katie before the service begins." Ella linked arms with Loraine and led her across the room.

～✑ ✑～

"How are you feeling, Mr. Lambright? Is the pain medicine working for you?"

Wayne grunted as a youthful-looking nurse with short brown hair stuck a thermometer under his tongue. How was he supposed to answer her question with something foreign in his mouth?

When she removed the thermometer, she asked again, "Is the pain medicine working for you?"

"It helps some, but it makes me real sleepy."

"That's to be expected." She slipped the blood pressure cuff around his arm. "Are you in pain right now?"

He shook his head.

When she removed the cuff, she listened to his heart and checked the bandages on the stub of his leg. "The doctor will be in later to examine your leg. Is there anything I can get for you?"

A new leg would be nice. "No, I'm fine."

"Would you like the TV turned on?"

"No, thanks. I have no interest in watching that."

"Oh, that's right. You Amish don't have TVs in your homes, do you?"

"No, and even if we did, I wouldn't be interested in watching it. I have better things to do with my time. At least I used to," he added bitterly.

The nurse quirked an eyebrow and placed the call button close to his hand. "Let us know if you need anything," she said before leaving the room.

Wayne reached for the Bible on the nightstand by his bed. Chaplain Taylor had left it there when he'd dropped by Wayne's room the other day.

Wayne opened it randomly, and his gaze came to rest on John 11:43–44: *"And when he thus had spoken, he cried with a loud voice,*

Lazarus, come forth. And he that was dead came forth, bound hand and foot with graveclothes: and his face was bound about with a napkin. Jesus saith unto them, Loose him, and let him go."

The page blurred, and Wayne blinked several times, hoping to keep the tears he felt pushing against his eyelids from falling onto his face. *Today, two of my good friends will be buried. Tomorrow is Paul's funeral. If Jesus were here, He could bring all three of them back to life. He did it for Lazarus; He could do it for my friends.*

Wayne's stomach twisted as his thoughts raced on. *I wish it had been me who'd been killed in the accident. It would have been better than living with only one leg. I can't marry Loraine. I won't be able to farm anymore, and I wouldn't be happy doing anything else.*

Wayne thought about the excitement he'd felt when he'd climbed into that van with Loraine and the others. The memory of how happy he and Loraine had been that afternoon shot through him like a knife. He was no longer a happy, excited, soon-to-be groom. He was an ugly half-man with a missing limb.

A huge knot formed in his throat as helpless fury swept over him. He grabbed his water glass and hurled it across the room, wincing when it smashed against the wall and broke. Nothing would ever be the same for him. Nothing!

CHAPTER 5

A feeling of heaviness settled on Loraine's chest as she looked out the front window of her father's buggy. A slow parade of black buggies inched their way up the hill toward the cemetery. Two funerals in one day; it was too much to bear. First Raymond's service this morning, and now they were about to bury Timothy.

She swallowed past the lump in her throat. Paul's funeral would be tomorrow, and many of the Amish from her community would attend his contemporary service as well. Paul and his wife, Rachel, had moved to Goshen five years ago, and he'd begun driving for the Amish soon after that. They were a middle-aged, childless couple, with no family living in the area. Loraine figured now that Paul was gone, Rachel would probably move back to Pennsylvania, where two of her sisters lived.

"We're here," Dad said as he guided their horse and buggy into the grassy area outside the cemetery.

When Loraine and her family climbed down from the buggy, her gaze came to rest on the open-bed hearse holding Timothy's coffin. Her heart pounded as the oilcloth cover was lifted and the coffin was carried to the gravesite. The mourners followed solemnly behind.

Once the coffin was set in place, the bishop read a hymn: "Ah, good night to those I love so; Good night to my heart's desire;

Good night to those hearts full of woe; Out of love they weep distressed. Tho' I from you pass away; In the grave you lay my clay; I will rise again securely, Greet you in eternity."

Loraine glanced at Timothy's parents, Calvin and Ruby. Calvin's shoulders shook as he struggled with his emotions, and Ruby, sobbing uncontrollably, had to be held up by her husband and oldest son, William.

A group of men sang a song while the grave was filled in by the pallbearers. Loraine's gaze went to Katie, leaning on her mother's shoulder. The poor girl's face looked drawn, and dark circles under her eyes underscored her exhaustion. She probably hadn't slept much since the day of the accident. Katie's vacant stare sent chills up Loraine's spine. It wasn't a look of acceptance; it was a look of defeat.

When the song ended, the bishop asked the congregation to silently pray the Lord's Prayer. As the others moved away from the gravesite, Katie remained near Timothy's grave, rocking back and forth on her heels. Finally, Katie's father led her away.

As Loraine walked back to her father's buggy, she lifted her tearful gaze to the cloudless sky. *Help Katie and all of us who are hurting today. I thank You, Lord, that Wayne's still alive. I don't know what I'd do if I lost him.*

~❧ ❧~

When Ella entered the Lehmans' house, where the second meal of the day would soon be served, she spotted Katie in one corner of the living room, standing in front of the window with a vacant stare.

Ella stepped up to her cousin and clasped her hand. "I'm sorry for your loss."

Katie blinked several times, as though waking up from a dream. *"Umkummes waar net not wendich,"* she said, as tears coursed down her cheeks.

Ella nodded. "I know his death was unnecessary, but—"

"It's my fault he's dead. I shouldn't have made such a fuss over that bee. If I'd kept quiet, Timothy would still be alive."

"It wasn't your fault. You were afraid of being stung." Ella slipped her arm around Katie's trembling shoulders. "Blaming won't bring my *bruder* or your *beau* back. We need to somehow move on with our lives and believe that God has taken our loved ones home to be with Him."

Katie's chin quivered. "Do we really know that? I mean, how can we know what was in their hearts the moment they died?"

Ella swallowed around the lump pushing against her throat. She missed Raymond so much. If she had the power to bring him back, she surely would. But heaven was a much better place. "We know that they lived like Christians and had acknowledged Jesus as their Savior when they joined the church." She squeezed Katie's fingers. "We have to believe that they're in heaven."

Katie pursed her lips and resumed staring out the window.

Ella gave Katie a hug and moved away. She'd been putting up a brave front all day and needed some time to be alone.

❧ ❧

"Are you all right?" Loraine asked when she stepped onto the porch and found Ella sitting on the porch swing, massaging her forehead.

"I have a headache. I think it's from holding back the tears."

"You shouldn't hold them back. It's okay to show your emotions, you know." Loraine took a seat beside Ella.

"I need to be strong for my mamm. If I give in to my tears, I'm afraid she'll fall apart." Ella rested her hand on Loraine's arm. "Will you be going to see Wayne soon?"

"Jah. Would you like to go along? It might do you some good to get away from here for a while."

"I can't. My family will be going home soon, and I need to stay close to Mama for the rest of the day. It wouldn't be right for me to desert her when she's grieving so hard."

"I understand."

"I spoke with Jolene's parents earlier. They said once Jolene's well enough to leave the hospital, she'll be going to Pennsylvania to stay with her aunt who teaches sign language."

Loraine nodded. "I heard that, too. Not being able to hear will be a challenge for Jolene. She'll be able to cope better if she's given the necessary skills."

"Jah."

"My ride should be here soon, so I'd better say good-bye to Timothy's family."

"When you see Wayne and Jolene, give them my love and let them both know that they're in my thoughts and prayers."

"I will." Loraine gave Ella a hug and went back inside.

She'd just told Timothy's folks good-bye, when Ada stepped up to her.

"I'd rather you not go to the hospital today."

"How come?"

"It upsets Wayne too much when he sees you."

Loraine's fingers curled into the palms of her hands until they dug into her flesh. "Wayne's upset about losing his leg. I don't think seeing me upsets him."

"Jah, it does. One of the nurses told me that he sinks into depression after your visits."

"Maybe that's because he misses my daughter so much," Loraine's father said, stepping between them.

Loraine smiled inwardly. Danki, *Dad. Thanks for sticking up for me.*

Ada's face colored a deep crimson. "My son's in a lot of pain right now—physically and emotionally." She looked at Loraine and squinted. "I think it would be best if you give him some time to deal with things on his own, don't you?"

Loraine shook her head. "I—I can't do that. He needs me!" She rushed out of the house before Ada could reply. She was Wayne's fiancée, and she would see him today no matter what his mother said!

CHAPTER 6

With a multitude of swirling emotions swimming in her head, Loraine entered Jolene's hospital room. She and Jolene had been close since they were little girls, just as they had been with Ella and Katie. Loraine hated to see Jolene leave, yet she knew going to Pennsylvania would probably be a good thing. She just hoped Jolene wouldn't decide to stay there permanently—she would miss her too much.

Jolene offered Loraine a feeble smile, and motioned her over to the bed.

Loraine took a seat and reached for the notebook and pen on the nightstand by the bed. *"How are you feeling?"* she wrote. *"Are you in much pain?"* She handed the notebook to Jolene.

"The pain's lessened some because the swelling's going down. I'm still taking pain medication, though," Jolene said in a voice louder than usual.

Loraine smiled and patted Jolene's hand. She knew her cousin had spoken loudly because she couldn't hear her own voice. Many elderly people who were hard of hearing did the same thing.

"I'm glad the pain isn't so bad anymore," Loraine wrote on the notepad.

"My balance is really off, though," Jolene said. "I have to hang on to things when I get out of bed and walk."

"I'm sure that will get better in time," Loraine wrote.

Jolene's eyes quickly filled with tears. "The hardest part of losing my hearing is knowing I won't be able to teach school anymore. I'll miss my scholars so much. They sent me a card they'd all signed, and I cried the whole time I read it." Her voice broke on a sob, and she swiped at the wetness on her cheeks.

Loraine took the notebook again. *"Maybe after you learn to read lips and talk with your hands, you'll be able to teach deaf students the way your aunt does."*

"I can't think about that right now." Jolene sniffed. "All I'm able to do is take one day at a time."

Loraine handed Jolene a tissue. *"That's all any of us should do,"* she wrote on the tablet.

Jolene nodded and blew her nose. "How's Wayne doing? Did you just come from seeing him?"

"I haven't been there yet," she wrote. *"I'll go to his room after I'm done visiting with you."*

"I'm sorry I couldn't be at Timothy's and Raymond's funerals today. How'd things go?"

Tears clouded Loraine's vision so she could barely see what she wrote. *"Ruby's taking Timothy's death pretty hard, and Katie's dealing with it by shutting everyone out. Ella's trying to be strong for everyone in her family—especially her mamm, who's grieving very hard for Raymond."*

"It must be terrible for all of them. I can't imagine how my family would feel if my bruder had been killed." Jolene yawned, and her eyes fluttered shut. "Forgive my rudeness. I guess the pain medicine's catching up to me."

"That's okay. I'll head over to Wayne's room now and let you sleep," Loraine wrote.

"Come back soon."

Loraine nodded and squeezed Jolene's fingers, and then she rose from the chair and slipped quietly from the room. It grieved her to think that Jolene would never hear again. No more listening to warbling birds, bubbling brooks, buzzing bees, the *clippety-clop* of horses' hooves, or the gentle whispering of tree branches blowing in the wind.

God, grant my deaf cousin a sense of peace, and keep her safe when she travels to Pennsylvania, Loraine prayed.

When she approached Wayne's room, she paused outside the door and whispered another prayer. "Dear Lord, give me the right words today, and help Wayne to be more receptive than the last time I was here."

❧ ❧

Wayne had been trying with little success to read a magazine, when he heard someone step into his room. He turned his head toward the door, and the rhythm of his heartbeat picked up speed. It was Loraine.

"How are you doing?" she asked, approaching his bed.

"About the same."

She pulled out the chair by the side of his bed and sat down. "I thought you might like to know how the funerals went today."

He nodded and set the magazine aside.

Tears clung to her lashes as she looked at him. "Timothy's and Raymond's families are deeply grieved, as is Katie. It was a sad time for all."

"Figured it would be." He winced and looked away.

"Are you in great pain?"

He shook his head. "The medicine they give me takes care of that fairly well, but I'm sure I'll have even more struggles once I'm home and the phantom pains begin."

"What's phantom pain?"

"I've been told that it feels as if the missing limb is still there. The doctor said it might feel like someone's twisting my foot up to my knees, even though there's no leg there."

Loraine grimaced. "That sounds baremlich! Isn't there something that can be done about it?"

"Just pain medicine, and that might need to be adjusted. I'll be going home in a few days." He sighed. "I guess that's when the challenges will really begin."

"So soon? I thought they might keep you longer—until you could be fitted for a prosthesis."

"If I decide to wear one, that'll come later. I'll have to use a wheelchair for now." He stared out the window, wishing she would stop asking questions and quit looking at him with such sympathy. It made him feel like even less of a man than he already did.

"Have you been to see Jolene?" Wayne asked, needing a change of subject.

"Jah. I went there before coming here."

"How's she doing?"

"As well as can be expected. She'll be getting out of the hospital soon. Then she'll be going to stay with her aunt in Pennsylvania who teaches the deaf." Loraine's eyebrows pulled together as she frowned. "So many changes for so many of our friends, and all because of one terrible, senseless accident."

He leaned into the pillow and groaned. "What's done is done. We're not God. We can't change the past."

Several minutes ticked by, then she reached for Wayne's hand. "When we get married and start our own family, I hope we can teach them to appreciate each other and make good decisions."

He pulled his hand away as he shook his head. "There will be no family for us because I can't marry you, Loraine."

"Why not?"

"I told you before." He grunted and motioned to his leg. "With only one good leg, how do you expect me to farm?"

"Well, maybe after you get a prosthesis—"

"If I can't farm, I can't earn a living!"

"There are other things you can do, Wayne."

He slowly shook his head. "I've never wanted to do anything but farm, and I won't burden my wife with having to care for an ugly, crippled, half-man."

"You're not ugly or half a man." She shook her head. "And you won't be a burden. Once you adjust to an artificial leg, you'll be able to do many things on your own."

42

"I won't hold you to your promise to marry me," he mumbled. He folded his arms and stared at the wall. "We're not getting married, so you're free to move on with your life."

"I don't want to move on with my life. Not without you, Wayne." A hint of sweet-smelling soap wafted to meet Wayne's nose as she stood and leaned close to him.

"I've made up my mind; we're not getting married," he said determinedly.

Her eyes filled with tears. "You can't mean that."

"Jah, I do."

"Has your mother been talking to you about us? Has she said something to turn you away from me?"

Wayne shook his head. "Mom has nothing to do with this. I make my own decisions."

She clasped his arm. "Don't shut me out of your life, Wayne. You need me now, even if you don't realize it, and I want us to get through this together."

"Well, I don't." He motioned to the door. "Please don't come back here to see me again. It's over between us."

Loraine sat several seconds, staring at him as though in disbelief. Then, with a childlike cry, she rushed to the door. She stood there a few seconds with her back to him, then turned and said, "I'm not giving up on us. We belong together!"

As the door closed behind Loraine, Wayne squeezed his eyes shut. *Oh, dear Lord, have I done the right thing?* The thought of living without Loraine was unbearable. It wouldn't be any life at all. Yet he couldn't ask her to marry him the way he was now. He had to remain firm in his decision.

CHAPTER 7

As Loraine stumbled down the hospital corridor, her breath burned in her lungs. She needed a place to be alone so she could gain control of her emotions before she went out to her driver's car.

She spotted a women's restroom and slipped inside. Good, no one was there. She leaned against one of the stalls, fighting back tears of confusion and frustration. She couldn't believe Wayne didn't want to marry her anymore. Didn't he realize she still loved him and wanted to be his wife? It didn't matter that he only had one leg. It didn't matter whether he farmed or not. They could work things out if he'd only give them a chance.

As Loraine's fears took hold, she burst into sobs and continued to sob until she could barely breathe. She went to the sink and splashed cold water on her face, and then she patted it dry with a paper towel.

I've got to get a hold of myself before I get into Marge Nelson's van. If I let her see me like this, she'll ask questions I'd rather not answer right now.

Once Loraine had composed herself, she left the restroom and headed outside. When she reached the parking lot and climbed into the front seat of Marge's van, tears welled in her eyes, despite her resolve not to break down.

Marge, who'd been reading a book, buckled her seatbelt and

44

turned to look at Loraine. "You seem upset. Is Wayne doing all right?"

Loraine shook her head. "He's very depressed and not thinking clearly right now." The tension in her throat rendered her words to a whisper, and a sense of helplessness crept through her body. If only she could make things better for Wayne. If only. . .

"Losing a leg has to be a terrible trauma." Marge turned on the ignition. "All that pain medication he's taking has probably made his brain fuzzy, too."

Loraine nodded. Maybe that was all it was. Once Wayne didn't have to be on so much medication for the pain, he would see things clearly again.

～✺ ✺～

As Priscilla sat at her kitchen table, drinking a cup of tea, her gaze came to rest on the quilting rack she kept in the sunroom next to the kitchen. Several months ago, she'd started making a quilt with the double-wedding-ring pattern to give to Loraine and Wayne when they got married. It wasn't quite finished, but she figured she had plenty of time, since the wedding would have to be postponed until Wayne was feeling better.

Priscilla's forehead creased as worry set in. *How will things be for my daughter after she marries Wayne? Will he be able to support her? Loraine would probably have to keep working at the hardware store, but her salary alone wouldn't provide enough for them to live on.*

She drank the last of her tea and set the cup aside, then turned in her chair and reached for the notepad on the counter. She needed to stop worrying and make out her grocery list before she went shopping in Shipshewana tomorrow morning.

Rice, pickles, potatoes, coffee, tea, laundry soap. . . Her list was quickly growing.

Let's see now. What else do I need?

Bam! The back door slammed shut, and Priscilla set the notepad aside.

"Oh, good, I'm glad you're home," she said when Loraine

45

entered the room. "I was just making out the grocery list and wondered if there was anything you'd like me to include."

"No, not really." Loraine draped her jacket over the back of a chair and sat down with a grunt. Her face looked pale and drawn. Her eyes were red and rimmed with tears. Alarm rose in Priscilla's chest.

"Daughter, what's wrong? Has something happened to make you feel *umgerennt?*"

"Jah, I'm feeling very upset. Wayne called off the wedding." Loraine caught her trembling lips between her teeth. "He—he thinks his life is over because he's lost his leg. He thinks he's only half a man."

"Is it because he won't be able to farm? Is that what's bothering him?"

"Partly."

"Is he afraid he won't be able to support you?"

"Jah, that too."

"Maybe it would be best if you didn't get married."

Loraine's eyes widened. "You can't mean that, Mom."

"I'm just trying to help you see the facts as they are." Priscilla's face grew warm as she fiddled with the edge of the tablecloth. She hoped she could say what was on her heart in a way that wouldn't upset Loraine any further. "If Wayne thinks you shouldn't be married, then maybe you ought to respect his decision. He might know what's best for both of you."

"Wayne's not thinking straight! He's *verhuddelt* about things." Loraine's hand shook as she swiped at the tears running down her cheeks. "He needs time to get used to the idea of having only one leg. I'm certain that after a time of healing, Wayne will change his mind about marrying me."

Priscilla reached over and took Loraine's hand. "I'm sure Wayne is feeling confused right now, but I want you to give serious thought to what I'm about to say."

"What is it?"

"Being married to a man with a handicap such as Wayne's

could put additional strain on your marriage. Do you really want to spend the rest of your life taking care of him and dealing with his melancholy moods?"

"He's only lost a leg, Mom. It's not like he's a helpless invalid, and I'm sure in time his moods will improve."

"I hope so, but there will still be some limitations as to what he can do."

"Some time ago, I read an article in the paper about a man who'd lost both of his legs, but thanks to a pair of artificial legs, he's actually running in races. And then there's a swimmer who—"

"I know there are many who have overcome great odds," Priscilla interrupted. "But even if Wayne does rise above his circumstances, he's got a long road ahead of him—both physically and emotionally."

Loraine's chair scraped across the linoleum as she pushed away from the table. "I know you mean well, but I promised to marry Wayne, and I intend to keep that promise. I don't care what sacrifices I might have to make, either." She moved toward the door. "I'd rather not talk about this anymore."

"I think we should talk about it. It's obvious that you're not thinking straight."

"Jah, I am." Loraine grabbed her jacket and outer bonnet. "I'm going for a ride!"

"But you just got home."

"I need to be alone for a while."

As the door banged shut behind Loraine, Priscilla made a decision. She would do everything in her power to make sure her daughter didn't make the biggest mistake of her life.

❧ ❀

Loraine headed for the barn to get her horse and shivered as a cluster of heavy, dark clouds moved across the sky. It looked like it might rain. "Well, let it pour," she mumbled when she reached Trixie's stall. "It can't dampen my spirits any more than they already are."

Memories of Wayne and all the good times they'd had in the past tugged at her heart. A sense of despair crept in, pushing through the tiny cracks of hope she'd been trying to conjure up. What if she couldn't get Wayne to change his mind about marrying her? How could she go to their biweekly church services and other community gatherings and not burst into tears every time she saw him?

In order to calm herself, Loraine let her mind wander back in time. Back to the night when Wayne asked her to marry him. . .

"Would you mind if we take a little detour before I take you home?" Wayne asked when they left the Essenhaus Restaurant parking lot.

Loraine looked up at him with curiosity. "Where are we going?"

"It's a surprise." He tweaked her nose. "You'll see soon enough."

She smiled. "Okay."

Half an hour later, Wayne pulled his horse and buggy into a grassy spot near the pond on the other side of his folks' property.

"How'd you like to live right here?" he asked, turning to face her.

She tipped her head in question.

"Wouldn't you like our home to be built so it overlooked the pond?"

"Our home?"

A wide smile spread across Wayne's face.

Loraine moistened her lips with the tip of her tongue. "Are—are you asking me to marry you?"

He nodded and slipped his arm across her shoulders. "I love you, Loraine. If you're willing to be my wife, I'd like to build our home right here."

Tears gathered in the corners of her eyes. "I'm more than willing, Wayne."

"Are you sure? I mean, if you still have feelings for—"

She shook her head vigorously. "It's you I love; no one else."

"I'm real glad to hear it. Can we be married this fall?"

"Do you think you'll have the house done by then? Since you're in the middle of spring planting, there won't be much time to build a house."

"That's true, but I'm sure we can live with my folks until the house is done. Would you be okay with that idea?"

"I—I guess so." The idea of living in the same house with Wayne's mother, who could sometimes be rather picky, didn't set too well with Loraine, but she was sure it wouldn't be for long.

Wayne pulled Loraine into his arms, and she melted into his embrace. She could hardly wait to become Mrs. Wayne Lambright.

A raw ache settled in the pit of Loraine's stomach, as her thoughts returned to the present. Would she and Wayne ever get married? Would they live together in the half-finished home he'd begun near the pond?

To dampen her spirits even further, the sky let loose. Rain pelted the front of her buggy. Her hands tingled as she gripped the reins and reminded herself to calm down. She needed to focus on the road ahead and make sure the horse obeyed her commands.

I hope Ella's at home; I really need to talk to her. I'm sure she'll be more supportive and understanding than Mom.

~≈ ≈~

Ella had just taken a batch of cinnamon rolls from the oven when she heard the whinny of a horse and the rumble of buggy wheels. She glanced out the window and noticed that it was raining heavily, so she hurried to the door and waited as Loraine climbed down from her buggy.

"Wie geht's?" Ella asked when Loraine stepped onto the porch a few minutes later.

"I've been better." Loraine removed her rain-soaked jacket, gave it a good shake, and entered the house. "Are you alone? I really need to talk."

"My mamm's not feeling well today, so I insisted she go to her room and rest." Ella motioned to the kitchen. "I just took some cinnamon rolls from the oven, so I'll fix us a cup of hot tea and we can have a snack while we visit."

"I'll pass on the cinnamon rolls, but a cup of tea sounds good." The chair creaked as Loraine slid it away from the table. She dropped into it with a sigh. "I went to the hospital to see Wayne this morning."

Ella poured tea into a cup and handed it to Loraine. "How's he doing?"

"Not so well. Besides the fact that he's still very depressed and is in a lot of pain, he called off our wedding."

Ella nearly dropped the teapot. "You're kidding!"

"No, I'm not. He also asked me not to visit him at the hospital again."

Ella took a seat beside Loraine. "Wayne's still in shock from losing his leg. I'm sure he'll change his mind once he's come to grips with his loss."

"I've been telling myself that, but it's getting harder and harder to have hope—especially when my own *mudder* isn't supportive."

"What do you mean?"

Loraine picked up a spoon and swirled it around in her tea, as she explained how her mother thought being married to a man with a handicap would be a burden. "Mom thinks Wayne did the right thing by breaking our engagement. How can it be wrong for two people who love each other to be together?" Her chin quivered. "At least, I think Wayne still loves me."

"Of course he does. He's just verhuddelt right now, that's all." Ella patted Loraine's arm in a motherly fashion. "You and Wayne are meant to be together."

"I think so, too." Loraine sniffed. "What would I do without you?"

Ella smiled. "That's what friends and family are for—to offer love and encouragement in the dark times, and to laugh and play together during the good times."

They sat quietly drinking their tea. The only sound in the room was the hiss and crackle of the log Ella had put on the fire a short time ago.

Finally, Loraine pushed her chair away from the table and stood. "I think I'll drive over to Aunt JoAnn and Uncle Jeremy's place and see how Katie's doing."

"I'd like to visit Katie, too," Ella said. "Would you mind if I tag along?"

"Of course not. We can go in my buggy, and I'll bring you back here on my way home."

Ella stood. "I'd better check on Mama first, and let her know where I'm going."

"Better take your umbrella," Loraine said as she peered out the kitchen window. "It's still raining pretty hard."

"Okay." As Ella left the room, she glanced over her shoulder. Loraine remained at the window with her nose pressed up to the glass.

I wish I could make things better for Loraine, Ella thought. *I wish I could think of some way to help ease her pain.*

CHAPTER 8

"We need to be careful today not to say anything that might upset Wayne," Crist said to Ada as they walked down the hospital corridor toward Wayne's room.

She halted and smacked one hand against her hip. "Are you insinuating that I upset our son the last time we came to see him?"

"I'm not insinuating anything." Crist shrugged. "As you well know, ever since the accident, Wayne gets easily upset. If either of us says the wrong thing, it might set him off."

"Well, no need to worry; I won't say anything to upset our son." Ada hurried down the hall. She couldn't believe the accusation she'd heard in Crist's voice. Why, he'd talked to her as if *she* were the reason Wayne had become upset on their last visit! Didn't Crist realize the reason for Wayne's sour disposition was because he'd lost his leg?

I've never been anything but supportive and helpful.

With her head held high and a smile on her face, Ada stepped into Wayne's room.

❦ ❧

When the door to Wayne's room swooshed open, he rolled onto his side and opened his eyes.

"How are you feeling today?" Mom asked, stepping up to his bed.

Pop was right behind her.

"About the same," Wayne mumbled.

"Are you in much pain?" Pop asked.

Wayne shook his head. "Only when the pain medicine wears off."

"Then how come you look like you're in pain?" Mom asked.

"Loraine was here awhile ago, and I—"

"Did she say something to upset you? Because if she did—"

"No, Mom. I broke things off with her, but now I'm having second thoughts."

"You called off the wedding?"

Wayne nodded. "But I love Loraine and can't imagine spending my life without her, so it's going to be hard for me to—"

Mom patted his shoulder. "You made the right decision. With your handicap, it would be hard for you to support a wife right now. Besides, Loraine's too demanding. She has high expectations and always wants her way." Deep wrinkles formed in Mom's forehead as she shook her head. "I never thought Loraine was the right woman for you."

Wayne grimaced. "I've never seen Loraine as demanding or having high expectations. She's sweet and even-tempered. She's—"

"I think we should change the subject," Pop said.

Wayne ground his teeth. "What shall we talk about—how lousy I feel, and how disappointed I am because God didn't answer my prayers for a safe trip to Hershey Park?"

Pop placed his hand on Wayne's shoulder. "Sometimes the answer to our prayers isn't what we expected. Sometimes God answers by giving us the strength to make it through trials. Other times, He sends someone to help us." He nodded his head. "Some of our greatest blessings can come because of a prayer that wasn't answered the way we'd hoped."

Wayne grunted and turned his head away. "I don't want any sermons today, and I sure don't feel blessed."

"I have some good news for you," Wayne's doctor announced as he entered the room, bringing their conversation to a halt.

"Barring anything unforeseen, you should be able to go home sometime tomorrow, Wayne."

"Oh, that's wunderbaar." Mom clasped Wayne's hand and squeezed his fingers. "I'm sure you'll be a lot more comfortable at home in your own familiar surroundings."

Wayne nodded mutely. Truth was, he was worried about how things would be for him at home. Would he be able to cope with his disability? Would he be able to farm again? Could he live without Loraine?

⁓❦⁓

Priscilla wrung her hands as she paced from the kitchen table to the window and back again. It gave her no pleasure to upset Loraine, but she felt she'd had the right to say what was on her mind. Loraine wasn't thinking straight and needed some guidance.

She glanced at the clock on the wall above the refrigerator. Where had Loraine gone, and when was she coming home?

"What time's supper?" Amos asked when he stepped into the kitchen a few minutes later.

"Whenever Loraine gets home."

"Where'd she go?"

Priscilla shrugged. "I don't know. She left several hours ago and hasn't returned."

Amos slid one of the chairs away from the table and took a seat. "Loraine's been through a lot lately. She probably needs some time alone."

Priscilla sucked in her lower lip. "We. . .uh. . .had a little disagreement. I think that's why she left."

Amos's eyebrows furrowed. "What was the disagreement about?"

She sat in the chair beside him and quickly related the story of how Loraine had gone to visit Wayne that morning and how he'd broken their engagement.

"I'm sorry to hear that." Amos looked at her with questioning eyes. "What'd *you* say that upset her?"

54

"I just said that I thought being married to a man with a handicap such as Wayne's could put a strain on their marriage."

"Well, no wonder she took off!" Amos glared at her. "You ought to stop meddling and let our daughter make her own decisions. You didn't interfere in our boys' lives like that when they all still lived at home."

Priscilla stiffened. "I wasn't meddling; I'm just concerned about Loraine and want her to be happy."

"Then you oughta realize that Loraine's happiness is with Wayne. She loves him, and that's why she agreed to marry him."

"I know that, but—"

"You oughta stop giving unwanted advice and just be supportive."

"I am being supportive."

"Whatever." Amos pushed away from the table. "Ring the bell when supper's ready." He rushed out of the house before Priscilla could respond.

～ ✢ ～

"I hope Katie's doing better than the last time we saw her," Loraine said as she and Ella headed down the road in her buggy.

Ella nodded. "Katie's always been kind of excitable, but I've never seen her so despondent and unresponsive, like she's been since Timothy died. I hope she snaps out of it soon."

"The accident affected everyone, but in different ways. I'm afraid some of us will never be the same."

Ella reached across the seat and touched Loraine's arm. "Are you thinking of Wayne?"

"Jah." Loraine blinked a couple of times, hoping to ward off the tears. Just thinking about the accident made her want to cry. Thinking about Wayne not wanting to marry her made her even more miserable.

"Things will work out between you and Wayne; you'll see."

"I—I hope so." A few tears leaked out and trickled down Loraine's cheeks. "Everything was going so well before the accident. Wayne and I had our wedding date set, my dress has been made, our home was getting close to being done, and we were moving along with our plans. Unless he changes his mind, there'll be no wedding for us at all."

Ella offered a reassuring smile. "We'll just have to pray that he does."

Loraine nodded and clucked to her horse to get her moving faster. At the rate Trixie was plodding along, it would be suppertime before they made it to Katie's, and then they'd have to turn right around and head back home.

They rode in silence the rest of the way, and Loraine forced herself to concentrate on driving her horse and watching out for any cars that might be going too fast or following too close on this rainy day.

When they arrived at the Millers', they found Katie's father in the barn, unloading a bunch of hay from the wagon he had parked there.

"Wie geht's?" he called with a friendly wave. "What brings you by this afternoon?"

"We came to see Katie," Loraine said. "We wanted to see how she's doing."

Uncle Jeremy's eyebrows furrowed. "She and her mamm took a trip to Sarasota, Florida, to visit Katie's grandparents. We decided the change of scenery might help Katie deal with the loss of Timothy."

"This is the first we've heard of it," Ella said. "How come no one told us until now?"

"It was a spur-of-the-moment decision, and I haven't had a chance to tell anyone yet," he said.

"How long will they be gone?" Loraine asked.

"Don't know for sure. Probably a few weeks." Uncle Jeremy glanced at the hay he'd already stacked along one wall. "I hope you don't mind, but I need to get back to stacking this hay so I can get some other chores done."

"Go right ahead. We need to get home and help start supper soon, anyway," Loraine said. "If you talk to Katie on the phone, would you please tell her that Ella and I said hello and that we're praying for her?"

"I sure will." Uncle Jeremy went back to unloading his hay, while Ella and Loraine climbed into the buggy.

"Would you mind stopping by Sara Bontrager's place on the way home?" Ella asked as Loraine guided the horse onto the road. "Since Sara's been recently widowed, I'd like to check on her and see if there's anything she needs."

"Jah, we can do that," Loraine replied. Besides doing a good deed for a neighbor, she figured it might take her mind off her own troubles for a while.

A short time later, they pulled into Sara's place. "If you want to head up to the house, I'll untie the horse and be in as soon as I'm done," Loraine said to Ella.

"That's fine." Ella climbed out of the buggy and sprinted to the house, rain pelting down on her umbrella as she dodged several puddles.

Once Loraine had the horse secured to the hitching rail, she followed. She found Ella and Sara sitting at the kitchen table, sharing a pot of tea.

"Come join us for some tea and banana bread." Sara motioned to the chair next to Ella.

After Loraine had taken a seat, Sara passed her a cup of tea and the plate of bread.

Loraine smiled. "Danki."

Sara smiled in return, revealing a set of crooked teeth.

Well, at least she still has all her own teeth, Loraine mused. *Many people Sara's age wear dentures.*

"How are things going with you?" Loraine asked the elderly woman.

"I'm getting along fairly well. Even though none of my family live close to me now, my good friends and neighbors check in on me regularly and make sure I have all that I need." Sara smiled again, a little wider this time. "Of course, once a month the widows in our community get together of an evening and either go out to supper or make a call on someone who's sick or isn't able to get out much. It makes me feel needed when I do something like that."

Ella reached over and clasped Sara's hand. "We all need to feel needed, and I think it's wunderbaar that you're still able to get around and do helpful things for others."

Sara looked over at Loraine and motioned to the loaf of bread on the table. "Before you came into the house, I was telling Ella that five different people dropped by this week, and each of them gave me some starter for friendship bread. I've made several loaves, but I have more starter than I know what to do with." She grinned at Loraine. "Ella's taking a loaf of bread and some starter home. Would you like some, too?"

"I'd appreciate the bread," Loraine said, "but I don't think I'll have time to tend the starter or make more bread, so I'd better pass on that."

"What about your mamm? Would she be able to tend the starter?"

Loraine shrugged. "I'm not sure, but I think I'll just take the bread if you don't mind. I will let Mom know that you have some starter, and if she wants any, I'm sure she'll be over to see you."

"That's fine." Sara took a sip of tea. "How are you two doing since that horrible accident? Are you fairly well healed of your injuries?"

"I wasn't seriously hurt," Ella said. "Just a mild concussion and some nasty bumps and bruises."

"Bumps and bruises were all I had, too, but I wish we could say the same for the others who were in the van." Loraine sighed. "We just came from our cousin Katie's, and her *daed* said Katie and her mamm went to Sarasota for a while."

"That's right," Ella interjected. "Katie's folks are hoping some time away might help Katie recover from the shock of losing Timothy."

"It's such a shame when someone so young passes on." Sara looked at Ella with sympathy. "I'm sure you and your family must miss your bruder."

A muscle on the side of Ella's cheek quivered. "My mamm's taken it the hardest, but in time, I'm sure she'll come to grips with Raymond's death."

Sara looked at Loraine. "How's your boyfriend doing? It must have been a real shock for him to lose a leg like that."

Loraine nodded. She glanced at Ella, hoping she wouldn't mention that Wayne had called off the wedding.

Sara patted Loraine's hand. "If you and Wayne commit everything to God, and if you'll seek His will in all things, I'm certain that it will work out just as it should."

Loraine dabbed at her damp cheeks with a napkin. She hoped Sara was right about things working out. She had so many doubts swirling around in her head. She'd never admit it to anyone, but Loraine's greatest fear was that she and Wayne might never get married.

CHAPTER 9

Are you warm enough, son?"

Wayne nodded as his mother draped a small quilt across his lap.

"Are you certain? I can add another log to the fire if you're cold."

"I'm fine, Mom."

"Are you sure you're comfortable enough lying on the sofa, or would you rather go to your room and rest awhile?"

Wayne gritted his teeth. Ever since he'd come home from the hospital this afternoon, Mom had hovered over him like a moth drawn to a flame. It was bad enough that he had to deal with the phantom pain he'd begun experiencing and try to get used to maneuvering around their house with his wheelchair. Did Mom have to smother him to death, as well?

Makes me wish I was back in the hospital, he thought. *At least there, they encouraged me to do some things on my own, and they didn't ask me every few minutes if I needed anything or was comfortable enough.*

Wayne stared at the flames rising from the wood in the fireplace across the room. *I wonder if anything in my life will ever feel normal again. Should I have let Loraine know I was coming home today? What if she goes to the hospital to see me and finds that I've gone?*

He scrubbed a hand down his face. *What am I thinking? I broke up with Loraine yesterday, so she'd have no reason to go to the hospital to see me today.*

∼✦∼

With a sense of urgency, Loraine hurried down the hospital corridor toward Wayne's room. She'd lain awake much of the night, thinking and praying about her situation with Wayne. She loved him and had made a commitment to become his wife. She wanted to rub away any tension Wayne felt today and hoped what she had to say to him might cause him to change his mind about marrying her.

As she approached Wayne's room, she said a quick prayer for guidance. Then, feeling a little more confident, she pushed the door open and stepped inside.

She blinked a couple of times and stared at his bed. It was empty and looked like it had been freshly made. Maybe Wayne was in another part of the hospital having physical therapy.

She left the room and hurried to the nurses' station. "Excuse me," she said to the nurse behind the counter. "I just came from Wayne Lambright's room, and he wasn't there. Do you know if he's having physical therapy right now?"

The nurse shook her head. "Mr. Lambright went home earlier today."

"He did?"

"Yes. His parents came to get him about two hours ago."

"Oh, I see." Loraine turned from the counter, feeling as if she were in a daze. She thought Wayne would have called and left a message on her folks' answering machine in the phone shed they shared with the neighbors. She thought he cared enough about her to let her know that he planned to come home, but apparently she was wrong.

Tears blurred her vision as she stumbled down the hall and out the door. As soon as they got back to Goshen, she'd ask Marge to drop her off at Wayne's. She needed to speak to him today!

~≈ ≈~

Loraine arrived at Wayne's house later that day, and her heart began to pound when his mother answered the door.

"Is—is Wayne here? When I went to the hospital, they said he'd gone home."

Ada nodded, a grim expression on her face. "Wayne's sleeping, and I don't want to disturb him right now. The trip home from the hospital took a lot out of him, and he's in a great deal of pain."

"I thought the pain medication took care of his pain."

"It did, but now he has more than the aftermath of his surgery pain to deal with."

"What do you mean?"

"The phantom pains have set in."

"Oh, I see. Wayne mentioned that those would likely occur."

Ada's pinched expression didn't change. "The doctor said it was likely to happen, but we had no idea it would start this soon or be this bad."

"I'm sorry to hear that. Is it all right if I come inside and wait until Wayne's awake? I really need to talk to him."

Ada shook her head. "That's not a good idea."

"Why not?"

"Do you really have to ask?"

Loraine leaned on the porch railing, feeling the need for some support. She didn't care for the cold reception she was getting from Wayne's mother. She'd been dealing with a lot of Ada's icy treatment since the accident.

Loraine moistened her lips. "You probably know that Wayne broke our engagement."

"Jah, and that means things are over between you and him." Ada folded her arms and glared at Loraine as if daring her to say otherwise.

Loraine grimaced. She didn't understand this sudden hostility. Until the accident, Ada had never acted like this toward her.

"I'm hoping Wayne will change his mind and realize that the

62

loss of his leg doesn't change anything between us." She moved away from the railing, feeling a bit more confident. "I want Wayne to know that I'm still his best friend, and that I love—"

"You can do that best by staying away from here. He needs time to heal without a lot of demands and expectations put upon him."

Loraine's skin prickled. "I wasn't planning to make demands or put expectations on Wayne. I just want him to know how much I love him and want to help in any way I can."

"Are you're hoping to change his mind about marrying you?"

Loraine nodded. She couldn't deny it, even though she knew it wasn't what Wayne's mother wanted to hear. "What have you got against me, Ada?" she dared to ask. "Have I said or done something to offend you?"

Ada's gaze dropped to the porch floor. "I—I just think my son has enough to deal with right now without taking on the responsibility of a wife and family."

"He wouldn't have to do it alone. I'm willing to help in any way I can."

Ada lifted her gaze. "Be that as it may, Wayne has a long road ahead of him. He won't be ready to even think about marriage for a long time to come."

"I realize that, and I'm willing to wait."

Ada rubbed her hands briskly over her arms. "It's getting cold out here, and I need to check on the chicken I have baking in the oven. So if you'll excuse me. . ."

Loraine gave a quick nod, turned, and started down the stairs. "Please tell Wayne I was here," she called over her shoulder. "Oh, and let him know that I'll be back tomorrow morning."

CHAPTER 10

Wayne squinted at the invading light streaming through his bedroom window, letting him know it was morning. He'd had a fitful night, tossing, turning, dreaming, and soaking his sheets with sweat. The pain he felt where his leg had once been was so intense at times he thought he'd go mad. The medicine they'd given him for pain had barely taken the edge off. He wished there was something he could do to alleviate his discomfort. He didn't think he could endure the pain if it went on too long.

Gritting his teeth, he pulled himself to a sitting position, took one step, and fell back on the bed with a groan. It had seemed so normal to be back in his own bed, he'd forgotten he only had one leg. He glanced at his stump and noticed that it had started to shrink. Another thing the doctor had told him would happen.

He reached for the handles of his wheelchair and swung it around. Then, hopping on one foot, he positioned himself in front of the wheelchair and sat down.

"Everything I do takes such effort," he mumbled. "I wonder if it'll ever get any easier for me." At least Mom had moved most of his things to the downstairs bedroom, and he didn't have to navigate the steps on one leg. The wheelchair wouldn't work on steps, either, which was why Pop had built a ramp leading to the back porch.

Mom and Pop have done all they can to make my life easier, Wayne thought as he slipped his arms into a long-sleeved cotton shirt. *I ought to be grateful and quit feeling sorry for myself, but in my circumstances, that's easier said than done.*

Wayne closed his eyes, and an image of Loraine popped into his head. It had only been two days since he'd last seen her, but already he missed her—more than he missed his leg. His arms longed to hold her. His fingers ached to stroke her soft skin. His lips yearned to kiss hers. If only they could be together. If things could just be as they'd once been. If he could only undo the past, he would. . . .

His eyes snapped open, and he shook his head. All the *if onlys* in the world wouldn't change a thing. He'd lost a leg, and he wouldn't be getting it back. He'd made a decision not to marry Loraine, and he wouldn't be changing his mind.

～✖※～

"I'm heading out now, Mom," Loraine said as she grabbed her jacket from the wall peg where she'd hung it the night before.

Mom's eyebrows raised. "Why are you leaving so early for work? You don't have to be at the hardware store for another couple of hours."

"I want to stop by the Lambrights' on my way to Shipshewana and see how Wayne's getting along. Since he was asleep when I stopped there yesterday, I didn't get the chance to talk to him."

"What are you going to talk about—your broken engagement?"

Loraine nodded. "That, plus a few other things."

Mom opened her mouth like she was going to say something more, but she snapped it shut and turned back to the dishes she'd been drying.

"I'll see you when I get home from work this afternoon." Loraine turned and headed out the door.

As soon as she started across the lawn, she spotted Dad coming out of the barn, leading Trixie.

"Figured you'd be leaving for work soon, so I decided to get your horse hitched to the buggy," he called to Loraine.

She stepped up to him and smiled. "Danki, Dad. That was thoughtful of you. Especially since I'm leaving earlier than usual today."

"Going by to see Wayne on the way to Shipshewana?"

She nodded. "He came home from the hospital yesterday, and I want to see how he's doing."

Dad placed a gentle hand on her arm. "I was sorry to hear Wayne called off the wedding. Sorry to hear you and your mamm had a disagreement about him, too."

"Mom doesn't understand how I feel about things." Tears welled in Loraine's eyes. "She's always had more understanding for James, Harold, Earl, and Ben than she has for me."

Dad shook his head. "I don't believe that. I just think that since your *brieder* are all married, and you're the only one of our kinner still living at home, your mamm worries about you more." He pulled Loraine to his side and gave her a hug. "Your mamm loves you a lot. Surely you know that."

"I do know it, but I wish she'd let me make my own decisions without interference. She doesn't think Wayne can take care of me now that he's lost a leg." Loraine sighed. "Of course, Wayne thinks he can't, either, so I'm really outnumbered."

"It'll all work out in the end; you'll see."

Loraine forced a smile. At least somebody was on her side.

❧ ❧

"Did you get enough to eat?" Mom pointed to Wayne's plate. "You hardly touched your poached eggs."

"I'm not that hungry this morning," he said. "The pain medicine has made my stomach upset."

"That's because you took it without eating first." Mom shook her head. "You need to follow the instructions on the bottle."

"Stop badgering him, Ada," Pop spoke up. "He's a grown man, not a little *buwe*."

She turned in her chair and glared at him. "Don't you think

I know that? I'm just trying to make things easier for him."

"Then stop badgering."

"I'm not."

"Jah, you sure are."

Unable to listen to his parents' squabbling a moment longer, Wayne pushed his wheelchair away from the table and propelled it across the floor. The biggest trouble with being an only child was that Mom had no one to fuss over but him, and sometimes she could be downright overbearing.

Wayne was almost to the hallway when a knock sounded on the door. "I'll get it!" he called before Mom could come running.

When he opened the back door, he was surprised to see Loraine on the porch.

"Wie geht's?" she asked with a smile.

"I'm doin' as well as can be expected."

"Can I come in? I'd like to talk to you."

"Jah, I guess it'll be okay." He opened the door wider. "My folks are about done with breakfast, but I'm sure there's still some coffee left if you'd like some."

"A cup of coffee would be nice."

Wayne pushed the door closed and headed back to the kitchen. He couldn't help but notice the scowl on Mom's face when Loraine entered the room with him. He hoped Loraine hadn't noticed.

"*Guder mariye*," Loraine said, smiling at Mom and then Pop.

"Morning," they said in unison.

"I invited Loraine in for a cup of coffee." Wayne looked at Mom. "Is there still some in the coffeepot?"

She nodded, frowned, and pushed away from the table. When she returned with a cup of coffee for Loraine, she was still frowning.

"Danki." Loraine took a seat at the table and looked over at Wayne. "I came by yesterday, but you were sleeping. So I decided to stop on my way to work this morning and see how you're doing."

"He's got an upset stomach," Mom said before Wayne could respond. "Didn't eat much breakfast because of it."

"I'm sorry to hear that. Do you think you're getting the flu?" Loraine asked Wayne.

He shook his head. "The pain medicine upsets my stomach."

"That's because you took it without eating first." Mom reached for the teapot sitting in the center of the table, poured some into a cup, and handed it to Wayne. "Drink some of this peppermint tea, and I'm sure it'll settle your stomach."

Wayne set the cup down. "I don't care for any tea—especially not peppermint. I never did like the taste of it."

"Well, I'd like you to at least try a little bit," Mom insisted.

Pop poked Mom's arm. "You're doing it again, Ada."

"Doing what?"

"Badgering."

"I'm only trying to make him feel better."

Loraine fiddled with the edge of the tablecloth, obviously uncomfortable. "When I was here yesterday," she said, lifting her gaze to meet Wayne's, "your mamm said you were in a lot of pain."

Wayne was about to speak when Mom butted in.

"Like I told you then, Wayne's been having some terrible phantom pains."

"How come you didn't tell me Loraine was here to see me yesterday?" Wayne asked, leaning close to Mom.

She shrugged. "You were asleep. By the time you woke up, I'd gotten busy and forgot."

Wayne ground his teeth. He had a feeling Mom had deliberately not mentioned Loraine's visit. Mom clearly didn't care for Loraine anymore, and he didn't understand why.

They sat in silence for a while; finally, Loraine drank her coffee and pushed away from the table. "I'd better go. I don't want to be late for work." She moved toward the door, but hesitated as though there was something else on her mind.

"I'll see you out," Wayne was quick to say. He sure didn't want Mom walking Loraine to the door.

Once they were on the porch, Loraine turned to him and said, "There was another reason I came by today, only I didn't want to say it with your folks sitting there."

"What's that?"

"I wanted to know if you've reconsidered your decision not to marry me."

Wayne's heart began to pound. Loraine was everything he wanted in a wife. Yet he loved her too much to strap her with a cripple who couldn't even support them by doing what he loved best.

"My answer's still the same," he mumbled. "And if you're gonna keep bringing up the subject, then I think it'd be best if you didn't come over here at all anymore."

"You can't mean that."

"I do mean it. In fact, it might be best for both of us if we didn't see each other except at church."

She stared at him several seconds, tears welling in her eyes. Then she sprinted down the stairs and raced to the hitching rail where her horse and buggy waited.

Exhausted and fighting the phantom pain once again, Wayne turned his wheelchair around and entered the house. With only a glance in Mom's direction, he wheeled down the hall and into his room. He didn't have the energy to deal with anything else.

⚡ ⚡

As Loraine guided her horse and buggy down the road, she replayed some of the things that had been said during her visit with Wayne. Every time she saw Ada, it became more obvious that the woman didn't care for her. And every time she saw Wayne, he seemed to withdraw from her all the more. Even so, Loraine's heart longed to be his wife.

How could he have suggested that I not come over to see him anymore? she fretted. *I was so sure if he had a few days to think things over he'd have changed his mind about his decision not to marry me.*

Tears stung the backs of her eyes, and she blinked multiple times in order to keep them from spilling onto her cheeks. *I still think that at least part of Wayne's rejection has something to do with*

69

his mother's dislike of me. If I could only think of something to do that would make Ada accept me, maybe Wayne would change his mind. Oh, I wish I knew what to do.

More tears came as Loraine passed the one-room schoolhouse where Jolene used to teach. Dorene Lehman, Timothy's thirty-year-old unmarried sister, taught there now, but it was just until the school board could find a permanent teacher. Dorene was planning to move to a small town in Montana soon.

My cousin was well liked at this place, Loraine thought as she slowed her horse and studied the two-story wooden structure where she, too, had gone to school. *The scholars must miss Jolene terribly. Jolene's probably missing them a lot, as well.*

Loraine gripped the reins a little tighter. *I, too, miss Jolene, and also Katie. We four cousins were always so close. In times past, I could go to any of them for comfort when I was upset about something. Now Katie and Jolene are gone, and Ella's so busy trying to comfort her mother and take care of things at their home that I feel guilty for bothering her with my problems. Wayne's pushed me away, and Mom doesn't understand me at all. I feel almost friendless right now.*

Beep! Beep! Loraine startled when she realized that her buggy had drifted into the wrong lane, and she gasped when she saw that a car was coming straight at her!

CHAPTER 11

Loraine jerked on the reins. The horse pulled out of the way just in time to avoid hitting the car coming toward her. "Thank You, Lord," she murmured. "That was too close for my comfort."

She gave Trixie the freedom to trot, and by the time they were halfway to work, the horse had worked up a sweat. Suddenly, a siren blared behind her, and she nearly jumped out of her seat. Thinking that a rescue vehicle must be coming down the road, she guided her horse and buggy to the side of the road. The next thing she knew, a police car had pulled in behind her. She gulped when a uniformed officer got out of the car and headed her way.

"Is there a problem?" Loraine asked when the policeman stepped up to her buggy.

"Someone called in a report about a horse and buggy that had nearly hit them on this stretch of road." He squinted over the top of his metal-framed glasses. "Since your horse and buggy is the only one I've seen on this stretch of road, I figured it had to be you."

Loraine hated to admit that she hadn't been concentrating on the road, but she didn't want to lie to the man, either. "I. . .uh. . . yes, it was me."

"Have you been drinking?"

"No, of course not! I was in deep thought about my fiancé having just lost his leg in an accident he and I were involved in

71

several days ago, and I didn't realize my horse had wandered into oncoming traffic."

His forehead wrinkled. "I should give you a ticket for reckless driving, but since I can see how distraught you seem to be, I'll let you off with a warning. However, I caution you to be more careful from now on."

"Yes. Yes, I will."

The officer glanced at Trixie and squinted. "I see your horse is pretty well lathered up, which tells me you must have been running it too fast. I really should call a vet to come check on the animal." His bushy eyebrows pulled together as he slowly shook his head. "There's too much animal abuse going on these days, and it's got to stop!"

"My horse is lathered up, but I haven't been running her too hard," Loraine said. "She's prone to sweating, so this is perfectly normal for her."

"Are you sure about that?"

She nodded. "If you don't believe me, you can call a vet to check Trixie over."

"Trixie, is it?" The officer chuckled. "Okay, I'm going to trust that everything you've told me is the truth." His smile faded. "Next time, though, you'd better keep a closer eye on your horse. Besides the fact that you should never run a horse too fast, there have been way too many accidents on this stretch of road, and we sure don't need any more."

"Thank you, sir."

His smile was back. "Now run along, and don't forget to rub that horse down good."

"Of course."

The officer returned to his vehicle, and Loraine breathed a sigh of relief. This was not starting out as a good day!

~⚹ ⚹~

Wayne closed his eyes and tried to sleep, but he couldn't stop thinking about Loraine and how dejected she'd looked when he'd said he hadn't changed his mind about marrying her. It almost killed him to give her up, but he saw no other way.

He curled his fingers into his palms as he stared at the stump of his leg. *I don't know if I'll ever be able to accept what's happened to me because I'll never be a whole man again.*

Tap! Tap! Tap!

Wayne turned his head toward the door and called, "Come in."

"I'm glad you're not asleep," Pop said when he poked his head into Wayne's room. "There's something I want to talk to you about."

"What's that?"

Pop stepped into the room and took a seat in the chair next to Wayne's bed. "I've been praying about something for sometime, and I've finally made a decision."

"A decision about what?"

"I'm going to quit farming and turn my hobby of taxidermy into a full-time business."

Wayne's teeth snapped together with a noisy click. "You're kidding!"

Pop shook his head. "This is something I've wanted to do for a long while, and I feel now's the right time."

"What about your land? Who's going to farm it if you open a taxidermy business?"

"I'm going to lease out the land to Harold Fry. I've already talked to him about it, and he's agreed to the arrangement."

Wayne's face contorted. It felt like someone had kicked him in the stomach. He had a hunch Pop's decision to quit farming and open his own taxidermy business was because of him and his missing leg.

Pop tapped Wayne's shoulder a couple of times. "If things go well, like I hope, then I might need a partner in my new business."

"I hope you're not thinking of me."

"I sure was. I think taxidermy would be a good thing for you to try, and it's something you can do from your wheelchair if necessary."

Wayne shook his head vigorously. "No way! Working with a

73

bunch of dead animal skins isn't for me!"

"How do you know that?"

" 'Cause it isn't, that's all. I'd rather be farming."

"But you can't farm anymore. You said so yourself."

Wayne jerked his head, feeling as if he'd been slapped. "I—I know what I said, but if I should get a prosthesis, and if we were both farming, then maybe—"

Pop held up his hand. "The decision's already been made about the farm, and I think I know what's best. You'll just have to accept things as they are." The floor squeaked as he rose from his chair. "Anytime you feel ready, I'll be happy to teach you what you need to know about taxidermy."

When the door clicked shut behind Pop, Wayne rolled over and punched his pillow. *If he wants to become a taxidermist, that's up to him, but he'll never talk me into messing with it!*

⚜

Priscilla had just taken a seat on the sofa late that afternoon when Loraine entered the room, her face pale and lips trembling. "You look so sad. Is something wrong?" Priscilla asked.

"*Es is mir verleed.*" Loraine sank into the rocking chair with a groan.

"Why are you discouraged?"

"I was so upset after I left Wayne's home that I almost got a ticket for reckless driving."

"I've never known you to drive the horse and buggy recklessly."

"I did today because I wasn't paying attention." Loraine gnawed on her lower lip. "Wayne hasn't changed his mind about marrying me, Mom. To make matters worse, he thinks it would be best if we didn't see each other anywhere except at church."

"Does that mean he doesn't want you to go over to his house anymore?"

"I believe it does." Loraine jumped out of her chair and began pacing. "I don't know how, but I have to get Wayne to change his mind about marrying me. I'll do whatever I have to in order to help us financially, too. I'll even work two jobs if that's what it takes."

Priscilla left her seat and stepped up to Loraine. "If Wayne feels he's made the right decision, then don't you think it's time for you to accept things as they are?"

"No, I can't accept Wayne's decision. I could tell from the tender expression on his face that he still loves me, and unless he says otherwise, I'm not giving up on us because I'm sure we're supposed to be together. I know I've got my work cut out for me, because Wayne keeps pushing me away when he needs me the most, but I can't give up on us."

Priscilla sighed deeply. "I know you care about Wayne, but you really should be taking care of yourself right now. You've been through a great ordeal, and you don't need to be worried about Wayne so much that you're getting yourself all worked up and upset." She patted Loraine gently on the back. "Give yourself a little time to get through all the emotional wounds, and then maybe—"

Loraine shook her head. "I don't care about my own needs right now. I only care about Wayne's needs, and I'll do what it takes to get through to him."

With tears streaming down her face, Loraine fled the room and dashed up the stairs.

Priscilla sank to the sofa and closed her eyes. *I think I ought to pay a call on the Lambrights, and it had better be soon.*

CHAPTER 12

As Priscilla guided her horse and buggy toward the Lambrights' place the next morning, she rehearsed in her mind what she was going to say when she saw Wayne. She had left home after Loraine had gone to work because she didn't want her to know where she was going.

She turned up the Lambrights' driveway, climbed down from the buggy, and tied the horse to a hitching rail near the barn. Then she hurried to the house. A few seconds after she'd rapped on the door, it opened, and Wayne's mother appeared.

"Guder mariye," Priscilla said.

Ada nodded. "Good morning. What brings you by so early in the day?"

"I came to see how Wayne's doing."

"He's having trouble adjusting to only one leg, but he's getting along as well as can be expected."

"Would it be all right if I came in and said hello to him?"

Ada glanced over her shoulder. "He's in the kitchen having a cup of coffee, but he didn't sleep well last night, so I don't know if he's up to any company this morning."

"I promise I won't stay long."

"All right then."

Ada led the way to the kitchen, where Wayne sat at the table in his wheelchair. His slumped shoulders and haggard expression gave indication that he really was tired.

"How are you feeling?" Priscilla asked, taking a seat in the chair beside him.

"I've been better," he mumbled.

"He's in a lot of pain yet." Ada handed Priscilla a cup of coffee.

"Danki." She turned to Wayne. "Doesn't the pain medicine help with that?"

He shrugged. "Sometimes."

"We're going to ask the doctor to try some other medicine for the pain Wayne's been having," Ada said. "There's just no good reason for him having to suffer like this."

Priscilla grimaced. She wished Ada would leave the room so she could speak to Wayne privately, but she didn't think she ought to come right out and make such a request.

"I'd like to talk to you about something," she said to Wayne.

"What's that?"

"It's about you and Loraine."

"What about them?" Ada butted in.

Priscilla gritted her teeth. She'd had just about enough of Ada's constant interrupting. "I understand that you broke things off with Loraine," she said, directing her comment to Wayne again.

"That's right," Ada said before he could respond. "Wayne doesn't feel that he can take on the responsibility of marriage right now."

"That's true," Wayne said. "With only one leg, I won't be able to farm. Besides, my daed's decided to lease out his land so he can become a full-time taxidermist. So even if I could still farm, I have no land to work anymore."

Priscilla couldn't help but notice the bitterness in Wayne's tone. She'd never seen him so negative before. Loraine was right about him being depressed, which was just one more reason Priscilla felt he wouldn't make a good husband.

Ada moved away from the table and turned on the water at the sink. "I don't see how my husband thinks he's going to earn a living making dead animals look like they're alive," she mumbled.

"But if that's what he wants to do, then I'll keep quiet about it."

I'll just bet you will. Priscilla noticed that she was gripping the handle of her cup really hard, and fearing it might break, she set it on the table. *I wish you'd be quiet right now, Ada, and let me speak to your son without your interruptions.* She looked at Wayne to gauge his reaction to his mother's comment, but his gaze remained fixed on his cup of coffee.

"I. . .uh. . .want you to know that I agree with your decision to break off your engagement to my daughter." Priscilla paused to wait for Wayne's response, but he said nothing.

"That's what I told him, too," Ada said over her shoulder. "I'm sure Loraine's upset about it, but she's a nice enough looking young woman. She's bound to catch the attention of some other fellow soon enough."

A muscle on the side of Wayne's neck quivered. "I won't hold Loraine to her promise to marry me, so if she wants to find someone else, she's free to do so." He backed his wheelchair away from the table and swung it around. "I'm tired. I think I'll go back to bed."

As soon as Wayne wheeled out of the room, Ada moved back to the table and leaned close to Priscilla. "I'm relieved to know you agree with me about Wayne breaking up with Loraine. I think it helps that we're thinking alike on this."

Priscilla nodded. "I only hope my daughter learns to accept things as they are and moves on with her life."

⁓ ✦ ⁓

"Guder mariye. How are things going for you?" Esther Lehman asked when Loraine entered the hardware store in Shipshewana.

"Okay." Loraine didn't think her boss needed to hear how she really felt this morning. Work wasn't the place to discuss her personal feelings.

"Are you ready for a busy day of stocking shelves and waiting on customers?"

"Ready as I'll ever be."

"Good, because we just got in a shipment of garden tools. There are also some boxes of weather vanes and birdhouses that need to be set out."

Loraine nodded. "That's fine. I'll do whatever needs to be done."

Esther motioned to the front counter. "You know where everything is, so I'd better get back to waiting on customers and let you get busy."

"Jah, I need to do that." Loraine hurried to the back room. She'd only been working a short time when her hands began to sweat and perspiration broke out on her forehead.

Maybe I shouldn't be working today. I can't seem to keep my mind off the situation with Wayne.

She reached for another birdhouse and was about to set it on the proper shelf, when it slipped from her fingers and crashed to the floor.

"What happened? I heard a clatter," Esther said, rushing up to Loraine.

"I—I dropped a birdhouse." Loraine motioned to the floor. "Thankfully, it doesn't appear to be broken." With a shaky hand, she wiped the perspiration from her forehead.

"Are you all right? Maybe you shouldn't have come to work today." Esther's pinched expression revealed her obvious concern.

Loraine shook her head. "I'll be okay."

Esther glanced over her shoulder. "Oh, there's someone waiting at the front counter, so I'd better go. Feel free to take a break if you need to."

"Danki."

Esther walked away, and Loraine bent to pick up the birdhouse. She was about to place it on the shelf when she heard someone call her name from behind her. She whirled around and was surprised to see Ella.

"I wondered if you'd be working today," Ella said.

"Jah, but I'm not doing a very good job of it." Loraine placed the birdhouse on the shelf and then pointed at it. "I dropped this because my hands are so shaky."

"How come they're shaky? Did something happen on the way to work this morning to get you upset?"

Loraine shook her head. "I didn't sleep well last night."

"Why not?"

"I went to see Wayne again yesterday, hoping he'd change his mind about marrying me." Loraine sighed. "He wouldn't budge and even said we should stop seeing each other socially."

"I'm sorry to hear that. What are you going to do?"

"For now, just try to be his friend. That's the only thing I can do, I guess, because if I keep pestering him about his decision, I'm sure it'll only drive him further away."

"I think you're right about that." Ella moved closer to Loraine. "Speaking of Wayne. . ." Her voice lowered to a whisper. "When I was on my way to town, I saw your mamm's horse and buggy pulling out of the Lambrights' driveway."

Loraine's forehead wrinkled. "Are you sure it was my mamm's rig?"

"Absolutely. She even waved as I went past."

"That seems a bit odd. Mom never mentioned to me that she'd be going over to the Lambrights' this morning." A spot on the side of Loraine's head began to pulsate, and she reached up to massage it. *I hope she didn't say anything to Wayne about him breaking up with me.*

Loraine moved over to a wooden bench that was on clearance and took a seat. "I know Ada doesn't want us to get married," she said after Ella had taken a seat beside her. "Maybe our mamms are in cahoots."

"You think they're working together to keep you and Wayne apart?"

"I wouldn't be surprised. Everything's been so verhuddelt since the accident, and nothing makes any sense. It seems like everyone's at odds with each other, too. It's very discouraging."

Ella took hold of Loraine's hand. "Is there anything I can do to help? Maybe speak to Wayne on your behalf, or have a talk with his mamm or your mamm?"

Loraine shook her head. "You've got enough to deal with in your own home right now. Besides, if anyone should speak to my mamm, it ought to be me." She drew in a deep breath. "In fact, I'm going to do that as soon as I get home. I need to know the reason she paid the Lambrights a visit this morning."

～ ✻ ～

As Jake Beechy drove through the town of Libby, Montana, he spotted a small store on the left. *Maybe I'll stop and see if they have anything to eat or drink. I need something to tide me over till I get back to the ranch.*

He pulled his truck into the parking lot and turned off the engine. A wave of homesickness washed over him when he entered the store and spotted a middle-aged Amish man behind the counter. He'd heard there were some Amish people living in Montana, but he hadn't seen any until today.

"Are you the owner of this store?" he asked the man behind the front counter.

"Yes. My wife and I are originally from Ohio, but we've been living here for the last ten years. I've been tempted to sell out a few times, yet here we still are."

"Fer was hoscht's net geduh?"

The man stared at Jake like he couldn't believe what he'd said. "Didn't you just ask me why I didn't do it?"

Jake nodded.

"You speak the *Dietch*?"

Jake nodded again. "I'm from Indiana. My family's Amish."

"But you're wearing English clothes. Does that mean you decided to go English?"

Jake raked his fingers through the ends of his short-cropped hair. "I left home almost two years ago and have never returned."

"Mind if I ask why?"

"Why I left or why I haven't gone home?"

"Both."

"I left to work on a horse ranch southeast of here. Figured it

81

was a quick way to make good money, but I still don't have enough to do what I want."

"And that would be?"

"I'd like to raise my own thoroughbred horses. Maybe train and board them, as well."

"Raising horses can be expensive."

"I know, and that's why I'm still working at the ranch here in Montana."

"And the reason you haven't been home?" the man asked as he leaned on the counter.

Jake shrugged. "I've thought about it plenty, and I might go back someday when I'm ready to settle down and my bank account is full of money."

"So what brings you to Libby?" the man asked.

Jake nodded toward the window where his truck and horse trailer were parked. "I'm on my way back from a horse auction, where I bought a couple of horses for my boss."

"I guess your boss must trust you, huh?"

Jake shrugged. "I hope so. As I was on my way out of town, I spotted your little store and decided to stop in and see if you had anything to eat or drink."

The man motioned to the back of the store. "There's water, juice, and soda pop in the cooler. You'll find some cheese and meat packages there, too."

"Sounds like just what I'm looking for." Jake hurried to the back of the store, knowing he needed to quit yakking and get back on the road.

He was about to open the cooler when a young Amish woman walked by. He stared at her a few minutes, then moved on. The woman's brown hair and brown eyes reminded him of Loraine.

Jake's heartbeat picked up speed. He hadn't thought of Loraine in a long while. Not since he'd started dating Roxanne, the boss's daughter. Jake and Roxanne had been dating for six months when she'd decided to go to some Bible college in Missouri. Said she wanted to be a missionary and had asked Jake to join her. He didn't feel called to mission work. For that matter, he wasn't sure his feelings for Roxanne went deep enough for a lasting relationship. In fact, he'd almost felt relief when she'd gone off to college.

Pulling his thoughts aside, Jake grabbed a package of cheese and a bottle of lemonade from the cooler. Then he found a box of crackers on a nearby shelf.

When he headed back to the counter to pay for them, he discovered the Amish man was reading a newspaper Jake recognized as *The Budget*.

"Looks like you found something to eat," the man said, looking up and setting the paper aside.

Jake nodded and chuckled. "This should provide me with enough fuel to get me up the road a few more miles at least."

"What part of Indiana did you say you were from?" the man asked as he put Jake's purchases in a paper sack.

"Northern Indiana. My folks live just outside of Goshen."

The man motioned to the newspaper. "Before you came in, I was reading in here about a vanload of young Amish people who were from Goshen, Middlebury, and Topeka. Guess they were involved in a bad accident a few weeks ago."

"Can I see that?"

The man handed Jake the newspaper.

Jake's lips compressed as he read the article that had been submitted by a scribe living in Middlebury. When he saw the names of those who'd been riding in the van, his heart nearly stopped beating. *Loraine. I've got to go home!*

~❧ ❧~

"I'm glad you're home. I could use some help cutting the potatoes I'll be using in a new casserole dish I want to try for supper," Priscilla said when Loraine came in the back door.

"I'd be glad to help, but first I'd like to ask you a question," Loraine said as she hung up her jacket and outer bonnet.

"We can talk while we do the potatoes."

83

"Okay. Just let me wash my hands and slip into my choring apron first."

By the time Loraine returned to the kitchen, Priscilla had everything ready.

"Mom, I—"

"Did you hear that—"

They'd both spoken at the same time.

Priscilla snickered. "You go ahead."

"No, you first, Mom."

"I was just going to say that when I went to the shoe and boot place in Topeka today, I overheard someone say that Paul's wife, Rachel, is moving back to Pennsylvania to be near her sisters."

"I guess that makes sense, since she has no family living here now that Paul's gone."

Priscilla nodded and handed Loraine a paring knife. "Now what'd you want to say to me?"

Loraine's mouth puckered. "Ella came into the hardware store this morning."

"That's nice. How's she doing these days?"

"As well as can be expected, under the circumstances." Loraine picked up a potato and started peeling it really fast.

"Slow down some, daughter." Priscilla touched Loraine's arm. "We're not in that big a hurry to get these potatoes done."

"Sorry, I'm just feeling a little frustrated right now."

"What are you frustrated about?"

Loraine started peeling again. "As I was saying, Ella came into the store, and she mentioned seeing you leaving the Lambrights' place this morning. Said you'd even waved at her."

Priscilla's neck grew warm, and the heat quickly spread to her face. "Uh. . .jah, I stopped by there on my way to Topeka."

"But the Lambrights' house isn't on the way to Topeka. You'd have had to go out of your way to drop by there."

"That's true enough, but I hadn't been over there since Wayne came home from the hospital, and I thought it would be good if I dropped by to see how he was doing."

Loraine tipped her head. "Did you talk to Wayne?"

"Jah. You're right about him being depressed."

Loraine flicked a potato peel that had landed on the counter into the sink. "Did he mention me?"

Priscilla shifted from one foot to the other and then leaned her full weight against the sink. "I. . .uh. . .guess your name did come up at some point during the conversation."

"You didn't say anything that would make things worse between me and Wayne, I hope."

"No, no, I'm sure I didn't." Priscilla glanced around, wishing she had some excuse to leave the room. If Loraine kept questioning her like this, she was likely to blurt out everything that had been said between her and Ada after Wayne had left the room.

"Well, I'm glad to know you didn't say anything that might hinder our relationship, because I'm going to try real hard to just be Wayne's friend and not pressure him about changing his mind." Loraine smiled, although it didn't quite seem genuine. "I think it's just a matter of time until Wayne and I are back together."

CHAPTER 13

Jake's heart pounded and his knuckles turned white as he gripped his steering wheel. Ever since he'd read about the accident several of his friends had been in, he hadn't been able to think of anything but how quickly he could get home. After he'd left the store in Libby, he'd gone to the ranch and dropped off the horses he'd bid on at the auction. Then, after explaining things to his boss and saying he wasn't sure when he'd be back, he'd thrown most of his things in his truck and started for Indiana.

As he neared the town of Middlebury, he had a decision to make. Should he stop and see Loraine first or go straight home to his folks?

I have to see Loraine, he decided. *I need to know if she was hurt in that van accident.*

Sweat dripped off Jake's forehead as he turned off the main road and started down the Millers' driveway.

Maybe I should have called first, he thought as he parked the truck near the barn. *No, they might not go out to their phone shed and check their answering machine regularly. Besides, after I've been gone so long, Loraine's probably angry with me and might have told me not to come by.*

Drawing in a quick breath to help steady his nerves, Jake stepped out of his truck and sprinted to the house. He'd just lifted

86

his hand to knock on the door when it swung open.

Jake moistened his lips with the tip of his tongue. "Is. . .uh. . . Loraine here?"

Priscilla's mouth hung slightly open as she gaped at him. "Jake Beechy. I—I didn't realize you'd come back to Indiana."

"I just got here. Read about the van accident and came right home. Is Loraine all right?"

"She's fine—only a few bumps and bruises." Priscilla's forehead wrinkled. "Some of the others didn't fare so well, though."

"Who all was hurt?"

Priscilla opened the door wider. "Let's go inside. It might be best if I let Loraine tell you about it."

Jake's heart hammered as he followed Priscilla down the hall. Just outside the kitchen door, she turned to him and said, "I'm sure whatever you have to say to my daughter you'd like to say in private, so I'll just leave you two alone."

When she disappeared into the living room, Jake wiped his sweaty hands on the sides of his blue jeans, sucked in a deep breath, and stepped into the kitchen.

～❧ ❧～

Loraine had just begun setting the table for breakfast when a young man with short-cropped, dark brown hair, dressed in blue jeans and a matching jacket, entered the kitchen.

Loraine's hands trembled so badly that the spoon she held clattered to the floor. "Jake."

He took a step toward her. "It's good to see you, Loraine. I came as soon as I found out about the accident."

Afraid she might topple over, Loraine sank into a chair at the table. "Wh–where have you been?"

"I've been working on a ranch in Montana. I had been to a horse auction and was on my way back to the ranch when I read an article in *The Budget* about a van accident in northern Indiana." He flopped into the chair across from her. "Your name was mentioned as one of those who'd been riding in the van, but it didn't say whether you'd been injured or not."

Loraine's head began to pound, and she closed her eyes tightly, hoping to halt the pain. In all the time Jake had been gone, he'd only written her two letters. He had promised he'd come back and would stay in touch, but he hadn't kept his promise. Of course, she'd promised to wait for him, and she'd broken that promise as well.

She could still see the way Jake had looked at her that last night they were together. She could hear his contagious laugh and even smell the licorice on his breath. . . .

"Loraine, there's something I need to tell you."

The urgency in Jake's tone caused Loraine to shiver.

"What is it, Jake? Why are you looking at me so seriously?"

Jake directed his horse and buggy to the side of the road and reached for Loraine's hand. "I. . .I'm planning to go away for a while."

"Go away?"

He nodded. "My cousin Sam, who used to live in Illinois, moved to Montana a few months ago, and. . .uh. . .I thought I'd spend the summer with him."

"Which Amish community in Montana did Sam move to?"

"None of them. Sam's working on a ranch in Montana for an English man who raises horses." Jake swallowed so hard that his Adam's apple bobbed up and down. "I want to try out the English way of life for a while—before I make a decision about joining the church." He paused and swiped his tongue across his lower lip. "The wages the man is offering per week is more than I can make working for my daed in a month, so I really can't pass on this opportunity."

Loraine's mouth hung slightly open. "What?"

"I said—"

"I heard what you said. I just can't believe you said it."

"It's not like I'll be gone forever. Probably just for the

summer, that's all." He squeezed her fingers and gave her one of his winning smiles. "You'll wait for me, won't you?"

Loraine sat, too numb to say a word. If Jake left now, what would it do to their relationship? She'd thought he'd been on the verge of asking her to marry him. She'd thought he would join the church this fall. If Jake went to Montana to work for an Englisher who raised horses, he might never come back.

"Say something, Loraine. Will you wait for me or not?"

Tears welled in her eyes. "For how long, Jake?"

"Until I come back to Indiana." Jake pulled her into his arms and kissed her on the mouth. "Just a few months, that's all," he whispered.

Loraine drew in a shaky breath and nodded slowly. "Jah, Jake. I'll wait for you."

"Loraine, did you hear what I said?"

Her eyes snapped open. "What was that?"

"The article in *The Budget* said that some people in the van had been seriously injured, and that three of them were killed. Who died, Loraine? Was it someone I know?"

Her throat constricted, and she had to swallow a couple of times before she could speak. "Katie's boyfriend, Timothy Lehman; Ella's brother, Raymond; and our driver, Paul Crawford are dead."

Jake groaned as he slowly shook his head. "I'm really sorry to hear that."

"Ella suffered a mild concussion, Andrew broke his arm, Jolene had damage to her auditory nerves, and Wayne lost one of his legs." Loraine paused a few seconds, hoping she wouldn't break down. "The rest of us had bumps and bruises. Oh, and Katie suffered great emotional distress."

"Hearing this news just makes me sick." Jake kept shaking his head. "I wish I'd stayed in better contact with everyone—especially you, Loraine. I should have been here for you."

"What happened, Jake? How come you quit writing and never came back until now?"

He dropped his gaze to the table. "I'm sorry, Loraine. I never meant to hurt you," he said, without really answering her question. "Seeing you now makes me realize what a fool I was. I never stopped caring for you. I was just so wrapped up in—"

"I'm engaged to Wayne."

"What?"

"I said I'm engaged to Wayne."

Jake's eyes widened as he lifted his gaze. "I had no idea you were seeing Wayne, much less planning to marry him. I—I can't believe it."

"When you quit writing, I was brokenhearted." Loraine paused again and drew in a shaky breath. "Wayne was there for me, first as my friend, and later, as the man I fell in love with."

"You're in love with Wayne?"

She nodded. "I wouldn't be planning to marry him if I wasn't."

Jake sat several minutes, staring at her in obvious disbelief. "Guess I don't have anyone to blame but myself for that." He plopped his elbows on the table and rested his chin in the palm of his hands.

"The accident changed everyone involved," Loraine said, unable to meet Jake's gaze. "I think it changed Wayne most of all."

"I imagine it's been hard for him to deal with the loss of his leg, huh?"

She nodded. "Wayne's been very depressed and negative ever since the amputation."

Jake tapped his finger against the little dimple in his chin, the way he'd always done when he was deep in thought. "If I hadn't left home, you and I would probably be married by now and maybe starting a family."

Loraine flinched. At one time, she had wanted a family with Jake; she'd loved him so much back then.

The sadness in Jake's blue-green eyes revealed the depth of his pain. "If I hadn't left home, that horrible accident might not have happened."

"Even if you'd stayed in Indiana, the accident might still have occurred. You could have been riding in the van with us that day."

Jake pulled his fingers through the top of his hair, causing it to stand straight up. Any other time, Loraine might have laughed, but not now.

"Where were you all headed to, anyway?" he asked.

"We were going to Hershey Park in Pennsylvania. It was supposed to be a fun day, but it turned into a nightmare."

"How'd the accident happen?"

Loraine quickly related the story, then said, "Paul ran off the road and hit a telephone pole." The memory of that day threatened to overtake her.

"If I'd known about it sooner, I would have come home right away."

"Are you here for good, or did you just come for a visit?"

He shrugged. "I–I'm not sure. Guess it all depends on how things go when I see my folks."

"You haven't been home yet?"

"Nope. Came here first thing. Guess I was hoping things would be the same between us and that we could start from where we left off."

She folded her arms. "That's not possible."

"I know." Jake rose from his seat. "I'm glad you're okay, Loraine, and I'm real sorry about the others." He moved quickly toward the door as though he couldn't wait to be on his way. "I'd better get going. See you around."

Jake disappeared out the back door, and Loraine moved over to the window and watched as he climbed into his truck. Seeing Jake again had stirred up feelings she thought were dead and buried. But exactly how deep the feelings went, she couldn't be sure.

Jake's hands shook as he headed down the road toward home. Seeing Loraine again had brought back a flood of memories. Hearing that she planned to marry Wayne had been like a kick in the belly.

It's my own dumb fault, he berated himself. *If I hadn't left home the way I did, she'd still be my girl, not Wayne's.*

He slapped the steering wheel with the palm of his hands. *I can't believe that two of my friends are dead or that Wayne lost one of his legs.* "It's not fair! Bad things shouldn't happen to good people!"

By the time Jake reached his folks' house, he was all worked up. He stopped the truck near the barn, wiped the sweat from his forehead, and headed for the house.

He found the back door open but stood on the porch a few minutes, rehearsing what he was going to say to his folks. Then, drawing in a deep breath, he stepped inside.

"Mom? Dad? Is anyone at home?"

"Jake? Oh Jake, is it really you?" Mom ran down the hall, her arms reaching for him.

"It's me all right." He gave her a hug.

"Ach! We've missed you so much," she said tearfully. "You've been gone such a long time, and we've been so worried. We— we were afraid something had happened to you." Mom's voice broke on a sob.

Jake kept his arms around her and patted her back until the sobs subsided. "I'm sorry, Mom. I didn't mean to make you worry."

"Well, you should be sorry!"

Jake whirled around and saw his father step into the kitchen. His face was red, and deep wrinkles creased his forehead. He obviously wasn't as happy to see Jake as Mom had been.

Jake took a step forward. "It's good to see you, Dad. I've missed you and Mom—and my brothers and sisters, too." He glanced around. "Where is the rest of the family? Are they at home?"

"Vern, Kyle, and Elmer are at school," Mom said. "Marilyn and Jeffrey both have jobs in Middlebury."

Before Jake could respond, Dad shook his finger at Jake and said, "Where have you been all this time?"

"I've been working at a horse ranch, just like I said in the letter I wrote when I first got to Montana."

Dad snorted. "One letter in nearly two years! You didn't even give us an address where we could write to you. What were you thinkin', Jake? Didn't you care enough about your family to keep in touch? How could you be so selfish and immature?"

Jake wiped the sweat from his brow. This was an inquisition—not the kind of homecoming he'd hoped for.

"I asked you a question!" Dad bellowed. "Why didn't you stay in touch with us?"

"I—I was afraid you'd pressure me to come home before I was ready."

"Are you ready now?" Dad stared at Jake through squinted eyelids.

"Maybe. If I can get my business going."

"What business is that?" Mom asked.

"I want to breed and train thoroughbred horses." Jake smiled. "That's what I've always wanted to do."

"Humph!" Dad grunted. "Shoein' horses isn't good enough for you anymore, huh?"

"It's never been about being good enough," Jake said. "I want to do something I enjoy, that's all."

Mom gave Jake a questioning look. "Does that mean you want to build your business here and join the Amish church?"

Jake tapped his chin as he contemplated the best way to answer her question. "I can't make a commitment yet. I need to wait and see how it goes."

"What's wrong?" Dad hollered. "Are you opposed to our plain and simple lifestyle now that you've been out in the modern, English world?"

"It's not that. I just can't make a decision about my future right now."

Mom gave Jake's shoulder a little pat, as if in doing so, he would know that what he'd said had been good enough for her. "Are you hungry, son? Would you like me to fix you something to eat?"

He smiled. "That'd be real nice. Danki."

"At least he hasn't forgotten how to speak the Dietch," Dad muttered.

Refusing to let his father's cool reception rile him, Jake followed his mother to the kitchen. He'd have a little something to eat, then head over to the Lambrights' to see Wayne. He only hoped he'd have a better reception there than he'd had here and at Loraine's.

CHAPTER 14

A knock sounded on the back door, but Wayne chose to ignore it. He'd been sitting in his wheelchair, staring out the living room window ever since breakfast, and he didn't want to be disturbed.

A few minutes later, Mom stepped into the room and touched Wayne's shoulder. "You have a visitor."

"Who is it?"

"Jake Beechy."

Wayne's eyebrows shot up. "Jake's back in Indiana?"

"Apparently so." Mom moved to stand in front of Wayne. "He's waiting on the porch."

Wayne's palms grew sweaty. If Jake had come home, he and Loraine might get back together. After all, she wasn't tied to Wayne any longer, and she had been Jake's girlfriend before he'd gone away. On the other hand, Jake might just be here for a visit and nothing more.

"Did you hear what I said, son?" Mom asked.

He nodded. "I guess you'd better let him in."

"Are you sure you're up to company?"

"Jah."

Mom left the room, and when she returned a few minutes later, Jake was at her side. He looked good—suntanned skin;

thick, shiny hair; and muscles in his arms that pointed to lots of hard work.

"I was sorry to hear about your accident," Jake said, stepping up to Wayne. "I came as soon as I heard the news."

"From what your folks have said, you haven't had much contact with them since you've been gone. How'd you find out about the accident?" Wayne asked.

"I read it in *The Budget*." Jake motioned to the sofa. "Mind if I take a seat?"

"Suit yourself."

Jake glanced at Wayne's missing leg and grimaced. "I'm real sorry that happened to you. Are you in a lot of pain?"

Wayne nodded. "Sometimes it feels like my leg's still there, and then the throbbing pain nearly drives me crazy. It's called phantom pain."

Jake winced as though he were the one in pain. "I've never heard of having pain where there's no limb."

"Guess most amputees experience it to some degree. It's supposed to get better in time, but I'm not holding my breath." Wayne shifted in his wheelchair. "My back's been hurting ever since the accident, too."

"Have you been to see the chiropractor?"

"Nope. Figured it would quit hurting on its own, but if it doesn't get better soon, I'll probably go in."

"That's a good idea." Jake cleared his throat a couple of times. "I. . .uh. . .went over to see Loraine awhile ago. I was surprised when she said you and she had been dating. I. . .uh. . .had no idea you were interested in her."

"Loraine was really hurt when you left the way you did, and if you'd continued writing to her, you would have known." Irritation bubbled in Wayne's soul. "'Course if you'd continued writing, then she probably never would have turned to me."

"I know what I did was wrong, but I can't undo the past. I just want Loraine to be happy." Jake tapped one finger along the edge of his chin. "She said you and she were engaged to be married."

"That's right, we were."

"What do you mean *were?*"

"After the accident, I broke our engagement."

"How come?"

Wayne motioned to his stump. "Thanks to losing this, I won't be able to farm anymore, which means I can't provide a decent living for us. That's why I called off the wedding."

Jake's eyes widened. "Loraine never said a thing about that. She made it seem like a wedding was being planned."

Wayne shrugged. "Guess she doesn't want to accept the fact that I'm a cripple and that I'm not going to be able to support her."

"But won't you be getting a prosthesis?"

"Maybe. If I decide to go that way."

"I'm sure you'll be able to do lots of things you used to do once you get an artificial limb."

"Maybe so, but it'll slow me down considerably. Besides, my daed's already leased out our land so there's nothing for me to farm."

"What's he going to do if he doesn't farm?"

Wayne glanced up at the wall where a mounted deer head hung over the fireplace. "He's opening his own taxidermy business." He grunted. "Pop wants me to learn the trade and go into business with him."

"Might not be a bad idea. Sounds like an interesting trade if you ask me."

"So, what brings you back to Indiana?" Wayne asked, changing the subject. He didn't want to talk about Pop's new business. "Are you here to stay, or did you come for a visit?"

"I may be staying—I don't know yet. I came back because I found out about the van accident. I was concerned about you and the others, and I wanted to see for myself how everyone was doing."

More than likely it was Loraine you were concerned about, since the two of you used to date, Wayne thought ruefully. "So what were you doing while you were gone so long?" he asked.

"I was working at a horse ranch in Montana."

"I heard something about that but figured you'd be back long before now."

"I would have, but—" Jake's voice trailed off and he stared at the floor.

Several minutes went by before Jake finally stood. "Guess I'd better get going. I still need to visit the Lehmans and Yoders and offer them my condolences. Then I'll probably swing by and see Katie and Jolene."

"You won't find 'em at home."

"How do you know that?"

"Jolene went to Pennsylvania to learn how to speak with her hands and read lips. The accident left her unable to hear."

"That's too bad."

"Jah, and Katie's in Sarasota with her grandparents, trying to come to grips with the loss of Timothy."

Jake slowly shook his head. "Seems like everyone riding in the van was affected in some way or another."

Wayne nodded. "None of our lives will ever be the same."

Jake edged toward the door. "It was good seeing you, Wayne. I'll stop by again soon."

"Before you go, there's something else I'd like to say," Wayne called over his shoulder.

Jake turned around. "What's that?"

"I hope you don't think I stole your girl while you were gone. Loraine and I didn't get together until you'd been gone a year and had stopped writing to her."

Jake's face turned crimson. "Don't worry about it. What's done is done. See you around, Wayne."

"Jah," Wayne mumbled as Jake went out the door, "what's done is done."

※ ⁂

As Jake drove away from the Lambrights', his stomach clenched so hard, he nearly doubled over. It was a shock seeing his friend sitting in a wheelchair with only one leg. It was a bigger shock to see the gloomy look on Wayne's face. He'd been so full of life when they were boys, always trying out new things and cracking one joke after another. Today he hadn't even cracked a smile.

Of course, Jake reasoned, *if it was me who'd lost a leg, I probably wouldn't be smiling or cracking jokes, either. I wish there was something I could do to make things better for Wayne. I wish I could undo the past.*

～⚬～

Ella had just taken a tray of peanut butter cookies from the oven when she heard a vehicle pull into the yard. She peered out the kitchen window. A blue pickup truck stopped near the barn, but she didn't recognize the dark-haired man who got out. When he sprinted toward the house, she wiped her hands on a towel and moved toward the door.

When Ella opened it, her heart felt as if it had jumped right into her throat. The man who stood before had short-cropped hair and tanned, muscular arms. He might not look the same as the young, impetuous teenager who'd left home a few years ago, but the deep dimple in the middle of his chin and his sparkling blue-green eyes gave him away. It was Jake Beechy.

"Hi, Ella," he said. "I came by to say I'm really sorry to hear about Raymond."

Tears sprang to Ella's eyes at the mention of her brother's name, and she blinked a couple of times to keep them from spilling over. "He was too young to die, and so were Timothy and our driver Paul." She swallowed hard. If she wasn't careful, it would be easy to let bitterness take over. "It's been a long time since we've seen you, Jake. Are you home for good?"

"I haven't decided yet."

"I guess you know that Loraine and Wayne got engaged while you were gone."

"Uh-huh. I also know they've recently broken up."

Ella's skin prickled as her face heated up. "I hope you don't have ideas about getting back with Loraine."

"Guess I'll have to see how it goes with her and Wayne first."

Ella clenched her fists so hard that her fingernails dug into her palms. "Things will work out for Wayne and Loraine, so don't even think about trying to get back with her."

"You don't have to get so riled up. I never said I was getting back with her. I just said I'd have to wait and see how it goes."

"So you came back here thinking you could pick up where you left off with Loraine?"

"It's not like that. I came back because I read about the accident. I never even knew Loraine and Wayne had started dating until I spoke with her earlier today."

"Jah, well, you'd be doing us all a favor if you got in that fancy truck of yours and went right on back to your horse ranch in Montana." Ella's hands shook, and her voice cracked on the last word. "You hurt Loraine once, and I won't let you hurt her again!"

Jake's eyes flashed angrily. "You may be Loraine's cousin, but you're not her keeper!"

"I never said I was. I care about Loraine. She's been through a lot lately, and I don't want to see her go through any more."

"I agree with you there. I really think Loraine needs all the support she can get right now." Jake looked Ella right in the eye, as if daring her to say more. "I'm going to give Loraine my support, no matter what you say!"

"You're just saying that because you think it's what I want to hear." Ella shook her finger at him. "I don't trust you as far as I can throw one of my daed's horses. I'll bet you came back home just to stir up trouble."

"You think you know everything, Ella. You were like that even when we were kinner." Jake turned and tromped down the steps.

Ella went back into the house, slamming the door behind her. "Jake Beechy, you're a selfish, immature man!"

CHAPTER 15

Wayne lay stretched out on his bed, watching the shadows of morning lurch off the ceiling and studying the tiny cracks where the ceiling met the walls. He'd had another rough night, tossing, turning, rumpling the sheets, and fighting the phantom pain, as well as a muscle spasm in his back. Around two o'clock, he'd finally quit fighting the pain and had taken a pill. He'd slept fitfully after that, but it was better than lying awake, thinking and brooding about the past. Life had no meaning for him anymore. He felt like he was merely going through the motions of living.

Wayne rolled over and gave his pillow a good whack. He'd been cheated out of a normal life, and it wasn't fair! He'd given up the only woman he'd ever loved, and he'd never love anyone that much again.

He covered his ears in an attempt to stop the agonizing thoughts raging in his head, but it did no good. Jerking the pillow out from under his head, he pitched it across the room. Then he grabbed the damp, wrinkled sheets and pulled himself to a sitting position.

"I need some air," he panted, lowering himself into his wheelchair. He rolled across the floor to the open window and drew in several deep breaths.

Finally, his anger faded to a sense of despair. He could fight this for all he was worth, but it wouldn't change a thing. No matter how much he longed for it, his leg would never grow back.

He rolled his wheelchair back to the small bedside table and picked up the glass of water. Tipping his head back, he allowed the cool liquid to trickle down his parched throat. *Maybe I'll feel better after I've had something to eat.*

He slipped on a clean shirt and struggled with his trousers. Seeing that he'd left the dresser drawer open, and knowing Mom would have something to say about it if he left it that way, he kicked it shut with his one and only foot. The dresser trembled and nearly toppled over. A simple thing like getting dressed, which he'd previously taken for granted, had become a tedious, frustrating chore, and it made him angry.

By the time Wayne wheeled himself out of the bedroom and made his way down the hall toward the aroma of spicy sausage sizzling in the frying pan, he was pretty worked up.

Mom turned from the stove and smiled when he entered the room. "I was wondering if you were up. I was just getting ready to come see if you needed my help getting dressed."

"I'm not a *boppli*!" he snapped. "I don't need anyone's help getting dressed!"

Mom frowned, and her forehead wrinkles ran together. "Of course you're not a baby, but I know how difficult it is for you to manage some things, so I just thought maybe I could—"

"You thought I needed babying. That's what you thought!" Wayne gripped the armrests on his wheelchair until his hands cramped. "Ever since I came home from the hospital, all you've done is hover over me and do everything I should be trying to do on my own!" His voice shook, and he nearly choked on the words.

Mom's eyes narrowed. "How can you say such a thing?"

He pushed his wheelchair up to the table. "Because it's how I feel."

A look of concern flashed in her eyes, and a few seconds ticked by before she spoke. "Maybe the problem isn't me trying to help you. Maybe the problem is you not wanting to rely on anyone for help."

Unable to meet his mother's piercing gaze, Wayne kept his eyes focused on the table. "Maybe. . .maybe. . . It's all just a bunch of *maybe*s," he muttered. "Maybe my pain will get better. Maybe I'll adjust to having only one leg. Maybe it would have been better if I had died in that accident. Then you wouldn't have to put up with my moods!"

She turned his wheelchair around to make him face her, grabbed his shoulders, and gave him a good shake. "Don't you talk that way, Wayne! You ought to thank the good Lord that you're still alive!"

Wayne opened his mouth to spew out more angry words but stopped when he felt a nudge at his heart. His self-pity was taking hold of him—making him say hurtful things, making him turn into a bitter, angry man. He pivoted the wheelchair back around, propped his elbows on the table, and let his forehead fall forward into his hands.

"I know you're hurting, son, but things will get better in time," Mom said in a voice that sounded more forced than cheerful. "You just need to be patient." She placed a glass of grapefruit juice on the table in front of him. "By the time your daed comes in from the barn, I'll have breakfast ready. In the meantime, why don't you have some of this?"

Wayne picked up the glass and flinched when the sharp taste of the tangy juice hit his tongue. "I'm really not hungry. I think I'll go out to the barn and see if Pop needs my help with anything."

"Oh, but you can't—"

"Jah, I can!" Wayne propelled his wheelchair across the room and went out the door. He needed time alone. Needed time to sort out his thoughts.

As he rolled down the ramp and headed across the yard, a brisk wind rustled the cornstalks in the fields and blew leaves from the trees. A wet, earthy smell wafted up to his nose. The falling leaves reminded him of a deer's ear flickering in the distance. It was

WANDA E. BRUNSTETTER

the first time since the accident that he'd really noticed what was going on outside. It was the first time he'd realized that fall had definitely made an appearance.

Wayne moved on until he came to the barn. When he opened the door, a shaft of sunlight filtered through the beams in the barn, and the smell of freshly placed hay assaulted his senses.

He wheeled across the floor and spotted his father coming out of one of the horse's stalls.

"How are you feeling this morning?" Pop asked with a smile. "Did you sleep any better last night?"

Wayne shook his head. "Besides the phantom pains plaguing me, my back went into spasms. Finally had to give in and take some medicine for the pain. Not that it helped very much."

"Hopefully, the phantom pains will go away soon, and then you won't have to take the medication anymore." Pop moved closer to Wayne and lowered himself to a bale of hay.

"Jah, I'm sure that things will go better for me soon." The words rang false, even to Wayne's own ears. He'd only said them because he thought it was what his dad wanted to hear.

Pop clasped Wayne's shoulder. "Maybe you ought to see the chiropractor and let him work on your back."

Wayne nodded slowly. "I've been thinkin' on that. Might call after breakfast and see if they can get me in sometime today."

"That's a good idea. When you find out what time, let me know, and I'll stop whatever I'm doing and take you in for the appointment."

Wayne cringed. He hated relying on others to take him everywhere. He'd never had to be so dependent before, and it stuck in his craw. "If you could hitch my horse to the buggy, maybe I can manage to drive myself to the chiropractor's office."

"No way!" Pop shook his head. "Your mamm would never go for that, and you know it."

Wayne grunted. "Mom thinks I can't do anything for myself. She treats me like a boppli, and I'm getting real sick of it!"

"I know she does, but I think in this situation, she would be right. If you're going to see the chiropractor, then I'd best take you there."

Wayne shrugged and blew out his breath. "Jah, okay…whatever you say."

Pop smiled and thumped Wayne on the back. "Is breakfast about ready? Is that why you came out to the barn?"

"Mom's still working on it." Wayne's shoulders tensed. "I really came out here to get away from her for a while."

A look of concern flashed across Pop's face. "Did she say something to upset you?"

"She hovers all the time." Wayne grunted. "She thinks I'm handicapped."

"Isn't that how you see yourself?"

Wayne shrugged. "Maybe so, but that doesn't mean I want to be treated like a boppli. I can still do some things on my own."

"I hear bitterness in your tone, son. Don't let it consume you," Pop said, gently shaking Wayne's arm. "Tragedies can either drive people away from God or draw them closer to Him."

"Jah, well, it would be a whole lot easier for me to feel close to God if He'd give me back my leg."

"You need to quit feeling sorry for yourself and ask God to help you be all you can be. He'll give you the grace to deal with your disability if you lean on Him and set your bitterness aside."

Wayne grunted in response.

Pop squeezed Wayne's shoulder. "Someone brought in a nice-looking turkey they'd shot the other day, and it needs to be stuffed. Why don't you join me in my shop later today and help with the procedure?"

"No, thanks."

"Have you got something better to do, or is your refusal to help me because you're hurting too bad?"

Wayne pulled his fingers through the ends of his thick, wavy hair. "After I call the chiropractor, I thought I might take a nap and try to get back some of the sleep I missed out on last night."

Pop gave a nod and rose to his feet. "I'm heading in to see about breakfast. Are you coming?"

"I'm not hungry. Just go on ahead without me."

"Suit yourself." Pop shrugged and headed out the door.

Wayne slouched in his wheelchair and closed his eyes. He wondered how he was going to get through another day.

~ ❦ ~

As Loraine headed down the driveway to get the mail, the wind rustled the leaves at her feet. The cool breeze carved a scent of damp, musty air to her nostrils. Fall was here; there was no doubt about it.

Until the accident that had changed the course of her life, she'd been looking forward to fall—and to her marriage to Wayne.

I have to keep my mind on other things, she chided herself. *It does me no good to keep dwelling on this.*

Her footsteps quickened. Fallen leaves crackled beneath her feet with each step she took. She opened the mailbox and was pleased to find two letters—one postmarked from Lancaster County, Pennsylvania, and the other one from Sarasota, Florida.

Hurrying up the driveway, she seated herself on the porch steps and tore open Jolene's letter from Pennsylvania:

Dear Loraine:

I wanted you to know that I've decided to stay with my daed's sister indefinitely. She's teaching me sign language and how to read lips, but I have so much to learn, and it's going to take some time. I miss you and everyone in my family, but I know I'm where I should be right now.

How are things going there with you? Is Wayne healing from his surgery? Has he gotten a prosthesis? Have you set another date for your wedding yet?

Loraine swallowed hard as hot tears pushed against her eyelids. She missed Jolene so much—missed not being able to talk with her and share her disappointment over Wayne breaking their engagement.

She finished Jolene's letter and opened the one from Florida. It was from Katie's mother:

Dear Loraine:

I'll be coming home sometime next week, but Katie won't be with me. She wants to stay with her grandparents awhile longer. She's still grieving over Timothy, and her depression and fear of riding in a car seem to have gotten worse. I pray that someday soon Katie will be happy and well-adjusted again, and then she'll return home.

Loraine's eyes glazed over, and she blinked rapidly to keep her tears from falling onto the paper. She placed the letters on the small table near the back door and covered her face with her hands. It wasn't right that Katie and Jolene had been forced to leave their homes and family. It wasn't right, what had happened to them.

Horse hooves clomped against the pavement like distant thunder, causing Loraine to open her eyes. She saw a horse and buggy rumbling down the street, then turning into their driveway.

She quickly dried her eyes and wiped her damp hands on her dress, waiting to see who'd come calling.

A few minutes later, Jake stepped out of the buggy, dressed in Amish clothes.

"I'm surprised to see you driving a horse and buggy," she said when he joined her on the porch. "Where's your truck?"

"I parked it behind my daed's barn." The stiffening breeze ruffled Jake's hair as he gave her a deep-dimpled smile. "I figure as long as I'm home, I oughta do what I can to keep the peace." He touched the brim of his straw hat. "I'll be wearing Amish clothes and driving a horse and buggy as long as I'm here."

A strange sensation prickled the wisps of hair on the back of Loraine's neck, and she shivered. If Jake had decided to stop driving his truck and had put on Amish clothes again, did that mean he was planning to stay permanently?

"If you're cold, maybe we should go inside," he suggested.

"I'm fine. Just felt a little chill from the wind, that's all."

"So you don't want me to go inside with you then?"

"It. . .it's not that. My mamm's busy cleaning, and the floors might still be wet."

"Okay." Jake plunked down on the step beside Loraine. "Looks like you've been out to the mailbox." He motioned to the letters on the table.

She nodded. "One's from Jolene, and the other one's from Katie's mamm. It looks like neither one of my cousins will be coming home anytime soon."

"Guess they're in the place they need to be for now." Jake leaned forward, resting his elbows on his knees. "Sure have been a lot of changes around here since I left home."

"Jah—especially since the accident."

"I should never have left home. If I'd stayed, a lot of things would be different."

Loraine looked away. She couldn't allow herself to think about how things would be if Jake hadn't gone. She couldn't afford to take her eyes off her goal to marry Wayne. She'd promised him her whole heart, and he needed her now, more than ever, even if he didn't seem to realize it.

A sharp wind blew under the eaves of the porch, whisking one of the letters away. Loraine jumped up and reached for it. Jake did the same. They grabbed the letter at the same time.

When their fingers touched, Loraine jumped back, feeling as if she'd been burned. "I've got it," she murmured.

"I can see that." Jake released the letter and jammed his hands into his trouser pockets.

They stood staring at each other until Jake's horse whinnied and stamped his foot.

"Looks like Midnight's getting impatient," he said, glancing over his shoulder. "I guess I'd better get going."

"What'd you come by for?" she asked. "Was it anything important?"

"Not really. I just wanted to see how you were doing."

I'd be doing better if you hadn't come back to Indiana. She forced a smile. "I'm all right; just taking one day at a time."

"That's the best way, I guess." Jake reached his hand out, like he might touch her, but he pulled it quickly away and turned toward his buggy.

She breathed a sigh of relief.

"See you later, Loraine," he mumbled as he walked away.

Loraine gathered up her letters and turned toward the door. *I hope it's awhile before I see you again, Jake,* she thought as she stepped into the house. *Being with you only confuses me.*

❧ ❧

"I'm a real idiot," Jake berated himself as he headed for home. "I shouldn't have tried to take Loraine's hand. I probably shouldn't have gone over there this morning."

Jake flicked the reins to get his horse moving faster and continued to fume.

He'd gone over to Loraine's place with the intent of telling her about his conversation with Wayne the day before and to see if he could tell if she might still have an interest in him. He'd changed his mind, though. If there was any chance at all of him rebuilding a relationship with Loraine, he'd have to go slow. For now, the best thing he could do was be her friend, and that's exactly what he planned to do.

❧ ❧

"I'm glad you were able to squeeze me in today," Wayne said as Dr. Hopkins helped him onto the table. "My back's so spasmed, I can barely move. Between that and the phantom pains I've been having, I'm about to climb the walls."

"I took a class not long ago and learned about a technique that involves something I think might be helpful in relieving not only your back pain, but the phantom pains you're experiencing, as well."

"Something besides chiropractic adjustments?" Wayne asked.

The doctor nodded. "Are you familiar with acupuncture?"

Wayne nodded. "I've never had it done to me, though."

"Well, there's a fairly new technique that involves tapping one's finger along certain acupuncture points, while stating an affirmation. If you're willing to give it a try, I'd like to show you how it's done."

"With the kind of pain I've been having, I'm willing to try most anything."

The doctor gave Wayne's arm a gentle squeeze. "All right then. I'll do some adjustments on your back, and then I'll teach you how and where to tap, and what you'll need to say while you're doing it."

Wayne rolled onto his side and closed his eyes. He didn't know what kind of weird thing he'd agreed to try, but if there was even a remote possibility that it might help relieve his phantom pains, he'd stand on his head and wiggle his ears.

CHAPTER 16

"Looks like we're gonna have ourselves one less sheep," Pop said when he entered the house after breakfast on Friday morning.

"What happened?" Mom asked. "Did some critter kill one of our sheep?"

"One of the young lambs got into the horses' pasture and got her left front leg stepped on pretty bad."

"Is she dead?" Mom asked.

Pop shook his head. "Nope, but her leg's badly mangled. I'm afraid she's gonna have to be put down."

"Did you call the vet to see if he can amputate the leg?" Wayne asked from where he sat in his wheelchair near the stove.

"Nope." Pop gave his beard a quick tug. "Even if the vet takes the ewe's leg, she won't be good for much."

The hair on the back of Wayne's neck bristled. "Did you put me down because I lost a leg? Do you think I'm good for nothing?"

Pop's face reddened, and a muscle on the side of his neck quivered.

"Of course you're good for something," Mom said before Pop could respond. "You're our only son, and we love you just as much now as we did before the accident."

Pop nodded vigorously. "You're mamm's right, and I didn't mean you were good for nothing, Wayne."

"What did you mean?" Wayne asked.

"I meant that you can't compare the lamb's situation to your having lost a leg or how it's dealt with."

"Well, I think that ewe has as much right to live as anyone." Wayne pointed to the stump of his leg. "I'm gonna have to adjust to only one leg, and so can the lamb."

Pop gave his earlobe a tug. "The lamb would need a lot of care, and with all the chores I have to do, I don't need another one right now."

"I'll look after it myself."

"Oh, Wayne, do you think you're up to that?" Mom asked.

Irritation flared in Wayne's chest. "I'm not a complete invalid!"

"I know that, but—"

"If he thinks he can do it, then maybe we should give him the chance." Pop squeezed Wayne's shoulder. "I'll go down to the phone shed and call the vet right now. If he thinks it's a good idea to take the ewe's leg rather than putting her down, then she's all yours."

Wayne smiled. It was the first genuine smile he'd been able to muster since the accident. He'd make sure that lamb survived, no matter what anyone said!

～❦ ❧～

Loraine had just left the hardware store to take her lunch break when she spotted Jake in the parking lot, getting out of his buggy.

Her mouth went dry, and her palms grew sweaty. So much for trying to avoid her ex-boyfriend. She wished she had gone out the back door, but the Wana Cup Restaurant was across the street, closer to the front of the shopping center where the hardware store was located. *Maybe Jake won't see me*, she thought as she hurried her steps. But it was too late. Jake was heading her way.

"Heard you were working here," he said, stepping up to Loraine. "I didn't think you'd be getting off work so early in the day, though."

She wiped her damp hands on the sides of her dress and forced a smile. "I work until four. I'm on way over to Wana Cup for some lunch."

Jake reached under his straw hat and scratched the side of his head. "I haven't had lunch yet, either. Mind if I join you?"

Truthfully, she did mind. Being with Jake after all this time made her feel uncomfortable and jittery. It hadn't always been so. Loraine used to long to be with Jake. She had felt happy and carefree back when they were together. Things were different now. She was in love with Wayne. It was too late for her and Jake.

Jake nudged her arm. "Your silence makes me wonder if you'd rather not have lunch with me."

"It's not that." She didn't want to appear rude. "I. . .uh. . .guess it would be okay."

A wide smile spread across Jake's handsome face. "Great! I'll even treat you to an ice cream cone for dessert."

She smiled, despite her reservations. "That does sound good."

He nudged her again. "We'd better get going before the restaurant gets too busy with the lunch crowd, and then there'll be no seats left for us."

～❧ ❧～

As Jake and Loraine sat at a small table near the back of the restaurant, eating burgers and fries, he studied the curves of her slender face, her ebony-colored eyes—even the smattering of freckles on her nose. Being with her again made him keenly aware that he'd missed her more than he'd realized. He knew he would have to work hard at rebuilding the walls of trust between them. Loraine had trusted him to come home, and he'd trusted her to wait for him. They'd both let each other down.

"This burger is sure good. I didn't realize how hungry I was until I started to eat." Loraine dabbed at the corners of her mouth with a napkin.

"You've got a spot of mustard on your chin." Jake reached across the table and blotted her chin with his napkin. He was pleased when she didn't pull away.

113

They ate in companionable silence for a while, and then Jake decided to bring up the subject of Wayne.

"I went to see Wayne the other day."

"Was he surprised to see you?"

He nodded. "You were right about him being depressed. He didn't seem like himself at all."

She reached for her soda and took a drink. "He's not the same. Because of the accident, none of us will ever be the same."

"I was surprised when he told me that you two had broken up. When you and I spoke, you never mentioned that."

"We…uh…didn't really break up. Wayne called off the wedding, but I'm sure when he feels better he'll change his mind."

"What if he doesn't?"

"He will."

"How do you know?"

"Because he loves me. Eventually, he'll realize that losing his leg doesn't mean we can't get married."

"What about you, Loraine? Do you love Wayne?"

"Of course I do. I wouldn't have agreed to marry him if I didn't."

"Do you love him as much as you did me?"

Loraine's face flamed. "That's not a fair question, Jake."

"I think it is."

She toyed with her knife and stared at the table.

He reached over and covered her hand with his. "I didn't mean to upset you. I just need to know if the love you feel for Wayne is stronger than what you felt for me."

Deep wrinkles formed in her forehead, and she pulled her hand away. "We shouldn't even be having this conversation."

"Why not?"

"Because you gave up your right to ask anything of me when you left home and didn't come back."

"I made a mistake; I realize that now."

"What's done is done. It's in the past."

"There's still the future." He laced his hands behind his head and stared at her.

"My future's with Wayne."

Jake was tempted to argue but decided it was best not to push. Even though Wayne had made it pretty clear the other day that he wasn't going to marry Loraine, she seemed convinced—almost determined—that he would change his mind.

The best thing I can do, Jake told himself, *is be patient and let Loraine know that I want to be her friend. Maybe after we spend a little more time together, she'll realize that she loves me more than she does Wayne.*

~❧ ❧~

When Ada stepped into the Wana Cup Restaurant, the tangy odor of cooked onions and grilling burgers wafted up to her nose. Her stomach rumbled. She'd been running errands all morning and had worked up quite an appetite. She was also desperately in need of a cup of coffee.

She headed for the back of the restaurant, thinking she'd use the restroom before finding a table, and screeched to a halt. Loraine sat at a table on the other side of the room, and Jake Beechy sat across from her!

That sneaky fellow wasted no time in trying to get her back, Ada fumed. *From the way she's looking at him, I'd guess she wants that, too. I knew Loraine wasn't right for my son. I've known it all along!*

Ada compressed her lips as she contemplated what to do. Should she go over to their table and say something—ask what they were doing together? Or would it be better to leave the restaurant and say nothing to Jake and Loraine?

Her hands trembled as she held them tightly at her sides. *I think it would be best if I don't make a scene here in the restaurant. I need to go home and tell Wayne what I've seen. He needs to know that the woman he loves was seen having lunch with another man—the man she used to date, no less.*

Ada whirled around and marched out the door.

CHAPTER 17

"Where's Wayne?" Ada called to Crist as she guided her horse and buggy up to the hitching rail near their barn.

Crist motioned to the barn. "He's in there with that crippled sheep he's taken on as a project."

"I need to speak to him." Ada stepped out of the buggy. "Would you mind taking care of my horse for me?"

"Sure, I can do that." Crist took the horse's reins, and Ada scurried into the barn. She found Wayne sitting in his wheelchair, holding the crippled lamb in his lap.

He turned his head and smiled at her. "Tripod's doing pretty good. I think she's gonna make it, Mom."

Ada tipped her head. "Tripod?"

"Jah. Just like a camera tripod that has three legs."

She lifted her gaze to the beams overhead and rolled her eyes. "If you ask me, Tripod's a silly name for a lamb."

He rubbed the lamb's ears, then patted its head. "I think it fits her just fine."

Ada shrugged, then lowered herself to a bale of straw, smoothing the skirt of her dress as she did so. "There's something I need to tell you."

"There's something I want to tell you, too."

"What's that?"

"When I was at the chiropractor's having him work on my back, he showed me a new technique to try for my phantom pain."

"Oh, what's that?"

"It involves tapping your fingers on different acupuncture parts of the body while you make an affirmation."

Ada's eyebrows lifted high on her forehead. "What kind of *narrisch* treatment is that?"

"It's not foolish. It's proven to work on a lot of different things, and Dr. Hopkins thought I should at least give it a try."

"And have you?"

He nodded. "It did bring some relief, so I'm going to keep doing it every day and see how it goes."

Ada clicked her tongue against the roof of her mouth. "I can't believe you'd actually try something like that! Sounds like a bunch of hooey to me, and it might even border on superstition."

"It's not superstition! I thought you'd be glad to know that I've had less pain."

"I am glad about that, but—"

"What was it you wanted to talk to me about?" Wayne asked, feeling the need for a change of subject.

Ada's eyes narrowed into tiny slits. "Before I left Shipshewana around noon, I decided to get some lunch at the Wana Cup Restaurant. You'll never guess who I saw there."

"Who was it?"

"Loraine and Jake Beechy—sitting at the same table together!"

"Why would I care about that? Loraine has a right to have lunch with anyone she pleases." Wayne's face reddened. "I broke up with her, remember?"

She nodded. "I just thought you'd like to know how fickle she is. Couldn't even wait a week before she took up with her old boyfriend."

"Like I said, she has the right to see Jake if she wants to. In fact, it's probably for the best. Since Loraine and I won't be getting married, she needs to move on with her life."

"Do you truly mean that?"

He gave a slow nod.

"I'm real glad to hear it." Ada smiled and touched his shoulder. "Since I didn't eat lunch in Shipshewana after all, I'm going into the house to fix myself something to eat. If you haven't eaten already, I'd be happy to fix something for you, too."

"No thanks. Pop and I had a ham sandwich about an hour ago."

"Wouldn't you at least like to come inside and keep me company?"

He shook his head. "You go ahead. I'm gonna stay out here with Tripod awhile longer."

"All right then." Ada patted the top of Wayne's head and left the barn, wearing a satisfied smile. It looked like she wouldn't have to do a thing to see that Wayne didn't marry Loraine. He'd taken care of that himself, and she was pleased that he seemed to have accepted the fact that he was better off without Loraine. She just wished there was some way to get him back with his old girlfriend again. Too bad Fern and her family had moved to Ohio.

❧ ❧

As Loraine pedaled her bicycle home from work that afternoon, she allowed her thoughts to wander. She had enjoyed being with Jake today. Sitting in Wana Cup, eating a juicy burger, had brought back memories of the days they'd been dating. Jake was fun to be with, and his lighthearted attitude made him easy to talk to.

Of course, she reasoned, *Wayne was easy to talk to before the accident. Now I feel like I'm talking to the barn wall whenever I visit with him. If he'd only take down the barrier he's erected and let me get close to him again.*

She blinked against stinging tears, remembering how peaceful and content she used to feel when she and Wayne were together. Now she felt as if she was skating on thin ice. Every time she opened her mouth, she was afraid she'd say the wrong thing. She thought about the verse of scripture that Ella had attached to the loaf of friendship bread she'd given her a few weeks ago. She wondered if she would ever really have the desires of her heart that Psalm 37:4 spoke of.

Of course, she thought, *I'm not sure what my desires are anymore.* A few months ago, Loraine had known exactly what she wanted and had looked forward to the future with gladness. Now she just felt confused and frustrated.

Wayne and I will never get back together if we don't see each other. I've got to go over to his place and check on him from time to time, even though he asked me not to. I'll just have to be careful what I say when I'm near him and make sure I don't bring up the subject of marriage.

Loraine turned her bike up the road leading to the Lambrights' place. She would stop there right now and say hello to Wayne before she went home.

She left the bike around the back of the house, stepped onto the porch, and knocked on the door. A few seconds later, Ada answered her knock.

"I came by to see how Wayne's doing," Loraine said. "Is he at home?"

"He is, but he doesn't want to see you." Ada's tone was about as cold as a block of ice. There wasn't even a hint of a smile on her face.

Loraine's jaw clenched. "I know what he said, but I thought—"

"I saw you with Jake Beechy at the Wana Cup Restaurant today." Ada's lips compressed tightly together. "Are you two dating again?"

"No, of course not. I was taking my lunch break when I ran into Jake. He asked if he could join me."

Ada folded her arms and leaned against the doorjamb. "Humph! You could have said no."

Irritation bubbled in Loraine's soul. "I didn't want to be rude. I thought—"

"What's going on?" Wayne asked as he wheeled up to the door.

Loraine smiled, feeling a sense of relief. "I'm glad to see you, Wayne. I came by to see how you're doing and ask if there's

119

anything I can to do to help."

"We're getting along just fine," Ada said in a none-too-friendly tone.

Wayne looked up at his mother. "If you don't mind, I'd like to talk to Loraine for a few minutes alone."

Ada's face blanched. "But you said you didn't want her coming over here again."

"I know what I said, but I want to talk to Loraine alone."

Loraine held her breath and waited for Ada's response.

After several seconds ticked by, Ada gave a muffled grunt, spun around on her heel, and marched into the house.

Wayne motioned to the wicker chair on one end of the porch. "Would you like to take a seat?"

"Okay." Loraine lowered herself into the chair, and Wayne maneuvered his wheelchair next to her.

"I'm surprised to see you here," Wayne said. "After what I told you last week, I didn't think you'd come over again."

She shook her head. "I can't stop coming to see you, Wayne. I care for you too much."

"Guess I can't stop you from coming over, but you need to know that we can never be more than friends."

"I wish you wouldn't say that. I wish—"

"I heard you had lunch with Jake today."

She nodded slowly, as a rush of heat cascaded up her neck and onto her cheeks. "I guess your mamm couldn't wait to tell you that she saw us at the restaurant, huh?"

"She did mention it."

"I hope you know there's nothing going on between me and Jake."

He shrugged. "Since we're no longer engaged, I have nothing to say about it. You have the right to see anyone you choose."

Loraine fought the temptation to say more on the subject but remembered her decision not to push Wayne or bring up marriage. "How are you feeling?" she asked. "Are you still having that phantom pain?"

He shook his head. "Not so much this week as I did before."

"That's good to hear. I guess the pain medicine must be helping."

He shrugged. "It's helped some, but I've had even less pain since I started using a new technique."

"What technique is that?"

"It involves tapping on various acupuncture points in the body."

Loraine listened with rapt attention as Wayne explained the principles of the tapping method he'd been shown and said his chiropractor had suggested that he give it a try.

"Then, too," he added, "I've been keeping busy taking care of Tripod, so that has helped to take my mind off my own problems for a while."

"Tripod?"

"She's one of our young ewes. Got her left front leg stepped on by one of our horses, and the vet had to take it off." He glanced at the place where his own leg had been. "My daed wanted to put her down, but I talked him out of it." He paused and stared off into space. Then he turned to look at her again. "Tripod and I have one thing in common."

"What's that?"

"We've both lost a leg and will have to learn how to walk all over again."

"Does that mean you've decided to get a prosthesis?"

"Haven't made up my mind yet. Those things are expensive. I was told they can run anywhere from three thousand dollars all the way up to fifteen thousand for the really fancy ones."

"I'm sure our community will help with your expenses. In fact, my daed mentioned the other night that some folks are making plans to hold a benefit auction to help with the medical bills for everyone who was involved in the accident." She smiled. "If you had a prosthesis, you might be able to farm again."

Deep creases formed across Wayne's forehead. "A lot of good that would do me, since Pop's already leased out our land."

"I'm sure you can find something else to do—something that's not as physical as farming. Or maybe you can farm for someone else."

"I don't know about that. Pop wants me to learn taxidermy, but I'm not so sure that kind of work's for me, either." He rubbed the bridge of his nose and grimaced. "I'll have to find something to do, though. Sure can't expect my folks to support me for the rest of my life. They won't be around forever."

The dejected look on Wayne's face was almost Loraine's undoing. She wanted to reach out to him—wrap her arms around him and assure him that everything would work out okay. She wanted to tell him that she thought he should take his father up on his offer to become a taxidermist and then they could be married as planned. She knew that would be a mistake, though, so she kept those thoughts to herself.

Finally, Loraine rose from her chair. "I'd better get going. Mom will be starting supper soon, and I should be there to help."

"I appreciate you coming by," he said. "Next time you come over, maybe I can introduce you to Tripod."

"I'd like that," she said, smiling down at him. "Good-bye, Wayne."

As Loraine hurried toward her bike, a renewed sense of determination welled in her soul. She could not allow her feelings for Jake to surface. She needed to concentrate on Wayne. With a little time and some patience, she was sure he would realize they were meant to be together. She hoped, however, that she wouldn't have to wait too long, because the more time she spent with Jake, the more confused she became.

CHAPTER 18

The following day, Loraine decided to stop and see Ella on her way home from work. It had been awhile since they'd had a good chat, and she was certainly in need of one.

She found Ella in the kitchen, stirring a batter of yeasty-smelling dough.

"It's good to see you." Ella smiled. "Are you ready for some more friendship bread?"

"If you have some made, I could take a loaf, but I'd prefer not to take home any starter."

Ella motioned to the stove. "There are a couple of loaves in the oven, and they should be done shortly, so I'd be glad to give you a loaf." She glanced at the table. "If you'd like to have a seat, I'll fix us some tea."

"That sounds nice. I'm in need of a good visit." Loraine pulled out a chair at the table and took a seat.

A few minutes later Ella placed a pot of tea on the table, along with two cups and a plate of ginger cookies. "Is there something specific you wanted to talk about?" she asked, seating herself in the chair beside Loraine.

Loraine nodded as she poured herself a cup of tea. "I'm really verhuddelt."

"What are you confused about?"

123

"I had lunch with Jake the other day, and being with him conjured up some feelings I thought I'd forgotten."

Ella gasped. "You're not in love with him, I hope."

"No, I'm not. It's just that being with Jake makes me think about the past and how happy we used to be when we were dating." Loraine took a sip of tea. "He's easy to talk to and so full of life. Being with him takes my mind off my troubles, and he makes me laugh, which is something I really need right now."

"Have you forgotten that he walked out on you so he could try out the English world and make lots of money?" Ella's face contorted. "Have you forgotten that he quit writing after only a few letters and didn't return home until he heard about the accident?"

"I haven't forgotten any of that, but it's not right to harbor resentment, and he did say he was sorry." Loraine sighed deeply. "I think Jake and I can still be good friends, and we are moving on from the past."

"I'm not saying you should harbor resentment. I'm reminding you not to get involved with Jake because he'll only hurt you again." Ella touched Loraine's arm. "And what about Wayne? Are you just going to walk away from him now that Jake is back?"

"No, of course not." Loraine frowned. "I went by to see Wayne after work yesterday. Would I do that if I planned to walk away?"

"I guess not." Ella drank some tea, set the cup down, and fiddled with the handle of her spoon. It seemed like she always had to be doing something to keep her hands busy. "How's Wayne doing? Is he still in a lot of pain?"

"He's said his pain's some better because of some new thing the chiropractor asked him to try, but I could tell that he's still struggling with depression. He's really upset because his daed leased out their land. That leaves Wayne no chance to farm even if he does get a prosthesis and learns to walk well with it."

"Does he plan to get one?"

"I don't know. He's concerned about the cost, but I know it'll be easier for him to adjust if he gets one soon."

"Maybe after the benefit auction, he'll have the money he needs."

"I hope so, but remember, whatever money's brought in will be divided among everyone who has hospital and doctor expenses due to the accident."

Ella nodded. "We'll need to pray that a lot of things will be auctioned off and that there will be plenty of money in the fund."

~≈ ≈~

When the back door swung open, Priscilla turned from peeling carrots to see who had entered her kitchen. "Oh, it's you, Amos. I thought it might be Loraine."

"She's not home from work yet?" he asked, removing his stocking cap and hanging it on a wall peg near the door.

Priscilla shook her head. "Maybe she stopped off to see Wayne on her way home from work. She went by there yesterday, you know."

He pulled out a chair at the table and took a seat. "Speaking of Wayne, I ran into his daed when I was Topeka earlier today."

"What'd you go to Topeka for?"

"Went to the shoe and boot store. I told you I was going there, remember?"

"Guess I must have forgotten." She reached for another carrot to peel. "Did you take time out to visit with Crist?"

"We talked for a few minutes." Deep wrinkles formed across Amos's forehead. "He said something kind of disturbing to me."

"What was that?"

"Said his wife saw Loraine having lunch with Jake Beechy yesterday." He grunted and slapped at the dirt on the sides of his trousers. "If she's in love with Wayne and hopin' to marry him someday, you wouldn't think she'd be having lunch with another man."

Priscilla leaned against the sink as she stared out the window. "Hmm…"

"Hmm, what?"

"Maybe Loraine and Jake will get back together. She was

pretty smitten with him when she was a teenager, you know."

"Maybe so, but she promised to marry Wayne."

"True, but he doesn't want to marry her now, and I think it might be for the best."

His eyebrows shot up. "How can you say that, Priscilla? I thought you liked Wayne as much as I do."

She pursed her lips. "He's a nice enough fellow, but he's become awful moody since the accident. Besides, I think dealing with his handicap would be hard on Loraine."

"Loraine's a strong woman. I'm sure she could deal with most anything if she wanted to badly enough."

She shrugged. "Jah, well, between you and me, I felt a sense of relief when Wayne broke things off with her."

"I think you're wrong, and it would be best if you kept quiet about this and let our daughter make her own decisions." Amos pushed away from the table. "I'll be out in the barn. Ring the dinner bell when supper's ready."

"Despite what you think, I do know what's best for our daughter," Priscilla mumbled as he rushed out of the room.

⊷ ❧

"This is sure not my favorite thing to do," Jake grumbled as he laid out some horse shoeing supplies. "I'd rather be breaking horses than shoeing 'em."

Jake knew he shouldn't complain. For as long as he chose to live at home, he'd need to work and contribute to the family's income. He just hadn't expected Dad to come down with the flu this morning, leaving him stuck shoeing all the horses lined up for the day. Charlie Albright, Dad's hired driver, would be here in a few hours to take him to several farms out of the area where horses needed to be shod. In the meantime, he had to shoe a couple of buggy horses that had been brought here to his dad's place. Their closest neighbor, Melvin Smucker, had dropped off his son's horse, as well as one of his own, while he ran some errands in Goshen. If Charlie arrived before Melvin got back,

Jake would leave Melvin's horses in the corral.

As Jake removed the old shoes from the first horse, he allowed his thoughts to wander. He'd enjoyed his lunch with Loraine the other day and looked forward to seeing her at church on Sunday. He'd like to have another lunch date with her or maybe take her for a ride in his buggy.

When I think the time is right and I've worked up my nerve, he decided, *I am going to ask her out for a real date.*

Years of regret tugged at Jake's heart. He'd been a fool to leave her the way he had. Jake gritted his teeth. *By staying away so long, and not keeping in touch, I opened the door for my best friend to swoop in and take my girlfriend away. Loraine's even prettier now than she was two years ago.* Jake frowned. *I wonder if it's really over between her and Wayne.*

He slapped the side of his head. *I've gotta quit thinking about this or I won't be able to concentrate on the job at hand.*

He set right to work on cleaning the horse's hoof and had just picked up the nippers to trim it, when the horse backed up and stepped right on his foot. Despite the fact that Jake wore boots, it hurt like crazy.

"Yeow!" Jake dropped the nippers and crumpled to the ground as searing pain shot from the top of his foot all the way up his leg.

He tried to stand, but the pain was so intense he just couldn't. Since his folks were in the house, and he was clear on the other side of the barn, he figured there'd be no point in hollering for help. Besides, Dad was sick in bed, and Mom sure couldn't carry him up to the house by herself.

There's only one thing I can do, he decided. *I'll have to stay on the grass and roll my way back to the house. I just hope I can get there before I pass out from the pain.*

By the time Jake made it up to the house, he was so exhausted he had to drag himself onto the porch.

Bam! Bam! Bam! Unable to stand, he reached up and pounded on the door with his fists.

Finally, the door swung open. "Jake! Why are you lying on the porch like that?" Mom asked.

"Stupid horse stepped on me when I was trying to clean his hooves." Jake moaned. "My foot hurts so bad I had to roll my way up to the house."

"Ach! Let's get you inside so I can take a look at your foot. It might be broken."

Jake shook his head as he gritted his teeth. "I think it's just a bad bruise."

"You're gonna have to help me now," Mom said, bending down and slipping her hands under Jake's arms.

Using every ounce of strength he could muster, Jake grabbed the edge of the chair near the door and pulled himself up. Then, using Mom as a support, he hopped into the house on one foot.

"Take a seat at the table," Mom instructed. "I'll get your boot off and see what I think."

Jake did as she asked and groaned when she tugged on the boot. "Not so hard, Mom! It hurts so bad I feel like I might pass out."

"Put your head between your knees," she instructed. "And take in a couple of deep breaths."

Jake complied, then winced when she pulled off the boot.

"It's already swollen," Mom said after she'd removed Jake's sock. "I think you need to go the hospital and have it x-rayed."

"It'll be fine," Jake argued. "I just need to put some ice on it and rest awhile."

Mom shook her head. "Resting it isn't good enough, son. You need to have it looked at."

Jake leaned over and stared at his purple, swollen foot. "I'm lookin' at it now, and I say it's not broken."

Mom gave him a light tap on the arm. "No funning around. If it's broken, it will need to be set and put in a cast."

Jake sighed. "Okay, okay. If it's not feeling better by the time Charlie gets here, I'll ask him to give me a ride to the hospital in Goshen."

CHAPTER 19

Loraine smiled when she saw Crist Lambright pushing Wayne's wheelchair across the grass. It was good to see Wayne attending church again. He needed to be in fellowship with his friends.

She was tempted to rush over but held herself in check, not wishing to appear overanxious or pushy. When Wayne looked her way and made eye contact, she offered him a smile and a friendly wave.

He lifted one hand and gave a quick nod. Then, grasping the wheels on his chair, he pushed himself up the path leading to the Lehmans' barn where several other men had gone.

Loraine headed for a group of women standing near the front porch but had only taken a few steps when she spotted Jake hobbling across the lawn.

"What happened to you?" she asked.

"I was getting ready to shoe a horse the other day, and the stupid critter stepped on my foot."

"That must have hurt."

"It sure did. It hurt so bad I couldn't even stand up or put any weight on my foot. I ended up having to roll my way to the house." He chuckled and gave his chin dimple a couple of taps. "Had to stop every few rolls in order to rest up for the rest of the trip."

Loraine could almost picture Jake lying on the ground, rolling across the grass. It brought a smile to her lips, even though she knew he must have been in a lot of pain.

"The whole episode is kind of funny now," Jake said, "but at the time, it sure wasn't. Thought for a while it was broken, but it turned out to only be a bad bruise."

"How do you know? Did you have it looked at right away?"

"Sure did. I looked at it every chance I got," Jake said with a wink.

She poked his arm. "You're such a tease. Seriously, did you have it x-rayed?"

"Jah, Charlie, my driver, was scheduled to give me a ride to shoe several horses. When he got to our house and took one look at my big foot, he said, 'Jake Beechy, you're going to the hospital to get that x-rayed, whether you like it or not!'"

Jake thumped his chin a couple of times. "I had it x-rayed and checked over real good, but the doctor said it was just a bad bruise and that a couple of blood vessels had busted." He tipped his head and gave Loraine a crooked grin. "Don't think I would have liked being laid up in a cast. It would've slowed me down too much."

Loraine's thoughts went to Wayne. *I can only imagine how he must feel being confined to a wheelchair. I'm sure he'd give just about anything to be in Jake's place right now.*

Jake nudged Loraine's arm and pointed to the Lehmans' house. "Guess you'd better go; your cousin's calling you."

Loraine turned her gaze in that direction and saw Ella on the porch, motioning for her to come.

"You're right; Ella does seem to want me. See you later, Jake."

❧ ❧

As Jake limped into the barn, he thought about Loraine and how pleasant she'd been to him. It seemed like each time they were together the barrier came down a little more. Maybe she was beginning to trust him again. Maybe he had reason to hope that they might get back together. He thought about asking her out right now but knew it wouldn't be the proper time. Oh, how pretty she looked this morning. It was enough to take a man's breath away.

"How come you're limping?" Wayne asked when Jake entered the barn and found him sitting off by himself.

Jake quickly related the story of how the horse had stepped on his foot and ended it by saying, "I'm just glad there was nothing broken. I can't afford to be laid up right now."

Wayne winced as though in pain, and Jake could have kicked himself. He didn't know what he'd do if he were in Wayne's place.

"So how are you doing?" Jake asked. "Are things going any better for you?"

Wayne shrugged. "My doctor talked me into getting a prosthesis, but now I'm having second thoughts."

"How come?" Jake asked as he lowered himself to a bale of hay.

"I've already gone through so much physical therapy and pain, and I'm not sure I want to go through any more."

"Guess I can understand that," Jake said. "As much as my foot hurts, I can't even imagine what all you've been through."

Wayne motioned to the men who'd begun heading into the buggy shed where their church service would be held. "Looks like church is about to begin, so I guess we'd better get in there."

Jake nodded and followed Wayne out of the barn.

≈ ≈

Ella grabbed Loraine's arm and pulled her close to her side. "What were you doing with Jake over there?"

"Don't look so worried; we were just talking."

"Humph!" Ella crossed her arms. "I thought you had better sense than to get involved with him again."

"We're not involved. I was just asking why he was limping."

"And why is that?"

"He got stepped on by a horse, but lucky for him, he only suffered a bad bruise." Loraine's eyebrows drew together. "It could have been much worse. It could have been broken or mangled like Wayne's sheep."

"What sheep is that?" Ella asked.

Loraine was about to reply when Ella's sister stepped between them and said, "Church is about to start. The men are heading for the buggy shed."

"Guess we'd better get in there, then." Ella led the way and quickly found a seat on one of the backless wooden benches on the women's side of the room.

During the service, Ella had a hard time concentrating. It was hard not to watch Jake as he kept looking over at Loraine.

Looks like I'd better have another talk with that fellow, she fumed. *He seems determined to get Loraine back.*

Ella's thoughts shifted gears when she noticed a little girl sitting on her mother's lap, holding a blanket while sucking her thumb.

A fly buzzed around the room, and some of the babies were getting fussy. A couple of the younger boys were bent over at the waist; it looked as though they might have fallen asleep.

Then Ella noticed her mother lift a shaky hand as she wiped her forehead with a handkerchief. Had the words from the song they were singing struck a nerve?

Ella glanced down at the *Ausbund* hymn book in her lap and figured the words from Song 76 had probably touched Mama's heart. *"Where shall I turn to, I the least of the brethren? Alone to God my Lord, Who will be my helper. In all my needs, I trust in you, O God! You will not forsake me; And will stand by me until death."*

Ella hoped her mother had decided to give God all of her needs and to trust only in Him. Mama would always miss Raymond, but with God's help, she could carry on.

❧ ❧

When church was over and everyone had eaten their common meal, Wayne decided to maneuver his wheelchair across the grass and find a spot near the pasture to look at the horses. It was nice to attend church service again, but ever since the accident, he'd had a difficult time socializing, so he preferred to be off by himself for a while.

He closed his eyes and lifted his face to the sky. It might be a bit chilly, but at least the sun was out.

"Are you sleeping?"

Wayne's eyes snapped open, and he turned at the sound of Loraine's voice.

"Uh. . .no. . .I was just sitting here, thinking."

She smiled. "I'm glad you felt up to coming to church today. You've been missed." Her expression was so intense it made his stomach lurch with nervous anticipation. Every nerve in his body tingled.

As Wayne turned back around, tension knotted his shoulders. He could almost feel her staring at him.

"You seem so tense." Loraine placed her hands on his taut shoulders. Fire flared up his arms as she made little circles along his shoulder blades. He feared if he didn't move away soon he might die from longing to hold her. Loraine's presence made Wayne feel like one of the old martyrs of Germany who had led the Amish to flee to America so many years ago.

"I. . .uh. . .have decided to go ahead and get a prosthesis," he mumbled, needing to get his mind on something else.

"Oh, that's good to hear." She continued to lightly massage his shoulders.

"I've got another doctor's appointment later this week, but I'm not looking forward to going."

"Would you like me to go with you?" she asked.

"That's not a good idea! Besides, my folks will be going with me."

"Oh." She stopped rubbing his shoulders and moved to stand near the fence. As she did so, an empty coldness swept over Wayne.

The silence settled around them, broken only by the whinny of the horses in the corral. As much as Wayne's heart cried out for Loraine to stay, he was anxious for her to leave him alone.

"I saw you talking to Jake before church started."

She fiddled with the strings on her head covering. "There was nothing to it; Jake and I are only friends."

He shrugged. "Whatever you say."

"It's true, Wayne. We—"

"It doesn't matter. You're better off with Jake than you would be with me. Now if you don't mind, I'd really like to be alone."

She blinked a couple of times, and then with a smile that appeared to be forced, she lifted her hand and bid him good-bye.

A lump formed in Wayne's throat as he watched her walk away. Even though he knew she'd be better off without him, it pained him to think of her being with Jake.

With fingertips pressed against his lips, he closed his eyes and relived the first kiss he and Loraine had ever shared.

CHAPTER 20

Wayne stared out the window of their English driver's van, watching the scenery go by and noting that many of the trees had dropped their leaves. It had been six weeks since he'd lost his leg, and this morning, he'd been given a new leg. The doctor had told him that the sooner he started to feel like the prosthesis was a part of him, the sooner he'd be able to adjust to the stride in his steps. He'd given Wayne instructions on how to attach the new leg, and then Wayne had been forced to take several agonizing steps between some parallel bars. He'd left the hospital with a pair of crutches, which he would use for support until he got used to walking with the new leg.

As Wayne stepped out of the van a short time later, he wobbled and gritted his teeth. Walking with his new prosthesis was no easy task.

"I'll probably never adjust to the artificial leg," he mumbled as Pop grabbed hold of his arm.

"Sure you will," Pop said. "Just give yourself some time."

"Would you prefer to ride up to the house in your wheelchair rather than trying to walk?" Mom asked.

Wayne shook his head and gritted his teeth. "I've got to get used to walking with this, so I may as well begin now."

As soon as they entered the house, Mom pulled out a chair

for Wayne. "You can sit here and rest while I get a pot of coffee going," she said, motioning to the kitchen table.

"I don't want any coffee," he mumbled.

"You look tired. Why don't you go to your room and rest awhile? I'll call you when I get lunch on the table."

Irritation welled in Wayne's soul. She was doing it again—smothering him. Truth was, he did feel pretty tired and was experiencing some pain. "Guess I'll go to the living room," he said. "I can rest on the sofa there." He hobbled out of the room before Mom said anything more.

❦

"You need to quit smothering him," Crist said after Wayne left the room.

Ada pursed her lips and glared at him. "How many times are you going to tell me that?"

"As many times as it takes." Crist helped himself to a cup of coffee and took a seat at the table. "If our son's ever going to adjust to his new leg, then he'll need to learn to do things on his own, and he doesn't need your suggestions."

Ada frowned. "I just wish—"

"Don't start with the wishing, now. All the wishing in the world won't change a thing. That young lamb Wayne's been taking care of for the last few weeks had to learn to adapt to its handicap, and Wayne's trying to do the same."

"Have you talked to him any more about becoming a taxidermist?"

He shook his head. "He knows the offer's open. I don't want to push him into something he'd rather not do."

"But he's got to do something. I mean, he can't spend the rest of his life taking care of a crippled sheep and feeling sorry for himself."

"I'm sure he won't—as long as we allow him to make his own decisions. Remember, it's his life, not ours, Ada."

Ada fiddled with the napkin beside her cup, finally crumpling it into a tight little ball. If she could have her way, she'd somehow make sure that Fern Bontrager was in Wayne's future. But she knew that wasn't possible, so she'd have to be happy taking care of Wayne for the rest of her life.

❧ ❧

"Have you decided yet whether you're going to stay in Indiana and join the church?" Jake's mother asked him during their evening meal.

Jake gave a noncommittal shrug and poked his fork into a thick slice of ham.

"Your mamm asked you a question, and I think she deserves an answer," Dad spoke up from his seat at the head of the table. "For that matter, I'd like to hear the answer to that question myself."

Jake chewed the piece of ham, then looked over at Mom. "I haven't made up my mind yet what I'm gonna do. I just know I'm where I'm supposed to be right now."

"You're right about that," Dad said with a nod. "And if you want my opinion, you should never have left home in the first place."

Jake ground his teeth. Not another lecture from Dad. Since he'd returned to Indiana, he'd had too many of them already.

"Jake's only hanging around because he's in love with Loraine," Elmer spoke up. "If she gets back with Wayne, he'll leave home again; you'll see that I'm right about that."

Jake glared at his twelve-year-old brother. "You think you know everything, don't you?"

Elmer took a drink and set the glass down so hard that some of the milk spilled out. "Do not. I just know you, that's all. When you set your sights on somethin', you go right after it and don't stop till you've got what you want." He swiped his tongue over his lip. "And when you don't get what you want, you run away."

Jake shook his head. "You don't know what you're talking about. When I went to Montana, it had nothing to do with me not getting something I wanted."

"Are you sure about that? As I recall, you wanted to quit shoeing horses and expected me to loan you the money to buy a herd of horses." Dad leaned his elbows on the table and stared at Jake so hard it made his toes curl inside his boots. "When I said if you wanted to start your own business you'd have to save up the money and do it on your own, you headed for Montana to play cowboy with a bunch of English fellows."

"That was different," Jake said in his own defense. "I knew I could make money quicker working at the horse ranch there than I could shoeing horses here."

Mom touched Jake's arm. "But you promised you'd be back, and you said you'd keep in touch." Her voice quivered, and she blinked a couple of times. "You didn't keep either of those promises."

"How'd that make you feel, Jake?" Dad asked. "Didn't you care that your family missed you and were worried because you didn't write or call?"

Jake's face heated up. "We've been through all this before, and I said I was sorry for not keeping in touch. Can't we just leave it at that?"

"We could if we had a guarantee that you were gonna stay here and join the church," Dad said.

"There are no guarantees in this world. That's evident by what happened to my friends when their van ran off the road and hit a pole."

"Can't we talk about somethin' else?" Jake's sister Marilyn spoke up. "All this arguing is making my stomach hurt."

"Well, don't let me stop you from eating in peace!" Jake pushed his chair aside and stood.

"Where are you going?" Mom asked.

"Outside to be with the horses!"

"But you haven't finished your meal."

"I've lost my appetite." Jake plunked his hat on his head and hurried out the door. He had some serious thinking to do.

Loraine's bare feet tingled as she hurried across the hay-strewn floor of their barn. There stood Jake leaning against one of the horse's stalls, a tender smile on his handsome face.

"I'm so glad you're here," she murmured. "I've been hoping you'd come."

Jake tipped his head and stared at her with such intensity that her toes curled. "I'm here forever and always." He reached for her hand and pressed it against his chest. "I promise never to leave you again, Loraine. I've always loved you, and I was a fool to leave the way I did. Will you please forgive me?"

Loraine's pulse hammered in her head. She tried to speak but couldn't get the words past the lump in her throat. How could she not forgive Jake? It wasn't right to carry a grudge.

Jake slipped his arms around Loraine's waist and held her so close that she could hear the steady beating of his heart.

She smiled, feeling all the tension in her body melt away. It felt right to be with Jake. He made her feel, not think.

His thumb stroked the top of her head with deliberate slowness, and her skin tingled with each light touch.

The barn door creaked open and slammed shut, shattering the pleasant moment.

"I should have known I'd find the two of you together! I'm so disappointed in you, Loraine."

Loraine pulled away from Jake and whirled around. Wayne hobbled toward them, shaking his head. "You'd rather be with him than me; isn't that right?"

Loraine opened her mouth to reply, but only a wordless squeak came out.

"I was a fool for believing you loved me." Wayne's eyes narrowed as he turned to look at Jake. "I thought you were my friend, but I was so wrong about that. Guess I was wrong about everything."

Stunned, and confused, Loraine waited for Jake's response. She could almost feel the sparks between the two men.

"You had your chance," Jake said, taking a step forward. "You pushed Loraine away because you lost your leg, and now she's with me."

Wayne's face turned bright red as rivulets of sweat beaded on his forehead. "I've changed my mind. Loraine belongs with me, and I want her back!"

Jake pulled Loraine to his side. "I think we should let her decide which one of us she wants."

Wayne's piercing eyes seemed to bore a hole right through her. "Who do you choose, Loraine?"

She looked at Jake, then back at Wayne, her heart beating furiously. Suddenly, her head jerked forward, as though she was a rag doll, and she toppled to the floor. . . .

Loraine's eyes snapped open. As the dim morning light filtered through the window, she lay on her bed, trying to shake off the dream that had left her sheets drenched with sweat. *"I love you, Loraine,"* she heard Jake's voice through the mist of her memory.

It had only been a dream, but it was a revelation. The thought that she might be in love with two men terrified her. How could she feel this way? How could she have allowed it to happen?

Loraine clambered out of bed and padded over to the window. She opened it quickly and drew in a couple of deep breaths. The only thing she knew for sure was that she couldn't let either Jake or Wayne know how she felt.

CHAPTER 21

"Y ou look awfully *mied* this morning," Mom said when Loraine entered the kitchen. "Didn't you sleep well?"

"I am tired. I had a bad dream, and it woke me up." Loraine yawned and stretched her arms over her head. "I couldn't get back to sleep after that."

"I'm sorry to hear it. Do you remember what the dream was about?"

"It's. . .uh. . .kind of vague." Loraine reached for her choring apron. She didn't want to talk about her conflicting emotions or the disconcerting dream she'd had—especially not with her mother. It would only bring about more questions—questions she wasn't ready to answer, questions she had no answers to.

"What would you like me to do to help with breakfast?" Loraine asked.

"Why don't you set the table while I keep an eye on the oatmeal cooking on the stove?"

"Okay." Loraine opened a drawer and took out the silverware.

"So you can't remember any of your dream?"

Loraine grimaced. Apparently Mom wasn't going to let this subject drop. "It was about Wayne." *At least part of it was.*

"Oh, I see." Mom took a box of brown sugar down from the cupboard. "Wasn't he supposed to get his prosthesis yesterday?"

Loraine nodded. "I think I might drop by there on my way to work this morning. I'd like to see how he's doing."

"Oh, Loraine, do you think that's really a good idea? Wayne did ask you not to go over there anymore."

Loraine didn't need that reminder—especially when she knew how Mom felt about Wayne's handicap and the pensive mood he'd been in since the accident. "I don't think he'll mind if I check on him," she said. "I just need to be careful what I say while I'm there."

"Because he's moody, you mean?"

Loraine replied with a shrug.

"Have you seen Jake lately?" Mom asked suddenly.

Loraine's face flamed. Did Mom suspect she might have some feelings for Jake? Not that Loraine was sure what those feelings were at this point.

She pulled three plates from the cupboard and placed them on the table. "I saw him for a few minutes the other day."

Mom smiled. "I always did like Jake. He seems so easygoing and is always full of humor and so polite."

Loraine couldn't argue with that, but then up until the accident, Wayne had been easygoing, full of humor, and polite, too. It was like he'd undergone a complete personality change.

"Is Jake planning to stay in Indiana and join the church?" Mom asked.

"I don't know what his plans are." Loraine took out some juice glasses and set them on the table. *But I do know that if Wayne and I don't get back together soon, I might succumb to Jake's attentions.*

❧ ❧

"Could you come in here a minute?" Pop asked as Wayne hobbled past the taxidermy shop.

With a muffled grunt, Wayne stepped into the room. "Did you need something?"

"Jah, I need another pair of hands."

Wayne shuffled over to the workbench where Pop sat on a

wooden stool. He'd help because Pop asked, but he really didn't want to. "What exactly do you need help with?"

Pop motioned to a deer hide stretched out on the bench. "I could use your assistance slipping this onto the molded form that'll become the deer's body."

"Can't you do it without my help? You've done deer bodies before, right?"

"Jah, but this one's bigger than most."

"Okay." Wayne sighed. He took a seat on the other stool, resigned to the fact that he was going to have to help Pop whether he liked it or not.

Pop handed Wayne one end of the hide, and he noticed how soft and pliable it felt. As they worked together getting it stretched over the mold, Wayne decided to ask a question.

"I've been wondering about something."

"What's that?"

"Did you give up farming and open this business because you thought I couldn't plow and plant anymore?"

Pop's face turned red as a radish. "That was part of the reason, but I really do enjoy this kind of work and have always wished I could do it full-time." He motioned to the deer hide. "For me, taxidermy work is a lot more enjoyable than farming ever was."

"Guess I never realized you were unhappy being a farmer."

"Oh, I wasn't, really. I just like this a whole lot more." Pop nudged Wayne's arm. "And you know what else?"

"What's that?"

"It wasn't so easy for us to visit when we were out in the fields. I rather like spending time with you like this."

"I enjoy spending time with you, too." Truth was, Wayne would rather be with Pop all day than spend five minutes in the same room with Mom. It wasn't that he didn't love her. He just couldn't deal with her constant hovering. It seemed that she was either trying to do everything for him or telling him what to do. It was enough to keep him on edge.

Pop picked up a pair of glass eyes that would be used in the deer's head. "These little things remind me of a joke I heard the other day."

"What was it?"

Pop scratched the side of his head and blinked. "You know—I can't remember it now."

"Don't let Mom hear you say that. She's likely to start accusing you of being forgetful."

Pop chuckled. "She already has—many times, in fact. And speaking of your mamm, our anniversary's coming up soon. I've been thinkin' I might like to take her on a trip to Sarasota."

"That's a good idea. Mom's been kind of edgy lately. A trip to Sarasota might be good for her." Wayne shifted on the stool, trying to find a comfortable position, and studied the deer hide. "Loraine's cousin Katie has been dealing with depression and fearful thoughts, and from what I hear, it's changed her disposition. That's the reason her folks sent her to Sarasota. They're hoping when she comes home she'll be her old self again."

"If going to Sarasota would change your mamm's disposition, I think I'd move us there permanently."

Wayne's head came up. "Would you want to live in Florida?"

"Not really. I like it here in Indiana." Pop gave Wayne's arm a light tap. "Don't worry, son. If we go to Sarasota, we'll only be gone a week or so."

"Who's going to Sarasota?" Mom asked, sticking her head into the room.

"You and me—for our anniversary." Pop grinned like a boy with a new toy. "What do you think of that idea, huh, Ada?"

Her lips compressed tightly as she stepped into the room. "There's no way we can go to Sarasota right now. I can't believe you'd even suggest such a thing!"

Pop raked his fingers through the ends of his beard. "Why not?"

Mom motioned to Wayne. "Our son just came home with his new leg, and you're asking why not?"

"I'll be fine on my own while you're gone," Wayne was quick to say. He wasn't so sure about that, but he didn't want to stand in the way of his folks taking a trip for their anniversary.

Mom shook her head so hard the ribbon ties on her head covering whipped around her face and into her eyes. "I wouldn't dream of running off to Florida and leaving you here alone." She flipped the ribbons to the back of her neck. "What if you needed something? What if—"

"You're smothering him, Ada." Pop frowned. "Can't you see that you're doing it again?"

She smacked her hand against her hip with a grunt and glared at him. "I'm not smothering him. I just think it's too soon for him to be at home by himself."

"I don't agree. He's got to learn to be independent and do things on his own. He'll never do that as long as you're hovering around trying to do everything for him."

"But I'm his mother, and I think—"

Unwilling to listen to any more of his parent's disagreement, Wayne grabbed his crutches and made his way quickly out the door. Once outside, he drew in a couple of deep breaths to help steady his nerves. It was bad enough that he had to deal with his handicap and Mom's smothering. Did he have to deal with his folks' bickering, too? Ever since the accident, his nerves had been frazzled, and listening to Mom and Pop arguing set his teeth on edge.

Guess I'll head over to the barn and check on Tripod, he decided. *That ought to help calm me down.*

Wayne was halfway there when he noticed a horse and buggy coming up the driveway. He recognized it right away: it was Loraine's. He clenched his fingers until his nails dug into his palms. *What's she doing here? I thought I told her not to come. This isn't doing either of us any good.*

He moved over to the hitching rail, and when her rig approached, he secured the horse for her. Maybe she had a good reason for being here. Maybe it had nothing to do with him.

"Wie geht's?" Loraine asked when she stepped down from the buggy. Her voice was sweeter than a bird calling to its mate.

"As well as can be expected, I guess." Wayne's heart pounded when she smiled at him, and that bothered him a lot. How was he ever going to let her go if she kept coming over here all the time, looking at him with such a sweet expression?

Loraine's gaze moved from Wayne's face to the pant leg that hid his artificial limb. "It looks like you got your new leg."

"Jah. Got it yesterday." Wayne lifted the end of one crutch. "I'm still pretty unsteady on my feet, so I'll be using these for a while, I guess."

"That's probably a good idea." She offered him another sweet smile, and his heartbeat picked up speed. He missed that smile. Missed their long talks. Missed going places with her. If only things could be different for him. If he just hadn't lost his leg.

"You look like you're in pain," Loraine said. "Would it help if we sat down?"

"I took something for the pain when I ate breakfast, so I'm doing okay." Wayne motioned to the barn. "I was heading in there to check on my lamb."

"Oh, how's she doing?"

"Would you like to go in with me and see for yourself?"

She nodded. "I can't stay very long, though. I'm on my way to work and don't want to be late."

"I understand." Wayne sucked in his breath. He understood why she couldn't stay long. What he didn't understand was why he'd invited her into the barn. How was he ever going to sever the ties between them if he kept weakening like this? He'd have to be on his guard from now on. He couldn't let her think there was even a chance of them getting back together.

Wayne entered the barn and led the way over to the stall where he kept Tripod during the night.

Loraine stepped up beside him and gasped. "Ach, that poor little thing! How does she manage to hobble around on three legs?"

"She just does. Tripod has a very determined spirit."

"But how's she ever going to make it with the other sheep in the pasture?"

"I guess she'll make it the same way I will—one step at a time."

146

Her forehead creased. "Do you really think she'll adjust to walking with only three legs?"

He grunted. "She's got two more'n me."

"That's true, but you have your prosthesis now, and that's going to help you get around much better than being in a wheelchair all the time."

"Maybe so." Wayne motioned to a bale of straw. "Should we sit a few minutes?"

When she nodded, he leaned his crutches against the stall door and lowered himself down, being careful not to lose his balance. It was bad enough Loraine had to see him limping around with a pair of crutches. He didn't want to make a complete fool of himself in front of her.

They sat quietly, watching Tripod bump around in her stall and nibble on the hay in her feeding trough. It was hard to come up with anything to say. What did they really have to talk about anymore? Wayne's missing leg? The pain medicine he'd been forced to take? How miserable he felt because they couldn't be together?

He gazed up at the beams overhead and pondered it some more. In the days before the accident, he and Loraine had always had plenty to say to each other. They used to talk about their future—who they'd invite to their wedding, who they'd ask to be their main attendants, how many children they might have. Even when they didn't talk—just sat quietly watching a sunset or took a walk to the pond—there had been a sense of peace between them. Now, everything seemed tense and unnatural, like they were just going through the motions of visiting with one another.

"Have you heard from Katie or Jolene lately?" Wayne thought to ask.

"I got another note from Jolene the other day, but Katie hasn't answered any of my letters."

"Guess some folks just don't like to write."

"I'm afraid with Katie it's a lot more than that." Loraine leaned her head against the barn wall and sighed. "When Katie's mamm came home from Sarasota, she said Katie had been shying away from riding in a car. She also doesn't want to go out—not even for shopping—and the only time she speaks is when she's asked a question. I'm concerned that if she doesn't snap out of it soon, she might never be the same."

"I guess that's possible." Wayne grabbed a piece of straw and snapped it in two. "I know I'll never be the same."

"I'm sorry," she murmured. "I hope what I said about Katie didn't upset you. I'm sorry for your loss, Wayne, really I am."

"Jah, well, I don't need your pity."

"I didn't mean it that way. I just meant that—"

Ma-a-a! Ma-a-a!

Wayne jerked his attention back to Tripod. The poor little critter had somehow managed to get one of her back feet stuck between a loose board and the wall in her stall.

"Guess I'd better see about getting Tripod set free from that board that's holding her captive." Wayne rose to his feet, and forgetting to use his crutches, he headed for the stall. He'd only made it halfway there when he stumbled and fell flat on the floor.

Loraine rushed forward. "Ach, Wayne! Did you hurt yourself?"

"I'm fine. Just lost my balance is all."

She bent down and placed her hands around his waist. "Here, let me help you up."

Wayne shrugged her hands away as his face heated up. "I'm fine. I can manage on my own." Gritting his teeth and using the wall for support, he rose, wobbled, and fell back down.

Loraine rushed forward again. This time he swallowed his pride and allowed her to help him. With Loraine's assistance, he made it over to the stall.

"If you have no objections, I'll try to get the lamb's leg free," she said, looking up at him with compassion on her face.

Wayne wanted to argue, but his hands shook so badly, he wasn't sure he could do what needed to be done. "Jah, okay," Wayne mumbled, flopping onto the bale of straw. He sat there feeling like a helpless little baby while Loraine freed his lamb.

"Now do you see why we can't be together?" Wayne asked when she returned to his side. "If you and I got married, you'd always feel obligated to help me, just like my mamm does now."

"I wouldn't mind helping at all."

"Well, I would mind!"

A look of bewilderment spread across her face. "I try to reach out to you, and what do I get? You look at me with anger and push me away. Why, Wayne? Why?"

He tried to speak but couldn't make his lips move. He wished he could run and hide, but he didn't know where to go. Loraine deserved so much more than he could offer. She deserved a man who could take care of her, not a one-legged cripple who couldn't even walk without falling on his backside.

With her gaze fixed somewhere near the center of his chest, Loraine whispered, "I love *you*, Wayne."

A vein in Wayne's temple began to throb. His arms ached to hold her. His lips yearned for the taste of hers.

Refusing to lose himself in the depths of her eyes, he stared at his hands, clasped tightly in his lap. "Why won't you let this go? I've told you and told you that it won't work for us anymore. You need to find happiness with someone else." He paused for a second. "You need someone like Jake. I'm sure he still loves you. That's why he came home, you know."

"No. No, he didn't. He said he came back because he heard about the accident and felt concern."

"Then why is he still here? He's seen how we all are and offered everyone his sympathies. He should have been gone by now—back to his horse ranch in Montana, don't you think?"

"Well, I don't know. I—"

Wayne pointed at Loraine. "You're the reason Jake is still here."

She slowly shook her head. "I don't think so."

Wayne shrugged. "Think what you want. I just know it's over between us, and you need to get on with your life—with or without Jake Beechy."

When tears pooled in Loraine's eyes, it was almost his undoing. He clasped his fingers tighter as he struggled with the urge to take her hand. He wished she would go before he said or did something really stupid.

"You can't mean that it's over between us, Wayne." She sniffed deeply. "I know you don't."

"Jah, I do mean it. I don't love you anymore." As the lie rolled off Wayne's tongue, a bitter taste was left in his mouth. Until the accident happened, he'd always been honest with Loraine. Now, he was not only a cripple, but a terrible liar as well.

Loraine stood there a moment, staring at Wayne as though in disbelief. With a deep moan, she whirled around and dashed out the door.

Wayne's head pounded as he watched her disappear. He knew he had hurt her, and it tore at his heart. Maybe someday when she was happily married to someone more deserving, she would realize he'd been right to end things as he had.

"She might even thank me for it," he mumbled.

"Jah, I think you're right."

Wayne's head snapped up. He was surprised when Mom stepped out of one of the empty horse stalls.

"How long have you been there?" he asked.

"Long enough to hear what you told Loraine about not loving her."

Anger boiled in him like hot coals on the fire. "You were spying on us?"

She shook her head vigorously. "No, of course not. I came into the barn to see what you were doing out here, and when I heard you talking to Loraine, I ducked into the stall."

"Why?"

Her face flamed. "Well, I—"

"You didn't want to make your presence known because you were spying on us."

She stared at him like he'd lost his mind, then she slowly shook her head. "This isn't about me, son. This is about you and Loraine."

"There is no me and Loraine anymore." Wayne grimaced. "I'm sure after me telling Loraine that I don't love her anymore, she finally believes it's over between us."

Mom nodded. "You did the right thing by being honest with her. A relationship built on pity would never last anyway."

Wayne tipped his head. "You think she pities me?"

"Jah, I sure do. I also think she feels guilty for talking you into going to Hershey Park. She knows if you hadn't gone along with her foolish idea that you'd still have both of your legs." Mom took a seat beside him. "If Loraine really loved you, she wouldn't be spending so much time with Jake." She patted his knee. "You're better off without her, son."

Wayne pressed his hands against his stomach, hoping he wouldn't get sick. He didn't know if the churning in his stomach was from the pain medicine or because he felt like such a heel for lying to Loraine. "I don't want to hear any more about Loraine! I just want to be alone."

Mom blinked several times. "Are you asking me to leave?"

He gave a quick nod.

She hesitated a minute, then fled from the barn.

Wayne remained on the bale of straw with his head in his hands. He had lied to himself, as well as to Loraine. He'd yelled at Mom and told her to go. He really was a poor excuse for a man!

CHAPTER 22

Loraine's horse stamped nervously and blew a burst of steam from its nostrils as she fumbled with the reins. Her hands shook so badly she could barely make them work.

Wayne's words resounded in her head: *"I don't love you anymore. You'd be better off with Jake."* The finality of his tone could have etched the words in steel.

A tremor shot through her body. It really was over between them. How could she go to work and put a smile on her face when her whole world was falling apart?

"This isn't how I wanted things to turn out!" she murmured tearfully as she guided her horse and buggy down the road.

How did you want them to turn out? an inner voice asked.

The buggy hit a pothole that jarred her, and she winced. "Jake and I are not supposed to be together! We're just good friends. I'm supposed to be with Wayne. I promised him I would always be his."

Loraine gripped the reins tighter, hoping to gain control of her swirling emotions, more than guiding the horse. No way could she allow herself to love Jake again. She couldn't let her guard down. She couldn't allow him to sweep her off her feet the way he'd done before. Wayne might not realize it, but he needed her now more than ever. Surely he couldn't have meant it when he said he didn't love her anymore.

A film of tears clouded Loraine's vision. Soon they started running down her cheeks. She sniffed and wiped them away. "Things have to get better," she mumbled, hoping to make herself feel more secure. "Wayne's bound to come to his senses, and I can't give up on him just because he said he doesn't love me anymore."

More tears fell, until Loraine couldn't see well enough to drive anymore. She guided Trixie to the side of the road, knowing she needed to get herself under control before she went any farther.

She reached for her handbag and fumbled inside until she found a tissue, and then she blew her nose. Leaning forward, and closing her eyes, she began to pray.

"Dear Lord, please give me some direction and a sense of peace. I know I can't keep pestering Wayne to change his mind about us, but should I give up and let him go? If Wayne and I are meant to be together, then help him see that. If we're not, then I need some assurance and confirmation."

~❦~

"Whoa!" Jake called to his horse after he spotted a horse and buggy parked along the side of the road. He wondered if the driver might have encountered some kind of problem. He pulled in behind it, climbed down from his buggy, and raced around to the driver's side of the other rig. When he saw Loraine sitting in the driver's seat with her head bowed, his heart gave a lurch. Had something happened to her? Could some impatient driver have run her horse and buggy off the road? He knew it happened at times when some wild teenagers decided it would be fun to have a good time at someone else's expense.

He jerked the door open, and her head snapped up. "Ach!" she gasped. "You scared me, Jake!"

"You scared me! When I saw you sitting here with your head down, I was afraid something terrible had happened to you."

"No, no. I'm fine." Her eyes glistened with tears, and her chin trembled like the petals of a flower on a breezy day.

"You're obviously not fine, or you wouldn't be crying." Jake flapped his hand at her. "Move over and let me come in."

Her eyes widened. "What for?"

"So we can talk about whatever made you cry."

With a wordless shrug, Loraine scooted to the passenger's side, and Jake climbed in beside her.

"So what's wrong?" he asked.

She sniffed and dabbed at her eyes with the tissue she held in her hand. "I. . .I've just come from seeing Wayne."

"Is he worse?"

"Not physically, but he's so negative, and he seems determined to push me out of his life."

"What do you mean?"

Sniff! Sniff! "He said he doesn't love me anymore, and—" Her voice cracked, and she sniffed a couple more times. "I just can't accept the idea that things are over between us. It doesn't seem right."

She blew her nose and put the tissue in her purse, bumping Jake's arm in the process.

Jake felt a jolt of electricity zip from his arm to the tips of his fingers. He wished he could tell Loraine how he felt about her—that he'd never stopped loving her, that he wished he could stay here in Indiana and ask her to marry him. He swallowed hard and resisted the urge to pull Loraine into his arms. "I can see how unhappy you are," he said gently. "Is there anything I can do to help?"

She shrugged.

"Would you like me to talk to Wayne—see if I can get him to rethink his decision?"

Her chin quivered. "You—you would do that?"

I don't want to, but I'd do it for you. He nodded. "If you want me to, I will."

Her lips curved into a smile. "Danki, Jake. You're such a good friend."

Good friend, Jake fumed. *Is that all I'll ever be to you?* "I'll do my best to get through to Wayne," he said with a nod.

She touched his arm, sending another jolt of electricity all the way to his fingers. "Before you stopped, I was praying for some direction. I think you might be the answer to my prayers."

He ground his teeth. *Maybe so, but I don't think it's the same answer I'm hoping for.*

～≈ ⁐～

As Jake headed down the road in his buggy awhile later, he rehearsed in his mind what he was going to tell Wayne. Should he come right out and say that he'd spoken to Loraine and knew that Wayne had cut her out of his life? Or should he engage Wayne in idle conversation for a while and see if he volunteered anything himself?

Jake knew if there was any chance of getting back with Loraine, he'd have to figure out a way to win her trust again. He also needed to be sure things were really over between her and Wayne before he made a move. If things were to work out like he hoped, he could end up staying in Indiana for good. Between what he made shoeing horses and what he'd saved up working at the horse ranch, he might be able to buy a couple of standard-bred racing horses that could be trained to pull Amish buggies. At least it would be a start, and once he got his business going good, he'd be ready to join the church and felt sure he'd be able to support a wife.

Jake flicked the reins to get his horse moving faster. The sooner he talked to Wayne, the sooner he'd know which direction to take with Loraine.

～≈ ⁐～

Wayne had just put Tripod in the pasture with the other sheep and was preparing to head back to the house, when a horse and buggy pulled up next to the barn. He was surprised to see that it was Jake.

"It's good to see you walking," Jake said after he'd climbed down from the buggy and secured his horse to the hitching rail.

"Got my new leg yesterday." Wayne pulled up his pant leg to reveal the prosthesis and lifted the end of one crutch. "My goal is to learn how to walk without using these for support."

Jake smiled. "I'm sure you will once you've gotten used to the prosthesis."

"I lost my balance in the barn awhile ago and ended up flat on my back. Had to rely on Loraine to help me get up." Wayne grimaced. "If she hadn't been there, I'd probably still be lying on the barn floor, feeling like a helpless invalid."

"It's good that Loraine was there. Does she come over to see you often?"

"She used to, but she won't be anymore."

"How come?"

"I told her to go—said things won't work between us, so she may as well get on with her life." Wayne leaned his crutches against the fence and wobbled a bit as he lowered himself to a wooden stool.

Jake took a seat on another stool. "Are you sure you really want to break up with her? I mean, don't you want to reconsider that decision?"

Wayne folded his arms and shook his head. "I made it clear that there's no future for us. Told her she ought to find someone else." He bumped Jake's arm. "I'm thinkin' that someone oughta be you."

Jake gave his earlobe a tug. "Wh–what makes you think that?"

"You and Loraine used to date. Fact is, if you'd come back from Montana sooner, you two might be married by now, and I wouldn't even be in the picture."

Jake popped a couple of knuckles on his left hand, and then he did the same to the knuckles on his right hand. "Wouldn't you be jealous if Loraine and I started dating again?"

Of course I'd be jealous; I'd hate seeing the two of you together. I'd hate the reminder that I'll never be with the woman I love.

Wayne forced a smile. "All I want is for Loraine to be happy. If she stayed with me, I'd only drag her down." He pointed to Jake. "I think you, on the other hand, have just what it takes to make her happy."

"How do you know that?"

"Because you're all she ever talked about when you first left home. She thought you were coming back. She thought you planned to marry her."

Jake's gaze dropped to the floor. "I did plan to come back and marry her, but then I met Roxanne."

"Who's Roxanne?"

"My boss's daughter. I thought for a time that I was in love with her, but after she went away to Bible college, I realized what I'd felt for Roxanne had only been an infatuation. To tell you the truth, I didn't even miss her that much."

"Then why didn't you come back for Loraine then?"

Jake shrugged his shoulders. "I don't really know. Guess I got so caught up in working with the boss's horses and tryin' to put money away that I lost track of my original goal."

"How do you feel about Loraine now that you're back at home? Could you begin a relationship with her now?"

Jake's face turned crimson. "Are you absolutely sure there's no chance of you and Loraine getting back together? Because if there is—"

Wayne held up his hand. "Things will never be the same for me and Loraine. It's over between us."

"Can you honestly say you don't love her anymore?"

"Jah, that's how it is." Each lie Wayne told seemed to get easier than the last. "Given a little time," he said, "I'm sure Loraine will come to realize that she's not in love with me, either."

Just then, Wayne's father stepped out of his shop and hollered, "Wayne, could you come here a minute? I need your help with something!"

Wayne reached for his crutches and grunted as he pulled himself up. "Guess I'd better go see what Pop wants." He bumped Jake's arm. "Think about what I said, okay?"

"Sure, I'll give it some thought." Jake stood and sprinted for his buggy.

As Wayne made his way up to Pop's taxidermy shop, a wave of nausea washed over him. He'd literally given Loraine over to Jake with his blessings. As much as it had hurt him to do it, he was convinced that it was for her own good.

CHAPTER 23

"Are you sure you don't want to take your wheelchair with you today?" Wayne's mother asked as they prepared to leave for the benefit auction on Saturday morning.

He shook his head and kept walking toward the buggy Pop had rolled out of the buggy shed. "I need to get used to walking with my artificial leg, and that won't happen if I sit around in my wheelchair all day."

She stepped in front of him and pursed her lips. "I understand that, but it's going to be a long day. If you get tired of standing or walking, you might wish you had your wheelchair."

"I won't be walking around that much. I'll find a seat and stay put most of the time."

"Even so, I think it would be good if you—"

"I'll be fine! Would you just stop mothering me?"

If Wayne thought the direct approach would put an end to his mother's nagging, he was sorely mistaken. "I'm your mudder, and I care about your welfare—even if you don't!" She pointed her bony finger at him. "I insist that you take your wheelchair!"

Despite the chilly fall morning, Wayne's face heated up. If he and Mom kept going on this way, they'd both be so upset that neither of them would want to go to the auction. Since Wayne was one of the benefactors of the money that would be taken in, he figured he ought to at least put in an appearance. He also knew that he should try to be in a halfway decent mood when he spoke to his friends who would be there.

Forcing a smile he didn't really feel, Wayne looked at his mother and said, "I'll ask Pop to put my wheelchair in the back of the buggy, but I won't use it unless I have to."

She smiled in return and gave a quick nod. "Danki. That's a wise decision."

I hope the rest of the day goes better than this, Wayne thought as he made his way to the buggy. *And I hope I can keep my emotions in check when I see Loraine, because I'm sure she'll be there.*

❦

"I figured I'd find you here," Loraine said when she entered the room inside the auction barn where baked goods were being sold and found Ella behind one of the tables.

Ella motioned to the tray of pumpkin bars in front of her. "You know how much I like to bake, so where else would I be but in a room full of baked goods?"

Loraine smiled, despite the misgivings she felt about being at the auction today. She dreaded seeing Wayne yet looked forward to it at the same time. "Are you working in here?" she asked Ella. "Or did you come in to buy something sweet to eat and get roped into working?"

"I came here to work—at least for the first half of the day, which I'm sure will be the busiest time."

Loraine moved closer to the table. "I'd be happy to help if you need me."

"We can always use another pair of hands," Ella's fourteen-year-old sister, Charlene, spoke up.

Ella bumped her sister's arm. "Why don't you work at that table over there?" She pointed across the room. "Then Loraine can take your place and be here with me."

Charlene wrinkled her nose and glared at Ella a few seconds before she finally moved away. It was obvious that she didn't like being told what to do by her older sister.

"I'd better go to the restroom and wash my hands before I start helping," Loraine said.

Ella nodded. "That's a good idea."

Loraine scurried off toward the women's restrooms. Halfway there, she spotted Wayne sitting in the big room where the auction had already begun. His parents sat on either side of him.

Loraine was tempted to go over there and say hello, but after the things Wayne had said to her the other day, she decided against it.

Just then, Wayne turned his head and looked in her direction. Their gazes locked for a few seconds, and then he quickly looked away.

A sense of hopelessness welled in Loraine's soul, causing her shoulders to droop. She bit her bottom lip in an effort to keep from crying. She ought to be a married woman by now, not a frustrated *maedel* forced to avoid the man she had promised to marry. She ought to be sitting beside Wayne right now, not standing on the sidelines, watching Ada fuss over her son.

❧ ❧

"Looks like there's quite a crowd here today," Jake said as he and his family entered the auction barn.

Dad nodded. "Not only is there a good crowd from our Amish community, but many of our English neighbors have come out as well."

The air rang with the sound of the auctioneer's booming voice mingled with the murmur of the crowd sitting or milling about. Mom motioned to the items at the front of the room—dressers, chairs, tables, quilts, and a whole lot of miscellaneous. "If most everything goes, there should be plenty of money brought in today, and that will help with everyone's hospital and doctor bills."

Jake nodded as he caught sight of Wayne and his folks across the room, sitting behind Bishop Hershberger and his wife, Sadie. He knew Wayne probably had a lot of medical bills and would likely have a lot more bills mounting up in the days ahead.

Jake shifted his gaze to the other side of the room and scanned the crowd. When he turned his head to the right, he saw Loraine walking toward the area where the baked goods were sold.

Mom nudged Dad's arm. "Should we have a seat or walk around and look at some of the things that'll soon be up for bid?"

"Let's walk around a bit," he replied. "If I sit too long, my back might cramp up on me."

"Can we get somethin' cold to drink?" Jake's brother Kyle asked, tugging on Mom's hand.

"Jah, sure we can." Mom looked over at Jake. "Are you coming with us, son?"

"Not right now. Think I'll get myself a doughnut or something else to eat. You and the rest of the family go ahead. I'll catch up to you later on."

"When we decide we're ready to bid on something, should we save you a seat?" she asked.

"No, that's okay. After I get my doughnut, I might wander around outside and see what kind of farm machinery's being auctioned off."

Dad's eyebrows shot up. "Why would you need any farm machinery?"

Jake shrugged. "I don't. Just thought I'd nose around. Besides, it's already hot and crowded in here. I don't like being stuck in a stuffy building with a bunch of noisy people."

Jake's brother Elmer poked Jake's arm with his stubby finger. "You never minded noise when you lived with us before you went to Montana."

"That was then; this is now," Jake mumbled.

"Maybe you just don't wanna be with us. Maybe—"

"Never mind, son." Dad gathered the other children together and hurried them in the direction of where the cold drinks were being sold. Mom shuffled behind them, unable to keep up with Dad's long strides.

Jake headed for the baked goods. As soon as he entered the

room, he saw Loraine behind one of the tables. Her cousin Ella stood beside her, making change for an elderly English woman who'd bought two loaves of bread.

"How's it going?" Jake asked, stepping up to Loraine.

"It's going okay. How are things with you?"

"Can't complain, I guess." He smiled. "Being at this benefit auction is a reminder for me that I have a lot to be thankful for. A day like this is a reminder that, but for the grace of God, it could be any of us in need of financial assistance."

She nodded. "I think we all tend to take life for granted at times."

Jake leaned against the table as he studied Loraine. She really was beautiful—inside and out.

She must have realized that he was staring at her, for her cheeks turned pink and she quickly averted his gaze. "Did you want to buy something?" she asked in a near whisper.

"Uh—jah. I'll take a couple of doughnuts."

"What kind would you like—sugar doughnuts, lemon-filled doughnuts, powdered sugar doughnuts, or doughnuts covered with chocolate icing and sprinkles?"

"I'll take a lemon-filled and one dipped in powdered sugar." Jake held up two fingers. "Better make that two powdered sugar doughnuts. I might save one for later."

Loraine snickered. "I guess some things never change. You always did have a sweet tooth, Jake Beechy."

He wiggled his eyebrows and grinned. "You know me so well. Or at least, you used to."

Loraine's face flamed, and when she picked up a powdered sugar doughnut, she gripped it so hard that it broke right in two. "Sorry about that. I'll pick out another one for you."

Jake dug around in his pocket for the money while she gathered up his doughnuts and put them on a paper plate.

"Here you go." He handed her a one-hundred-dollar bill.

"Oh, I'm not sure I have enough change for a bill that size."

"No problem; keep the change. You can call it my donation to

162

the benefit auction, 'cause I probably won't bid on anything here today."

She smiled. "That's so nice of you, Jake. Danki."

"It's the least I can do to help out my friends." Jake turned and started to walk away; then, gathering up his courage, he turned back around. "I thought I might go outside and walk around for a bit. Would you like to walk with me?"

"She's busy helping me," Ella cut in.

The color in Loraine's cheeks deepened. "I did say I'd help sell the baked goods."

Jake bumped her arm with his elbow. "We won't be gone very long."

"We need her help here." Ella shot Jake a look that could have stopped a runaway horse.

Loraine's cousin doesn't like me anymore, Jake thought. *Come to think of it, maybe she never did. Even before I left for Montana, she was never all that friendly toward me. I wonder if I've done something to offend her.*

"How long do you need to help out here?" Jake asked, directing his question to Loraine.

"For as long as we need her." Ella motioned to a group of English people who had just entered the room. "Looks like we're going to be busy for quite a while yet."

Jake looked back at Loraine, and when she said nothing, he decided it was probably time to head outside. "See you later, Loraine."

He made his way quickly through the crowd and was almost to the door when he heard a shrill voice.

"Wait a minute, Jake!"

He spun around with a feeling of dread. "What do you want, Ella?"

"I want to talk to you about Loraine."

"What about her?"

"I hope you have no ideas about you and Loraine getting back together."

"Well, I—"

"She's still in love with Wayne, and once he realizes they can work things out, they'll get married, just like they'd planned."

"You need to get right in your thinking," Jake said through clenched teeth. "Wayne broke up with Loraine, so he has no plans to marry her now."

"That doesn't mean he won't change his mind." Ella's forehead puckered. "If you start seeing Loraine again, everything will get all messed up. Loraine thinks—"

"Fire! Fire! Someone—put out the fire!"

Jake whirled around. He spotted several of the women who'd been selling baked goods running out of that room. With heart pounding and sweat rolling down his face, he tore across the building.

CHAPTER 24

By the time Jake arrived at the baked good's room, all the women were gone. Some of the men were leading the women and children from the main part of the auction barn outside, where they would be safe should the fire start to spread.

As sparks and shooting flames exploded from the light fixture hanging above one of the tables, Jake jumped into action.

"What's going on?" Andrew Yoder asked as he dashed into the room.

Jake pointed upwards. "Looks to me like it's an electrical problem. We need to get the fire out as quickly as possible!"

By this time, the sparks had ignited a pile of cardboard boxes that had now begun to burn. Jake feared if they didn't get the fire out soon, it would become uncontrollable. He looked frantically around the room. "Andrew, do you know where there might be a fire extinguisher?"

"Maybe there's one in the kitchen!" Andrew shouted. "I'll hurry and check!" He rushed out of the room.

"I'd better call 911!" Jake reached into his pocket and pulled out his cell phone.

By the time he'd finished making the call, Andrew was back with a fire extinguisher. Several other men had arrived on the scene, as well.

Once the fire was out and the power had been turned off, Jake breathed a sigh of relief. Everyone had been evacuated from the building, which meant the auction would have to be put on hold until the fire department had arrived and made sure it was safe to resume.

"Maybe we should check the conduit pipe in other parts of the building to be sure that there aren't any hotspots," Jake said to Loraine's father, who'd come into the room to see if his help was needed.

Amos nodded. "It's a dangerous thing when a fire starts like this."

"I'm just glad no one was hurt and that we didn't lose the building," Jake said.

"My daughter was in here selling baked goods, so I appreciate what you did in getting the fire out so quickly." Deep wrinkles formed across Amos's forehead. "Last year during the Mennonite Relief Sale in Goshen, there was a fire. Two of the buildings at the fairgrounds went up in smoke because it wasn't caught in time."

"I didn't know about that," Jake said.

"Guess you wouldn't, since you weren't living here at the time and didn't keep in touch with anyone."

Jake winced at the remark. He wondered if Loraine's dad thought he was a terrible person because he'd taken off to Montana and had quit writing to Loraine.

Just then, a group of firemen swarmed into the building. Jake quickly explained what had happened and suggested they check for possible hotspots in other parts of the building.

"We appreciate the information, and we'll take it from here," one of the firemen said with a nod.

Jake, Amos, and the other Amish men joined the crowd waiting outside. A light rain had begun to fall, and many of the people hovered under umbrellas or one of the tents that had been set up to house some of the farming equipment.

Jake scanned the area until he spotted Loraine. She was talking to Ella and her mother. As much as Jake wanted to speak with Loraine, after the encounter he'd had with Ella awhile ago, he figured he'd better not engage Loraine in conversation in front of her take-charge cousin.

He glanced in another direction and noticed Wayne sitting in his wheelchair across the way. *I think I'll go talk to him,* he decided.

❦ ❧

"I wonder if they'll let us back in the auction barn soon," Wayne's mother said as she pushed his wheelchair under one of the tents.

"I don't know, but I'm glad I took your advice and brought my wheelchair along. I wouldn't want to have to stand out here all this time while we wait to find out."

She nodded soberly. "All the chairs are inside, too. Guess we should have thought to bring some out with us."

"There was no time for that," Wayne said. "It wasn't safe to stay in the building."

Mom glanced over her shoulder. "I see your daed's talking to some of the men in charge. Maybe he has some news to report. I think I'll go find out." She opened her umbrella and scurried away.

Wayne was about to follow when he saw Jake heading his way, so he decided to stay put.

"I hear you're the one who put out the fire," Wayne said when Jake approached.

Jake nodded. "Andrew Yoder helped by getting the fire extinguisher, and then we turned off the power." He motioned to the fire trucks lined up in the parking lot. "Now the firemen are checking things over in other parts of the building, looking for hotspots."

"Guess that makes good sense."

"I saw you walking earlier, but I see that you're in your wheelchair now," Jake said. "Does that mean you haven't adjusted to your new leg yet?"

"No, I haven't. It's a struggle to get my balance, but I'm forcing myself to wear it several hours every day." Wayne frowned deeply. "If I could hobble around on one leg as well as my lamb does on three, I'd have no need for a prosthesis."

"I guess not."

"Have you talked to Loraine today?" Wayne asked, taking their conversation in a different direction.

"I spoke with her for a few minutes when I went into the room where she was selling baked goods. Why do you ask?"

"I was wondering if you've given some thought to what I said the other day about asking her out."

"I didn't talk to her long enough for that." Blotches of red erupted on Jake's cheeks. "Besides, I'm still a little concerned that things aren't really over between you two."

"I told you before, Loraine and I are—"

"I just spoke with some of the firemen," Wayne's father said, stepping between them. "It looks like the auction is over for the day. They want to call in an electrician to check things out and make sure everything in the barn is up to code." He tapped Wayne's shoulder. "It's probably for the best, son. You look really tired, and I've come down with a sore throat, so I think we ought to head for home."

Wayne nodded. "Where's Mom? Does she know we're leaving?"

"I spoke with her a few minutes ago. She's saying good-bye to some of her friends and will meet us out by the buggy." Pop swallowed a couple of times and grimaced. "I can't remember the last time my throat hurt this bad. Sure hope I'm feeling better by Monday, because I've got a lot of work to be done in my shop, and this is no time for me to be getting sick."

"I'm sorry to hear your throat hurts, Pop." Wayne motioned to Jake. "As soon as Jake and I have finished our conversation, I'll meet you and Mom at the buggy."

"Oh, okay." Pop hurried off, and Wayne turned to face Jake again.

"As I was saying before my daed showed up—Loraine I are

not getting married, so you have free rein to ask her out whenever you choose."

Jake hesitated a moment, but then, what Wayne could only classify as a look of relief spread over his face. "All right, I just might ask her out."

"Since that's all settled, I'd better get going. Don't want to keep my folks waiting any longer." Wayne forced a smile and turned his wheelchair toward the opening of the tent. He had to get out of here quick, before Jake saw the look of regret that no doubt showed on his face.

Wayne was almost to the area where the horses had been tied, when Ella rushed up to him, waving her umbrella.

"Hold up a minute, would you, Wayne? I need to talk to you about something!"

Wayne halted and waited for her to catch up to him. "What's up, Ella?"

She stopped in front of his wheelchair and bent down so her umbrella covered both of them. "I need to talk to you about Jake Beechy."

"What about Jake?"

"He's been hanging around Loraine a lot lately. I think he wants to date her again."

Wayne shrugged. "So, what's that to me?"

Her eyes widened. "Are you kidding? Up until the day of our accident, you and Loraine were a happy couple looking forward to your wedding, and—"

"Things are different now. I'm not the man Loraine needs anymore."

"How can you say that? Don't you know how much she loves you?"

"I'm not sure she ever really loved me." Wayne couldn't keep the bitterness out of his tone. "As I'm sure you already know, she used to love Jake. I was only her second choice."

"It may seem that way, but—"

"Loraine feels sorry for me now that I'm a cripple, and she

169

thinks she has to keep her promise to marry me." He shook his head. "But she doesn't. I've released her of that promise and told her that she's free to get back with Jake."

"What if she doesn't want Jake? What if she wants you?"

"Then she'll have to make *him* her second choice, because we're not getting back together so we won't ever be getting married!"

Ella released an exasperated sigh. "I see your mamm's waving for you to come, but I just want to say one more thing before you go."

"What's that?"

"If you want my opinion, you're full of *hochmut*."

"I am not full of pride; I'm just doing what I think is best."

"Jah, well, if you don't wake up and come to your senses soon, you're going to live to regret it!"

Ella dashed off, and Wayne sat in the pouring down rain, shaking his head and feeling sorry for himself. "I already do regret it," he mumbled, "but it's the only way."

CHAPTER 25

"How's your throat feel today?" Ada asked when Crist entered the kitchen on Monday morning.

"Not so good. It's even worse than it was two days ago." He touched his throat and winced. "I can barely swallow."

"Open your mouth and let me have a look-see," she said, standing on her tiptoes.

He shook his head. "No need for that; you're not a doctor."

"I just want to see if your throat is red or swollen. If there are any white patches, it could mean that you have an infection." Ada hurried across the room and opened a kitchen drawer. She returned, holding a flashlight. "Now, open real wide."

Crist stood like a statue for several seconds, but finally grunted and opened his mouth.

Ada squinted as she shined the flashlight inside. "Umm...I'm afraid your throat doesn't look good at all. After breakfast, you'd better go on back to bed while I run out to the phone shed and call the doctor's office."

"Does my throat look that bad?"

She gave a slow nod. "You'll probably need some antibiotics to get it under control."

He groaned. "Oh, great. This is just not what I need this morning."

"What's not what you need?" Wayne asked, wheeling into the room.

"Your daed's throat is still sore, and I think he needs to see the doctor."

Wayne looked over at Crist. "That's too bad, Pop. I was hoping you'd feel better this morning."

"You and me both."

Ada motioned to Wayne's wheelchair. "How come you're not wearing your prosthesis?"

"My leg's kind of sore from where the appliance rubs, so I decided not to wear it today."

"Maybe you need to have it adjusted," Ada said. "Want me to see if Dr. Bower can take a look at it if I'm able to get an appointment for your daed today?"

"That's okay," Wayne said. "I have an appointment to see the specialist next Monday, so I'll talk to him about my problem when I go in then."

"You mean you're not going to try that silly tapping method?" Ada still couldn't believe her son thought something like that could actually work. But then, maybe it was a mind over matter kind of thing, and if that was the case, then he could have talked himself out of the pain.

Wayne shook his head. "The tapping method helped my phantom pains, but I don't think it'll take the place of an adjustment on my prosthesis."

"So what are you going to do until next Monday—sit around in your wheelchair all the time?" Crist asked, giving Wayne a look of disapproval.

"I'll try wearing the prosthesis again later today or tomorrow at the latest. It might feel better by then." Wayne rolled his chair up to the table. "Is breakfast ready yet, Mom?"

"Not quite. The bacon's still frying, and I have to do up some eggs."

"No bacon for me," Crist said. "I'd never be able to eat it."

"How about some oatmeal?"

"That sounds good."

She touched his arm. "If I do get an appointment for you, would you like me to go along?"

"No, thanks. I'll probably run a few errands while I'm in town, so I might be gone awhile."

"I wouldn't mind running some errands with you," she said.

He shook his head. "Thanks anyway, but I'll go alone."

"Whatever you say." Ada shuffled over to the stove. It was obvious that Crist didn't want her to go with him. Could he still be upset because she'd refused to go to Sarasota to celebrate their anniversary? Or was he worried that she might embarrass him by asking too many questions of the doctor?

She looked over at Crist and then at Wayne. *Men can be so hard to figure out at times.*

~ ❧ ~

"Are you feeling okay this morning?" Ella asked her mother as they cleared the breakfast dishes from the table. "You look really tired, and I noticed during breakfast that your hands were shaking."

"I think it's all the excitement of the weekend. I was feeling pretty keyed up when we left the auction on Saturday, and then, with Sunday services being held here, it left me a bit drained." Mom placed the plates she was holding into the kitchen sink. "I had a hard time sleeping last night, too, which didn't help, either."

"I'm sorry to hear that. Why don't you go rest while Charlene and I do the dishes?"

"I really should go to Shipshewana this morning. I need to get some sewing notions at Spector's."

"Just give me a list of what you need, and I'll run to town for you," Ella said.

Mom smiled wearily. "Oh, I'd appreciate that. You're such a thoughtful *dochder.*"

"Ella can go to town right now if you want her to," Charlene spoke up as she brought the rest of the dishes to the sink. "I can manage to wash and dry the dishes on my own."

"Are you sure you don't mind?" Ella asked.

"Don't mind a bit."

Mom patted Charlene's back. "Danki. You're a thoughtful daughter, too." She yawned noisily. "Now, I think I'll go rest."

"I'm worried about her," Ella whispered after Mom had left the room. "She hasn't been the same since Raymond died."

Charlene wrinkled her nose. "Of course she hasn't. What mother could be the same after one of their kinner passed away?"

Ella gave her sister a little nudge. "When did you get to be so *schmaert*?"

"I've always been smart," Charlene said with a smirk. "You've just been too busy to notice."

"Jah, maybe so." Ella grabbed her sweater and black outer bonnet and hurried out the door.

After the heavy drizzle they'd had for the past two days, a thick layer of fog covered much of the land. Ella shivered and quickened her steps. She didn't look forward to going anywhere in this chilly weather but figured the sooner she got it over with, the better it would be.

She hitched her horse to the buggy and was preparing to back away from the hitching rail when—*whack!*—something bumped the rear end of her buggy. Her head snapped forward and she gasped. "What on earth was that?"

She jerked the door open and was just getting ready to climb down, when Jake stepped up to her buggy. Ella squinted at him. "Did you have anything to do with that jolt I just felt?"

Jake nodded. "Afraid so. The front of my rig caught the back of your rig as I was pulling in. You ought to take a look behind you before you pull out."

"Well, you shouldn't have snuck up behind me like that. What are you doing here, anyway?"

"I wasn't sneaking. I came to shoe one of your daed's horses. Didn't he tell you I was coming?"

"No, he sure didn't." Ella wrinkled her nose. "You shouldn't have come barreling in here, smashing into my buggy."

"I didn't barrel or smash your buggy. It was only a little tap." Jake thumped the spot where his chin dimple was and scowled at her. "Who gave you driving lessons, anyhow?"

"My daed, that's who."

"Well, he must have been wearin' blinders."

Refusing to let Jake get the best of her, Ella folded her arms and glared at him.

He motioned to the back of her buggy. "I don't think any damage was done, so you needn't look at me as though I'm your enemy."

"There better not be any damage," Ella said through tight lips. She rushed around to the back of the buggy and was relieved to see that there was no dent. Even so, she was irked at the way Jake kept smirking at her.

"You're very inconsiderate, you know that, Jake?"

His eyebrows lifted. "You think I'm inconsiderate because I accidentally bumped your buggy?"

"I'm not just talking about the fact that you bumped my buggy."

"What then?"

"I think you were very inconsiderate when you took off for Montana two years ago and left Loraine in the lurch. Don't you know that it almost broke my cousin's heart?"

Jake opened his mouth as if to defend himself, but Ella rushed on. "Your lack of consideration proves what kind of a person you are. I hope Loraine never believes anything you have to say, because I sure don't!"

Ella thought she would feel better for spouting off like that, but all it had done was leave her with a sick feeling in the pit of her stomach. She had watched Loraine mope around for months after Jake left Indiana. When he'd quit writing and didn't return home, Ella was afraid Loraine might never get over being jilted by her first love. But then Wayne, bless his heart, had become Loraine's good friend. Ella had been real pleased when the couple had fallen in love and become engaged to be married. She just wished Wayne hadn't ruined things by breaking up with Loraine.

Couldn't he see that she would be better off with him than she would be with self-centered, selfish Jake?

Jake cleared his throat a couple of times and stared at the ground. "I know what I did was wrong, but I've grown up and changed since then."

"Have you really? From what I heard, the only reason you came home at all was because you heard about the accident my cousins and I were in. If it hadn't been for that, I'll bet you'd still be in Montana playing cowboy."

"Well, I—"

"You'd better not break Loraine's heart again. I mean it, Jake." Ella's hand shook as she pointed at him. "Because if you do break my cousin's heart, then you'll have to answer to me!"

"I won't break Loraine's heart. I care about her a lot."

"If you care about her so much, then you'll leave her alone. She and Wayne are meant to be together, and if you'll just stay out of the picture, I'm sure in time they'll get back together."

Jake looked like he was going to say something more, but Ella's father showed up just then.

"Glad to see you made it here early," he said, thumping Jake on the back. "I have a chiropractor's appointment this morning and have to be there soon, and I'd like to get my horse shod before I go." He looked over at Ella and smiled. "Your mamm said you were going to pick up some things for her in town, but I can do it if you'd rather stay home."

Ella shook her head. "Since today's my day off from working in your shop, I don't mind going. In fact, getting away from here for a while might be just what I need." She glanced over at Jake, but he shrugged and walked away.

Ella climbed into her buggy again, gathered up the reins, and headed down the driveway at a pretty good clip. She wished Jake would leave Indiana for good!

❧ ❧

"Where are you going?" Wayne's mother called as he headed for the back door, wearing his prosthesis.

"I'm sick of sitting around. I'm going outside to check on my lamb."

"But I thought your leg was bothering you. You said earlier that you weren't going to wear the prosthesis today."

"I said I might try it later on, and I've decided to give it a try now." Wayne hurried out the door before Mom could respond.

Once outside, he drew in a couple of deep breaths. The air felt clean and fresh after the rain they'd had. Even though the rain had stopped, the sun had tried all morning to make an appearance but never quite overcame the low-hanging clouds. He guessed that was better than chilling rain.

Wayne hobbled out to the fence that separated their yard from the pasture and stood watching the sheep graze. He couldn't help but smile when Tripod let out a loud *baa* and headed straight for him. He bent over and reached through the fence so he could pet the sheep's head. "You've accepted your plight in life, haven't you, girl?" he murmured. "Sure wish I could do the same."

Tripod turned and rubbed her side against the wooden boards on the fence.

"What's the matter, girl? Have you got an itch?" He rubbed her wooly back and sides and snickered when she closed her eyes, obviously enjoying the attention.

He glanced over at the watering trough and noticed that it was almost empty. "Guess I'd better give you and the other sheep some fresh water to drink."

Tripod let out a loud *baa* as Wayne moved away from the fence.

"Don't worry, girl; I'll be back."

Wayne made his way over to the hose, turned on the water, and then hauled the hose back across the yard. That seemed easier than having to walk back to the spigot and turning the water on after he'd placed the hose in the trough.

Poking the hose through the fence slats, he let it drop into the trough. He then stood back and watched as Tripod and the other sheep eagerly drank their fill.

One of the more aggressive rams pushed two ewes out of the way and bunted the hose with his nose. The next thing Wayne knew, the hose was on the ground with water shooting into the air.

"Oh, great," Wayne moaned. He reached through the slats to grab the hose, and at the same time his hat fell off his head and landed in the pasture on the other side of the fence.

He winced as he hobbled over to the gate and stepped into the pasture. The part of his leg where the prosthesis was attached had begun to throb.

Wayne leaned down to retrieve the hat, when—*whoomp!*—the rambunctious ram butted him from behind, sending him into the watering trough with a *splash*!

Wayne gasped as the chilly water hit his body. Gritting his teeth, he grabbed the edge of the trough and tried to pull himself up. *Splash!*—he fell right back in.

He tried two more times to get out of the water, but with no success. He realized that he had no other choice but to call for help and hope that Mom would hear him hollering from inside the house.

Just then, a van pulled into the yard and stopped near the fence. A middle-aged English man got out.

"Looks like you're in need of some help," he said, stepping into the pasture.

Wayne accepted the man's hand, despite the humiliation he felt over being found in such an awkward, embarrassing position.

"Thanks," he mumbled as the man pulled him to his feet. "I was stuck in there and couldn't get out."

The man chuckled. "If it was a warm summer day, I might have thought you were trying to cool off, but since winter will be coming soon, I'm guessing you didn't purposely take a dip in that old water trough."

"No, I sure didn't." Wayne shook his head, spraying water everywhere. "One of our rams knocked me into the trough when I was trying to pick up my hat. I never even saw it coming."

The man's gaze traveled around the pasture. "Say, did you know that one of your ewes is limping real bad?" he asked, pointing to Wayne's crippled lamb.

"That's Tripod. She had one of her legs amputated not long ago." Wayne pulled up his pant leg, exposing his prosthesis. "See, just like me."

A look of shock registered on the man's face. "I didn't realize you had only one leg."

"Lost it in an accident a few months ago. If you live around here, I'm surprised you didn't hear about it."

"Actually, I'm new to the area," the man said. "One of my friends told me that an Amish man runs a taxidermy shop here, so I brought over a couple of pheasants I'd like to have stuffed."

"It's my dad's business, but he's not here right now," Wayne said. "You can leave the birds with me if you like, and I'll see that he gets 'em." He motioned to the house. "If you'd like to put the pheasants on the back porch and come inside with me, I'll take down your information and give it to Pop as soon as he gets back."

"Oh, okay."

The man followed Wayne up to the house. When they stepped into the kitchen, Mom greeted them with a frown. "What happened to you, Wayne? Your clothes are sopping wet!"

"I fell in the watering trough, and this nice man was kind enough to help me out."

Mom regarded the Englisher with a curious stare. "I don't believe I've met you before."

He extended his hand. "My name's Howard McKenna. I brought some pheasants by to have them stuffed."

"Oh, I see. Well, my husband's not here right now."

"Yes, I know. I'm going to leave the pheasants, as well as my name and phone number. He can call me whenever they're done."

Mom nodded. Then she turned to look at Wayne. "I'll take care of getting the details from Mr. McKenna. You'd better get out of those wet clothes before you end up sick like your daed."

Wayne didn't argue with her. His teeth had already begun to chatter.

~≈ ≋~

When Wayne returned to the kitchen, the man was gone, and Pop was sitting at the table holding a cup of tea.

"What'd the doctor say about your sore throat?" Wayne asked as he took a seat beside his dad.

Pop grimaced. "Said it's strep."

"Ach, no!"

"He gave me a prescription for an antibiotic, but I was feeling so rough, I didn't even go to the pharmacy; just came straight home."

Mom reached over and touched Pop's forehead. "You're running a fever, Crist, and you don't look well at all! I insist that you go right to bed. I'll head to town and get the medicine for you."

"My horse is in the pasture, and the buggy's put away, so you'll have to get them both out again."

Mom shook her head. "That'll take me too much time. I'll just ride my bike to the pharmacy. It shouldn't take long at all."

~≈ ≋~

As Loraine sifted flour into a bowl and added some sugar, her thoughts carried her back to the auction on Saturday. Even though they hadn't been able to resume the auction after the fire was put out, she'd learned that they'd taken in a pretty good sum of money that morning, and it had been decided that another auction wouldn't be necessary at this time. Loraine was glad for that, because she didn't think she could go to another auction any time soon and watch Wayne at a distance, feeling that she couldn't even speak to him. It was ridiculous for him to think they couldn't be together just because he'd lost his leg. And him saying he didn't love her anymore made no sense at all. How could a person love someone one day and not the next?

Loraine stirred the cookie batter so hard that her fingers began to ache. *Why, God, why? Why did Wayne have to lose his leg? Why can't he accept the fact that I still love him and want to be his wife?*

An image of Jake flashed into her mind. She had wanted to be his wife once, too. Had she loved him more than she did Wayne? Could she let herself love Jake again?

"You'd better let me take that job over for you," Mom said when she stepped into the kitchen. "It's almost time for you to go to work, and if you don't leave now, you'll probably be late."

Loraine glanced at the clock on the far wall. She'd been asked to work the afternoon shift today, and it was nearly one o'clock. She did need to get going.

She handed Mom the wooden spoon she'd been using and removed the apron she wore to do her household chores. "I guess I should have started the cookies sooner," she said. "I don't know what I was thinking."

"It's all right; I'll do them. You run along and have a good day at work."

"Danki, I'll try." Loraine slipped into her jacket and outer head covering and headed out the door. When she stepped outside, the cold, damp air sent a shiver through her body. She pulled her jacket tightly around her neck, hurried to the barn, and took out her horse.

A short time later, she was headed down the road toward Shipshewana. She'd only gone a short ways when she spotted Ada Lambright pedaling her bicycle along the shoulder of the road. Suddenly, Ada's bike started to wobble. It looked like she had hit a patch of loose gravel. Loraine shrieked when the bike toppled over and Ada fell to the ground.

"Whoa!" She halted the horse and clambered out of the buggy. Then she raced over to Ada.

A thin, wordless cry tore from the poor woman's lips as she looked up at Loraine.

Loraine dropped down beside her. "Are you hurt, Ada?"

"I think my leg's broken. I've never had such horrible pain." Ada's voice sounded muffled, as if she were trying to talk under water.

That's when Loraine noticed that Ada's left leg was bent at a very odd angle.

She knew she needed to make Ada as comfortable as possible, and the hard ground was anything but comfortable.

"I'm going to my buggy to get some blankets," Loraine said. "Just hold real still and I'll be right back." She hurried off, and returned with two blankets. She folded one and put it under Ada's head and draped the other one over Ada's shivering body.

"Can you hang on here while I'll go to the nearest phone shed and make a call for help?" Loraine asked, touching Ada's shoulder.

Ada nodded, as tears seeped out from under her lashes. "Guess I don't have much choice."

"I'll be back as quick as I can." Loraine hurried to her buggy and tore off down the road.

CHAPTER 26

Loraine paced from the row of chairs in the hospital waiting room over to the window and back again. It wasn't that long ago that she'd been in another hospital waiting room, waiting to hear how Wayne and the others were doing after their accident. Now she waited impatiently for some news on Ada's condition.

Loraine had called the paramedics from Sandy and Glen Pritchard's house, then left a message on the answering machine in the Lambrights' phone shed. The Pritchards had dropped Loraine off to wait with Ada until the ambulance came and had taken Loraine's buggy home to their house, where she would pick it up later. If she hadn't been in such a hurry to get back to Ada, she might have stopped at the Lambrights', but the Pritchards' place was a lot closer, and Loraine knew she needed to get back to Ada as quickly as possible.

During the time Loraine and Ada had waited for the ambulance to arrive, Ada had told her that Crist was in bed with a bad sore throat and that Wayne had been having trouble with his prosthesis. Loraine figured it wasn't likely that either Wayne or Crist would check for phone messages today, so they'd have to be told about Ada when Loraine brought her home.

After they'd arrived at the hospital emergency room in Goshen, Loraine had called her boss and explained what had happened, asking if she could be excused from work today. She was pleased that Esther had said yes and had seemed so understanding. Then she'd called Marge Nelson and alerted her to the fact that they would need a ride home once Ada's leg had been taken care of.

If things had gone as Wayne and I had originally planned, we'd be married now, Loraine thought painfully. *I'd be here at the hospital waiting for news on my mother-in-law, not my ex-fiancé's mother, who didn't even tell me thanks for seeing that she got help today.*

Tears sprang to Loraine's eyes. *I shouldn't expect any thanks for what I've done. It's my Christian duty to help others, whether they thank me or not.*

"You look tired," Marge said, when she entered the room. "Have you had any news on Ada yet?"

"No, and I'm beginning to worry. It's been over an hour since they took her back to be examined." Loraine sighed and flopped into a chair. "I wonder what could be taking so long. I hope it's not a bad sign."

"I'm sure everything will be fine," Marge said in her usual positive tone. "You just need to sit there and relax."

Loraine plucked a magazine off the table and pretended to read it. She wasn't just worried about Ada; she was worried about Wayne and how he would manage with both of his parents laid up.

"Maybe I should have gone over to the Lambrights' and told them about Ada instead of coming here," Loraine said. "I'm sure Wayne and his dad are wondering why she hasn't returned home, and I doubt that either of them has checked their answering machine."

Marge opened her purse and removed her cell phone. "I'll give my husband a call and ask him to stop by their place on his way home from work and explain things to them."

"Thanks. That's a real good idea."

Marge punched in a few numbers and lifted the cell phone to her ear. Several seconds went by before she clicked off the phone and dropped it back in her purse. "I should have remembered."

"Remembered what?"

"Brian didn't answer because he left his cell phone at home this morning, so it wouldn't make any sense for me to leave a message on his voice mail."

"I'm Dr. Gaylord," a middle-aged man announced as he stepped into the room. "Are you a relative of Ada Lambright?" he asked Loraine.

She shook her head. "I'm just a friend of the family, and I'm waiting to take Ada home."

"I'm afraid she won't be going home until sometime tomorrow," the doctor said. "She's suffered a bad break in her leg, and we're going to have to do some surgery before we can set it."

"I'm real sorry to hear that. Her family has no idea she's here, so I think we should let them know right away." She looked over at Marge.

Marge nodded. "I'll drive you there now if you like."

"I appreciate that, but I'd like to see Ada first and let her know that I picked up Crist's prescription and will stop by the house and let her family know what's happened to her."

"Mrs. Lambright's being prepared for surgery right now," the doctor said, "but I'll see that she gets your message."

"Thank you." Loraine stood and moved toward the door. Marge joined her.

"With Ada being laid up for the next several weeks, she's going to need a lot of help," Loraine said as she and Marge headed down the hall toward the exit.

"I'm sure the women in your community will chip in and do whatever they can."

Loraine nodded. "I'll help out as much as possible, too."

❧ ❧

Wayne glanced at the clock on the kitchen wall and frowned. Mom had been gone several hours already. It shouldn't have taken her this long to pick up Pop's prescription.

Maybe she stopped off to visit one of her friends, he thought as he peered out the window. *Maybe I should go to the phone shed and*

*check the answering machine. If she did stop somewhere, she might
have called and left a message.*

He slipped into his jacket, grabbed his crutches for support,
and headed out the door.

~·~

As Loraine neared the Lambrights' house, her heartbeat picked
up speed. She had wanted to see Wayne again, just not under
these circumstances.

She clucked to her horse and guided him off the road and onto
the Lambrights' driveway. Smoke curled from the chimney of the
house, so she figured either Wayne or his dad must be tending the
fire.

She spotted Wayne on the porch, with a pair of crutches under
his arms. He stood motionless until she pulled her rig up to the hitching rail, and then he headed her way. By the time he reached her, she
was out of the buggy and had tied the horse to the rail.

Deep wrinkles formed in Wayne's forehead when he stepped
up to her. "What are you doing here? I thought I told you—"

"I came to let you know that your mamm's been in an accident.
She's in the hospital in Goshen with a broken leg."

Wayne's eyebrows shot up. "What happened?"

Loraine quickly explained the details of how she'd seen Ada
fall off her bike and had then gone to call for help. "When Marge
and I left the hospital, I asked her to drop me off at my house so
I could tell my folks what was going on and let them know I was
coming over here. I figured you'd be worried about your mamm."

"Jah, I sure was."

"I also came over to fix you some supper," she said.

"You're here to fix supper?" His mouth gaped open.

She nodded. "Your mamm told me about your daed being
sick, so I figured since you—"

"I may be handicapped, but I'm not an invalid! I'm perfectly
capable of fixing Pop and me something to eat."

Loraine cringed, and the pressure behind her eyes signaled

that tears were forthcoming. Until the accident had occurred, Wayne had never been so sharp with her. Now, he always seemed to be full of anger and resentment.

With a sigh of resignation, Loraine turned toward her buggy. "If you don't want me to fix supper, then I'll just take the chicken and potatoes I was planning to prepare and head for home."

Wayne stepped in front of her, and she noticed that his expression had softened a bit. "Did you say, 'baked chicken'?"

Loraine nodded. She knew baked chicken was one of Wayne's favorite dishes, so hopefully, he might change his mind.

She wasn't disappointed when he gave her a bird dog look and said, "I've. . .uh. . .changed my mind. If you're still willing, then I'd appreciate having you fix my supper."

"I'm more than willing." Loraine reached into the buggy and pulled out a cardboard box.

"I'd help you with that, but I don't think I could manage it and hold onto my crutches, too," he said.

"It's not heavy. I'll do fine on my own."

Wayne started moving toward the house, and she walked beside him. They were halfway there when he halted and drew in a quick breath.

"Are you okay?" she asked with concern.

"I've been wearing my prosthesis most of the day, and the stump of my leg is really sore."

"Do you need my help, because if you do, then I'll just—"

"I can manage fine on my own!"

Loraine bristled. "Why must you always be so defensive?"

"I just don't need you treating me like a boppli. I get enough of that from my mamm."

"I'm not your mamm."

"Never said you were. Just said you were treating me the way she does."

Loraine kept walking. There was no use arguing with him; it wouldn't solve a thing.

When she stepped into Ada's kitchen, she was surprised to see that the dishes were done and the room looked clean and orderly. *Of course,* she reasoned, *Ada probably cleaned it this morning. It's not likely that Wayne cleaned the kitchen—not with his leg hurting.*

"I'm going to let Pop know about Mom, and see if he feels up to eating anything for supper," Wayne said.

Loraine reached into the box and withdrew the container of cut-up chicken. "I can fix him some soup if his throat's too sore to deal with baked chicken."

"Okay, I'll tell him that." Wayne hobbled out of the room, and Loraine set right to work in Ada's kitchen.

Wayne didn't return until the chicken was almost done. This time he was in his wheelchair. "Pop's throat still hurts real bad, so he'll just have some soup," he said.

"That's fine. Oh, I almost forgot." Loraine reached into the cardboard box and pulled out a paper sack. "At your mamm's request, I picked up your daed's prescription. If you'd like to take it to him, I'll bring in the soup as soon as it's ready."

Loraine's fingers brushed Wayne's as she handed him the bottle of pills. The innocent contact brought warmth to her cheeks.

Apparently unaffected by her touch, Wayne placed the bottle of antibiotics in his pocket and rolled out of the room, mumbling something under his breath that she couldn't understand.

Oh, how Loraine wished things could be as they once were. The tension she felt between her and Wayne and the anger and despondency she heard in his voice made it difficult not to be snappish with him in return. It grieved her to realize that, unless God brought a miracle, things would never be the same between her and Wayne.

CHAPTER 27

Rivulets of sweat poured off Wayne's forehead as he tossed and turned in his rumpled sheets. It would be time to get up soon, and if he didn't get a few more hours' sleep, he wouldn't be worth anything all day. He'd had trouble falling asleep, thinking about Loraine and how wonderful the supper she'd fixed had tasted. He hated to admit it, but he'd enjoyed being with her. As they'd shared a meal at the table, it was a taste of what it would be like if they were husband and wife. Wayne had been careful to keep his distance, however, and spoke only when she'd asked a question. No point in letting her think there was even a chance of them getting back together.

If only I felt capable of supporting her and being able to meet all of her needs, he thought with regret. *That fall I took in the water trough only confirms that I'm not able to care for myself, much less look after a wife and children.*

He punched his pillow and rolled onto his side. *I love Loraine too much to let her spend the rest of her life taking care of a cripple. She needs a whole man—one she can count on to always be there for her. She needs to get back with Jake.* He gave his pillow another good punch. *I need to keep after Jake and make sure that it happens.*

❧ ❦

"You're up earlier than usual this morning," Priscilla said when she

189

stepped into the kitchen and found Loraine in front of the sink.

"I want to stop by the Lambrights' and check on Wayne and his daed before I head to work, so I need to get an early start on my day." Loraine placed the last of her dishes in the dishpan and dried her hands on a clean towel. "I've already eaten, so unless you need my help fixing breakfast for you and Dad, I'll be on my way."

Priscilla shook her head. "I don't need your help with breakfast, but I don't see why you have to go over to the Lambrights' again this morning."

Loraine's forehead creased. "With Ada being laid up with a broken leg, Crist having strep throat, and Wayne dealing with the loss of his leg, they need someone to help out over there."

"I realize that, but does that *someone* have to be you?"

"Maybe not, but since they have no other family members living nearby, I thought—"

"There are others in our community who I'm sure will help." Priscilla pulled the pot of coffee off the stove and poured herself a cup. "I'm wondering if the real reason you're going over there isn't just so you can spend more time with Wayne. Are you hoping you can get him to change his mind about marrying you?"

Loraine's face flamed. "I do want to be with him, and I'm hoping that he will change his mind about marrying me, but that's not the reason I said I would help."

"Are you hoping Ada will become friendlier toward you if you do all her chores? Is that the reason you're overextending yourself?"

"I'm not overextending myself, Mom, and I'm not helping out in order to impress Ada or anyone else."

"You don't plan to go over there every day, I hope."

"I'll go before and after work, and on my days off, I'll probably be there most of the day. That way, I can wash clothes for them, and also clean their house."

"As I said before, I'm sure someone else can do all that." Priscilla took a drink from her cup and winced when it burned her lips. "It doesn't have to be you!"

"But I want it to be me. I still care about Wayne, and I want to help him and his family."

Priscilla lowered herself into a chair. She knew if she said too much, she would only drive her daughter away. "You can do whatever you like; just don't expect any thanks from Ada. She's been in a foul mood ever since Wayne's accident, and I doubt that your helping out there will change her attitude any."

"I don't care about that. I'm not helping to make Ada like me." Loraine slipped into her jacket and picked up her purse. "See you later, Mom. Have a good day."

When the back door clicked shut, Priscilla ambled over to the window. "What a dreadful day," she mumbled, peered out at the dismal-looking gray sky. It looked like there was more rain coming, which she could certainly do without. The dreary day clearly matched her mood.

❦ ❦

As Loraine headed to the Lambrights', a sense of excitement welled in her soul. She was anxious to see Wayne. He'd been awfully quiet during supper last night, but at least he'd seemed to enjoy the meal she'd prepared and had even thanked her for it. When she'd said she would be back this morning to fix his breakfast, she was grateful that he hadn't argued with her. At least that was a step in the right direction.

As Loraine neared the crossroad leading to the Lambrights', she spotted another buggy up ahead. When she drew closer, the driver pulled to the side of the road and stopped. Jake climbed down and signaled her to pull over.

"I thought that was you behind me," he said after he'd come around to the driver's side of her buggy. "Where are you heading so early this morning?"

"I might ask you the same thing."

"I have a horse to shoe for an English fellow who lives nearby. He wanted it done right away this morning, so I'm heading there now." Jake offered Loraine a sincere-looking smile. "You can't be heading to work this early. Am I right?"

"I'm going over to the Lambrights' to fix Wayne and his daed some breakfast. When I'm done, I'll be going to work."

"Why would you be fixing breakfast for the Lambrights?" Jake asked. "Isn't that Ada's job?"

"Ada's not there. She fell off her bicycle yesterday and broke her leg. She won't be going home from the hospital until sometime today."

"Too bad about her leg. That family's sure had their share of troubles, haven't they?"

Loraine nodded. "Since Ada won't be able to do much for the next several weeks, I've decided to help out whenever I can."

"That's real nice of you, but can't Wayne or his daed fix their meals?"

"Under normal conditions they probably could, but Crist has strep throat, and Wayne's having a hard time adjusting to his prosthesis."

Jake thumped his chin a few times. "I'll bet they could probably use some help with the outside chores. Maybe I'll swing by there after I finish shoeing the horse and see what needs to be done."

"I'm sure they'd appreciate it." Loraine started to turn away but turned back. "By the way, have you talked to Wayne yet about his decision to break up with me?"

Jake scuffed the toe of his boot in the dirt, and his cheeks turned pink. "Well, I tried to once, but Wayne didn't give me much chance to say a whole lot, and what I did say didn't seem to be appreciated."

Loraine dropped her gaze to the ground. "Oh, I see."

"I can try again if you like."

She lifted her gaze to meet his. "No, don't bother. If Wayne thinks he's being pushed, he might never change his mind."

"I guess you're right." Jake gave the dirt another pass with his toe. "Guess I'd better go. See you later, Loraine." He gave her a quick smile and sprinted for his buggy.

As soon as Jake pulled out, Loraine got her horse moving again. *Despite what Ella says, Jake really does seem to care about other people,* she thought. *I just wish I knew whether he'll be sticking around this time or not.*

CHAPTER 28

Loraine had just returned to the kitchen after taking Crist some poached eggs on a tray and was getting ready to serve Wayne a plate of eggs, when a knock sounded on the back door.

"I'll get it!" Wayne wheeled his chair out of the room before Loraine could respond.

He returned a few seconds later with Jake at his side.

"I heard that your mamm broke her leg and your daed's down with a sore throat," Jake said to Wayne. "Thought I'd come by and see if you need my help with anything."

"Guess I could use some help feeding the livestock, but I'm feeling so hungry it's making me a bit shaky, so no chores will be done till after I've eaten." Wayne motioned to the table. "Would you like to join us for breakfast?"

"My mamm fed me a decent breakfast before I left home, but I worked up an appetite shoeing Milo Watkin's horse, so if you've got enough to go around, I think I could eat a bit more." Jake looked over at Loraine, as if needing her approval.

"There are plenty of eggs," she said with a nod. Maybe with Jake here, Wayne would be more talkative than he had been last night.

"How bad is your daed's sore throat?" Jake asked Wayne.

"Still pretty sore, and he's got about as much energy as an old hound dog on a hot summer day."

Jake chuckled. "Speaking of hound dogs, one of the fellows at the ranch where I worked in Montana told me a story about a very smart hound dog. Want to hear it?"

Wayne shook his head. "Not really."

"I'd like to hear it," Loraine said as she placed a platter of scrambled eggs and some bacon on the table. She took a seat between the two men. "Let's pray first; then Jake can tell us his story."

All heads bowed, and when their prayers were done, Loraine handed the platter of eggs to Wayne. "I hope these are the way you like them."

"I'm sure they're fine." Wayne spooned some onto his plate and handed the platter to Jake.

"Mmm, these sure do look good." He helped himself and passed the eggs to Loraine. "Now about that story.... An Englisher had a sign in his front yard that read: TALKING HOUND DOG FOR SALE—$5.

" 'Who do you think you are, advertising a talking dog?' the man's neighbor asked. 'There's no such animal!'

"Just then the dog looked up at the man and said, 'I used to be the richest dog in the world, but my owner took all my money and won't buy me any food.'

"The neighbor's mouth dropped open. 'Well, what do you know? That dog really can talk!' He looked at the dog's owner and said, 'How come you're selling this remarkable dog for only five dollars?'

" 'Because,' said the dog's owner. 'I'm gettin' real tired of listening to all his lies!'

"The hound dog looked up at the neighbor, tipped his head back, and howled. 'I'm not a liar; I just remember real big!' "

Loraine laughed and was pleased when Wayne actually snickered. It was good to see him relax a bit and respond to Jake's humor.

Jake told a couple more jokes, and they visited about the weather and various other things as they ate. When the meal was over, Loraine cleared the table and ran warm water into the sink. She was surprised when Jake followed her across the room.

"Why don't you wash, and I'll dry?" he suggested.

Loraine glanced at the clock on the far wall. "I need to leave for work soon, so I appreciate your offer of help." She turned to face Wayne. "Is there anything else you'd like me to do before I have to head out?"

He shook his head.

"Okay, then. I'll come back after work and fix your supper." Loraine smiled. "Hopefully, your mamm will be home from the hospital by then."

Wayne nodded. "Our main driver isn't available right now, but I called Marge Nelson last night. She said she'll go to the hospital and get Mom whenever she's ready to come home. She'll be checking with the hospital sometime this morning."

Loraine smiled. "Marge is usually available whenever we need a driver."

"I still have my truck," Jake put in. "So I could drive you, or anyone in your family, anywhere you need to go."

"I thought you'd been driving a horse and buggy since you came home," Wayne said without commenting on whether he'd accept a ride.

Jake nodded. "I have been driving a horse and buggy most of the time, but I still have my truck. Until I'm ready to join the church, I plan to keep it."

"I'll bet your folks aren't too happy about that," Wayne said.

"You're right. My daed's been giving me a hard time about joining the church, but I told him I won't do it until I feel ready."

You were ready once, but you ran off to Montana and never looked back, Loraine thought with regret. The sponge she held slipped from her fingers and plopped into the water, splashing water and soapy bubbles onto the front of her dress.

Jake chuckled. "You'd better be careful or you'll be washin' yourself instead of those dishes."

She laughed, and swatted his arm with her wet, soapy hand.

"You'd better watch it now, or this could get ugly." The twinkle in Jake's eyes let Loraine know he was only teasing. It was nice to have someone to kid around with again. Wayne sure wasn't in the mood to tease her these days. In fact, the last time she remembered him teasing her was the day they'd been riding in Paul Crawford's van, heading for Hershey Park.

With a grunt, Wayne pushed his wheelchair away from the table. "I'm going down the hall to check on Pop, and then I guess I'll head outside to feed the sheep."

"I'll be leaving as soon as I'm done with the dishes, but I'll see you later today," Loraine called as he went out the door.

"Wayne seemed kind of edgy during breakfast, don't you think?" Jake asked.

She nodded. "I wonder if he's in pain."

"That could be, or maybe watching the two of us together made him feel uncomfortable."

"Do you think he's jealous?"

"Could be." Jake shrugged. "You know how it is—people always take for granted what they have until they don't have it anymore."

Hope welled in Loraine's soul. "If Wayne is feeling jealous, do you think that might be enough to make him realize he and I are supposed to be together?"

Jake grabbed a glass from the dish drainer and dried it with the towel before he replied. "I think he wouldn't have called off your wedding if he really cared. Makes me wonder if you two were ever supposed to be together."

Loraine nodded slowly. As much as she hated to admit it, Jake could be right. What if she and Wayne had gotten married, and then he'd decided he didn't love her? It hurt to know he didn't love her anymore, but it was better to find that out now than to find out after it was too late.

❧ ❧

"I was hoping I'd find Loraine here today," Ella said to Esther

Lehman when she entered the hardware store in Shipshewana and found her moving several things around on one of the shelves.

Esther turned to Ella and smiled. "Loraine is scheduled to work today, so she should be in soon, I expect. Is there anything I can help you with?"

Ella shook her head. "I need to talk to Loraine about something."

"You're welcome to wander around the store and wait, or you can have a seat on one of the benches outside the store."

"I think I'll wander around awhile." Ella moved away and busied herself looking at the various wind chimes her father had made and sold to the store. They were very well built and had a much prettier sound than any of the other wind chimes she'd seen for sale in town.

She was getting ready to head over to the book rack when Loraine showed up.

"I'm glad to see you," Ella said, clasping Loraine's arm. "I came in early, figuring you'd be here already."

Loraine shook her head. "My shift begins now, and I work until three; then I'm going over to—"

"I wanted you to know that I put Jake Beechy in his place during the auction the other day."

Loraine's eyebrows furrowed. "What did you say to Jake?"

Ella pulled Loraine off to one side and lowered her voice. "I let him know what I thought about him running off to Montana the way he did. I said I didn't trust him, and that I didn't want him hanging around you so much. I also made it clear that I didn't want him trying to come between you and Wayne."

Loraine's lips compressed into a thin, tight line. "You had no right to say those things, Ella—especially when they're not even true."

"Do I need to remind you that when Jake ran off to Montana, he left you in the lurch?"

"I don't need the reminder. Besides, Jake's back now, and he's trying to be a good friend to Wayne and to me. I'm sure he's not trying to come between us, either."

"Oh, really? Then how come he hovers around you all the time?"

"Jake doesn't hover around me!"

"Jah, he sure does. I've seen that hound-dog look he gets whenever he's anywhere near you."

Loraine turned away, and Ella, determined to make her cousin see the truth for what it was, moved in front of Loraine. "I'm only saying these things because I care about you. I don't want Jake to hurt you again."

Loraine's eyes filled with tears. "I couldn't be hurt any more than I already am."

"You mean because of Wayne breaking up with you?"

"Jah."

"That's why I'm concerned. If Jake keeps hanging around, Wayne's bound to see it, and then the two of you will never get back together."

"I don't think Wayne cares about getting back together." Loraine sniffed. "At least he's changed his mind about me coming over to his house, though."

"That's a real good thing. What brought about that change?"

"His daed's down with a bad sore throat, and his mamm broke her leg yesterday. I'm planning to go over there and help out before and after work every day."

"Now that is good news!" Ella's face heated up. "I don't mean Ada's broken leg or Crist being sick is good news." She grinned widely. "Ada's probably going to be laid up for several weeks, which means if you go over to their place every day, you'll see Wayne a lot, and he might finally come to his senses before it's too late."

"That would be nice, but it's not the reason I'm doing it. I just want to do the right thing and be helpful." Loraine smiled. "Jake's promised to help out, too. He came over this morning to do some of the outside chores, and he's going back there again this evening."

Ella grimaced. "That's just great. Now he'll have even more

of a chance to hover over you. Can't you discourage him from helping out?"

"I doubt it. He seemed determined, and Wayne was more than willing to accept his help." Loraine shrugged. "Besides, it's not my place to discourage Jake. The Lambrights need all the help they can get right now."

"I'm sure there are others in our community who will help."

"That may be so, but there's no reason for Jake not to help if he wants to."

"Then *you* ought to stay home." Ella smiled as an idea popped into her head. "I know what—I'll go over to the Lambrights' in your place. I'm only answering the phone and doing some paperwork in my daed's business, and I'm sure he wouldn't mind if I took a few hours off every day to help out at the Lambrights'."

"But you've said several times before that your mamm needs you around at home to help her out."

Ella nodded. "That's true, but she's got Charlene to help, and I'll be around most of the time, so I'm able to go over to the Lambrights' whenever I'm needed."

Loraine shook her head. "But you said a few minutes ago that my helping out would be a good way for me to spend more time with Wayne. How am I going to do that if you're taking my place?"

"I know what I said, but that was before I realized Jake was going to be there messing things up between you and Wayne."

"He's not messing things up. He's going to talk to Wayne, and hopefully he'll get him to change his mind about us." Loraine grunted and picked up a box of nails that had been sitting on the floor. "I need to get busy working, so let's drop this discussion!"

Ella felt like a glass of cold water had been thrown in her face. In all the years she'd known Loraine, she'd never spoken to her in that edgy tone of voice. It appeared that Jake was not only coming between Loraine and Wayne, but he was coming between two cousins who used to be such good friends.

CHAPTER 29

As Loraine headed to the Lambrights' that evening, she thought about her conversation with Ella. Could it be true? Was Jake trying to worm his way back into her life? Could he have offered to help at the Lambrights' just so he could be near her?

She shuddered as the thought shook her clean to her toes. Did she want to get back with Jake? Would she be happier with him than she had been with Wayne?

No, no, I mustn't think like that, she chided herself. *It would hurt Wayne too much if Jake and I got back together.* Her fingers gripped the reins until they began to ache. *At least, I think Wayne would be hurt. If he really doesn't love me anymore, then he might be relieved if I found someone else.*

The multitude of confusing thoughts continued to swirl in Loraine's head like a windmill turning at full speed in a heavy wind. As she approached the Lambrights' driveway, she directed the horse to turn in and, at the same time, reined in her thoughts. She was here to help Wayne and his family and needed to keep her focus on that.

As Loraine drew closer to the house, she saw Marge's van parked in the driveway. Ada was obviously home from the hospital, hopefully in less pain than she'd been in yesterday.

⁓⁂⁓

"Does your leg hurt much?" Wayne asked as Mom hobbled over to the sofa, using the pair of crutches she'd come home with.

She nodded and gritted her teeth. "Never had such pain before. Even childbirth was less painful than this."

Wayne had no firsthand experience with the pangs of childbirth, but he was no stranger to pain. "Maybe you ought to try the tapping method I've used for my phantom pains," he suggested.

"Puh!" Mom flapped her hand like she was shooing away a pesky fly. "Like that's going to help with anything!"

"It might, and you'll never know if you don't give it a try."

"I won't be doing any tapping because I'm just not interested in anything of that nature." She collapsed against the sofa pillows, then pointed to Wayne's empty pant leg. "I see you're not wearing your prosthesis again. Are you still having pain?"

"Not the phantom pain; just the spot on my stump where the prosthesis has rubbed it sore," he replied. "When I see the doctor on Monday, he'll probably suggest some adjustments be made to the appliance."

"I'm free on Monday," Marge spoke up, "So if you need a ride, I can take you to your appointment."

"I appreciate that," Wayne said, "but Jake was here earlier today, and he said he'd be glad to take me there."

"I can't believe you'd go anywhere with that fellow!" Mom's eyes narrowed. "If you ask me, Jake Beechy's not to be trusted!"

Before Wayne could comment, a knock sounded on the back door. "I'll see who that is," he said, wheeling quickly out of the room.

When he opened the door, he found Loraine on the porch, holding a cardboard box. "I wasn't sure what your mamm had on hand for supper, so I picked up a few things at the grocery store after I got off work." She scurried into the kitchen and set the box on the table. "Does stew and dumplings sound good to you?"

Wayne's mouth watered with anticipation. "Next to baked

chicken, stew and dumplings is one of my favorite meals."

Loraine snickered. "I can think of lots of things you've told me that you like to eat, so I'm sure you have more than one or two things you'd like to call your favorite meal."

He nodded. "I've gotta be careful how much I eat now, though. Since I'm not farming anymore, I don't get the exercise I used to get, so it would be easy for me to put on some extra pounds."

Marge stepped into the room just then. "I'm heading for home now, Wayne. You know my number, so give me a call if you need anything."

"I will, thank you."

Marge smiled at Loraine. "Are you here to fix supper?"

"I am, and you're welcome to join us if you like."

"I appreciate the offer, but Brian should be home from work by now. I don't think he'd be too pleased if I ate supper here and he had to fend for himself."

"I suppose not. Most husbands I know want their wives cooking for them when they come home from work." Loraine glanced at Wayne, but he looked away. He couldn't risk her seeing the look of longing he figured must be on his face.

"I'd better go back to the living room and check on Mom," Wayne said, wheeling quickly away. If he didn't get out of the kitchen soon, he might say or do something he would later regret.

"I'll get the stew going," he heard Loraine call over her shoulder. "Then I'll be in to say hello to your mamm."

When Wayne returned to the living room, he found Mom stretched out on the sofa with her eyes closed. Figuring she needed to sleep, he started to leave, but her eyes snapped open.

"You looked so comfortable there, I thought you might be sleeping," he said.

"Not yet, but I am kind of drowsy." She yawned. "I think it must be from the pain medicine they gave me at the hospital."

"Maybe I should leave so you can sleep."

She shook her head. "No, stay and keep me company."

"Okay, Mom." Wayne maneuvered his wheelchair close to the

sofa and tried to relax. It was hard to think about anything other than Loraine in the next room, making supper.

"Loraine came over. She's making stew and dumplings for our supper." He smiled at Mom.

"With all this pain I'm having, I hope I can eat," she said, making no reference to Loraine's good deed.

"She fixed supper for Pop and me last night, too."

A deep wrinkle formed above Mom's nose as her eyebrows pulled together. "And what do you suppose her motive was for that?"

Wayne shrugged. "Because she knew we'd be hungry?"

"Humph! I'm guessing her coming over here to fix supper last night and then coming back again this evening has more to do with her wanting to get you to change your mind about marrying her than it does with the fact that she knew you'd be hungry."

Wayne's skin prickled. He didn't understand why Mom was always so quick to criticize Loraine. Even though he'd done what he felt was right by breaking up with Loraine, he figured her motive for helping out was pure and right.

When Wayne looked over at Mom, prepared to tell her what he thought about her comment, he noticed that her eyes were closed again. This time, however, Mom's heaving breathing and soft snoring indicated she'd fallen asleep.

It's probably for the best, he decided. *If I said what I really thought, we'd only have ended up in an argument. I may as well go back to the kitchen and see if Loraine needs my help with anything. It'll be better than sitting here, watching Mom sleep.*

Wayne wheeled into the hallway and halted just outside the kitchen door, watching as Loraine took a kettle out of the cupboard, set it on the stove, and put the meat inside. His chest tightened as he continued to watch her. He marveled at her easy, efficient movements. She was capable, intelligent, and a hard worker. She also looked pretty good in the face. He wanted to melt in the warmth of Loraine's ebony eyes, but cold reality stabbed him before he allowed his thoughts to carry him away. He gripped the arms on his wheelchair. Loraine really would make a wonderful wife. Just not his wife.

Loraine turned toward him just then, and the seconds ticked by as they stared at each other. What was going through her mind? Did she know what was going through his?

"I didn't realize you were there," she said, touching her flushed cheeks.

Wayne's face heated up as well. The chemistry between them was still there, although he wished it wasn't. "I was wondering if you needed my help with anything," he mumbled.

She hesitated a moment, then shook her head. "I've got the meat going now, and after I've said hello to your mamm, I'll add in the vegetables."

"Mom's asleep right now, and my daed was sleeping the last time I checked on him, too, so you'll have to wait awhile to say hello."

"Oh, I see. I guess there's really no hurry. I just wanted to see how she's doing today." Loraine headed for the pantry, and when she bent down and lifted the bulky sack of potatoes sitting on the floor, her face turned red and she grunted.

Wayne grimaced. He wished he'd been able to lift the sack for her. If he had two good legs, he surely could have. If he was wearing his prosthesis, he might have been able to lift the heavy sack, too. But no, he was stuck in a wheelchair, unable to do much at all.

"You look tired. Why don't you go back to the living room and relax?" Loraine suggested. "I'll call you when supper's ready."

"If that's what you'd prefer."

She nodded. "I think it would be best."

Wayne whipped the wheelchair around and rolled quickly out of the kitchen. Maybe Loraine didn't want to be alone in the same room with him. Maybe she was sickened by seeing him in his wheelchair. She seemed to be pulling away from him more all the time.

Isn't that what you were hoping for when you broke up with her?

his conscience reminded. *Jah, I just didn't know it would hurt this much.*

❦

Jake smiled when he pulled his horse and buggy up to the Lambrights' barn and saw Loraine's rig. She'd no doubt come to fix supper.

Jake hated the inner battle he'd been fighting since he'd come home—one minute anxious to make some headway with Loraine, the next minute feeling guilty for wanting the woman who had fallen in love with and planned to marry his best friend. It gave him no pleasure to feel happy at his friend's expense, but he felt a sense of relief and had to keep reminding himself that Wayne had given his permission for him to pursue a relationship with Loraine. That must mean Wayne actually wanted them to get back together. Or at least, it seemed that way. Maybe Wayne was hiding behind the mask of self-pity and depression he seemed so determined to wear. Maybe one of these days, he would wake up and wish he hadn't foolishly pushed Loraine away.

Despite all the misgivings running through his head, Jake knew that, if he really wanted to get back with Loraine, he'd have to get past the guilty feelings and work up the nerve to ask her to go out with him. He just hoped she wouldn't turn him down when he finally did.

Jake eased his horse up to the hitching rail, climbed out of the buggy, and unhitched the horse. He figured he'd probably be awhile, so it would be best to put Midnight in the corral.

When that was done, Jake sprinted to the house and rapped on the back door.

"We're in the kitchen, so come on in!" Wayne called from the other side of the door.

When Jake stepped into the room, he was surprised to see Wayne, Loraine, and Ada sitting at the table. He figured they would have been done with supper by now.

A delicious aroma filled the room, and Jake sniffed deeply.

"Did I interrupt your supper?" he asked.

Wayne waved a hand. "Not so much."

"If you want to tell me what chores need to be done, I'll just head back outside and let you eat your meal in peace."

"No, no. Why don't you join us?" Wayne motioned to the large bowl of stew sitting on the table. "Loraine made plenty, and I'm sure you'll work a lot harder if your belly's full."

Jake chuckled and rubbed his chin. "You've got a good point there." He looked over at Loraine and grinned. "That stew does smell mighty *gut*."

Her cheeks reddened. "It's just an ordinary stew; nothing fancy, that's for sure."

"Stew always sounds good to me—especially on a chilly evening such as this." Jake pulled out the chair next to Wayne and sat down.

When Jake had finished his silent prayer, Loraine passed him a bowl of stew, topped with two plump dumplings. He smacked his lips and took a bite. "Mmm, this is sure tasty."

"Danki," she said, without glancing his way. He wondered if having him here made her nervous. Maybe she felt uncomfortable eating supper with her two ex-boyfriends. Come to think of it, she'd seemed a lot more relaxed this morning. But then, Wayne's mother hadn't been sitting at the table with them.

"I was sorry to hear about your broken leg," Jake said, looking over at Ada. "Is it causing you much pain?"

Ada nodded and reached for her glass of water. "I never knew anything could hurt so bad. The doctor gave me something for the throbbing, but it doesn't help that much."

"I'm sure in a few days you'll be feeling better," Loraine spoke up.

Ada shot her a look of obvious displeasure. "How would you know that? Have you ever broken a bone?"

Loraine slowly shook her head.

"I didn't think so."

The room got deathly quiet. Jake didn't care for the serious expressions he was seeing. He figured it was time to ease the awkward tension, so he quickly launched into the talking hound-dog story he'd told during breakfast, hoping he might get at least one smile from someone around the table.

When Jake finished the story, Ada sat, stony-faced, without uttering a word. To Jake's surprise, however, Wayne leaned his head back and roared. "Ha! Ha! Ha! That sure was a good one, Jake! It was even funnier hearing it tonight than when you told it this morning. You're sure good at making people laugh, and you're such a hard-working fellow. I'll bet you'll make a good daed someday."

Now where did that come from? Jake wondered. *Is Wayne trying to make a point, or is he just making polite conversation, hoping to take his mother's mind off the pain in her leg?*

"Speaking of daeds, how's your daed feeling?" Jake asked, looking at Wayne.

"Crist's throat has improved some from what it was two days ago," Ada said before Wayne could even open his mouth. "But he's still hurting and doesn't feel up to being out of bed much yet."

"Sorry to hear that." Jake reached for a hunk of celery from the vegetable platter and took a bite. He was beginning to think Wayne had done Loraine a favor by breaking their engagement. Putting up with an irritable busybody like Ada Lambright would have been hard on Loraine and probably wrecked havoc on her and Wayne's marriage.

They ate in silence for a time; then Jake, unable to stand the quiet, spoke again.

"I told Wayne that I'd help out for as long as it's needed," he said, looking at Ada, "so Crist won't need to be in a hurry to get back to his chores."

Ada nodded. "I'll be sure and tell him that." She glanced at the calendar across the wall. "Looks like Crist and I are going to be laid up on our anniversary tomorrow."

"When you're both feeling better, maybe you can go to the Blue Gate or one of the other nice restaurants for a meal," Loraine suggested.

"We'll have to wait and see how it goes," Ada mumbled around a mouthful of stew.

"Say, Jake," Wayne spoke up, "when Loraine's ready to go home, would you mind following her in your rig? The last time I looked outside, it had started to rain real hard, so the roads might be kind of slippery, not to mention that it'll be pitch dark."

Jake looked over at Loraine to gauge her reaction. He was relieved when she offered him a little smile and nodded.

"Jah, sure. I'd be happy to see that Loraine gets home."

CHAPTER 30

J ake squinted against the pouring rain, and turned on his battery-operated windshield wipers. If not for the flashing red lights up ahead, he wouldn't have known Loraine's buggy was ahead of his. He'd never cared much for rain, but since it was a common occurrence during the fall, he'd just have to deal with it. He guessed he shouldn't complain. If he was still in Montana, he might be dealing with bitter cold, snowy weather by now.

I wonder if Loraine will invite me in when we get to her house. That would be nice, but if her folks are around, it won't give us the chance to be alone. Jake had been hoping for the opportunity to ask her out and thought maybe tonight would work out.

Swish! Swish! The noise of the wiper blades pulled Jake's thoughts aside. It was raining harder, and he squinted to see out the window.

Blink. . .blink. Blink. . .blink. . . At least he could still see the lights on Loraine's buggy up ahead.

When the headlights of a car that had decided to pass shone on Loraine's buggy, Jake noticed that one of the back wheels on her rig was wobbling. After making sure that no other cars were coming, he eased his horse into the other lane, passed her buggy, and pulled onto the shoulder of the road. As soon as she pulled in behind him, he hopped out and sprinted around to the driver's side of her rig.

"What's wrong?" she asked when he opened her door. "Why'd you pass me like that?"

"Your left back wheel seems to be loose. It's been wobbling really bad."

"I did notice the buggy bumping, but I thought it was just the rough road."

Jake shook his head as he swiped at the raindrops splashing on his face. "It's the wheel all right, and if I don't fix it now, you'll never make it home."

"Oh, okay." She stepped out of the buggy. "What can I do to help?"

"I don't know yet. Let me get a flashlight, and then I'll take a look and see whether a nut fell out or if something might have broken."

Jake sprinted back to his buggy and got a flashlight, then he handed it to Loraine. "Shine it right there," he said, pointing to the hub of the wheel.

She did as he asked, and he squatted down to inspect things. "The wheel nut's missing all right, and—"

Whack! They bumped heads as he stood.

"Are you okay?" A jolt of electricity shot through Jake's fingers as he reached out and touched Loraine's forehead.

"I'm fine. How about you?" Loraine's voice trembled, and Jake wondered if she'd felt the same connection between them as he'd felt.

"I'm okay." He laughed. "Don't think any permanent damage was done."

"None for me, either."

They stood staring at each other for several seconds. Jake was on the verge of taking Loraine in his arms and kissing her, when she turned her head away. "If the nut's missing, how are we going to fix my wheel?"

"I could look for it along the road, but since we don't know when or where it fell off, that wouldn't make much sense. Especially since it's dark and raining." Jake motioned to his own rig. "I've got some extra wheel nuts in my toolbox."

"I guess you'll need this then." She handed him the flashlight.

Jake hesitated a minute, then ran back to his rig. A few minutes later, he was back with the nut and necessary tools.

Loraine held the flashlight while Jake worked, and in short order he had it fixed. "There you go; it's good as new."

"Danki, Jake."

He smiled. "You're welcome." *Should I ask her out now? Would this be a good time?*

"Well, we'd better get going. It's raining harder, and I'm really getting wet standing out here like this."

Jake nodded and swiped a hand across his damp face. Maybe he'd have a chance to ask Loraine out when they got to her place.

~❧ ❧~

As Loraine climbed back in her buggy and took up the reins, she thought about the way Jake had looked at her after they'd bumped heads. Had he been about to kiss her? Did she want him to?

Pushing her thoughts aside, she focused on the road ahead and concentrated on keeping her horse from losing its footing on the slippery, wet pavement. She'd have time to think about all this later on—after she was home safely and had changed out of her wet clothes.

Loraine was glad Wayne had suggested that Jake follow her home. She didn't know what she would have done if she'd been all alone when the nut had fallen out of the buggy wheel. If she'd gone much farther with it that way, the wheel would probably have fallen off, and she might have ended up in a serious accident.

As Loraine approached her folks' place, she clicked on the right-turn blinker and guided the horse up the driveway. She halted it near the barn, and when she climbed down, she was surprised to see Jake pull his rig in beside hers. She figured he would have gone on his way home once he'd seen her turn up the driveway.

"Danki for seeing me home," she said when he stepped up to her. "And again, I appreciate your help with the buggy wheel."

"No problem. Glad I could do it." He fiddled with the flashlight in his hands, turning it over and over a couple of times. "Uh, Loraine, there's something I want to ask—"

"What are you two doing out there in the rain?"

Loraine looked toward the house. There stood Mom with her hands cupped around her mouth.

"Jake followed me home from the Lambrights'!" Loraine called back.

"Bring him in for some hot coffee!"

Loraine looked over at Jake. "What do you think?"

"I think a cup of coffee sounds pretty good about now," he said with a nod. "If you want to get in out of this cold, I'll take care of putting your horse away, and then I'll be up as soon as I'm done."

"I appreciate that." Loraine shivered. "I really do need to get out of my wet clothes."

"You go ahead then, and I'll be in shortly."

Loraine hurried into the house, shivering all the way.

When she stepped into the kitchen, Mom handed her a towel. "Where's Jake? Isn't he coming in for coffee?"

Jake? Was he all Mom could think about? Didn't she even care that Loraine was sopping wet and shivering from the cold?

"Jake's putting Trixie away for me, and he'll be in as soon as he's done." Loraine turned toward the door leading to the stairs. "I'm going up to my room to change out of these wet clothes."

"That's a good idea. I'll set things out and have them on the table by the time you get back." Mom motioned to the living room door. "Your daed's in there reading the newspaper. I'll go see if he wants to join us in the kitchen."

"Okay." Loraine hurried from the room.

When she returned sometime later, she found Mom, Dad, and Jake sitting at the kitchen table, eating thick slices of apple pie and drinking coffee.

Mom motioned to the chair next to Jake. "Have a seat, Loraine."

Loraine hesitated a minute, then pulled out the chair and sat down.

"I told your mamm I was awfully wet and probably shouldn't sit at her table," Jake said, smiling at Loraine. "But she just plopped a towel down and told me to take a seat and that between the fire in the wood burning stove and a hot cup of coffee, I'd warm up and dry off real quick."

Loraine smiled. "The heat from the stove does feel good."

Mom handed Loraine a piece of pie. "Jake explained about the missing wheel nut on your buggy."

Loraine nodded. "It was Wayne's idea for Jake to follow me home."

"It's a good thing he did," Dad said. "Otherwise you might have had a serious problem out on the road by yourself. I'll have to keep a better check on our buggy wheels from now on. Wouldn't want to see an accident happen because I was negligent about checking."

Mom poured more coffee into Jake's cup. "Would you like another piece of pie?"

He nodded with an eager expression. "Jah, sure, why not?"

"Jake was also telling us that he plans to raise and train horses," Mom said as she cut a large piece of pie and handed it to Jake.

"What kind of horses did you say you want to raise?" Dad asked.

"Standard-bred racing horses, because they're good for pulling our buggies." Jake took a drink of coffee and swiped his napkin across his lips. "When my business gets going good, I may want to raise some Percheron workhorses, too."

Loraine ate her pie and drank her coffee as she listened to Jake talk about horses and answer all of Mom and Dad's questions. Every once in a while, Mom would compliment Jake on something—how much he knew about horses, how helpful he was, and what an easygoing, pleasant person he seemed to be.

Jake's cheeks reddened, and he quickly launched into a couple of humorous stories, which Mom especially seemed to enjoy.

214

Finally, Jake pushed back his chair and stood. "Guess I'd better get home before my folks start to worry." He looked over at Mom and smiled. "Danki for the pie and coffee, Priscilla. It was just what I needed."

She grinned at him. "You're quite welcome. Come by and see us anytime."

Jake looked over at Loraine. "Guess I'll see you soon."

She nodded. "Jah, probably so."

When the door clicked shut behind Jake, Mom turned to Loraine and said, "I think that young man likes you."

"What makes you think that?"

"The way he kept looking at you and telling those funny stories. I think he was trying to make you laugh."

"You seemed to be enjoying Jake's stories more than Loraine." Dad nudged Mom's arm with his elbow.

She smiled and nodded. "I think an encouraging, positive thinker like Jake would make a real good husband."

Loraine couldn't argue with that. She just wasn't sure she'd want Jake to be *her* husband.

~❧~

"You look mied," Wayne said when he entered the living room where Ada sat on the sofa with her leg propped on a pillow.

She yawned. "I am tired, but I dread going to bed."

"How come?"

"The cast on my leg is so cumbersome, and it's hard to find a comfortable position." She leaned her head against the sofa cushion and sighed. "I can't wait until my leg's healed and I can finally get this cast taken off. It's so heavy and awkward."

Wayne lowered himself into a chair. "This prosthesis I'm expected to wear weighs about four pounds, and since it doesn't feel like my own leg, I wonder if I'll ever fully adjust to walking with it."

"Just give it some more time and try to be patient." Ada stretched her arms over her head and released another noisy yawn. "One of the biggest reasons I can't wait to get my cast off is so I can take over my household chores again. It's hard to sit around and watch someone else come in here and do everything the wrong way."

"Who's doing things the wrong way?" Wayne asked.

"Loraine."

"What did she do that was wrong?"

"For one thing, she put my frying pans and kettles in the cupboard on the left-hand side of the sink." Mom grunted. "They're supposed to go in the drawer beneath the stove."

"It's not the end of the world, Mom. Once you're able to take over in the kitchen again, you can put the frying pan and kettles back exactly where you want them to be."

Ada pursed her lips and folded her arms. "She left dust on the bookcase, too—which she said she had cleaned, and then she—"

"I think Loraine's doing the best she can," Wayne interrupted. "She doesn't have to take time out of her busy day to come over here and help, you know. I think you ought to appreciate what she does instead of complaining and finding fault all of the time."

"I'm not complaining or finding fault; I'm just stating facts." Ada wrinkled her nose. "If you want my opinion, I think Loraine only comes over here so she can make you jealous."

Wayne's eyebrows furrowed. "Jealous of what?"

"Not what—who. Haven't you seen the way Loraine hangs on Jake's every word? I think she's using him to try and get to you. And Jake's no better," she quickly added. "He hovers over Loraine all the time, and hangs on her every word. He's out to get her back as his girlfriend. Mark my words, before this year's out, they'll be announcing their engagement."

Wayne shrugged. "That's fine with me. Fact is, I'm hoping Loraine and Jake get back together."

"You. . .you are?"

He nodded. "Why else would I have suggested that Jake follow Loraine home tonight?"

As Wayne's words set in fully, Ada smiled to herself. *It's amazing how when you want something badly enough, it all works out for the good. And to think, I didn't even have to make this happen myself.*

CHAPTER 31

For the last two weeks, Loraine had gone over to the Lambrights' every morning before work and every afternoon on her way home. She still hadn't won Ada over, but at least the difficult woman was willing to accept Loraine's assistance. Some of the other women, including Loraine's mother, took turns helping out, too.

Wayne's father was feeling better, so he'd taken over his chores again. For some reason, Jake thought his help was still needed, though, so he came over nearly every day. When he was finished with the chores, he hung around Loraine. That made her nervous.

On Saturday, Loraine had the day off from her job at the hardware store, so she was free to spend most of the day at the Lambrights'. She'd just begun baking some bread when Jake entered the kitchen.

"I'm done cleaning the barn, and Wayne's in his daed's shop helping him with some taxidermy stuff, so I thought I'd see if you needed my help with anything." He stopped and sniffed the air. "Whoa! Something sure smells good in here!"

"I'm baking bread."

"What kind?"

"I've already made one loaf, using the basic recipe for friendship bread, but I'm planning to add some nuts and chocolate chips to this next batch, hoping to make it more interesting for finicky taste buds."

Jake snickered. "Can't imagine who'd have finicky taste buds in this family."

Loraine put her fingers to her lips. "*Shh.* . .she'll hear you."

He glanced around. "Where is the old grouch?"

"In her bedroom, resting her leg. She was up on it quite a bit yesterday, and I'm afraid she's paying the price for it today."

"She's had you and several other ladies from our community helping out, so why was she doing too much?"

"It's her home, and she wants to help. You can't really blame her for that."

"No, I guess not." Jake frowned deeply. "I sure can't figure out why Ada's so grouchy all the time. You must be a saint for helping someone who doesn't even appreciate it. For all the mean things that woman has said to you, I'd think you'd want to stay as far away from her as you possibly can."

Loraine shook her head. "I'm no saint; I just care about people and want to help whenever I see a need. Even if Ada never comes to like me, I won't regret having helped during her time of need." She stood on her tiptoes, reaching for the jar of nuts on the top shelf of the cupboard.

"Here, let me get that for you." Jake rushed forward and grabbed the jar at the same time as she reached for it. Their heads collided, the jar slipped out of his hands, and it tumbled to the floor. Crushed walnuts scattered everywhere!

"Rats!" Jake dropped to his knees and picked up the jar. "Well, at least it's not broken."

Loraine sighed. "No, but now I have no nuts to add to the bread dough."

"Sorry about that. Guess that's what I get for trying to help you get the jar down. I should have minded my own business."

Jake's sheepish look brought a smile to Loraine's lips. He'd always been a bit accident prone. "If you really want to help," she said, motioning to the utility room, "you can get a broom and dustpan and sweep up this mess while I finish mixing my bread dough."

"Sure, I can do that."

Loraine turned back to the counter and had just begun adding the chocolate chips when she heard a *crunch*, then a *crash*!

She whirled around. Jake sat on the floor in the middle of the scattered nuts, wearing a bewildered expression.

"I can't believe it," he groaned. "I really am a big *dummkopp*!"

"You're not a dunce. You're just a little clumsy at times, but that doesn't mean you're stupid." She held out her hand. "Here, let me help you up."

Jake reached out his hand, and as their fingers touched, Loraine felt a tingle shoot all the way up her arm. A familiar longing crept into her heart as she remembered how she used to feel when she and Jake had been dating. *Why does his touch send my heart flying up to my throat?* she wondered. *It's over between us and has been for some time.*

With Jake standing so near, Loraine could feel his warm breath on her neck and smell a minty aroma. It made her light-headed. Jake's face was so close to hers that she noticed the fine lines etched around his eyes and saw a look of longing on his face.

She drew back, her heart hammering fiercely in her chest. "I'd better get busy on the bread or it'll never get baked." She couldn't let him know how being this close to him had affected her. She couldn't—wouldn't—admit it to herself.

"I'd better try once more to get this mess cleaned up. Sure wouldn't want Ada to come in here and see her kitchen floor littered with nuts. She might have a conniption." Jake wiggled his eyebrows and gave her a playful wink.

Loraine quickly turned her back on him. Was he flirting with her? Worse yet, did she want him to? Jake had such a pleasant way about him, and he'd always been able to make her laugh. But the look of longing she'd seen a few minutes ago frightened her.

She braced herself against the counter, her pulse hammering in her head. *Dear God, please make me strong. Help me not to lose my heart to Jake and forget the promise I made to Wayne.*

"What's going on in here?" Ada asked, hobbling into the room on her crutches. "I was napping in my room, until I heard a crash, and then—" Her mouth opened wide. "Ach, my! Why are those nuts scattered all over my kitchen floor?"

Loraine quickly explained what had happened and said that Jake was getting ready to sweep the floor.

"If you're the one who dropped the jar, shouldn't you be the one cleaning up the mess?"

"She didn't drop the jar, Ada. I did," Jake was quick to say.

"Whatever." Ada's eyes flashed as she stared angrily at Loraine. "I thought you came here to help, not wreck havoc with my kitchen!"

Loraine opened her mouth, ready to spew out angry words, but a verse of scripture, Matthew 5:44, came to her mind: *"But I say unto you, Love your enemies, bless them that curse you, do good to them that hate you, and pray for them which despitefully use you, and persecute you."*

I need to pray for Ada, she reminded herself. *I'll never win her over with angry, spiteful words.*

Forcing a smile to her lips, Loraine looked at Ada and said, "It was an accident, and I'm sorry about the mess. Jake and I will get it cleaned up as quickly as we can, so why don't you go back to your room and rest?"

Ada stood staring at the floor several seconds, then with an undignified grunt, she turned and hobbled out of the kitchen.

Jake poked Loraine's arm with his elbow. "I don't care what you say, you really are a saint."

She grinned and poked him right back. "You'd better hurry and get that broom before Ada decides to come back in here and chew me out some more."

⁓ ⁔

As Jake carried the broom and dustpan into the kitchen, he glanced back at Loraine. The memory of the way she'd smiled at him earlier sparkled like a moment in a pleasant dream. When he'd smiled at her in return, he'd seen a flicker of something. There'd been a flush on her cheeks and a sparkle in her heavily fringed eyes that he hadn't seen for a long time. Was it a look of longing, or was it merely his own wishful thinking?

Jake leaned against the doorjamb, watching as Loraine poured the bread dough into two pans. For the nearly two years Jake had been living in Montana, he'd been running from what he wanted most and hadn't even realized it. He couldn't deny his feelings—he was still in love with Loraine. The question was, what should he do about it?

Ask her out, prompted a little voice in his head. *Do it now, before you lose your nerve.*

He quickly swept up the nuts, deposited them in the garbage can, and put the broom and dustpan away. The whole time, he rehearsed what he should say to Loraine. *I've never stopped loving you. I think we're meant to be together. Would you go out with me?* No, it would be too bold to declare his feelings right out. If he said he loved her too soon, it might push her away.

He wiped his sweaty palms on the knees of his trousers and stepped up beside her. "Loraine, I was wondering—"

"Oh, look, there's Wayne and that cute little ewe of his." Loraine pointed out the window. "I can't get over how well that sheep gets around on only three legs."

"Jah, and the critter likes to follow Wayne everywhere he goes."

"Have you noticed that Wayne seems to be walking better with his prosthesis now?"

Jake nodded. "Since he had it adjusted a few weeks ago, he's walking more normally and, from what I can tell, with less pain." Jake transferred his weight from one foot to the other and moistened his lips with the tip of his tongue. *Ask her now, before you lose your nerve. What are you waiting for, anyway?*

"This bread's ready to go in the oven now," she said, picking up the two pans. "And I think it'll be good, even without the nuts."

"Anything you make is bound to be good."

Her cheeks reddened, and she looked away.

"Sorry if I embarrassed you. I was just remembering how you used to make ginger cookies for me when we were going out together, and they were always so good."

Loraine moved over to the stove and put the bread pans in.

"Do you remember how much fun we used to have when we were together?"

She gave a slow nod and closed the oven door.

Jake grabbed a glass from the cupboard, filled it with water, and took a drink. As he let the cool liquid trickle down his throat, he contemplated what to say next. "Uh. . .I was wondering, would you like to have supper with me on Friday evening?" There, it was finally out.

Loraine's eyes widened as she turned to face him. "Are you asking me out on a date?"

"Jah, I am. I thought we could go to Tiffany's in Topeka. We used to like going there to eat, remember?"

"I do remember, but—" She slowly shook her head. "I couldn't go out with you, Jake. It wouldn't be fair to Wayne."

"You've been working real hard here these last few weeks, and I think you should go."

Jake whirled around. He hadn't realized Wayne had come into the house, much less had entered the kitchen. "Are you sure you don't mind? I mean, if—"

"Don't mind at all."

A look of shock registered on Loraine's face. "But, Wayne, we're—"

"Just friends. That's all we'll ever be, Loraine." Wayne's words were crisp and to the point. Apparently, he'd meant what he'd said to Jake about dating Loraine. Could it be that Wayne had been telling the truth when he'd said that he really didn't love her anymore? Jake wondered. Or was he only giving Loraine over to Jake because he no longer felt like a man?

"We're more than friends, Wayne." Doubt tinged Loraine's voice, and there was no sparkle in her eyes. She'd been clearly hurt by Wayne's remark.

"We used to be more than friends, but not anymore." Wayne moved over to the refrigerator and took out a gallon of apple cider.

Then he grabbed two paper cups from the pantry and turned them upside-down over the lid on the cider. "My daed sent me in to get us something cold to drink, so I'd better get back out to his shop with this." Without so much as a backwards glance, he shuffled from the room.

Loraine looked at Jake like she couldn't quite believe what had just happened. Then, with a smile that held no sparkle at all, she said in a voice barely above a whisper, "I'd be happy to go out to supper with you on Friday night."

Jake stood there, too stunned to say a word. As much as he wanted to take Loraine out, he'd really expected her to say no. *I guess I have Wayne to thank for her change of heart, but I hope she's not going out with me just to spite him. I'd feel a lot better if I knew she really wanted to be with me.*

"I'll pick you up at your house at five o'clock," he said. "Does that sound all right?"

She nodded slowly. "Five o'clock is fine for me."

꧁ ꧂

A raw ached settled in the pit of Wayne's stomach as he headed to his dad's shop. Even though he'd convinced himself that breaking up with Loraine was for her own good, he felt miserable. It was obvious from the look on Jake's face whenever Loraine was near that he'd never stopped loving her, but he wasn't sure how Loraine felt about Jake.

Wayne stopped walking and rolled his shoulders in order to loosen his stiff muscles and erase the tension he felt. Loraine had been happy with Jake once; she could be happy with him again.

He kicked at a fallen tree branch with the toe of his boot and groaned. *I love her too much not to let her go. I just wish I didn't have to see her and Jake together.*

As Wayne started walking again, an idea popped into his head. After their accident in Paul's van, Katie and Jolene had left home in order to find healing. Maybe he should go away, too.

CHAPTER 32

Y ou seem to be having a hard time keeping your mind on the job at hand," Pop said, nudging Wayne's arm. "Are you bored with working on animal skins?"

Wayne shook his head. "Not really. I thought I'd hate it at first, but after working here awhile, I realize it's not so bad."

Pop's face broke into a wide smile. "I'm real happy to hear that. Someday, when I'm too old to do this anymore, maybe you can take over the business."

Wayne shrugged his shoulders. "I don't know about that. I've been thinking I might want to do something else."

Pop's eyebrows furrowed. "Are you still wishing you could farm? Because if you are, and you think you're up to it, I can let you have a few acres of land and see how it goes."

Wayne shook his head. "I'm thinking I might want to move to Arthur, Illinois, and stay with Uncle Ezra and Aunt Evelyn awhile. Maybe Uncle Ezra would be willing to teach me something about the woodworking trade."

Pop's mouth formed an O. "I had no idea you were thinking of leaving home. I thought you were happy here."

Wayne gripped the piece of deer hide in his hands so hard his fingers began to ache. "Happy? Pop, I haven't been happy since I lost my leg!"

"You need to give it more time, son. Healing, emotionally and physically—that's gonna take some time."

"That's why I want to move away and leave all the memories behind."

"What about your leg? Don't you think you need to stay close to your doctors until it's sufficiently healed?"

"I'm sure there are plenty of good doctors in Illinois who can take over my case."

Pop dropped the piece of deer hide he'd been working on onto the workbench and massaged the bridge of his nose. "You can't run from your past, son. It won't solve a thing."

"I wouldn't be running. I just need a fresh start."

"What about Loraine and your plans to be married? Have you spoken to her about the idea of moving to Illinois?"

Wayne shook his head. "I've told you this before, Pop—Loraine and I will not be getting married. She's moving on with her life. In fact, she'll be going out to supper with Jake this evening."

Pop continued to rub his nose. "So that's the reason you want to go away. You're still in love with Loraine and can't stand the thought of her seeing someone else."

Wayne offered no reply.

"If you're in love with her, then you shouldn't let her go." Pop made a sweeping gesture of the room. "If you keep working here with me, you can make enough money to support a wife. There's no reason you and Loraine can't be married like you'd planned."

"Even if I could provide a decent living for a wife and family, I'll always be handicapped, and I don't want to be a burden."

"I'm sure Loraine wouldn't see being married to you as a burden. For goodness' sake, Wayne, there are folks with worse handicaps than yours, and many have gotten married and lived a normal life."

"There's nothing *normal* about losing a leg." Wayne couldn't keep the bitterness from his tone. "Besides, Loraine doesn't love me anymore. She used to love Jake before he went to Montana, and I've seen the way the two of them look at each other." He slowly shook his head. "I won't stand in the way of their happiness, and I won't hold Loraine to her promise to marry me just because she feels sorry for me now. I've made up my mind to leave, and I plan to contact Uncle Ezra next week."

Pop clasped both of Wayne's shoulders and turned him so they were eye to eye. "I can't keep you from going to Illinois, but I think it would be best if you waited until your mamm gets her cast off and is able to take over the cooking and household chores again."

"Loraine and some of the others in our community are helping out. Mom doesn't need me here for that."

"That's true, but your mamm's been an emotional wreck ever since your accident, and breaking her leg has only added to her frustrations." Pop blew out his breath as he whacked the edge of his workbench with his knuckles. "I think it would put her over the edge if you took off for Illinois right now."

Wayne stared at the workbench, contemplating his father's words. As much as he needed to get away, he didn't want Mom to feel any worse than she already did. Pop was right; she hadn't been the same since the accident. No one had, really.

"All right then, I'll wait until Mom gets her cast off and is getting around well enough on her own, but then I'll be heading for Illinois."

"You won't say anything about these plans to her now, I hope. It would really upset her, you know."

Wayne shook his head. "For the time being, I'm not going to mention it to anyone else."

~ ❧ ❦ ~

Loraine peeked out the kitchen window, watching for Jake's buggy to come into the yard. She could hardly believe she'd agreed to go out with him this evening. Would it be like old times, or would she feel stiff and uncomfortable eating supper with him at Tiffany's? They used to go there a lot when they were dating—sometimes with other couples, sometimes just the two of them.

Their times together had always been relaxed yet exciting. Back then, Loraine had believed that she and Jake would eventually marry. Now she wasn't sure what she wanted or how she felt about much of anything.

Is going out with Jake tonight what I really want to do? she asked herself. *Or am I only going out with him because Wayne wants me to? Why does Wayne want me to go out with Jake, anyway? Could he really have stopped loving me, or is he just feeling sorry for himself and thinking this is the best thing for me?*

"Are you watching for Jake?" Mom asked, stepping up to Loraine.

"Jah, and I'm feeling a bit *naerfich* about going out with him this evening."

Mom gave Loraine's arm a gentle squeeze. "Don't be nervous. Jake's so pleasant and easygoing; I'm glad you're seeing him again."

"He is easy to be with, but I can't forget the promise I made to Wayne."

"He broke up with you, Loraine. That means you're no longer bound by your promise."

Loraine blinked against the tears that threatened to spill over. "Can we please change the subject? I'd rather not talk about this anymore."

"Jah, sure. I need to get supper started for me and your daed anyway." Mom went to the refrigerator.

"I think I'll wait out on the porch for Jake," Loraine said.

"Oh, okay. Have a good time, and tell him I said hello and to come by again soon for more pie and coffee."

Loraine nodded, grabbed her jacket and bonnet, then scurried out the door. She'd no more than taken a seat on the porch swing when a horse and buggy rolled into the yard. Only it wasn't Jake who climbed down from the buggy—it was Ella.

"I went over to the Lambrights', thinking you'd be there," Ella said when she stepped onto the porch. "I found Aunt Leah there, fixing supper for them instead." She scowled at Loraine. "I was shocked when Ada said you weren't there because you were having supper with Jake this evening."

Loraine nodded. "That's right. He's taking me to Tiffany's, and he should be here any minute."

Ella grunted as she plopped down beside Loraine. "After the way Jake hurt you before, I don't understand how you could even consider going out with him now."

Loraine gripped the armrest of the swing, hoping to gain control of her emotions. It seemed that every time she spoke to Ella these days, they ended up in an argument over Jake.

Ella bumped Loraine's arm. "Can you explain why you've ignored my advice and accepted a date with Jake?"

"I enjoy being with him. And he's apologized for what he did."

"Puh!" Ella's nose crinkled as though some foul odor had permeated the air. "I've said it before, and I'll say it once more, that fellow's not to be trusted. How do you know he won't run off again?"

"I don't know that. There are no guarantees in this life."

"What about Wayne? Does he know you're going out with Jake?"

"Jah, he knows, and he seems to be perfectly fine with the idea." Loraine blew out her breath. "In fact, he actually said I should go."

"What?" Ella's eyes widened. "You've got to be kidding!"

"No. Not only has Wayne said several times that it's over between us, but the other day, he came right out and said he thought Jake and I should get back together."

Ella sat several seconds, rubbing her chin and tapping her sneaker against the weathered porch floor. "I can't believe it. It doesn't make sense that Wayne would want you and Jake to get back together."

"It makes sense if Wayne doesn't love me anymore." Loraine swallowed hard, hoping she wouldn't break down in tears. "And he obviously doesn't, or he wouldn't be trying to push me and Jake together, now would he?"

"I don't know. I mean—"

A horse whinnied, and Loraine turned to look toward the driveway. A buggy rolled in. The door on the driver's side was open, and she could see Jake sitting inside with one foot hanging out the opening. He had always liked to ride in his buggy like that, even in colder weather.

She watched as he pulled alongside the barn, but instead of getting out and tying his horse to the rail, he just sat there.

"Jake's here now, so I'd better go," Loraine said, rising to her feet.

Ella jumped up from the swing. "Look at him—he's just sitting there like a bump on a log. Isn't he coming up to the house to get you?"

"Maybe he thinks there's no need since I'm out here waiting for him."

"That's baremlich! If he wants to take you on a date, then the least he can do is come up to the house and get you."

Loraine started off the porch, but Ella grabbed her arm. "Don't you dare go out there!"

"Why not?"

"You'll look overanxious, and it won't teach Jake anything about proper manners." Ella's nose wrinkled. "That fellow is so into himself, which I just don't understand, since it's not the way he was raised!"

Irritation welled in Loraine's soul as she looked Ella in the face. "I am not Jake's mamm, and it's not my place to teach him good manners. Besides, I think you're wrong about Jake. He's kind and helpful and not at all into himself."

Ella's eyes squinted into tiny slits. "If you go out there, I'll never speak to you again!"

Loraine sighed. "Don't be lecherich. When we were little girls and you didn't get your way, you used to threaten not to speak to me. Don't you think it's time for you to grow up and stop trying to control every situation?"

Ella's face flamed. "I'm not being ridiculous or trying to

control every situation. I just care about you too much to stand by and watch you get hurt by the likes of him." She stared across the yard, where Jake still sat in his buggy. "But if you want to ruin your life, then go ahead; don't let me stop you."

Loraine took a step forward, but halted. She didn't want Ella to be mad at her, but at the same time she didn't want to keep Jake waiting. Maybe if she didn't rush out to his buggy, he would take the hint and come up to the house to get her. On the other hand, if she did go out to him, she'd never hear the end of it from Ella, even if she had threatened not to speak to her again.

❧ ❦

Jake shifted on the buggy seat, trying to decide what to do. He wanted to go up to the house and see if Loraine was ready for their date, but with Ella standing there, it might be best to let Loraine come to him. The last time he'd talked to Ella, they'd ended up in an argument. He didn't want to risk that again. At the same time, he didn't want to offend Loraine. He'd worked too hard at gaining her trust to ruin things now.

Gathering up his courage, Jake hopped down from the buggy and started for the house.

When he stepped onto the porch, he smiled at Loraine and said, "Are you ready to head to Topeka?"

She smiled. "I'm more than ready."

Jake glanced over at Ella and forced a smile. "Wie geht's?" he asked.

"I'm doing fine. I was at the Lambrights' and decided to stop by here and see Loraine for a few minutes before I went home." She turned to Loraine and gave her arm a little squeeze. "Think about what I said, okay?"

Loraine gave a quick nod, stepped off the porch, and hurried toward Jake's buggy. It made him wonder if she was as anxious to get away from Ella as he was. At least this time Ella hadn't said anything mean to him.

He helped Loraine into his buggy and went around to untie

231

the horse. When he climbed into the driver's seat, he noticed Loraine looking over her shoulder with a worried expression.

"Is everything all right?" he asked.

She nodded. "I'm just worried about Ella. She's been trying to be everything to everyone ever since her bruder died, but sometimes she's just too pushy."

"You won't get any argument from me there." Jake snapped the reins and directed his horse onto the main road. "Now, can we forget about Ella and concentrate on the two of us having a good time this evening?"

Loraine smiled. "That's exactly what I plan to do."

CHAPTER 33

"The fried chicken here at Tiffany's is sure good," Loraine said, then took another bite and savored the delicious taste.

Jake smiled. "Jah, but not nearly as good as yours."

Loraine's cheeks warmed. "Danki."

"I mean it, Loraine, you're really a good cook. That bread you baked for Ada the other day was real tasty."

"I think Ada must have liked it, too, because she ate most of one loaf." Loraine's eyebrows squeezed together. "Of course, she'd never say it was good or give me a compliment for anything. I've come to accept the fact that she's probably never going to like me."

"That's too bad. I guess she doesn't know when she's met a good person."

Loraine shrugged and forked some mashed potatoes into her mouth.

As they continued to eat their meal, Loraine listened with interest while Jake told her more about the horse ranch in Montana where he'd worked and how he'd purchased a couple of thoroughbred horses the other day and hoped to breed them.

"I've worked with horses ever since I was a buwe, and I've had the dream of owning my own business since I turned sixteen." Jake leaned forward, his elbows resting on the table and a serious expression on his face. "That's the reason I went to Montana—so

I could make more money."

"Money isn't everything," she said with a catch in her voice. "Being with family and friends—that's what's important."

"I agree, but a fellow can't provide for a wife and family if he doesn't have enough money."

"Weren't you making a decent living working for your daed?"

Jake shook his head. "Not enough to save up much money. Besides, I don't want to shoe horses for the rest of my life. It's hard on the back and not nearly as much fun as training them."

Loraine took another bite of chicken and washed it down with a swallow of water. "Your daed must enjoy shoeing horses. He's been doing it for quite a few years."

Jake nodded and swiped his napkin across his chin where some juice from the chicken had dribbled. "That doesn't mean I want to follow in his footsteps."

"Who's going to take over the business when your daed retires?"

"Maybe my younger brother Elmer. He's only twelve, but he's already taken an interest in helping Dad." Jake reached for his glass of water and took a drink. "I just know it won't be me takin' over my daed's business."

"I guess if you don't like it that well, then it's not something you should do for the rest of your life."

"How about you?" he asked. "Do you enjoy your job at the hardware store in Shipshewana?"

"I like it well enough, but it's not something I'd want to do forever," she replied.

Jake jiggled his eyebrows. "Nothing's forever. Nothing here on earth, at least."

"That's true. We won't know eternity until we get to heaven."

Jake's gaze shifted to the other side of the room. "Say, isn't that Fern Bontrager sitting over there? I haven't seen her in a good long while."

"I don't think so. Fern and her folks moved to Ohio a few months after you left for Montana, and they've not been back since."

Jake continued to stare. "Sure does look like her. Same mousy blond hair and turned-up nose. Jah, that's gotta be Fern."

Loraine's head snapped to the right, and her breath caught in her throat when she saw the young woman Jake was referring to. "It's her, isn't it?"

Loraine nodded slowly. "I wonder what she's doing here, and who's that young man sitting with her?"

"Maybe she's gotten married since she moved to Ohio."

"Or maybe he's a friend or a relative."

"There's only one way to find out. Let's go over there and ask." Before Loraine could respond, Jake pushed his chair away from the table and started across the room.

With a sigh of resignation, Loraine rose from her seat. The idea of talking to Wayne's ex-girlfriend held no appeal, but it wouldn't be right to remain at the table while Jake went over to say hello. Besides, Loraine was curious as to what had brought Fern back to Indiana.

By the time Loraine reached the table, Jake had already pulled out a chair and taken a seat next to the young man with a thick crop of sandy brown hair.

"Hello, Fern," Loraine said, forcing a smile. "I'm surprised to see you here. I thought you were living in Ohio."

"We have been, and my folks are still there, but I've been asked to teach the older grades at the schoolhouse where your cousin Jolene used to teach, so I'm moving back here."

Loraine's heart started to pound. "Y–you're going to be teaching here now?"

"That's right." Fern motioned to the young man sitting across from her. "My brother Freeman came along to see about opening a bicycle shop here similar to our Uncle John's bike shop, where he's worked for the past several years." She smiled at her brother. "Freeman misses Indiana and wants to get settled in here. Since our Grandma Sara is widowed and has plenty of room, we'll be staying with her, at least for now."

Jake thumped Freeman on the back. "Wow, you've sure grown

up since I last saw you. I didn't even realize it was you."

"I'm almost twenty-two years old now," Freeman said with a grin.

Fern motioned to the empty chair beside her. "Would you like to have a seat, Loraine?"

Loraine shifted uneasily, wishing Jake would say they ought to return to their table. He made no move to get up, however, because he was deeply engaged in conversation with Freeman.

Reluctantly, Loraine pulled out the chair and sat down. Other than the fact that she and Fern had both dated Wayne, they really had nothing in common. She didn't have a clue what to talk about, either.

Fern seemed equally uncomfortable, as she fiddled with the fork beside her plate. "I. . .uh. . .heard about the accident you, Wayne, and the others were in. It must have been horrible for him, losing a leg like that."

"Jah, it was quite a shock."

"How's Wayne getting along now?"

"As well as can be expected." Loraine saw no need to tell Fern how depressed Wayne had been or that he'd called off their wedding. Since Fern was moving here, she would probably hear all about that soon enough anyway—especially if she talked to Ada.

I wonder how things will be once Ada finds out Fern's moving back? Loraine wondered. *It would be just like Ada to try and get Wayne and Fern together again. But then,* she reasoned, *if Wayne thinks he's not capable of taking care of a wife and family, it's not likely that he'd start going out with Fern—especially since he was the one to break up with her.*

"I'll try to get over and see Wayne sometime this week," Fern said, scattering Loraine's thoughts. "I'd like to see how he's doing and offer a few encouraging words."

"I'm sure he'd appreciate that." Loraine looked over at Jake again, silently begging him to say that they needed to return to their table. If he didn't say something soon, maybe she'd say it herself.

After what seemed like an eternity, Jake rose to his feet. "I guess Loraine and I should get back to our table before our food gets cold." He smiled at Fern and her brother. "It's been nice seeing you both. If you ever have a horse in need of some shoes, just give me or my daed a call."

～❦❀～

Jake glanced at Loraine out of the corner of his eye. She hadn't said more than two words since they'd left Topeka. In fact, ever since their brief visit with Fern and her brother, Loraine had been quiet.

"It was sure strange seeing Fern again, wasn't it?" he said, hoping to break the silence between them.

Loraine nodded.

"Her brother's sure changed. I wouldn't have recognized him if Fern hadn't said his name."

"Uh-huh."

"While Freeman and I were gabbing, what'd you and Fern talk about?"

"Not much. Just said a few things about the accident."

"It's good that the school board's found someone to take your cousin's place, don't you think?"

"I suppose, although the older scholars are doing okay with their temporary teacher, and I know from what I've heard that they really do miss Jolene." Loraine sighed. "She was a good teacher, and it's a shame she won't be able to teach school again because of losing her hearing."

"Maybe she'll find something else to do—something that doesn't require her to hear."

"Jah, maybe so."

"Getting back to Fern," Jake said, "as I recall, she always had an easygoing way about her. Hopefully, she'll get along well with her students."

"Time will tell, I guess."

"I overheard her say something to you about visiting Wayne. Are you bothered by that?"

237

Loraine shook her head. "Why should I be?"

"I just thought since he and Fern used to date that you might—"

"Wayne and I aren't engaged anymore, so he can see whomever he pleases."

Jake decided to drop the subject. From the responses Loraine had given, he figured she wasn't too excited about Fern moving back, and he had a hunch she hadn't gotten over Wayne yet, either. Could she be jealous of Wayne's old girlfriend? Or could Loraine's coolness toward Fern have something to do with the fact that she'd be taking over Jolene's teaching position?

"Are you warm enough?" Jake asked. "Because if you're not, there's a buggy robe under the seat."

"It is a little chilly." She reached under the seat but came up empty-handed. "There's no buggy robe there, Jake."

He scratched the side of his head. "Maybe my mamm washed it and forgot to put it back. She said something about washing all the buggy robes the other day." He patted the empty space beside him. "You could move closer to me if you're cold. There's nothing like a little body warmth to chase away the chill."

Loraine didn't make a move at first, but then to Jake's surprise, she scooted a little closer. So close, in fact, that their shoulders touched.

Jake smiled. The warmth of her arm against his brought back memories of their courting days. They'd been so happy and carefree. It felt good to be out with her again—almost like old times. He wished the evening never had to end. He wished they could get back to where they'd once been. Well, given some time, maybe they could.

"Look at that starry sky." Loraine pointed out the front window. "It almost seems as if the stars are hung on invisible threads."

Jake nudged her arm gently. "Listen to you now. All those flowery words make you sound like a poet."

She nudged him back. "For your information, I have written a few poems."

"Oh, really? Why don't you let me hear one of them?"

"Are you sure? I mean, some people aren't interested in poetry."

"Well, I'm not *some* people. I'm interested in any poem that was written by you." Throwing caution to the wind, Jake reached for her hand and was pleased when she didn't pull it away.

"All right then. . ." Loraine cleared her throat. "My poem goes like this:

"I looked up at the sky one night;
    across the horizon, clouds were bright
with streaks of red and pink hues,
    and the sky was a brilliant blue.
I gazed upon this glorious sight,
    and knew the Artist had done it all right.
God had painted the sky for everyone to behold,
    so that His glory could always be told!"

Jake gently squeezed Loraine's fingers. "That was really good. I think you have a talent for making up poems."

"Really?"

He nodded. "Maybe you ought to quit your job at the hardware store and become a poet."

She snickered. "Jah, right."

"No, I mean it, Loraine. You ought to at least try to get some of your poems published."

She shook her head. "I'm not interested in that. I only write poems when the mood hits, and I doubt that anything I've written would be considered good enough to publish."

"You'll never know unless you try. Want me to check at the library and see if there's any information available about where you could send your poems?"

She shook her head. "I appreciate the offer, but I think not."

He shrugged. "If you change your mind let me know."

They rode in silence the rest of the way home, but Jake found that words weren't needed when he was with Loraine. It felt so natural and pleasant, sitting here beside her like they were meant to be together.

"I wish I'd thought to bring my harmonica along," he said, breaking the silence. "It would have been fun to play it on the drive home."

"You'll have to bring it next time," she said.

He nodded. *Next time. Why did that sound so good?*

"I had a nice time tonight. Danki for inviting me to have supper with you, Jake." Tenderness laced Loraine's words like a soft blanket against rough, calloused skin.

"You're welcome; I had a good time, too."

Jake smiled to himself. If Loraine's response on this drive home was any indication of how she felt toward him, then he was confident that they were making some headway toward getting back together. The expression he'd seen on her face during supper and the way she'd listened so intently to his description of Montana and life on the horse ranch had made him think she still cared for him, too. She'd seemed happy and relaxed while they were eating—at least until they'd talked to Fern and her brother.

Jake guided his horse and buggy up the driveway leading to her place and stopped it on the side of the barn, facing the pasture, where he knew they couldn't be seen from the house.

His stomach lurched with nervous anticipation as he slid his hand under Loraine's chin. Should he tell her about Roxanne, and how they'd almost become engaged? Was there any reason she needed to know? Pushing the thought aside, he slowly lowered his head and captured Loraine's lips with a kiss that stole his breath away.

She leaned closer and placed both hands around his neck.

Caught up in the moment, he moaned and deepened the kiss.

With a sudden gasp, she pulled away, trembling like a blade of grass shaken by the wind. "I'd better go." Without waiting for

Jake's reply, she hopped out of the buggy and made a beeline for the house.

"Maybe I shouldn't have done it," Jake mumbled. "I hope that kiss won't keep Loraine from going out with me again."

CHAPTER 34

Loraine's legs shook like a newborn colt as she stumbled into the house. She could hardly believe Jake had kissed her. She could hardly believe she'd let him.

She leaned against the door, her heart racing so hard she feared she might pass out. Gulping in several deep breaths, she tried to calm herself.

Should I have agreed to go out with Jake tonight? Am I falling for him again? Oh Lord, how could I have let this happen? If I allow myself to fall in love with Jake, how can I ever face Wayne?

Loraine remained slumped against the door, breathing deeply and replaying Jake's kiss in her mind. At first it had taken her by surprise, but then she'd begun to relax, and had found the kiss to be comforting and kind of nice. Then, when he'd deepened the kiss, it had taken her breath away. That frightened her a lot!

She stayed at the door for several more minutes. Once she'd calmed down enough to walk without shaking, she tiptoed up the stairs and into her room. Thankfully, Mom and Dad's bedroom door was shut, so she assumed they were asleep. Good. She didn't feel up to engaging in any small talk or answering anyone's questions about her date with Jake. She needed to be alone to think, pray, and read her Bible.

Loraine found the Bible lying in the drawer of her nightstand.

She'd been negligent in reading it regularly, using the excuse that she was too tired by the time she went to bed each night. Tonight, however, she needed some answers and knew they'd best come by filling her mind with God's Word.

She took a seat on the bed, opened the Bible, and turned to Psalms, one of her favorite books. She thumbed through a few pages, until her gaze came to rest on verse 4 of chapter 37. It was the same verse that had been attached to a loaf of friendship bread she'd gotten from Ella several weeks ago. "Delight thyself also in the Lord: and he shall give thee the desires of thine heart."

I don't know what my desire is, Lord, Loraine silently prayed. *I used to think I wanted to be married to Jake, but after he left, I fell in love with Wayne. Now Jake's back, and I'm having some feelings for him again. Yet whenever I see Wayne, I long to be with him. Is what I'm feeling for Jake really love? Or am I merely attracted to Jake because Wayne's pushed me away? If I continue to see Jake, will he think we're back together? Do I want us to be? Wayne says he doesn't love me anymore, but I can't seem to let go of what we once had. Oh Lord, what do I want? What should I do?*

No answers came; just the steady *tick-tock* of the clock by her bed.

She stood and moved over to the window. The bright, full moon she'd seen earlier was now hidden behind the cloudy night sky. As she stared into the yard, she saw nothing but darkness. Even the stars she'd made comment about on the drive home had disappeared.

She pulled the window open, and a chilly breeze blew in, causing her to shiver. She didn't care. The cold air might help clear her head. Leaning against the windowsill, she drew in several deep, even breaths.

Still, no clear direction as to what she should do.

With a sigh of resignation, she closed the window and returned to her bed.

Flopping against the pillows, Loraine closed her eyes. Almost immediately, an image of Jake popped into her head—playful, teasing, full of laughter and life. Then she saw Wayne in her mind's eye—not the way he used to be, but the way he was now: somber, pessimistic, full of self-doubt.

What happened to you, Wayne? Loraine's soul cried out. *Why'd you have to stop loving me? Have you given up on life? What happened to our plans to live together as husband and wife for the rest of our lives?*

Tears coursed down her cheeks, and she sniffed and swiped them away with the back of her hand. *Maybe I should give Jake a chance. That's what Wayne wants, after all. I may not love Jake in the same way I love Wayne, but I do enjoy being with him more than I care to admit. Maybe it's okay to settle for second best.*

⁂

Feeling a tug at his heart to spend some time in God's Word, Wayne lifted his Bible off the nightstand and took a seat on his bed. He opened it to the book of Proverbs, and his gaze came to rest on chapter 3, verses 5 and 6: "Trust in the Lord with all thine heart; and lean not unto thine own understanding. In all thy ways acknowledge him, and he shall direct thy paths."

Wayne swallowed against the lump in his throat. He knew he hadn't been trusting in God these last few months. He'd been wallowing in self-pity and was full of doubts. His understanding of things had pulled him down to the pit of despair. He hadn't acknowledged God or allowed Him to direct his paths, either. He'd been trying to do everything in his own strength, irritated when others wanted to help. He'd been ashamed of his appearance and embarrassed and concerned about what others thought because he only had one leg. He'd felt incapable of becoming a husband because he thought he was only half a man.

Wayne turned over to the book of Isaiah and read chapter 50, verse 7: "For the Lord God will help me; therefore shall I not be confounded: therefore have I set my face like a flint, and I know that I shall not be ashamed."

He set the Bible aside and closed his eyes. *Maybe my situation isn't hopeless, Lord. Just as the stump of my leg has begun to heal, my emotional wounds need to heal as well. I realize now that You've been with me all the time, helping me to get through each day. Please help me learn to accept my limitations and be thankful for the things I'm able to do.*

Wayne thought about how, for the last few weeks, he'd been helping Pop in his taxidermy business. To his surprise, he'd found that he rather enjoyed the work, and they were making a decent living. He'd adjusted fairly well to the prosthesis, too, so maybe getting married and raising a family wasn't an impossible thing.

He winced as he pulled the covers aside and crawled into bed. *Loraine's the only woman I'd ever want to marry, but it's too late for us now that she and Jake are back together. She deserves to be happy, so I won't come between them. Loraine and Jake will never know how I feel.*

 ❦

Tears sprang to Ella's eyes as she sat near the fireplace, rocking in her chair, and thinking about Loraine and the things she'd said when Jake had come to pick Loraine up for their date.

I only want to help her, she silently moaned. *I don't want to see her get hurt again.* Ella's tears trickled down her cheeks and splashed onto the front of her robe. She was glad the rest of the family had gone to bed. She was supposed to be the strong one and didn't want anyone to see her give in to her tears.

Loraine and I have always been so close, but since the accident, we've been drifting further and further apart. She squeezed her eyes shut. *Is it my fault, Lord? Am I the reason Loraine's been pulling away?*

When Ella opened her eyes, she saw Dad's Bible lying on the coffee table, where he'd placed it after they'd done their family devotions earlier this evening. *What was that verse of scripture Dad read?* Ella had been so upset with Loraine and Jake when she'd come home, she hadn't really listened to much of anything during devotions.

Ella rose from her chair and picked up the Bible. Then, taking a seat on the sofa, she opened it to the place that had been marked with a narrow piece of ribbon. It was the book of Proverbs, and Dad had underlined verse 24 of chapter 18. "A man that hath friends must shew himself friendly: and there is a friend that sticketh closer than a brother."

The words swam on the page because of Ella's tears. She'd been trying to be a good friend to Loraine, but everything she said seemed to be taken the wrong way. *Why can't Loraine see that Jake isn't the right man for her? Why won't she listen to my warnings? Doesn't she realize she's walking on dangerous ground?*

Ella flipped through a few more pages, until her gaze came to rest on another verse Dad had underlined: "A word fitly spoken is like apples of gold in pictures of silver."

She continued to read several more verses that had been underlined, and swallowed on the sob rising in her throat when she read Proverbs 27:15: "A continual dropping in a very rainy day and a contentious woman are alike."

"I've been a contentious woman and have been going about trying to help Loraine in all the wrong ways," she murmured. "If I want Loraine to remain my friend, then I need to keep quiet about Jake. It's Loraine's life, and she has to make her own decisions without interference from me. From now on, I'll keep my opinions and concerns to myself."

❦

As Jake headed down the road toward home, he couldn't stop thinking about Loraine and the way he'd felt being with her tonight. He only hoped his unexpected kiss hadn't driven her away. Since he'd recently purchased a couple of thoroughbred horses, he figured if things went well with Loraine and he was able to get his business going soon, in a few more months, he might be in a position to ask her to marry him. The question that nagged him the most, though, was whether Loraine might still be in love with Wayne.

Directing his focus on the road ahead, Jake decided he would stop worrying and commit his future to God.

He was almost home when he spotted a couple of horses running down the road. It was too dark to see what color they were, but he had a sinking feeling they were his.

He pulled his horse and buggy onto the shoulder of the road and was about to get out and investigate, when he spotted a semi-truck barreling down the road in the opposite lane.

Jake's heart leaped into his throat. Before he had the chance to react, the truck slammed on its brakes, skidded several feet, and plowed into the first horse, knocking it to the side of the road. The second horse, obviously panicked, reared up, and rammed into the side of the truck.

Jake let out a yelp, jumped from his buggy, and dashed into the road, where the truck had stopped.

The driver got out, and stood there, shaking his head. "I didn't see the horses until it was too late." He looked over at Jake. "Are they yours?"

Jake nodded, as the headlights from the truck made the horses clearly visible. They were his! What a horrible ending to an otherwise perfect day!

CHAPTER 35

"I still can't believe my horses got out on the road last night," Jake said as he took a seat at the breakfast table. "One horse is dead, and the other one injured so bad it might never fully recover." He groaned. "I'll never get my business going at this rate."

"Maybe you need to accept the fact that you might not be able to have your horse ranch here," Dad said. "You oughta be thankful you've got a job working for me."

"I've already told you, I don't want to shoe horses for the rest of my life. I want to raise and train horses." Jake looked over at his three younger brothers. "When I left to take Loraine out to supper last night, my horses were both in the corral, and the gate was closed. Did any of you open the gate?"

Vern and Kyle, the two youngest boys, shook their heads.

"I never went near the corral last night, either," Elmer said.

"Well, somebody had to open that gate!" Jake frowned. "It sure didn't open itself and let the horses out."

"Maybe it blew open in the wind," Jake's sister Marilyn spoke up.

Jake shook his head. "That's not likely since there wasn't any wind last night. I'm sure someone in this family opened that gate and they're just sittin' here, afraid to tell." He eyeballed his brothers again.

"That's enough with the blaming," Dad said in a stern voice. "The horses got out, and we don't know how, so let's just leave it at that."

"That's easy enough for you to say," Jake mumbled. "They weren't your horses."

"Even if they had been my horses, I wouldn't be trying to put the blame on someone else for what happened." Dad put both hands on the table, and locked his fingers together. "Now, let's pray."

As Jake bowed his head with the others, all he could think to pray about was his situation with Loraine. He had to see her today. Had to find out if she was upset with him for kissing her last night. Had to know if there was any chance that they might have a future together.

I'll go over to her place later today, he decided. *Or maybe I'll stop by the Lambrights' around five o'clock. Loraine might be fixing dinner for them.*

～⚹～

"I'll be going over to the Lambrights' after I get off work again today," Loraine told her mother as she set the table for breakfast.

"I wish you wouldn't go over there so often," Mom said, reaching for her choring apron.

"Ada still needs help." Loraine grabbed three napkins from the basket in the center of the table.

"I realize that, since I, too, have been helping out there. Even so, I don't think it's good for you to hang around Wayne so much." Mom sighed. "I know the main reason you keep going over there is because you're hoping he'll change his mind about breaking up with you."

Loraine let the napkins fall to the table and whirled around to face her mother. "I'm not trying to get Wayne to change his mind. Fact is, I've changed *my* mind."

"What do you mean?"

"I've decided to give Jake a chance. If he asks me out again,

I'm going to say yes."

Mom smiled and moved over to the stove. "Now that is good news."

Loraine took a pitcher of grape juice from the refrigerator and set it on the table. She could understand why Mom might like Jake better than Wayne. He was a lot more pleasant to talk to, and he always had a joke or funny story to tell. Still, Wayne had his good points, too—or at least he used to before the accident. Too bad Mom couldn't be more supportive of Wayne. Maybe with a little encouragement, Loraine might not have given up on Wayne herself. Maybe Mom could have even put in a good word with Ada on Loraine's behalf. But no, she just took her turn at helping and never said a thing.

Loraine poured juice into one of the glasses and took a drink, hoping to push down the lump that had lodged itself in her throat. Ella, who was supposed to be one of her best friends, wasn't supportive or understanding, either. Mom wanted her to get together with Jake, and every chance Ella got, she tried to convince Loraine that Jake was no good for her. Well, Ella and Mom could think whatever they wanted. After mulling things over last night, despite the fact that she'd gotten no clear answers from God, Loraine had made her decision.

~⚹~

Wayne poured the last bit of coffee from his cup down the sink and glanced out the window just as a young Amish woman pedaled up the driveway on a bicycle. He squinted, trying to make out who she was, but she was too far away to know for sure.

He waited at the window until she drew closer, and when she stopped her bike near the house and got off, he realized it was Fern Bontrager.

What's Fern doing here? he wondered. *Last I heard, she was living in Ohio.*

He went to the door and opened it just as she stepped onto the porch.

"Hello, Wayne." Fern smiled shyly. "It's good to see you again."

He gave a nod. "I didn't realize you were in the area. Has your family moved back to Indiana?"

Fern shook her head. "My folks still live in Ohio, but my brother Freeman and I are moving here."

"Oh?"

She nodded. "I'll be teaching at the schoolhouse where Jolene Yoder taught before she lost her hearing, and Freeman hopes to open a bike shop."

"I see." Wayne leaned against the doorjamb, feeling the need for a little support. He remembered how, when he and Fern had been going out together, Mom had said she really liked Fern and hoped she and Wayne might get married someday. He figured Mom would probably be happy to hear that Fern was moving back, but he hoped she wouldn't have any ideas about him and Fern getting together again. He wasn't sure why Mom had always liked Fern so well. Maybe it was because she was such a compliant person and had always agreed with everything Mom said.

"I heard about the horrible accident you and your friends were in," Fern said. "I felt bad when I learned that you'd lost a leg because of it."

Wayne lifted his pant leg enough to reveal his prosthesis. "Thanks to this, I'm able to walk at least."

"It's really good that things like that are made available to people who lose a limb."

Wayne nodded. "They're expensive, though."

"I can only imagine. Did you have help from the community paying for it?" she asked.

"Jah. They held an auction, and even though it was cut short because of a fire in the building, enough money came in to help with everyone's medical expenses."

"That's good to hear." Fern's forehead wrinkled. "I saw Loraine Miller and Jake Beechy at Tiffany's restaurant last night. I was surprised to see them together. The last I'd heard, you and Loraine were engaged to be married, and Jake was living in Montana."

Wayne shrugged. "Loraine and I broke up, and now she's seeing Jake again."

"Oh, I see."

A harsh wind whistled under the eaves of the porch, causing Fern to shiver and pull her jacket tightly around her neck. "The weather sure is unpredictable these days. One day it's too warm for fall, and the next day it almost feels like winter."

Wayne nodded. "Why don't you come in out of the cold? I'm sure my mamm will be glad to see you."

"I'd like to see her as well." Fern stepped into the house, and Wayne shut the door.

"Mom broke her leg a few weeks ago, so she's not up to doing much yet." Wayne motioned to the door leading to the living room. "You'll find her in there."

Fern gave him a curious stare. "Aren't you coming in to visit with us?"

Wayne shifted uneasily. He had no desire to listen to Mom gush over Fern, but he didn't want to appear impolite, either. "Jah, sure," he said, feigning a smile. "I guess I can sit and visit awhile."

When they stepped into the living room, Mom's face broke into a wide smile. "Fern Bontrager! What a pleasant surprise! I had no idea you were back in town."

"I've been hired to teach at the schoolhouse in this district," Fern explained.

"Ach, that's wunderbaar!" Mom patted the sofa cushion beside her. "Come, sit and tell me all about it."

Fern removed her jacket and took a seat beside Mom. Wayne seated himself in the recliner across from them. For the next several minutes he listened to Fern tell about her folks and how much they enjoyed living in Ohio. When Fern finally came up for air, Mom jumped right in.

"Did you hear about the accident Wayne and his friends were in?"

Fern nodded soberly. "My folks found out when they read

about it in *The Budget*. We were sorry to hear that some lost their lives."

"It's been a sad time for all." Mom looked over at Wayne with a doting expression. "We're very grateful that our son is alive, even though his leg had to be amputated because of his injuries."

"She knows about that, too," Wayne said, "But let's not go into the details, okay?"

Mom's pinched expression let him know that she'd planned to do just that, but he was relieved when she nodded and relaxed against the sofa pillows.

"I can't tell you how much I've missed our visits," she said, patting Fern's arm. "As soon as you get settled in, you'll have to come over for supper some evening." She glanced back at Wayne. "It'll give you two a chance to get reacquainted."

Fern said nothing, and Wayne looked around the room, wishing there was a hole in the floor so he could crawl right in it.

"Do you need a place to stay while you're here, Fern?" Mom asked. "Because if you do—"

"My bruder, Freeman, and I will be staying with our grandma, Sara Bontrager."

"Is Freeman moving here with you?"

Fern nodded. "He's hoping to open his own bike shop."

Mom smiled. "That sounds exciting. We can always use another bike shop in the area."

For the next several minutes, Wayne listened to Mom and Fern gab on and on, but when Mom started dropping hints about what a good wife Fern would make for some lucky fellow, he decided it was time to take his leave.

"If you two will excuse me," he said, rising to his feet, "I need to get out to the taxidermy shop. Pop's planning to work on a baby fox that was brought in by one of our English neighbors, so I'd better not keep him waiting."

Mom pursed her lips. "Oh, but I thought—"

"It's been nice seeing you again, Fern." Wayne hurried from the room.

~€ ℈~

When Ella entered the hardware store, she was relieved to see Loraine behind the counter waiting on a middle-aged English woman. After the decision she'd made last night, she needed to talk to Loraine and make things right.

She waited over by the rack of books until the customer had paid for her purchases and left the store, and then she quickly stepped up to the counter. "I'm glad you're working today, because I need to tell you something," she said, leaning as close to Loraine as the counter between them would allow.

Loraine tapped her fingers along the edge of the cash register. "If you're here to give me another lecture about Jake, you can save your breath; I've already made my decision."

"What decision?"

"About me and Jake." Loraine's voice lowered to a whisper. "Since Wayne has made it more than clear that he doesn't love me anymore, I've decided to give Jake a chance. That is, if he wants to continue seeing me," she quickly added.

Ella leaned against the counter, too dumbfounded to say a word. Even though she'd planned to tell Loraine that she wouldn't say negative things about Jake anymore, she hadn't expected to hear such a declaration.

"Aren't you going to say something?" Loraine asked, nudging Ella's arm. "I'm sure what I said is not what you were hoping to hear; am I right about that?"

Ella slowly shook her head. "It's not what I'd like to hear, but I've been doing some thinking and praying, and I've come to realize that it's your life, not mine." She forced a smile. "So if you think Jake will make you happy, then it's none of my business."

Loraine's mouth gaped open as she stared at Ella in disbelief. "Do you really mean that?"

"Said so, didn't I?" Tears welled in Ella's eyes. "We've been best cousin-friends since we were little girls, and I don't want anything or anyone to come between us. I'm sorry for the things I said

254

before. From now on, I'm behind you one hundred percent."

Loraine stepped out from behind the counter and gave Ella a hug. "You really are my best cousin-friend."

Ella grinned. She might not like the idea of Jake dating her cousin, but she felt good about her decision to stop nagging Loraine and just be her friend.

❧ ❧

"Pop's gonna run to town for a few things we need in his shop, and I'd like to go with him," Wayne said when he stepped into the living room where Ada sat on the sofa with a basket of mending beside her. "Will you be okay here by yourself until we get back? I don't think we'll be gone for more than a few hours."

"Jah, sure, I'll be fine." She lifted the pair of trousers she'd been mending. "I'll stay busy with these for a while, and then I may take a nap."

"That's a good idea. I'm sure one of the ladies in our community will be over later with some supper for us, so there's no reason you can't rest until we get back from town."

As Wayne started to leave the room, she called out, "Were you as surprised to see Fern this morning as I was?"

He turned and nodded. "I guess the members of the school board will be happy to have another full-time teacher."

"What about you, son? Aren't you happy to have your girlfriend back in town?"

Wayne's eyes narrowed. "Ex-girlfriend, Mom. Fern and I haven't dated each other in several years."

"That's true, but since she's back now, I thought maybe—"

"You thought you could figure out some way to get us back together?"

Ada's face heated up. "Well, I—"

"If that's what you had in mind, you can forget about it." Wayne shook his head. "I'm not interested in a relationship with Fern or any other woman. I've come to realize that staying a bachelor's the best thing for me."

"Oh, but—"

"I've gotta go. Pop's waiting in the buggy, and the sooner we get going, the sooner we'll be back. See you later, Mom." Wayne hurried from the room, leaving Ada shaking her head.

"I wish men weren't so stubborn," she mumbled as she threaded her needle. "And I wish my son would realize that I only want what's best for him."

Ada's stomach rumbled, and she looked at the battery-operated clock across the room. It wouldn't be suppertime for several more hours, but she was hungry now.

She set the sewing aside, grabbed her crutches, and stood.

When she entered the kitchen, she headed straight for the refrigerator, thinking she'd get a jar of canned peaches.

"Oh, bother," she said when she realized there were no peaches. "I really wanted some of those."

She turned toward the basement door. *There's more downstairs. I wonder if I can get myself down there without breaking another bone.*

With sheer grit and determination, Ada opened the basement door, and using one crutch and the handrail, she started down the stairs. She'd only made it halfway, when she lost her grip on the crutch, and it slipped out from under her arm. With only the handrail for support, she quickly lost her balance. The next thing she knew, she was tumbling down the stairs.

CHAPTER 36

As Loraine headed to the Lambrights' place, she wondered if she would see Jake. He often dropped by when he was done working for the day. Since she'd ridden her bike and not come by horse and buggy, she knew she'd have to get home before it got too dark. Even though she had a battery-operated light on her bicycle, it wasn't good to be out in the dark of night. That meant she'd have to hurry and fix supper for the Lambrights and be on her way.

She pedaled up their driveway, parked her bike near the barn, and hurried up the steps. No one answered the door on her first knock, so she knocked again.

Still no answer.

Maybe no one's at home, she thought. *They could have had errands to run in town, or maybe Ada had a doctor's appointment and Crist and Wayne went with her.*

She was about to head back to her bike when she noticed that the kitchen window was wide open. Since a breeze had come up, and it smelled like rain was coming, she decided to go inside and close the window.

Loraine hurried to the kitchen and had just shut the window when she heard a noise.

She tipped her head and listened. There it was again—a soft

moan. It sounded like it was coming from the basement.

When she discovered that the basement door was partially open, she grabbed the flashlight hanging on a nail near the door and descended the stairs. As her foot touched the bottom step, she gasped. Ada lay in a heap on the floor.

Loraine rushed over to the woman. "Ada, can you hear me? Are you hurt?"

No response.

She touched Ada's forehead and felt something warm and sticky ooze between her fingers. A quick glance with the flashlight, and she knew it was blood. Ada must have fallen down the stairs and hit her head on the floor.

"Ada, can you hear me?"

Ada moaned slightly but didn't open her eyes.

"Oh, dear Lord," Loraine prayed out loud. "Please let Ada be all right. This family's been through so much; they don't need anything more."

Suddenly, Ada's eyes popped open. "You—you were praying for me?"

Loraine nodded as a sense of relief flooded her soul. "I'm so glad you're awake."

Ada tried to sit up, but Loraine kept her from moving by placing a gentle hand on her chest. "Better not move just yet. There's a gash on your head, and it's bleeding. I can't tell how bad it is, but you might have a serious injury."

"I can move my arms and my one good leg, so I don't think I broke any more bones." Ada groaned. "But my head sure hurts. I think I hit it pretty hard when I fell down the stairs."

"What were you doing coming down here, and where's the rest of your family?"

"I came to get a jar of peaches. The menfolk went shopping in Shipshewana."

"Oh, Ada," Loraine said, shaking her head, "you should never have come down here alone. Not with a cast on your leg!"

Ada's chin quivered, and she blinked a couple of times like

she might be on the verge of tears. "I know it was a stupid thing to do, but I was hungry for peaches and there weren't any in the refrigerator."

Loraine glanced around, searching for something she could put under the poor woman's head. When she spotted a laundry basket full of towels, she wrapped a smaller towel around Ada's head where the gash was and put another one under Ada's head as a cushion. "You need to lie very still while I go out to the phone shed and call for help."

Ada clasped Loraine's hand. "Please, don't leave me here alone."

"I promise, I won't be gone long. We need to get you to the hospital so you can be checked over by a doctor."

"What time is it?" Ada asked.

"When I left home, it was two thirty, so it's probably sometime after three."

"Crist and Wayne left around two, and Wayne said he thought they'd only be gone a few hours. I'm sure they'll be here soon. Then Crist can see that I get to the doctor's."

Loraine nibbled on her lower lip as she contemplated the problem. "I don't know, Ada. I'm really worried about you, and—"

"You prayed for me, and now you're worried about me?"

"Jah."

"I can't believe it." A few tears slipped under Ada's lashes and splashed onto her cheeks. "You're the one who got help for me when I fell off my bike and broke my leg, and you're the one who's been coming over here regularly to help out ever since."

Loraine nodded.

"Why, Loraine? Why have you been so nice to me when all I've done is to treat you unkindly?"

Loraine blinked against her own set of tears. "I did it because I care about you, Ada."

"But how could you care when I've been so mean and unappreciative of the things you've done?"

"It's not always easy, but it's our duty as Christians to do what we can to help others, regardless of how they might treat us."

"I'm sorry, Loraine. Sorry for all the nasty things I've said to you and about you. I haven't been thinking clearly since Wayne lost his leg. I was wrong when I blamed you for asking him to go to Hershey Park." Ada sniffed deeply, as more tears fell. "Can you find it in your heart to forgive me?"

Loraine nodded and squeezed Ada's fingers. "I forgive you."

"What can I do to make it up to you?"

"Nothing. I don't expect you to do anything at all."

"But I messed things up between you and Wayne. If I hadn't interfered and said I disapproved of you, he might have—"

"No, Ada." Loraine shook her head. "Wayne broke our engagement of his own free will. He doesn't love me anymore. He thinks I'd be better off with Jake." She swallowed hard and nearly choked on the sob rising in her throat. "It took me awhile, but I've finally come to terms with the way things are. I'm now trying to move on with my life, and I hope Wayne will do the same."

"Are you in love with Jake?"

"I do care for him, but—"

Ada squeezed Loraine's fingers. "You're a good woman. Any man would be pleased to have you for a wife, so I hope Jake appreciates what he's found."

Thunk! Thunk! Thunk! Loraine heard footsteps upstairs. "That must be your men," she said to Ada. She cupped her hands around her mouth and shouted, "We're down here! Ada's fallen and needs to see a doctor right away!"

⁓⁜⁓

Taking the stairs as carefully as he could, Wayne followed his father to the basement. When they reached the bottom, he saw Mom lying on the concrete floor. Loraine was kneeling beside her.

"What happened here?" Pop hollered as he hurried toward Mom. "Why's my *fraa* lying on the floor?"

"Silly me. I decided to come to the basement to get a jar of peaches. When I was halfway down, my crutch sailed right out from under me." Mom looked up at Loraine and smiled. "Loraine found me here, and she put a towel under my head." *Sniff! Sniff!* "She even prayed for me. Can you believe that, Crist? Loraine actually petitioned God on my behalf."

"I'm glad Loraine came by when she did." Pop knelt on the floor beside Mom and took her hand, and then he looked up at Wayne. "We need to get your mamm to the hospital right away. Would you please go to the phone shed and call 911?"

"Nee," Mom shook her head. "I don't think I'm seriously hurt."

"There's a gash on your head, and it's bleeding. I think you should listen to your husband and let Wayne call for help," Loraine said.

Wayne nodded. "I agree. You need to be seen by a doctor."

"Oh, all right; I can see that I'm outnumbered in this," Mom said. "Go ahead and call for help."

Wayne chuckled, despite the seriousness of the situation. Leave it up to Mom to have the last word, even when she was lying on a cold, hard floor with a cut on her head.

Loraine looked at Wayne. "Once the ambulance shows up, I'll head for home while you and your daed go with your mamm to the hospital."

"Absolutely not!" Mom shouted. "Crist can ride to the hospital with me, while Wayne sees that you get safely home!"

CHAPTER 37

Would you like me to fix you something to eat before I head for home?" Loraine asked Wayne after the ambulance had pulled away.

"I'm not all that hungry." He moved toward the door, feeling suddenly uncomfortable in her presence. He was tempted to ask about how her date went with Jake, but thought better of it. No point in rubbing salt in his own wounds.

"I'll get your bike and put it in the back of my buggy," he mumbled.

"I'm sure it's heavy; you might need some help." Loraine rushed out the door before he had a chance to respond.

Wayne frowned. *Doesn't she think I'm capable of doing anything?*

He stepped out the door and watched from the porch as she grabbed the handlebars of her bike and started wheeling it toward his dad's buggy, which was parked near the barn.

The light rain that had begun falling during their trip home from Shipshewana had now turned to hail.

As Wayne started moving across the yard, the hail stopped as abruptly as it had started. A short period of calm followed. Then a loud roar that sounded like continuous thunder split through the air. The sky had darkened to a sickly green color, and a gust of wind whooshed through the yard so hard that Wayne could barely stay on his feet.

The whine of warning sirens blared in the distance—the kind that only went off in emergencies.

Wayne looked into the yard to see how Loraine was dealing with the harsh wind and gasped when she tripped and fell.

"Look up!" she shouted, pointing to the sky. "A funnel cloud's coming!"

Wayne's heart thumped wildly, and he rushed forward, almost falling himself.

Loraine struggled to get back on her feet, but the force of the wind dragged her across the yard and into the woodpile.

"Oh, no! Oh, no!" Wayne stumbled forward as quickly as he could. He reached Loraine just as the roof of the barn was ripped off and tossed into the air. They needed to find a safe place quickly, and the only one he could think of was the root cellar.

He bent down, grabbed Loraine under her arms, and lifted her up and into his arms.

"I'm too heavy. Put me down; I can walk," she panted.

Ignoring her pleas, Wayne started to run as fast as he could. A few feet from the root cellar, he stumbled and lost his grip on Loraine.

She screamed and fell to the ground.

With a sense of determination and a whispered prayer, Wayne grabbed Loraine's arms and dragged her over to the cellar. As he struggled to open the door, he heard a terrible crack. Glancing over his shoulder, he watched in horror as Pop's barn was torn asunder.

With his heart pounding so hard he feared it might burst right through his chest, Wayne grasped the cellar door handle and gave it a jerk.

It didn't budge.

He grabbed it again, pulling harder this time. *Snap!*—the handle broke off in his hand.

He looked up at the approaching funnel cloud and knew if they didn't find shelter immediately, they would surely perish.

CHAPTER 38

With a strength Loraine didn't know Wayne had, he reached into the seam of the door and pried it open. As they stumbled inside, Loraine sent up a silent prayer. *Oh Lord, please see us through this unexpected storm!*

Wayne turned and pulled the inside handle on the door, but the wind was so strong he couldn't get it to close. "Help me get this door shut!" he shouted. "We've got to get it closed now, or we'll be blown away!" A look of determination mixed with fear etched Wayne's face. He'd used all of his strength to get the door open so they could get into the root cellar; now she needed to help him get it closed.

Loraine scrambled to her feet and grabbed hold of the handle. Wayne did the same.

"Lord, give us strength," he prayed out loud.

Straining against the wind and blowing debris, Loraine gritted her teeth and pulled for all she was worth.

"Ugh!" She lost her grip and fell backwards, crashing into a box of potatoes. She tried to stand up, but the force of the wind whipping into the cellar held her down. Wayne, with another apparent burst of strength, braced his feet on either side of the doorjamb and pulled with all his might.

With one quick—*snap!*—the door slammed shut, and the room went dark.

Loraine's chest heaved up and down as she gasped for breath. "Th–this can't be happening! It's not tornado season, and there was no warning at all."

"Doesn't have to be. From what I've read about tornados, they can hit just about anytime," he panted.

A beam of light broke through the darkness as he shined a flashlight on her.

"Wh–where you'd get that?"

"Found it on the shelf behind me. We keep it in here for emergencies."

"Are we gonna be all right? Will the door stay shut?"

Wayne handed her the flashlight. "Hold this while I look for something I can use to secure the door." He scanned the room with a frantic expression and finally located a hammer.

Loraine held the flashlight so the beam of light shone on the door. She sucked in a deep breath and watched him struggle with the hammer, and she breathed a sigh of relief when he managed to wedge it in the handle of the door.

"We'd better pray that the handle holds, because if this door blows open, the wind could suck us right out." He pointed to the corner of the cellar. "We'd better get over there so we're not near the door!"

"O–okay."

Wayne grabbed an empty wooden box and turned it over and then lowered himself onto it and leaned against the wall. Loraine crouched on her knees in the corner beside him.

"Are you okay?" she asked with concern. "You didn't hurt your leg, I hope."

"I'm fine. Just tired and out of breath." He took the flashlight from her and snapped it off. "I don't know how old the batteries are, but we don't want to wear 'em down."

"I guess that makes sense." Loraine couldn't see Wayne's face anymore, but she was comforted by his voice. She didn't like being in the dark and wished she could throw herself into his arms and stay there until this nightmare was over.

"You're amazing, Wayne," she whispered.

"What do you mean?"

"You may only have one leg, but you're strong as an ox."

He snorted. "Don't think I've ever been compared to an ox before."

Loraine shifted, trying to find a comfortable position, and winced when a searing pain shot through her right leg. She reached down and touched the spot that hurt. Something wet and sticky oozed between her fingers. "I think my leg's bleeding. Can I see the flashlight a minute?"

Wayne snapped on the light and pointed it at her leg. "Ach, Loraine, you're cut!"

"I must have scraped it on something—maybe it happened when I fell into the woodpile."

"I can't tell for sure, but the cut doesn't look too deep. Might not even need any stitches." He reached into his pants pocket, withdrew a handkerchief, and handed it to her. "You can wrap this around your leg. It hasn't even been used," he added.

"Danki." Loraine wrapped it securely around her leg and tried to relax.

They sat in the darkness as the wind roared and shook the cellar door. "I'm scared, Wayne." Loraine's voice came out in a squeak, and fear churned like bile in her stomach. "I can't remember ever being in a tornado before, and I'm not ready to die."

"If your heart's not right with the Lord, then you need to pray and ask His forgiveness."

"I've done that already. I'm just not ready to leave this world yet. I want to get married and have children."

"Jake's children, you mean?"

Loraine's mouth went dry. Did she dare tell Wayne how she felt about Jake?

She drew in a quick breath and decided to plunge ahead. "I do care about Jake, but—"

"Figured as much."

"But not in the same way I used to."

"What do you mean?"

"When Jake and I were going out before he left for Montana, I used to think we'd get married some day."

The wooden box creaked beneath Wayne's weight. "Because you loved him, right?"

"Yes. No. Well, I thought I did." Loraine paused, searching for the right words. "I enjoy being with Jake; he makes me laugh and forget about my troubles." She reached over and touched Wayne's hand, sending a wave of warmth up her arm. "But it's not the same as when I'm with you."

"No, I don't suppose it would be. Jake's a whole man; I'm sure not."

"Jah, you are, Wayne. When we were out there in the midst of the storm, could you have carried me all that way if you weren't a whole man?"

"I stumbled and dropped you, remember?"

"But you dragged me to safety, and that took a lot of strength. Then when the door handle broke off, you pried it open and got us inside." She paused for a breath. "Then you closed and bolted the door all on your own. You were calm the whole time, and I have to think that you can do most anything you set your mind to do." She gulped on a sob and paused to gain control of her emotions. "Even if you couldn't do anything at all—even if you were confined to your bed—I would love you for the caring, gentle man you really are."

"You—you still love me?"

"Jah, and truth be told, I've never loved anyone the way I love you, and I never will."

"What about Jake? He's in love with you, Loraine. I can see it on his face when you're together. I can hear it in his voice when he talks about you."

"I don't know. I don't want to hurt Jake, but I know now that I can never make a permanent commitment to him because my heart will always belong to you."

❧ ❧

Wayne sat very still as he let Loraine's words sink into his head.

The breath he'd been unconsciously holding came out in a sigh of relief. *She loves me, not Jake. Even with Jake's good looks and playfulness, she'd rather be with me than him.* The revelation was almost too much to comprehend.

"You're awfully quiet. What are you thinking about?" Loraine's sweet voice cut into Wayne's thoughts.

"I'm thinking what a fool I've been for pushing you away. I'm thinking that I wish I could take back all the things I've said to you since the accident. I'm thinking that I made a big mistake even thinking I should move to Illinois."

"You were planning to move?"

"Jah. I thought if I moved away I could leave my past behind, and I wouldn't have to suffer the torment of seeing how happy you and Jake were together." He swallowed hard as his throat constricted. "All those things I've said about not loving you, they were lies. . .just a bunch of lies. I never stopped loving you, Loraine. I only suggested that you go out with Jake because I wanted you to be happy—to have a full life with a man who could give you all the things you deserve, a man who didn't have to rely on others for help."

"So you were giving me up so that I could be happy with Jake?"

"Jah."

"Oh, Wayne, don't you know I'd never truly be happy without you? If I chose Jake, I'd be choosing second best."

Wayne got quiet again, as he continued to mull things over. Could he and Loraine be together again? He'd proven today that he could be there for her in a time of need. In his own strength he could do little, but with God's help, he could do much. He thought of the words from Philippians 4:13: *"I can do all things through Christ which strengtheneth me."*

He reached through the darkness and took hold of her hand. "I love you, Loraine, and I want to spend the rest of my life with you. Will you marry me?"

He heard her sharp intake of breath, followed by a sob. "Jah, Wayne, I'd be honored to be your wife."

He squeezed her fingers as they sat quietly together, waiting for the storm to subside.

"What about Jake?" she whispered. "I don't want to hurt him, but I can't give my heart to him because it belongs to you."

"Want me to tell him?"

"No, I need to be the one."

"Maybe we can tell him together."

"Jah, okay."

Wayne stirred restlessly. "It seems quiet out there. I think I should open the cellar door and check on things."

"Are. . .are you sure?"

"Tornados happen fast and don't normally last too long. I think it's safe to go out." Wayne turned on the flashlight and made his way across the small room. He removed the hammer from the handle and pushed on the door.

It didn't budge.

Loraine jumped up. "I'll help you push."

They leaned their weight against the door and pushed with all their might, but it wouldn't open.

Wayne groaned. "Something must be blocking the door." He didn't say anything to Loraine, but he wondered how long it might take for someone to find them down here. He thought about an article he'd read in the newspaper awhile back about an Amish man who'd hit his head, passed out, and fallen on top of his wife, pinning her to the floor. It had taken several hours before someone came to help.

Bam! Bam! Bam! Loraine banged on the door. "We're stuck down here! Somebody help!"

Wayne pulled her to his side and held her tightly. "There's no point in banging on the door. There's no one out there to hear us. Pop took Mom to the hospital, and no one else is around." He gently stroked the side of her face. "All we can do is pray."

269

CHAPTER 39

A s the wind whipped furiously against his body, Jake lay huddled in a ditch. He'd been heading to the Lambrights' to see if they needed help with their chores, when he'd heard a deafening roar that reminded him of a jet plane. Then he'd seen it—a huge funnel cloud heading his way. He'd pulled the buggy over, unhitched the horse, and then hurried to take cover in the ditch along the shoulder of the road.

With his arms over his head, Jake lay unmoving, praying for all he was worth.

When the storm finally subsided, he lifted his head and rose to his feet. The first thing he saw was pieces of his mangled buggy that had been scattered around like matchsticks.

Jake's horse was nowhere to be seen. Hopefully, he'd run somewhere safe and had escaped the wrath of the storm.

As Jake started walking along the edge of the road toward the Lambrights', his legs shook so badly he thought he could hear his knees knocking. He didn't know what might lie ahead, but he knew he had to keep going.

The tornado had whipped through with lightning speed, and what Jake saw along the road told him it had left a trail of destruction. Telephone poles had been knocked over; the roofs on several houses were missing; many barns had been knocked flat;

trees had been uprooted; and animals milled about in the fields, making pitiful noises.

Shivers rippled along Jake's spine as sirens wailed in the distance. With a sense of urgency, he picked up his speed.

By the time he reached the Lambrights' place, he was exhausted. The shock of what he saw there caused him to drop to his knees; everything seemed surreal. Crist and Ada's home had been leveled by the tornado, and so had their barn. A few sheep, including the ewe with three legs, milled about the place, apparently unharmed.

Jake looked around frantically. Nothing but rubble lay where the house had once been. Where were the Lambrights? Had they gotten out alive—maybe run to a neighbor's before the storm hit? Or were their dead bodies hidden under the pile of debris?

He cupped his hands around his mouth and hollered, "Is anyone here? Can anybody hear me?"

No response. Nothing but the moaning of the wind mingled with the animals' pathetic cries.

Jake's palms grew sweaty as he walked from one section of the farm to the other, searching for bodies. When he spotted a man's boot sticking out from under a pile of bricks, he halted. *Oh dear Lord, could it be Wayne or Crist?*

With his heart pounding and his mouth so dry he could barely swallow, Jake bent down and gave the boot a little tug. He heaved a sigh of relief when he discovered that it wasn't attached to anyone's foot.

He kicked at the ruins as he continued walking along, praying with each step he took that the Lambrights weren't here.

"Help!"

Jake tipped his head and listened. It sounded like someone calling for help. He looked all around but didn't see anyone or anything that looked like it might have trapped a victim.

"Help!"

There it was again.

Jake spotted a huge tree branch pushed up against the door of

271

an old root cellar. Could one of the Lambrights be in there?

He moved toward the door and listened.

"Help! If anyone's out there, we're trapped down here!"

With his heart beating so hard it seemed to be echoing in his ears, Jake grabbed the end of the branch and pulled.

It didn't move an inch.

"Dear Lord in Heaven," he prayed out loud, "I need the strength of Samson right now!"

He gritted his teeth and yanked even harder. This time, he was able to pull the branch far enough away from the door that he could see that the handle was missing.

He stuck his fingers under the seam of the door and pried it open. A beam of light greeted him, and he saw two figures huddled together inside the cellar, one holding a flashlight, the other with eyes full of fear. Wayne and Loraine!

They scrambled out, clinging to each other as though they were each afraid to let go.

"Jake, what are you doing here? How'd you know we were in the cellar?" Wayne asked, clasping Jake's shoulder with one hand, while he held onto Loraine's hand with the other.

"I was on my way over here to see if you needed help with your chores, and the tornado struck," Jake said. "I jumped out of my buggy and took cover in a ditch. When the funnel cloud passed, and the wind had settled down, I came over here on foot." He drew in a quick gulp of air. "When I got here and saw the devastation, I was afraid you and your family might be dead. I searched through the rubble and found nothing. When I heard your cries for help, I discovered a tree branch had blocked the cellar door. I asked God to give me the strength of Samson so I could move it, and He did. Are you two all right?" Jake asked breathlessly.

"We are now," Wayne said.

"We didn't know how long we might be trapped down there, and I was getting more frightened by the minute," Loraine added tearfully.

Jake was relieved to have found Wayne and Loraine, but there were still two more people on this farm who were not accounted for. "Where are your folks? I looked everywhere for them, but found nothing," he said to Wayne.

"Mom fell down the basement steps trying to get some peaches, so Dad called 911, and the ambulance came and took her to the hospital to be checked over. Hopefully, they weren't in the path of the tornado." A look of shock and disbelief spread over Wayne's face as he gazed at the ruins of his folks' farm. "Ach! I'm so thankful they weren't in the house when this hit!"

Jake's mouth went dry. It didn't take a genius to see the look of love on Wayne's face as he gazed into Loraine's eyes. And it was more than obvious that Loraine felt the same way about Wayne. At that moment, Jake made a decision—one that would change the course of his life.

Loraine let go of Wayne's hand and moved toward Jake. "Wayne saved my life when he helped me get into the cellar, and now you've saved our lives by getting us out of the cellar." She blinked several times, and more tears gathered in her eyes. "There's something I need to tell you, Jake."

He held up his hand. "If you don't mind, I'd like to say something first."

She nodded. "Go ahead."

"I've. . .uh. . .changed my mind about staying in Indiana. I've come to realize that my place is back on the horse ranch in Montana." He looked over at Wayne and forced a smile, even though his heart was breaking. "It's obvious that you and Loraine love each other very much. I think the two of you are meant to be together."

Wayne's cheeks turned crimson. "You really mean that?"

Jake swallowed hard. "Jah, I really do." There was no way he could tell Loraine the truth—that he'd come over to the Lambrights' hoping she'd be here, that he'd planned to ask her out again, that he loved her and hoped someday they could be married.

"Danki, Jake," Loraine murmured. Tears flowed freely down

273

her face, and as much as it hurt, Jake knew he'd made the right decision.

"The tornado turned my buggy into matchsticks, and my horse took off, but I've gotta get home and find out how my folks fared the wrath of the tornado," Jake said, feeling an immediate need to go.

"I need to check on my family, too." Loraine looked up at Wayne. "There are so many in our community who might have been affected by this awful storm, but we have no way to get there except on foot."

"One of us could ride that." Wayne pointed to a bicycle lying in the middle of the yard.

Jake dashed over to the bike and picked it up. "It seems to be in pretty good shape," he called to Loraine and Wayne. He climbed on the bike and rode it back to where they stood. "How about if I ride this and you two wait here? I'll come back as soon as I know something."

"I guess we don't have much choice," Wayne said. He motioned to Loraine. "She's got a cut on her leg, and she probably wouldn't be able to walk very far. For that matter, neither could I."

"I'll be back as quick as I can." Jake started pedaling the bike down the driveway, but he'd only made it halfway when a van pulled in. It was Marge Nelson and her husband, Brian.

Marge rolled her window down and stuck out her head. "Is everyone all right here? Was anyone hurt?"

"Wayne and Loraine were the only ones here when the tornado struck. Loraine's got a cut on her leg, but I don't think it's serious." Jake turned and motioned to the farm. "As you can see, there's not much left of the Lambrights' place."

Brian nodded grimly, a pained expression on his face. "Our place is fine, but we saw destruction all up and down the road as we headed this way."

"I'm going home now to check on my folks and some of the others," Jake said, "but Wayne and Loraine are stuck here until I get back with some news."

"We'd be happy to give all of you a ride," Brian said. "You can put the bike in the back of my van if you like."

"It's not mine, so I'll just leave it here." Jake dropped the bike to the ground and climbed into the back of the Nelsons' van. Then Brian headed up the driveway to where Loraine and Wayne stood huddled together.

❦ ❧

"I can't believe all this devastation!" Loraine exclaimed as they traveled down the road in the Nelsons' van. "So many people left without their homes. So many will have to rebuild."

Wayne squeezed her hand as they passed farms, homes, and places of business that had been affected in some way by the wrath of the tornado.

Brian steered the van around a large tree branch lying in the road and pulled into the driveway were Jake's family lived. "Looks like your house and barn are still standing," he said as he came to a stop.

Jake pointed out the window. "There's Mom, Dad, and the rest of my family. Thank God, none of them seem to be hurt." He looked over at Loraine, who sat between him and Wayne. "If you need me to come with you to your folks' place, I'll just check on my family and be right back."

Loraine shook her head. "You go ahead, Jake. I'm sure your family needs you right now."

"Okay. Let us know how everyone fared, and if you need anything, don't hesitate to ask." Jake whipped the door open and hopped out. "Thanks for the ride, Brian!" he called.

When they continued their drive toward Loraine's house, her heart began to pound as she thought about what they might find. The newfound joy she and Wayne had found when they'd expressed their love in the root cellar could be over if she found that anyone in her family was dead.

CHAPTER 40

"Look, there's a buggy that's smashed up pretty bad!" Wayne shouted as they continued down the road. "I wonder if it belongs to someone we know."

"You'd better stop and see if there's anyone inside," Marge told her husband.

Brian pulled the van over behind the buggy and hopped out.

Wayne looked over at Loraine. "Sit tight while I check things out with Brian."

Loraine nodded as tears welled in her eyes. "I'm so afraid of what we're going to find at my place. What if—"

"Try to think positive." He gave her arm a gentle squeeze and stepped out of the van.

"There was no one inside the buggy," Brian said when he and Wayne returned a few minutes later. "I'm guessing whoever was in the buggy probably got out and ran for cover as soon as they saw that funnel cloud coming."

Wayne nodded. "That's what Jake did. He jumped into a ditch, covered his head, and waited out the storm." He looked out the window and scanned the area. There wasn't a soul in sight. "Whoever was in the buggy probably headed for home on foot as soon as they knew it was safe."

"I think you're probably right about that," Brian said as he pulled back onto the road.

They'd only gone a short ways when Loraine spotted three Amish people walking along the side of the road—an elderly woman, a younger woman, and a young man.

"Isn't that Sara Bontrager?" Loraine asked, looking at Wayne.

He nodded. "And that's Fern and Freeman walking with her."

"We'd better stop and see if they need any help," Brian said over his shoulder.

Loraine knew they were doing the right thing by stopping, but she was anxious to get to her house and wished they could keep on going. What if something had happened to Mom and Dad? She'd had a disagreement with Mom this afternoon. She needed to make things right—needed to explain about her and Wayne getting back together.

When Brian pulled over, Marge rolled down her window again. "Do you folks need some help?" she asked.

Sara nodded but seemed unable to find her voice.

"We were heading home from Shipshewana when the tornado struck, and we had to take cover in a ditch by the side of the road," Freeman said. "Our buggy's wrecked, and our horse is missing, so we were on our way home on foot."

"We've got room for three more," Brian said. "So if you'd like to get in, we'll give you a lift."

"We'd be grateful for the ride." Fern motioned to her grandmother. "It's a long walk to Grandma's house, and she's already tired and pretty well shaken up by the unexpected storm."

Brian hopped out of the van and went around to open the back door. Fern and Freeman climbed into the seat at the very back of the van, and Sara sat on the seat beside Loraine and Wayne.

"How are things at your place?" Fern asked, tapping Wayne's shoulder.

"Not so good." He slowly shook his head. "The house and barn are gone."

"I'm sorry to hear that." Sara clutched Wayne's arm. "Where are your folks? Are they okay?"

"I hope so," Wayne replied. "Pop took Mom to the hospital in Goshen after she fell down the basement stairs, so unless the tornado hit there, they should be okay."

Sara looked over at Loraine. "How about your folks?"

"I…I don't know. We're on our way there now to see." Loraine's voice cracked on the last word.

Just then, they came across another buggy going in the opposite direction, a horse being led behind it.

"That's Ella and her daed!" Wayne shouted. "We'd better stop and check on them, too."

Loraine was tempted to argue, since Uncle Rueben's buggy looked perfectly fine; but he or Ella might have information to give them about Loraine's folks, so she didn't give a word of argument when Brian pulled alongside the buggy and signaled it to stop. "Are you folks okay?" he asked. "Did the tornado do much damage to your place?"

Uncle Rueben shook his head. "We're all fine. Nothing at our place was even touched." He and Ella stepped down from the buggy and came over to the van.

"We were heading to the Lambrights' to check on them and found this horse running along the side of the road," Uncle Rueben said. "Do any of you recognize it?"

"I think that's Jake's horse," Loraine said, looking out the window.

"I believe you're right." Wayne opened the door of the van and quickly told Ella and her father what had happened at their place and ended by saying, "We dropped Jake off at his house and were relieved to see that everything there looked all right."

"Have you heard anything about my folks?" Loraine called to Ella.

Ella shook her head. "We were going to go there after we stopped by the Lambrights' place."

"I'll tell you what," Uncle Rueben said, looking at Loraine, "Ella can ride with you over to Loraine's house, while I take Jake's horse over to him. Then when I'm done, I'll swing over to check on things at your place and pick Ella up."

Wayne opened the door, and Ella climbed in beside Loraine. "What a horrible day this has turned out to be," she said with a catch in her voice. "On the way here, we saw so many houses and barns that had been leveled. It will take a lot of rebuilding to get things back to the way they used to be."

"The community will work together," Wayne said.

"That's right," Freeman agreed from the backseat. "That's how it was for us in Ohio when several places were flooded out last year. Everyone pulled together."

"I'm sure a lot of the English men in our area will help with the rebuilding, too," Marge put in.

Brian nodded. "And I'll be one of them."

Ella nudged Loraine's arm. "How come you're holding Wayne's hand?" she whispered.

Loraine explained about being trapped in the cellar with Wayne, and said that even though they were scared, it had given them the time they needed to talk things through. "Wayne and I realize now that we've never stopped loving each other," she said.

"I'm so happy for you." Ella squeezed Loraine's hand. "I always did think you and Wayne belonged together."

"We both know that with God's help, we can work things out." Loraine's eyes misted. "I just hope that—"

"Hey, that's my daed's driver, Stan Burnet." Wayne leaned over the seat and tapped Brian's shoulder. "Would you stop and see if that's my folks he has with him?"

"Yeah, sure."

Loraine gripped the edge of her seat. She was anxious to see if Ada and Crist were okay, but every stop they made meant it was that much longer before she knew how her folks were doing. All she could do was to wait, hope for the best, and pray.

Brian honked his horn and motioned for Stan to pull over. Once both vehicles had stopped, Wayne climbed out and hurried to the other car.

Loraine watched as the backseat window rolled down and Crist stuck his head out.

"Looks like it is Wayne's folks," Marge said. "From what I can tell, they seem to be okay."

Loraine breathed a sigh of relief.

A few minutes later, Wayne climbed back into the van. "Dad said they were at the hospital when they heard about the tornado, but it didn't strike in Goshen at all."

"What about your mamm?" Loraine asked. "Is she doing okay?"

Wayne nodded and smiled. "I guess she suffered a mild concussion, and that cut on her head required a few stitches." He glanced down at Loraine's leg. "Looks like the bleeding has stopped on your leg. Does it hurt much?"

She shook her head. "I don't think it's anything to worry about." Her forehead wrinkled. "I am worried about Mom and Dad, though. Could we go there now?"

"Jah, sure." Wayne reached for her hand again. "I told my folks where we're headed and what to expect when they get to our place. Dad said he wants to see things for himself, and then they'll be over to your folks' right after that."

"We'd better get going then." Brian pulled onto the road again, and Loraine tried to relax.

When they finally pulled into her folks' driveway, her mouth went dry. Several big trees were down, the roof of the barn was gone, and the house was damaged extensively.

As soon as the van stopped, she jerked open the door and stepped out. She scanned the yard, and seeing no one, dashed across the grass, and was about to step onto what was left of the porch, when she heard Dad call, "Loraine! We're over here!"

She whirled around and was relieved to see Mom and Dad come around the side of the house. She rushed forward and grabbed them both in a hug.

"Are you all right?" they asked at the same time.

Loraine nodded. "How about you?"

"We're fine," Dad said. "When the tornado hit, we took cover in the basement."

Loraine quickly told them what had happened to her and Wayne, and how he'd saved her life by getting her into the root cellar.

"I'm so relieved." Mom's eyes filled with tears. "I've been feeling so bad about the disagreement we had earlier and have been praying that I'd get the chance to say how sorry I am for upsetting you like that."

Loraine clung to her mother, as tears splashed onto her cheeks. "I'm sorry for my part in all of it, too."

Wayne stepped up to them then, and Dad clasped Wayne's shoulder. "Danki for saving our daughter's life."

Wayne's face turned red. "No thanks is needed, Amos. I would have done anything to save the life of my future wife."

Loraine held her breath as she waited for her mother's response.

The minutes ticked by as Mom stood staring at Loraine in disbelief. Then she looked over at Wayne and said, "It does my heart good to see my daughter looking so happy, and I want you to know that I'd be real pleased to have someone as devoted as you for my son-in-law."

Wayne's smile stretched wide. "Danki. And I'll be real pleased to become part of your family."

As Loraine stood in the yard, holding Wayne's hand, she thought about Psalm 37:4, the verse that had been attached to the loaf of friendship bread Ella had given her several months ago—the same verse she'd read the other night. She realized now that God had truly given her the desire of her heart, and she determined that she would remember to pray for Jake in the days ahead.

Loraine inhaled deeply, feeling peace enter her like the fragrance of fresh roses. She wasn't sure exactly when she and Wayne would be married or where they would live, but she knew she'd be keeping the promise she'd made to Wayne last spring. For the moment, that was all she needed to know.

LORAINE'S FAVORITE CHICKEN

6 chicken breasts, skinned and boneless
1 (8 ounces) whipped carton cream cheese with onion and
    chives
1 tablespoon butter
Salt and pepper to taste

Preheat oven to 400 degrees. Flatten chicken to ½ inch thickness.
Spread 3 tablespoons cream cheese over each. Dot each with butter
and sprinkle with salt and pepper. Place in a greased 9 x 13 inch
baking dish. Bake uncovered for 35–45 minutes or until juice runs
clear.

AUTHOR'S NOTE:

NORTHERN INDIANA AMISH

In 1841, four Amish families moved from Pennsylvania to northern Indiana. In the succeeding years, that Amish community grew rapidly. Now, more than twenty thousand Amish live in Elkhart and LaGrange counties, making this area the third-largest Amish settlement in the United States. The population doubles about every twenty years.

While the majority of northern Indiana's Amish live on farms, few Amish men farm full-time anymore. In order to support their families, most Amish men either work in factories, a variety of stores, workshops, or in home-based businesses.

Elkhart and LaGrange counties have a large variety of Amish businesses, including quilt shops, buggy shops, furniture stores, bulk food stores, variety stores, window manufacturing, horseshoeing, bicycle shops, and numerous other stores. The Midwest's largest flea market is held in Shipshewana, where many Amish and English go to buy and sell their wares. A favorite place for tourists to stop when they travel to the area is Menno-Hof, a Mennonite-Amish interpretative center, also in Shipshewana. There, one can learn about the Amish and Mennonite way of life and discover how and when the Plain People came to America as they fled persecution.

The Old Order Amish living in northern Indiana use bicycles and horses and buggies for their transportation when traveling locally. The larger buggies are referred to as "queen buggies." For longer trips, they hire an English driver. While telephones and electricity are not permitted in their homes, the Amish make use of phone sheds and, in some cases, they use cell phones or have telephones in their places of business.

Amish young people in Elkhart and LaGrange counties often have Saturday get-togethers, where they play volleyball or table games. Some groups of young Amish women raise money for people in need by having candle parties or volleyball tournaments. Some meet to make things for Christian Aid Ministries.

Ice cream suppers are a tradition among the northern Indiana Amish. They fellowship with one another as they share a casserole dish or hot dog meal that is furnished by the hostess. Others who come to the supper bring things like chips, fruit, cookies, and cake. The evening is ended with servings of ice cream.

The Amish of northern Indiana strive to maintain their heritage. They believe it's important for Christians to be separate from the world, which is reflected in their dress, their language, their form of worship, and their minimal use of technology. They value hard work, simplicity, and a closeness to God, as well as to their families.

DISCUSSION QUESTIONS

1. A tragic accident can change the course of a person's life. Of the six people who survived the van accident in this story, whose lives do you think were the most affected?

2. There was a lot of blaming going on after the accident. Was Loraine justified in blaming herself for suggesting that she and her friends take a trip to Hershey Park? Was her guilt self-inflicted, or did it come about because of the comments Wayne's mother made?

3. There are times in people's lives when they become consumed with guilt over something they think they should or shouldn't have done. What are some ways we can work through such guilt? How can we help someone who is riddled with guilt and blames themselves unnecessarily for something that happened?

4. When Wayne learned that he'd lost a leg as a result of the accident, he fell into depression and called off his wedding, thinking he was less of a man and could no longer provide for a wife and a family. What, if anything, did Wayne's friends and family do to help him come to grips with his loss?

5. Some people might have a tendency to over-protect or smother someone who has gone through a tragedy such as Wayne did. What are some things that Wayne's mother could have done differently to help Wayne deal with his loss?

6. Even though Wayne seemed determined to push Loraine away, she was equally determined to keep her promise to marry him. Do you think this was a result of her guilt over the accident, or did she love Wayne unconditionally and want to be his wife despite his handicap?

7. When Jake Beechy, Loraine's old boyfriend, returned to Indiana, she felt comforted, yet confused. She'd been in love with Jake once and wondered if she could love him again, yet she still had feelings for Wayne. The more Wayne pushed Loraine away, the closer she got to Jake and the guiltier she felt. Were Loraine's feelings for Jake deep enough that she

should have been able to let go of the promise she'd made to Wayne? Or should Loraine have kept her promise to Wayne despite her past feelings for Jake?

8. If Loraine decided to choose Wayne because she felt sorry for him, how do you think it might have affected their future?

9. Is there ever a time when it's all right to break a promise you've made? If so, what are some examples of when it might be all right?

10. Was Loraine's mother right in thinking that Wayne would be a burden to Loraine if she married him? How might Priscilla have been more supportive to her daughter during such a difficult time?

11. Loraine's cousin Ella was opposed to Loraine going out with Jake. What were her reasons and were they justified? How did Ella's attitude toward Jake affect her relationship with Loraine? How might Ella have been more supportive?

12. What life's lessons did you learn from reading *A Cousin's Promise* and which scripture verses from the story spoke to your heart the most?

A Cousin's
PRAYER

INDIANA COUSINS | BOOK 2

DEDICATION/ACKNOWLEDGMENTS

To Mary Alice and Doretta Yoder, two special Amish friends who have patiently answered my many questions.

In appreciation of the Oaklawn therapists who offer spiritual and emotional help to many patients.

With special thanks to Lovina Petersheim for sharing her recipe for Banana Nut Cake.

Peace I leave with you, my peace I give unto you:
not as the world giveth, give I unto you.
Let not your heart be troubled, neither let it be afraid.

JOHN 14:27

PROLOGUE

Katie Miller's stomach churned as she read the letter she'd just received from her cousin Loraine:

> *Dear Katie,*
> *Wayne and I will be getting married the last Thursday of April. I'd like you to be one of my attendants.*

Katie's heart pounded. There was no way she could go to her cousin's wedding, much less be one of her attendants.

"Who's the letter from?" Katie's grandmother asked, taking a seat on the porch swing beside Katie.

"Loraine. She's getting married in April, and she wants me to be one of her attendants." Katie almost choked on the words.

"That's *wunderbaar*. I'm sure you're looking forward to going."

Katie shook her head. "I don't want to go."

"Think how disappointed Loraine would be if you weren't at her wedding."

Katie's gaze dropped to the floor. "I can't go back to Indiana, Grammy."

"Loraine and Wayne have been through so much. Don't you want to be there to share in their joy?"

Katie shivered despite the warm Florida breeze. If Timothy hadn't been killed on their way to Hershey Park last fall, she'd be

293

planning her own wedding right now.

"Katie, did you hear what I said?"

Katie nodded, hoping she wouldn't give in to the tears pushing against her eyelids. "If I hadn't freaked out about a bee in the van, Timothy, Paul, and Raymond would still be alive." Katie drew in a shaky breath. "Jolene wouldn't have lost her hearing, either, and Wayne would still have both of his legs."

"You're not to blame, Katie. It was an accident. It might have happened even if you hadn't been afraid of the bee." Grammy touched Katie's arm. "You need to accept it and go on with your life."

"I—I don't know if I can."

"Timothy wouldn't want you to continue grieving for him. He wouldn't want you to blame yourself for the accident."

"You've said that before."

"Then you ought to listen." Grammy took hold of Katie's hand. "Let's go inside so you can write Loraine and let her know you'll be at the wedding."

"I–I'm afraid to go. The thought of traveling alone scares me. I don't think I can deal with all the painful memories that are there."

"Will you go to Loraine's wedding if I go with you?"

"What about Grandpa? Would he go, too?"

Grammy shook her head. "He has things to do here."

Katie couldn't imagine what things Grandpa would have to do. He was retired and spent a good deal of his time at the beach.

"What about it, Katie?" Grammy asked. "Will you go to the wedding if I go along?"

Katie sat for several seconds, thinking things through. Finally, she gave a slow nod. It would be easier going back to Indiana with Grammy along, and as soon as the wedding was over, they'd come back here.

CHAPTER 1

"It sure is good to have you home," Katie's father said as they headed down the road in his buggy toward Uncle Amos and Aunt Priscilla's house. He glanced over at Katie and smiled. "Your *mamm* said Loraine was real pleased when she got your letter saying you'd be one of her attendants."

Katie clutched the folds in her dress as she stared out the window. She didn't know why she felt so edgy. She hadn't felt like this when she was in Florida. She'd been depressed after Timothy died, but not quivery inside the way she'd been since she'd climbed into Dad's buggy. She was grateful they didn't have far to go.

Dad motioned to what was left of the barn they were passing. "Take a look at the devastation from the tornado that hit this past winter. That terrible storm affected nearly everyone around these parts in some way or another."

"No one was killed, though, right?"

"No, but some were injured, and the damage was great. Many, like Wayne's folks, lost their homes, barns, and shops. It's a good thing the house Wayne started building before he lost his leg didn't sustain any damage from the tornado," Dad said. "Several of the men in our community finished it for him, and Wayne's folks have been livin' in it ever since."

"Will they continue living there after Loraine and Wayne get married?" Katie asked.

Dad nodded. "At least until their own house is done."

Katie knew from some of the things Loraine had said in her letters that she and Ada hadn't always gotten along so well. She wondered how things would be with them both living under the same roof.

"Look at the Chupps' place." Dad pointed to the left. "They lost their barn, his buggy shop, and the house. Only those who've actually seen the destruction of a tornado like we had here can even imagine such a sight."

Katie gripped the edge of the seat. "I don't understand why God allows such horrible things to happen."

He shrugged his broad shoulders. "It's not our place to question God. His ways are not our ways."

Katie clamped her teeth together in an effort to keep from saying what was on her mind. Dad wouldn't understand if she told him how angry she was with God for taking Timothy. He'd probably give her a lecture and say it was Timothy's time to die, as he'd said to her on the day of Timothy's funeral.

"Do you know how long you'll be helping at Loraine's?" Dad asked.

"Probably most of the day, since I'm sure there's a lot to be done before the wedding. You can come by sometime before supper and pick me up, or I can ask someone to give me a ride home."

"I don't mind coming back for you. I'll be here around four, okay?"

"That's fine, but if we get done sooner, I'll just ask for a ride home."

"Sounds good." Dad guided the horse up Uncle Amos's driveway and directed him toward the barn. When they stopped at the hitching rail, Dad turned to Katie and said, "Have a good day, and don't work too hard. You're lookin' kind of peaked today."

"I'll be fine, Dad." Katie climbed out of the buggy and headed to the house. She wasn't fine at all. It seemed strange being back here again. She'd only been gone from home a little over six months, but it seemed a lot longer.

She noticed several people in the yard pulling weeds and

planting flowers but didn't see any sign of Loraine or her folks. She figured they must be in the house.

When she stepped onto the back porch, she drew in a shaky breath. She wished Grammy or Mom would have come with her today instead of going shopping in Shipshewana. Katie figured since Mom and Grammy hadn't seen each other for several months, they probably wanted to spend some time alone.

Just as Katie lifted her hand to knock on the back door, it swung open. Loraine stepped onto the porch and gave Katie a hug. "It's so good to have you home! *Danki* for coming. It means a lot for me to have you and Ella as my attendants."

"Danki for asking me." Katie forced a smile. In some ways, it was good to be here, but she felt as out of place as a chicken in a duck pond.

"I just wish Jolene could be here, too."

"She's not coming?"

"Huh-uh. Her aunt's been dealing with carpal tunnel on both of her wrists, and she recently had surgery to correct the problem. Jolene thought it'd be best if she stayed in Pennsylvania to help out."

"That makes sense. But do you think Jolene will ever come back to Indiana?" Katie asked.

"I hope so." Loraine opened the door and motioned Katie inside. "Ella and her sister Charlene are in the kitchen. We decided to have a snack before we head out to the barn to help decorate the tables for the wedding meal."

When Katie entered the kitchen behind Loraine, she saw Ella and Charlene sitting at the table.

Ella jumped up, raced over to Katie, and gave her a hug that nearly took Katie's breath away. "It's so good to see you! We've all missed you so much!"

Katie smiled. "I've missed you, too."

"Would you like a glass of iced tea?" Loraine asked.

Katie nodded and took a seat at the table.

"How about a piece of my sister's *appeditlich* friendship bread?" Charlene motioned to the plate of bread on the table.

"I'm sure the bread's delicious, but I'm not really hungry right now."

"As skinny as you are, you oughta eat the whole loaf." Charlene's eyebrows lifted high. "Are you sure you're not hungry?"

Katie shook her head.

Ella shot her sister a look of disapproval, but Charlene didn't seem to notice. She was busy cutting herself another hunk of bread.

"Didn't you have a birthday last month?" Charlene asked, her mouth full.

Katie nodded. "I turned twenty."

Charlene grabbed her glass and took a drink. "You'd sure never know it. Why, you don't look like you're more than sixteen." She pointed to herself. "I look older than you."

Katie groaned inwardly. She didn't need the reminder that she looked young for her age. She couldn't help it if she was short, petite, and had the face of a teenager. *At least I act more mature than my sixteen-year-old cousin,* she thought.

"I got a letter from Jolene last week," Ella said. "She won't be coming to Loraine's wedding because—"

"She already knows," Loraine interrupted. "I told her about Jolene's aunt when we were out on the porch."

"I wonder if Jolene's using her aunt's surgery as an excuse not to come home. She might be afraid that she won't fit in with the rest of us now that she can't hear," Charlene put in.

Ella shot her sister another look. "I'm sure that's not the reason. Jolene would never make up an excuse not to come to the wedding."

Katie's shoulders tensed as she shifted her gaze to the window. What would her cousins think if they knew she hadn't wanted to come home for the wedding? Did they have any idea how hard it had been for her to make the trip? Even with Grammy along, Katie had felt anxious on the bus ride. Every horn honk and sudden stop had sent shivers up her spine. She knew she couldn't have made the trip home alone. Even though she wasn't looking forward to riding the bus again, she looked forward to going back to Florida where there were no painful reminders of the past.

Loraine stood. "Would anyone like to see my wedding dress?"

Charlene's hand shot up. "I would!"

"Me, too," Ella said.

Katie nodded as well.

"I'll be right back." Loraine scurried out of the room.

Charlene nudged Katie's arm. "What's it like in Pinecraft? That's where your *grossmudder* lives, isn't it?"

Katie nodded as she fiddled with the edge of the tablecloth. "As you know, Pinecraft is the section of Sarasota where many Plain People have homes or come to rent. It's a nice community."

"Is it true that there are no horses and buggies?" Charlene asked.

Katie nodded. "Unless they're going out of the area and need to hire a driver, everyone either walks or rides a bike."

"Do you go to the beach very often?" Ella questioned.

"*Jah.* Grandpa and I go there a lot. We enjoy looking for shells, and Grandpa likes to fish."

Charlene sighed. "I wish I could visit Florida sometime. I'm sure I'd enjoy being on the beach."

"Maybe you can visit me there sometime."

Ella's eyes widened. "You're going back?"

"Of course. My home's in Pinecraft now."

The room got deathly quiet. Ella and Charlene stared at each other as though in disbelief.

Katie figured it was time for a change of subject. "Who did Wayne choose to be his attendants?" she asked.

"Jolene's *bruder,* Andrew, and Freeman Bontrager," Ella replied. "Wayne and Freeman have become good friends since Freeman and his sister, Fern, moved back to Indiana a few months ago."

"Freeman opened a bicycle shop," Charlene added. "Mom and Dad bought me a new bike for my birthday in February."

"Oh, I see." Katie stifled a yawn. She'd had trouble falling asleep last night.

"Freeman won't be helping here today because he has lots of work at the shop." Charlene sipped her iced tea. "You should see all the bikes he has. I'll bet he'd do real well if he had a shop in Sarasota, since so many people ride bikes there."

"Here it is," Loraine said, sweeping into the room with a khaki green dress draped over her arm. "I'll wear a full white apron over the front of the dress, of course." She held it out to Katie. "What do you think?"

With trembling fingers and a wave of envy, Katie touched the smooth piece of fabric. "It–it's very nice."

"Are you okay?" Loraine asked with a look of concern. "Your hand's shaking."

Katie dropped both hands into her lap and clutched the folds in her dress. "I'm fine. Just a bit shaky because I didn't have much breakfast."

"Then you oughta have a piece of this." Charlene pushed the plate of friendship bread toward Katie. "You'll blow away in a strong wind if you don't put some meat on your bones."

Katie ground her teeth until her jaw began to ache. One of the first things Mom had said to her when she'd arrived home was that she needed to gain some weight. Of course, Dad had mentioned it, too.

"Charlene's right." Ella spoke up. "If you're feeling shaky, then you should eat something."

"Maybe you're right." Katie grabbed a piece of bread and took a bite. Then she washed it down with a sip of iced tea.

Bam! The screen door swung open, causing Katie to nearly jump out of her seat. Walking with a slow, stiff gait, Wayne entered the room. His face broke into a wide smile when he saw Katie. *"Wie geht's?"*

"I'm fine." The lie rolled off Katie's tongue much too easily. She was getting used to telling people what she thought they wanted to hear.

Wayne moved across the room and stood beside Loraine's chair. "We're sure glad you could come for the wedding."

Katie forced a smile and nodded.

"Would you like to see my new leg?" Before she could respond, Wayne pulled up his pant leg, exposing his prosthesis.

Katie bit back a gasp. "D–does it hurt?" She could hardly get the words out.

"It did at first, but I've pretty well adjusted to it now." Wayne took a seat beside Loraine. "It could have been worse, and I'm grateful to be alive."

Uneasiness tightened Katie's chest, and she blew out a slow, shaky breath. Seeing him like this was a reminder of what she'd caused—and what she'd lost.

Wayne reached around Ella and grabbed a piece of bread. "Looks like you've been baking again, huh, Ella?"

She nodded. "It keeps me busy when I'm not helping my *daed* in his business."

"Those wind chimes he makes are so nice," Loraine said. "I might buy one soon, to hang on our porch."

"You won't have to do that," Charlene said. "Dad and Mom are planning to give you one of his nicest sets of wind chimes for a wedding present."

Ella poked her sister's arm. "It was supposed to be a surprise."

Charlene covered her mouth. "Oops."

Loraine poured another glass of iced tea and handed it to Wayne. "How are things going outside?"

"Pretty good. By the end of the day, I think your folks' yard will look like a park." He grinned and lifted his glass to take a drink. "This sure hits the spot. It's getting mighty warm out there. Much warmer than normal for April, I think."

"That's fine with me," Loraine said. "A warm spring day is exactly what I wished we'd have on our wedding day. I hope the weather stays just like it is—at least until Thursday."

Katie stared out the kitchen window, blinking back tears of envy and frustration. *I'd give anything if it were me and Timothy getting married in two days. Oh Lord, please give me the strength to get through Loraine's wedding.*

CHAPTER 2

Katie squinted against the sunlight streaming through the open window of her bedroom. Today was her cousin's wedding day, and no matter how much she dreaded going, she knew she was expected to be there on time.

Forcing herself to sit up, she swung her legs over the edge of the bed. Shuffling across the room, she peered out the window. The sky was a deep indigo blue, and the sun shone so brightly she had to shield her eyes from its glare. Loraine had gotten her wish—it was going to be another warm day. Katie wished she could spend the day sitting on the grassy banks by the pond behind their house instead of going to the wedding and putting on a happy face. No matter how bad she felt, though, she couldn't let on to Loraine or anyone else in her family. Only Grammy knew that Katie hadn't fully recovered from Timothy's death, and even she didn't know the full extent of Katie's emotional state.

She sighed and turned away from the window. It was time to get dressed and help Mom with breakfast.

❧ ❦

"Are you sure you really have to leave the day after tomorrow?" Katie heard Mom say as she approached the kitchen.

"Jah, I need to get back home in time for my friend Anna's birthday," Grammy said. "Anna's a recent widow, and several of her friends are getting together to take her out for lunch, and then I'll need to. . ." Grammy's voice lowered, and Katie couldn't hear the rest of what she said. Well, it didn't matter; Katie was relieved to know they'd be returning to Sarasota soon. Even though she didn't look forward to riding on the bus again, it would be a welcome relief to get back to a place where she felt free from so many reminders of the past.

When Katie stepped into the kitchen, she was greeted by a friendly smile from Grammy, who stood at the sink filling the coffeepot with water.

"Didn't you sleep well, Katie?" Mom asked, moving away from the stove, where she'd been frying a slab of bacon. *"Du bischt awwer verschlofe heit."*

Katie yawned and stretched her arms over her head. "I guess I am sleepyheaded. I had trouble sleeping."

"You were probably excited about the wedding today, jah?"

Katie nodded and forced a smile. She felt nervous about being one of Loraine's attendants, but if she admitted that to Mom, she'd probably be given a bunch of suggestions on how to relax.

"I know I've said this before, but it's awfully good to have you home." Mom gave Katie a hug. "Your daed and I have missed you so much. So have your brothers and their families."

"I. . .I missed you all, too." Katie looked around, anxious for something to do—anything to keep her hands busy. "Is there something you'd like me to do?" she asked.

"Why don't you scramble up some eggs?" Mom pointed to the refrigerator. "Your daed brought in some fresh ones earlier, so there should be plenty."

Katie took a carton of eggs from the refrigerator and set it on the counter. When she removed a bowl from the cupboard she bumped her arm. The bowl slipped out of her hand and crashed to the floor.

"Ach, Katie, watch what you're doing!" Mom's forehead wrinkled. "Are you feeling *naerfich* about the wedding? Your hands are sure shaking."

"Guess I am a little nervous. This is the first wedding I've been asked to take part in."

Katie went down on her knees to pick the bowl up, relieved that it hadn't broken.

When she stood, Mom said, "Are you okay?"

"I'm fine."

"I've got the coffee going now, so Katie, why don't you let me scramble the eggs?" Grammy smiled. "Then you can have a seat at the table and visit with your mamm and me until your daed comes in to eat."

Katie shook her head. "I don't need to sit. I want to help with breakfast."

"Then why don't you run down to the basement for me? I'd like to have a jar of my homemade salsa to put on the table." Mom smiled. "You know how much your daed likes salsa on his eggs."

"Okay." Katie grabbed a flashlight from a wall peg near the door and hurried from the room. When she reached the basement, she lit a gas lamp and made her way to the area where Mom kept all her canning goods. Several shelves were loaded with an array of jars filled with peaches, pears, beets, carrots, and several other fruits and vegetables, as well as the salsa. As she reached for some salsa, something furry brushed her bare foot.

Katie jumped as a little gray mouse skittered past her and ducked into a hole across the room. *Calm down,* she told herself. *It's just a little* maus.

She grabbed the jar of salsa, turned off the gas lamp, and hurried up the stairs.

"I think Dad needs to set some mousetraps in the basement," Katie said to Mom when she entered the kitchen. "I saw a maus down there."

Mom pursed her lips. "I thought he had set some traps. Guess he'll need to set a few more."

"A few more what?" Dad asked, walking through the doorway.

"Mousetraps," Mom said. "Katie saw a maus in the basement."

"I'll take care of it after we get home from the wedding." Dad hurried to the sink and washed his hands. "Is breakfast ready? We'll need to get going soon."

304

Mom nodded. "Sit yourself down, and we'll put things on the table."

After everyone was seated, they bowed their heads for silent prayer. Katie prayed for strength to get through the day and asked God to calm her racing heart.

When the prayer was done, they hurried through their meal, although Katie only picked at the food on her plate. How could she eat when it felt as if a brigade of butterflies was fluttering around in her stomach?

She pushed her chair away from the table and was about to grab her plate when Mom said, "You'd better eat more than that if you're going to make it through the day, Katie."

"I can't eat any more."

"It'll be a long time until the first wedding meal's served. I really think you should—"

"Let the girl be, JoAnn," Dad said. "If she's hungry, she'll eat."

Katie was relieved when Mom didn't press the issue. It was bad enough that her stomach was tied in knots; she didn't need Mom pestering her to eat.

When the kitchen had been cleaned up and dishes were done, Katie and her family hurried outside and climbed into Dad's buggy.

The buggy horse stamped nervously, obviously anxious to be on his way. Katie sure wasn't anxious to go. The more she thought about her part in Loraine's wedding, the more nervous she became. The only thing that might make it a little easier to get through the day was knowing that in just a few days, she and Grandma would be on their way to Florida.

❧ ❦

"Are you *naerfich?*" Freeman asked Wayne when he joined him and Loraine's cousin Andrew outside the Hershbergers' buggy shed where the wedding service would be held.

Wayne gave a quick nod and clasped his hands together. "I've never felt more nervous, but I'm feeling *glicklich* to be marrying the woman I love."

"So if you're feeling lucky, then you must not be gettin' cold feet."

"Just one cold foot." Wayne pointed to his artificial limb. "This foot doesn't feel anything at all." He chuckled and punched Andrew's arm.

Andrew snickered. "I've never known anyone who liked to joke around the way you do."

"What about Jake? He always has lots of funny stories."

"Speaking of Jake," Freeman spoke up, "will he be coming today?"

Wayne shook his head. "I got a letter from him last week. Said he was busy at the horse ranch in Montana and wouldn't be able to make it to our wedding."

Freeman had a feeling the reason Jake wasn't coming to this special event had more to do with the fact that he used to date Loraine than it did with him being too busy. He couldn't really blame him. It would be hard for any man to watch the woman he loved marry someone else. Not that Freeman knew anything about that personally. He was twenty-two years old but had only had a couple of girlfriends so far. He'd never been serious about either of them.

"Looks like Loraine and her attendants are heading this way," Andrew said, nudging Wayne's arm.

Freeman glanced to his left. Ella walked beside Loraine, and he recognized Katie Miller, the shorter of the two, walking with her. He hadn't seen Katie since he'd moved to Ohio with his family several years ago, but he didn't think she'd changed much. Same emerald green eyes, shiny brown hair, and turned-up nose. She was only two years younger than him, but she looked more like a fifteen-year-old girl than she did a woman.

"Are you ready for this?" Loraine asked, stepping up to Wayne.

He grinned down at her. "I'm a bit naerfich, but I'm more than ready to make you my *fraa*."

Loraine's cheeks turned pink when she smiled at her groom. Then she turned to Freeman and said, "You remember my cousin Katie, don't you?"

"Of course." He smiled at Katie. "It's good to see you again."

She gave a nod but averted her gaze.

Freeman remembered how when they were children, Katie had been a little chatterbox. She'd always asked their teacher a lot of questions and often whispered to her friends when she should have been paying attention.

Freeman heard some laughter and glanced to his right. Eunice Byler was walking across the yard with her parents and twelve-year-old brother, Richard. The Bylers had moved to Indiana a few weeks ago, after leaving Pennsylvania in search of more land. Eunice's dad had stopped by Freeman's bicycle shop a few days after they'd moved and purchased bikes for Eunice and Richard. Since that time, Eunice had come by the shop a couple of times to ask Freeman some questions about her bike.

"It's time for us to go in now." Wayne leaned closer to Loraine. "Just think, by this time next year, we'll be celebrating our first anniversary."

"You might even have a *boppli* by then," Ella said with a twinkle in her eyes.

~ ❧ ~

The wedding service seemed to drag on and on as the congregation sang songs and listened to the messages being preached by some of the visiting ministers. It was so hot inside the building that steam had formed around the edges of the windows.

When Loraine and Wayne finally stood in front of the bishop to say their vows, Katie noticed that Wayne's eyes glistened with tears, although his face wore a broad smile, as did Loraine's.

"Can you confess, brother, that you accept this, our sister, as your wife, and that you will not leave her until death separates you?" the bishop asked Wayne.

Without hesitation, Wayne nodded and said, "Yes."

Katie blinked against a rush of tears as a sense of unease grew within her like a gathering storm. She attempted to focus on what the bishop was saying to Loraine, but the rapid rhythm of her heartbeat made it difficult to stay focused. The unexplained fear she felt increased, and a nauseous bile rose in her throat.

I need to concentrate on something else. Katie glanced to the other side of the room where several young boys sat. They looked bored. One of them chewed gum. Another twiddled his fingers. A third boy stared out the window with a look of longing on his face. Did he wish to be outside as much as Katie did?

She looked at the section where the men sat. One young father held his sleeping young son in his lap. Another sat with a restless baby in his arms.

Her gaze swung to the other side of the room. Some of the younger girls sat quietly whispering to one another, and a few of them held their dolls in their laps.

Hearing a baby cry, Katie's attention was drawn to the benches where some of the young mothers sat. One woman held a baby against her shoulder and was gently patting its back. Another, whose baby had fallen asleep, stroked the infant's flushed cheek with her thumb.

" 'Husbands love your wives, even as Christ also loved the church, and gave himself for it,' " the bishop quoted from Ephesians 5:25.

Katie's face heated up then broke into a cold sweat. Her hands felt frozen, yet the air in the room was stifling. It felt as if something heavy was pushing on her chest. Her stomach clenched. She needed some air. She needed to get out of this room!

With no thought of what anyone might think, Katie jumped up and raced out the door.

CHAPTER 3

Katie's legs shook as she stood outside the Hershbergers' buggy shed trying to cool off and calm her racing heart. The fresh scent of earth coming from the first warm days of spring offered little comfort. She couldn't believe she'd gotten up in the middle of Loraine and Wayne's wedding vows and rushed outside. She couldn't believe she was such a ball of nerves.

There must be something wrong with me. Am I losing my mind? A shudder rippled through Katie. When she had been sitting in that buggy shed, she'd felt as if she was going to die. Was that how Timothy had felt right before his life was snuffed out?

A gentle hand touched Katie's shoulder, and she whirled around. Ella stood behind her with a worried expression.

"Are you okay? You look *umgerennt.*"

Katie shook her head. "I'm not upset. It was so hot in there, and I—I needed some fresh air." She fanned her face with her hands and blew out a quick breath.

"Your face looks flushed. Maybe you should go up to the house and get a drink of water."

"I'm okay now. I just need to stay out here awhile so I can cool down."

"The wedding will be over soon, and then we'll be heading over to Aunt Priscilla and Uncle Amos's place for the first meal of the day. Maybe you'll feel better once you've had something to eat."

"Jah, maybe so." Katie wished she didn't have to go to even one of the wedding meals, but with her being one of Loraine's attendants, she didn't see any way she could get out of it.

Ella slipped her arm around Katie's waist. "Are you sure you're all right?"

"I'm fine. I just need to be alone for a while."

Ella looked stunned. "You're not going back inside for the rest of the wedding?"

"No."

"I'll wait out here with you then."

Katie shook her head. "It wouldn't look right if we both stayed out here. Everyone will wonder what's going on."

"You're probably right. Guess I'd better get back inside."

When Ella left, Katie decided to start walking up the road to Uncle Amos and Aunt Priscilla's house. Maybe her help would be needed in the kitchen. At least that would occupy her hands and hopefully keep her from thinking too many negative thoughts.

❧ ❧

"How come you left the wedding?" Loraine asked when she stepped into her mother's kitchen and found Katie mixing a fruit salad.

"It was too warm in there, and I needed some air." Katie glanced past Loraine's shoulder. "Where's Wayne? Shouldn't the two of you be seated at your table by now?"

Loraine nodded. "And so should our attendants."

Katie's face flamed. "I'm—uh—busy helping here."

"You're not one of the cooks, you know. You're supposed to be with the wedding party."

Katie dropped her gaze to the floor. "I'll be there as soon as I'm done with the salad."

"I can do that for you." Selma Hershberger scurried across the room and took the spoon from Katie.

As Loraine followed Katie out the door, she felt concerned. Not only had Katie run outside in the middle of the wedding, but she was acting awfully strange. It seemed as though she'd rather be helping in the kitchen than joining the others at the wedding meal. What happened to the old Katie who used to be full of laughter and enjoyed being with people?

When they entered the barn where the tables had been set up a few days before, Loraine took a seat on the left side of her groom, while Ella seated herself beside Loraine, with Katie next to her. Andrew and Freeman took seats on the right side of Wayne.

Loraine looked over at Ella and said, "I've smiled so much already today that the muscles in my cheeks are beginning to ache."

"It's been a happy, blessed day, and you have every right to smile." Ella squeezed Loraine's arm. "Seeing two people I care so much about come together as husband and wife brought tears to my eyes."

"It brought a few tears to my eyes as well," Loraine said.

"Same here." Wayne leaned closer to Loraine. "When the bishop asked if I'd accept you as my wife and never leave until death separates us, I got so choked up I wasn't sure I could answer his question."

Loraine reached under the table and clasped Wayne's hand. "When I think of how close I came to losing you, I get choked up, too."

He squeezed her fingers in response. "I hope we never take each other for granted. I want us to teach our *kinner* to appreciate their family and live each day to the fullest."

"I agree with that." Loraine glanced over at Katie. She still seemed sad and nervous. She hadn't said more than a few words to anyone since they'd sat down at the table. Was she missing Timothy? Was she thinking about the wedding they'd never have?

As they bowed their heads for silent prayer before the meal began, Loraine thanked God for her new husband and asked Him to bless all of her family—especially Katie.

~ ❧ ~

"With all this food being served here, I hate to think of how full we'll be by the end of the day," Freeman said to Andrew.

Andrew chuckled and reached for the bowl of fruit salad

one of the waiters had just put on the table. "Think maybe I'll run around awhile between each of the meals that will be served throughout the day. When I get tired of that, I might make some animal balloons for some of the kinner."

Freeman's interest was piqued. "I didn't know you could do that. Is it hard to learn?"

"Some of the basic balloon animals are fairly easy, but a few of them are pretty difficult to make." Andrew shoveled a heaping spoonful of fruit salad onto his plate. "The hardest part of making balloon animals is blowing 'em up."

"Does it take a lot of air?"

"Sure does, which is why I usually use the hand pump when I've got a lot of balloons to blow up."

"Making balloon animals sounds like fun," Freeman said as Andrew passed him the salad bowl.

"It is, and so are balloons I make look like flowers. The beagle on a bike is my favorite one, though."

"Beagle on a bike, huh? Now that sounds like the kind of balloon I should to learn to make."

"I'd be glad to show you sometime," Andrew offered.

Freeman shrugged. "Guess we'll have to see how it goes. Between my job at the bike shop and your job at the harness shop in Topeka, neither one of us has a lot of free time."

"That's true, but I'll make the time if you're interested."

"I'm definitely interested, so I'll let you know when we can." Freeman glanced at the tables where some of the young women sat and caught Eunice looking at him. He smiled and gave her a nod. She returned his smile with one of her own. Her shiny blond hair and vivid blue eyes made her stand out in the crowd. He figured it wouldn't take her long to find a boyfriend. Next year at this time, she could even be the one getting married.

He looked past the bridal couple and noticed Katie. There wasn't much food on her plate, and what was there looked like it had hardly been touched. *I wonder if she's on a diet.*

Freeman shook his head. Katie Miller didn't need to lose any weight. If anything, she needed to gain a few pounds. He had a feeling something was going on with Katie. She'd been acting kind of strange all day. The way she'd run out during the wedding made him wonder if she might be sick.

"Here you go," Andrew said, handing Freeman a platter of fried chicken.

"Danki." Freeman forked a piece onto his plate and handed the platter to Wayne. Then he turned his attention back to Katie again. She fidgeted in her chair, and her hand shook as she reached for her glass of water and took a drink.

She's either sick or nervous about something, he decided. *The way she's acting makes me think. . .*

"Here's some more food to put on your plate." Andrew handed Freeman a bowl of mashed potatoes and then some gravy and bread filling.

Freeman helped himself and passed the bowls along. As he ate his meal, he kept glancing at Katie. She didn't look well at all.

⟶ ❧ ❧ ⟵

The napkin in front of Katie bore nothing but crumbs, and she didn't even remember eating the roll that had been on her plate. That same panicky feeling she'd had during the wedding was coming over her again. She didn't want to make a fool of herself by rushing outside, so she reached for her glass of water and took a drink. *I'll never make it through the rest of the day. Help me, Lord.*

She glanced at the smiling newlyweds and wondered how she could make her escape without arousing too much suspicion. Leaning close to Ella, she whispered, "I'm not feeling so well. I think I'd better go home."

Deep wrinkles formed across Ella's forehead. "What's wrong. Are you *grank*?"

Katie's chin quivered, and her throat felt so clogged she could barely speak. "I. . .I'm not sure."

"Do you want me to see if I can find your folks?"

"No, I can do that. Please explain things to Loraine for me, would you?"

"Sure." Ella patted Katie's arm in a motherly fashion. "I hope you feel better soon."

Katie was on the verge of saying she hoped so, too, when she was hit by a sudden wave of nausea. She covered her mouth, jumped up, and bolted from the room.

Outside, she drew in a couple of deep breaths and was relieved when the nausea finally subsided. Then her head started to pound. Maybe she really was sick. She might be coming down with the flu.

She glanced around the yard and spotted her father standing near the barn talking to Uncle Amos. She hurried over to him and said, "Can you take me home, Dad? I'm not feeling well."

"Are you grank?" he asked with a look of concern.

She nodded. "I've got a *koppweh,* and my stomach's upset."

"Maybe it's one of those sick headaches," Uncle Amos spoke up. "My fraa gets 'em sometimes when she's feeling stressed out."

"Are you feeling stressed?" Dad asked Katie.

She shook her head. "I think I might be coming down with the flu."

"I'd better take you home then." Dad motioned to the long line of buggies parked in the field. "You can wait in our buggy while I get your mamm and grossmudder."

"Why don't you let them stay awhile? You can take me home and then come back here to enjoy the rest of your day."

Dad frowned. "Your mamm wouldn't like the idea of you goin' home alone if you're sick."

"I'm not that sick, and there's no reason for her to know."

"You sure about that? I mean, if you think you need—"

"I'll be fine once I'm home and can lie down awhile."

"Okay." Dad started walking toward the horses, and Katie sprinted for their buggy. She could hardly wait to get home.

As they headed down the road, Katie spotted an Amish couple sitting under a gazebo in their front yard. Two small children played nearby. Katie's heart ached at the sight of them. She longed to have a husband and children of her own.

When Dad turned off the main road and into their driveway, the horse picked up speed and headed straight for the barn. As soon as the buggy came to a stop, Katie hopped out. "I'll see you later, Dad!"

Her feet churned against the grass as she raced for the house. Flinging the door open, she leaned against the wall and drew in a couple of deep breaths. Her head still hurt, and her stomach hadn't completely settled, but she felt safer and calmer than she had all day.

The stairs creaked as Katie made her way up to her room. When she opened the door, a blast of warm air hit her full in the face. She hurried to open the window, and when a trickle of air floated into the room, she breathed deeply. She stood there several seconds then flopped onto her bed.

Plumping up the pillow, she closed her eyes and tried to relax. She hoped Loraine wasn't too upset that she'd skipped out like that. She'd really had no other choice, for if she'd stayed at the table, she might have thrown up or even passed out.

Uninvited tears seeped from under Katie's lashes. She'd never felt sick enough to run away from a gathering like that, and the fearful thoughts she'd had today made no sense at all.

She opened her eyes and dabbed at the wetness beneath them. She tried to pray, but no words would come. Looking ahead to the future caused Katie's feelings of anxiety to return. After all, what kind of a future was there for someone like her?

CHAPTER 4

When Katie came downstairs the following morning, she heard whispered voices coming from the kitchen. A sense of dread balled in her stomach when Grammy said, "I agree with you, Jeremy. Katie's been living with us long enough. Under the circumstances, I think it's best if she remains here with you and JoAnn."

Katie rushed into the kitchen, but before she could open her mouth to protest, Mom turned in her chair and said, *"Mir hen yuscht vun dir ghat."*

Katie's head bobbed up and down as she swallowed around the lump in her throat. "I know you were talking about me. I heard Grammy say she didn't want me to go back to Florida with her."

Grammy shook her head. "I never said that, Katie. I said I thought under the circumstances that you need to stay here."

"What circumstances?"

Grammy rose from her chair and slipped her arm around Katie's waist. "Grandpa and I won't be living in Florida much longer, so—"

Katie's mouth fell open. "What? Where are you going?"

"We're moving to Wisconsin to be closer to my sister, Mary. She's been widowed for sometime and is having some health problems, so we've decided to move there and help her out."

"That's the reason my daed didn't come to Indiana with my mamm," Mom said. "He needed to stay in Sarasota and get the

316

house ready to rent out."

Katie groaned as she sank into a chair at the table. "Why wasn't I told about this sooner?"

Grammy's face turned crimson. "We didn't want to upset you. Your grandpa and I thought that after you came back here and saw everyone again, you'd be more receptive to the idea of staying."

Katie folded her arms and frowned. "I was looking forward to going back to Florida. I. . .I like it there."

"We know you do, but we're not going to be there, and it's best that you stay here with your folks."

Katie gave a woeful shake of her head. "I can't stay. There are too many painful memories here."

"You can't run from the past for the rest of your life," Mom said.

Katie clasped Grammy's arm. "Can't you just go to Wisconsin to help Mary for a while and then move back to Florida when she's better?"

"I'm not sure she'll ever be better, and we're going to do what we think is best for Mary," Grammy said.

Doesn't anyone care what's best for me? Katie bit her bottom lip in an effort to keep from crying. She knew she was being selfish, but the thought of Grandpa and Grandma leaving Florida, where she'd felt safe these last several months, made her nausea return. She'd be happier in Florida. She'd even made a few friends there. How could they expect her to stay here with all her painful memories?

"Maybe I could get a job and rent your house in Pinecraft," Katie said, feeling more desperate by the minute.

Grammy shook her head. "We've already found someone to rent it."

"Now that we've got everything settled," Dad said before Katie could protest further, "let's eat breakfast so I can get to work making windows in my shop, and you and your mamm can open your stamp shop."

Mom looked over at Katie. "I was hoping you could work by yourself for a few hours this afternoon while I go to my dental appointment."

A sense of panic seized Katie, and she gripped the edge of her chair. "You want me to work there alone?"

Before Mom could reply, Grammy spoke up. "If there's anything I can do at the shop, I'd be happy to help out."

Katie breathed a sigh of relief. She hadn't worked in the stamp shop for several months. The thought of waiting on customers made her feel apprehensive. "I'd appreciate the help," she said with a nod.

※ ※

"Would you like some more eggs?" Freeman's grandmother asked, smiling at him from across the table.

He shook his head. "No thanks. I've got lots to do today, so I'd better get out to my shop." He stood.

"How late do you plan to work today?" Grandma asked.

Freeman shrugged. "Don't know. Guess that all depends on how much work I get done."

"I hope you'll be finished in time for us to take Fern out to supper like we'd planned."

Freeman's forehead wrinkled. "We're taking Fern to supper?"

Grandma sighed. "I'm glad she went to town early this morning to do some shopping. I wouldn't want her to hear that her bruder has obviously forgotten that today's her birthday."

Freeman's face heated up. "Oh, that's right. Guess it must have slipped my mind."

Grandma held up her hand. "No need to offer an excuse. Just make sure you're done working in time to take us to supper."

"Okay." Freeman started across the room and was about to pluck his hat off the wall peg when he turned back around. "Do you have any idea what Fern might like for her birthday? Has she dropped any hints?"

Grandma shook her head. "She's given me no hints, but I know she's been working on a scrapbook the last few months. Maybe some rubber stamps would be appreciated."

"Is that what you planned to give her?"

"No. I made her something for her hope chest." Grandma sipped her coffee. "If you can spare the time, why don't you go over

318

to the Millers' stamp shop today and see what you can find."

Freeman nodded. "I'll try to do that during my lunch hour."

Grandma smiled. "Would you like me to take a sandwich out to you shortly before noon so you can eat while you're riding over to the Millers'?"

"That won't be necessary. I'll pick something up on my way back home." Freeman plopped his hat on his head and hurried out the door.

When he entered his shop a few minutes later, he lit the gas lamps then quickly set to work on a bike one of their English neighbors had brought in for repairs.

He'd only been working a short time when the shop door opened and Eunice stepped in.

"Wie geht's?" she asked with a cheerful smile.

"Can't complain. How about you?"

"I'm doing well." Her smile widened as she moved closer to him. "Looks like you're hard at work."

He nodded. "Always have something to do, it seems."

"I'm still enjoying the bicycle my daed bought for me."

"Glad you like it."

She squatted down beside him and leaned so close that he could see the smattering of light-colored freckles on her nose. "The bike you're working on looks like a nice one. How many speeds does it have?"

"It's a 21-speed, just like yours."

"What's wrong with it?"

Freeman motioned to the back of the bike. "The wheel's bent, the chain's messed up, and one of the pedals is broken."

"What happened?"

"Wally Andrews, the owner of the bike, took a bad spill the other day."

"Was he hurt?"

"Just a few scrapes and bruises." Freeman grimaced. "The bike took the worst of it."

"You sure seem to know what you're doing. How long have you been repairing bikes?"

"Since I was sixteen. My uncle in Ohio trained me well." Freeman reached for the wrench lying on the floor beside Eunice. "The last time you were here, you mentioned that you'd been looking for a job. Have you found one yet?"

She shook her head. "No one seems to be hiring right now. Things are tight all over."

"I know. Hopefully, once the tourists begin pouring into Shipshewana when the flea market opens next month, some jobs will come open."

"I hope so." Eunice offered him another pleasant smile. "If you're not too busy this afternoon, would you like to come over to my house for lunch? My mamm fixed too much chicken corn soup for supper last night. You'd be doing us a favor if you helped us eat some of it for lunch."

"I appreciate the offer, but I have an errand to run during my lunch hour."

Her pale eyebrows furrowed. "That's too bad. If you came for lunch, it would give us a chance to get better acquainted."

"Maybe some other time."

A light danced in her eyes. "You mean it?"

He nodded.

"How about coming over for supper this evening?"

"I can't. Today's my sister's birthday. I'll be taking her and my grossmudder to supper."

"Oh, I see." Eunice sighed. "I'm going to be busy helping my mamm with the garden the first part of next week, but what about Saturday? Would you be free to have lunch with me then?"

Freeman shook his head. "That's the day of the school program and potluck meal. Since my sister's one of the teachers, I think she'd like me to be there."

"Oh, that's right, I'd forgotten about the program. When would you be free?"

"How about the following Saturday?"

"All right then." Eunice stood and smoothed the wrinkles in her dress. "Guess I'd better let you get back to work. See you at church tomorrow, Freeman."

As the door shut behind Eunice, Freeman slapped the side of his head. "I hope she doesn't think we're a courting couple just because I agreed to have lunch with her in a few weeks."

⚜ ⚜

By the time Katie and Grammy had been working in the stamp shop a few hours, Katie had begun to relax. She'd almost forgotten how much she enjoyed the work.

Grammy placed a stack of off-white cardstock on one of the shelves. "There are so many interesting things in this shop. I think it must be a fun place to work."

Katie nodded. "I was just thinking that. When I worked here with Mom before I went to Florida, and we weren't waiting on customers or stocking shelves, we used to take a few minutes out to work on our own scrapbooking projects. We also liked to make cards that we could give to our friends and family on special occasions."

Grammy nodded. "Your mamm has sent me several of her homemade cards over the years, and I've always enjoyed getting them. I think a homemade card's so much more personal than one that's bought in a store."

Katie was about to comment when the bell above the shop door jingled and Loraine walked in. "How are you today?" she asked, stepping up to Katie. "I was worried when you left the wedding meal."

"Didn't Ella tell you I left early because I wasn't feeling well?"

Loraine nodded. "But I wanted to come by and find out if you're okay."

"I'm fine now."

"Glad to hear it." Loraine slipped her arm around Katie's waist. "It's good to see you working in the stamp shop again."

"Looks like I'll be working here from now on, because Grammy and Grandpa are planning to rent their place out and move to Wisconsin. That means I won't be going back to Sarasota."

Grammy explained about her sister's ill health then turned to Katie and said, "It's almost lunchtime. If you don't need me

321

for anything right now, I think I'll go up to the house and fix us something to eat."

"That's fine," Katie said with a nod. "We can eat it out here so I won't have to close the stamp shop."

Grammy smiled at Loraine. "If you're not here when I get back, I'll see you at church tomorrow. I'll be leaving for Florida on Monday morning to finish getting ready for the move, so Sunday will be my last chance to say good-bye to everyone."

"It's been nice seeing you again," Loraine said. "I hope things go well with your move."

After Grammy left the shop, Katie started putting some stamps on the shelves. "Are you and Wayne getting settled into your new house?" she asked Loraine.

"Pretty much. We moved our wedding gifts over there yesterday after we'd finished helping clean things up at my folks' place. You probably heard that Wayne's parents lost their house when the tornado hit last winter, so they've been living in Wayne's house ever since. They'll continue to do so until their new house is finished."

"How long do you think that will be?" Katie asked.

Loraine shrugged. "Don't know. Crist and Wayne have been so busy in the taxidermy shop that they haven't had much free time to work on it. Now that spring's here, many of our Amish neighbors are busy planting their fields, so I doubt they'll get much help on the house from them, either."

"I hope it goes okay with you and Ada living under the same roof. I know you two didn't always get along so well."

"Things are better between Ada and me now. I don't think it should be too difficult to have her and Crist staying with us."

Katie motioned to the stamps she'd put on the shelf. "Mom said these recently came in, so if you need any new stamps, you might wanna choose 'em now before they're all picked over."

"Actually, I need to run some errands in Shipshe right now," Loraine said, "but maybe I'll come by sometime next week and take a look."

"Okay. I'm sure they won't all be sold by then."

Loraine gave Katie a hug. "I'm glad you're feeling better, and I'll see you at church tomorrow morning. It'll be at Ella's folks' place."

Katie nodded. She hoped sitting in her uncle's barn with a crowd of people wouldn't bother her as much as it had during Loraine's wedding.

Loraine waved as she went out the door. A few minutes later, the bell above the door jingled again. Thinking it might be Grammy with their lunch, Katie continued to stock the shelves and didn't look at the door.

"Can ya help me find something my sister might like?" a deep voice asked.

Startled, Katie dropped the stamps she'd been holding. When she turned and bumped into Freeman, she gasped.

CHAPTER 5

I. . .I didn't realize you were here," Katie stammered. "I mean, I thought it was my grossmudder who'd come into the shop."

Freeman smiled. "Nope, just me. Today's my sister's birthday, so I came in to see if I could find her a gift."

Katie's hand shook as she motioned to the stamps she'd already put on the shelf. She didn't know why she felt so nervous all of a sudden. She'd been perfectly calm a minute ago. "We just got in a new supply of stamps. Maybe she'd like one of them."

"This one's kind of nice." Freeman picked up a large rubber stamp with a hummingbird on it. "Ever since Fern was a *maedel*, she's liked to feed the hummingbirds that come into our yard. I'm thinkin' she'd probably like this."

"There're a couple other hummingbird stamps over there." Katie pointed to the shelf a few feet away. "They're older ones, though, so she may already have them."

"She couldn't have gotten much, since we've only been back in Indiana a few months ourselves," he said.

"My mamm's not working here today, but if you'd like to come back tomorrow, we can ask if she knows what stamps Fern has bought."

"I can't wait that long. We're going out to celebrate Fern's birthday this evening, and I'm sure she'd be real disappointed if I didn't have a gift to give her."

"Guess you'd better buy one of the newer ones then."

"I'll take the humming bird stamp, and also this one," he said, reaching for one of the larger stamps with a sunflower on it.

The bell above the door jingled once more, and Katie turned. Rita Howard, one of their English neighbors, stood in the doorway. Rita was a robust woman with curly red hair and deeply set blue eyes. As she ambled across the room toward Katie, the floor vibrated.

"I left my boys outside to play while I look around," Rita said. "I hope that's okay."

"It's fine." Katie figured having the rambunctious boys playing outside would be better than having them in the shop where they were likely to run all over the place and mess with things.

"When I was in here on Monday, your mother said she'd be getting some new stamps by the end of the week. Did they come in yet?" Rita asked.

Katie motioned to the shelf she'd been stocking. "They're right here."

"Oh good." Rita rushed toward Katie, nearly knocking her over.

Katie stepped back and bumped into Freeman. "Excuse me."

Wham! A baseball crashed through the window and hit one of the shelves, knocking several stamps to the floor. Katie screamed, and Rita rushed outside. At least no one had gotten hurt, and from what Katie could tell, nothing had been damaged, but her legs shook so badly she could barely stand.

Freeman grabbed Katie's arm. "You're trembling like a newborn colt tryin' to stand. Maybe you ought to sit down."

Feeling very unsteady, Katie wobbled across the room and sank into the chair in front of her mother's desk.

"I'll get you something cold to drink." Freeman hurried into the bathroom and returned with a paper cup full of water. "Here you go," he said, handing it to Katie.

"Danki." She took the cup and gulped down some water.

"Feel better?"

"A little."

"Take a few deep breaths. That should help you relax."

Katie did as Freeman suggested.

Ding! The shop door opened and Rita stepped in. "Sorry about the broken window," she said, stepping up to the desk where Katie sat. "Guess my boys were playing too close to the store." She reached up to rub her forehead. "I should have left 'em home with their dad today."

"Other than the broken window, no harm was done," Katie said.

"I'm glad of that, and I'll pay for whatever it costs to replace the window." Rita glanced toward the door. "I'd better gather up my boys and head for home. I'll come by sometime next week when the kids are in school and look at the new stamps you got in. Maybe by then you'll have a new window and will know how much I owe you." Without waiting for Katie's reply, Rita scurried out of the store.

Katie remained at the desk while Freeman picked up the stamps that had been knocked to the floor. When he was done, he handed Katie the stamps he'd chosen for Fern. "I'd better pay for these and get back to work. I've been gone longer than I'd planned."

Katie rang up his purchase and had just put the stamps in a paper sack when Grammy burst into the room. "A *deichel* broke, and there's water running all over your mamm's kitchen floor!"

"What pipe?" Freeman asked.

"It's under the sink. I tried to shut it off, but the valve wouldn't budge, and I don't know where Katie's daed keeps his tools."

"I'd better take a look." Freeman rushed out the door, and Grammy and Katie followed.

When they entered the house, Grammy halted inside the utility room. "We'd better take off our shoes. The kitchen's turned into a flood zone."

Katie slipped off her shoes, and when she entered the kitchen, she gasped. Water shot out from under the sink, and the floor looked like a small lake.

"You two had better wait out here while I check things out,"

Freeman said. "It wouldn't be good for either of you to slip and fall on the floor." He plodded through the water and squatted in front of the sink. "Ah, I see the problem. The pipe has a huge hole in it. Must have rusted out." He glanced over his shoulder at Katie. "If you'll find me a wrench, I'll get the water turned off."

Katie sloshed through the water and opened the drawer where Dad kept his tools. She grabbed the wrench, sloshed back, and handed it to Freeman.

"If your daed has another pipe and some plumbing supplies, I think I can fix this," he said after he'd shut off the water.

"I think there might be some plumbing tools in the shed, but I don't know if there's any pipe or not," Katie said.

"Shouldn't we get this water cleaned up first?" Grammy asked, sticking her head through the open door.

Katie nodded. "I'll work on getting the water off the floor while Freeman looks for the plumbing supplies."

Freeman hurried out the door, and Katie got out the mop. By the time he'd returned to the kitchen, she had some of the water mopped up.

"Found a pipe that I think will work," he said, going down on his knees in front of the sink.

While Katie finished mopping and towel-drying the floor, Freeman installed the new pipe.

Grammy stepped into the room and pointed to the water marks that had been left on the wall. "Your daed will have a conniption when he gets home and sees this, not to mention the broken window that'll have to be replaced in the stamp shop."

"You're right," Katie agreed. A horse and buggy pulled into the yard, and she glanced out the window. "Someone just pulled up in front of the stamp shop. Guess I'd better go see who it is." She hurried out the door and stepped onto the porch in time to see Ella climb down from her buggy.

"What happened to the window in the stamp shop?" Ella asked when Katie joined her on the lawn.

"Rita Howard was here with her boys. She left them outside to play while she came in to look at stamps." Katie grimaced.

"Between that and a broken pipe under our kitchen sink, this has not been a good day."

Ella draped her arm across Katie's shoulders. "You look upset. Don't let a few mishaps ruin your day."

"My day's not ruined. I'm just frustrated, that's all."

Ella motioned to the other horse and buggy tied to the hitching rail near the shop. "Whose rig is that?"

"It belongs to Freeman Bontrager. He came by to get some stamps for his sister's birthday. He's in the house putting a new pipe under the sink."

Ella smiled. "I'm surprised Freeman isn't married already. A man as helpful as him will probably make someone a real good husband."

Katie stared at Ella. "Are you interested in Freeman?"

Ella's mouth opened wide. " 'Course not. I was just saying that he'll make a good husband." She motioned to the stamp shop. "Are you open yet, or have you closed for the day?"

"We're still open. Is there something you need?"

Ella nodded. "I need a stamp pad with blue ink for my daed's business invoices."

"No problem. We have plenty." As Katie led the way to the stamp shop, she thought about Ella's comments concerning Freeman making a good husband. *I hope she wasn't hinting that I should take an interest in him, because I'm not interested in any man.* Uninvited tears blurred Katie's vision. *I'm in love with Timothy, and I always will be.*

CHAPTER 6

When Fern entered the hardware store in Shipshewana, she noticed Eunice standing in front of the book rack.

"Is there anything new to read?" Fern asked, stepping up to Eunice.

Eunice pointed to one of the books. "I thumbed through several pages of this children's book. It's about a young Amish girl and her brother who live in Pennsylvania. I think it might be something your scholars would enjoy reading."

Fern picked up the book and read the description on the back cover. "You're right. This could be a nice addition to the fiction I have available at the schoolhouse. Since school will be out for our summer break next week, I may as well wait and get the book when it's closer to the next school term in August."

"I guess that makes sense." Eunice smiled. "I understand that the end-of-the-year school program is next Saturday. Your bruder mentioned that he plans to attend."

Fern nodded. From the hopeful expression she saw on Eunice's face, she had a suspicion that Eunice might have more than a passing interest in Freeman. "As far as I know, my bruder and our grossmudder are both planning to go to the program."

"I hope to come, too, since my brother, Richard, will no doubt have a part in the program."

"Good, I'd like you to come."

Eunice gave Fern's arm a gentle squeeze. "By the way, happy birthday!"

"How'd you know?"

"When I spoke with Freeman this morning, I invited him to come over to our place for supper this evening. He said he couldn't, though, because he was taking you out to celebrate your birthday."

"Why don't you join us?" Fern suggested. "We're going to Das Dutchman, and we could pick you up on our way there."

Eunice's face broke into a wide smile. "Danki for inviting me; I'd love to go!"

⋇ ⋇

After Freeman left and Katie was sure that all the water was off the kitchen floor, she and Grammy ate a quick lunch; then Katie returned to the stamp shop while Grammy did the dishes.

Katie flopped into the chair at her mother's desk and yawned. She felt weak and kind of shaky and wished she could close the shop and take a nap. She stared at the stack of invoices lying on the desk. She should file them away but wasn't in the mood. *Maybe I'll make a few cards instead.*

She'd just pushed back her chair when the shop door opened and Mom stepped in.

"What happened to our window?"

Katie quickly explained and then told Mom about the broken pipe in the kitchen.

Deep wrinkles formed above Mom's brows. "Were you able to get the water shut off?"

Katie nodded. "Freeman Bontrager was here, so he turned off the valve and put a new pipe under the sink."

"That's good to hear." Mom smiled. "Freeman's such a nice man. I wouldn't be surprised if some young woman doesn't come along soon and snag him for a husband."

"Well, it sure won't be me!"

Mom looked at Katie as if she'd taken leave of her senses. "I wasn't suggesting that at all. Why are you acting so defensive?"

330

"Sorry," Katie mumbled, "but I think you should know that I'm not interested in any man. I'm still in love with Timothy."

Mom pursed her lips. "Timothy's dead, Katie, and you need to—"

"I'll never stop loving Timothy, and you can't make me!" Katie rushed out of the shop and raced to the house, leaving Mom to manage the stamp shop by herself.

❧ ❧

When Freeman entered the house, he found Fern and Grandma sitting at the kitchen table.

"Are you two ready to head out for supper?" he asked.

"In a minute. Let's give Fern her gifts before we leave." Grandma gestured to Freeman. "Do you want to go first, or shall I?"

He shrugged. "Doesn't matter to me."

"I'll go first then." Grandma stood, pulled open one of the kitchen drawers, and removed a package. She placed it on the table in front of Fern.

Fern grinned. "I may be a twenty-four-year-old woman, but I still like getting presents." She pulled the tissue off and removed two embroidered pillowcases and a quilted table runner. "They're beautiful, Grandma. Danki."

Grandma's pale blue eyes twinkled as she patted Fern's hand. "I made them for your hope chest."

Fern smiled. "That's a nice thought, but I'll probably never get married."

"What makes you say that?" Grandma asked.

Fern shrugged. "Just don't think I will, that's all."

"You're not pining for your old boyfriend, I hope." Grandma's brows furrowed when she frowned. "Wayne chose Loraine, and you need to come to grips with that."

Fern shook her head. "I'm not pining for Wayne. I just have no interest in getting married."

"Don't you want to have kinner someday?"

"I'm happy being a schoolteacher; the scholars are almost like having my own kinner."

Grandma shook her head. "It's not the same as having your own, and I'm sure you'll change your mind about marriage someday when the right man comes along. In the meantime, if you want to make use of the pillowcases and table runner, that's fine with me."

Freeman stepped forward and handed Fern a paper sack. "Here you go. Happy birthday."

Fern opened the sack, and a smile spread across her face as she pulled out two rubber stamps. "These are so nice. I'll use them when I do scrapbooking. Danki, Freeman."

"You're welcome." Freeman moved toward the door. "Now can we go eat? I didn't have any lunch today, so I'm starving."

"How come you didn't eat?" Grandma asked.

"Because I ended up replacing a broken pipe during my lunch hour."

Fern's eyebrows puckered. "Was it a pipe in your bike shop?"

"No, it wasn't. I'll tell you about it on our way to Das Dutchman." Freeman grabbed his hat and hurried out the door with Fern and Grandma following.

They were almost to Freeman's buggy when Andy Weaver, one of Fern's students, walked into the yard carrying a cocker spaniel puppy in his arms. "We had five *hundlin* at our house, and this one's the last to go." He held the pup out to Fern. "Happy birthday, Teacher!"

Fern's eyes widened, and she looked over at Freeman as if she hoped he'd come to her rescue.

Freeman just shrugged and folded his arms.

"I named the *hundli* Penny 'cause she's copper-colored like a penny." Andy grinned up at Fern. "I hope you'll take good care of her."

Fern nodded and took the puppy from him. "Danki, Andy."

"You're welcome." Andy gave Penny a quick pat then headed down the driveway. "See you at school, Teacher."

"What are you going to do with the dog while you're teaching school?" Grandma asked. "I hope you don't expect me to care for it, because I've got enough to do already."

Fern looked at Freeman. "Will you keep an eye on Penny for me when I'm away from home?"

"I guess the mutt can hang around with me in the bike shop, just as long as she doesn't cause any trouble." He took the pup from Fern. "In the meantime, I'll put her in the barn where she'll be safe while we're gone to supper."

"Danki, Freeman."

Freeman grunted in reply. He wasn't thrilled about babysitting the puppy but didn't have the heart to tell Fern no. As soon as he had some free time, he'd build the pup a dog run; then he wouldn't have to worry about playing babysitter.

He hurried to the barn and put Penny in one of the empty horse stalls. When he went back outside, he found Fern and Grandma sitting in his buggy.

"Oh, I almost forgot to mention something," Fern said after Freeman had climbed into the driver's seat.

"What's that?"

"I ran into Eunice when I was in Shipshe earlier today, and I invited her to join us for supper." Fern smiled. "I said we'd pick her up on the way to the restaurant."

"How come you invited her to go along?" Freeman asked.

"Eunice told me she'd invited you to her house for supper tonight, but you said you couldn't go because you were going out with Grandma and me. I figured I was doing you a favor by asking Eunice to join us."

"You did it as a favor to me, huh?"

"That's right, and I hope you don't mind."

Freeman shrugged and guided the horse and buggy down the driveway. "It's your birthday, so you can invite whomever you please."

As they headed down the road, Freeman told Grandma and Fern about the broken window in the Millers' stamp shop and the broken pipe in their kitchen.

"Sounds like you had an interesting, busy day," Fern said.

"Guess you could say that." Freeman grunted. "It was busy, at least."

Grandma reached across the seat and patted Freeman's knee. "It was nice of you to help out at the Millers. You've turned into a fine young man."

"I sure couldn't leave 'em with water running all over the kitchen floor." Freeman flicked the reins to get the horse moving faster. "Katie acted real nervous after the ball sailed through the shop window. If she'd had to deal with the broken pipe on her own, she'd probably have fallen apart."

Fern leaned over the seat and poked his shoulder. "Don't *iwwerdreiwe* now."

"I'm not exaggerating; it's the truth. Katie was shaking so badly I was afraid she might cave in."

"As I recall, Katie took it real hard when her boyfriend died," Grandma said. "I spoke to Katie's mamm at Loraine and Wayne's wedding, and she said Katie's still having a hard time with it."

"That's too bad, but what I saw today seemed like it was more than just somebody grieving over someone who'd died."

"Did you do anything to try and calm Katie?" Fern asked.

Freeman nodded. "Told her to take a couple of deep breaths, and I got her a glass of water. Guess there might have been more I could have done, but it felt kind of awkward, and I really wasn't sure what to say or do."

"When put in the position of comforting someone in pain, what often needs to be said can best be said with a listening ear or a comforting touch." Grandma smiled. "It might not seem like much to the person offering comfort, but it can be more effective than you may ever know."

"Grandma's right," Fern agreed. "When one of my scholars gets hurt on the playground or becomes upset over something, I give them a hug and let them know that I care. It seems to help a lot."

Freeman grunted. "Jah, right. Like I was gonna give Katie a hug. She probably would've thrown me out of the stamp shop if I'd tried something like that."

"I wasn't suggesting that you hug her," Fern said. "I was merely saying that a person doesn't always have to say something to make someone who's hurting feel better."

"That's right," Grandma agreed. "But I'm sure you handled it the best way you could."

As they approached the driveway leading to Eunice's house, Freeman's hands grew sweaty. The way Eunice had looked at him this morning made him wonder if she had more than friendship on her mind.

CHAPTER 7

Everything we ordered sure looks good." Eunice smiled so sweetly at Freeman that he couldn't help but be drawn to her luminous blue eyes.

"You're right; it does." He reached for a roll from the bread basket and slathered it with apple butter.

"Did you get any more bikes in for repair today?" Eunice asked Freeman.

He nodded and forked some mashed potatoes into his mouth.

"I'm glad you're keeping busy with work," Grandma said. "Some folks in our area aren't so fortunate right now."

Fern nodded. "That's true. When I was at the hardware store in Shipshe today, Esther mentioned that several of the trailer factories have shut down. That means many of our Amish friends are now out of work."

"You're fortunate to have a business of your own," Eunice said to Freeman. "Especially one that seems to be doing so well."

He nodded. He hoped his business would continue to do well, but with the economic slump, there were no guarantees.

"After I left the hardware store, I did some shopping in the fabric store," Fern said. "I found some material for a new dress, and then. . ."

Freeman listened halfheartedly as Fern told about the events

336

of her day. He was really more interested in filling his empty stomach than engaging in idle chitchat. As he continued to eat his meal, he glanced at Eunice and noticed that she seemed to be watching him. Was she expecting him to say something to her? Maybe when he was done eating, he could think of something to talk about, but right now he needed to eat.

"Oh, I almost forgot. I have a birthday present for you." Eunice reached into her purse and handed a small package to Fern.

Fern smiled. "You didn't have to get me anything."

"I know, but I wanted to." Eunice motioned to the gift. "I hope you like it."

Fern opened the package and removed a leather journal. "Danki, it's very nice. I'll use this to record my thoughts about teaching school."

"I'm glad you like it." Eunice looked over at Freeman and smiled. "You mentioned earlier today that you plan to be at the school program next Saturday."

Freeman nodded.

"I wanted you to know that I'll be there, too. Your sister said she'd like me to be there."

"I'm sure you'll enjoy it." Freeman grabbed a chicken leg and took a bite. First Fern had invited Eunice to join them for supper, and now the school program. He wondered if she'd decided to play matchmaker all of a sudden. Maybe Fern thought he and Eunice would make a good pair. The question was, did he think that, too?

~✖ ✖~

Loraine smiled at Wayne as the two of them sat at the kitchen table drinking coffee. Wayne's dad had gone to the barn after supper to feed the horses, and his mother was in the living room doing some sewing. It was the first chance Loraine had had to be alone with her husband all day, and she was glad they could spend a few minutes alone.

"I stopped by the stamp shop today to check on Katie," Loraine said. "I'm worried about her."

"How come?"

"She seems sad and kind of jittery."

He nodded soberly. "I noticed that on our wedding day. Do you think seeing us get married brought back memories of Timothy?"

"I'm sure it did, but she wasn't herself at the stamp shop today, either."

"Maybe she just needs more time to adjust to being home again. She might miss Florida and those sunny beaches."

"I suppose that could be part of it, but I think there might be more going on with Katie than we know."

"Like what?"

"I'm not sure." Loraine sighed. "I just wish there was something I could do to help her, but if she won't open up and tell me what's wrong—"

"My advice is to give her some time and be as supportive as she'll let you be." Wayne took hold of Loraine's hand. "Remember how things were with me when I first lost my leg?"

"Jah."

"Even though it took me awhile to work through the pain and frustration of it all, with God's help and the support of my family, I came through it, and I believe my faith was strengthened, too."

"I know it was, and so was mine." Loraine gave his fingers a gentle squeeze. "I'm glad I married such a *schmaert* man."

Wayne chuckled. "I'm smart all right. Smart because I woke up and realized I was going to lose you to Jake Beechy if I didn't let you know how much I loved you."

Loraine leaned her head on his shoulder. "If I'd had my way, we would've been married even sooner." She glanced around their cozy kitchen. "I'm glad you had this house started and that it didn't take long to finish it after the tornado struck."

He nodded. "My folks were glad, too, because if we hadn't invited them to move here after their place was destroyed, they wouldn't have had a place to live."

"Do you think they'll be here much longer?"

Wayne shrugged. "My daed wants to start working on their new house again, but my mamm says they should wait until they have more money to finish the house. I've heard 'em go back and forth about it several times."

"Every couple disagrees sometimes, but they need to work things out so no misunderstandings occur."

Wayne grunted. "Tell that to my mamm. You know how determined she can be."

Loraine wondered if Ada and Crist were having marital problems. She was about to ask when Crist entered the room. "Sorry to bother you, but I could use your help with something in the barn," he said to Wayne.

"Okay." Wayne stood, dumped the rest of his coffee in the sink, and left the room with his dad.

Loraine closed her eyes. *Lord, if Crist and Ada are having marital problems, then please help them work things out on their own or seek help through one of our ministers.*

❧ ❧

"Supper's going to be awhile yet, so if you want to go out and feed the cats now, go ahead," Mom said after Katie had finished setting the table.

"All right, I'll do it now." Katie slipped out the door.

As she stepped onto the porch, a gentle breeze caressed her face. She breathed deeply, listening to the sounds of the night: an owl hooting from a nearby tree; their hound dog's loud snores coming from his pen; and a chorus of sweet music from crickets and frogs settling in for the night.

Unexpectedly, the breeze turned blustery as it whipped through the trees and under the eaves of the house. Katie hurried across the yard and into the barn. A fluffy gray cat darted out from behind a bale of hay as soon as she poured food into one of the feeding dishes. A few seconds later, two more cats showed up.

Katie put the food away and took a seat on a bale of hay. A shaft of light filtered through the beams above, but it seemed dark inside the barn.

She leaned her head back so it touched the wall and closed her eyes. For an unguarded moment, she allowed herself to imagine what it would be like being married to Timothy. She could see herself sitting with him on the sofa, holding a baby boy in her lap. He looked like Timothy.

Tears pushed against Katie's eyelids, threatening to spill over, while a surge of frustration washed over her like angry waves on the beach.

"I still love him," Katie murmured, "but he's gone, and wherever he is, he's not coming back." She drew in a deep breath and hiccupped on a sob when she released it. *What a battle I'm having with bitterness, guilt, and confusion.* Katie wished she could share her deepest feelings with someone, but there was no one she felt she could trust.

The wind howled, and Katie found the drumming of the rain against the roof to be an annoyance.

She stood. *Mom's probably got supper ready by now, so I'd better get inside.*

She left the barn and headed for the house, stepping carefully around the mud puddles that had already formed. The wind blew against her back like an angry crowd pressing her forward, and her stiff white *kapp* hung limp against her head from the rain.

When Katie stepped into the kitchen, the strong smell of onions fastened itself to her face, and she nearly gagged. "What kind of onions are you using? They smell so strong."

"They're yellow onions. The smell lingered even after I added them to the stew." Mom pointed to Katie's dress. "From the looks of your clothes, I'm guessing it must be raining pretty hard."

Katie nodded. "It came up quick, too."

"Supper's almost ready, but I think you'd better change before we eat."

Katie started for the steps but turned back around. "It's fine if you and Dad want to start without me."

"There's no need for that. Your daed's still taking a shower."

Katie hurried up the stairs, relieved that Mom hadn't noticed her tears. The last thing she needed was a bunch of questions.

As Freeman helped Eunice into the buggy, she shivered with excitement. The tingle she felt when his hand touched hers made her want to be his girlfriend.

If Fern and Freeman's grandma weren't with us tonight, this would seem like a real date, she thought. *Freeman acted as if he was having a good time during supper, and he kept looking at me. Maybe he is interested in me.*

Eunice smiled to herself and settled against the seat. *If I can get Freeman to ask me out, by this time next year we might be married.*

CHAPTER 8

The tantalizing aroma of bacon and eggs floated up to Freeman's nose, and he sniffed appreciatively. He enjoyed having breakfast out with his friends and hoped they could do it on a regular basis.

Freeman looked across the table at Wayne and Andrew. They seemed as eager to eat their breakfast as he was.

"Let's pray so we can eat," Wayne said. "I'm as hungry as a mule that hasn't been fed for a week."

Freeman chuckled then bowed his head. *Dear Lord, bless this food to our bodies, and be with those who are in need.*

An image of Katie Miller popped into his head. *And please give Katie a sense of peace today. Amen.*

"How are things going at your place?" Andrew asked Wayne. "Are you happy being married? Is my cousin treating you okay?"

Wayne nodded and reached for his glass of juice. "Loraine's a good wife, and I couldn't be happier." A smile stretched across his face as he winked at Andrew and then Freeman. "I'd recommend married life to both of you."

"Gotta find the right woman first." Andrew bumped Freeman's arm. "How about you? Is there anyone special in your life these days?"

Freeman's face heated up. "Uh, no, not really." He wasn't about to admit that he might be interested in Eunice. There'd be no end to the teasing he'd have to put up with from these two.

Wayne dipped the end of his toast into the egg on his plate. "From the looks of your red face, I'm guessing there's someone special in your life. Come on now, *raus mitt*!"

"Jah, out with it now." Andrew bumped Freeman's arm again. "Don't keep us in suspense. Who is she?"

Freeman took a bite of his toast and washed it down with a drink of juice. "I don't have an *aldi*, but I probably could have if I wanted one."

Andrew leaned his elbows on the table and looked at Freeman with interest. "Who is she—this aldi you don't have but could?"

"Eunice Byler." Freeman reached for the jar of apple butter and slathered some on his toast, thinking he ought to come up with something else to talk about real quick.

"So tell us, what's going on with you and Eunice?" Wayne chuckled.

"Nothing's going on. I just have a feeling that she likes me."

"How do you know?" Andrew asked.

Freeman told them how Eunice had come by his shop a couple of times, and how she'd joined them for supper on Saturday evening.

"Maybe she likes bikes," Andrew mumbled around a mouthful of bacon.

"That could be, but why'd she accept Fern's invitation to join us for supper?"

"Maybe she enjoys your sister's company." Andrew added some salt and pepper to his eggs. "Just because she's been to your shop a few times and went out to supper with you doesn't mean she wants to be your aldi."

"Well, she invited me to her house for supper, too." Freeman rubbed the bridge of his nose. "And you should have seen the way she looked at me when we were at the restaurant."

"How was that?" Wayne asked.

"Like she wanted to be my aldi." Freeman groaned. "Eunice seems nice enough, and she looks pretty good, but I'm not sure if I'm interested."

Wayne chuckled again, a little louder this time. "I'll just bet you're not sure."

Freeman shook his head. "I really don't have time to be courting anyone right now. I've got a business that needs my attention, not to mention a little thing named Penny."

"Who's Penny?" Andrew asked.

Glad for the change of subject, Freeman explained how the cocker spaniel pup had come to live at their house. "She spent the last two nights in an empty stall in our barn, but I'll have to make the hundli a pen pretty soon, I expect."

"That's probably a good idea," Wayne agreed. "A horse stall's really not the place for a growing puppy."

"Fern expects me to babysit the dog while she's teaching school, but I'm not sure I want a lively little mutt underfoot in the bike shop." Freeman shook his head. "My customers might not like it, either."

"You never know," Wayne said. "It might bring in more customers if you have a cute little pup for folks to pet."

A shrill horn honking, followed by screeching brakes, drew Freeman's attention to the window.

"Looks like someone riding a bike got hit!" Wayne pushed back his chair and stood. Freeman and Andrew did the same.

They and several others in the restaurant hurried outside to see what had happened.

A young English man lay in the middle of the road, his mangled bike nearby. Several people were gathered around, and the English driver stood beside his car with a cell phone up to his ear.

"Can you tell what's going on?"

"Is he hurt bad?"

"Did you see how it happened?"

Everyone spoke at once, until a middle-aged man who said he was a doctor pushed his way through the crowd.

Freeman stood on the sidewalk with the others, watching as the doctor checked the injured biker. "Has someone called 911?" the doctor asked.

"I just did," the English driver said. "An ambulance is on its way." He slowly shook his head. "That fellow was weaving in and out of traffic. He obviously doesn't know a thing about bicycle safety."

Freeman thought about how Wayne's mother had been riding her bike a few months ago and had skidded in some gravel. She'd fallen and broken her leg. Then a few weeks ago, a young Amish girl had lost control of her bike and run into a tree. She'd been lucky to have endured only a mild concussion.

As Freeman heard the wail of sirens in the distance, he made a decision. If Fern was agreeable, he planned to give her scholars a lesson on bicycle safety.

～≈～

As Katie stood with Grammy on the porch waiting for Marge Nelson to take Grammy to the bus station in Elkhart, a lump formed in her throat. "I wish you didn't have to go. I wish you and Grandpa were moving here instead of Wisconsin."

Grammy reached for Katie's hand. "We'll come for visits whenever we can, and you and your folks can visit us, too."

Mom nodded as she and Dad stepped onto the porch. "We haven't been to Wisconsin for a long time, so we'd enjoy a trip there."

Marge Nelson's car came up the driveway just then, and Dad picked up Grammy's suitcase. "Looks like your ride's here, so I'll carry this out to the car for you."

Grammy hugged Mom and Dad; then she turned to Katie and said, "I love you. Take care of yourself, you hear?"

Katie nodded. "I. . .I love you, too. Write to me, okay?" She nearly choked on the words, holding back her tears.

"Of course I will, and I expect you to do the same." Grammy gave Katie a hug and hurried toward the car.

Katie's shoulders tensed as she watched Marge's car pull away. She was trying not to cry, but when she heard Mom sniffle, she finally gave in and wept.

"It's been good having my mamm here for a visit, even though it was just a short one." Mom dabbed at her tears.

All Katie could do was nod.

Dad stepped back onto the porch and slipped his arm around Katie's shoulders. "How'd you like to take a ride with me?"

"Where to?" she asked.

"I have some errands to run in Topeka today. Thought you might like to go along." He looked over at Mom. "Can you get by without Katie's help in the stamp shop for a few hours?"

"I managed on my own while she was living in Florida, so I'm sure I can manage fine now." She touched Dad's arm. "Oh, and since you'll pass by Clara Smucker's place on the way to Topeka, would you mind dropping off a couple of things she ordered from the stamp shop? I left a message on her answering machine the other day, but she hasn't returned my call."

"Sure, we can do that." Dad stepped off the porch behind Katie. "I'll hitch my horse to the buggy while you get Clara's stuff put together. I'll be ready to go in ten minutes."

꧁ ꧂

Loraine plunged her hands into the dishpan full of soapy water and sloshed the sponge across a plate coated with sticky syrup. It had just been her, Ada, and Crist for breakfast this morning, since Wayne had gone out to eat with Andrew and Freeman. Both Ada and Crist had been unusually quiet during the meal, and Loraine wondered if her suspicions were right about them having marital problems. She'd intended to talk to Wayne more about it but hadn't had the chance. She'd thought she could bring up the subject last night before bed, but Wayne fell asleep before she'd been able to say anything. Then this morning, he'd left early to have breakfast at a restaurant in Middlebury.

The *clip-clop* of horse's hooves and the rumble of buggy wheels drew Loraine's attention to the window. She smiled when she recognized her mother's horse and buggy pulling up to the hitching rail.

Loraine dried her hands on a towel and hurried to the door.

"Wie geht's?" Mom asked as she stepped onto the porch a short time later.

"I'm fine. How are you?"

"Other than sniffling because of my spring allergies, I can't complain."

Loraine opened the door and motioned Mom inside. "Come on in, and let's have a cup of tea."

"That sounds good." Mom followed Loraine into the kitchen and took a seat at the table. "Where's Ada? Isn't she going to join us?"

"She had an appointment with her chiropractor this morning, and I think she planned to do some shopping afterwards." Loraine's forehead wrinkled. "I'm worried about her and Crist. I think they're having marital problems."

Mom sucked in her breath. "Ach, my! Do you know what the problem is between them?"

"Not really, but they were both very quiet during breakfast this morning, which is unusual, especially for Ada."

Mom blew on her tea and took a sip. "Communication is the key to a successful marriage. Maybe I should talk to the bishop's wife and see if she knows anything. She and Ada have been good friends for a long time. Ada might have confided in her."

Loraine nodded. "That's a good idea. In the meantime, we'd better both be praying."

~❧ ❧~

As Katie and her father headed for Topeka, her head lolled against the seat, and she closed her eyes. Ever since the accident, riding in any vehicle made her feel nervous. She wished she could make the anxious feelings stop, but she didn't know how. "You're awfully quiet." Dad nudged Katie's arm. "Are you sleeping?"

Katie opened her eyes. "I'm awake; just trying to relax."

"Are you still feeling sad about your grossmudder and *grossdaadi* moving to Wisconsin?"

"Jah." No point in telling Dad that she was nervous about riding in the buggy. She was sure he wouldn't understand.

They traveled in silence until they came to Clara's driveway. When Dad pulled the buggy up to the hitching rail, he motioned to the package sitting on the floor by Katie's feet. "Would you mind taking Clara's things in to her?"

"Okay." Katie picked up the package, sprinted for the house, and knocked on the door.

When Clara didn't answer, she knocked again.

Still no response.

The door squeaked when she opened it and poked her head inside. "Clara, are you at home?"

No reply.

Figuring Clara might be upstairs or out back in the garden, Katie decided to leave the package on the kitchen table. She stepped into the room and halted when she saw Clara lying on the floor. Katie's heart pounded. She was sure the woman must be dead!

CHAPTER 9

Katie raced outside, hollering, "*Kumme,* Dad, *schnell!*"

"What's wrong?" Dad asked as he scrambled out of the buggy. "What are you hollering about?"

"Clara's lying on the kitchen floor, and I. . .I'm sure she's dead!" Katie shook so hard that her teeth chattered.

Dad quickly tied his horse to the hitching rail and raced for the house.

Katie lowered herself to the grass and drew in a couple of deep breaths, hoping to calm her racing heart.

Several minutes passed before Dad came out of the house and hurried toward Katie. "Clara's not dead. She was only sleeping."

Katie's brows furrowed. "Why would she be sleeping in the middle of the kitchen floor?"

"She said she'd been mopping the floor and got a kink in her back. Said it hurt so bad she had to lie down on the floor and ended up falling asleep."

"If she was only sleeping, why didn't she hear me knock or call out to her?"

"Said she didn't have her hearing aid in."

"Will she be all right?"

Dad nodded. "I helped her up, and she's resting on the sofa. We'll stop by her daughter's place on the way home and let her know what happened. I'm sure she'll see that Clara gets to the chiropractor's right away." He untied the horse and motioned to the buggy. "We'd better get going."

~ ❧ ~

Woof! Woof!

Freeman glanced down at the eager-looking pup staring up at him and groaned. When he'd returned from having breakfast with Wayne and Andrew, he'd brought Penny out to the bicycle shop, but all the dog had done since then was either whine or bark. Freeman had quit working to take the dog outside a few times, and he'd stopped to pet the mutt more times than he cared to admit.

Woof! Woof! Woof!

"Go lie down; I've got work to do." Freeman pointed to the braided throw rug across the room.

Penny looked up at him and whimpered pathetically.

Freeman knelt on the floor to begin work on a bike that had been brought in last week. He should have finished it by now.

Slurp! Slurp! The puppy swiped Freeman's hand with her warm pink tongue.

Freeman picked Penny up, carried her across the room, and placed her on the rug. "Now go to sleep!"

The pup wagged her tail and pawed at Freeman's leg.

Freeman grimaced. If he couldn't get the pup to settle down soon, he'd never get any work done. "Maybe I should put you back in the barn."

"Put who in the barn?"

Freeman whirled around and was shocked to see Eunice standing there. He hadn't even heard her come in.

"I'm babysitting the pup Fern got for her birthday." Freeman motioned to the dog. "The little *pescht* won't let me get any work done."

"What's the puppy's name?" Eunice asked.

"Penny."

"She's sure a cute little thing." Eunice bent over and scooped the pup into her arms. "If you like, I'll keep an eye on her for you."

350

"Do you want to take her home?"

Eunice shook her head. "I thought I'd stay and keep the pup occupied right here."

Freeman gulped. If Eunice hung around his shop all day, he'd never get anything done. "I appreciate the offer, but I think I'll put Penny back in the barn."

"You don't want me to stay?"

"It's not that. I'm sure you have better things to do with your time."

"Not really, but do whatever you think's best with the dog." She stood and brushed a clump of dog hair off her dress. "The reason I came by is because my bike's been making a strange grinding sound when I try to shift gears. I was wondering if you could take a look at it."

"I guess I could do that right now. Why don't you bring the bike in?"

"I don't have it with me. I walked over here."

"Oh, I see. Well, whenever you can bring in the bike, I'll take a look and see if I can locate the problem."

"I thought maybe you could come over to my house this afternoon. Afterwards, you can stay for supper."

A trickle of sweat rolled down Freeman's forehead. He was attracted to Eunice, but things were moving a bit too fast. Besides, he'd already agreed to have supper at her place next Saturday, so he didn't see why she was asking him to go there today.

He motioned to the line of bikes that had been brought in for repair. "I appreciate the offer, but I have a lot of work to do, and I'll probably be working late every night this week. If you're not able to bring the bike into my shop, then when I come for supper next Saturday, I'll take a look at it."

Eunice dropped her gaze to the floor. "I don't want to ride the bike the way it is, and I don't want to wait that long, so maybe I'll just ask my daed to haul it over here. See you later, Freeman." Eunice hurried out the door before he had a chance to respond.

Woof! Woof!

Freeman looked down at Penny and slowly shook his head.

351

"Some women are sure hard to figure out. That goes for you, too." He leaned over and patted the dog's head.

～ ❦ ～

JoAnn glanced out the kitchen window. It was nearly lunchtime, and still no sign of Jeremy and Katie. *I wonder what's taking them so long.*

She moved away from the window and over to the stove to check on the chicken soup that was heating.

She hoped nothing had happened to them. There'd been several buggy accidents on the stretch of road between their place and Shipshewana lately, and she couldn't help feeling some concern.

The whinny of a horse drew her attention back to the window, and she breathed a sigh of relief when she saw Jeremy's horse and buggy roll into the yard.

A few minutes later, Katie entered the house, her face as pale as fresh-fallen snow.

"What's wrong, Katie?" JoAnn asked. "Aren't you feeling well?"

"I've got a koppweh, and I feel kind of shaky."

"Maybe some food will make your headache better." JoAnn gestured to the stove. "The soup should be hot enough now, so as soon as your daed comes in, we can eat."

Katie shook her head. "I'm not hungry. I need to lie down." She hurried up the stairs to her room.

～ ❦ ～

A cool breeze trickled through the open window in Katie's bedroom as she sat on the edge of her bed. She wished she could tell someone what was on her mind, but no one would understand. How could they when Katie herself didn't?

She flopped onto the pillow and released a puff of air as she thought about finding Clara on the kitchen floor. What if she had been dead? What if she'd died with no one with her? What if—

Katie rolled onto her side and squeezed her eyes shut. She didn't want to think about death. She didn't want to think about anything at all. She just wanted to sleep.

An image of Timothy popped into her head, so real she could almost feel his warm breath on her face and see the twinkle in his eyes when he teased her.

Tears stung Katie's eyes, and she clutched the edge of her mattress. It was bad enough when a person got old and died, but to have someone snatched off the earth in the prime of life wasn't fair! How could God be so cruel? Why did bad things happen to good people?

Katie curled into a tight ball and sobbed until no more tears would come.

～❦ ❦～

JoAnn sighed as she stood at the stove stirring the soup. It upset her that Katie didn't want to eat lunch. She'd been eating like a bird ever since she came home, and she was too thin for her own good.

The back door swung open, and Jeremy stepped into the room. He sniffed the air. "Somethin' smells good in here. I hope whatever you've fixed is ready, because I need to eat and get out to my shop and start workin'."

"The soup's ready, and I'll dish it up while you wash your hands."

When they were seated at the table a few minutes later, Jeremy looked at Katie's empty chair and frowned. "Where's our *dochder?*"

"Our daughter's upstairs in her room. She said she had a koppweh and wasn't hungry." JoAnn slowly shook her head. "I'm worried about her, Jeremy. I don't think she's happy being home. Maybe we should have sent her back to Florida with my mamm."

"But your folks are moving to Wisconsin."

"I know, but maybe Kate could have moved there with them."

Jeremy shook his head. "We've had this discussion before, and I don't think Katie's behavior has anything to do with her not

353

being happy here. I think she's still grieving over Timothy."

"How do you know?"

"There was an incident over at Clara's place this morning. Seeing how shaken Katie was made me realize that she's not come to grips with Timothy's death."

"What are we going to do about it?"

"If she doesn't snap out of it soon, we might have to make her an appointment to see one of the counselors at the mental health facility." He bowed his head. "In the meantime, we need to pray and eat our lunch."

CHAPTER 10

Katie squinted against the intense morning sun as she stepped into the yard to feed the chickens Saturday morning.

The hens followed her, clucking in anticipation of what was to come.

"You're all greedy, you know that?" Katie mumbled as she threw some corn on the ground.

Weep! Weep! She looked up and spotted a cardinal in the tree overhead. It amazed her how cheerful the birds in their yard seemed to be. She wished she could sing the way they did when she really felt like crying.

She threw out some more food for the chickens then headed for the house.

When she stepped into the kitchen, the fragrant aroma from whatever Mom was baking lingered in the air.

Mom gestured to the teapot on the table. "Pour yourself a cup of tea, and we can visit while my cookies are baking."

Katie thought it was too warm for tea, so she filled a glass with water and took a seat at the table.

"You haven't forgotten about the program and potluck lunch at the schoolhouse, I hope," Mom said, taking a seat beside Katie.

"No, I haven't forgotten." Truth was Katie wasn't in the mood to go to the program, but she knew if she didn't go, Mom would pressure her.

"We'll leave in about an hour," Mom said. "I should be done with my baking by then."

A trickle of fear meandered through Katie's mind until it turned into a torrential flood of negative thoughts. She hated feeling so nervous about things. She wished she could be strong, confident, and happy again.

"Don't look so down-in-the-mouth," Mom said. "Today will be fun. You'll see."

When Katie and her mother stepped into the schoolhouse, Katie quickly found a seat near the back of the room. She wanted to be close to the door in case she felt the need to escape.

She looked around and spotted several people she knew—Loraine and Wayne; Ella, Charlene, and their folks; Freeman and his grandmother; and her cousin Andrew.

Katie wondered if being here today and seeing Fern at the front of the room, taking the place of his sister, made Andrew feel sad. It made Katie sad. The accident she and her cousins had been in had turned everyone's lives upside-down. It must be awful for Jolene to have lost her hearing, as well as her job. She'd been forced to move away so she could learn to read lips and talk with her hands. Then there was Ella's family, Timothy's family, and Paul's wife, who had each lost a loved one because of the accident. Katie hadn't suffered physically, but she wasn't sure her emotions would ever be the same.

"Before we begin our program today," Fern said, drawing Katie's attention to the front of the room, "my brother, Freeman, has asked if he can speak for a few minutes about bicycle safety." She smiled at the scholars seated on one side of the room. "Many of you own bikes and will be riding them a lot this summer, so please listen to what Freeman has to say."

Fern took a seat, and Freeman walked to the front of the room. "All bicycles should be adjusted to the size of the rider, and the bike should have properly adjusted brakes and a bell that can be heard from one hundred feet away," he said. "Red reflectors should be mounted on the rear of the bike, as well as the spokes of the rear wheel. White reflectors should be mounted on the front of the bike and also in the spokes of the front wheel. During low-light situations, the bike should have a white lamp visible from five hundred feet to the front, and a red lamp visible from five hundred feet to the rear."

Katie tuned Freeman out as she glanced at the closest window. It was warm and stuffy in the building. *I wish someone would open at least one of the windows. I feel like I can't breathe.*

She looked around the room, wondering if anyone else felt the way she did. Everyone seemed to be listening to what Freeman had to say. Everyone appeared to be calm and relaxed. Everyone but her.

Katie looked out the window again, praying for the strength to stay in her seat. She couldn't embarrass herself by getting up and leaving before the program had begun. *I can do this. I just need to think about something else.*

A pesky fly buzzed overhead, and when it landed on Katie's arm, she flicked at it.

The fly zipped across the room and back again; then it landed on the windowsill behind Katie. Wayne must have spotted it there, for he turned and opened the window.

Katie breathed deeply as a breeze floated into the room. It smelled as if rain might be coming soon. Hopefully, not until later in the day, as she knew the older scholars had planned a game of baseball with some of the men.

Katie turned her attention to the front of the room. Freeman had finally finished his talk, and several of the younger students had begun reciting poems. Katie thought about the programs she'd taken part in as a girl. School days had been fun and carefree, and when she'd graduated after eighth grade, she'd been happy to help Mom in the stamp shop full-time. Soon after Katie had turned sixteen, she and Timothy had begun dating.

Katie closed her eyes as she thought about Timothy and how happy they'd been together. He'd always been able to make her laugh and had treated her as if she was someone special. He'd teased her a few times about looking like a little girl, but it was only in fun. How she missed his dimpled smile and laughing blue eyes.

Someone poked Katie's arm, and her eyes snapped open.

"Katie, wake up. The program's over," Mom whispered.

"I wasn't sleeping. I was just resting my eyes."

Mom motioned to the back of the door leading to the basement. "Let's go downstairs and help set out the food."

Katie followed Mom out of the room. The sooner they ate, the sooner they could go home.

~ ❧ ~

After the meal was over, Freeman wandered outside to watch the baseball game the older boys and some of the men had begun playing.

"Aren't you gonna join us?" Andrew called from where he stood near second base.

Freeman shook his head. "I have to leave soon, so I'll just watch until it's time for me to go."

Andrew shrugged. "Suit yourself."

Freeman heard voices nearby and noticed Ella and Loraine visiting a few feet away.

"What's Wayne have to say about his folks having marital problems?" Ella asked Loraine.

Loraine shrugged. "I was finally able to talk to him about it the other night, but he said he doesn't think it's anything serious and that he's sure they'll work things out." She clutched Ella's arm. "I've heard Ada raise her voice at Crist several times in the last few weeks, and I can't help but be concerned."

Freeman wondered if he ought to say something to Wayne about what he'd heard but decided it was none of his business. Besides, whatever Loraine had witnessed between Crist and Ada might be nothing more than a little spat.

Freeman was about to walk away when Eunice showed up.

"The program went well, didn't it?" she asked, smiling up at him.

He nodded. "I thought all the scholars did a good job with their parts."

"I was hoping to talk to you after lunch, but you got away too quick."

"It was hot and stuffy, even in the basement, and I was anxious to get some fresh air." Freeman glanced to the left and saw Wayne heading his way. "I'd better go. I've got a customer coming to the bike shop soon." The last thing he needed was more ribbing from his friend about him being sweet on Eunice.

"Oh, okay." Eunice turned with the grace of a bluebird floating on the wind and walked away.

Freeman was halfway to his buggy when he spotted Fern trying to convince one of her students to join the water balloon game. "Why don't you let the little fellow alone?" He stepped up to her. "It upsets a man to be ordered about, so just let go of his hand and let him decide for himself if he wants to play the game or not."

Fern squinted as she pursed her lips. "I think I know the best way to handle things with my students."

Freeman shrugged. It was obvious that Fern wasn't going to listen to anything he had to say. Even when they were kinner, she thought she knew more than him and often bossed him around. "I'm leaving now," he mumbled.

"So soon? But we're having ice cream after the games, and I'd hoped you could help me with the water balloons."

"I've got a customer coming to pick up a bike this afternoon. I need to be there when he shows up." Freeman hurried off before she could say anything more.

He found Grandma sitting in a chair on the lawn, visiting with a couple other women her age. "I'm heading for home," he told her. "Do you want to come along, or would you rather stay and ride home with Fern?"

Grandma smiled sweetly. "I think I'll ride home with Fern. I'd like to stay and watch the kinner play their games."

"Okay, I'll see you later on." Freeman hurried toward his buggy, anxious to be on his way.

❧ ❧

As JoAnn sat on a bench outside the schoolhouse with several other women, she glanced across the yard and noticed Katie sitting on the lawn by herself. She'd been quieter than usual today and hadn't eaten much lunch or visited with her cousins during the meal. JoAnn figured Katie ought to be with Ella and Loraine right now as they sat on the grass watching the younger children toss water balloons back and forth. For some reason, she obviously preferred to be alone.

I remember when my daughter was a little girl, JoAnn thought. *She used to be a happy, curious child, full of fun and looking for adventure around every corner. She's changed since the accident. Makes me wonder if she'll ever be the same.*

She tapped her chin. *If what Jeremy said about Katie grieving for Timothy is true, then it might be good for her to visit his grave. Hopefully, it'll help Katie come to grips with Timothy's death.*

An unexpected puff of wind rattled the leaves on the trees, and the next thing JoAnn knew, a few sprinkles of rain fell. She knew if she was going to stop by the cemetery she'd better do it soon before the rain got any worse.

She hurried over to Katie. "We'd better go. I think we might be in for some heavy rain."

Katie followed JoAnn to their buggy and climbed in without a word.

JoAnn untied the horse from the hitching rail and took her seat on the driver's side. As she headed the horse in the direction of the cemetery, she glanced over at Katie. "You seemed awfully quiet today and kept to yourself. Didn't you visit with any of your friends?"

"Not really."

"How come?"

"I didn't have anything to say."

"Did you enjoy the program?"

"It was okay."

"I thought the skit the older scholars put on was quite funny, didn't you?"

"Uh-huh."

JoAnn sighed. She'd hoped going to the program might give

her daughter a reason to smile, but it seemed as if Katie didn't want to have a good time.

As they pulled onto the grassy spot outside the cemetery, Katie stiffened. "What are we doing here?"

"I thought it would be good for you to visit Timothy's grave."

"I don't want to."

"It's stopped raining now, so let's take a walk over there."

Katie shook her head.

"I really think it will help you—"

"What I've lost will never be returned." Katie's voice shook as she stared at the graveyard.

"You're right," JoAnn agreed. "Timothy's not coming back, but your life's not over, Katie. God might have someone else for you in the days ahead."

"I don't want anyone else!"

JoAnn touched her daughter's trembling shoulder. "It's perfectly normal for a person to grieve when they lose someone they love, but it's not normal to carry on like this for such a long time. I'd hoped that the months you spent with my folks in Florida would help you come to grips with your pain, but apparently it did no good at all."

Katie shook her head in short, quick jerks. "That's not true. I felt a lot more peaceful when I was living with Grammy and Grandpa than I do here."

"Why don't you feel peaceful here?"

"Because there are too many reminders of Timothy."

JoAnn felt deeply troubled by her daughter's dark mood and wished there was something she could do or say to make things easier for Katie, but she didn't know what. It might have been better for Katie if she could have stayed in Florida, but she was here now, and they'd need to find a way for her to work things through.

CHAPTER 11

Katie squinted against the invading light shining in her bedroom window. It had rained most of the night. Now her room felt hot and sticky. She hadn't slept well last night and wished she could spend the day in bed. But this was Sunday, and she was expected to go to church with her folks.

Katie rolled out of bed, plodded across the room, and opened her window, hoping to let in a cool breeze. What she got was a blast of hot air. The sun had risen over the horizon like a giant ball of fire.

Last spring they'd had some muggy days like this, with high temperatures in the eighties. She wondered if it would be like that again and whether it meant they were in for a very hot summer.

With a weary sigh, Katie moved away from the window. She needed to get dressed and go downstairs to help Mom with breakfast. She picked up the hand mirror on her dresser and grimaced. Her eyes had an almost distant look to them. Her face looked thinner than it used to be. Her hands shook as she placed the mirror back on the dresser.

There must be something wrong with me. Should I talk to Mom about it?

Katie shook her head. *Bad idea. Mom will probably say I need to eat more and get out of the house more often. She might even make me go to the doctor. If that happens, the doctor might run all sorts of tests.*

If he finds something seriously wrong with me, he'll say I'm going to die, and then—

Tap! Tap! Tap! "Katie, are you up?" Dad hollered through the closed door. "Your mamm's got breakfast ready."

"I'm coming!" Katie pinched her cheeks to give them more color and set her covering in place.

When she stepped out of the room, the aroma of sausage and eggs floated up the stairs to meet her. She would force herself to eat something this morning even if she didn't feel hungry.

As Katie descended the stairs, she heard whispered voices coming from the kitchen. She halted on the bottom step and tipped her head and listened.

"I can't help but be worried about Katie," Mom said. "She's been acting so strange since she got back from Florida. She didn't visit with anyone at the school program yesterday, and when I took her by the cemetery, she refused to get out of the buggy." She made a clicking noise with her tongue. "She'll hardly eat a thing and jumps at the slightest noise. I want to help her, but she won't open up to me."

"Do you think it's something physical going on with her, or is it a mental problem she's dealing with?" Dad asked.

"I don't know. It could be either or both."

"Maybe we should take her to see Dr. Baker and ask him to run some tests. If he doesn't find anything, then we'd better see about getting her some counseling at the mental health facility." Dad grunted. "If you'll recall, I suggested taking her there after Timothy died, but you insisted on sending her to your folks, for all the good it did."

Katie froze as a wave of nausea rolled through her stomach. She couldn't let them send her there. She didn't want to know what was wrong with her, and she didn't want anyone to think she was crazy. She'd do whatever she could to make Mom and Dad think she was okay. No matter how nervous or sickly she felt, she would pretend that she felt fine.

⊷ ⊶

During the church service that morning, which was held in

WANDA E. BRUNSTETTER

the Lehmans' buggy shop, the room had become so warm that someone finally passed out the lids from ice cream pails to use as fans. Even with the makeshift fans, Katie felt hot, confined, and woozy.

She gripped the edge of her bench and forced herself to focus on the message the bishop was giving. She couldn't give in to these feelings, so she would remain seated instead of rushing outside for fresh air like she wanted to do. Katie had noticed Mom watching her and knew if she did anything out of the ordinary it might be just what Mom needed to haul her off to the doctor's office. Worse yet, Mom might insist that Katie see someone at the mental health facility where she'd be expected to tell them things she didn't understand and could barely deal with herself.

A wave of dizziness washed over Katie, and she grabbed the edge of her bench for support. *I can do this. I can do this. The service is almost over. I can make it through okay.*

Katie blinked a couple of times as the bishop's face began to blur. Her head tingled, and she felt as if she were being pulled into a long, dark tunnel. She swayed unsteadily; then everything went black.

CHAPTER 12

"Wake up, Katie. Can you hear me? Are you all right?"

Katie blinked as her mother's face came into view. She saw Dad, Ella, and several others looking down at her, too. "Wh—what happened? Where am I?"

"You passed out just as church was about to end." Dad's forehead wrinkled as he stared at Katie. "Are you feeling grank?"

Katie shook her head and slowly sat up. "I'm not sick. It was hot in there, and I felt kind of woozy."

"I think you'd better see the doctor tomorrow," Mom said. "You haven't felt well since you got back from Florida, and something could be seriously wrong."

Katie's heart pounded, and her mouth went dry. She didn't see how she could be seriously ill when she'd felt fine while she was in Sarasota. But then there had to be something wrong with her, or she wouldn't keep having these strange attacks.

"You didn't eat a lot for breakfast this morning," Dad said, helping Katie to her feet. "Maybe that's the reason you passed out."

She nodded, hoping that was all there was to it.

Mom slipped her arm around Katie's waist and led her toward the Lehmans' house. "I think you ought to lie down awhile. I'll come and get you after lunch is set out."

Katie didn't argue. The way her legs were shaking and her heart was pounding, she knew she really did need to lie down.

～≫≪～

Soon after the common meal had been served, Loraine sought out Ella and suggested that they check on Katie. "I haven't had a chance to speak with her since we ate lunch," she said to Ella. "I want to see how she's doing."

"That's a good idea. She's sitting under the maple tree over there."

They headed across the yard, and when they reached the tree, they knelt on the ground beside her.

"Mind if we join you?" Ella asked.

Katie smiled, although her expression appeared to be forced. " 'Course not."

"It really scared us when you passed out during church," Loraine said. "How are you feeling now that you've had something to eat?"

"I'm better."

Ella touched Katie's shoulder. "Your daed said he thinks you didn't have enough to eat for breakfast. What do you think?"

Katie shrugged. "I guess that might have been part of the problem, but I was doing okay until the room got so warm."

"Have you ever passed out like that before?" Loraine asked.

"Huh-uh, but I've felt dizzy a couple of times."

Ella and Loraine's worried expressions made Katie wish she could put their minds at ease, but that was hard to do since she was worried herself.

"Are you going to see the doctor like your mamm suggested?" Ella questioned.

"Not if I can help it."

Tiny wrinkles formed in Loraine's forehead. "Why not? Don't you want to find out what's wrong with you?"

Katie shook her head.

Ella looked at Katie as if she'd lost her mind. "You're kidding, right?"

"No, I'm not. If there's something seriously wrong with me, then I don't want to know about it." Katie sighed. "Now, can we please change the subject?"

Ella looked at Loraine as if she was hoping she might say something more, but Loraine just shrugged and looked away.

"Let's talk about the stamp shop then," Ella said. "Are you and your mamm keeping busy there, or are you getting fewer customers now that jobs are scarce and money's tight for so many people?"

"We're still busy," Katie said. "I think more people are making cards rather than buying them. Since we have a good variety of rubber stamps and other card-making supplies, we're hoping the business will keep going."

"Say, I have an idea," Loraine said. "Why don't the three of us get together one of these days and do some stamping like we did when we were teenagers?"

Ella nodded. "That sounds like fun. What do you think, Katie?"

"I guess it would be all right, but it'd have to be after the shop's closed for the day. I don't think my mamm would appreciate me fooling around with stamping projects when I'm supposed to be working."

"Aren't there days when you're not so busy?" Loraine asked.

"Jah, but Mom usually finds something for me to do."

"That's fine," Ella said. "We can get together some evening."

As they continued to visit, Loraine was pleased that Katie seemed more talkative, even though she did seem to be on edge.

"I got another letter from Jolene yesterday," Ella said. "She's doing well with her classes on sign language and thinks when she's done she might want to teach deaf children."

"That'd be good," Loraine said. "I know how much she's missed teaching school, and she really does need a purpose."

"Speaking of purpose," Ella said, "I need to buy a few things in Goshen later this week, and I was wondering if you two might be free to go with me. We can have lunch afterwards—maybe go to that restaurant where they serve barbecued ribs."

Loraine nodded. "Sounds like a fun day to me."

Ella turned to Katie. "How about you?"

Katie shook her head. "I don't think my mamm can spare me that long."

Just then Eunice showed up. "I hope I'm not interrupting anything," she said.

"We were just catching up with each other's lives." Loraine patted the ground beside her. "Have a seat; you're welcome to join us."

"I think I will." Eunice lowered herself to the ground. "Are you okay?" she asked, looking at Katie. "You gave us all a scare when you fell off the bench like that."

"I'm fine."

"Are you sure? Your face still looks awfully pale."

Katie's lips compressed together. "I'm feeling much better now."

"Glad to hear it."

"We've been talking about getting together to do some stamping," Ella said. "If you like to stamp, maybe you'd like to join us."

"That sounds like fun. When did you plan to get together?"

"We haven't picked a date yet," Katie said, "but we'll let you know when we do."

Loraine smiled. It was good to see Katie taking an active part in their conversation. She'd been quiet and kept to herself much of the time since she'd been home. Maybe she was beginning to adjust.

When Loraine heard her name being called, she glanced over her shoulder and saw Wayne heading her way.

"My mamm's got a headache and wants to go home," he said when he approached her. "Since my folks rode in our buggy today, we're kind of obligated to take them home."

Loraine stood and pressed the wrinkles from her dress. "That's fine. I'm ready for a little nap myself." She said her good-byes and hurried off with Wayne.

~※ ※~

Eunice leaned back on her elbows and stared at the sky. "It's another warm day—too warm for spring, if you ask me."

Ella nodded. "Makes me wonder what summer will be like."

Katie grimaced. "Probably hot and sticky."

"After living in Florida, I'd think that you'd be used to hot and sticky," Ella said.

"It was different there. I could cool off whenever I went to the beach."

"I've never been to Sarasota, but I hear the sand is white, and someone told me that there are lots of interesting shells on the beach," Eunice said.

Katie nodded. "I would have brought some home with me, but I didn't know I'd be staying."

"You were planning to go back?" Eunice asked.

"Jah, but things have changed."

Eunice glanced over her shoulder and saw Fern standing near the Lehmans' back porch. When Fern motioned to her, she clambered to her feet. "Fern's waving at me, so I'd better go see what she wants. Let me know when you're ready to do some stamping."

Ella smiled. "We will."

Eunice hurried off and took a seat beside Fern on the porch.

"I was hoping to talk to you after the program yesterday," Fern said when Eunice joined her. "But things got busy with the games, and you left before I had the chance to say anything."

"Was there anything in particular you wanted to talk to me about?" Eunice asked.

"I wanted to see if you'd be free to come over to our place for supper tomorrow evening."

"I'd like that." Eunice moistened her lips with the tip of her tongue. "Will Freeman be there?"

Fern nodded. "I thought it would give the three of us a chance to get better acquainted. I think our grossmudder would enjoy visiting with you, too."

"That'd be great." Eunice didn't know if she'd enjoy visiting with Fern's grandmother, but she was eager to spend more time with Freeman. Even though he'd be coming to her place soon, she wasn't about to turn down Fern's invitation.

～⚹～

"That was a real good service we had today," Grandma said as Freeman drove their buggy toward home later that day. "I enjoyed visiting afterwards, as well."

369

"It was a nice day," Fern agreed. "I had a short visit with Eunice Byler, too." She tapped Grandma lightly on the shoulder. "I invited Eunice to join us for supper tomorrow night. I hope that's all right with you."

"Won't bother me any," Grandma said with a chuckle, "because I won't be at home."

Freeman gave her a sidelong glance. "Where will you be?"

"Several of us widows are going out for supper. I thought I'd mentioned that to you both a few days ago."

"Guess we forgot," Fern said.

Freeman glanced over his shoulder. "What made you decide to invite Eunice over for supper, Fern?"

"She seems like a nice person, and I thought it would give us a chance to get to know her a little better."

"Hmm. . .I see." Freeman had to admit the idea of spending the evening with Eunice held some appeal, but he'd promised to have supper at her place next Saturday and hadn't expected they'd be getting together quite so soon. He had a feeling Eunice might be looking for a husband, and since he wasn't ready to settle down yet, he hoped it wasn't him she had in mind for the job.

"I don't know about you two, but I'm feeling hungry," Grandma said when Freeman guided the horse and buggy onto their driveway. "Think I'll fix myself a little snack."

Freeman chuckled. Grandma might be a small woman, but she could pack away food like a full-grown man. It seemed as if she was always snacking on something.

"I'll drop you off here, and then I'll put the horse and buggy away," Freeman said, pulling the buggy up close to the house. "Oh, and Grandma, if you want to fix a snack, I think I could manage to eat a little something, too."

"Will do." Grandma climbed down from the buggy with the ease of a woman much younger than her seventy years. Fern stepped out behind her.

When they stepped onto the porch and opened the back door, Grandma let out a high-pitched screech. "Ach, what a *marascht*!"

Freeman jumped out of the buggy and sprinted for the house.

"What's a mess?" he asked, leaping onto the porch.

"Come in here and look for yourself," Grandma hollered from the kitchen.

Freeman rushed in and screeched to a stop just inside the door. Grandma and Fern stood there shaking their heads.

Penny lay curled up on the braided throw rug by the kitchen sink, sleeping peacefully. The room, however, was a disaster! A box of cereal must have fallen off the table, for the contents were dumped on the floor. Several plastic sacks that had been in a box in the utility room were ripped up and strewn about. Some of Grandma's dish towels were shredded, and a wad of napkins lay clumped together on the floor near the pup.

"This doesn't set well with me at all," Grandma grumbled. She pointed to Freeman. "I want you to get that hundli out of my kitchen right now!"

When Freeman started across the room, Penny's eyes snapped open. She leaped up and darted under the table.

"Nemm ihn fescht!" Fern hollered.

"Penny's a she, and I'm trying to take hold of her like you asked." Freeman lunged for the pup, but she slipped through his fingers. The pup's toenails clicked against the linoleum as she raced out of the room.

Freeman tore after the animal, hollering, "Come back here, you troublesome mutt!" He rounded the corner just in time to see Penny collide with the cardboard box on the utility porch.

Yip! Yip! Yip! The pup shook her head and looked up at Freeman with a pathetic whimper.

Freeman bent down and scooped Penny into his arms. "You're nothing but trouble; you know that? How'd you get in the house and manage to make such a mess?"

Slurp! Slurp! The pup swiped her tongue across Freeman's chin.

"You're going back to the barn!" Freeman pushed the screen door open with his knee. "I'll be back to help clean up the mess in a few minutes," he called over his shoulder. "First thing tomorrow morning, I'm gonna build this mutt a dog run with a sturdy gate!"

CHAPTER 13

Katie picked up the heavy braided throw rugs she'd taken from the living room and lugged them out to the porch. She'd been cleaning the house while Mom did the laundry. Because the stamp shop was always closed on Mondays, it was the best time to get things done around the house. She'd been relieved this morning at breakfast that neither Mom nor Dad had said anything more about her seeing the doctor. Since she'd eaten most of the food on her plate and had forced herself to smile and appear relaxed, maybe they'd decided there was nothing wrong with her and she didn't need to see the doctor.

Katie draped the rugs over the porch railing and beat them with a broom. Dust flew in all directions, causing her to sneeze. She set the broom down, leaned against the railing, and sighed. It was too warm to be cleaning house.

The back door opened, and Mom stepped onto the porch holding a basket of laundry. "If you feel up to it, would you mind hanging these clothes on the line for me while I wash another load?"

"Sure, I can do that." Katie took the basket and plodded down the stairs. She trudged across the lawn and set the basket under the clothesline.

By the time she'd hung the last sheet, she was sweating, and her back ached from stretching to reach the line.

Bzz. . .bzz. . .

Katie looked up and gasped. A swarm of bees was heading her way!

Bzz. . .bzz. . .

They landed on the sheet overhead.

Katie raced across the yard, screaming, "*Iemeschwarm!*"

The back door flew open, and Mom rushed outside just as Katie leaped onto the porch. "What's going on, Katie? What swarm of bees are you hollering about?"

"Th–they landed on one of the sheets!" Katie's voice trembled, and so did her legs. She leaned against the porch railing and drew in a shaky breath. "I. . .I feel sick to my stomach, and I can hardly breathe."

Mom took hold of Katie's arm. "This has gone on long enough. I'm making you a doctor's appointment today!"

Katie shook her head. "I don't want to see the doctor, and you can't make me go!"

She dashed down the stairs and raced into the field.

With tears coursing down her cheeks, she ran until her sides began to ache. She stopped at the edge of the road and sucked in several deep breaths of air. Then she started walking along the shoulder of the road.

The sun burned furiously, but Katie hurried on, paying no attention to where she was going. When she came to the entrance of their Amish cemetery, she halted. *Should I go in? Would I feel better if I visited Timothy's grave like Mom wanted me to do? Would seeing it again make me feel better or worse?*

Katie stood several minutes, shifting from one foot to the other. Finally, she gathered up her courage, opened the gate, and stepped inside. When she found Timothy's grave, she dropped to her knees. It didn't seem possible that the man she loved and had been planning to marry was lying dead beneath the mound of dirt by his headstone.

Katie's eyes and nose burned; she held her breath until her lungs screamed for air.

Where are you, Timothy? Where'd your spirit go when it left your body?

A strange prickling sensation came over Katie, and her heart started to pound. Suddenly, everything seemed unreal—as if she no longer existed.

Katie jumped up and started to run. She needed to get away. Needed to find a place where she felt safe.

᎗᎗᎗

When JoAnn entered the health food store, she noticed Eunice Byler talking to one of the English women who worked there, so she decided to look around on her own, hoping to find a remedy that might help Katie relax. There was no doubt in JoAnn's mind that Katie had some sort of physical or emotional health issue. But if Katie refused to see the doctor, what could be done for her? Katie was a woman now, and JoAnn couldn't force her to go to the doctor. Maybe, though, she could convince Katie to take one of the natural remedies found here.

As JoAnn headed down the aisle where the herbs and homeopathic remedies were displayed, she spotted Loraine's mother, Priscilla.

"Wie geht's?" JoAnn asked when Priscilla stepped up to her.

"I'm fine, but Amos isn't doing so well. He's come down with a cold." Priscilla frowned. "Told me this morning that he felt stuffed up like a rag doll, so I came here to see what I could find to help with his symptoms. What brings you here today? Is someone in your family grank?"

"I'm not sure. Katie might be, but she refuses to let us take her to see the doctor."

"Is she still feeling dizzy like she was on Sunday?"

"I don't think so, but this morning she freaked out over some bees that landed on one of the sheets hanging on the clothesline. Said she felt sick to her stomach and could hardly breathe. She got real upset when I tried to talk to her and ran off into the field." JoAnn motioned to the bottles of herbs. "I figured if I could get her calmed down, she might listen to reason about seeing the doctor, so I came here looking for something that might help."

"Maybe you should try this." Priscilla handed JoAnn a bottle of valerian root. "This herb is supposed to act as a natural sedative.

There's also a remedy in the homeopathic section that's used for calming."

"I appreciate the suggestions, and I'll see if Katie's willing to try them." JoAnn smiled. "How are things with Loraine and Wayne? Are they enjoying married life?"

"Except for Loraine's concerns over Crist and Ada, I believe things are going well."

"What concerns? Are there problems between Loraine and Ada again?"

Priscilla shook her head. "From what I understand, Crist and Ada are having marital problems."

"What a shame. Has our bishop or one of the other ministers counseled with them?"

"Not that I know of. I'm not sure any of the ministers knows about the problem."

"Divorce is not an option for Ada and Crist, so I'd think they would seek help if their marriage is strained."

"I'm not sure Crist would admit to such a thing, and you know how stubborn Ada can be."

"You're good friends with Sadie," JoAnn said, thinking of their bishop's wife. "Maybe you should talk to her about the situation with Crist and Ada."

Priscilla nodded. "I've thought of that, and I may drop by to see her on my way home."

"I think you should. No point in letting this go on until things get worse."

"You're right. It's stressful enough for the newlyweds to be sharing their house with Wayne's folks. They don't need any arguing going on."

"Let me know how it goes." JoAnn turned toward the counter where the cash register sat. "Guess I'd better pay for my things and be on my way. Hopefully by the time I get home, Katie will be there, too."

❧ ❧

Freeman whistled as he headed for home with his horse and

buggy. He'd just come from Shipshewana, where he'd picked up the things he needed to finish the dog run he'd started building. He'd be glad to get it done so the pup could be in a safe place, away from the house and his bike shop.

Freeman glanced to the right and was surprised to see Katie Miller running along the shoulder of the road. He guided his horse and buggy alongside of her and stopped. "What are you doing out here so far from home?" he called.

She didn't answer, just kept on running.

Freeman followed her down the road and stopped his horse again when he got ahead of her. This time he got out of the buggy and waited for her. "Katie, what's wrong?"

She finally stopped running and stared up at him like a frightened child. "I. . .I'm going home."

"You're a long ways from home. Where have you been?"

She dropped her gaze to the ground and kicked at the pebbles beneath her feet. "I was out for a walk and ended up at the cemetery."

Now it made sense. Katie's strange behavior had something to do with her visit to the cemetery. "Did you go there to visit Timothy's grave?"

She nodded slowly, and when she lifted her head, tears gathered in her eyes. "I. . .I started to feel funny while I was there, and I knew I needed to go home."

"Funny in what way?"

She shrugged. "Just funny, that's all."

It was obvious that she didn't want to talk about it, so Freeman decided not to press the issue. He motioned to his buggy. "I'm on my way back to my shop, so why don't you let me give you a ride?"

She shifted uneasily but finally nodded.

When they climbed into his buggy, Freeman noticed that Katie had started to shiver. He reached under the seat and pulled out a buggy robe. "If you're cold, here's something you can wrap around your shoulders."

She took the robe but gave no reply.

As they rode along, Freeman asked God to give him the right

words to say to Katie. She was clearly upset, and he didn't want to say anything that might upset her even more.

"Do you have a dog?" he asked.

She gave a quick nod.

"Full grown or still a pup?"

"Full grown."

Not much information, but at least she was talking.

"What kind of dog do you have?"

"Just an old hound, but he's really my daed's dog."

"One of Fern's students presented her with a cocker spaniel puppy for her birthday. She's real cute but can sure be a pescht." Freeman grimaced. "One of us must have left the back door open yesterday morning, because the pup got into the house without our knowing it. When we came home from church, she was in the kitchen and had made a big mess."

"Puppies are known for that. Timothy had a puppy that chewed nearly every one of his socks." Katie's chin quivered. "I. . .I miss him so much."

"I'm sure you do. It's always hard to lose a friend or family member."

"We were going to be married this fall." Katie's voice broke, and she covered her mouth with the back of her hand.

Freeman reached across the seat and touched her arm. "I'm sorry, Katie."

"Can we talk about something else?"

"Jah, sure. If you'd rather, we don't have to talk at all."

She nodded and sighed.

Lord, please be with Katie, Freeman prayed. *I can see that she really does need a friend.*

❧ ❧

"Danki for the ride," Katie said when Freeman pulled his horse and buggy to a stop near their barn.

"You're welcome."

She slipped the buggy robe he'd given her under the seat and stepped out of the buggy.

"Take care, Katie," Freeman called as she sprinted toward the house.

When Katie entered the kitchen, she found Mom making a sandwich. "Where have you been, Katie? I've been so worried about you."

"I went to the cemetery."

"On foot?"

Katie nodded.

"But that's a long way to walk."

"I needed to be alone, and I wasn't thinking about how far it was." Katie glanced out the window and watched as Freeman's buggy headed down the driveway. "As I walked home, Freeman came along and offered me a ride."

"That's good. I'm glad you didn't have to walk all that way." Mom moved closer to Katie. "You still look distressed. Are you still upset over that swarm of bees, or is it because you went to the cemetery?"

Katie nodded. "It was a mistake to go there. I won't go again."

"Avoidance isn't the answer, Katie." Mom opened one of the cupboard doors and took out two bottles. "I went to the health food store while you were gone and got these."

"What are they for?"

"One's valerian root, and the other's a homeopathic remedy. Both are supposed to have a calming affect, and I thought they might help you feel better."

Katie shook her head. "I won't take them."

"Why not?"

"Because I don't need them; I'm fine."

"You don't look fine to me. Your face looks strained, and I can see from the red around your eyes that you've been crying."

"I don't need any herbs or homeopathic remedies. I just need to be left alone!"

"You're being stubborn," Mom said. "Just because you still look like a little girl doesn't mean you have to act like one."

"I'm not a little girl, but you're treating me like one!" Katie turned and dashed up the stairs.

When Eunice returned home from the health food store, she found her mother sitting in a chair on the front porch with a basket of mending in her lap. "Here's the chickweed salve you asked me to get for Richard's poison ivy." She handed the paper sack to her mother and took a seat in the chair beside her.

"Danki. I appreciate your going after it. I'm sure your little bruder will, too."

"While I was at the health food store, I heard Priscilla and JoAnn talking about a couple of things that were very surprising."

"Like what?"

Eunice leaned closer to Mom. "For one thing, Priscilla said that Ada and Crist Lambright are having some marital problems."

"Are you sure?"

Eunice nodded. "Priscilla said she's planning to speak with the bishop's wife about it."

"You shouldn't listen to idle chitchat, Eunice."

"It wasn't chitchat. Loraine's mamm is worried about Crist and Ada."

"Even if it's true, it's none of our business."

"You want to know the other thing I heard that really surprised me?"

"What was that?"

"JoAnn was talking to Priscilla about Katie, and she said that she needed to get a remedy to help Katie calm down." Eunice crinkled her nose. "You know what I think, Mom?"

"What's that?"

"I think Katie might be pregnant."

CHAPTER 14

Supper's ready," Mom called through Katie's bedroom door.

Katie groaned. She'd been taking a nap and didn't want to be disturbed.

Tap. Tap. Tap. "Katie, are you awake?"

Katie nestled under her covers like a kitten burrowing into a pile of straw. She didn't want to eat supper, but she knew if she didn't, Mom would probably badger her some more about taking the remedy she'd bought at the health food store.

Tap. Tap.

"I'll be right there!" Katie pushed the covers aside and climbed out of bed. Using her fingers, she tried to smooth the wrinkles from her dress, but it was no use; she looked a mess. She was tempted to change clothes but figured that if she took the time to do that, Mom would knock on her door again.

She set her head covering in place, tucked a few stray hairs under the sides, and left her room. Pulling her shoulders back, she hurried down the stairs.

When she entered the kitchen, she couldn't help but notice the impatient look on Mom's face.

Dad tapped his foot a couple of times. "It's about time," he mumbled. "I'm hungry, and the food's gettin' cold."

"Sorry." Katie slipped into her chair and bowed her head.

After their time of prayer, Dad looked over at Katie and said,

380

"Your mamm told me what happened earlier today. You shouldn't have run off the way you did. Don't you know how worried your mamm was when you didn't come back right away?"

"I didn't mean to make her worry; I just needed to be alone."

"Jah, well, you could've gone to your room instead of takin' off like that." Dad helped himself to a slice of ham. "And what's all the fuss about a few bees?"

"It wasn't a few bees, Dad. It was whole swarm." Katie forked a piece of ham onto her plate and handed the platter to Mom. "I'm sorry for not helping with supper. I fell asleep in my room."

"Don't worry about it," Mom said with a wave of her hand. "When we're finished eating, you can clear the table and wash the dishes."

Dad looked over at Katie and frowned. "Your mamm also said that she bought something at the health food store to help calm your nerves, but you refused to take it."

Katie slowly nodded. She didn't like being questioned like this. It made her feel like a little girl.

"Why didn't you give one of the remedies a try?"

"I didn't think I needed it. I just needed to rest awhile." Katie took a drink of water. "I feel much better after my nap."

"Glad to hear it." Dad shoveled some mashed potatoes onto his plate and dropped a pat of butter on top. "Your mamm and I have been very worried about you, Katie."

She gave a shaky laugh. "Well, you don't need to be. I'm fine."

"Are you sure about that?"

Katie nodded.

"You weren't fine when you passed out during church," Dad said.

"That was because it was so warm in the buggy shop, and it may also have been because I hadn't had much breakfast."

"What about how upset you got today?" Mom asked. "You sure weren't fine when you ran off the way you did."

"I was upset about the bees, and I'm sorry if I upset you."

Mom's disbelieving look made Katie even more determined

381

to prove to her folks that she didn't need any kind of remedy to settle her nerves.

~≈ ≈~

Loraine had just set a kettle of water on the stove to boil when Wayne stepped into the kitchen.

"What's for supper?" he asked, sniffing the air. "I don't smell anything cooking."

She pointed to a package of noodles on the counter. "I'm just getting started. We should be ready to eat in a half hour or so."

"I'm surprised my mamm's not in here helping. Where is she anyway?"

"She spilled coffee on her dress and went to her room to change."

Wayne's forehead puckered. "I hope she didn't burn herself."

Loraine shook her head. "It was a cup she'd forgotten to drink, so it wasn't hot."

"That's good." Wayne looked over his shoulder. "My daed came in behind me, but I think he headed down the hall to the bathroom."

Loraine lowered her voice to a whisper. "By the way, have you had a chance to speak to your folks about their problem?"

"What problem?"

"Their marital problem."

Wayne shrugged. "I'm not sure they're having a problem. I mean, I haven't heard them raise their voices for a couple of days."

"*Absatz!* Stop badgering me, Ada!" Crist rushed into the kitchen, his face bright red. He halted in front of Wayne. "Your *mudder* just won't leave me alone!"

"That's because he won't listen to reason!" Ada shouted as she followed him into the room. She frowned at Crist. "If he *could* listen, that is."

Crist took a step back from her. "You don't have to yell! I'm standing right here!"

"If I didn't yell, you wouldn't hear what I was saying!"

Wayne held up his hand. "Don't you two realize how it makes us feel when you argue like this?"

"We wouldn't argue if your daed wasn't so stubborn." Ada motioned to Wayne. "Can't you talk him into getting his hearing tested?"

Wayne's eyes widened. "Is that why you've been hollering at each other so much lately?"

Ada nodded. "I'm surprised you and Loraine haven't been yelling so your daed could hear you, too."

Wayne gave a nod. "Now that you mention it, I have had to repeat myself to Pop several times lately."

Ada nudged Crist's arm. "Uh-huh, I knew it."

Loraine heard a buggy rumble into the yard, and she glanced out the window. "Looks like we've got company."

"Now who's come here this close to supper? I hope it's not someone bringing another dead animal hide to your taxidermy shop." Ada craned her neck to look around Crist. "Ach, it's the bishop! I wonder what he wants."

Loraine's mouth went dry. *What if Mom spoke to the bishop's wife like she said she might do? What if Sadie told James, and he's come here to speak to Ada and Crist about their marital problems?*

"There's only one way we'll know what Bishop James wants, and that's to open the door and let him in." Wayne ambled out of the room and, moments later, returned with the bishop.

The bishop pulled his fingers through his thick, full beard and looked right at Crist. "I heard some rather distressing news today. Figured I'd better come over here and find out if it's true."

"What good news did you hear?" Crist asked.

The bishop's bushy eyebrows shot up. "I said *distressing* news, not *good* news."

"What distressing news?" asked Ada.

Loraine's heart started to pound, and she stepped between Ada and the bishop. "I. . .uh. . .think there's been a mistake."

"What kind of cake?" Crist scratched his head. "Are we having cake for dessert tonight?"

Ada groaned. "No one said anything about cake." She turned

to the bishop. "What kind of distressing news did you come to give us?"

The bishop shook his head. "Didn't come to give you any news. Came to see if I could help with your marital problems."

Ada's mouth formed an O. "Crist and I aren't having marital problems. Who said we were?"

The bishop motioned to Loraine. "Her mamm told my fraa that you and Crist have been hollering at each other a lot lately."

"I holler because he can't hear." Ada needled Crist in the ribs. "He needs to get his hearing tested, but he refuses to go."

"That's all there is to it?"

Ada nodded.

A look of relief flooded the bishop's face. "You come with me later this week," he said to Crist. "I'll take you to my doctor to get your hearing tested."

Crist moved closer to the bishop. "What was that?"

"Said I'll be by later this week, and we'll get your hearing tested!"

Crist nodded and smiled. "Jah, sure; I'd be happy to go along when you get your hearing tested."

Loraine looked at Wayne; Wayne looked at Ada; and they all laughed. It was a relief to know that Ada and Crist's marriage wasn't in trouble. And if the bishop could get Crist to have his hearing tested, then Loraine was sure all the shouting would end.

~❧ ❧~

"Where are you going?" Fern called to Freeman as he started out the back door.

"I'm headin' to the phone shed to call a few customers. Need to let 'em know that their bikes are ready."

"Well, don't be too long. Eunice will be here soon, and supper's almost ready."

"No problem. I'll be back in short order. Wouldn't risk missing out on your baked ham and mashed potatoes." He winked at Fern and went out the door.

As Freeman headed down the path leading to the phone shed,

he thought about Katie and wondered how she was doing. After seeing how she'd acted this afternoon, he was sure something was weighing on her mind besides missing Timothy. If there was just some way he could get her to open up about her feelings. If he could get her to do that, maybe he could find out what was at the root of her nervousness.

I'll just have to keep praying for her, and whenever I get the chance, I'll offer an encouraging word, he thought as he stepped into the phone shed.

Since the small building had no windows, it was dark inside. Freeman left the door open and turned on the battery-operated lantern sitting on the small table beside the phone. Then he took a seat in the folding chair, placed his notebook on the table, and punched in the phone number of the first customer he needed to call.

He got a busy signal, so he tried the next number. There was no answer there, so he left a message on the customer's voice mail.

He'd just started dialing the third number, when a gust of wind came up. *Bam!* The door blew shut.

A sense of uneasiness tightened Freeman's chest as he thought about the discomfort he felt whenever he was in a confined place like this.

He moved away from the phone and grabbed the doorknob. When he turned it, the knob fell off in his hand.

"Oh no!" Sweat beaded on Freeman's forehead and ran down his nose. His shoulders tensed, and he drew in a quick breath.

Don't panic. Relax. Stay calm.

He placed the doorknob on the phone table, took a couple more deep breaths, and closed his eyes.

An image from the past leaped into his head. He'd been seven years old and had gone down to the cellar to get a jar of peaches for his mother. He hadn't been afraid at first—not until he couldn't get the door open. Then when his flashlight batteries died, Freeman had panicked. He'd pounded on the door and hollered until his throat hurt, certain that no one would find him and he'd die in the cellar. By the time Mom realized he was missing and come looking for him, he was bawling like a newborn calf.

Freeman's eyes popped open, and his mind snapped back to the present. *I'm not a little boy anymore. I'm a grown man, and I know how to diffuse my fear.*

Breathe deeply. . .move through the anxiety. . .float with it. . .get mad at it. . .do whatever it takes.

He stared at the doorknob, wishing he had the tools to put it back on. "This is really dumb," he muttered. "All I need to do is call someone and say I'm locked in the phone shed."

He dialed the number of their closest neighbor, got their answering machine, and left a message. Then he called another neighbor, but there was no answer there, either.

After making five calls and getting nothing but voice mails and answering machines, he was more than a little frustrated.

Stay relaxed, he told himself. *If someone gets my message soon, they'll rescue me. Or else when supper's ready and I'm not at the house, Fern will come looking for me.*

Freeman drew in another deep breath and rested his head on the table. *While I'm waiting, I may as well try to take a nap.*

CHAPTER 15

As Eunice guided her horse and buggy in the direction of the Bontragers' house, her excitement mounted. She could hardly wait to see Freeman again and hoped he would enjoy the pie she'd brought for dessert.

An unexpected gust of wind pushed against the buggy, and it started to rain.

She leaned forward, straining to see through the rain-spattered windshield. At this rate, it would take forever to get to Freeman's house.

Eunice didn't like driving in the rain, but fortunately she didn't have far to go. She hoped that by the time she was to return home this evening the weather would improve.

A pair of wide-beamed headlights went by; then she saw the red taillights as the car disappeared. Eunice leaned over and flipped the button to turn on the windshield wipers, keeping her focus on the road.

As Eunice passed the Millers' place, she thought about Katie and the way she'd fainted in church. Between that and the things she'd heard Katie's mother say at the health food store, Eunice was almost sure Katie must be pregnant. She wondered if anyone else thought that, too. Mom had cautioned her not to mention her suspicions to anyone since she didn't know for sure that Katie was pregnant, but it was going to be hard to keep quiet about this.

Soon the Bontragers' place came into view, and she breathed a sigh of relief. She turned up the driveway, drove past the phone shed and the bike shop, and halted the horse near the barn. Then she climbed out of the buggy, unhitched the horse, and put him in the corral.

Returning to the buggy, she grabbed the plastic container with her pie inside and sprinted for the house.

When she stepped inside, she was greeted by Fern.

"It's good to see you; you're right on time," Fern said, glancing at the clock on the kitchen wall.

Eunice smiled and handed her the container. "I brought a strawberry-rhubarb pie for dessert."

"Umm. . .that sounds good. Strawberry-rhubarb's one of Freeman's favorites. It's also one of mine."

Eunice glanced around. "Where is Freeman? I didn't see any light coming from his shop, so I figured he must have quit working and was here at the house."

"He was here, but he went out to the phone shed to make a few calls." Fern's forehead wrinkled as she looked at the clock again. "That was quite awhile ago. He should have been back by now."

"Maybe he went out to his shop after he made the phone calls."

"That could be."

"Want me to go check?"

"If you don't mind going back outside. It's raining pretty hard out there."

"It started coming down soon after I left home." Eunice motioned to her rain-soaked dress. "I'm already wet, so I guess a little more rain won't matter."

"There's an umbrella hanging on the wall peg by the back door," Fern said. "You can borrow that if you like."

"Danki." Eunice grabbed the umbrella and scooted out the door.

She'd only made it halfway to the bike shop when a gust of wind came up and turned the umbrella inside-out.

"I don't need this kind of trouble," she mumbled as she hurried along.

Her feet slipped on the wet grass, and she went down on her knees. With a sense of determination, she scrambled to her feet. When she finally reached the bicycle shop, she discovered that the door was locked. Freeman was obviously not inside.

He must still be in the phone shed. Eunice quickened her steps and headed in that direction.

❧ ❧

Freeman lifted his head from the table and stared at the phone, wondering if he should make another call. He was sure someone would eventually hear one of the messages he'd left, but in the meantime, his rumbling stomach kept reminding him that it was time for supper.

I wonder if Eunice has arrived yet. He hadn't heard her horse and buggy come up the driveway, but then the wind and rain were making so much noise, he probably couldn't have heard a dump truck if it had roared past the shed.

A knock on the door pulled Freeman's thoughts aside. "Are you in there, Freeman?"

Freeman was relieved to hear Eunice's voice. "Jah, I'm here. The doorknob came off, and I'm trapped."

He heard a rattling noise; then a few seconds later, the door opened. When Eunice stepped inside, he noticed that her dress was sopping wet and her kapp had gone limp from the rain. Even so, he thought she looked like an angel.

"How long have you been in here?" she asked.

He shrugged. "Too long. I don't like small places."

She motioned to the phone. "Why didn't you call someone for help?"

"I did, but all I got were folks' answering machines or voice mails." Freeman groaned. "I was beginning to think I'd have to spend the night out here."

She snickered. "I'm sure your sister would have eventually come looking for you."

389

"Jah, I suppose."

"We'd better get up to the house right away, or she'll probably come looking for both of us."

Freeman pointed to the doorknob lying on the phone table. "Guess I'll worry about fixing that later. It's not likely that anyone will come by wanting to use the phone shed in this crummy weather."

As they stepped outside, Freeman wrapped his hand around hers and gave it a gentle squeeze. "Danki, for coming to my rescue, Eunice."

"You're welcome," she said smiling up at him sweetly.

They hurried across the yard, and when they entered the house, Fern gave Eunice one of her dresses to change into.

While Eunice changed clothes, Freeman told Fern about his ordeal in the phone shed.

"I had no idea you were trapped in there. I wondered why it was taking so long for you to make a few calls." Fern touched his shoulder. "Did it bother you being stuck in that small shed?"

"It did at first, but I worked through it okay."

Fern smiled. "And then Eunice came along and rescued you."

"That's right, and I'm grateful she did."

Fern gestured to the stove. "Supper's ready now, so as soon as Eunice comes out of the bathroom we can eat."

❧ ❧

Freeman stared into his nearly empty glass. Throughout the meal he'd become acutely aware that Fern approved of Eunice and was making every effort to get them together. No doubt that was the reason she'd invited Eunice to join them for supper this evening. Well, that was okay with Freeman. He could enjoy Eunice's company, even though he had no plans to settle down to marriage for a good long while.

"Now it's time for us to eat the dessert I brought." Eunice smiled at Freeman, her eyes sparkling in the light of the gas lamp hanging above the table.

He patted his full stomach and groaned. "I ate so much supper,

I'm not sure I have any room for dessert."

Eunice's chin jutted out, and her nose crinkled. "You have to try some of my strawberry-rhubarb pie. I baked it just for you."

Freeman smiled. "That's my favorite kind of pie, so I guess I can't say no."

~≈ ≉~

"You ought to see how hard the wind's whipping the trees in our backyard," Katie's mother said, staring out the kitchen window. "I hope your daed's not having any trouble getting the horses put in the barn."

Katie stepped up beside Mom and peered out the window. It was hard to believe the warm weather they'd been having had changed so drastically and in such a short time.

She caught sight of Dad struggling to get one of their horses into the barn. If Katie's four brothers weren't married and still lived at home, they'd be outside helping him right now.

Maybe I should go out and help. Katie hurried across the room and plucked her jacket off the wall peg near the back door. "I'm going out to help Dad," she called to Mom before she rushed out the door.

Katie fought against the harsh wind as she made her way to the corral. Two of Dad's newer horses that weren't fully trained hadn't gone into the barn yet. They stamped their hooves, reared up, and kicked out their back legs, obviously frightened by the howling wind.

Dad had a rope and was trying to fasten it around one horse's halter, while the second horse ran around the corral in circles.

Katie darted into the buggy shed and grabbed a buggy whip. Dad never used a whip on any of his horses unless it was absolutely necessary. Katie figured she could put the whip to good use without hitting the horse, so she snapped it behind the horse a couple of times, and that did the trick.

By the time they got both horses into the barn, Katie was out of breath, and her dress was soaking wet from the rain.

"Danki for your help." Dad gave Katie an appreciative smile.

"I think those two were really spooked by this nasty weather."

Katie nodded. "The wind and rain are enough to spook anyone."

"I'd better get the door shut or we'll have rain and wind in here." Dad grabbed the handle of the barn door and gave it a tug. He almost had it closed when a gust of wind whipped against the door, and it slammed shut, smacking him in the head.

Dad let out a moan and crumpled to the floor.

CHAPTER 16

I wish I could stay and visit awhile longer," Eunice said, rising from the sofa. "But since there's a break in the rain, I'd better get home before it starts up again."

"That's probably a good idea. I'll get the rest of your pie for you to take home," Fern said, heading for the kitchen.

"No, that's okay. You can keep what's left of the pie." Eunice looked over at Freeman and smiled. "Maybe I'll bake another pie when you come over for supper on Saturday."

"That'd be nice."

Eunice started for the door but turned back around. "Oh, I almost forgot. . . I left my dress hanging in the bathroom. I'd better check and see if it's dry so I can give you back your dress."

"It's probably still wet, but you can wear my dress home. I'll get it from you later in the week." Fern gave Eunice a hug. "I'm glad you were able to join us for supper."

"Me, too. Well, I'll get my dress and put it in a plastic bag, then I'll be on my way." Eunice hurried down the hall to the bathroom.

When she returned to the living room a short time later, she was disappointed to see that Freeman wasn't there.

"Freeman's outside getting your horse hitched to the buggy," Fern said. "You might want to wait in here until it's ready."

"It shouldn't take him too long, so I'll wait out on the porch.

393

Thanks again for supper. It was delicious." Eunice smiled and scooted out the door.

She was pleased when Freeman brought the horse and buggy close to the house and called, "She's hitched up for you and ready to go!"

Eunice left the porch and hurried up to Freeman, who stood by the horse stroking it behind the ears. "Seems like a nice mare," he said. "What's her name?"

"Dolly."

He grinned. "Did you name her that, or did she already have the name when you got her?"

"Dolly was her name when my daed bought her for me." Eunice put her purse and the bag with her dress in it inside the buggy; then she turned to face Freeman. "I appreciate your getting my horse and buggy ready. Danki."

He pulled his fingers through the sides of his hair and gave a quick nod. "Sure, no problem."

She hesitated, hoping he might say something more, but he just stood, scuffing the toe of his boot on the ground.

"Guess I'd better go." Eunice stepped into the buggy and took up the reins.

"I'll see you next week," he called as she turned toward the driveway.

She smiled and lifted her hand with a wave.

~🙢 🙠~

When Freeman returned to the house, he found Fern sitting at the kitchen table drinking a cup of tea.

"Would you like another piece of pie?" she asked.

He shook his head.

"How about some tea?"

"No thanks."

Fern motioned to the chair beside her. "Then have a seat, and we can visit while I drink my tea."

Freeman bristled. He didn't care for her bossy tone.

As if sensing his irritation, Fern said in a much softer tone,

"Please, have a seat. I'd like to talk to you a minute."

The chair scraped against the linoleum as Freeman pulled it away from the table. "What'd you want to talk about?"

"Eunice."

"What about her?"

"I think she's nice, don't you?"

He nodded.

"She's very pleasant and easy to talk to."

Freeman propped his elbows on the table. "Are you trying to make a point?"

Fern took another sip of tea. "Grandma and I were talking the other day, and we're both hoping you'll join the church this fall."

"Uh-huh, I probably will."

"We're also hoping that you'll find the right girl, and that you might—"

"Get married and settle down?"

"Jah."

"Don't tell me—you think Eunice is the girl I should marry."

Fern nodded. "From what I can tell, I think she'd make a good wife."

Irritation welled in Freeman's chest. He didn't appreciate his sister trying to choose a mate for him. If and when he felt ready for marriage, he'd do his own choosing.

He glanced at the clock above the refrigerator. "It's getting late. Shouldn't Grandma be home by now?"

Fern shook her head. "She told me this morning that after she was done eating supper with her widowed friends, she'd be going to Sharon Hershberger's to spend the night."

"How come?"

"Because Sharon's feeling very lonely—it's only been a month since her husband died. Some of Sharon's friends and relatives have been taking turns spending the night with her. Tonight is Grandma's turn."

"Oh, I see. That's nice of her."

Fern nodded. "Getting back to Eunice, what did you think of her pie?"

"It was good. If you'll recall, I had two pieces." Freeman pushed his chair away from the table. "I'm tired; think I'll go on up to bed."

Fern opened her mouth as if to say something more, but Freeman hurried from the room.

~ *≈* ~

Katie squirmed in her chair as she sat beside her mother in a waiting area outside the emergency room at the hospital in Goshen, awaiting some news on her dad's condition.

Please, God, Katie prayed, *don't let my daed die.*

Tears stung her eyes, and she could barely swallow because her throat burned so much. Even though this wasn't the same hospital she and her cousins had been taken to after their accident last fall, she felt as if she were reliving the moment. She could see herself sitting in the waiting room after she'd been given the news that Timothy was dead. She could hear Loraine's voice as she tried talking to her, and she remembered how unresponsive she'd been.

Katie could almost smell the hospital smells and feel the cold metal of the chair she'd been sitting in. She'd withdrawn into her own little world and hadn't emerged until she'd move to Florida to be with Grammy and Grandpa.

Mom touched Katie's shoulder. "Did you hear what I said?"

"What was that?"

"I asked if you'd like something to drink."

Katie shook her head. "I just want to know how Dad is doing. I hope he's not going to—" Her voice faltered, and she nearly choked on a sob.

Mom grasped Katie's hand. "We have to trust God and keep praying for your daed."

I prayed for Timothy, and what good did that do? Katie thought bitterly. She glanced at the clock on the far wall. It had been almost two hours since Dad had been taken in to be examined. What could be taking so long?

At the sound of a siren approaching, Katie jumped up. She went to the window and looked out. An ambulance had pulled up to the emergency room entrance. Two paramedics rushed in, pushing a man on a gurney. He was covered in blood!

A rush of heat flooded Katie's face, her heart thudded, and a wave of nausea rolled through her stomach. Everything felt unreal—as if she no longer existed. She could see and hear what was going on around her, but it felt as if it were all a dream. She whirled around and raced out the door.

Leaning heavily against the side of the building, she closed her eyes and gulped in some air. Her legs wobbled, and she felt weak and light-headed, as if she might pass out.

The rain had stopped, and a cool breeze blew, but it didn't help at all. She wanted to run and keep on running but didn't know where to go.

"Katie, are you all right?"

Katie's eyes snapped open, and she blinked a couple of times. She could see by the pinched expression on Mom's face that she was worried about her.

"I. . .I'm fine. The sight of all that blood made me feel woozy." No point in telling Mom about the feeling of unreality that had converged on her. Mom wouldn't understand. Besides, the strange feelings Katie had experienced were too difficult to explain.

Mom slipped her arm around Katie's waist. "I just spoke with one of the doctors."

"What'd he say?"

"He said your daed has a mild concussion, but he's going to be okay. The doctor wants to keep him overnight for observation, so I'll call our driver to take us home, and then we'll come back tomorrow to get your daed."

Katie nodded as a sense of relief flooded her soul. Dad wasn't going to die. At least one of her prayers had been answered. Now if God would only answer her most recent prayer and take away the anxious feelings she'd been having since she had returned home.

CHAPTER 17

The month of June brought hot days and humid nights, causing Loraine to feel wet and sticky. That, coupled with nausea, made it hard not to be cross. But this morning, as she returned home from her doctor's appointment, she felt better than she had in days. Her heart pulsed with joy as she held both hands against her stomach. She was carrying Wayne's child. In seven months she was going to be a mother. She could hardly wait to see Wayne and share the good news.

Loraine was tempted to go out to the taxidermy shop where Wayne was working with his dad, but she didn't want to disturb them. Besides, what she had to say was for Wayne to hear in private. He had the right to know he was going to be a father before his parents heard the news. She hoped he'd be as happy about becoming a parent as she was but was worried that he might not feel ready to take on the responsibility. With their business slacking off some in the last few weeks, he might feel that they couldn't afford to have a baby right now.

Well, it's too late for that, Loraine thought as Marge Nelson pulled up in front of the house. She paid Marge for the ride, said good-bye, and hurried up the stairs.

When Loraine entered the kitchen, she found Ada filling a cardboard box with dishes and towels. "What are you doing?" she asked.

Ada smiled. "Since Crist and I will be moving next week to the little house we found to rent, I figured I'd better get some things packed up."

"Are you getting tired of waiting for your new house to be built? Is that why you've decided to rent?"

Ada nodded. "That, and we came to the conclusion that it's time for us to leave you and Wayne alone to enjoy each other and raise your family without us in the way."

"You're not in the way," Loraine said with a shake of her head.

"That's nice of you to say, but we feel that moving into the rental will be best for all." Ada pulled out a chair at the table and sat down. "How'd your doctor's appointment go? Did you find out why you've been feeling sick to your stomach so often lately?"

Loraine's face flamed. "You know about that?"

Ada chuckled. "You can't hide things like that from a woman who's had a boppli herself."

"No, I suppose not."

"So what'd the doctor say?"

"I'd like wait and talk to Wayne about my appointment before I say anything to you and Crist," Loraine said.

"I understand. Sorry for putting you on the spot like that. Sometimes I shoot off my big mouth before I think about what I should say."

Loraine smiled. Wayne's mother had changed in the last several months. There was a day when Ada wouldn't have admitted to any of her shortcomings. She wouldn't have spoken so kindly to Loraine before, either.

"How's Crist adjusting to his new hearing aid?" Loraine asked. "I haven't had the chance to ask him about it."

"He's hearing much better these days, although there are times when I think he turns it off so he won't have to listen to me."

Loraine chuckled. Ada had even developed a sense of humor that she hadn't had before.

She took a glass from the cupboard and filled it with water. "Do you think Crist will move the taxidermy shop to one of the buildings on your property when your new house is finally finished?"

Ada shrugged. "I don't think so. Crist mentioned keeping the shop here because it's closer for Wayne. After all, he'll be taking it over someday."

"Did Wayne tell you that?"

"Tell me what?" Wayne asked as he stepped into the kitchen.

"We were just talking about the taxidermy business," Loraine said. "Your mamm mentioned you'll be taking it over someday."

"Maybe so, but there's still a lot I don't know about the business, and I hope Pop will be working with me for a long time." Wayne joined Loraine in front of the sink. "How'd your doctor's appointment go? Did you find out why you've been feeling so tired and queasy?"

Loraine glanced over at Ada, hoping she wouldn't say anything about what she suspected.

"Think I'll leave you two alone while I take something cold to drink out to your daed." Ada opened the refrigerator and removed a container of lemonade. Then she grabbed two paper cups and scurried out the door.

Loraine motioned to the table. "Let's have a seat, and I'll tell you what the doctor said."

Wayne pulled out a chair for Loraine, and after she sat down, he seated himself in the chair beside her. "You look so solemn. Please don't tell me there's something seriously wrong."

She shook her head. "No, no, I'm fine." She placed both hands on her stomach. "I'm in a family way, that's all."

Wayne's eyebrows met between the bridge of his nose, and he stared at her with a look of disbelief.

Loraine wondered if he was unhappy about becoming a father. She remembered how reluctant he had been to marry her after he'd lost his leg. Maybe he was afraid his disability would keep him from being the kind of father he felt he needed to be.

"Are you disappointed?" Her question came out as a squeak.

Wayne shook his head. "Of course not; I'm just surprised. We've only been married a few months, and I didn't think we'd be starting our family so soon." He sat motionless for several seconds, then reached for her hand. "I'm glad you're with child. I can't wait to be a father."

She leaned her head on his shoulder and breathed a sigh of relief. Now they could tell the rest of their family.

～∂ ⅏～

As Freeman sat on the Bylers' back porch with Eunice's twelve-year-old brother, he couldn't help but smile. The boy was a regular chatterbox, and he couldn't sit still for more than a few minutes. Freeman remembered Fern mentioning that she'd had trouble dealing with Richard in class. Watching the way the boy carried on, Freeman could understand why. He didn't envy Fern her job as Richard's teacher.

"Sure is hot out tonight." Richard swiped at the sweat rolling down the side of his face. "Makes me wish I could go swimmin' in our pond." He frowned. "I'll probably have to spend my whole summer workin' for Papa in the fields. Probably won't get to do much swimmin' at all."

"I'm sure you'll get some time off so you can have a little fun." Freeman leaned back in his chair, put both hands behind his head, and rested his head in his palms. He knew how important it was for a young boy to have some time to himself. Even though Freeman had enjoyed working in his uncle's bike shop when he was a teenager, he'd anxiously awaited his days off so he could fool around and have some fun.

Freeman reached into his pocket and pulled out a long, slender yellow balloon. Andrew had come by the bike shop a few days ago and taught Freeman how to make a few simple animal balloons, like a giraffe and a weiner dog.

Richard tipped his head. "Whatcha doin' with that balloon?"

"I'm gonna blow it up and make a giraffe for you."

"Oh, ya mean like Andrew Yoder does?"

Freeman nodded and stretched the balloon. "It takes a lot of air to blow one of these up, but it helps if the balloon's stretched well first."

"I'll bet I could blow the balloon up without stretchin' it."

"You think so?"

Richard bobbed his head. "Sure do."

"All right then." Freeman pulled another balloon from his pocket and handed it to Richard. "Here you go."

Freeman quickly blew up his balloon; then he sat back and waited to see what the boy would do.

Richard put the end of the balloon between his lips and blew. Nothing happened. He blew again and again until his face turned red. Finally, he stretched the balloon a few times and tried once more. The balloon still didn't inflate.

Freeman chuckled. "Looks a lot easier than it is, doesn't it?"

With a look of sheer determination, Richard blew again. Finally, the balloon inflated.

"Now watch what I do with my balloon and then try to do the same with yours." Freeman twisted a bubble for the giraffe's head. When that was done, he twisted several more bubbles, until the balloon looked like a giraffe.

"Whew! That was hard work," Richard said once his giraffe had been formed. "Sure hope Mama and Eunice have supper ready soon, 'cause I'm more hungry now than I was before!"

Freeman laughed as he nodded his head. "Me, too. I'm lookin' forward to trying out some of your sister's cooking."

"*Sie is en gudi koch,*" Richard said.

"I'm sure she is a good cook. I had some of her strawberry-rhubarb pie last week, and it was wunderbaar."

"Sure hope Mama don't fix her green bean casserole." Richard wrinkled his nose. "I don't like green beans!"

Freeman leaned closer to the boy and lowered his voice. "Can you keep a secret?"

"Sure can, but if you've got a secret, then you'd better not tell Eunice, 'cause she blabs everything she hears."

"I do not!"

Richard's face blanched, and Freeman whirled around at the sound of Eunice's shrill voice. He'd been so engrossed in his conversation with her brother that he hadn't heard her come out to the porch. He'd never heard her shout like that, either. It made him wonder what kind of a mother she would make.

Eunice gave her brother a nasty look then quickly covered it with a smile in Freeman's direction. "What was the secret you wanted to tell my little bruder?"

"It's not really a secret," Freeman said. "I was just going to say that I don't care much for green beans."

A look of relief spread across Eunice's face. "No problem. There will be no green beans on the table this evening."

Richard clapped his hands. "That's a relief!"

"I came out here to tell you that supper's almost ready." Eunice looked over at Richard. "Run out to the barn and tell Papa that we'll be ready to eat in five minutes."

The boy frowned. "Can't ya just ring the dinner bell? Freeman's been showin' me how to make an animal balloon." He held up the giraffe. "And we've also been busy gabbin'."

Eunice shot him another look. "Do as I asked or I'll tell Mama that you're being uncooperative again! You know how she feels about kinner who don't listen. If you're not careful you might get a *bletsching.*"

"Don't want no whippin', so I'll be goin' right away!" Richard jumped out of his chair, leaped off the porch, and raced for the barn.

Eunice shook her head as she lowered herself into the chair he'd been sitting on. "That ornery bruder of mine has a mind of his own."

"I think most boys his age do," Freeman said.

"Maybe so, but he's more headstrong than most boys his age." Eunice gave Freeman a heart-melting smile. "I'm glad you were able to come for supper this evening."

He returned her smile. "I hear you're a good cook, so I'm sure it was well worth the wait."

⁓ ⁓

"Are you sure you won't change your mind and come with us to Ohio for my cousin's funeral?" Mom asked when she stepped into the garden where Katie had been weeding.

Katie shook her head. "You and Dad will be gone several days, and someone needs to be here to run the stamp shop."

Mom's eyebrows furrowed. "We can close the shop if you'd like to come along. It's not like we're running a business that requires someone to be here all the time."

"No, that's okay; I'd rather stay here and keep working."

Mom squatted beside Katie. "I'm worried about you staying here by yourself."

"I'll be fine. I'm looking forward to some quiet time on my own." Katie hoped Mom believed her. She needed her folks to think she was doing okay, and she was determined to put on a brave front. Besides the fact that Katie couldn't deal with the thought of going to another funeral, she really did look forward to being alone for a few days. It would be a welcome relief not to have Mom fussing over her all the time, asking how she felt, and suggesting that she see a doctor or take some herbs.

Katie brushed the dirt from her hands and stood. "You and Dad go on to Ohio and stay as long as you need to. I'll be fine on my own while you're gone."

As Katie thought about spending the next several nights alone, a ripple of apprehension shot up her spine. *At least I hope I'll be fine.*

CHAPTER 18

Breathing the damp aroma of the moist soil where she'd been pulling weeds, Katie let her fingers trail along the stem of a flower. She lifted her head and watched as the puffy clouds shifted across the sky. Simple pleasures, she knew, were the most satisfying, and working in the garden was a simple pleasure.

An oppressive hot wind whipped against Katie's face, but she kept pulling weeds. She wanted to get this done before it was time to fix supper, and she hoped, if there was enough time before it got dark, she could take a walk out back to the pond.

The *clip-clop* of horse's hooves drew Katie's attention to the road. When a horse and buggy started up their driveway, Katie slapped her hands together to remove the dirt and stood. She figured it was someone coming to the stamp shop, and she'd need to tell them that the shop was closed for the day.

Katie was surprised when the buggy pulled up to the barn and Loraine and Ella got out.

"We heard your folks had gone to Ohio and that you'd stayed here by yourself," Ella said when Katie stepped up to Loraine's buggy.

Katie nodded. "They left this morning after breakfast."

"Ella and I decided to come by and see if there was anything you needed," Loraine said.

"That's nice of you," Katie replied, "but I'm getting along fine on my own."

Ella handed Katie a small paper sack. "I brought you some of my friendship bread. Should we go inside and have a piece?"

Katie hesitated but finally nodded. "Jah, sure. It'll be good to get out of this heat for a while."

They hurried into the house, and while Loraine and Ella took seats at the table, Katie washed her hands and then poured them each a glass of iced tea and cut Ella's bread.

They sat across from each other, talking about ordinary things like the hot, humid weather and Ella's job doing the books at her dad's wind chime business.

"There's another reason we came by," Ella said.

"What's that?" Katie asked.

Ella looked over at Loraine. "You'd better tell her. After all, it's your surprise."

Loraine's cheeks turned pink as she placed both hands against her stomach. "Wayne and I are expecting a boppli."

"A baby? When?"

"It's not due until the end of February, but we can hardly wait."

"I'm looking forward to being a second cousin." Ella reached for another piece of bread. "I think it'll be fun to have a sweet little boppli we can all fuss over."

Loraine chuckled. "Between Wayne's mamm and my mamm, we might have to stand in line to hold the boppli."

Katie sipped her iced tea as she listened to her cousins talk about the baby. She was happy for Loraine but couldn't help feeling a bit envious. She longed to be a wife and a mother, but that dream had been snatched away the day Timothy died. She'd have to spend the rest of her life enjoying other people's babies.

Loraine pushed her chair away from the table and stood. "I think we'd better go. It'll be time to start supper soon, and I should be there to help Ada."

Ella nodded. "My mamm will be expecting my help, too."

Katie followed them to the door. "Danki for coming by. It was nice to take a break from what I was doing."

As they started down the porch steps, Loraine turned to Katie and said, "I forgot to mention that I attached one of my poems to the loaf of friendship bread Ella made. Did you see it on the wrapping paper when you opened the bread?"

Katie nodded. "I didn't take time to read it, but I left it on the counter, so I'll read it later when I'm done with my weeding."

"Say, with your folks gone, maybe one evening this week we can do some stamping like we'd talked about," Ella said.

"I'll have to see how it goes," Katie replied. "If I'm real busy in the stamp shop, I may be too tired to do any stamping at the end of the day."

"Well, let us know," Loraine said.

"I will."

As Loraine and Ella headed for their buggy, Katie returned to her job in the garden. By the time she'd finished weeding, she was more than ready for a walk to the pond. She gathered up her gardening tools, put them in the shed, and headed across the field behind their house.

Soon she saw the water from the pond glistening in the sunlight, offering her a welcome relief.

Katie flopped onto the ground, leaned her head against the trunk of a tree, and closed her eyes. A cool breeze caressed her face, and she was soon asleep.

~❦~

Katie sat up with a start and looked around. It was almost dark. The sun had spread its palette of warm hues across the darkening sky, and one by one, the fireflies were beginning to appear.

Katie's stomach growled, and she realized that it was past time to fix supper. She scrambled to her feet and hurried across the field.

By the time she reached the house, the sky had darkened. She paused on the porch and peered up at the twinkling stars, enjoying a sense of calm. She hadn't felt this peaceful since she'd come home from Florida. Maybe all she'd needed was a little time alone, away from Mom's constant hovering.

When Katie's stomach rumbled again, she scurried into the

kitchen and lit the gas lantern hanging above the table. She'd just put some leftover soup in a kettle and was about to set it on the stove when she spotted the poem Loraine had written. She picked it up and read it out loud:

> *"Pleasant thoughts are being sent your way;*
> *I know that God is with you every day.*
> *Remember to thank Him for being by your side;*
> *No matter the circumstance, in Him you can abide."*

The words blurred as Katie blinked against a film of tears. Oh, how she wanted to believe that God was by her side. She felt alone and frightened much of the time.

Thump! Thump!

Katie jerked her head.

Thump! Thump! There it was again. It sounded like footsteps on the front porch.

Dad's dog howled from his dog run outside. Katie's heart pounded, and her palms grew sweaty. She hadn't heard a car or a horse and buggy come into the yard. Maybe someone had ridden in on a bike or come on foot.

She left the kitchen and headed for the living room. *Maybe it's someone wanting something from the stamp shop.*

"Who's there?" Katie called through the closed door.

No response. Nothing but the whisper of the wind.

She grasped the doorknob and slowly opened the door.

Waaa! Waaa!

Katie sucked in a startled breath and gasped. On the porch sat a wicker basket with a baby inside!

When Katie bent down, she spotted a note attached to the baby's blanket. She plucked it off and silently read it: *I can't take care of my baby, so I'm giving her to you. Her name is Susan. Please take good care of her.*

"It's a miracle," Katie murmured as she carried the baby into the house. "God's given me the thing I long for the most."

She soon discovered that whoever had put the baby in the

basket had included a few diapers, a baby bottle, and a can of formula.

Katie picked up the baby and took a seat in the rocking chair. She stroked the baby's pale, dewy skin as she rocked and hummed. Katie knew she should notify someone, but holding the precious baby girl felt so right, she couldn't even think about notifying anyone right now.

She kissed the top of the baby's downy, dark head and whispered, "I'll take care of you, baby Susan."

As Katie lay in her bed that night, she heard the downstairs clock chime twelve times and realized it was midnight. She was tired and needed to sleep but kept getting up to check on the baby, who was asleep in her basket at the foot of Katie's bed. Little Susan had only been there a few hours, but already Katie had grown attached and didn't know if she could bring herself to part with her.

The diapers and formula that had been left with the baby wouldn't last long. If Katie kept the baby awhile, she would need to get more formula, as well as some diapers and a clean set of clothes for Susan to wear.

But how am I going to go shopping? Katie wondered. *I'm scared to drive the buggy alone. Even if I were brave enough to take it out, I'd have to take the baby along, which would bring all sorts of questions from anyone I might know.* She grimaced. *I sure can't leave the baby alone by herself.*

Katie heard the crickets singing through her open window. She drew in a deep breath and tried to relax. *I'll deal with all this in the morning. Maybe by then I'll be able to think more clearly.*

❧ ❧

Freeman flexed his shoulders and reached around to rub a kink in his back. He'd been working all morning on the broken gears of a bike and still didn't have it fixed. He didn't know if it was because the gears were harder to fix than some he'd worked on or if it was simply because he couldn't stay focused. He'd been thinking about Eunice and the way she'd looked at him last night when they'd sat on her porch before supper.

She was attracted to him; he was sure of it. He was attracted to her, too. But was attraction enough to build a relationship on? Was he even ready for a relationship with Eunice?

Freeman thought about the chicken and dumplings Eunice had made, and his mouth watered just thinking about how good they had tasted. The chocolate cream pie she'd served for dessert had been equally good.

Eunice not only looks good in the face, but she's a fine cook, he told himself. *But is that reason enough to start courting her?*

Woof! Woof! Woof!

Freeman groaned. "There goes that mutt again." Ever since he'd put Penny in her dog run, all she'd done was whine and bark.

The shop door opened just then, and Wayne stepped in. "How's it going?" he asked. "Are you keeping busy enough?"

Freeman nodded. "I'm keepin' plenty busy, but things aren't goin' so well."

"What's the problem?"

Woof! Woof!

"That pup's the problem." Freeman pointed to the window. "Guess she doesn't like her dog run so well."

"You had her in here when Fern first got her, so why not bring her back in?"

"Because she's nothing but a pescht." Freeman grimaced. "She wouldn't leave me alone—kept following me around, lickin' my hand and whimpering when I didn't stop to pet her often enough."

"She's probably just lonely and needs some attention. It's hard for a pup to be taken from its mamm."

"I realize that." Freeman pulled his fingers through the ends of his hair. "Maybe I'll bring her in after you leave. No point in her

411

making a nuisance of herself while you're here. What brings you into the shop this morning, anyway? Do you need a new bike, or are you needing an old one fixed?"

Wayne shook his head. "Neither. I'm heading to the hardware store and figured I'd stop by and share some good news with you."

"What's the good news?"

"Loraine's expecting a boppli at the end of February." A wide smile stretched across Wayne's face. "Six months ago I didn't think I'd even be marrying Loraine, much less that we'd become parents so soon."

Freeman smiled. "God is good, jah?"

"He sure is. God opened my eyes so I'd realize that I could marry Loraine in spite of my handicap, and He provided a way for me to support my family by giving me a job in my daed's taxidermy shop."

"Do you like working there?"

Wayne nodded and moved closer to where Freeman knelt beside the bike. "Seems to me that you like your work, too."

"You're right. I do. Wouldn't want to do anything else for a living."

Wayne smiled. "Guess most of us who have a business to run like what we're doing or we wouldn't be doing it."

"That's true enough." Freeman reached for a pair of pliers. "My grossmudder mentioned the other day that your folks are planning to move into a small rented house soon. What made them decide to do that?"

"Guess they want to give Loraine and me some space, and since their new house isn't done yet, they're renting a place and moving out on their own." Wayne glanced at the door. "Guess I'd better get going. If I have time, I might stop by the Millers' place and check on Katie after I'm done with my errands."

"How come you need to check on Katie? Is she feeling sick again?"

"I don't think so, but she's alone at the house this week. Her folks went to Ohio for JoAnn's cousin's funeral and left Katie behind."

"I didn't know that."

"Guess Katie didn't want to go." Wayne turned and headed for the door. "I'd better head out or I'll never get to the hardware store. See you later, Freeman."

As the door clicked shut behind Wayne, Freeman made a decision. He'd close his shop at noon and go check on Katie.

※ ※

Eunice opened the door to Freeman's shop and stepped inside. It was dark, and she detected no sign of Freeman.

That's strange, she thought. *It's past one, and if he'd gone to lunch, I would think he would have put the CLOSED sign in his window.*

She glanced up at the house, thinking Freeman might have gone there to eat lunch. That made sense since the door to his shop wasn't locked.

She debated about waiting for him in the shop but decided to go up to the house instead.

When Eunice knocked on the door a few minutes later, she was greeted by Fern.

"This is a pleasant surprise." Fern motioned Eunice into the house. "Would you like a glass of lemonade or some iced tea?"

"That'd be nice." Eunice wiped the perspiration from her forehead. "It's such a warm day. A cool drink would sure hit the spot."

"What would you like—iced tea or lemonade?" Fern asked, leading the way to the kitchen.

"Whatever you're having is fine for me." Eunice glanced around the kitchen and was disappointed when she saw Fern's grandmother sitting at the table. There was no sign of Freeman.

"How are you, Sara?" Eunice asked, taking a seat beside the elderly woman.

"Doing okay. Just trying to stay cool in this hot weather we've been having." Sara fanned her face with her hand. "It's too warm for this early in the summer." She yawned. "When it's hot and sticky like this, I have a hard time sleeping at night."

"I set one of our reclining lawn chairs under the maple tree awhile ago," Fern said, placing a pitcher of iced tea on the table. "Why don't you go out there and try to take a nap, Grandma?"

"Jah, I think I will." Sara poured herself a glass of iced tea and stood. "Don't let me sleep too long, though. I need to be awake in time to help you with supper."

"If you sleep that long, I'll be sure to wake you," Fern said with a grin.

Sara shuffled out the door, and Fern took a seat at the table.

"I heard the supper you fixed for Freeman last night was real tasty." Fern bumped Eunice's arm. "I think my bruder likes you."

"Maybe it's my chocolate cream pie Freeman likes. He ate two pieces."

Fern snickered. "Well, you know what they say about the way to a man's heart."

"Guess I'll have to keep inviting Freeman over for supper. I was hoping to see if he'd be free to eat with us again one night next week." Eunice frowned. "But when I stopped at his shop to ask, he wasn't there. I figured he must have come here to have lunch."

Fern shook her head. "He told me he had an errand to run and would grab a bite to eat along the way."

"Did he say where he was going?"

"No. Just said he'd be back around one."

Eunice motioned to the clock on the far wall. "It's almost one thirty now."

"Guess his errand must have taken longer than he expected. I'm sure he'll be back soon if you want to wait."

"I'd like to, but I need to pick up some material for my mamm at the fabric shop in Shipshe. Then I may stop by the Millers' stamp shop on my way home to buy some cardstock." Eunice pushed away from the table and stood. "Would you tell Freeman that I dropped by?"

"Of course, and if you like, I'll put in a good word for you, too."

Eunice smiled. "I'd appreciate that."

❧ ❧

When Freeman pulled his horse and buggy up to the Millers' hitching rail, he noticed that there was a CLOSED sign on the door of the stamp shop. He figured Katie might be at the house having lunch, so after he tied his horse up, he headed that way.

He was surprised to discover that all the doors and windows on the house were shut. It was a hot, humid day—must be even hotter inside.

Freeman rapped on the door. When no one answered, he knocked again. "Katie, are you here? It's Freeman Bontrager."

Several seconds went by, and then the door opened slowly. Katie, looking rumpled and flushed, stepped onto the porch and closed the door partway. "If you need something from the stamp shop, it's closed today." Wearing an anxious expression, she glanced over her shoulder.

"Didn't come to get anything from the stamp shop," Freeman said. "I heard you were alone, so I came by to see if you needed anything."

"I'm fine. Danki for stopping." Katie turned, and was about to enter the house, when what sounded like a baby's cry floated out the door.

Katie's face flamed, and she quickly shut the door.

Freeman took a step forward. "Are you watching someone's boppli today?"

"Uh. . .jah." Katie dropped her gaze to the porch floor.

"Who's baby are you watching?"

Katie cleared her throat a couple of times. "It's. . .uh. . .no one you know."

"How do you know that? Does the boppli belong to someone who lives close by?"

"Uh, maybe."

"I don't get it, Katie. What's the big secret? Why won't you tell me whose boppli you're watching?"

Tears pooled in Katie's eyes, and her chin quivered slightly. "Can you keep a secret?"

415

He shrugged. "Depends on what it is."

"I've gotta go." Katie whirled around and stepped into the house. Freeman quickly followed.

"Listen, Katie," he said, "if you've got a secret—" Freeman halted when Katie bent down and picked up a baby from the basket. Most people he knew didn't keep their babies in baskets.

Katie turned to face him. "Please don't tell anyone about the boppli."

He squinted at her. "Tell 'em what? Whose baby is that, anyway?"

"She was left on our front porch last night. A note was attached to her blanket, and—" The words poured out of Katie like a leaky bucket. Her lips trembled, and she stopped talking long enough to draw in a quick breath. "Are you going to tell my folks?"

Freeman scratched the side of his head. "What are you talking about? Your folks will be home in a few days, and then you'll have to tell 'em yourself." He pointed to the baby, who was now fussing and squirming in Katie's arms. "A squalling boppli isn't something you can hide for very long."

"I. . .I know that." Katie took a seat in the rocking chair, cradling the baby in her arms.

"Have you let the sheriff know about this yet?"

"No."

"Why not?"

"The phone in our shed's not working right now."

"Then why didn't you drive over to one of your neighbors and phone him from there?"

"I don't know."

"Why don't you know?"

"I feel anxious, and I—" A shadow of fear covered Katie's words, and she looked at him with a painful openness, as though she wanted to say more but couldn't.

"Why do you feel anxious?"

Katie tensed but gave no response.

Freeman moved closer and took a seat on the sofa. "You don't have to be afraid to talk to me. I'd like to be your friend."

Katie looked at him like a frightened child. "I get so jittery whenever I ride in any vehicle, and the thought of driving the buggy myself scares me real bad."

"I'd be happy to drive you and the boppli to the sheriff's office, or even over to your neighbor's house so you can use their phone."

Katie shook her head. "I'm not ready to notify the sheriff yet. Besides, whoever left the boppli on our porch must have wanted us to have her, because they left a note asking us to take care of her."

"You can't keep what isn't yours. You've got to let the sheriff know about the boppli."

Tears welled in Katie's eyes. "I just want to keep her awhile— until right before my folks come home." She stroked the top of the baby's head. "Please don't tell anyone about the boppli."

Freeman drummed his fingers along the arm of the sofa as he mulled things over. Finally, he gave a nod. "I'll keep your secret, but only if you promise to let me take you to the sheriff before your folks get home."

"I promise."

"Now that we've got that settled, is there anything I can do for you while I'm here?"

"I don't think so. Well, maybe there is."

"What?"

"I need formula, diapers, and at least one outfit for the boppli. Would you mind going to the store to get them for me?"

Freeman's eyebrows shot up. "What kind of reaction do you think I'll get if I walk into the Kuntry Store and ask for baby things?"

Katie shook her head. "I thought you could go to one of the stores where the English mostly shop. Maybe pick one that's out of our district. That way you'll be less apt to run into anyone you know."

Freeman glanced at the clock across the room. If he took time to go the store for Katie, he'd be late getting back to his shop. If he didn't go, she'd be here alone trying to care for a baby without the things she needed.

"Okay," he said, rising to his feet. "Make me a list, and I'll get whatever you need."

"Danki. You don't know how much this means to me."

The look of gratitude Freeman saw on Katie's face was all the thanks he needed.

CHAPTER 20

There's no way I can work today and take care of the baby, Katie thought as she peered out the kitchen window at the Closed sign she'd put on the door of the stamp shop early that morning. So far only Wayne had come by, and since the baby had been sleeping, she'd stepped onto the porch to speak with him. She hoped no one else would show up and worried that, if they did come to the shop and saw the Closed sign in the window, they might stop at the house. She couldn't risk anyone else knowing about the baby.

Katie moved back to the stove, where she'd started heating some soup for lunch. She dipped the ladle into the kettle and stirred it around, then held her hand beneath the ladle and took a sip. It wasn't quite warm enough, so she turned the gas burner up a bit. Freeman should be back from the store soon, and she figured he might want something to eat, since he'd given up his lunch hour to check on her.

The sound of a buggy approaching pulled Katie's thoughts aside.

She peered out the window, but the sun's glare prevented her from seeing who it was. She wiped her hands on her apron and moved over to the door. When she opened it, she was surprised to see Loraine getting out of her buggy.

Katie quickly shut and locked the door; then she rushed to the living room, where the baby lay in her basket. The last thing Katie needed was for Loraine to find out about the baby. She'd probably insist that Katie call the sheriff.

Katie stiffened when the doorknob rattled and Loraine called, "Katie, are you here?"

Tap! Tap! Tap!

The baby stirred restlessly and gave a pathetic whimper.

Please, don't start crying. Katie bent down and scooped the baby into her arms. *Shh. . . Shh. . .* She gently patted the baby's back.

Loraine called Katie's name once more; then Katie heard footsteps tromping down the steps.

She listened until she heard the whinny of a horse followed by hoofbeats.

Whew! She's gone!

Katie placed the baby back in the basket and hurried to the kitchen. She peeked out the window and saw Loraine's buggy moving down the driveway. Just then another buggy turned in.

Katie froze. *What if it's Freeman? Can I trust him not to tell Loraine that I'm here and that there's a baby with me?*

Keeping to the right of the window so she wouldn't be seen, Katie watched Eunice get out of her buggy and go around to Loraine's buggy. They visited for several minutes; then Eunice got back in her buggy and drove off. Loraine's rig pulled out behind her.

Katie gulped in some air. She hadn't realized that she'd been holding her breath until her chest started to burn. Feeling the need for a cool drink, she grabbed a glass from the cupboard and turned on the faucet at the kitchen sink. She took a couple sips of water then held the glass against her hot cheek, wondering how much longer she could keep little Susan a secret.

❧ ❧

Just before Loraine pulled onto the road, she turned in her seat and glanced over her shoulder. It seemed odd that Katie wasn't at the stamp shop or in the house. She knew from what Katie's mother had told her mamm that Katie hardly went anywhere by herself. With Katie's folks gone, Loraine figured Katie would be working in the stamp shop most of the day.

Maybe Katie needed some things from one of our local Amish-run stores. Or maybe she hired a driver to take her shopping in Goshen.

Loraine flicked the reins to get the horse moving in the direction of home as she made a decision. Since tomorrow was an off-Sunday from church in their district, rather than visiting a neighboring church, as they often did, she would stop by and check on Katie again.

❧ ❧

Freeman glanced at the sack full of baby things sitting on the floor of his buggy. He wondered if he was doing the right thing by keeping Katie's secret. He knew they should notify the sheriff, but Katie had been extremely upset when he'd mentioned it earlier and he didn't want to upset her any more. Maybe a day or two with the baby wouldn't hurt. Katie had seemed calmer when she was holding the baby than he'd seen her in a good long while. Maybe what Katie needed was to find herself a man, get married, and have some babies of her own. There was no way she could keep the baby she'd found. The infant belonged to someone else and wasn't Katie's to keep.

As Freeman approached the Millers' place, he spotted Eunice's buggy on the other side of the road. When his buggy passed hers, she waved and motioned for him to pull over.

"Oh great," Freeman mumbled. "I don't need this right now." He hoped whatever Eunice had to say wouldn't take too long, because he needed to be on his way.

Freeman turned his horse and buggy around and stopped behind Eunice's rig, which she'd pulled onto the shoulder of the road. Then he climbed down, tied his horse to a nearby post, and went around to see what she wanted.

"I stopped by your bike shop earlier, but you weren't there," Eunice said.

"I had some errands to run."

"Are you on your way home now?"

"Uh—jah." It wasn't exactly a lie. He would be on his way home as soon as he delivered the baby things to Katie. Of course, he wasn't about to tell Eunice that.

Eunice offered Freeman one of her most pleasant smiles. "I was wondering if you'd be free to come over to our place for supper again next week."

He scratched the side of his head. "Uh, I'm not sure. Maybe."

"Is there any particular night that would work best for you?"

"I don't know. It'll depend on how much work I have in the shop. Can I let you know?"

She nodded slowly. "I hope you can make it. I really enjoy spending time with you, Freeman."

Freeman figured she was waiting for him to say that he enjoyed spending time with her, too, so he gave a quick nod and mumbled, "Same here."

"Guess I'd better let you go so you can get back to your shop." Eunice gathered up the reins. "See you soon."

As she drove away, sweat beaded on Freeman's forehead. Despite his feelings of attraction to Eunice, he didn't care for her pushy ways. If he accepted her invitation to have supper with her again, he hoped she wouldn't expect to make it a weekly event. If he did decide to start courting her, he wanted it to be his idea, not hers.

~≈ ≈~

Katie swallowed down the last of her soup and put her bowl in the sink. She glanced out the window, hoping that Freeman would pull in soon, but there wasn't a buggy in sight.

What could be taking him so long? she fretted. *Did he change his mind about helping me?* She clutched the edge of the counter and frowned. *If Freeman doesn't bring the things I need for the baby, it won't be long before I'll run out of formula and diapers. Then what'll I do?*

The baby started crying, and Katie hurried from the kitchen. She was halfway there when she heard hoofbeats coming up the driveway. She halted and tensed. How long could she keep hiding here in the house whenever a customer showed up at the stamp shop?

She rushed back to the kitchen and took a peek out the window.

A feeling of relief washed over her when she saw Freeman climb down from his buggy.

She hurried back to the living room, picked up the crying baby, and opened the door for Freeman.

"Sorry it took me so long. I got waylaid talking to Eunice not far from here." He held out a paper sack. "Where would you like me to put this?"

Katie motioned to the kitchen. "You can set it on the counter. As soon as I put the boppli down, I'll get my purse and pay you for the things you bought."

Freeman shook his head. "That's okay. I'm not worried about it."

"I had some soup earlier, and there's still some on the stove," she said. "At least let me feed you some lunch before you go."

"I appreciate the offer, but I've been gone from my shop much longer than I planned to be, so I'd better go." Freeman hurried into the kitchen to drop off the sack and returned a few seconds later. "Is it all right if I come back this evening to see how you're doing?"

Katie gave a nod, already looking forward to his return.

CHAPTER 21

As Freeman drove in his open buggy toward Katie's that evening, a warm breeze blew against his face. He was awed by the way the rim of the sun spread rosy color across the sky like a drop of dye. Whenever he saw a pretty sunset like this, he felt closer to God. Not tonight, though. Because of the promise he'd made to keep Katie's secret about the baby she'd found, he felt as if he'd erected a wall between him and God. He knew what he and Katie were doing was wrong, and he didn't like being deceitful. Yet he didn't feel that he could renege on the promise he'd made to her.

Maybe I can talk Katie into notifying the sheriff this evening, Freeman thought as the Millers' place came into view. *I need to convince her that it's the best thing to do.*

Freeman guided his horse up the driveway. As he pulled his rig up close to the Millers' barn and climbed down, their old hound dog howled from his pen. Not knowing how long he'd be staying, Freeman led his horse to the corral and put him inside. After he'd shut the gate, he sprinted for the house.

He knocked several times before Katie answered the door.

"I—I wasn't sure you'd come." She nibbled on her lower lip. "You haven't told anyone about the boppli, I hope."

Freeman shook his head. He was about to suggest that Katie should call the sheriff, but the painful expression he saw on her

424

face clutched at his heart and kept him from telling her what he thought. *Maybe later,* he thought.

"How's the boppli?" he asked.

"Fine. She's sleeping peacefully right now." Katie pointed to a couple of wicker chairs on the other end of the porch. "Would you like to have a seat?"

He nodded and sat down. Katie took the seat beside him.

Freeman leaned forward and rested his elbows on his knees. "Can you tell me about the anxiety you feel whenever you think about traveling in a car or a horse and buggy?"

Katie's hands shook as she fanned her flushed cheeks. "I don't know how to put this into words, but I get these strange sensations sometimes. They come out of nowhere when I least expect them." Her eyes glistened with tears. "I get so scared when I can't make them stop."

Freeman listened as Katie gave a detailed account of the sensations she experienced.

"The thing that scares me the most is when everything feels unreal and I have no control over what's happening to me." She dabbed at her tears.

"Have you told your folks about these feelings of unreality?" he asked.

Katie shook her head, discouragement and frustration clearly written on her face. "They know I've felt light-headed and shaky, but I haven't told them about my other symptoms." She sniffed. "I'm afraid if I tell Mom and Dad, they'll think I'm going crazy."

"Is that what you think, Katie?"

"I. . .I'm not sure. Maybe."

"You're not crazy."

"How do you know?"

"I believe what you've been having are anxiety attacks." He shifted in his chair, trying to find a comfortable position. "Some people call 'em panic attacks."

"What's that?"

"It's when a person gets a sudden attack of fear and nervousness, followed by some physical symptoms that could include sweating, a racing heart, nausea, trembling, dizziness, and a sensation of feeling as though nothing is real."

A look of surprise flashed across Katie's face, and she blinked a couple of times. "I've been having several of those symptoms."

"Panic disorders affect more people than you might realize, and everyone's symptoms aren't always the same," Freeman went on to say.

"Do. . .do you know what causes a panic attack?"

Freeman nodded. "Stressful events and major changes in a person's life are usually the cause, and panic attacks can hit a person at any time, anywhere." He tapped his fingers along the arm of the chair. "Once a panic attack strikes, the person becomes afraid and often tries to avoid situations that they think might bring on another attack."

Katie pursed her lips. "You sound like a doctor, Freeman. How do you know all that?"

Freeman drew in a breath and released it slowly. "Because I used to suffer from panic attacks."

Katie's face registered confusion as her eyebrows squeezed together. "Are you serious?"

He nodded. "When I was seven years old, I went to our cellar to get something for my mamm, and I got trapped down there because the door wouldn't open." Freeman gave his earlobe a tug. It wasn't easy to talk about this, but if it might help Katie to know that someone else had gone through something similar to what she was going through now, he would bare his soul. He wanted her to know that he understood her symptoms. "It wasn't long after I got trapped that I started having some weird symptoms that really scared me."

"What kind of symptoms?"

"Shortness of breath, pounding heart, a choking sensation. I felt like I was losing control and was gonna die."

"Did you tell anyone about it?"

"Not at first. Later—soon after we moved to Ohio—the horrible symptoms got worse, so I finally told my folks."

"What'd they say?"

"They were concerned and took me to the doctor. He ran all kinds of tests, but he couldn't find anything physically wrong with me, so he told my folks that he thought I was having anxiety attacks and suggested that I see a counselor." Freeman pulled his fingers through the back of his hair as memories from the past flooded over him. "At first Mom couldn't accept the idea that I was having emotional problems, but then she went to the library and got a book on the subject of panic attacks, which helped us understand things better."

"Did anything in the book tell how to make the panic attacks stop?" she asked.

Freeman nodded. "I tried some of the things suggested, but then my daed decided that I should see a Christian counselor someone had told him about."

"I hope you're not suggesting that I see a counselor, because I don't think I could do that."

"Why not?"

"He might expect me to talk about things I don't want to discuss." Tears trickled down Katie's cheeks. "He might put me on medication."

"Sometimes medication can help, and it's nothing to be ashamed of if you have to take it for a while." Freeman shrugged. "Then again, you may not need medication. Everyone's different, and one thing might work for one person, while something else works for another. It'll all depend on what works best for you."

"Did you take medication?"

Freeman shook his head. "Since my aunt runs a health food store in Ohio, she suggested I try a homeopathic remedy first. If that hadn't helped, my counselor probably would have suggested medication."

"Did the remedy work for you?"

He nodded. "It helped me feel calmer, and I took it until I learned how to manage the attacks."

"How'd you manage them?"

"I did some relaxation and deep-breathing exercises, and I learned how to face my fears without letting them control me."

Waaa! Waaa! Waaa!

Katie jumped up. "I'd better tend to the baby. If you're still here when I get back, we can talk about this some more."

"I'll be right here."

⟶⁕⟵

While Katie changed the baby's diaper, she thought about the things Freeman had said to her. It felt good to talk to someone about the weird sensations she'd been having. It was a relief to know that what she'd been experiencing actually had a name. If Freeman had gotten over his attacks, maybe she could, too.

When Katie finished diapering little Susan, she returned to the porch with the baby in her arms. She was relieved to see that Freeman was still there.

"I made some banana nut cake earlier today," she said. "Would you like to try some?"

"Sure, that sounds good."

"Would you mind holding the boppli while I go inside and get the cake?" Katie asked.

Freeman's eyebrows shot up. "You. . .you want me to hold that tiny little thing?"

She gave a nod. "I'll only be gone a few minutes."

"I'm not sure me holding the boppli's such a good idea. I may be able to fix bikes, but I know little or nothing about *bopplin*."

"I'm sure you'll do okay. All you have to do is hold her." Katie placed the baby in Freeman's arms and hurried into the house.

A few minutes later, she returned with two glasses of milk and some slices of banana nut cake. "Want me to take the boppli now?" she asked.

He shook his head. "We're just starting to get acquainted. Believe it or not, I kind of like holding her."

Katie smiled. A warm breeze moved with the sound of the baby's breathing, and she relaxed in her chair. She drank some milk and ate a piece of cake, savoring the sweetness.

Freeman reached for a piece of cake and popped most of it into his mouth. "Umm. . .this is appeditlich. You're a good cook, Katie."

"Danki." As Katie glanced into the yard, she saw a host of fireflies rise out of the grass, twinkling like tiny diamonds. She never got tired of watching the fireflies. When she and her older brothers were children, they used to have a contest to see who could capture the most fireflies in one of Mom's empty canning jars. One time her brother Harold had been fooling around and knocked over Katie's jar. The fireflies had escaped, of course. It had taken almost an hour to get them all out of the kitchen. Harold had gotten in trouble with Mom for being so careless.

"Sure is a nice evening, isn't it?" Freeman asked, halting Katie's musings.

She nodded. "I like watching the fireflies as they flutter all over the yard."

"Me, too."

As they watched the sun go down and the fireflies disappeared, Freeman entertained Katie with a couple of jokes.

"Do you know who the most successful physician was in the Bible?" he asked.

Katie shook her head.

"It was Job, because he had the most patience." Freeman slapped his knee. "Get it—the most patients?"

Katie laughed. "I've never heard that one before."

"I've never heard you laugh like that before," Freeman said. "At least not since we were kinner."

"Laugh like what?" she asked.

"Like a rippling brook."

"There hasn't been much for me to laugh about. Not since the accident, anyhow."

"Sometimes we need to look for things to laugh about." He looked down at the baby, asleep in his arms. "Won't be long, and this little girl will be laughin' and gurglin' for no reason at all."

"I guess you're right about that." Katie sighed. "Too bad she won't be with me then so I can see her laugh and gurgle."

The baby started to fuss, and Katie reached for her. "I think she probably needs to be fed."

Freeman handed the baby to Katie. "I probably should head

for home. I told Grandma I wouldn't be gone long, and I don't want her to worry."

A ripple of fear shot through Katie. "You didn't tell her you were coming over here, I hope."

"Jah, I did," Freeman said, "but I just said I was going to check on you since your folks were gone. I didn't say a word about the boppli you found."

Katie blew out a quick breath. "Danki for keeping my secret. . .and for everything else you've done."

"You're welcome. I'll try to drop by again tomorrow and see how you're doing." Freeman hesitated a minute as if he might have more to say, but he stepped off the porch with only a wave.

As Katie watched him head for his buggy, tears slipped out of her eyes and spilled onto the baby's head. She wiped them away with the corner of her apron. It had been such a long time since she'd felt this peaceful and content. She wished she could make the feeling last forever.

CHAPTER 22

The following morning, as Katie stepped onto the lawn, she appreciated the coolness beneath her bare feet. It had been much too warm last night, and she was glad for the chilly morning. She knew she couldn't linger outside very long. Even though it was Sunday, the animals needed to be fed, and she wanted to get that done before the baby woke up.

Katie was also glad that this was an off-Sunday from church. There was no way she could have gone to the service alone, much less with a baby she'd found on her porch. And she certainly wouldn't have left little Susan alone.

An image of Freeman popped into her head. He'd looked so natural holding the baby last night. Freeman might not realize it, but he'd make a good father. He had a gentleness about him, and Katie couldn't get over the compassion and understanding he'd shown when she'd told him about her anxiety attacks. She'd seen some of those same qualities in Timothy, although Timothy had been more spontaneous than Freeman and had always liked to tease. Freeman might not be as spontaneous, or a teaser, but he was a hard worker. A few weeks ago, Dad had stopped by Freeman's shop to buy a new headlight for his bike. When he'd gotten home, he'd mentioned how busy Freeman was and what a hard worker he seemed to be.

Katie shook herself mentally. *Why am I thinking about Freeman*

431

or comparing him to Timothy? I'm not interested in a relationship with Freeman, and I'm sure he wouldn't be interested in anyone like me.

Determined to think about something else, Katie hurriedly fed the horses. When that was done, she tended to the dog and cats, then went to the coop to take care of the chickens. She stepped out of the chicken coop just in time to see a horse and buggy rumble up the driveway. It was too late to make a run for the house, so she waited near the barn to see who it was. When the horse came to a stop, Loraine stepped down from the buggy.

"I'm surprised to see you this morning. I figured you and Wayne would be visiting a neighboring church district today," Katie said when Loraine joined her by the barn.

"Wayne woke up with a *buckleweh,* so when he decided that we should stay home today so he could rest, I figured it'd be a good time for me to check on you."

"I'm sorry to hear Wayne has a backache. Will he see the chiropractor tomorrow?"

"If he's not feeling better, probably so." Loraine motioned to the stamp shop. "I came by to see you yesterday, but the stamp shop was closed, and when I went up to the house, you didn't answer my knock."

Katie's mouth went dry. She didn't feel right about lying to her cousin, but she didn't want to admit the truth, either.

"Where'd you go, Katie? Did you have errands to run?"

"Uh, no, I didn't go anywhere yesterday."

A deep wrinkle formed above the bridge of Loraine's nose. "Were you sleeping when I knocked?"

Katie shrugged. "I. . .uh. . .may have been."

"Were you feeling grank or just tired?"

"I was tired. Didn't sleep well the night before."

"Would you like to come over to our place and stay until your folks get home?"

"I appreciate the offer, but I'm doing fine here on my own." Katie glanced toward the stamp shop. "Besides, I'll need to be here tomorrow morning, in case anyone comes to the shop." She knew she wouldn't be opening the stamp shop tomorrow morning, but she wasn't about to tell Loraine that.

"You can stay at our place tonight and then come back here in the morning."

Katie nibbled on the inside of her cheek. She needed to come up with a better reason than the one she'd offered. "You have enough people at your house right now," she said. "You don't need one more."

"Ada and Crist moved into a rental yesterday." Loraine smiled. "So it's just me and Wayne now, and we've got plenty of room."

"I'm sure you'd like some time alone with your husband since you've only been married a few months and haven't had much time to be by yourselves."

"We really wouldn't mind the company."

"I'd better stay here."

"Are you sure you'll be okay?"

Katie nodded, glancing nervously toward the house. She hoped the baby wasn't crying.

Loraine touched Katie's arm. "Am I keeping you from something?"

"I. . .uh. . .was just getting ready to head inside and fix myself some breakfast."

"That's fine. I'll go in with you. We can visit while you eat."

A sense of urgency settled over Katie. She couldn't let Loraine come inside with her. She'd find out about the baby. "I'm not good company right now." Katie massaged her forehead. "I've got a koppweh, and I need to be alone."

"If you have a headache, I'd be happy to fix you something to eat, and you can lie down and rest while I'm making it."

"No, really, I'll be fine."

Loraine hesitated a moment then finally nodded. "Guess I'll be on my way home then." She gave Katie a hug. "If you need anything while your folks are gone, be sure to call and leave us a message."

"I will, danki."

Loraine climbed into her buggy, and Katie hurried to the house.

"How's your back?" Loraine asked Wayne when she stepped onto the porch where he sat drinking a glass of orange juice.

"Doin' a little better than when I first woke up."

"That's good to hear. Do you think you'll need to see the chiropractor tomorrow morning?"

He shrugged. "Maybe so. I'll just have to wait and see how it goes. How are things with Katie?"

"I'm not sure."

"What do you mean?"

Loraine lowered herself into the chair beside him. "She turned down my offer to stay with us until her folks get home."

"How come?"

"She said she was getting along fine on her own and that she didn't want to impose." Loraine frowned. "I think she was using it as an excuse. I think something else is going on."

"Like what?"

"I don't know. Katie acted nervous and kept glancing at the house as though she was eager to get inside."

"Didn't she invite you in?"

"Huh-uh. She said she had a headache, and when I volunteered to fix her some breakfast, she said she wanted to be alone. I got the feeling that she really wanted me to go."

"Well, now that my folks have moved out, I'm enjoying the time we have to ourselves, so to tell you the truth, I'm not too upset that Katie turned down your offer."

Loraine glanced down at her stomach, which was still quite flat, and nodded. "I think that we'd better enjoy our alone time now, because once the boppli comes, things will definitely change for us."

He grinned. "Are you hoping for a *buwe* or a *maedel*?"

"I don't care whether it's a boy or a girl. I just want our boppli to be healthy."

Wayne reached for Loraine's hand and gave her fingers a gentle squeeze. "Same goes for me."

Freeman thumped the arm of his chair as he stared at the Scrabble pieces lying before him. It would be hard to make a word when he had no vowels, and he couldn't use the ones already on the board because of how they'd been placed.

"Gebscht uff?" Fern asked, reaching down to pet Penny, who'd crawled under the card table they'd set up on the back porch.

"Jah, I give up. You beat me real good this time."

"You seemed like you didn't really have your mind on the game. If you'd just concentrated harder you might have won."

"I doubt that." Freeman stood up and started down the stairs.

"Where are you going?" Fern asked. "Don't you want to play another game?"

"Not right now. Think I'll go over to the Millers' and check on Katie."

"But you were just over there last night."

"I know that, but I want to see how she's doing today."

"I doubt she's even at home."

"What makes you think that?"

"She probably went to church at a neighboring district, or she could have gone to spend the day with one of her cousins."

"Maybe so, but I'm still going over to check on her." There was no way Freeman could tell Fern that he knew Katie would be home today because she was taking care of the baby she'd found. If he told her that, he'd be breaking his promise to Katie to keep quiet about the baby, and Fern would insist that he notify the sheriff. She'd always been the kind of person who wanted to do everything just the right way, and Freeman was sure she wouldn't understand why he hadn't told her about the baby.

Fern stared at Freeman with a strange expression. "Are you starting a relationship with Katie? Is that the reason you're going over there again so soon?"

Freeman shook his head forcefully. "I'm not starting anything with Katie. I only want to be her friend."

She lifted her brows with a disbelieving look. "Are you sure about that? The look I saw on your face when you got home from Katie's last night made me think you might be falling for her."

"I'm not falling for her, and I don't have a *look*."

Fern frowned. "I'd appreciate it if you didn't speak to me in that tone of voice. I'm older than you, and I think you should show me a little respect."

"Sorry," he mumbled, "but you shouldn't worry about what I do. I'm a grown man, not a little buwe you can boss around."

"I'm not trying to boss you, but I can't help but worry when I see you hanging around someone who's bound to break your heart."

"What's that supposed to mean?"

"Everyone with eyes and ears knows that Katie has some kind of emotional problems. She hasn't been acting right since she came back from Florida."

"So Katie has a few problems. As you well know, I had some problems of my own a few years back, but I came through them okay."

"That was different. You got help for your problems."

"Katie's getting help, too."

"How do you know?"

"Because I'm trying to help her."

"How?"

"Just listening and letting her talk things through."

"What about Eunice?"

"What about her?"

"I thought you liked Eunice. When you came home after eating supper at her place the other night, you said you enjoyed being with her and might ask her out sometime soon."

"I do like Eunice, and I might ask her out, but that's got nothing to do with me helping Katie."

Deep wrinkles formed across Fern's forehead. "How do you think Eunice would feel if she knew you were going over to see Katie so often?"

"I'm sure she wouldn't have a problem with it. Besides, I've made no commitment to Eunice, so it doesn't matter what she thinks." Freeman tromped down the steps and sprinted for the buggy shed, glad to be away from Fern and all of her questions.

Woof! Woof! Woof! Penny raced after him, nipping at his heels.

Freeman halted, scooped the pup into his arms, and headed to the dog run. "Why do you have to hang around me all the time?" he mumbled. "You're supposed to be Fern's dog, not mine!"

Slurp! Slurp! Penny swiped her pink tongue across Freeman's chin.

"Yuk!" Freeman put the dog inside the run and shut the gate. "Starting tomorrow, I'm gonna start teaching you some manners!"

CHAPTER 23

Since there wasn't much traffic on the road, Freeman gave his horse the freedom to trot. It was a nice day to be out for a ride, and if he wasn't in such a hurry to get to Katie's house, he'd have taken it slower, like the open buggy up ahead was doing.

Impatient to pass, Freeman pulled his horse into the opposite lane. When he came alongside of the other rig, he realized that it belonged to Eunice.

"Seems like we've done this before," she hollered, motioning for him to pull over.

Freeman pulled his buggy in behind hers and brought the horse to a stop. Then he climbed down and tied the horse to a nearby tree. Some well-trained, docile horses might stay put, but not his.

"Where are you headed?" Eunice asked when he came around to the driver's side of her open buggy.

"I'm goin' over to Jeremy Miller's place."

"How come you're going there?"

"Katie's folks are gone, and I thought I ought to check and see how she's doing."

A look of disappointment flashed across Eunice's face, but she quickly replaced it with a hopeful smile. "Mind if I go along?"

"Huh?"

"I can follow you there, and after we've checked on Katie, we can go over to my house for a piece of pie. I made two coconut cream pies the other day, and I think you ought to try a piece."

Freeman sucked in a deep breath. He knew he'd better think of a good excuse, and real quick. He couldn't have Eunice going over to Katie's with him. The last thing Katie needed was Eunice finding out about the baby she'd found. "I. . .uh. . .shouldn't be at Katie's too long." He rubbed his chin as he mulled things over. "Tell you what—after I leave Katie's place, I'll come over to your house for a piece of pie. How's that sound?"

"Is that a promise?"

"Sure. See you soon." Freeman untied his horse and climbed back in his buggy.

Eunice looked over her shoulder and waved; then she snapped the reins and went on her way.

❧ ❧

As the day wore on, it had become hot and stuffy in the house. Katie was tempted to take the baby outside until the sun went down and it had cooled off some, but that might be too risky. Loraine had showed up unannounced, and someone else might come by.

A horse whinnied, and Arnold, their hound dog, let out a howl. Katie hurried to the kitchen window and glanced outside. She was relieved to see Freeman climbing down from his open buggy.

She opened the door and stepped out onto the porch. *"Hoscht du schunn gesse?"* she asked as he came up the steps.

He nodded. "Jah, I ate lunch a short time ago, but if you haven't eaten yet, don't let me stop you. I just came by to see how you're doing."

"I'm doing okay." Katie opened the door wider. "Why don't you come inside? You can keep me company while I feed Susan and fix myself a sandwich."

"Guess I will." Freeman entered the house and followed Katie to the kitchen. "How's the boppli doing today?" he asked.

"Just fine. She's eating well and doesn't cry much at all."

"Have you thought any more about notifying the sheriff?"

Katie shifted uneasily as she struggled to put her thoughts into words. "I know I'll have to eventually, but I want a few more days with the boppli. I promise I'll do it before my folks get home, though."

"When will that be?"

"Friday. At least that's what they said when they called to let me know they'd gotten there okay."

"Should I come by on Thursday and take you to the sheriff's?"

Katie nodded and sank into a chair at the table. She hated the thought of giving up the baby, but she'd definitely have to do it before Mom and Dad came home. In the meantime, though, she planned to enjoy every minute she had to care for little Susan.

⁓ᵉ ᵍ⁓

Eunice paced from the porch swing to the steps and back again, stopping every once in a while to scan the road out front. The air was so hot and humid she could smell the musty odor coming from the garden. She'd spent most of the afternoon waiting for Freeman and was worried that he'd changed his mind and wouldn't come at all.

The screen door squeaked, and Eunice's mother stepped out. "I set some lunch meat and cheese on the table," she said. "Why don't you come in and fix yourself a sandwich?"

Eunice shook her head. "I'm not hungry."

Mama stepped up to Eunice and placed both hands on her shoulders. "Pacing the porch and watching the road won't bring Freeman here any quicker."

"I know that." Eunice sighed. "When I met up with him earlier, he acted kind of strange."

"In what way?"

"Like he might be keeping something from me." Eunice glanced at the road again. "I wonder if he knows that Katie's pregnant and is keeping her secret."

"Now, Eunice, you don't know for sure that she's pregnant."

"Why else would she be feeling sick to her stomach and passing out in church like she did?"

"I don't know. It does seem rather odd." Mama's lips compressed. "If Katie is pregnant, do you think Freeman might be the father?"

Eunice gasped. "There's no way, Mama! Freeman's not the kind of man who would—" She sank to the porch swing with a moan. "Ach, Mama, if Freeman is the father of Katie's baby, what am I going to do?"

"Do about what?" Eunice's little brother asked, poking his head out the screen door.

"Never mind!" Eunice shook her finger at Richard. "You're too nosy for your own good, and you shouldn't be listening in on other's people's conversations."

"I was just gettin' ready to ask Mama where the mustard is, and I heard you say that you didn't know what you was gonna do." He tipped his head and looked at her with a curious expression. "Do about what, Eunice?"

"It was nothing important." Eunice flapped her hand at him. "Now go get the mustard."

"I just told ya—I don't know where it is."

"It's in the pantry," Mama said.

"I looked there already." Richard wrinkled his nose. "I think someone must've hid it."

Eunice rolled her eyes. "Don't be *lecherich*! No one hid the mustard!"

"Your sister's right," Mama said. "It's ridiculous to think that anyone would hide the mustard."

"Did you look in the refrigerator?" Eunice asked.

He bobbed his head. "It ain't there."

"Isn't," Eunice corrected. "Haven't you learned anything in school?"

"I've learned plenty!" Richard darted into the house and returned a few minutes later with a jar of mustard. "Found it!" He marched up to Eunice, opened the jar, and stuck it under her nose. "Want some?"

"No, I don't want any mustard!" Eunice's jaw clenched as she pointed to the door. "Now go fix your sandwich and quit bothering me!"

441

"Aw, you're no fun!" Richard snickered, passed the mustard under Eunice's nose one more time, and scurried into the house.

Mama sighed. "Is it any wonder that my hair's turning so gray? That buwe can be such a challenge sometimes."

Eunice grimaced. Poor Mama. Just when she'd thought she was done having children, Richard had come along. He could be a little pill at times, but Eunice knew her folks loved him just the same.

Eunice glanced anxiously toward the road. "If Freeman doesn't stop by like he promised, then I think I'll just go over to his shop tomorrow and find out what happened."

Mama's eyebrows furrowed. "Are you planning to ask if he's the father of Katie's boppli?"

Eunice sucked in her breath. "Do you think I should?"

Mama shook her head. "I wouldn't if I were you. You don't know for sure if Katie's in a family way, and if you wrongly accuse Freeman of fathering Katie's boppli, it could ruin your relationship with him."

"Hmm. . . Maybe you're right." Eunice tapped her chin a couple of times. "I don't want to lose Freeman to Katie, the way I lost Sam to my so-called friend Amanda."

"Just be nice to Freeman, and I'm sure you won't lose him." Mama gave Eunice's arm a squeeze. "I'm going inside to see if your daed wants a sandwich. If you get tired of waiting for Freeman, come join us."

"I'm already tired of waiting, so I think I'll join you now." Eunice left the swing and followed her mother inside.

~❧ ❧~

For the last hour, Katie and Freeman had been sitting on the back porch enjoying the cool breeze as the sun went down. The silence between them was as comfortable as an old pair of shoes, and Katie felt more relaxed than she had in months.

She leaned her head back and sighed. Being with Freeman lifted her spirits and gave her a sense of hope. Maybe if she learned what to do, she could overcome her panic attacks and feel normal again. Truth was, she hadn't felt normal since Timothy died.

"Sure is a peaceful evening." A single dimple showed in Freeman's left cheek as he reached over and laid his hand on Katie's arm.

His unexpected touch gave Katie goose bumps, and she shivered.

"Are you cold?" he asked, pulling his hand aside. "Should we go back inside?"

"No, I'm fine." There was no way Katie could tell Freeman how she'd felt when he'd touched her arm. He might misread what she said and think she was interested in him.

Am I? She mentally shook her head. *Of course not. I'm still in love with Timothy. I'll never love anyone else. Besides, Freeman could never love someone like me.*

"Are you hungry?" she asked, needing to get her mind on something else. "I can fix us a sandwich or heat up some leftover soup."

"That sounds good." Freeman stood. "I'll come inside and make the sandwiches while you heat the soup."

Katie smiled. Even Timothy hadn't been that kind and helpful.

❦

By the time Freeman left Katie's, it was dark outside. He hadn't meant to stay so long, but the time seemed to fly by as he got to know Katie a little better. He knew she had some serious issues she needed to deal with, which were probably the root cause of her anxiety attacks. Maybe he could do something to help Katie deal with the attacks. She had a sweet, gentle spirit; he'd seen that when he'd watched her care for the baby. She deserved to be free of the anxiety attacks and free to live a happy, peaceful life again.

Freeman gave his horse the freedom to trot. As he looked up at the star-speckled sky, he thanked God for the beautiful world He'd created. Sometimes when Freeman thought about God's majesty and power, he felt overcome with emotion. The thought that God could love the people He'd created so much that He'd sent His only Son to die for them was too much to comprehend. Freeman was thankful that he'd accepted Christ as his Savior not long ago. He wondered if Katie had done the same.

As Freeman drew closer to home, he suddenly remembered his promise to stop by Eunice's for a piece of the pie she'd baked.

It's too late for that now. She's probably gone to bed already. Guess that's what I get for staying at Katie's so long. He groaned and thumped the side of his head. "Sure hope I'm not falling for two women at once."

CHAPTER 24

For the next few days, Freeman went over to check on Katie regularly. He decided not to let Grandma or Fern know where he was going so he wouldn't arouse any suspicion. He'd gone to the store for Katie again and picked up a few more things she needed for the baby. But he'd made sure he went to stores where none of their Amish friends shopped.

The previous night when Freeman had gone to check on Katie, he'd given her a book about anxiety attacks. She hadn't seemed that interested, though. Her focus had been on the baby. He guessed he couldn't blame her for that. She'd grown attached to little Susan. Maybe after Katie turned the baby over to the sheriff, she'd be more receptive to reading the book.

Freeman grabbed the handlebars of the bike that had been brought in for repairs earlier that morning and rolled it across the room, knowing he needed to quit thinking about Katie and get back to work.

As he set the bike into position to begin working on it, Fern's puppy zipped across the room and leaped on his foot. *Woof! Woof!*

"Not now, Penny. I've got work to do, and I don't have time to be playin' with you."

Penny grabbed his shoelace in her mouth and gave it a shake.

"Knock it off!" Freeman pushed the puppy aside. "Go lay down, or I'll put you back in your dog run!"

Freeman had started working with Penny a few days earlier, but he hadn't made much progress. He figured he had his work cut out for him if he was going to get the pup fully trained, but he didn't have time to bother with her now.

Penny slunk away with her tail between her legs, and Freeman got busy on the bike. He'd just taken the tires off when the shop door opened and Eunice stepped in. Her pinched lips and deep frown let him know she was unhappy about something.

"I came by on Monday morning, but there was a CLOSED sign on your door!" She stomped up to him with her hands on her hips. He'd never seen her look so disgruntled before.

"I was away from the shop for a while."

"Where'd you go?"

"Had some errands to run."

"What kind of errands?"

"Just errands." Freeman squeezed the rim of the tire. He didn't like being quizzed like this. The look on Eunice's face reminded him of Fern whenever she found something to scold him about.

"I need to talk to you about something," Eunice said.

"Go ahead, but I'll have to keep working." Freeman gestured to the bike. "I need to have this done by two o'clock."

"That's fine." Eunice knelt on the floor beside Freeman.

Woof! Woof! Penny jumped up, zipped across the room, and leaped into Eunice's lap.

Eunice frowned and pushed the dog away. "Get away from me! You're getting dog hair on my dress!"

Penny crept back to the place where she'd been sleeping.

"I'm surprised by your reaction to the pup," Freeman said. "The last time you were here, you acted like Penny was your best friend."

Eunice's cheeks turned pink. "I like the dog well enough; I just don't want to be bothered with her now. I came here to ask you a question, not to play with your hundli."

"What do you want to know?" Freeman asked.

"The reason I came by on Monday was to ask why you didn't stop by my place on Sunday like you promised," Eunice said in a little softer tone.

446

A surge of heat cascaded up Freeman's neck. "Sorry," he mumbled. "Katie and I started talking, and I lost track of time. I meant to swing by your place yesterday and apologize for not showing up on Sunday, but I got busy here and forgot."

"Are you interested in Katie?"

"I'm interested in helping her."

"I think it's more than that. I think you're falling for her."

"Huh?"

"If you didn't have more than a passing interest in Katie, you wouldn't be going over there so much or staying so long." Eunice pursed her lips. "That tells me you must have an interest."

Freeman shook his head. "Katie and I are just friends."

"Is it because she's pregnant? Is that why you've been going over there so often?"

"What?" The heat on Freeman's neck spread quickly to his face. "Where'd you get the notion that Katie's expecting a boppli?"

Eunice folded her arms and glared at him. "It's not hard to figure out. She's been sick to her stomach, and she even fainted during church a few weeks ago."

"That's because she's been having—" Freeman clamped his mouth shut. If he told Eunice about Katie's anxiety attacks, she might blab that around. But if he didn't tell her, she might think Katie really was pregnant and start a rumor about that. It was a no-win situation.

"Katie's having what?" Eunice asked.

"Nothing."

Eunice's eyes flashed angrily. "I wasn't going to ask you this question, but I've changed my mind."

"Ask me what?"

"Are you the father of Katie's boppli?"

Another jolt of heat shot up Freeman's neck, and sweat broke out on his forehead. "You think I got Katie pregnant?"

"I don't know; I'm just asking is all."

"As I said before, Katie and I are friends, but I've never touched her in an inappropriate way, and I'm sure she's not pregnant!"

Eunice leaned away from him. "You don't have to yell."

"I can't believe you'd accuse me of such a thing. I thought we were beginning to build a relationship." He slowly shook his head. "If you really believe Katie's pregnant and that I'm the father, then there's no chance of you and me ever having a relationship!"

Eunice's face softened, and she touched his arm. "I'm sorry. If you say you're not the father, then I believe you, Freeman."

"Do you still believe Katie's in a family way?"

Eunice shrugged. "I don't know. The symptoms she has sure makes me believe she is, and today I heard someone at the health food store talking about a young woman who's pregnant, so I'm thinking it's Katie."

"I don't see how she could be. I mean, her boyfriend died eight months ago, and Katie's skinny as a twig. If she did get pregnant before Timothy died, then she'd be eight months along. Don't you think she'd be way out to here by now?" Freeman clasped his fingers together and held his hands about a foot from his stomach.

Eunice nodded. "She's obviously not that far along. I suppose she could have gotten pregnant when she was living in Florida."

"I don't think so."

"How can you be sure?"

"Because Katie's—" Freeman blew out his breath. "Can we just drop this subject? It's lecherich."

"I don't think it's ridiculous at all!" Eunice scrambled to her feet. "I can see that you're busy, so I'll leave you alone to do your work!" She hesitated a minute, then started across the room, her shoulders drooping.

Freeman knew she was upset and probably still thought he had an interest in Katie. He needed to convince her that she was wrong about that so she wouldn't spread any rumors about Katie.

"I hope you're not gonna say anything to anyone else about your suspicions that Katie's pregnant," he called after her.

She shrugged her shoulders and kept moving toward the door.

"Would you like to go out to supper with me on Friday night," he called, feeling a sense of desperation.

She halted and turned back around. "You mean it?"

"Wouldn't have asked if I didn't."

"Which restaurant?"

"Which one's your favorite?"

"I like eating at the Blue Gate, but then Das Dutchman's really good, too."

Freeman shrugged. "Either one is fine with me, so you can choose if you like."

"Let's go to the Blue Gate."

"Okay. I'll come by your place around five and pick you up."

"I'll see you on Friday then." Eunice flashed him a smile and went out the door.

Penny left her spot on the rug and ambled over to Freeman. He reached out and stroked the pup's silky ears. "Sure hope Eunice is wrong about Katie. It'd be a real shock to everyone, especially me, if she really is pregnant."

~⚹~

Like all the other days since Mom and Dad had been gone to Ohio, Katie kept the stamp shop closed and stayed in the house with the baby. Twice that morning someone had stopped at the stamp shop and then come to the house and knocked on the door. Katie hadn't answered, even though the baby was asleep. It was too risky to answer the door to anyone but Freeman.

Katie took a seat in the rocking chair and placed the sleeping baby in her lap. She nuzzled the top of the infant's head, wishing she could keep her, but knowing it was an impossible dream. There was no way Mom and Dad would let her keep the baby; they'd notify the sheriff for sure.

Tears welled in Katie's eyes as she was overcome with a sense of guilt. The precious little girl in her arms wasn't hers to keep. She'd been wrong to keep Susan this long.

I won't wait until Wednesday to notify the sheriff, she decided. *The next time Freeman comes by, I'll ask him to take me there.*

~⚹~

Eunice knocked on Sara Bontrager's door. When no one came, she peered in through the screen. "Is anybody here?"

No response.

Maybe they're upstairs or somewhere out back.

Eunice turned and was about to step off the porch when the screen door swung open and Sara stepped out. "Fern's not in the house. She's working out back," she said.

"Oh, okay. I'll go there now."

Eunice found Fern bent over a row of peas in the garden. *"Guder mariye,"* she said, stepping carefully between the rows.

Fern looked up and smiled. "Good morning, Eunice."

"Are you weeding or picking?"

"A little of both." Fern motioned to the plastic pail nearby. "I should have a nice mess of peas we can have with our supper this evening."

"The peas in our garden have all shriveled up from the hot weather we've been having," Eunice said with a shake of her head. "Keeping the garden watered is nearly a full-time job."

"I know what you mean. I usually water every other day, and sometimes that doesn't seem to be enough." Fern stopped picking and wiped her forehead with the corner of her choring apron. "Should we go up to the house and have something cold to drink? I'm more than ready for a little break."

"A cold drink sounds good to me."

Fern picked up the bucket of peas, and she and Eunice headed for the house.

"If you'd like to have a seat on the porch swing, I'll go inside and get us some iced meadow tea. Or would you rather have a glass of lemonade?"

"Meadow tea's fine for me. I like the minty taste." Eunice lowered herself to the swing.

Fern disappeared into the house and returned a few minutes later with two glasses of iced tea and a plate of oatmeal cookies. She set the cookies on the small table nearby, handed one of the glasses to Eunice, and took a seat beside her. "What brings you by this morning? Have you been out to the bike shop to see Freeman?"

Eunice nodded. "I went there to ask why he didn't come by to see me on Sunday like he promised."

Fern's brows lifted slightly. "I thought he went to see Katie. At least that's where he said he'd gone."

"Freeman passed my buggy Sunday afternoon, and we stopped and talked for a few minutes. He said he was going over to check on Katie but that he'd stop by my place for a piece of pie on his way home." Eunice frowned. "Of course, he never showed up." She took a sip of tea and held the cool glass against her forehead. "Freeman's sudden interest in Katie has me worried. One minute he acts as if he likes me, and the next minute he's running off to check on her."

Fern patted Eunice's arm in a motherly fashion. "I don't think you have anything to worry about. My bruder has always liked to fix broken things, and I believe he thinks Katie needs fixing."

"Why would he think Katie needs fixing?"

"She's been carrying around a lot of emotional baggage since the accident that took her boyfriend's life. I'm sure Freeman sees Katie as someone who needs his help, but certainly not as his aldi."

"I hope you're right, but with her being pregnant—" Eunice covered her mouth. "Oops! Guess I shouldn't have mentioned it."

Fern's eyes widened. "Are you serious?"

Eunice nodded.

"Where'd you ever get an idea like that?"

Eunice told Fern about the conversation she'd heard at the health food store awhile back and then mentioned the symptoms Katie had been having.

Fern's lips compressed into a thin, straight line. "Have you said anything to Freeman about this?"

Eunice nodded. "I mentioned it to him when I was in the bike shop awhile ago. We almost ended up in an argument when I asked if he was the father of Katie's boppli."

Fern blinked a couple of times and jerked her head. "You accused my bruder of that?"

"I did, but Freeman denied it."

Fern's head moved slowly from side to side. "If Katie's pregnant, which I'm not convinced that she is, there's no way that Freeman could be the father."

"How can you be so sure?"

"Think about it, Eunice. The only time Freeman's been alone with Katie is the few times he's stopped to check on her since her folks left for Ohio."

Eunice tapped her chin as she thought things through. "Maybe the father is someone Katie met while she was living in Florida. It's the only logical conclusion."

❧ ❧

Shortly after noon, Katie glanced out the kitchen window and spotted Freeman getting out of his buggy. She wiped her wet hands on a dish towel and hurried to the door.

"How are you doing?" Freeman asked when he entered the house a short time later. "Do you need anything else for the boppli?"

"I've still got plenty of everything." She motioned to the counter where she'd begun making a sandwich. "I was about to fix myself some lunch. If you haven't eaten yet, maybe you'd like to join me."

Freeman smiled. "I haven't eaten, so I'd be glad to join you."

Katie buttered the bread and was getting ready to cut some ham slices when she heard the baby crying in the other room. "I'll be right back. I need to see about the boppli."

Freeman stepped up to the counter. "I'll take over the sandwich making."

Katie smiled as she left the room. She couldn't get over how helpful Freeman seemed to be. Each time she was with him, she found herself longing for the one thing she wanted most but was sure she'd never have—a husband and children.

When Katie returned to the kitchen, she found two ham and cheese sandwiches sitting on the table.

"Is the boppli doing okay? I don't hear her crying anymore," Freeman said.

"She's fine. I changed her *windle*, and she went right back to sleep." Katie pulled out a chair and sat down. After they'd said their silent prayers, she looked over at Freeman and said, "I did some serious thinking this morning, and I've decided that it's time to take Susan to the sheriff."

"But you said before that your folks won't be back until the end of the week. What made you decide to see the sheriff today?"

"I'm growing attached to the boppli. It's only making me feel worse because I know I can't keep her." Katie groaned. "I should have notified the sheriff right away. Keeping the baby wasn't right, and I feel guilty about it."

"When do you want to go?"

"As soon as we're done eating, if you have the time."

"I'll make the time." Freeman looked away and dropped his gaze to the floor.

"Is something wrong? You look kind of thoughtful."

He pulled his fingers through the back of his hair and grimaced. "Something's bothering me, Katie, and I'd like to talk to you about it, but I'm not sure how."

"What is it?"

"Well, someone mentioned. . ." He cleared his throat a couple of times. "This is so hard for me to say."

"Did someone mention something about me?"

He nodded.

"Is it about the boppli?"

"Jah."

"Does someone else know that I found little Susan on the porch?"

"Uh, no. . ." Freeman blew out his breath in a puff of air that sent the napkin on his knees floating to the floor. He lifted his gaze and looked at her. "Are you in a family way, Katie?"

She sucked in her breath, and her face heated up. "Who—who told you that?"

"I'd rather not say." He looked at her with such intensity that her heart started to pound. "Is it true?"

She shook her head so hard that the ties on her covering whipped around her face. "I've never been intimate with any man, and I can't believe someone would spread such a rumor about me." Tears stung her eyes, and she nearly choked on the sob rising in her throat.

"I didn't want to believe it, Katie, but I had to ask so I could put a stop to any rumors that might be going around."

"Who told you that I'm pregnant? I need to know."

"It doesn't matter who told."

"It matters to me!"

"I shouldn't have said anything. I'm sorry I've upset you."

"So you're not going to tell me who told you I'm pregnant?"

He shook his head.

Bitter disappointment weighed Katie down. She couldn't believe Freeman wouldn't tell. With a sense of irritation, she pushed her chair aside and jumped up. "I'll get the boppli ready now. As soon as you're done with your sandwich, we can head to the sheriff's."

Freeman blinked a couple of times. "Are you sure you want to do this right now? Your face is awfully pale, and you look kind of shaky. Maybe you should eat something before we go."

"I'm not hungry!" Katie's legs wobbled as she raced from the room.

When she returned with the baby several minutes later, Freeman had finished eating and was washing the dishes.

"We're ready to go," she said in a voice barely above a whisper.

Freeman dried his hands and reached for the diaper bag Katie held under one arm. Then he opened the door and waited for Katie to go out first.

She hesitated a minute, drew in a quick breath, and plodded down the stairs.

As they were headed to Freeman's buggy, a car came up the driveway. When the back door opened, two people got out.

Katie gulped. "Oh no. It's Mom and Dad!"

CHAPTER 25

"Katie, whose boppli is that you're holding?" Mom asked as their driver pulled his car away.

Katie's mouth felt so dry she could barely swallow. She glanced over at Freeman, hoping he might say something, but he stood beside her with a blank expression.

"Katie, answer your mudder's question," Dad said sternly. "Whose boppli are you holding?"

Katie moistened her lips with the tip of her tongue. "I. . . uh. . .found her on our front porch the night you left for Ohio."

"What?" Mom's eyes widened, and Dad looked like he'd been hit over the head with a hammer.

Katie quickly explained about the note that had been attached to the baby's blanket and how she'd taken care of little Susan for the past several days.

"Did you notify the sheriff?" Dad asked.

She shook her head. "Freeman and I were—"

"I can't believe you kept the boppli all this time and didn't let the sheriff know about it!" Mom's shrill voice sent shivers up Katie's spine. "What on earth possessed you to do such a thing?"

"I was afraid to drive the buggy, and I—well, I became attached to the boppli and didn't want to give her up."

Mom glared at Katie. "What an upheaval you've caused by your immature actions!"

"Calm down, JoAnn. You're gettin' yourself all worked up." Dad touched Mom's arm. "We just need to take the boppli to the sheriff, and that'll be the end of it."

Mom shook her head forcefully. "No, it won't. What if the sheriff puts Katie in jail?"

Katie's heart pounded, and her throat constricted. The thought that she might be put in jail for keeping the baby had never entered her mind.

As if sensing her fears, Freeman touched her arm and said, "It's gonna be okay, Katie. I'm sure once we explain things to the sheriff and he sees that the boppli's unharmed, he won't—"

Dad moved closer to Freeman. "How long have you known about the boppli?"

"Since the morning after Katie found her," Freeman replied. "I came over to see if Katie was doing all right, and she told me about the boppli."

"So you've kept Katie's secret the whole time we've been gone?"

Freeman's face flamed as he nodded.

"Didn't you even think to suggest that she take the baby to the sheriff?"

"I did. Even said I'd take her myself, but she didn't feel ready to go there until now." Freeman gestured to his horse and buggy tied to the hitching rail. "We were getting ready to go to the sheriff's office in Middlebury when you and JoAnn showed up."

Dad gave his beard a tug. "You can go home now, Freeman. Katie's mamm and I will see that the baby is taken to the sheriff."

"I'd like to go along," Freeman said.

Dad shook his head. "No need for that. I'm sure you've got things you need to do at your shop."

"Besides," Mom put in, "this is *our* problem, not *yours*."

"Okay." Freeman offered Katie a sympathetic smile. "I'll be praying for you."

❧ ❧

As Freeman drove away from Katie's house, he couldn't help but feel concerned. She was not only upset with him for asking if she was pregnant, but now she was faced with going to the sheriff's, fearful that she might be arrested. She'd looked so pathetic trying to explain things to her folks. Seeing the way her eyes glistened with tears had tugged at his heartstrings.

I should have insisted that she notify the sheriff right away, Freeman berated himself. *The longer she kept the baby, the more attached she became. Now she's in trouble with her folks and could be in trouble with the sheriff.*

Freeman thumped his head a couple of times. "I'm as much to blame for all this as she is." He knew that keeping quiet about the baby was wrong, but he'd gone along with it in order to appease Katie.

Maybe I'm too softhearted for my own good. Maybe Fern's right. I might need someone to tell me what to do.

Freeman thought about the look of agony he'd seen on Katie's face when he'd asked if she was pregnant, and he wondered if she'd ever trust him again.

By the time Freeman turned onto his driveway, he'd gotten himself all worked up.

Pray for Katie. Pray for Katie.

Freeman halted his horse in front of the buggy shed and bowed his head. *Heavenly Father, please be with Katie when she goes to the sheriff's. Give the sheriff an understanding heart, and may Your will be done for Katie and the boppli she found.*

～❧❦～

Katie sank to her bed with a moan. They'd returned from the sheriff's office a short time ago, and she'd gone straight to her room. She could still see the shocked expression on the sheriff's face when she and her folks had walked into his office with little Susan. After Katie had told him the story of how she'd found the baby, he'd told them an equally surprising story. Three days ago, he'd gotten a call from an English woman who'd said that their teenage daughter had told them she'd given birth to a baby the week before while she was staying with a friend. The young woman knew she couldn't care for the baby, so she'd left it on an

Amish family's front porch. When her parents asked where the house was, she'd said it was dark outside and she couldn't remember exactly where she'd gone. She just knew it was an Amish home because she'd seen a buggy parked outside by the barn.

Katie let her head fall forward into her hands and gave in to the tears she'd been holding back all day. She was relieved that she hadn't been accused of any crime, but it had hurt to see the compassion in the sheriff's eyes when Mom said, "Our daughter suffered a tragic loss several months ago and hasn't been the same since, so she wasn't thinking clearly."

Katie squeezed her eyes tightly shut as tears trickled down her cheeks. It seemed as if every time she opened her heart to someone, she lost that person. She'd not only lost little Susan, but thanks to Freeman's accusations, she'd lost him as a friend, too. After all, why have a friend who wouldn't tell her who'd been saying she was pregnant? Who was Freeman protecting, anyway?

A knock sounded on Katie's bedroom door, pulling her thoughts aside.

"Supper's ready," Mom called.

"I'm not hungry."

"You need to eat."

"I don't want any supper. Please leave me alone."

Katie felt relieved when she heard Mom's footsteps clomping down the stairs.

She stretched out on her back, staring at the ceiling and searching for a ray of hope that would offer comfort yet finding none. Sometime later the shadows in Katie's room faded into darkness, and she fell asleep.

CHAPTER 26

As Katie hung a towel on the clothesline the following morning, a pang of regret shot through her like a knife. It was the same towel she'd used when she'd bathed little Susan. It seemed like everything she did caused her to think about the baby.

I need to keep busy and try not to think about the boppli. It'll only make me sadder if I think about how awful I felt having to give Susan up to the sheriff. Katie swallowed past the lump in her throat. *How could any mother leave her little girl on the porch of a complete stranger like that? If I had a boppli, I'd never give it up.*

Forcing her thoughts to come to a halt, Katie hurried through the process of hanging the clothes and was getting ready to head back to the stamp shop when Dad came out of the house and motioned to her.

"I was wondering if you'd do me a favor," he said when Katie joined him near the porch.

"What do you need?"

"I'd like you to go to the Kuntry Store and pick up the clock I ordered for your mamm. Since tomorrow's her birthday and we've made plans to eat supper out, I want to be sure I get the gift on time."

"Can't you pick it up?"

He shook his head. "I don't have the time for that today. I've got several customers coming to pick up windows they ordered,

459

and I need to get out to my shop right away."

"Can't your helper take care of the shop while you're gone?"

Dad shook his head. "Alvin's sick, so he won't be in today."

Katie shuffled her feet a few times and stared at the ground. The thought of driving the buggy anywhere made her feel sick to her stomach. "I. . .I don't have the time, either," she mumbled. "Mom needs my help in the stamp shop."

"You haven't been that busy all week. I'm sure your mamm can manage fine on her own for an hour or so."

"But what am I supposed to tell her? I mean, you don't want her to know about the clock you ordered, right?"

"Just tell her you're running an errand for me. She doesn't have to know where you'll be going or what you're getting."

Katie kicked at a clump of dirt with the toe of her sneaker as she mulled things over. She didn't want to go anywhere in the buggy alone. Just the thought of it made her face feel hot and her stomach churn.

Dad nudged her arm. "What's it going to be? Will you pick up the clock for me or not?"

Katie didn't want to disappoint Dad, and she wanted Mom to have her birthday present on time, so she gave a slow nod and said, "I'll go right after lunch."

Dad smiled and patted Katie's shoulder. "Danki, I appreciate it very much."

❧ ❧

Katie's arms ached as she guided her horse, Dixie, to pull the buggy slowly down the road. She clung to the reins so tightly that her fingers felt numb, but she wouldn't relax her grip. She had to keep the horse from going too fast; she had to stay focused on the road.

Things went along fairly well for a while—until they came to a bend in the road. A car whipped around them, blasting its horn. The horse whinnied, reared up, and then bolted down the road.

A shrill scream tore from Katie's throat, and she jerked on the reins.

Dixie kept running, full speed ahead.

Katie's face flooded with heat, and her heart thumped furiously; then she was hit with a wave of nausea. The dreaded feeling of unreality converged on her like a dark cloud, ready to snuff out her life. Everything seemed to be moving in slow motion. She could see things around her, but they didn't seem real. She gulped in a quick breath of air and looked around frantically, searching for something that would help her gain some control.

Katie grabbed the lever on the windshield wipers and pushed it back and forth. Anything to bring her back to reality. *Squeak! Squeak! Squeak!* The wipers scraped noisily against the front window.

She could see Dixie's rear end, but the horse seemed far away, as though Katie was seeing her in a dream. She gulped in a few more breaths and started counting. *One. . .two. . .three. . .four. . .* There, that was a little better. She could see things clearly again, although her heart still pounded and her hands felt so clammy she could barely hold on to the reins.

"*Sachde!*" Katie shouted as her senses returned. "Slowly, Dixie! Go slower, now!"

Dixie finally slowed to a trot, and then she continued with a normal walk.

Katie was tempted to turn around and head straight for home but knew she'd have to answer to Dad if she showed up without Mom's gift.

"I have to go on," she told herself. "I need to get to the store and get back home."

By the time Katie arrived at the Kuntry Store, she was shaking so badly she could hardly walk. Gritting her teeth, she tied the horse to the hitching rail and forced herself to go into the store.

"Do you have the clock my daed ordered?" Katie asked Laura Petersheim, the middle-aged Amish woman behind the counter.

"Got it right here." Laura bent down, picked up a cardboard box, and placed it on the counter.

Katie reached into her purse and handed Laura the money Dad had given her.

Laura's forehead wrinkled. "Are you all right, Katie? Your hands are shaking."

"My horse spooked on the way here, and it. . .it upset me real bad." Katie picked up the package, and was almost to the door when she bumped into Ella, who was just coming in.

Ella's forehead wrinkled as she stared at Katie. "Are you okay? Your face is nearly as pale as goat's milk."

"I'm fine." Katie pushed past Ella and hurried out the door. She'd just placed the box in the back of the buggy when Ella stepped up to her.

"Are you feeling grank?"

"No. I said I'm fine."

"I don't believe you. Tell me what's wrong."

Katie knew she would never get away from Ella if she didn't offer some sort of explanation, so she told her about the horn honking and Dixie getting spooked, but she left out the part about her panicking and the strange sensation of things being unreal that had followed.

"That must have been frightening. I wish folks wouldn't honk their horns when they pass." Ella grimaced. "I think some people get impatient with our buggies."

"You're probably right." Katie shifted uneasily, thinking about the trip home. She dreaded getting back into the buggy. What if she had another panic attack? What if she couldn't control the horse? What if the buggy flipped over or ran into a car? What if she were killed?

Ella bumped Katie's arm. "Did you hear what I said?"

"Uh, jah. You said some people get impatient with our buggies."

"That wasn't the last thing I said."

"What'd you say?"

"I was telling you about an article I read in today's newspaper. I wondered if you'd read it, too."

"What article?"

"It was about a teenage English girl who'd given birth to a boppli, kept it for a week, and then left it on some Amish family's porch." Ella slowly shook her head. "Can you imagine such a thing?"

462

Katie swallowed hard. Did Ella know that she was the one who'd found the baby? Should she say anything?

"Did you read the article?" Ella asked.

Tears welled in Katie's eyes. She figured she may as well own up to it, because the newspaper might have given her name. "I'm the one who found the boppli," she murmured.

Ella gasped. "Seriously?"

Katie nodded.

"Tell me about it."

Katie quickly related the story of how she'd found little Susan and had taken care of her for several days.

"Why'd you keep the boppli so long?"

"I was lonely with my folks gone, and the boppli kept me company. Besides, she was so sweet, and it was hard to let her go."

Ella's disapproving frown made Katie cringe. "If you were lonely, you should have let me know. You could've come over to our place to stay, or I could've stayed with you. Didn't you realize that the sheriff needed to be told about the boppli right away?"

Katie sniffed, trying to hold back her tears. "You don't have to be so judgmental. Freeman understood why I kept the baby so long. He didn't try to make me feel guilty."

Ella's eyes opened wide. "Freeman knew you had the boppli, and he kept quiet about it?"

Katie nodded once more. "He went to the store to get me some things for the boppli, and then the day Mom and Dad got home, he was going to—"

"I can't believe you'd do something like that, Katie. I'm really disappointed in you."

Katie's throat clogged, and her eyes stung with tears. "I—I need to go." She stepped up into the buggy, gathered the reins, and clucked to the horse. She wished she'd never run into Ella. She wished she hadn't agreed to pick up the clock for Dad. She wished she'd told him she had a headache, because she had one now!

~❧ ❧~

JoAnn glanced out the window of the stamp shop and frowned.

Katie had been gone a long time, and she was beginning to worry. What if something had happened to her as she was out running the errand for Jeremy? Ever since the accident Katie and her cousins had been involved in last fall, JoAnn had worried about Katie.

But for the grace of God, it could have been Katie's life that was taken that day, she thought ruefully. But the Lord had spared Katie, and even though she'd suffered from the emotional effects, she hadn't been physically hurt. At first JoAnn had thought Katie just needed some time to get over the shock of losing Timothy. But when she'd tried to get Katie to visit Timothy's grave and seen her reaction, she'd realized that Katie had a long way to go in overcoming her grief over losing Timothy. Now, with Katie having all sorts of physical and emotional problems, JoAnn was even more concerned. What if Katie never snapped out of it? What if she got worse instead of better?

The *clip-clop* of horse's hooves drew JoAnn's attention to the window again. She was relieved to see Katie climb down from her buggy. Now she could stop worrying and get back to work.

When Katie entered the stamp shop a few minutes later, JoAnn said, "That errand your daed sent you on must have taken some time."

"Jah, it did," Katie said with a nod.

"Wouldn't have anything to do with my birthday, would it?"

Katie grimaced as she rubbed her forehead. "I really can't say."

"What's wrong? Aren't you feeling well?"

"I have a koppweh. Seems like I've been getting a lot of them lately."

"I'm sorry to hear that. Why don't you go up to the house and lie down for a while?"

"Don't you need my help this afternoon?"

"Things have been slow here today, so I'm sure I can manage on my own." JoAnn smiled and patted Katie's arm. "Run along now, and take a couple of white willow bark capsules before you lie down."

Katie nodded and hurried out the door.

When Freeman looked up from the bike he'd been working on and saw Ella enter his bicycle shop with a pinched expression on her face, he knew she must be upset about something.

"What's wrong? Is there a problem with your bike?" he asked, picking up the wrench lying beside the bike's back wheel.

She shook her head.

"Do you need some part or new reflective tape?"

"No."

"What'd you come in for then?"

"I just came from the Kuntry Store, and while I was there, I saw Katie. She told me about the boppli."

Ella's word pierced Freeman like a knife, and he dropped the wrench on his toe. A shooting pain zinged up his foot, causing him to grimace. A cloud of doubt settled over him. Could Katie really be pregnant?

"What boppli are you talking about?" he rasped.

"The boppli Katie found on her porch." Ella leaned against Freeman's desk. "She said you knew about the boppli but kept quiet about it."

Freeman nodded, feeling a sense of relief. At least Ella wasn't saying that Katie was pregnant. "Katie asked me not to tell anyone about the boppli she found."

"And you agreed to that?"

"Jah, I did."

Ella's face flamed. "What in all the world were you thinking?"

"I wanted to help her, and I figured—"

"What you did was wrong! You didn't help Katie one little bit by protecting her, either." Ella eyed him critically. "I hope you're not leading Katie on."

"What's that supposed to mean?"

"Katie might think the interest you've taken in her goes deeper than friendship, and I don't want her to get hurt." Ella shook her head. "She's already been hurt enough, and I hate to see how naerfich she's become."

Freeman tapped his foot, feeling more frustrated by the minute. "I'm not leading Katie on. I just want to help her deal with her panic attacks."

Ella drew back like she'd been stung by a bee. "Katie's having panic attacks?"

A burst of heat shot up Freeman's neck and spread quickly to his cheeks. "I—I figured from what you said about Katie being nervous that she must have told you she was having panic attacks."

"I knew she was nervous and had been struggling with some health issues, but I had no idea she was having panic attacks."

Freeman groaned. "Guess I shouldn't have opened my big mouth."

"I'm glad you told me. Now that I know, maybe I can help Katie."

"Have you ever had a panic attack?"

"No."

"Then what makes you think you can help her?"

Ella blinked in rapid succession. "Well, I—"

"Unless you've had panic attacks and have been treated for them, I doubt you could help her at all."

"I care about Katie, so as soon as I have the chance, I'm going over to see her, and if there's any way I can help, I surely will."

Freeman knew he had to talk to Katie before Ella did. "Sorry, Ella, but I can't talk anymore. I've got an errand to run." He grabbed his hat and rushed out the door.

～ ❧ ～

As Freeman headed over to Katie's on his bike, he rehearsed what he was going to say. He'd been wanting to see how she was doing since she'd turned the baby over to the sheriff, and now he needed to let her know that he'd blabbed to Ella about her panic attacks. It seemed that he'd been messing up a lot lately where Katie was concerned, and he needed to make things right.

When Freeman entered the Millers' stamp shop a short time later, he spotted JoAnn stacking some scrapbook paper on one of the shelves, but he didn't see Katie anywhere.

"Is Katie here?" he asked.

"She has a headache and is up at the house resting." JoAnn frowned deeply. "With all the problems Katie's been having, it doesn't surprise me that she's been getting so many headaches lately."

Freeman nodded and shuffled his feet. "Would you mind giving Katie a message?"

"Of course."

"Would you tell her that I'm sorry for blabbing to Ella about her panic attacks?"

JoAnn tipped her head. "Ella's having panic attacks?"

"No, I'm talking about Katie."

"Katie?"

"Jah. While you and Jeremy were gone, she told me about her panic attacks."

JoAnn sank into the chair at her desk. "I. . .I had no idea!"

Freeman groaned. He couldn't believe he'd blown it again.

CHAPTER 27

The following day while Katie emptied the trash and rearranged some of their older stamps, JoAnn sat at her desk filling out an order for some supplies they needed. She had a hard time concentrating though. Ever since Freeman had come by and said that Katie was having panic attacks, JoAnn had been thinking about things and fretting over whether she should mention it to Katie or not. She'd planned to speak to Jeremy about the situation last night, but he'd gone back to work in his shop right after supper. By the time he'd come in, she'd fallen asleep. As soon as they had the opportunity to hash things over, she wanted to discuss it with Katie. If Katie really was having panic attacks, they needed to get her some help.

❦

As Eunice stood at the kitchen window waiting for Freeman to pick her up for their date, a sense of excitement welled in her soul. The fact that he'd invited her out for supper gave her hope that he might be looking for more than friendship. She certainly hoped so, because she really wanted to get married.

"Staring out the window isn't going to bring your date here any quicker," Mama said, joining Eunice at the window.

Eunice smiled. "I know, but I'm anxious for Freeman to get here."

"You don't want to appear too anxious." Mama gestured to the table. "Why don't you sit and try to relax? We can visit while you wait for Freeman."

Eunice took a seat. Mama was right; she was overanxious, but it was hard not to be when she wanted to be with Freeman so badly. She hadn't had any steady boyfriends since Sam had broken up with her two years ago. Freeman was the first man who'd showed an interest in her since they'd moved to Indiana. He was nice-looking, had a pleasant personality, and owned his own business. What more could she ask for in a husband?

"Would you like a glass of lemonade or something to snack on while you're waiting for Freeman?" Mama asked.

Eunice shook her head. "I'm holding out for the meal we'll be having at the restaurant."

"I guess that makes sense." Mama took a seat beside Eunice and picked up the newspaper that had been lying on the table. "Did you read the article in here about the English boppli that was left on an Amish woman's porch?"

"No, I didn't. What'd it say?"

"See for yourself." Mama handed the paper to Eunice.

Eunice read the article and frowned. "That's *baremlich*!"

"I think it's terrible, too."

"I wonder if the family who found the boppli is anyone we know."

"As a matter of fact, it was Katie Miller."

"Seriously?"

Mama nodded. "When I was outside the Kuntry Store yesterday, I overheard Ella and Katie talking. Katie said she'd found a boppli on her porch and had kept it several days before taking it to the sheriff."

Eunice sucked in her breath. "No wonder the stamp shop was closed when I went by there. Katie must have been in the house with the boppli."

"That's not all," Mama said. "Katie said that Freeman knew about it and had bought some baby items for her."

Anger boiled up in Eunice. "Now I know why Freeman's been

acting so secretive lately. He told me he'd gone over to check on Katie once, but I'll bet he was going over there all the time so he could play with the boppli and hold Katie's hand."

"Now you don't know that for sure."

"I know he was over at Katie's last Sunday." Eunice ground her teeth together. "At least he admitted that much."

"If I were you, I wouldn't say anything to Freeman about this," Mama cautioned.

"Why not?"

"It might make him angry if he thinks you don't trust him."

"Well, I don't trust him. Not anymore."

"Even so, if you're hoping for a relationship with Freeman, you ought to tread lightly, don't you think?"

Eunice shrugged.

"A man doesn't like it when a woman pushes too hard or becomes demanding. If you want to have a meaningful relationship with Freeman, you need to be careful about what you say and do."

"You may be right, but if I'm given the opportunity this evening, I'm going to tell Freeman that I know about the boppli Katie kept hidden." Eunice stood and rushed to the window. "I think I hear a horse and buggy coming up the driveway. I hope it's Freeman."

❧ ❧

"Are you hungry?" Freeman asked as he and Eunice were ushered to their seats at the restaurant.

She nodded. She'd been quiet on the way to the restaurant, trying to think of how to broach the subject of Katie. She knew she'd have to handle it tactfully so that Freeman didn't get upset.

"I think I'll have the baked chicken." Freeman licked his lips and pointed to the menu. "Maybe I'll have some ham to go with it. What appeals to you, Eunice?"

She studied her menu a few minutes. There were so many choices that it was hard to decide. "Guess I'll have the turkey dinner."

They placed their orders with the waitress then bowed their heads for silent prayer.

When Eunice opened her eyes, she found Freeman staring at her.

"What's wrong? Why are you looking at me like that?" she asked.

"I was just thinking what pretty blue eyes you have."

"Danki." Eunice smiled as her face warmed. Freeman had never given her such a nice compliment before. She felt like she was floating on a cloud. *Maybe he does care for me*, she thought. *He might have been helping Katie with the baby only because he felt sorry for her.*

"The weather was much cooler today than it has been lately." Eunice continued to smile at Freeman. "Maybe we'll get some rain."

He nodded. "We could probably use some, all right."

While they waited for their food, they talked about the weather, Freeman's bike shop, and Eunice's inability to find a job.

"I'm thinking I might try selling candles and scented soaps," she said. "Maybe I can get some of the women in our community to host some parties in their homes."

"That might be a good idea," he said. "Guess it's worth a try at least."

"That's what I think, too."

Soon after the waitress brought their meal, Eunice noticed Freeman staring across the room. Her gaze followed his, and heat flushed her cheeks. Katie and her folks sat at a table on the other side of the room, and Freeman was looking at Katie!

❧ ❧

Katie reached for her glass of water and glanced across the room. Her hand froze in midair when she spotted Freeman sitting at a table with Eunice. A wave of envy washed over her. Freeman and Eunice were obviously on a date.

Katie knew she had no reason to be jealous, because she had no claim on Freeman. He had every right to date Eunice or anyone else he chose, so it was useless to think about her having a relationship with Freeman. *Then why does it make me feel sad to see him with her?*

"Aren't you hungry?" Mom pointed to Katie's plate. "You've hardly touched your chicken."

"I'll eat it. I just need a drink of water right now." Katie gulped down some water and set her glass on the table. Then she cut a piece of chicken and popped it into her mouth.

"Are you enjoying your birthday supper?" Dad asked Mom.

She nodded. "Everything's real *gut*."

Katie glanced across the room again and was surprised when she saw Freeman heading their way. Eunice remained at their table with a glum expression on her face.

"How are you doing, Katie?" Freeman asked as he strode up to her side of the table.

"Okay."

"I came by the stamp shop to see you yesterday, but your mamm said you had a headache and were in the house resting. Are you feeling better now?"

"I'm fine."

"How'd things go with the sheriff?"

"He was very understanding after we explained things to him," Mom said before Katie could respond.

Dad nodded in agreement.

Freeman pulled out the empty chair next to Katie and took a seat. "I also wanted to apologize to you."

"For what?"

"For blurting out to your mamm that you've been having panic attacks. I thought your folks probably both knew by now."

Dad's face turned bright red, and he looked at Katie in disbelief. "Is this true?"

Tears sprang to Katie's eyes as she slowly nodded.

"Why didn't you tell us?"

"I. . .I was afraid to."

"Afraid of what?"

"Afraid you wouldn't understand. Afraid you might think I was crazy."

Freeman's face turned bright red. "I'm real sorry, Katie," he said. "I assumed that your folks both knew by now, and after all the things you and I discussed about your panic attacks, I'm surprised you didn't tell 'em."

Katie looked away. She felt betrayed by Freeman. She'd thought he was her friend, but he'd been saying and doing things lately to prove that he was anything but.

"Will you accept my apology?" Freeman asked.

She gave a noncommittal shrug.

Dad cleared his throat and looked at Freeman. "I think my fraa and I need to talk to Katie alone."

"Oh, okay."

Katie felt Freeman's eyes on her, but she refused to look at him. She didn't want him to see the tears burning her eyes, and she didn't want his pity. She felt relief when Freeman pushed his chair aside and stood. "I'm really sorry, Katie," he said once more. Then he walked back to the table where Eunice waited for him.

❧ ❧

On the drive home, Freeman kept berating himself. He felt like a heel for hurting Katie. If he'd known she hadn't told her folks about her panic attacks, he never would have said anything. Maybe in some ways it was good that the truth had come out. Katie's folks might insist that she get some help. Freeman wished he'd been able to help her, but they hadn't spent enough time together for that. Besides, he wasn't a trained counselor. The only thing that made him qualified to discuss Katie's panic attacks was that he'd suffered from them, too.

"What's wrong?" Eunice asked, giving Freeman's arm a light tap. "You've been awfully quiet ever since you went over to the Millers' table at the restaurant."

Freeman shrugged.

"Did Katie say something to upset you?"

"No."

"Do you wish you'd been having supper with her instead of me?"

Freeman turned to face her. " 'Course not. I just went over there

473

to find out how Katie was doing and to apologize for something I said."

"What'd you say?"

"I'd rather not talk about it."

"Does it have anything to do with the boppli she kidnapped?"

"She didn't *kidnap* the boppli; she found it on her porch." Freeman glared at Eunice. "How'd you find out about it, anyhow?"

"It was in the newspaper. I'm sure everyone in our community knows about it by now."

Freeman gripped the reins a little tighter. "I read the article in the paper, too, and it didn't give the name of the woman who found the boppli."

"Well, my mamm overheard Katie and Ella talking about it yesterday. Katie came right out and said that she was the one who found the boppli. She also said that you were in on it the whole time."

"I wasn't *in* on it. I just helped Katie out by buying some things she needed for the boppli."

"Humph! At least now I know why you've been acting so secretive and why you stayed at Katie's so late last Sunday. Are you in *lieb* with Katie?"

"No, I'm not in love with her! Now, can we just drop the subject?" Freeman's face heated up, and a trickle of sweat rolled down his forehead. He didn't like being grilled like this. It made him feel like he was a little boy.

They rode in silence the rest of the way home, and when Freeman pulled into Eunice's yard, she hopped down from the buggy and sprinted for her house without saying good-bye.

"Wish I'd never asked her out for supper," Freeman mumbled as he drove away. "Wish I'd never gone over to the Millers' table tonight and shot off my big mouth!"

By the time Freeman arrived at his house, he was quite worked up. Instead of having a pleasant evening with Eunice, he'd upset both her and Katie, and now he was upset as well.

He hurried to get the horse and buggy put away and then headed for the house.

When Freeman stepped into the living room, he halted. Fern knelt on the floor sobbing like a child.

"What's wrong?" He moved quickly toward her.

With a shaky finger, she pointed across the room to where Grandma lay on the sofa. "I. . .I think she's dead!"

CHAPTER 28

Katie groaned and shielded her eyes from the ray of sun streaming through the curtain in her bedroom window. It was time to get up and help Mom with breakfast, but she didn't want to leave her bed. On Sunday they'd gotten word that Sara Bontrager had died from a heart attack. Today was Sara's funeral. Even the thought of going sent shivers up Katie's spine. She hated funerals. Hated anything that reminded her of death.

With a weary sigh, she climbed out of bed, plodded over to the window, and stared out at the cloudless sky. *I wish I had a good excuse not to go to Sara's funeral.* She dug her nails into the soft wood of the windowsill. *Mom and Dad will expect me to go, and I don't think they'll let me stay home no matter what I say.*

Katie thought about Freeman and Fern and wondered how they were dealing with the loss of their grandmother. She thought about how horrible she'd feel if either of her grandparents died, and she remembered the agony she'd felt when Timothy died. Even though she was still angry with Freeman for telling Mom and Dad about her panic attacks, her heart went out to him today.

On the way home from Mom's birthday supper last night, Dad had quizzed Katie about the panic attacks and said he thought they needed to get her some help. Katie had responded by saying that it wasn't as bad as Freeman made it seem, and she was sure she could handle the panicky feelings on her own. Dad's response to that was, *"We'll talk about it later."*

With the news of Sara's death, Mom and Dad had other things on their minds. At least, Katie figured, they wouldn't bring up the subject of her panic attacks for a while.

～✲ ✲～

Freeman stood with his family in front of Grandma's coffin, gazing at her softly wrinkled face. They'd had a short service that morning for their closest relatives. Soon the main service would begin, with everyone else in their community invited.

"I'll miss you, Grandma," Freeman whispered, swallowing around the lump in his throat.

Freeman's mother placed her hand on his shoulder. "We'll all miss her, but we can take comfort in knowing she's in a better place."

He nodded slowly. "I. . .I still can't believe she's gone."

"Me neither." Tears ran down Fern's face, and she swiped them away with a trembling hand. "It was a shock to find her lying dead on the sofa." She sniffed and blew her nose on her hanky. "Grandma hardly ever got sick, and she rarely complained about anything. I had no idea she had a weak heart."

"None of us did," Dad said with a shake of his head.

Freeman moved away from the coffin, leaving Mom, Dad, and his brothers and sisters who'd come from Ohio and several other states to say good-bye to Grandma. Some of their church members had begun to arrive, and he knew it would soon be time to close the casket before the main service began.

～✲ ✲～

A few minutes past nine o'clock, Katie and her folks arrived at the Bontragers' place for Sara's funeral. Katie took a seat beside Ella and prayed for the strength to make it through the day.

Ella reached for Katie's hand and gave it a gentle squeeze. "Are you okay?" she whispered.

Katie nodded and forced a smile. She couldn't let on how uneasy she felt. She needed to keep her emotions under control and stay as relaxed as she could.

She glanced around the room at the people who'd come to this somber occasion—men and women dressed in black—young children and teens, all sitting quietly on their backless wooden benches.

The service began at nine thirty, with one of the ministers speaking about creation. He quoted from John 5:20–30 and from the latter portion of 1 Corinthians 15. Both passages dealt with the resurrection of the dead.

Then another minister preached for twenty minutes more, and the final message was delivered by the bishop, followed by some scriptures and a prayer.

Katie closed her eyes, determined to focus on something else. She thought about the baby she'd found on her porch. She thought about Florida and warm sunny beaches. She thought about the pond out behind their house, wishing she could be there instead of here.

Katie heard someone sobbing, and her eyes snapped open. Fern and Freeman were sitting with their family, and Fern's shoulders shook as the bishop read Sara's obituary. Then the casket was opened, and the viewing began. The home church men went into the room where Sara's body lay. The home church women followed so they could help the men sing a few songs while the people filed through.

As Katie approached Sara's casket, she choked back a sob. Sara, lying still and pale inside her plain, simple coffin, wore a peaceful look. Did that mean crossing from this life to the next had been a joyful occasion for her? Had Sara gone to heaven to be with Jesus, or had her spirit merely vanished into nothingness when it left her body?

That's how I feel whenever I'm having a panic attack, Katie thought as she made her way out of the room. *It's like I'm floating away into nothingness.* Just thinking about the experience made her tremble.

She stepped quickly out the door and drew in a couple of deep breaths.

"Are you okay?" Ella asked, coming up behind Katie. "You

look like you might pass out."

"I. . .I'm fine. Just need to breathe in some fresh air."

"It was quite stuffy in there," Ella said. "When you get that many bodies in one place, it's bound to be warm." She touched Katie's arm. "When I saw how pale and shaky you looked, I was worried that you might be having a panic attack."

Katie gulped. "Where'd you get that idea?"

"Well, after what Freeman said to me the other day—" Ella's face flamed. "Did you know he spoke to me about you?"

Katie's fingers clenched as she shook her head. "What did he say?"

"Said you've been having panic attacks, and I said I wanted to help you." Ella frowned. "But between my job helping Dad, and Mom not feeling well again, I haven't been able to speak to you until now."

Irritation welled in Katie's soul. "Freeman had no right to tell you that. I wouldn't have told him about my panic attacks if I'd known he was going to blab it all over the place."

"I'm sure he wasn't trying to be malicious. He's concerned about you, and he thought I knew."

"I never told anyone until the night I admitted it to Freeman, and now he's told you, Mom, and Dad." Katie grimaced. "Who knows who else he's told about my panic attacks?"

"Who's having panic attacks?" Loraine asked as she joined them on the lawn.

Katie dropped her gaze to the ground. "Apparently Freeman's been telling everyone, so I guess you may as well know that I've been having panic attacks."

Loraine touched Katie's arm. "Ach, I'm so sorry. Do your folks know about this?"

Katie nodded. "Freeman blabbed to them, too."

"What are you going to do?" Loraine asked.

Katie opened her mouth to reply, but Ella bumped her arm and motioned to the long line of buggies in the yard. "Looks like we're getting ready to head to the cemetery for the graveside service, so we'd better go."

❦ ❧

Katie had been holding things together fairly well until they gathered at the cemetery. When the men set the casket in place over the freshly dug hole, she struggled to keep her composure. She felt shaky and hot, as if she might pass out, and her legs felt like two sticks of rubber.

Could this be the beginning of another panic attack? Help me, Lord. Help me to stay calm and in control.

As several men who were related to Sara began to fill in her grave, Katie swayed unsteadily. With every clump of dirt that hit the coffin, she thought of Timothy and the horrible feeling she'd had in the pit of her stomach the day he was buried.

Katie gulped in a quick breath of air and squeezed her eyes shut. *Think about something else. Breathe in. Breathe out.*

When the graveside service was finally over, Katie relaxed a bit. Now they could go back to the Bontragers', eat the simple meal that had been prepared, and head for home.

❦ ❧

After the funeral dinner was over, Loraine decided to have a talk with Ella. She was worried about Katie and hoped Ella might have some idea as to what they could do to help her. She'd been watching Katie throughout the graveside service and had noticed how nervous and wobbly she seemed to be. No doubt she'd been remembering the day Timothy was buried.

Loraine didn't know much about panic attacks, other than the little bit she'd read in a magazine one day. What she'd read had made her realize that anyone dealing with panic attacks needed some kind of help.

Loraine spotted Ella talking with her sister Charlene near the barn.

"How are you feeling?" Charlene asked when Loraine walked up to them. "I hear you've been having some morning sickness."

Loraine nodded. "Some days it's worse than others, but today it hasn't been so bad."

"I hate feeling sick to my stomach." Charlene wrinkled her nose. "If I ever get married and am expecting a boppli, morning sickness is the one thing I won't like."

Ella tapped her sister's shoulder. "That's a ways off for you, and maybe by then you'll have gotten used to the idea."

Charlene shook her head. "I doubt that very much."

They engaged in small talk for a while; then Charlene left to visit some of her friends.

Loraine moved closer to Ella and lowered her voice. "I'm really worried about Katie."

"Me, too. She made it through the funeral okay, but at the graveside service, she looked so shaky I was afraid she might pass out." Ella's expression was full of compassion. "I was thinking about my bruder Raymond's funeral, so I'm sure Katie was thinking about Timothy's funeral, too."

"Can you think of anything we can do to help with her emotional problems?" Loraine asked.

Ella shrugged. "I don't know much about panic attacks, so I'm not sure we can help her get over them, but maybe we can help in some other way."

"Like what?"

"Let's think of something fun we could do. Maybe if her mind's off herself, she'll learn to relax and won't have so many panic attacks."

"We still haven't gotten together to do any stamping," Loraine said. "Let's try to do that with Katie soon."

Ella nodded. "It'll be like old times."

"Except Jolene won't be with us." Loraine sighed. "I sure do miss her."

"So do I."

"Do you think she'll ever come home?"

"Maybe for a visit, but now that she's deaf and can't teach school, I doubt she'd stay for good."

"You're probably right. Jolene was very happy being a teacher, and I'm sure she still misses her students." Ella glanced across the yard. "I haven't seen Katie in a while. Do you know if she's still here?"

Loraine shrugged. "I'm not sure."

"Let's go see if we can find her," Ella suggested. "I want to see when she might be free to do some stamping."

~•≈•~

As soon as Katie finished eating, she headed for the creek behind Sara's house. She needed to be alone for a while to think and calm down. During the meal, she'd noticed a few people staring at her. She wondered if they knew about her panic attacks. Worse yet, what if they thought she was pregnant? Oh, how she wanted to know who'd told Freeman such a thing. She wished she could have made an announcement—tell everyone she wasn't pregnant and that she wasn't the only person in the world suffering from panic attacks.

When the water finally came into view, Katie was relieved that no one else was around. She took a seat on the grass, removed her shoes, and dangled her feet in the water. Then she closed her eyes and lifted her face to the sun. She sat like that for several minutes until a twig snapped from behind.

Katie jumped.

"Sorry, I didn't mean to startle you," Freeman said, taking a seat beside her. "Are you all right?"

"I'm fine." Katie shifted uneasily. She was still upset with Freeman for revealing her secret, but the sympathy she felt for him losing his grandma overruled her anger. "I'm sorry about your grandma. She was a kind woman, and she'll be missed by everyone."

He nodded. "The house will sure seem empty with her gone."

"Will you and Fern continue to live there?"

"Jah. She left the place in both of our names."

"That's good." Katie wondered what would happen if either Freeman or Fern got married. Would one of them move out? But she didn't voice the question.

Freeman rubbed the bridge of his nose and squinted. "I hope you're not still mad at me, Katie."

"You mean for telling Ella and my folks about my panic attacks?"

He nodded. "I never would have said anything if I'd known you hadn't told 'em."

Tears burned Katie's eyes and trickled down her cheeks.

Freeman touched her arm. "Will you forgive me?"

"The truth's out now, and I guess it wouldn't be right if I didn't forgive you." She sniffed and swiped at her tears. "I. . .I'm really scared."

"Of what?"

"I'm scared that I'll never get over my panic attacks. I'm scared that people will think I'm crazy, or worse, that I'm pregnant." Katie choked on a sob.

"Don't cry, Katie. It's gonna be okay. No one else has mentioned it to me, and if they do say anything, I'll nip it right in the bud." Freeman touched her arm. "You can find things to help overcome the panic attacks, and I'll help in any way I can." He slipped his arms around her waist, and she clung to him as if her life depended on it. "It'll be okay. Just give it some time," he whispered in her ear.

~⚜~

Eunice had seen Freeman heading for the creek, so a bit later she decided to follow. She was almost there when she caught sight of him sitting on the grass, hugging Katie.

Eunice ground her teeth together. *He takes me out for supper and says nice things about my pretty eyes, and now he's hugging her! How could he do this to me? Is Freeman planning to drop me for Katie the way Sam did when Amanda started hanging around?*

She tapped her foot and continued to watch Freeman and Katie. *Maybe it was Katie who initiated the hug. I'll bet that's exactly what happened.*

Eunice whirled around and started back toward the house. *I should find a way to get even with Katie Miller. I ought to tell everyone I know about the baby Katie found, and how I'm almost sure that Katie's pregnant.*

CHAPTER 29

"Did you see how sullen Katie was on the way home from the Bontragers'?" JoAnn asked Jeremy as they sat on the porch swing together that evening.

He nodded soberly. "When I helped her into the buggy, I noticed that her eyes were red and swollen. She seemed kind of shaky, too."

"Katie didn't know Sara that well, but she seemed to take her death pretty hard."

"She takes everything hard these days. Makes me sad to see her acting so naerfich all the time." Jeremy's nose crinkled when he frowned. "Do you really think she's suffering from panic attacks?"

JoAnn shrugged. "Freeman said so, and Katie admitted it, too."

"If that's the case, don't you think we oughta get her some help?"

"What kind of help?"

"I think we should talk to the bishop about Katie's problem."

"When did you want to speak with him?"

"How about now? Since Katie went to bed soon after we got home, she's probably asleep by now and won't even know we're gone."

JoAnn nodded slowly. "I suppose you're right; we shouldn't put this off."

Katie had just slipped into her nightgown when she heard the sound of buggy wheels rolling along the driveway. She figured either they had some late evening company or Dad had decided to go someplace.

She yawned and stretched her arms over her head. The events of the day had left her feeling exhausted. She glanced at the clock on her nightstand and realized it was only eight o'clock. Even so, she was more than ready for bed.

She stood in front of the dresser and removed the pins from her hair. She was about to pick up her hairbrush when she caught sight of a pink baby bootie sticking out from under her bed.

Katie bent to pick it up, slipped it in the bottom drawer of her dresser, and sank to the edge of her bed with a moan. One more reminder of the baby she'd had to give up.

Her thoughts shifted gears as she remembered the way Freeman had hugged her today. Was it possible that he had feelings for her that went beyond friendship?

She shook her head. *I'm being stupid for even thinking he might be interested in me. What man would want to marry a woman who can't go anywhere on her own without having a panic attack? He needs someone strong and stable like Eunice, not an immature woman who's afraid of her own shadow. As long as I'm trapped in my fears, I can't live a normal life.*

It was probably for the best, Katie decided. The thought of falling in love again frightened her. If she were to love another man and lost him the way she's lost Timothy, it would be too much to bear.

"What's that hundlin got under her head?" Freeman's dad asked when he took a seat on the porch beside Freeman.

"It's one of Grandma's slippers." Freeman grunted. "Come here, Penny. Get your head off that slipper."

The puppy just lay there, staring up at him.

He reached over and pulled the slipper out from under the pup's head. "Give that to me now!" So much for trying to train the mutt to do what he said.

Penny whimpered and stared longingly at the slipper.

"I don't think she was hurtin' it any," Dad said. "She's still a pup and doesn't understand. Maybe she misses my mamm the way we all do and the slipper brings her comfort."

"Guess you're right. I might be expecting too much from the hundli." Freeman tossed the slipper back on the porch.

Penny flopped her head down on Grandma's slipper and let out a grunt.

Freeman rolled his eyes and shook his head.

The screen door creaked open just then, and Fern, Mom, and two of Freeman's other sisters stepped onto the porch.

"Mind if we join you?" Mom asked, taking a seat in the chair on the other side of Dad.

" 'Course not." Freeman motioned to the remaining folding chairs on the porch. "You'll be leaving for home soon, so we need to take every opportunity we have to visit."

They began sharing their memories about Grandma and some of the things she'd said or done over the years that had been special to them.

When the women started singing "Glory Gates," which had been one of Grandma's favorite songs from the *Heartland Hymns* book, Freeman leaned his head against the wall and closed his eyes. He thought about Grandma for a while, until an image of Katie popped into his mind. He could still see the pathetic way she'd looked at him when they'd visited at the creek. He thought about how he'd impulsively hugged her and wondered if he'd been too forward. She hadn't pulled away, and the gesture had seemed to help calm her down. Truth be told, the hug had made Freeman feel comforted, too. He hoped Katie hadn't misread his intentions, though.

Woof! Woof!

Penny leaped into Freeman's lap, and he jumped.

"What do you want, girl?" He patted the dog's head. "Are you feeling lonely without Grandma to rub your belly and stroke your ears?"

Penny whined and nuzzled Freeman's hand with her nose.

"I think that pup really likes you," Mom said with a smile.

Freeman nodded. "I've finally accepted that fact."

～ ❧ ～

The following morning as Katie and her mother worked together in the stamp shop, Katie decided to try making some cards using one of their new paper punches.

Katie felt safe here among the stamping supplies, but she wished she could work here alone without having to wait on customers.

"How's that punch working out for you?" Mom asked.

Katie sighed. "It keeps slipping, and I'm having a hard time getting it set straight on the paper."

"Just keep on trying," Mom said. "Everyone feels better when they know they've done their best."

Katie frowned. "Are you saying I'm not trying to do my best?"

"That's not what I'm saying at all." Mom stepped up to the table where Katie sat and put her hands on Katie's shoulders. "You feel so tense. If you're having that much trouble with the punch, then you ought to set it aside and do something else."

Katie pushed her chair away from the table and stood.

"Where are you going?"

"I need a drink of water." Katie hurried to the bathroom, grabbed a paper cup, and filled it with water from the sink. As she took a drink, she made the mistake of looking in the mirror. Her eyes looked bloodshot, and there were dark circles beneath them. She obviously needed to get more sleep.

When Katie stepped out of the bathroom a few minutes later, she discovered Mom standing just outside the door with her arms folded.

"Since we have no customers at the moment, I'd like to talk to you about something," Mom said.

"What about?" Katie moved back to the table and took a seat.

Mom sat in the chair on the other side of her. "Your daed and I went to see the bishop last night after you'd gone to bed."

"How come?"

"We went there to talk to him about the panic attacks you've been having."

Katie's spine stiffened. "You told the bishop about that?"

Mom nodded. "He said we should take you to see one of the counselors in the place dedicated to us Amish at the mental health clinic in Goshen."

"You want to send me away because you think I'm going crazy, don't you?"

Mom shook her head. "Of course not! We just want you to get help. You wouldn't have to stay there. You could be seen as an outpatient."

"I don't want to go. Freeman gave me a book about panic attacks, and I think I can get better on my own by reading that."

"Your daed thinks it's a good idea for you to go to the clinic, and he plans to talk to you about it this evening. I just thought it would help if I explained things to you first."

Katie leaped out of her chair, sending it crashing to the floor. "I'm not going to the clinic! And he won't talk me into it!"

CHAPTER 30

Katie raced from the stamp shop, tears streaming down her cheeks. She needed to be alone. Needed time to think. The best place to do that was at the pond, so she tore off in that direction.

It was another warm day, and the unrelenting grip of the summer heat wave made her feel as if she couldn't breathe. Farm fields had been baked brown, and everyone's gardens were withering badly. They needed some rain, and they needed it soon.

When Katie reached the pond, she removed her shoes and waded into the water, letting it cool her feet. She plodded back and forth along the shallow edge, kicking and splashing the way she'd done as a child. If only her life could be as simple and happy as it had been back then. She still couldn't believe Mom and Dad were trying to force her to go for counseling. Didn't they realize how frightening it would be for her to talk about her problems with a stranger, not to mention the stress of having to hire a driver for getting to and from the clinic?

She flopped onto the grass with a weary sigh. The sun glinted off the water, and she looked up, shielding her eyes from the glare. She tried to pray, but words wouldn't come. What was the use of praying, anyhow? It seemed that God answered so few of Katie's prayers.

I wish there was someone I could talk to about this, she thought. *Maybe I should have begged Grandma and Grandpa to let me move to*

Wisconsin with them. At least they didn't try to make me do things I didn't want to do. I was much happier living in Florida with them.

The more Katie mulled things over, the more agitated she became. It made no sense that the panic attacks came at certain times and not others. It made no sense that the symptoms she'd been experiencing were so weird and left her feeling weak and confused.

Freeman had told Katie that he'd gotten over his panic attacks, so there must be a way. *Oh Lord, please let there be a way.*

Katie thought about the book Freeman had given her about panic attacks. She'd stuck it away in her dresser and hadn't even looked at it, but since she'd mentioned it to Mom, she guessed she'd better start reading it right away. Maybe there was something in the book that would help her. If she could get over the horrible attacks on her own, maybe Mom and Dad wouldn't insist on her seeing a counselor.

Katie scrambled to her feet and started walking toward the house. She was halfway there when she spotted Loraine heading in her direction.

"I stopped by the stamp shop to see you," Loraine said when she caught up to Katie. "Your mamm said you'd gotten upset about something and had run out of the shop. I checked the house first, and when I didn't find you there, I figured you might have gone to the pond."

Katie nodded. "I needed some time alone."

"If you'd like to talk about whatever's bothering you, I'm willing to listen. In fact, that's why I'm here—so we can talk about some things."

Katie hesitated a minute then nodded. "Let's go back to the pond where we can sit and visit."

"Sounds good to me. I might even decide to go wading."

When they reached the pond, they took seats under the shade of a maple tree.

Katie leaned back on her elbows and sighed. "I envy you, Loraine."

"Why's that?"

"You're married to the man you love, and—"

"Your time will come. Someday you'll find the right man and get married."

Katie shook her head. "I found the right man once, but he was taken from me. Besides, I can't even think about getting married as long as I'm having panic attacks."

"There must be something you can do to get over them."

Katie shrugged. "Mom and Dad want me to go for counseling, but I don't want to go."

"How come?"

"The thought of riding in a car makes me naerfich enough, but the idea of having to share my innermost thoughts with a total stranger makes me feel like I could throw up." Katie groaned as she touched her cheeks. "Do you know how embarrassed I feel because of my panic attacks? I'm afraid people are looking at me, thinking what a crazy person I am."

Loraine shook her head. "No one thinks you're crazy. And you might feel like you stand out or that people are looking at you, but don't let that give you an excuse to hide your embarrassment."

"I do look for excuses," Katie admitted. "Sometimes I look for reasons not to go places or do certain things. I feel safer when I'm at home."

"I hope you don't mind, but I discussed your panic attacks with Wayne, and he gave me some information to give you."

"What kind of information?"

"Wayne's chiropractor taught him to use a tapping method on certain acupressure points to help his phantom pains after his leg was removed."

"Did it work?"

Loraine nodded. "The chiropractor told Wayne that some people have used the tapping method as a way to relax and deal with their panic attacks."

Katie nibbled on the inside of her cheek. Between the book Freeman had given her and the information about tapping, maybe she could get on top of her anxiety attacks. "Do you have the tapping information with you?" she asked.

"Jah. It's in my buggy. I'll get it for you before I leave." Loraine touched Katie's arm. "There are a couple more things I wanted to talk to you about."

"Like what?"

"Ella and I want to get together with you to do some stamping. Can we do it one evening this week after the stamp shop is closed?"

"I guess that would be okay. How about Friday?"

"Friday should work." Loraine smiled. "It's been a long time since the three of us did anything fun together. It'll be like old times."

"Uh-huh." Katie shifted her legs to a more comfortable position. "How are you feeling these days? Is your morning sickness any better?"

"Some. The tea I got at the health food store has helped."

"Maybe I should try some of that, too."

"What for?"

"I get waves of nausea sometimes."

Loraine fidgeted with the ends of her head covering ties and sucked in her lower lip. "I'm, uh, not quite sure how to say this, but when I was at the health food store today, I heard someone say something I just couldn't believe."

"What was it?"

"They said you'd planned to keep the boppli you found on your porch, and that you only gave it up because your folks came home and made you take it to the sheriff."

Katie's face felt like it was on fire. "That's not true! Freeman and I were getting ready to go to the sheriff's when Mom and Dad showed up." Her eyes narrowed. "Who said that, anyhow?"

Loraine pulled on a piece of grass and twirled it around her fingers. "I'd rather not say."

"I think I have the right to know who's spreading rumors about me, don't you?"

"Maybe you're right." Loraine sighed. "It was Eunice."

"How would she know anything about what I'd planned to do with the boppli?" Katie clenched her teeth so hard that her jaw ached.

"Maybe Freeman said something to Eunice. From what I've been told, he and Eunice are pretty good friends."

Katie knew that Freeman and Eunice were good friends, although she couldn't understand what Freeman saw in Eunice. She seemed pushy and spoiled, used to having her own way.

"Did Eunice say anything else about me?" Katie asked.

Loraine nodded slowly. "She said that you're expecting a boppli."

Katie balled her fingers into the palms of her hands. "Awhile back, Freeman told me that he'd heard the same thing, only he never said who'd been spreading that rumor." Tears welled in Katie's eyes. "I don't know what I'll do if Mom and Dad get wind of this."

Loraine clasped Katie's hand. "Please tell me it's not true."

Katie shook her head real hard. "It's a lie, plain and simple!"

"Then why were you asking me about raspberry tea, and how come you're suffering from bouts of nausea?"

"It's one of the symptoms I've been having with my panic attacks." Katie frowned. "Sometimes I feel lightheaded and like I'm not really here."

"That sounds strange. What exactly do you mean?"

"It's a strange sensation—like things aren't real."

"Ach, that's baremlich, and it must be very frightening!"

Katie nodded. "It's the most terrible, scary feeling I've ever had, and it makes me feel like I'm losing control."

"I can only imagine."

Katie leaned closer to Loraine. "You don't believe I'm pregnant, I hope."

Loraine shook her head. "I never really thought you were, but I felt that I should let you know what's being said so you didn't hear it from someone else."

"I'm glad you did."

"If I hear any more such talk, I'll make sure they know it's not true."

"Danki, I appreciate that."

The more Katie thought about things, the more agitated she

became. She jumped up and started pacing. If Freeman had told Eunice that she'd planned to keep the baby, then he wasn't her friend at all! And if Eunice was telling folks that she thought Katie was pregnant, she needed to be stopped!

CHAPTER 31

As long as you're living in this house, you'll do as I say!"

Katie cringed as Dad's fist came down hard on the table. Ever since they'd finished supper, he and Mom had been talking about the need for Katie to get help for her panic attacks. She'd tried to explain to her folks that she planned to read the article on tapping from Wayne, as well as the book Freeman had given her, but Dad said he thought it was all a bunch of hooey and insisted that she needed to go for counseling.

"You were very depressed after Timothy died," Dad said. "Now that you're having these panic attacks, your mamm and I feel that it's time for you to get some professional help."

Katie wasn't ready to accept that. She was afraid to speak with a counselor, and she was afraid to ride in a car to the clinic. It seemed as if her whole world was falling apart and she was powerless to stop it. "I. . .I don't know why you're making me do this," she said sniffling.

"It's because we love you and want to see you happy and well adjusted again." Mom slid her chair a little closer and draped her arm across Katie's shoulders. "I know you're feeling naerfich about riding in a car, so I've decided to close the stamp shop and go with you on Friday."

Katie grabbed a napkin from the basket in the center of the table and wiped her tears. Short of moving out of Mom and Dad's house, there was no way she could get out of seeing the counselor, so she may as well resign herself to the fact.

Dad pushed away from the table. "Now that we have everything settled, I'm going out to the barn."

"I guess we'd better get these dishes cleared off the table." Mom grabbed their plates and took them over to the sink.

"Do you want me to wash or dry? Katie asked, picking up the silverware and glasses.

"Whatever you prefer."

"Guess I'll wash." Katie placed the dishes into the sink and turned on the water. *At least I'm still allowed to make some choices of my own,* she thought bitterly. *I wish I'd never come home for Loraine's wedding. If I could have stayed in Florida. . .*

A knock sounded on the back door.

"I'll see who that is." Mom hurried from the room and returned with Freeman.

Katie stiffened and looked away. "What are you doing here?" she mumbled.

Mom frowned. "Is that any way to speak to your friend?"

"He isn't my friend." Katie grabbed a glass and poked the sponge inside. "Not anymore."

❧

Freeman glanced at JoAnn, wishing she'd leave so he could speak to Katie in private.

As if sensing his need, JoAnn gave Freeman a nod and quietly left the room.

"What'd you mean when you said I'm not your friend?" Freeman asked, moving closer to the sink.

Katie shrugged and kept washing the dishes.

Freeman grimaced. Something wasn't right. Katie had been friendly enough when they'd visited at the creek yesterday, even letting him hug her. Maybe that was the problem. Katie might have misunderstood his intentions and thought he was being too forward.

"I owe you an apology," he said.

Katie glanced over her shoulder. "I know you do."

"I'm sorry for hugging you yesterday. It wasn't right for me to—"

"Is that all you're sorry for?" She whirled around to face him. Her face had turned red, and her eyes held no sparkle. "Eunice has been spreading rumors about me. She told my cousin Loraine that I'd planned to keep the boppli I found, and she even told someone that she thinks I'm pregnant."

Freeman's jaw dropped. "I can't believe she would spread rumors like that."

Katie dropped the sponge into the soapy water, sending bubbles up to the ceiling. "Eunice is the one who told you I was pregnant, isn't she?"

He nodded slowly. "I didn't think any good could come from me telling you that, Katie. Figured it would only make things worse if you knew who'd told."

"You're not my friend, and neither is Eunice!" Katie's chin trembled, and her eyes filled with tears. "The next time I see her, I'm going to tell her what I think about the lies she's been telling."

"Let me talk to Eunice," Freeman was quick to say. "I'm sure I can get her to listen to reason and stop spreading such rumors."

"You can do whatever you want, but I doubt it'll do any good." Katie turned and fled the room.

Freeman froze. Then he rushed out the door. He planned to stop by Eunice's place on the way home and have a little talk with her!

⁓ ⁑ ⁓

For the last twenty minutes, Eunice had been sitting on the front porch watching the sun go down and thinking about Freeman. When she spotted his horse and buggy pull into the yard, her heart lurched. She hadn't expected to see him this soon, so this was a pleasant surprise.

She resisted the urge to run out to his buggy but remained where she was so she wouldn't appear too eager.

Freeman stepped onto the porch, scowling.

"What's wrong?" she asked. "You look *uffriehrisch*."

"I am agitated." He flopped into the chair beside her and tapped his foot. "I just came from seeing Katie. She told me something I didn't like at all."

"What was that?"

"She said you told Loraine that Katie was planning to keep the baby she found, and worse than that, you said you thought Katie might be pregnant." He frowned deeply. "You shouldn't start rumors like that—especially when they're not true."

"I wasn't trying to start a rumor. I was only repeating something I'd heard someone else say." Eunice flapped her hand like she was shooing away a pesky fly. "As I said before, Katie's symptoms make me think she's definitely pregnant."

Freeman shook his head. "I'm sure she's not, but I'm really worried about her."

"How come?"

"She's going through a rough time right now and doesn't need anything more to feel stressed about."

"What about me?" Eunice's throat constricted. "Doesn't it matter if I feel stressed out when I see Katie in your arms?"

"What?"

"I saw the two of you at the creek the day of your grossmudder's funeral, and you were hugging her." Tears welled in Eunice's eyes.

"It's not what you think. I need you to understand how things are with me and Katie."

"How are things, Freeman?"

"Katie and I are just good friends. I didn't mean anything by the hug; I was only comforting her."

"Why would she need comforting? It was you who lost your grossmudder, not Katie."

A muscle in Freeman's jaw quivered. "Katie's going through some emotional problems right now, and since I've been through something similar, I think I can help her."

Eunice tipped her head and squinted at him. "What are you talking about?"

"I used to have anxiety attacks."

Her eyebrows shot up. "Huh-uh!"

"It's true. When I was a buwe I had panic attacks just like Katie's having now."

"Katie's having panic attacks?"

He nodded. "I figured you probably knew, since you seem to know everything else."

Eunice shook her head. "How would I know that? It's not like Katie and I are best friends or anything. She doesn't confide in me the way she does you."

Freeman's face turned red, and he looked at Eunice with a pleading expression. "Maybe I shouldn't have said anything, but I wanted you to realize that Katie's not pregnant. I'm sure her symptoms are caused by the panic attacks she's been having. Please don't tell anyone what I told you about Katie."

She gave a noncommittal shrug.

"I mean it, Eunice. Katie's had enough gossip spread about her."

"What about you, Freeman?" she asked. "You wouldn't want anyone knowing you used to have panic attacks, would you?"

"It's no big secret, and there's no shame in admitting you've had some emotional problems, so if you feel the need to tell others about me, then go right ahead."

Eunice knew she'd never have Freeman for herself if she did that, so she smiled sweetly and said, "Don't worry, I won't say a word about you or Katie."

CHAPTER 32

Katie's heart pounded as she sat beside Mom in the counselor's office on Friday morning. She'd done okay on the drive here, but now, faced with talking about things she'd rather not talk about, to a man she didn't know, she felt on the verge of another panic attack.

She glanced around the room, which was decorated in a western theme. It was neat and orderly, and the leather furniture had a strong odor. She felt uncomfortable.

To make matters worse, ever since they'd come into the room, Mom had interrupted several times and kept answering most of the questions Dr. Coleman, the counselor, had asked Katie. Only a few times had Katie been able to respond herself, and that made her feel even more on edge.

"What are you feeling right now?" Dr. Coleman asked Katie.

"I. . .I'm nervous, and I hope that I'm able to get over my panic attacks, but I feel that—"

"Hope isn't a feeling, Katie. Hope is something you do." Mom looked over at the counselor and smiled. "Isn't that right, Dr. Coleman?"

"Yes, of course, but I think we should hear what your daughter has to say." He nodded at Katie. "Go ahead."

Katie twisted her fingers around the narrow ribbon ties on her head covering. It wasn't easy to talk about her feelings, especially to someone she'd just met.

Mom nudged Katie's arm. "You were saying that you hope you can get over the panic attacks."

Katie nodded. "But I have this feeling that I never will."

"Why do you think that?" Dr. Coleman asked.

"Because the strange sensation I get when I have an attack seems to be getting worse, and—and it is happening more often."

"Maybe that's because you're thinking about the panic attacks so much," Mom said. "You might be bringing the attacks on by doing that. Don't you agree, Dr. Coleman?"

"It's possible." He looked back at Katie. "Could you describe the feelings you get when you have an attack?"

Katie explained about the feelings of unreality, and how she often felt dizzy, nauseous, shaky, and like she couldn't get her breath. "I just don't understand why these feelings come on so quickly and with no warning." She sighed as she shrugged her shoulders. "Then they disappear as quickly as they came. Whenever I'm expected to go anywhere, I get scared because I'm afraid it'll happen again."

Dr. Coleman explained that everyone's symptoms are different, and that Katie's symptoms were fairly common among those who experienced panic attacks. "One of the strange things about a panic attack is that it usually subsides as quickly as it started." He tapped his pen against the edge of his desk a few times. "Feeling short of breath is a common symptom of panic attacks, but it's not dangerous."

"What causes that to happen?" Mom wanted to know.

"It happens when a person breathes from the chest and not the diaphragm." He looked at Katie again. "What is the worst thing a panic attack ever did to you, Katie?"

She shrugged. "I guess it was when I passed out in church."

"That could have been because it was such a warm day," Mom put in. "You've never fainted before, so I'm sure the heat we had that day was the cause."

"Jah, maybe so," Katie mumbled. Why did Mom think she had all the answers?

WANDA E. BRUNSTETTER

Dr. Coleman looked at Katie. "Is there anything else you'd like to tell me about your panic attacks?"

"I. . .I don't think so."

"I mentioned that panic attacks can trick a person's mind into thinking there's danger. Do you have any questions about that?" he asked.

Katie opened her mouth to respond, but Mom cut in again. "I read a little in a book about panic attacks that Katie got from one of her friends. It said that a person's supposed to decide whether the feelings they have during a panic attack are dangerous or just uncomfortable."

Dr. Coleman nodded. "That's true. Most of the feelings a person might encounter during a panic attack are uncomfortable but not dangerous. So asking yourself that question is a good way to gauge whether you should be concerned about the feelings you're having."

"That makes sense to me," Mom said. She asked Dr. Coleman a few more questions and gave her opinion on several more things.

Katie frowned. *Why is Mom talking so much and answering questions that are meant for me? It's as though Mom thinks she's the patient instead of me.*

Katie leaned her head back and let her mind wander as Mom went on and on about some other things she'd read in the book on panic attacks. *I wonder if Freeman talked to Eunice about the lies she's been telling about me. Should I say something to Mom about this, or would it be better to wait until I talk to Freeman again to find out how things went? If I tell Mom, she'll probably say more on the subject than I want her to say, and she might want to talk to Eunice herself. That would really be embarrassing.*

Dr. Coleman cleared his throat loudly and looked at his watch. "We're almost out of time for this session, but I'd like to see Katie again next Friday, and then we'll delve deeper into the mystery of panic attacks." He handed Katie a notebook. "I'd like you to make a list of the fears you have during a panic attack, and it's also a good idea if you keep a panic journal and record every panic attack you have and how you feel during the attack."

502

"We'll be here next Friday, and I'll make sure Katie does her homework," Mom said before Katie could respond. She rose from her chair and motioned for Katie to do the same.

Katie stood and started for the door, more than anxious to go. Today had gone even worse than she'd expected.

"Why don't you wait out in the waiting room, Katie?" Dr. Coleman said. "I'd like to speak with your mother for a few minutes."

Katie gave a quick nod and hurried from the room. She was glad the session was over and wished she could talk Mom into staying home next week. But that would mean she'd have to come alone, and that thought caused her stomach to plummet like a roller coaster ride.

～✸～

JoAnn seated herself and waited for Dr. Coleman to speak.

He folded his hands on his desk and leaned slightly forward. "When you bring Katie here next week, I think it would be best if you stay in the waiting room while she's in talking to me."

JoAnn bristled, and she clenched her fingers so hard that they turned numb. "How come?"

"I know you're concerned about your daughter, but if Katie's going to make any kind of progress, she needs to feel free to say what's on her mind without interruptions or distractions."

"Did I talk too much today? Is that the problem?"

"You did tend to monopolize the conversation quite a bit." He picked up his pen and tapped it against the edge of his desk. "Katie needs the freedom to express herself without fearing that you might disapprove. She needs to know that—"

"I don't disapprove! I'm just concerned about my daughter and want her to get better."

"So do I," he said with a nod. "However, I think we'll make more headway if I'm able to speak with Katie alone."

"I. . .I see. I'll do as you wish." JoAnn stood and hurried from the room. Maybe she'd made a mistake in bringing Katie here!

When she entered the waiting room, she found Katie standing

in front of the window with her head bowed and her hands folded as if she was praying.

JoAnn touched Katie's shoulder. "I'm ready to go. Our driver should be waiting for us."

Katie turned around. "What'd Dr. Coleman say to you?"

JoAnn tucked a stray hair under the side of Katie's head covering. Katie had obviously not done a good enough job with her hair this morning. "He asked if I'd wait out here during your next counseling session," she said with a huff. "I'm not the least bit happy about it, either. I'm your mudder, and it's my place to be with you when you're talking to him."

"I think you should stay home next week, Mom."

"What?"

"It made me feel naerfich having you here today. I felt like I couldn't really say what was on my mind."

"I'll do as Dr. Coleman suggested and wait out here so you'll be free to say whatever you want to him, but I won't stay home."

Katie dropped her gaze to the floor. "You need to take care of the store."

"That's not as important as being with you. I'm sure our customers will understand if the stamp shop is closed for a few hours. Besides, we haven't been that busy lately."

Katie's jaw clenched, and a muscle in her cheek quivered. "I. . .I'd rather come here alone."

JoAnn was tempted to argue further, but she didn't want to make a scene in front of the other people waiting in the room. She slipped her arm around Katie's waist and whispered, "We can talk about this later."

≈❦❧≈

When Katie opened the door to the stamp shop that afternoon, she discovered an envelope with her name on it.

"Who's that from?" Mom asked, following Katie into the shop.

"I don't know." Katie tore open the envelope, slipped behind the counter, and silently read the note:

Dear Katie,

I spoke with Eunice the other day, and she said she wasn't trying to start a rumor about you and that she won't tell anyone else. I hope you believe that I didn't betray your trust. I'm really sorry if I said anything to upset you. Seems like I've been opening my big mouth a lot lately, saying things that get me in trouble.

Freeman

Mom stepped up to Katie and nudged her arm. "Well, who's it from?"

"Freeman Bontrager."

"What'd he have to say?"

"He. . .uh. . .just wanted to explain something to me." Katie quickly slipped the note into her purse, hoping Mom wouldn't press for details. She was relieved when Mom said she had some things to do in the house and left the shop.

Katie leaned against the counter and folded her arms. *Guess I'd better accept Freeman's apology. He did sound sorry, and it's the right thing to do. I just hope Eunice stops gossiping about me.*

The bell on the shop door jingled, and Ella and Loraine stepped in. "We came a little early to look around before we do our stamping together," Ella said.

Katie's face warmed. Thanks to the stress of the day, she'd forgotten about their plans.

"I invited Eunice to join us this evening, but she's selling candles and scented soaps now, and she said she has a party to do somewhere out of our district," Ella explained.

"Ada's hosting one of Eunice's candle parties next week," Loraine said. "Would either of you like to go?"

Ella smiled. "I might go and buy a few candles. How about you, Katie?"

Katie shook her head. "I'm not that interested in candles or scented soaps." She motioned to the worktable. "Since I have no customers at the moment and Mom's up at the house, I guess we could start stamping now." Katie was glad Eunice hadn't been able to come, and she sure didn't want to go to one of her parties.

"I've been looking forward to this all day." Ella pulled out a chair and sat down. "We have several birthdays coming up in our family, so it'll be fun to make a few cards."

Loraine reached for the stack of cardstock in the center of the table. "I think I'll make Ada and Crist a card to go with the gift Wayne and I are giving them for their new house. I might include one of my poems on the inside of the card."

"What'd you get them?" Katie asked.

"Wayne made a coffee table. He says he's not an expert carpenter, but I think he did a good job. I'm sure his folks will be real pleased."

"Due to our current economic situation, a lot of people are making more things rather than buying store-bought items," Ella said. "My folks have decided to stay home for more meals instead of eating out so often."

"Guess everyone needs to do their part to help out when money's tight," Loraine said.

"That's true," Ella agreed. "Charlene and I have been helping our mamm put up a lot more produce this summer. It'll save us a lot of money at the grocery store come winter." She looked over at Loraine. "Changing the subject, I've been wondering how Wayne's three-legged sheep is getting along."

"Tripod's doing real well. The critter still follows Wayne all over the place like she's his pet."

"I guess she is," Ella said with a nod.

"Listen to us going on and on about so many unimportant things." Loraine leaned closer to Katie and tapped her arm. "Didn't you have a counseling session today?"

Katie nodded.

"How'd it go?"

"Okay." Katie hoped Loraine wouldn't question her about what had been said during her session with Dr. Coleman. She didn't want to talk about it. She just wanted to spend a few hours having some fun.

For the next half hour, Katie worked quietly on some cards

while she listened to Ella and Loraine visit. Every once in a while, she left the table to wait on a customer.

Soon after Katie took her seat again, she noticed Loraine clenching her teeth as she clutched her stomach.

"Are you okay?" Ella asked.

"I've been having a few stomach cramps off and on all day. They weren't too bad at first, but they seem to be getting worse." Loraine grimaced as she pushed away from the table and stood. "I think I'd better use the bathroom."

When Loraine left the room, Katie looked over at Ella and said, "Sure hope it's nothing serious."

"It's probably indigestion. My mamm had that a lot when she was carrying Charlene."

A few minutes later, Loraine returned, looking pale and shaken. "I. . .I need to go home. I'm bleeding!"

CHAPTER 33

Katie's chair squeaked as she took a seat at the kitchen table. She had no appetite for food. How could she think about eating supper when she was worried about Loraine? They hadn't heard anything for several hours—not since Loraine had been taken to the hospital.

"Let's pray," Dad said after he'd taken his seat at the head of the table.

Katie bowed her head and closed her eyes. Searching for the right words, she silently prayed, *Please, God, don't let Loraine lose her boppli. She and Wayne have been through a lot, and they deserve to be happy. Take away my fears, and help me with my panic attacks. And please bring all the gossiping about me to an end.*

Dad rustled his napkin, and Katie's eyes snapped open. Mom took a spoonful of potato salad and handed the bowl to Katie. Katie stared at it a few seconds then handed it to Dad.

Mom nudged Katie's arm. "Aren't you having any potato salad? I made it with plenty of mustard, just the way you like."

Katie passed the plate of ham to Dad as she shook her head. "I'm too worried about Loraine to think about food."

"You don't have to *think* about food; just eat it." The lines running across Dad's forehead deepened. "You eat like a bird, and you're way too skinny."

"Your daed's right," Mom agreed. "You'll end up sick if you

508

don't start eating more."

Katie's skin prickled. She was tired of Mom and Dad badgering her all the time.

"Have some of this." Mom plopped a huge spoonful of coleslaw in the middle of Katie's plate.

"I'm not hungry!" Katie leaped out of her chair and was almost to the stairs leading to the second floor when a knock sounded on the back door. She opened the door. The bishop stood on the porch, and he wasn't smiling.

"Mom and Dad are in the kitchen," Katie said.

He shook his head. "Didn't come to see them. Came to see you."

"Oh? What about?"

"There's a rumor going around that you're expecting a boppli. Is it true?"

"Is what true?" Dad questioned as he came to the door. "What's this all about?"

"Can I come in?" asked the bishop.

Dad nodded and led the way to the kitchen. Katie followed, her legs trembling like a newborn colt. Eunice had obviously taken her story to the bishop, probably hoping to make Katie look bad for trying to hide her pregnancy from everyone.

"Now what's this all about?" Dad asked again.

The bishop pulled out a chair at the table and sat down. "I'm not here to be judgmental, but there's a rumor going around that your daughter's in a family way. I came to find out whether it's true or not."

"Of course it's not true," Mom said with a quick shake of her head. "I don't know why anyone would think Katie's pregnant."

Dad touched Mom's shoulder. "Now don't get yourself all worked up, JoAnn. As the bishop said, it's only a rumor." He turned to face Katie. "Tell the bishop what he needs to hear."

"It's not true," Katie said, slowly shaking her head. "Eunice made it up, but Freeman said she wasn't going to keep the rumor going. I guess he was wrong about that."

Mom rubbed the bridge of her nose as she stared at Katie. "How long have you known about this rumor?"

Katie shrugged. "Awhile."

"And you never said a word to us? Why, Katie?" Dad asked.

"I didn't want you to be upset or think that I might be—"

"We know you're not pregnant, Katie." Mom looked at the bishop. "As you know, Katie's dealing with some emotional issues." He gave a nod.

"One of her anxiety symptoms is nausea, and another one's feeling lightheaded and shaky. Maybe Eunice assumed Katie was pregnant because of her symptoms."

"That could be." The bishop pushed his chair back and stood. "Well, I won't take up any more of your time." He smiled at Katie. "If I hear any more rumors about you, I'll put an end to them real quick."

"We appreciate that," Mom said before Katie could respond.

After the bishop left, Katie decided that she needed to be alone by herself for a while, and some fresh air might help clear her head. "I'm going outside," she said.

"Please come finish your supper first," Mom said, motioning to Katie's plate.

Katie shook her head. "I told you before, I'm not hungry." She turned and rushed out the door.

~≈≈~

JoAnn looked over at Jeremy and frowned. "I don't know what we're going to do about Katie."

"Surely you don't think she's lying about not being pregnant."

She shook her head. "I wasn't talking about that. I was talking about the symptoms she's been having. Some might be related to her panic attacks all right, but being nauseous and shaky could be because she doesn't eat enough."

Jeremy lifted his broad shoulders. "Not much we can do about that. It's not like it was when she was a maedel and we could take away her desert if she didn't eat supper."

"I'm hoping Katie's counseling sessions will bring her back to us." JoAnn sighed deeply. "I won't be there to hear what Dr. Coleman has to say when Katie goes next week."

"How come?"

"He asked me to wait outside, and even though I wasn't thrilled about the idea, I agreed." She frowned. "But then Katie said she wants me to stay home next week, and if I agree to that, she'll be all alone."

Jeremy drank some of his water. "Might be for the best. Katie needs to learn to go places by herself and do things on her own. She'll never be able to function as a woman if she doesn't."

"Jah, well, Katie might be able to do that once she's feeling better emotionally. Right now, though, I feel she needs someone to go with her to offer moral support and to ask Dr. Coleman questions she might not think of."

He set his glass down and frowned at her. "You're overprotective where Katie's concerned, and you have been ever since she was a boppli. I don't know if it's because she's our only maedel or because she's the youngest of our kinner, but it's gotten worse since she came back from Florida. You hover over her all the time and offer way too many suggestions."

Irritation welled in JoAnn's soul. "I'm not overprotective, and I don't hover! I care about our daughter and want what's best for her."

"Then let her stand on her own two feet, and offer support through your love and prayers instead of pushing so hard. If Katie needs something, I'm sure she'll ask. If Katie's hungry, I'm sure she'll eat." Jeremy slid his chair away from the table. "I'm goin' outside on the porch to read the newspaper!"

"But you haven't finished your supper."

"I ate as much as I want, and I'm not a little buwe, so stop tellin' me what to do!" Jeremy strode across the room and jerked open the back door.

JoAnn cringed when the door slammed shut. Was she the only one who cared about Katie?

❧ ❧

As soon as Freeman pulled his bike into the Millers' yard, he spotted Katie's dad sitting on the porch.

"Is that an English or Amish newspaper you're reading?"

Freeman asked as he stepped onto the porch.

"English. This one's out of Goshen." Jeremy motioned to the chair beside him. "Take a seat if you like."

"Anything interesting in there?" Freeman asked as he sat down.

"Lots of bad news, including more about our depressed economy and how it's affecting us here." Jeremy frowned. "Seems to be gettin' worse all the time."

Freeman nodded slowly. "I know. With so many of the RV factories either shut down or having cut way back, a lot of men in our area have lost their jobs or have had their hours cut back."

Jeremy crossed his legs. "A man can't support a family when he has no work. Some may have to move if things don't improve. I don't know an Amish man who won't do whatever it takes to provide for his family."

"Guess some might need to look at other options for making money," Freeman said.

"Like what?"

"Maybe making birdhouses, wooden plaques, baked goods, or anything handcrafted that could be sold at the Shipshewana flea market or in some of our local shops. The Amish probably won't buy 'em, but maybe the tourists would."

Jeremy nodded. "It doesn't help the economy any when our property taxes keep going up, either." He pointed to the newspaper. "Yet it looks like they're planning to raise 'em again."

"It amazes me that some people think we Amish don't pay any kind of taxes, when we pay most of the same taxes as the Englishers."

"That's true, and besides paying taxes, we fund our own schools." Jeremy heaved a sigh. "All that said, if we Amish stick together, I'm sure we'll survive any crisis that comes our way. Always have; always will."

"Guess you're right about that." Freeman glanced over his shoulder. "Is Katie in the house? I'd like to know if she got the note I left her at the stamp shop."

Jeremy gestured toward the barn. "She was wandering around out in the yard when I came out here awhile ago, but then she went in there. Think she was lookin' for a place to be alone."

"Maybe I shouldn't bother her then."

Jeremy shook his head. "I'm pretty sure it was her mamm she was trying to get away from. Don't think she'd object to seein' you, though."

Freeman wasn't sure if he should comment on that, so he stared at the barn, trying to decide whether he should bother Katie.

"JoAnn took Katie to see one of the counselors at the mental health facility today." Jeremy sighed loudly. "It didn't go so well with JoAnn bein' in there while the counselor was trying to talk to Katie. She said he asked her to wait outside the next time they come."

"Guess it makes sense that he'd want to speak with Katie alone."

"She'll be alone all right. Told her mamm she didn't want her going to the next session with her at all." Jeremy gestured to the barn again. "Feel free to visit with Katie if you like. I'm sure she'll be glad to see you."

Freeman wasn't so sure about that, but he said good-bye to Jeremy and headed for the barn. He found Katie inside, sitting on a bale of hay with a fluffy gray cat curled in her lap.

"How are you doing?" Freeman asked, taking a seat beside her.

"Okay," she mumbled without looking up.

Freeman cringed. Was she still mad at him?

"I. . .uh. . .was wondering if you got the note I left for you."

She nodded and stroked the cat's head. It began to purr and nestled deeper into her lap.

"Are you still angry with me, Katie?"

"I guess not."

"Then what's wrong? I can see that you're unhappy about something."

"I'm upset about several things."

"Like what?"

"For one thing, our bishop was here awhile ago, asking if I was in a family way."

"Are you kidding?"

"No, I'm not. He said he'd heard a rumor that I was pregnant, and he wanted to find out whether it was true or not." Katie frowned. "It was Eunice who started the rumor, of course."

"I'm really sorry, Katie. Were you able to convince him that the rumor's not true?"

She nodded. "He said if he hears any more gossip about me, he'll put a stop to it."

"That's good."

"Then to make my day even worse, Loraine's at the hospital, and she may lose her boppli."

"I'm sorry to hear that. I know how excited she and Wayne were about becoming parents, so I hope and pray it'll go okay for her."

"Me, too."

Freeman reached over and stroked the cat's head. "Before I came in here, I was talking to your daed, and he said you went to see the counselor today."

"Uh-huh. I saw Dr. Coleman."

"How'd it go?"

"Okay, I guess, but he didn't really say much to help me."

"It's gonna take time, Katie. It took awhile for your panic attacks to start, and it'll take awhile for you to learn how to deal with 'em."

"I hope you're right. I have another appointment with Dr. Coleman next week, and I asked my mamm not to go with me again."

"How come?"

"She kept answering all the questions Dr. Coleman asked me, and when she wasn't answering questions, she was asking them. I could hardly get in a word." Katie shuddered and sighed. "I'm already feeling naerfich about going there alone, but I don't want Mom to go with me again."

"Would you like me to go with you? I'd stay in the waiting room while you're in with the counselor, of course."

"You. . .you'd be willing to do that?"

"If it'd make you feel more comfortable, I'd be glad to ride along."

"What about your work? I wouldn't want you to get behind on

things at the bike shop because of me."

"I'm pretty well caught up right now, so it shouldn't be a problem if I'm gone for a few hours once a week."

Katie smiled. "Danki, Freeman. I would like you to ride along with me."

Just then Katie's dad stepped into the barn, shaking his head and wearing a frown. "I just checked the answering machine, and we got some bad news. Loraine lost the boppli."

Katie pushed the cat aside, jumped off the bale of hay, and stormed out of the barn. "That's it!" she shouted. "I'm done praying for things!"

CHAPTER 34

Are you sure you're feeling up to doing that?"

Loraine turned from the stove where she'd been heating some soup, as well as some water for tea. "I'm fine," she said, smiling at her mother.

"But it's only been a few days since you miscarried, and I don't want you overdoing it."

"I'm not. Besides, cooking a meal gives me something to do. It's better than sitting around feeling sorry for myself."

The teakettle whistled, and Loraine removed it from the stove and dropped in a couple of tea bags.

Mom opened the cupboard door and started setting the table. "I know how disappointed you must feel, because I felt the same way when I miscarried."

Loraine's eyes widened. "When was that? I never knew you had a miscarriage."

"It was before you were born, and I never saw a need to mention it until now." Mom stared out the window.

"Was it your first pregnancy?"

"Jah." Mom sighed. "Have you ever had the feeling that something in your life was too good to be true?"

Loraine nodded.

"Well, that's the way I felt when I first learned I was pregnant—I was bursting with happiness. But then when I lost the boppli,

516

your daed and I felt so disappointed I wondered if either of us would ever feel happy again." Mom smiled. "But God was good, and within a year, I got pregnant again. I finally came to realize that the boppli I'd lost might have been born with serious problems and that losing it might have been God's will for me."

Loraine turned down the gas on the stove and took a seat at the table. "I've been telling myself that, too. As Wayne said last night, 'God knows our needs, and for whatever the reason, He chose to take our boppli to heaven.' "

Mom placed the rest of the dishes on the table and sat across from Loraine. "No one ever said life would be easy, but if we keep God in the center of our lives, with His help, we can make it through."

Loraine nodded. "That's the only way for me."

A knock sounded on the back door, and moments later Ella stepped into the kitchen.

"Sorry I didn't get over here sooner, but Mama came down with a bad cold, so Charlene and I have had to take over all the household chores." Ella handed Loraine a paper sack. "I baked you a loaf of friendship bread, and there's a scripture verse attached to the plastic wrap."

"Danki, I appreciate that." Loraine opened the sack and removed the bread. Then she read the verse out loud. " 'And we know that all things work together for good to them that love God, to them who are the called according to his purpose.' Romans 8:28."

Tears welled in her eyes. "Mom and I were just talking about how God knows our needs. This scripture verse goes along with that."

Mom gestured to a chair. "We won't be eating for another half hour or so. If you have the time, why don't you sit and visit with us awhile?"

"Sure, I've got a few minutes to spare." Ella offered Loraine a sympathetic smile. "How are you feeling physically?"

"I'm doing okay. Since I came home from the hospital, Mom's been coming over every day to fix our meals. She's also done the laundry and some cleaning, so I've been able to rest a lot."

"That's good. Rest is what you need right now." Ella gave Loraine a hug. "I'm real sorry you lost the boppli. It must be very disappointing."

Loraine swallowed around the lump in her throat. "It is, but Wayne and I are trusting that God will allow us to have other bopplin in the future."

~⁂~

"Are you feeling naerfich?" Freeman asked as he helped Katie out of the van.

She shook her head. "Not so much. I appreciate your riding with me, though. I was trying to be brave when I asked Mom to stay home, but I don't think I could have gone to my counseling session alone today."

"I'm glad to do it." Freeman stuck his head into the van. "Can you pick us up in an hour and a half?" he asked Mary Hertz, their driver. "I think we should be ready to go by then."

Mary nodded. "I'll be waiting right here when you come out."

As Katie walked to the building, she noticed that she felt a bit more confident than she had last week. Something about being with Freeman made her feel a sense of calm.

She was surprised when Freeman held the door and let her walk in first. No one had done that for her since Timothy died.

They took seats in the waiting room, and Freeman found a magazine to read. A few minutes later, Katie was called into the counselor's office. She glanced at Freeman, and he gave her a reassuring smile. Drawing in a quick breath, she stepped into Dr. Coleman's office.

He motioned to the chair on the other side of his desk, and she took a seat.

"How did your week go, Katie? Did you have any anxiety attacks?"

She shook her head. "I don't understand why I have them at certain times and not others. Or for that matter, why I started having them in the first place."

"There's no set time for an anxiety attack to occur, but they do seem to happen more often when a person's under a lot of stress. Panic onset can be caused by many things, such as the death of a loved one or trying too hard to please someone."

Katie nodded. "I felt depressed after my boyfriend died, but the panic attacks didn't start until I left Florida and came home."

"Is there someone you're trying too hard to please?"

"I. . .I don't think so. Well, maybe my folks, but it's always been that way."

"You'll need to work on that, Katie. We can't always please other people, and you can stress out if you try too hard."

Katie sat staring at her folded hands as she mulled things over.

"Where do your panic attacks seem to happen the most often?" he asked.

"When I'm riding in a car or our buggy. They've also happened when I'm in a stuffy room with a lot of people." Katie smoothed the wrinkles in her dress, a nervous gesture she'd had since she was a young girl. "Do you think I'll have panic attacks for the rest of my life?"

He rested his elbows on his desk and smiled at her. "Take heart, Katie. You *can* recover from panic attacks; it's just going to take some time and a lot of patience on your part. There are several things you can try, and it may take awhile before you find one that works best for you."

Katie gripped the edge of her chair. "Another thing I don't understand is how come the panicky feelings make me feel like everything's unreal."

"You mentioned that in our last session. Is it sort of like you're dreaming?"

"Kind of. It's hard to describe. I get this warm prickly sensation, and then it's as though nothing seems real anymore." She shivered, remembering the fear she'd felt the last time she'd had an attack. It had left her feeling confused and shaky for nearly an hour.

"Have you made any changes in your daily routine in order to avoid having another panic attack?" Dr. Coleman asked.

She nodded. "I look for excuses not to go places, and the thought of driving the buggy by myself makes me feel like I'm going to throw up or even faint. After passing out in church not long ago, I'm afraid to go there, too."

"Do you force yourself to go places?"

"Sometimes. Church is one of the places where I make myself go, but it's getting harder all the time. I have trouble concentrating on the service because I'm so afraid that I'm going to feel panicky again."

"Fear of a potential attack can almost paralyze a person," Dr. Coleman said. "Struggling against the fear is like trying to put out a fire with a can of gas."

Katie reached into the canvas tote bag she'd brought along. "One of my friends gave me this." She placed the book Freeman had given her about panic attacks on the counselor's desk. "It's the book my mother was telling you about last week. And my cousin gave me this." She handed him the article on tapping that Loraine had given her.

Dr. Coleman read the article and scanned through the book. "I'm familiar with the things mentioned in this book. It has many good points that we'll be talking about here, and you can put them into practice right away. I'm not that familiar with the tapping method, but you're welcome to try it. Before you leave today, I'll give you a few other things you can try, as well." He folded his hands. "Of course, you also need to trust God and ask Him to calm your heart and give you a sense of peace as you practice the things I'm going to suggest."

Katie frowned. "It's my feeling of fear that keeps me from trusting God."

"It's your choice to trust in God that will change your feelings of fear," he said, motioning to the Bible on his desk. "Remember this: The beginning of anxiety is the end of faith, and the end of anxiety is the beginning of faith."

Katie nibbled on her lower lip as she fought against the urge to chew her nails.

"Is there something else bothering you?"

"I think one of the reasons I feel so anxious is because I can't forgive myself for causing the accident that killed my boyfriend."

"What makes you think you're to blame?"

"A bee got in the van, and I freaked out. Our driver turned around to see what the commotion was about, and he lost control of the van." Katie blinked against the tears stinging her eyes. It was hard to talk about that day.

"You're not to blame for the accident, and you shouldn't let yesterday's regrets or tomorrow's anxieties get the best of you. You need to give them over to God."

Katie wasn't sure she could give anything to God, because ever since the accident, she'd been mad at Him for letting Timothy die.

Dr. Coleman picked up the Bible. "Before I give you some breathing exercises to do this week, I'd like to read you a verse of scripture found in 2 Timothy 1:7." He opened the Bible and read the verse out loud. " 'For God hath not given us the spirit of fear; but of power, and of love, and of a sound mind.' " Then he wrote the verse on a slip of paper and handed it to Katie. "If you memorize this, you'll be reminded that God doesn't want you to be fearful. He wants you to get well, Katie."

Katie swallowed around the lump in her throat. "I. . .I want that, too."

⚜ ⚜

Freeman glanced at the clock above the receptionist's desk. Katie had been in with the counselor almost an hour, so he figured she should be out soon. He hoped the counselor would be able to help Katie get her panic attacks under control soon. On the other hand, if she recovered quickly, then she wouldn't need him anymore. He didn't know why that thought bothered him so much. Was it because, like Fern often said, he liked to fix broken things? Or was he drawn to Katie for some other reason? He had been interested in Katie when they were children, but that was a long time ago, and she'd been a different girl back then.

Guess it really doesn't matter, he thought as he turned to look out the window. *Katie's still pining for Timothy and has no interest in me. Besides, I'm supposed to be courting Eunice. Despite my irritation with her at times, I must admit that I'm physically attracted to her.*

❧ ❧

As Eunice pedaled her bike up to Freeman's shop, excitement welled in her soul. She knew she probably shouldn't come over here so often, but she couldn't seem to help herself. From the way Freeman often looked at her, she was sure he was interested in her. She definitely liked him.

Eunice found the Closed sign on the shop door. Disappointed, she glanced at her watch. It was nearly three o'clock, so Freeman wasn't out for lunch. Maybe he'd had an errand to run or had gone to pick up some parts.

Guess I may as well stop at the house and see if Fern's at home. Eunice climbed back on her bike and pedaled up the driveway. She found Fern sitting under a maple tree in the front yard with a basket of mending in her lap.

"Are you too busy to visit?" Eunice asked as she rolled her bike across the lawn.

"I'm never too busy for you." Fern smiled and motioned to the house. "Grab a chair from the porch and bring it over."

Eunice parked the bike near the porch, picked up a chair, and hauled it over to the tree. "Whew, it's another warm day, isn't it?"

Fern nodded. "That's why I'm doing my mending out here. It's too warm in the house, and I'm sure not looking forward to cooking supper this evening."

"Maybe Freeman will take you out to eat," Eunice said as she took a seat.

Fern shook her head. "I don't think so. Thanks to Katie Miller, my bruder will be working late tonight."

Eunice puckered her lips. "What's Katie got to do with Freeman working late?"

"She had an appointment with one of the counselors at the mental health facility in Goshen, and Freeman went along as moral support." The tiny lines in Fern's forehead deepened when she frowned. "Seems like fixing bikes isn't good enough for my bruder these days. He's got it in his head that he can help Katie get over her panic attacks."

"Do you think he can?" Eunice asked.

Fern shrugged. "I don't know, but I think he'll keep trying as long as he thinks Katie needs his help."

Eunice bit her bottom lip until she tasted blood. Every time she turned around, Freeman was with Katie. It had to be more than him just trying to fix her problems. Katie was probably trying to win Freeman's heart.

If I don't do something about this soon, it might be too late, she thought. *I need to come up with some way to make Freeman spend more time with me and less time with Katie.*

CHAPTER 35

June quickly slipped into the more humid days of July and August. Katie was still plagued by panic attacks, but as Freeman continued to accompany her to the counseling sessions, she found herself drawn to him and wishing that he might see her as more than a friend. He'd dropped by the stamp shop several times and had come over to the house some evenings just to visit. Katie kept reminding herself that Freeman was going out with Eunice. He'd given no indication that he felt anything for Katie other than friendship, and if he ended up marrying Eunice, then the friendship he and Katie had now would be over.

Katie wondered if Freeman might see her as more than a friend if she were prettier and more outgoing like Eunice. Or maybe he'd be attracted to her if she was emotionally stable and didn't have panic attacks.

As Katie sat in Dr. Coleman's office one afternoon, she told him that she was getting impatient in her search for something that would put an end to her panic attacks and that she was about to give up.

"We've talked about this before, Katie," he said. "Impatience shows a lack of faith. You must be willing to tell God that you surrender your will to His and that you'll trust Him and not lose heart. When we ask God to do something, we often want to tell Him how and when to do it. We want it to be done our way. In the end, though, it must be God's will, not ours."

It sounded so easy, but Katie had never felt close enough to God to surrender her will to Him. She didn't tell Dr. Coleman that, though. Instead, she sat with her hands folded, staring at the floor.

Dr. Coleman handed her a slip of paper. "Here's another verse for you to memorize and use whenever you start to doubt. 'What time I am afraid, I will trust in thee.' Psalm 56:3." He smiled. "As you practice some of the suggestions I've given you, trust the Lord and visualize Him helping you."

Katie swallowed hard, hoping she wouldn't break down and cry. If only it were that simple.

"Have you been keeping a panic journal like I suggested?" he asked.

She shook her head. "I've written down a few things, but I usually forget."

"I believe it will help if you write down where you were and what was happening during an attack, then record your level of discomfort, the thoughts you had, and your behavior during the attack."

"I'll try to do better with that."

"What about the breathing techniques I asked you to try? Are you practicing them regularly?"

She nodded. "I have been doing those, and I've been trying to relax the parts of my body that are the tensest during a panic attack."

"Are you making yourself do things that frighten you, or are you still avoiding them?"

"I. . .I'm avoiding them whenever I can, and I get nervous just thinking about going anywhere alone."

"The goal of exposing yourself to the things that frighten you is to bring on an attack so you can practice responding to it in a more comfortable way."

"That sounds hard."

"It won't be easy at first, but it's important for you to acknowledge your urge to flee, yet stay in place and work through the panic attack."

Katie clenched and unclenched her fingers. Just thinking

about an attack made her feel as if she could have one right now.

"Have you tried getting angry at the attacks—talking back to them, telling them to do their best?"

"No, I haven't tried that yet."

"Have you taken the horse and buggy out alone?"

"I'm too scared to try driving the buggy alone. The last time I took it out by myself, I had a very bad panic attack." Katie shuddered, and tears blurred her vision. "Now I'm afraid of losing control."

"Maybe it's time for you to try some medication to help you feel calmer."

"I don't want that."

"Why not?"

"I'm afraid I'll become dependent on it or that it'll make me feel sleepy." She blotted the tears on her cheeks and sniffed. "If at all possible, I want to do this without medication."

He stared at the notes on his desk. "What about the homeopathic remedy you said your mother got from the health food store? Have you tried taking that to see if it makes you feel calmer?"

She shook her head.

His eyebrows furrowed as he leaned forward and looked at her intently. "Do you want to get better, Katie?"

She stiffened. "Of course I do!" She couldn't believe he'd even asked her that question.

"Then you need to practice the things I've suggested, and if you're not going to let me prescribe some medication, I want you to try the homeopathic remedy." He glanced at his watch. "Our time is up for today, but when you come back next week, I'll expect a progress report."

Feeling as though she'd been thoroughly scolded, Katie gave a quick nod and hurried from the room.

❧ ❧

When Katie stepped out of the counselor's room, her head was down and her shoulders were slumped. Freeman knew immediately that she was upset. He was tempted to ask how it had gone but decided that if Katie wanted to talk about it she would. It might upset her more if he pressed for details.

Freeman opened the door for Katie, and they walked silently across the parking lot.

"How'd your appointment go, Katie?" Mary Hertz asked when they climbed into her van.

"Okay," Katie said with a shrug.

Freeman hoped Mary wouldn't question Katie further, and he decided to try to get her talking about something else. "Did you get some shopping done?" he asked.

Mary shook her head. "Decided there wasn't anything I needed right now, so I stayed in the van and got caught up on my reading." She lifted a copy of *The Budget* newspaper. "I read several of the articles written by various Amish scribes around the country. Many related to accidents that had occurred last month."

Freeman glanced at Katie, who sat staring out the window as though deep in thought.

Mary pointed to the newspaper and frowned. "In Ohio, a young Amish woman was hit by a car when she was crossing the street to get to a phone shed." She pointed to another article. "Someone's buggy in Pennsylvania was hit when a car failed to stop at a stop sign." Her finger slid down the page. "Then in Illinois, a young boy was killed when he fell from the hayloft." She shook her head slowly. "Guess one never knows when their time will be up."

Freeman glanced at Katie. Her chin quivered, and her fingers were curled tightly into the palms of her hands. She was obviously distressed. Was it the things Mary had shared from *The Budget*, or was Katie upset about whatever had been said during her counseling session?

Usually Freeman headed straight to his shop after they dropped Katie off at her house, but today he thought he'd better stick around for a while and see if she would tell him what was bothering her.

❦

As they headed down the road, Mary continued to comment on

the accidents she'd read about in *The Budget*, and Katie felt like she could scream. By the time they got to her house, she was on the verge of a panic attack. She paid Mary for the ride, said good-bye to Freeman, and stepped out of the van.

"Wait up, Katie!" Freeman called as Katie hurried toward the stamp shop.

Katie halted and turned around. "I need to help my mamm."

"I'd like to talk to you a few minutes, and I promise I won't keep you long." Freeman motioned to the pond beyond their barn. "Why don't we take a walk out there so we can visit in private?"

Katie glanced at the parking area on the side of the stamp shop. She saw only one car and no buggies, so she figured Mom wasn't that busy at the moment. "I guess I can take a few minutes to talk, but maybe we should sit on the porch so I can watch the stamp shop in case more customers show up and Mom gets real busy."

Freeman nodded. "That's fine with me."

They stepped onto the porch. Katie took a seat on the swing, and Freeman leaned against the porch railing.

"What'd you want to talk to me about?" Katie asked.

"I noticed when you came out of the counselor's office that you seemed upset."

Katie's face heated up, and perspiration beaded on her forehead.

"If you'd rather not talk about it, I'll understand."

"It's all right. I might feel better if I do talk about it." Katie sighed as she massaged the back of her neck. "Dr. Coleman got after me for not doing some of the things he'd suggested, and then he accused me of not wanting to get better. He also said I might need to try medication."

"Are you going to?"

She shook her head. "I think I'll try the homeopathic remedy my mamm bought at the health food store some time ago."

"That's a good idea. Remember, a remedy worked well for me."

The swing squeaked as Katie pushed it back and forth with her feet.

"Were you upset only because of what Dr. Coleman said, or did something that Mary mentioned reading about in *The Budget* upset you?"

"I. . .I don't like hearing about people dying," Katie mumbled.

"Death is part of life," Freeman said.

"I know that, but I don't have to like it."

"That's right—you don't, but you shouldn't get upset just because someone talks about dying."

She nibbled on the inside of her cheek, wondering how much she should say. Freeman might not understand the way she felt about things. "Can we please change the subject? I really don't want to talk about death."

"How come?"

"I just don't, that's all."

"You're not afraid of death, are you, Katie?"

Tears clung to her lashes, and her throat felt so clogged she could barely swallow. "Jah. To be honest, I'm afraid of dying."

"I think most everyone fears death a little, but that's because the process of dying is something we haven't experienced before. But if we know where we're going, then—"

Katie shook her head vigorously. "I don't."

"Don't what?"

"I don't know where I'm going." She drew in a shaky breath. "If I died tomorrow, I don't know if I'd go to heaven."

"You'd go there if you believe that Jesus is the Son of God and have invited Him into your heart." Freeman took a seat on the porch swing beside her. "Didn't you make that commitment and profession of faith when you joined the church?"

She shrugged. "I'm not sure. I just said what was expected of me, and I've never really understood it or felt as if I know God in a personal way."

"Have you ever read John 11:25–26, about Jesus being the resurrection and the life?"

"I don't know."

"It says: 'I am the resurrection, and the life: he that believeth in me, though he were dead, yet shall he live. And whosoever liveth and believeth in me shall never die.' "

Katie shifted on the swing. She didn't think she'd ever heard those verses before. If she had, she must not have been paying attention.

"In order to make it to heaven, we have to accept Christ as our Savior and believe that He died for our sins." Freeman touched Katie's arm. "Have you ever accepted Christ as your Savior and asked Him to forgive your sins?"

Katie shook her head.

"Would you like to do that now?"

She nodded, for she didn't trust her voice.

"All you need to do is tell Jesus that you believe in Him and acknowledge that He's the Son of God, who died for you."

"I'd like to do that right now." Katie bowed her head and silently prayed, *Heavenly Father, I believe that Jesus is Your only begotten Son, and that He died on the cross for me. I believe that He rose from the dead to give me a new life. I confess my sins and ask You to wash them away. Amen.*

When Katie opened her eyes, a gentle breeze caressed her face, and she drew in a deep breath. Her heart was raised to God in joyful adoration and thankfulness. She wanted to bask in this comfortable feeling forever. She was filled with an overwhelming sense of gratitude to Freeman for helping her finally see the truth. She wondered if her fear of death could have been the root cause of her panic attacks. She couldn't help but think that God knew all about her anxiety attacks and that He would help her find a way to overcome them. It was the first time she'd felt any real sense of hope that she might get better.

She looked over at Freeman and smiled. "Danki for being my friend."

He returned her smile. "You're welcome."

≈ ≈

That afternoon while Katie was in the stamp shop organizing some colored pens and pencils they'd recently gotten in, she thought about the time she'd spent with Freeman on the porch and how, for the first time in her life, she no longer feared death. Her only concern was the panic attacks that plagued her. Maybe she needed to force herself to do things, like Dr. Coleman had said. She would keep doing her breathing exercises for relaxation, try out the tapping method Wayne had used for his phantom pains, write down her thoughts, and face her fears head-on. She knew it would take courage to drive the buggy by herself, but with God's help, maybe she could.

"Ach, Katie, kumme. . .schnell!" Mom hollered from the back room where she'd gone to cut some cardstock.

Katie raced into the room, wondering why Mom was telling her to come quickly. When she saw Mom's hand covered with blood, her breath caught in her throat.

"What happened?"

Mom teetered unsteadily. "I cut my hand on the paper cutter, and it's bleeding really bad."

Fearful that Mom might pass out, Katie grabbed a clean towel from the bathroom and wrapped it around Mom's hand. Then she pulled out a chair so Mom could sit down.

"I think it's going to need stitches," Mom said shakily. "You'd better get your daed and tell him to call one of our drivers."

Katie slowly shook her head. "Dad's not in his shop right now. He went to Shipshe to pick up some supplies at the hardware store, and his helper went home already."

"Oh, that's right." Mom's face was as pale as a bedsheet, and blood had begun to seep through the towel wrapped around her hand.

"I'll run down to the phone shed and call for help. Just sit right there and apply pressure to the wound." Katie rushed out the door.

When she reached the phone shed a few minutes later, she was nearly out of breath. She dropped into the folding chair inside the shed, picked up the receiver, and was about to dial Mary Hertz's number when she realized that the phone was dead. The wind storm they'd had the previous night must have knocked out the power.

Katie's stomach churned, and her mind spun in circles. The only way she could get help for Mom was to go over to the Andersons', their closest English neighbors. It was too far to walk, and she knew she couldn't take the time to hitch a horse to the buggy, so she decided to ride her bike over there.

She left the phone shed and raced back to the stamp shop. Mom was slumped over the table, looking even paler and more shaken than she had before.

Katie grabbed another towel from the bathroom and wrapped it around Mom's hand. "The phone's dead, so I'm going to bike over to our neighbor's and get help."

Mom nodded. "Schnell, Katie. Schnell!"

CHAPTER 36

Katie yawned and rolled out of bed. Dark still covered the window, but she needed to get up. She'd gone to bed early last night, exhausted after the ordeal with Mom's hand. Mom's thumb had required several stitches, and she'd been given a tetanus shot, but there was no permanent damage, and Katie was grateful. She'd been so concerned about Mom that she hadn't even been nervous when she'd ridden her bike to the Andersons' place. Peggy Anderson had given Mom and Katie a ride to the hospital, and while Mom was getting her hand worked on, Katie had waited and prayed. The whole ordeal had made Katie realize all the more that she needed to practice doing the things she was afraid of, regardless of whether she had a panic attack or not.

Katie had set her alarm clock to go off at four, knowing her folks wouldn't be up until six. She figured that should give her enough time to hitch her horse to the buggy and go out on the road for half an hour or so. There wouldn't be much traffic, and she hoped that would help her not to be quite so nervous.

Katie padded across the room, pushed the curtain aside, and opened the window. Outside, everything was calm and still. Stars twinkled in the sky, crickets sang, and a gentle breeze caressed her face. God seemed very near. Surely He would see her through the coming days.

Filled with a sense of peace she hadn't known in many months,

Katie hurried to get dressed and slipped quietly from her room. She tiptoed down the stairs, being careful not to step on any that squeaked.

When she reached the first floor, she ducked into the kitchen and took one of the homeopathic tablets for calming. Then she grabbed a flashlight and opened the back door.

The sky was still dark, but the moon shone brightly, so she didn't need the flashlight until she got to the buggy shed. Being careful not to make too much noise, she opened the door and pushed one of their smaller open buggies into the yard. Then she hurried into the barn to get Dixie, their gentlest mare.

By the time Katie had the horse hitched to the buggy, her hands had begun to shake. This was going to be a lot harder than she'd thought it would be.

"You need to face your fears," Dr. Coleman had said during one of her counseling sessions. *"Don't avoid situations where you've had a panic attack before."*

Katie leaned against the buggy, closed her mouth, and inhaled slowly through her nose, pushing her stomach out like Dr. Coleman had instructed her to do. Then she opened her mouth and exhaled by pulling her stomach in. "I'm afraid, Lord," she whispered. "Help me overcome these horrible panic attacks. My future looks dark and impossible, but I know You are with me."

A verse of scripture she'd read before going to bed popped into her head. *"What time I am afraid, I will trust in thee."*

My choice to trust God will help calm my feelings of fear, Katie told herself.

Two more verses came to mind: *"I can do all things through Christ which strengtheneth me"—Philippians 4:13;* and *"Peace I leave with you, my peace I give unto you: not as the world giveth, give I unto you. Let not your heart be troubled, neither let it be afraid"—John 14:27.*

A sense of calm stole into Katie's heart again. It was the same peaceful feeling she'd had in her bedroom. Surely God wouldn't forsake her. She needed to trust Him and keep asking for strength and courage.

Katie opened the flap on the driver's side of the buggy so she'd have plenty of fresh air, climbed inside, and took up the reins.

There's nothing to be afraid of. With God's help I can do this. I'll just go as far as I feel comfortable, she told herself. *If I start to panic, I can turn around and come back home.*

In Katie's mind's eye she pictured the Lord gathering her up in His strong arms. He loved her. He cared for her. He was here with her now.

Katie felt more confident as she guided Dixie down the driveway, but when she came to the road, her heart started to pound and her hands grew so sweaty she could barely hang on to the reins.

"Stop it! Stop it! Stop doing this to me!" she shouted.

Katie mentally shook herself. That was the wrong approach. What was it that Dr. Coleman had suggested she say and do? When she was frightened like this, it was hard to think.

Oh yes, now I remember. "Panic attack, you can't control me anymore!" she shouted. "Go ahead and do your best!"

Katie's horse whinnied and twitched her ears.

"It's all right, Dixie, I'm not hollering at you." Feeling a little more relaxed, Katie clucked gently to the horse and eased her onto the road.

They'd only got a short ways when Katie noticed a blinking light on the shoulder of the road to her right. She hadn't expected to see anyone on this stretch of the road in the wee hours of the morning. As her buggy drew closer she realized it was their English paperboy delivering the morning newspaper on his bike. She'd only met the young man once, when he'd come to the house to collect the money he was due. Katie didn't know his name but figured from his youthful appearance that he was probably in his late teens or early twenties.

"You're out early. Where are ya headed?" he called to her.

"Just taking a ride." She flicked the reins and got the horse moving faster. There was no time for idle chitchat. Especially not with someone she barely knew.

As Katie continued down the road, things went along fairly well. She felt more relaxed driving the buggy than she thought she would. Maybe there was some hope of her living a normal life without fear of panic attacks.

She relaxed against the seat, enjoying the cool, early morning breeze.

Ribet! Ribet! A chorus of frogs serenaded her.

When the sun peaked over the horizon, Katie decided it was time to head for home. Since things had gone so well, she thought she might take the buggy out early every morning this week.

She turned up their driveway, put the horse and buggy away, and entered the house just in time to see Dad step out of his and Mom's room.

"I'm surprised to see you up and dressed already," he said, passing her in the hall.

"I woke up earlier than usual this morning," Katie replied. Did Dad suspect that she'd been outside? She hoped he wouldn't question her further.

"Since you're up already, would you mind putting the coffee on?" he asked. "Your mamm's still getting dressed."

"Sure." Katie picked up the coffeepot and filled it with water from the sink.

"Guess I'll head outside to do my chores," Dad said.

"I'll have breakfast ready when you get back," Katie called as he went out the door. She breathed a sigh of relief.

～❧ ❧～

As Katie headed for the stamp shop later that morning, she stopped in the garden, bent down, and plucked a leaf from one of their mint plants. She rubbed the leaf between her fingers, relishing the sharp aroma. She hadn't noticed things like this in such a long time.

She turned, closed her eyes, and stood with her face lifted to the sun. It felt good to be alive.

A horse whinnied, and Katie opened her eyes just in time see Ella's buggy come up the driveway, headed toward the stamp shop.

Katie hurried to the shop and stopped just outside the door to wait for Ella.

"How are things with you?" Ella asked. "Are you still seeing the counselor at the clinic once a week?"

Katie nodded and smiled. "Freeman's been riding with me, and that's helped me feel more confident about going."

Ella's brows puckered. "Are you in love with him?"

" 'Course not. Why do you ask?"

"You got a dreamy-eyed look on your face as soon as you mentioned his name."

"I did not."

"Jah, you did." Ella poked Katie's arm. "Does he feel the same way about you?"

"He sees me as a friend, nothing more."

"That's good, because from what I've heard, Freeman's been going out with Eunice, and after talking to her the other day, I realized that she's convinced that she and Freeman are going steady."

Katie shrugged, but her skin prickled. "What's that got to do with me?"

"It could have everything to do with you if you're in love with Freeman."

"I'm not."

Ella gave Katie's arm a light tap. "You do like him, though, don't you?"

"I like him as a friend." Katie quickly opened the door to the stamp shop, needing to change the subject. "Let's go inside so you can buy whatever you came here for."

⚜

Freeman pulled out his set of tools to begin working on a bike, but he hadn't been at it long before he found himself thinking about Katie. He was pleased that she'd accepted Christ as her Savior. It had to be a relief for her to know that her heart was right with God and that if she died, she would go to heaven.

Freeman wasn't sure why, but Katie's sweet response to the things he'd shared with her yesterday had stirred up a longing in his heart for more than friendship. But it seemed like an impossible dream,

537

because as far as he knew, she hadn't stopped loving Timothy or grieving for him. Until she did, Freeman saw no way they could be together. Besides, Katie was still struggling with her panic attacks, and that was enough for her to deal with right now.

Then there was Eunice. From the way she looked at him and the comments she made whenever they were together, Freeman knew she was getting serious about him. Probably thought he was serious about her, too. Might even be hoping for a marriage proposal. Trouble was, he wasn't sure how he felt about Eunice. She had a pretty face, cooked well enough, and had a way of flirting that made him feel like a man. But he didn't think he was in love with her. At least not like he was with—

Woof! Woof! Penny raced across the room and slurped his hand. He patted the pup's head and smiled. "What do you want, girl? Do you need to go outside for a while?"

Penny whined and raced for the door. Freeman followed.

When he opened the door, Ella stepped in. Penny darted between her legs and dashed into the yard, yipping and wagging her tail.

"What can I do for you?" Freeman asked, smiling at Ella. "Do you need something for your bike?"

She shook her head. "I'm here because I'm concerned about Katie."

"What do you mean?"

"I don't think it's a good idea for you to see Katie so much."

"I don't see her that much—just every Friday when she goes for her counseling session."

"Katie's dealing with a lot of things right now, and I don't want her to get hurt."

Freeman frowned. "How's she gonna get hurt? What exactly are you saying?"

"I'm saying that I think you're seeing too much of her, and she might begin to think you care for her."

"I do care for her; we're good friends." Freeman wasn't about to admit to Katie's cousin how he felt about Katie. She was likely to blab it to Katie.

"She might think it's more than that, and with you going steady with Eunice and all—"

The shop door opened again, and an English customer stepped in.

"I can see you're busy, so I'll just say one thing before I go. Please don't lead Katie on." Ella hurried out the door before Freeman could respond.

He turned to his customer and said, "Can I help you with something?"

CHAPTER 37

Katie clucked to her horse and turned onto the road. For the last two weeks, she'd been taking her family's open buggy out every morning to practice driving alone. In between those times, she practiced her breathing exercises and affirmations, wrote her thoughts in a journal, prayed, and read her Bible regularly. She'd had a couple of panic attacks, but they'd been mild, and she was determined to keep trying. If she didn't, she'd never get better, and if she never got better, there would be no chance for her and Freeman.

Katie thought about the way Freeman had looked at her on their way home from her counselor's appointment yesterday afternoon. Was it a look of longing she'd seen on his face, or had it just been the friendly smile of a good friend? She wished she felt free to tell Freeman how much she'd come to care for him, but that would be too bold. Besides, if he wasn't interested in her romantically, she'd be opening herself up for rejection, which she knew she couldn't handle right now. Katie wasn't really sure where things stood with Freeman and Eunice, but if they were serious about each other, it wouldn't be right to do or say anything that might come between them.

As Katie turned down County Road 13, she saw a flashing light, and as she drew closer, she realized that a bicycle was lying on its side. A young man stood beside it. When she slowed the horse, she recognized their paperboy. "Are you having a problem with your bike?" she asked, pulling the buggy alongside him.

"Yeah. I've got a flat tire." He motioned to the canvas satchel lying beside his bike. "I haven't finished delivering my papers, so this wasn't a good time for something like this to happen."

Katie thought about offering to give him a ride so he could make the rest of his deliveries, but that would take up more time than she had. The sun would be up soon, and she needed to get home before Mom and Dad got up.

"I think there's room for your bike in my buggy, so if you want to put it in the back, I can give you a ride home," she said.

"Thanks, I appreciate that." The young man lifted his bike into the back of her buggy then climbed into the passenger's seat up front. He looked over at Katie and said, "My name's Mike Olsen, and you're Katie Miller, aren't you?"

She nodded. "How'd you know my name?"

"I make it my business to know the names of every pretty girl along my route." He chuckled and bumped her arm.

Katie's face warmed. She was glad it was too dark for him to see her blushing. No one except Timothy had ever called her pretty.

"Sure will be glad when summer's over and I can head back to Florida," Mike said.

"Are you from Florida?" Katie asked with interest.

"Yeah, my folks live just outside of Sarasota."

"Then what are you doing here?"

"I got into some trouble this spring, and they sent me up here to stay with my grandparents for a while, hoping it'd straighten me out." Mike snorted. "Like a few months of mending fences and delivering papers is gonna make me a better person."

Katie wondered what kind of trouble he'd been in, but she didn't voice the question, since it was really none of her business.

"Do you like Florida better than here?" she asked.

"Sure do. I hope to be on my way back there before fall. Can't wait to say good-bye to boring Indiana and hello to Florida's white sandy beaches."

Katie had never thought of Indiana as boring, but she'd enjoyed spending time on the beach near Sarasota, looking for shells and wading near the shore. "I lived in Sarasota for seven months," she said.

"By yourself?"

"No, with my grandparents."

"Did you like it there?"

"Yes, I did."

"Then why'd you leave?"

"I came home for my cousin's wedding, and then my grandparents moved to Wisconsin, so I had to stay here."

"Who says you have to stay here?" Mike reached in his shirt pocket and pulled out a cigarette. "Want one?" He waved it in front of Katie's nose.

She shook her head. "No thanks."

"If you liked Florida so much, why don't you go back?"

"I just told you, my grandparents moved to Wisconsin."

He lit the cigarette and took a puff. "Who says you have to live with them?"

"Well, I'd need a job and a place to stay."

"You can always find a job in Sarasota, and if you need a place to crash for a while, you can stay with me." He patted his pocket. "By the end of this summer, I'll have plenty of money, so I won't have to rely on my folks anymore, and I'll get my own place."

Katie's mouth went dry. A few months ago, she'd have given most anything to go back to Florida. But with Grandma and Grandpa not there, the idea didn't have quite as much appeal. Besides, it wouldn't be proper for her to stay with Mike. "I appreciate the offer," she said, "but I'm happy staying here right now."

He blew a puff of smoke in her direction. "A lot can happen between now and fall, so if you change your mind, just let me know."

～≈ ❧ ～

Eunice groaned as she climbed out of bed. She'd been drifting in and out of sleep most of the night, thinking about Freeman and wondering why he seemed to be cooling off toward her lately. The last time he'd taken her out to supper, he hadn't said more than a few words, and she was worried that he might be losing interest in her.

Since I can't sleep, I may as well get up and start some coffee going, Eunice decided. She slipped off her nightgown, put on a dress, and headed outside to see if the newspaper had been delivered yet.

As Eunice walked down the driveway, her thoughts remained on Freeman. Tonight there would be a young people's gathering at Ella's, and Freeman had agreed to take her. Of course, she'd been the one to bring it up. In fact, she'd suggested several of their outings and had invited him to her house for supper at least once a week. She'd been trying to keep Freeman too busy with her to think about Katie. Eunice thought if she spent more time with Freeman, he would realize that they were meant to be together. If things went as she planned, by this time next year, they could be married.

As Eunice approached the paper box, she heard the rhythmic *clip-clop* of horse's hooves. She squinted at the flashing lights coming down the road, but as the buggy drew closer, she couldn't make out who was inside.

When Eunice heard a woman's voice, she froze. It sounded like Katie Miller, and she was talking to a man.

Eunice quickly stepped behind a bush and strained to listen as the buggy went past.

Eunice caught just a few of their words, but she was sure now that the woman speaking was Katie. She didn't recognize the man's voice, though. What she couldn't figure out was why Katie would be out on the road so early—and with a man, no less!

Maybe Katie's seeing someone and doesn't want her folks to know, Eunice thought. *She might have snuck out of bed so she could be with him. Or maybe they've been out all night together.*

Eunice was relieved that Katie wasn't with Freeman. If Katie had a boyfriend, Eunice had nothing to be concerned about. Now all she needed to do was let Freeman know that Katie had a boyfriend.

CHAPTER 38

"Aren't you going to play anymore?" Ella called to Eunice as she stepped away from the volleyball net after the last game had ended.

Eunice fanned her cheeks. "It's hot, and I'm tired! Think I'll take a break from playing for a while." She found a chair under a leafy tree and flopped down. She'd only been sitting there a few minutes when she spotted Freeman talking to Katie on the other side of the yard.

What's he doing with her? she fumed.

Eunice leaped out of her chair and rushed over to where they were standing. "I'm really thirsty, Freeman," she said, stepping between them. "Would you mind getting me something cold to drink?"

Freeman nodded. "Sure, I can do that." He looked over at Katie and smiled. "Would you like something, too?"

"Jah, that'd be nice," Katie replied.

As soon as Freeman moved away, Eunice turned to Katie and said, "Can you keep a secret?"

Katie nodded.

"Freeman plans to join the church this fall, so by next spring we'll be planning our wedding."

Katie blinked a couple of times. "Oh, I. . .didn't realize he'd asked you to marry him."

"It's not official yet, so we're keeping it quiet until we're published." Eunice smiled. "Of course, since you're one of Freeman's closest friends, I figured you'd want to know."

"I hope you'll be very happy." Katie gave a quick nod and hurried away. Eunice sighed, feeling pleased with herself. She may have lost one boyfriend, but she wouldn't lose another.

A few minutes later, Freeman returned with two paper cups. He handed one to Eunice. "I brought you both some punch."

"Danki."

He glanced around. "Where's Katie?"

Eunice shrugged. "I really couldn't say. She rushed off without a word." Freeman turned his head to the left. "Oh, there's Katie, walking toward the barn. Guess I'll head over there and see if she wants some punch."

He hurried away quickly, and Eunice followed. She'd only taken a few steps when she stumbled, spilling punch all over the front of her dress.

"Ach!" she cried. "My ankle!"

"Are you all right?" Andrew asked, catching hold of her arm as he walked by.

"I was going after Freeman, and I think I must've stumbled on a rock." Eunice grimaced.

Andrew called to Freeman, and he turned around.

"What happened?" Freeman asked, hurrying to Eunice's side.

"I. . .I tripped on a rock, and—" Eunice winced as she bent down and touched her ankle. "I don't think I can walk by myself."

"We'll help you," Andrew said.

Freeman nodded. "Jah, of course."

Eunice hung on to Freeman's arm with one hand and Andrew's arm with the other as they helped her to the nearest chair.

"I'll run into my aunt's house and get you some ice." Andrew glanced down at Eunice with a look of concern; then he sprinted across the lawn.

Freeman knelt beside Eunice. "Maybe we should call someone to take you to the hospital so you can have your ankle x-rayed."

She shook her head. "I'm sure it's just sprained. As soon

as Andrew gets back with the ice, I think you should take me home."

Freeman nodded. "Whatever you think is best."

❦

When Katie saw Andrew coming out of the house, she hurried up to him. "I'm not feeling well. Would you mind taking me home?"

"Sure, I can do that as soon as I take this out to Eunice." He lifted the bag of ice in his hand.

"Why does Eunice need ice?"

"She stumbled on a rock and twisted her ankle."

"That's too bad," Katie mumbled. It was hard to feel sorry for Eunice when she acted so superior all the time. It was especially hard now that Katie had admitted to herself that she was in love with Freeman, yet she had no chance with him because he loved Eunice.

That's what I get for letting myself fall in love again, she berated herself. *I lost Timothy to death, and now I've lost Freeman to Eunice. Guess he's better off without me as his friend. Why would he want to tie himself down with someone like me when he can have her?*

"If you'd like to wait for me in the barn, I shouldn't be long," Andrew said.

"Okay." A lump formed in Katie's throat as she moved away. It had been a shock to hear that Freeman had asked Eunice to marry him, although she should have seen it coming. After all, Freeman had been going out with Eunice all summer, and he hadn't asked Katie out even once.

Well, why would he? she asked herself. *He's only spent time with me because he's been trying to help me get over my panic attacks. He's probably been so nice only because he feels sorry for me.*

Katie stared out across the field behind Ella's house and winced as a hawk swooped down and snatched a field mouse. She felt as helpless as the poor, defenseless mouse. *If Freeman marries Eunice, the friendship we have now will be over.*

Katie pushed her shoulders back as she made a decision. *As soon as I have enough money saved up, I'm going back to Florida.*

CHAPTER 39

As Freeman drove Eunice home, he thought about the decision he'd made earlier to break up with her and wondered if this was the right time to bring up the subject. She'd hurt her ankle, and he was sorry about that, but he couldn't let that stop him from telling her the way he felt. If he kept going out with Eunice, it would be even harder to break up, and Eunice might expect a marriage proposal.

Eunice fidgeted on the seat beside him and leaned down to reposition the bag of ice Andrew had given her.

"How's your ankle?" Freeman asked. "Does it feel any better?"

"A little. I think the ice has helped some." She moved closer to him and rested her head on his shoulder. "Sure is a pretty night, isn't it?"

"Jah. Lots of stars and a bright full moon."

"It's the perfect night for a buggy ride."

"Uh-huh."

They rode in silence the rest of the way, and Freeman wondered if Eunice had fallen asleep.

Maybe I'd better not say anything about breaking up with her tonight, he decided. *I can talk to her about it another time when her ankle's feeling better.*

When Freeman guided his horse and buggy up Eunice's driveway, she sat up and looked around. "Are we here already?"

"Jah. I think you slept part of the way home."

She touched his arm. "Would you like to come in for a piece of pie and a glass of milk?"

"I'd better not. Tomorrow's Sunday, and we'll have to get up early."

"It's not that late. Surely you can come in for a few minutes."

"I really can't. I've got a stop to make on my way home."

Her eyebrows furrowed. "Whose house are you stopping at?"

"Just have a delivery to make."

"What kind of delivery would you have to make on a Saturday night?"

"One of my customers ordered a part for his bike, and I said I'd drop it off this afternoon, but I got busy in the shop and never made it there. Figured I could do it on my way home tonight."

"You're going over to see Katie, aren't you?" Eunice's shrill voice and pinched expression let Freeman know she was angry with him.

"I'm not going to see Katie," he insisted.

"Right."

"I said I'm not. Now can we please drop the subject?"

Eunice sat with her arms folded, staring straight ahead. "Are you still riding to the mental health clinic with Katie every week?"

"Jah. Why do you ask?"

"I don't want you to go with her anymore. She's not a boppli; she ought to be able to ride there by herself."

"I've explained this to you before, so I don't know why you're bringing it up again. Katie feels better about riding in the van if someone's with her."

"Well, it doesn't have to be you! She can find someone else to ride with her!"

Freeman knew if he didn't leave soon he'd say something he might regret. He hopped down from the buggy and held his hand out to her. "I'll help you into the house, and then I need to be on my way."

"Do you like her more than you do me?"

"Who?"

"Katie, of course. Who else were we talking about?"

Freeman grunted. "Not this again."

"Just answer me. Do you like her more than you do me?"

"I've said this before, but apparently you need me to say it again. Katie and I are just good friends."

"She has a boyfriend, you know."

Heat radiated up the back of Freeman's neck. Was Eunice trying to get a rise out of him? "Are you getting out of the buggy or what?"

"Don't you want to hear about Katie's boyfriend?"

"Her boyfriend's dead."

"Not that boyfriend. She has a new one now."

"Katie's never mentioned having a boyfriend to me."

"Maybe she doesn't want anyone to know. That could be why she's been sneaking around in the wee hours of the morning with him."

Freeman's heart pounded like a trotting horse. "What are you talking about?"

"I went out to get the newspaper early this morning, and a horse and buggy came by the front of our house. I heard talking and recognized Katie's voice. The other person was a man, but I don't know who it was." Eunice leaned close to Freeman. "I smelled smoke when the buggy went past, so I'm sure that either Katie or her boyfriend was smoking."

"Katie doesn't smoke."

"How do you know?"

"I would have smelled it on her if she did."

"Then I guess her boyfriend must have been smoking."

Freeman grimaced. Did Katie really have a boyfriend? Was it possible that she'd been out in the fellow's buggy? *Who can it be?* he wondered. *Should I come right out and ask Katie who she was with this morning?*

Eunice tugged on his arm. "I'm sorry if I upset you, but I thought you had the right to know that Katie's not the innocent girl you think her to be."

Anger boiled in Freeman's chest. He'd had enough of Eunice

putting Katie down! He turned to her and said, "It's over between us, Eunice."

Her chin trembled, and her eyes filled with tears. "You—you can't mean that!"

"Jah, I do."

"It's because of her, isn't it? She's made you think that she's a nice girl, but she's really—"

"That's enough!" Freeman shouted. "I won't listen to another spiteful word about Katie!"

"You'll be sorry for breaking up with me. Someday you'll be very sorry." Eunice stepped down from the buggy and ran to her house.

"Guess her ankle's not hurtin' quite as bad as she let on," Freeman mumbled as he climbed into the buggy and got the horse moving again. "Maybe I'll head over to Katie's and see what I can find out about the fellow she was out riding with this morning."

❧ ❧

Katie had just taken an aspirin for her headache and was getting ready to go upstairs to her room when a knock sounded on the back door. "I'll get it," she called to her folks, who were in the living room playing a game of Dutch Blitz.

When Katie opened the door and saw Freeman on the porch, she froze. "What are you doing here? I thought you were still at the gathering."

"I left early after Eunice twisted her ankle."

Katie peered around him, into the yard. "Is Eunice with you?"

Freeman shook his head. "I took her home." He shuffled his feet a few times. "Came here to ask you a question."

"What's that?"

"Eunice said that she'd heard a buggy coming down the road near her house early this morning and that you and some man were in it. I. . .uh. . .wondered whether that was true or not."

Katie nodded. "It was me all right. I was giving our paperboy a ride to his grandparents' house because the tire on his bike was flat."

Freeman gave his earlobe a tug. "Mind if I ask what you were doing out on the road so early?"

"I was doing what Dr. Coleman said I should do—facing my fears." Katie massaged her throbbing head. "I figured the easiest way to do that was to practice driving the buggy when there aren't so many cars on the road."

"Guess that makes sense." Freeman took a step closer. "Katie, I—"

"I don't mean to be rude, but I have a koppweh, and I'm really tired, so I need to go to bed."

"Sorry to hear you have a headache. I'll let you go then." Freeman started down the stairs but halted and turned around. "I'll see you on Sunday, and then again on Friday for your counselor's session."

"That's okay," Katie was quick to say. "I won't need you to go with me next time."

He tipped his head. "How come?"

"I need to start doing things on my own. *Gut nacht*, Freeman." Katie hurried inside and shut the door.

"Calm down, Eunice, and tell me why you're crying like a wounded heifer," Mama said as she took a seat beside Eunice on the sofa.

"Freeman broke up with me!" Eunice hiccupped on a sob.

"What happened?"

"It—it's all because of Katie. He cares more about her than he does me." *Hic! Hic!*

"What makes you think that?"

"He's always talking to her when he should be talking to me." Eunice hiccuped again and wiped away her tears. "I tried telling him that Katie has a boyfriend, but he wouldn't believe me. He never believes anything I say about Katie."

Mama reached for Eunice's hand. "I know how badly you want a husband, but it was wrong for you to try to turn Freeman against Katie in order to get him for yourself." She clucked her tongue. "I hate to say this, but you're getting just what you deserve."

"What's that supposed to mean?"

"It means you set yourself up for this when you spread rumors about Katie wanting to keep that boppli she found on her porch, not to mention your telling everyone that you thought Katie was pregnant. Hopefully, you'll learn a lesson from this and will wait for your true love to come along instead of trying to force it to happen."

"You don't understand how I feel," Eunice wailed. "Don't you even care how miserable I am?"

"I do care, but I can't condone your actions. It's time for you to grow up and face the fact that you can't always have what you want."

"Jah, I can! I'll give Freeman some time to think about things, and then I'll talk to him again. Hopefully, I can get him to change his mind about us." Eunice pulled the quilt off the back of the sofa and draped it across her lap. "I sprained my ankle at the gathering, and it hurts too bad to walk up the stairs, so I'm sleeping here tonight!"

CHAPTER 40

For the next several weeks, Katie got up early every morning and took her horse and buggy out on the road. Each time, her confidence grew, and when she felt nervous or afraid, she prayed, did some deep breathing, repeated her affirmations, and talked back to the panic attacks.

One morning, as Katie was about to pull out onto the road, she spotted Mike peddling his bike up to their paper box. "I see you're up early again," he said, shining his flashlight on her.

Katie shielded her eyes from the light and nodded. "I see you got your bicycle fixed."

"Sure did." He climbed off his bike, leaned it against the wooden post, and walked to her buggy. "I'll be leaving for Florida soon. Think you might want to ride along?"

"Are you planning to take the bus there?"

"No way! I came by bus, but I'm goin' back in style. Should have the money I need to buy a car by the end of next week, and I'll leave soon after that." He pulled a package of gum from his pocket and stuck a piece in his mouth.

"I'd like to go," she said, "but like I said, I'd have no place to stay until I found a job."

"And if you'll recall, I said you could stay with me."

"I couldn't do that."

"Why not?"

"It wouldn't be proper."

His jaw moved up and down as he chomped on his gum. "Well, give it some thought. If you change your mind, you can leave me a note in your paper box." Mike slapped his hands together and grinned. "See you later, Katie!"

❦

"Did you see any sign of Katie outside?" JoAnn asked Jeremy when he entered the kitchen after doing his chores.

He shook his head. "She wasn't in the barn or the yard, so she's probably still in her room."

"No, she's not. I checked there already."

"Guess she could be in the bathroom."

"I looked there, too."

Jeremy reached under his hat and scratched the side of his head. "That makes no sense. She's either got to be in the house or outside somewhere. Want me to go back out and take a look around?"

"Maybe you should." JoAnn sighed. "You know, Katie's been acting kind of peculiar ever since she went to that young people's gathering at Ella's. It makes me wonder if she's keeping secrets from us again."

"What kind of secrets?"

"I don't know, but she's been very quiet, and when I mentioned the other day how nice it is to have her working in the stamp shop with me, she got all teary eyed."

"You worry too much." He gave her shoulders a squeeze. "You need to give Katie some space and stop mothering her so much. If she has something she wants to tell us, she'll say it in her own good time."

She sighed. "That remains to be seen."

He turned toward the back door and was about to open it when Katie stepped in, red-faced and looking very flustered.

"Ach, you scared me, Dad! It's still early, and I didn't think you were up yet."

"As you can see, both me and your mamm are up, and she's been lookin' for you."

Katie's face turned crimson. "I. . .I was outside."

"That's obvious, since you just came inside." JoAnn stepped up to Katie. "What were you doing outside so early?"

Katie shifted from one foot to the other and stared at the floor.

"I just came from the barn and you weren't there." Jeremy quirked an eyebrow. "Didn't see you in the yard, either."

Katie lifted her gaze and pushed her shoulders back. "Guess I can't keep it a secret any longer. For the past few weeks, I've been taking the horse and buggy out early every morning, before you and Mom got up."

"What for?" JoAnn questioned.

"So I could practice driving the buggy."

Jeremy's eyebrows furrowed. "You already know how to drive a buggy, so why would you need to practice?"

"Dr. Coleman said the best way for me to get over my panic attacks is to face my fears and force myself to do what I'm most afraid of."

"That makes sense," JoAnn said, "but why so early in the morning?"

"Because there are fewer cars on the road, and I didn't want you and Dad to know what I was doing."

"Why not?" Jeremy asked. "Didn't you think we'd approve?"

"It's not that. I wanted to be sure I was getting better before I told you, and I wanted it to be a surprise."

"If I'd known what you were doing, I'd have offered to ride along with you," JoAnn said.

Katie sank into a chair at the table. "I need to make a life of my own and stop relying on you and Dad for everything. In fact, I've been thinking about going back to Florida."

"What?" JoAnn grabbed the edge of the nearest chair so hard that her fingers ached. "Where on earth did that idea come from?"

"I. . .was happier living in Florida."

"You weren't happier; you were hiding from your past." JoAnn shook her head. "And where would you stay?" JoAnn looked at

Jeremy. "Tell her how *narrish* she's being for thinking she should move back to Florida."

He took a seat across from Katie and pulled his fingers through the ends of his beard. "Your mamm's right. Moving back to Florida would be a foolish thing for you to do."

"I don't see why. I've saved up some money working in the stamp shop, and I'll look for a job when I get to Sarasota."

"Puh!" JoAnn flopped into the chair she'd been gripping. "Jobs are hard to find these days, and you'll be out of money in short order if you don't find a job right away. Besides, you have a good job right here in our stamp shop, and I thought you enjoyed working there."

"I do, but—"

"What about your counseling sessions?" Jeremy asked. "If you move back to Florida, you might lose all the ground you've gained."

Katie fiddled with the edge of the tablecloth. "I can practice the things Dr. Coleman suggested while I'm living in Florida just as well as I can here."

JoAnn reached over and clasped Katie's hand. "What's the reason behind this decision? Are you that unhappy living here with us? Have I said or done something to turn you against me?"

Tears welled in Katie's eyes and dribbled onto her cheeks. She sniffed and swiped them away. "It's not you, Mom."

"Then what is it that's driving you away?"

"I. . .I'm in love with Freeman, but he loves Eunice, and I can't stand the thought of seeing them get married next spring."

JoAnn's mouth dropped open. "Oh, Katie, I had no idea you'd fallen in love with Freeman. Are you sure he's planning to marry Eunice?"

Katie nodded. "Eunice told me that Freeman's going to join the church this fall and that they're planning a spring wedding."

"Have you talked to Freeman about this?" Jeremy asked.

Katie shook her head. "I'd be too embarrassed to admit that I love him. He's never seen me as anything more than a friend." She reached for a napkin and dabbed at her tears. "It hurts so bad to know that he loves Eunice. She's not a nice person and doesn't deserve someone as kind as Freeman."

"That may be true, and I'm sure that it hurts, but you can't spend the rest of your life running from things you don't like," JoAnn said. "I think you need to stay right here and deal with the situation."

Jeremy shook his head. "No she doesn't, JoAnn. If Katie can't stand the thought of seeing Freeman and Eunice together, then we need to support her decision to move." He touched Katie's arm. "My cousin Clarence and his wife, Mae, will be moving to Sarasota, probably next month. Would you like me to ask if they'd be willing to let you stay with them until you find a job and are able to rent a small place of your own?"

"Would you really do that for me?" Katie asked with a hopeful expression.

"Wouldn't have suggested it if I wasn't willing."

JoAnn stood up and pushed her chair aside so quickly that it toppled to the floor. "I can't go along with this! Katie's place is here with us, plain and simple!"

CHAPTER 41

"*Sell kann ich mir gaar net eibilde!*" Katie's dad said as he stared at the newspaper.

"You can't conceive of what?" Mom asked, peering over his shoulder.

"The young English man who delivers our paper every morning was arrested for robbing a convenience store in Goshen. Guess he told the sheriff he needed the money to buy a new car." Dad slowly shook his head. "The fellow had a gun and threatened the store clerk with it, but then another customer came in, saw what was happening, and called for help."

"That's too bad. When a young person does something like that, it hurts not only him but his whole family." Mom clicked her tongue as though she were scolding someone. "Sure wish we could read some positive news in the paper once in a while. It's depressing to hear so many negative things, and it makes me sad to know that there's so much crime and corruption in our world."

Katie cringed. She was glad she hadn't taken Mike up on his offer to ride with him to Sarasota. He was obviously not as nice as he seemed to be. It was better that she'd be traveling with Dad's cousin and his wife.

Mom still wasn't in favor of Katie moving back to Florida, but at least she'd stopped hounding her about it. Since Clarence and Mae wouldn't be moving for another month, that gave Katie plenty of time to get ready to go. She would need to tell Loraine and Ella, too. She just wasn't sure what to do about saying good-bye to Freeman.

Mom touched Katie's arm. "Will Freeman be going to your counseling session with you again today?" she asked, pulling Katie's thoughts aside.

"I'll be going by myself from now on," Katie said. "It's better that's way."

"Would you like me to go with you?"

Katie shook her head. "If I'm going to move back to Florida, I'll have to learn to go places and do things on my own."

Mom opened her mouth as if she might say something more, but she closed it again and reached for her cup of coffee.

Dad looked over at Katie and winked. At least he understood why she needed to move.

~※ ※~

"Are you sure you have time to trim the trees in our yard this morning?" Fern asked Freeman during breakfast.

Freeman bobbed his head. "I'm caught up on things in my shop, so this is as good a time as any to get the trimming done."

She smiled. "If you can get started before I leave for school, I'll hold the ladder for you."

"That's okay," he said with a shake of his head. "I'll make sure the ladder's secure."

"Even so, I'd feel better if someone was here to help."

Freeman clenched his teeth. "I'm not a boppli, Fern, so stop treating me like one."

"I'm not."

"Jah, you are." He reached for a piece of toast. "Sometimes I think you just like telling me what to do."

"I do not! I just don't want to see you get hurt."

"I'll be fine on my own, so just go ahead to school and teach your scholars. By the time you get home, all the trees in our yard will have had a nice haircut."

"All right then," Fern said with a nod, "but please be careful."

"I will."

She pushed her chair away from the table, picked up her dishes, and carried them to the sink. "Oh, I forgot to mention that I talked to Eunice the other day, and she said that since she hasn't been able to find a job, she's decided to start selling candles and scented soaps. I think I might book a party with her soon."

"That's nice," Freeman mumbled around a mouthful of cereal.

Fern glanced over her shoulder. "Have you made any plans to go out with Eunice soon?"

He shook his head. "We broke up a few weeks ago. I thought I'd told you that."

"You did, but I was hoping you'd change your mind and get back together with her."

"Nope."

"Why not?"

"She's too much of a gossip, and she's pushing to get married." He gulped down the rest of his juice and swiped his tongue across his lip. "I'm not ready for marriage. At least not with her."

Fern's forehead wrinkled. "Are you thinking about marrying someone else?"

"Maybe. When the time's right."

"It's not Katie Miller, I hope."

Freeman blew out his breath. "What have you got against Katie?"

Fern shrugged. "I don't have anything against her personally, but I don't think she's the right woman for you." Fern glanced at the clock. "We can talk about this later. I need to go or I'll be late for school." She grabbed her canvas satchel and black outer bonnet then hurried out the door.

❧ ❧

"How are things going for you?" Dr. Coleman asked Katie as she took a chair on the other side of his desk.

"I've been driving the buggy more, and I'm having fewer panic attacks."

"That's good to hear. Are you going places that have caused

you to feel nervous in the past?"

Katie nodded.

"What do you feel has helped the most in conquering your panic attacks?"

"The tapping method, breathing exercises, and homeopathic remedy are helping me relax, and I think facing my fears and talking back to the panic attacks are keeping them from happening so often or lasting so long." Katie clutched the folds in her dress, wondering if she should bring up the subject of moving back to Florida.

"You look kind of thoughtful. Is there something on your mind?"

Katie nodded. She figured she may as well tell him now. "My dad's cousin and his wife will be moving to Florida soon, and I'm planning to go with them."

His eyebrows rose. "How come?"

Katie shifted in her chair, too embarrassed to tell him the reason she was planning to move. "Well, I like it in Florida, and I think I'll be happier there."

Dr. Coleman wrote something on his notepad. "Does this decision have something to do with your mother?"

Katie blinked. "No, of course not. Why would you think that?"

"I saw the way you responded during your first counseling session with me. It was obvious that your mother wouldn't let you speak for yourself, and whenever you did get in a word, she kept interrupting." He placed both hands on his desk and clasped his fingers together. "That's why I asked her not to sit in on any future sessions."

"My mother is overprotective, but that's not the reason I want to go back to Florida."

"What is the reason?"

Katie squinted against the ray of light streaming in the window as she struggled with what she wanted to say. "There are too many things here to remind me of my past. Too many things I'd rather forget."

"You can't run from your past. You'll only take your problems with you." He leaned forward and looked at her so intently that she squirmed in her chair. "You're just beginning to make some progress in dealing with your panic attacks. If you move now, you might lose ground."

"I'll still be able to do the things I'm doing now," she said.

"That may be true, but I think you'll do better if you keep coming here awhile longer. Will you at least think about it, Katie?"

She nodded, although as far as she was concerned, the decision had already been made. When Clarence and Mae were ready to move, Katie would be going with them.

~✖ ✖~

Later that afternoon while Katie was working in the stamp shop by herself, Ella showed up. "Is it true?" Ella asked, frowning.

"Is what true?"

"Are you really moving back to Florida?"

Katie nodded. "How'd you find out?"

"My mamm said your mamm told her when they saw each other at the Kuntry Store a few days ago."

"Oh, I see."

Ella folded her arms. "How come you didn't tell me about this, Katie?"

Katie swallowed hard, hoping she wouldn't cry. "I was going to tell you. I've just been busy and haven't had the chance to speak with you yet."

"Does anyone else know?"

"Just Mom and Dad. Of course I don't know who else Mom might have told."

Ella frowned. "What would make you decide to move back to Florida? I thought things were going better for you and that you were happy living here."

Tears welled in Katie's eyes, and she blinked to keep them from spilling over. "Freeman's going to marry Eunice next spring."

"What's that got to do with—" Ella's forehead puckered. "Oh, now I get it. You're in love with him, aren't you?"

Katie nodded slowly. "I. . .I didn't think I could ever love anyone but Timothy, but I feel so peaceful and content when I'm with Freeman." She reached for a tissue from Mom's desk and blew her nose. "At least, I used to."

Ella slipped her arms around Katie and gave her a hug. "I was afraid you were falling for him, and I tried to warn him not to lead you on, but—"

Katie pulled away. "You—you've talked to Freeman about me?"

"Jah. I knew he was going out with Eunice, and I was afraid if you fell in love with him, you'd end up getting hurt."

"What'd he say when you talked to him?"

"That I was worried for nothing, that you and he were just friends."

Katie swallowed several times until the lump in her throat disappeared. "I. . .I'm so embarrassed. I wish you hadn't talked to him. He probably thinks I'm a foolish little girl who's been trying to take him away from Eunice. I'll bet he wishes that he'd never befriended me." She leaned her head on Ella's shoulder. "I wish I'd never come back to Indiana!"

~≈ ≈~

Freeman had just finished writing up an ad he planned to place in *The People's Exchange* when Penny darted up to him with a ball in her mouth.

He leaned down, grabbed the ball, and tossed it across the room. "Go get it, girl!"

Woof! Woof! Penny raced after the ball, scooped it up in her mouth, and dashed back to Freeman. She dropped the ball in front of Freeman and looked up at him with her tail wagging and her head cocked.

Freeman chuckled and threw the ball again. Penny darted after it.

He was amazed at how quickly she caught on to things. He'd been able to teach her several tricks already—to fetch the ball, roll over, play dead, and sit up and beg. Besides the pleasure it had brought him to train Penny, his customers seemed to enjoy the pup's antics, too. Freeman had begun to wonder if some people came into the shop just to play with Penny.

Woof! Woof!

Freeman chuckled when she dropped the ball at his feet again. "Okay, but this is the last time, girl. I've got to get this ad written up; then I need to get outside and trim up some trees." Freeman tossed the ball, and Penny scampered after it.

He hurried to finish the ad; then he put the CLOSED sign in the window and went out the door. Penny raced out with him and found a place to sleep on one end of the porch.

Freeman went to the barn to get the ladder and lopping shears; then he hauled them across the yard and leaned the ladder against the most overgrown tree. Holding the shears in one hand, he climbed the ladder, reached up, and cut the nearest branch. Then he trimmed two more and leaned out farther to trim a third branch.

"Whoa!" Freeman clung to the ladder as it began to sway. He leaned to the left, trying to regain control, but it was too late. The ladder shifted again; then it toppled over. Freeman tossed the shears aside and reached for the closest branch. He missed and fell to the ground with a *thud*.

A searing pain shot through his chest, and he gasped for breath. *Dear God, send someone to help me, please.*

CHAPTER 42

Eunice was not looking forward to going to the stamp shop, but that's exactly where she was heading. She'd just come from the Lambrights' place, where she'd delivered some candles Ada had ordered. Mama had asked her to stop by the stamp shop on her way home to pick up some cardstock and a few scrapbooking supplies. Eunice dreaded seeing Katie because she knew that Katie was in love with Freeman. She could tell by the look on Katie's face whenever she and Freeman were together.

Eunice had hoped that after she'd told Katie that she and Freeman planned to be married, it would discourage her from hanging around Freeman so much. What Eunice hadn't expected was that Freeman would break up with her that very same night. She hoped she could get him to change his mind, but in the meantime, she was worried that Freeman might start going out with Katie.

When Eunice entered the stamp shop, JoAnn was busy waiting on an English woman, but there no sign of Katie. That was a relief. Maybe Katie wasn't working today. Maybe she wouldn't have to speak to Katie at all.

Anxious to be on her way, she hurried over to the scrapbooking supplies and picked out what Mama needed; then she grabbed a package of cardstock. As soon as the English woman left, Eunice placed the items on the counter.

JoAnn smiled. "Looks like you're going to be busy for a while."

"These aren't for me," Eunice said. "They're for my mamm."

"Oh, I see." JoAnn placed everything in a plastic bag. "Is there anything else you need?"

"No, but I was wondering where Katie is. Isn't she working here today?"

JoAnn shook her head. "Katie's up at the house, packing her suitcase."

"Is she going on a trip?"

"No, she'll be moving back to Florida tomorrow morning."

"Now that's sure a surprise."

"It was to us, too. She'll be living with Jeremy's cousin and his wife until she finds a job."

Eunice smiled to herself. With Katie out of the picture, Freeman was bound to take her back.

~ ❧ ~

Slurp! Slurp! Slurp!

Freeman moaned as Penny continued to lick his face. He tried to sit up, but the burning pain in his chest wouldn't allow him to move. He tried to talk, but he could barely breathe. All he could do was lie on the ground and pray.

Clip-clop. Clip-clop. Someone was coming up the lane. *Clip-clop. Clip-clop.* The sound of horse's hooves drew closer.

Freeman gritted his teeth and tried to get up, but it was no use.

Woof! Woof! Penny darted away.

Freeman lay there helplessly as Penny continued to bark. Even if he'd been able to holler for help, no one could have heard him with the dog yapping like that. Well, at least she'd quit licking his face.

Several minutes went by; then someone shouted his name.

"Oh, Freeman, what happened to you?" Eunice dropped to her knees beside him, her eyes wide with fear.

"F—fell," he rasped.

Eunice stared at him with a blank expression for several

seconds. Then she pointed to the ladder nearby. "Did you fall from that?"

He managed a slow nod. "C–can't breathe."

"I'm going to the phone shed to call for help!" Eunice leaped to her feet and hurried away.

Penny flopped down beside Freeman, whimpered, and licked his nose.

Freeman closed his eyes and said a prayer. *Thank You, Lord, for sending help.*

Several minutes went by; then Eunice knelt beside him again. "I called 911, and an ambulance is on the way." She took hold of Freeman's hand. "I was heading to your bike shop to tell you something, but Penny kept barking and looking up this way, so I decided I'd better see if something was wrong."

Freeman's chest hurt so bad, he could only nod in reply. He was relieved when he heard the wail of a siren.

"I'd better go to the schoolhouse and let Fern know what's happened," Eunice said after the ambulance arrived.

Freeman nodded and closed his eyes, thankful to God that Eunice had come along when she did.

CHAPTER 43

Would you like another pillow?" Fern asked as Freeman settled himself on the sofa.

He winced as he shook his head. "One's enough."

"Are you in pain?"

"A little."

"Should I get you some water and a pain pill?"

"Not right now. I had a pill before we left the hospital."

Slurp! Slurp! Penny, who'd been lying on the floor in front of the sofa, lifted her head and swiped her tongue across Freeman's hand.

"You're a good girl," Freeman mumbled.

Fern took a seat in the rocking chair across from him. "I'm so thankful that Eunice found you when she did. No telling what would have happened if she hadn't come along."

Freeman nodded. "I'm very grateful."

Fern's nose crinkled. "When Eunice came to the schoolhouse to tell me what happened, I could see how concerned she was. It's obvious that she cares for you, Freeman."

"I know." Freeman leaned his head against the pillow and closed his eyes. "I'm really tired. Could we talk about this later?"

A knock sounded on the door. Freeman opened his eyes and groaned. "I hope it's not someone who went looking for me at the bike shop."

"I'll see who it is." Fern hurried from the room, and when she returned a few seconds later, Eunice was with her.

"I was hoping you'd be home from the hospital by now," Eunice said, moving quickly across the room.

"I have something to do in the kitchen, so I'll leave you alone." Fern smiled at Eunice, and then she scurried from the room.

"How are you feeling?" Eunice asked, stepping into Freeman's field of vision.

"Fair to middlin', all things considered."

She took a seat on the end of the sofa by his feet. "I was really scared when I found you lying on the ground."

"I was scared, too." He grimaced as he tried to find a comfortable position. "Don't know what I'd have done if you hadn't come along when you did."

She nodded. "Guess it's a good thing Fern's puppy was barking like that, or I might not have come up to the yard."

Just then Penny leaped into Eunice's lap and swiped her tongue across Eunice's nose.

"Get down!" With a disgruntled look, Eunice pushed Penny to the floor.

Freeman smiled despite the pain in his chest. "Guess I'm not the only one that pup likes to kiss."

They spent the next several minutes in silence. The only noise in the room was the steady *tick-tock* of the clock on the far wall. Freeman wondered if Eunice felt as uncomfortable as he did. Was she expecting him to say that he'd changed his mind about breaking up with her?

Should I change my mind? he asked himself. *She did come to my rescue yesterday, and she does seem to care about me. Still, I'm not sure that's a good enough reason to keep going out with her.*

Eunice inched a little closer to Freeman. "When you're feeling better, maybe you can come over to my place for supper again."

The expectant look he saw on Eunice's face made him want to jump off the sofa, run out to the barn, and hide in the hayloft. But he was in no position to jump or run. "Since I'm gonna be laid up for the next several days, I probably won't be going anyplace," he said.

"I meant after you're feeling better."

"Maybe Fern and I can both come to supper after I catch up with things in the shop," he said, hoping to appease her.

Her mouth turned up at the corners. "That would be nice."

～≈ ≈～

Loraine's steps slowed as she neared the stamp shop. When Ella had told her that Katie was leaving for Florida tomorrow, she'd decided to come over and see if she could talk Katie out of going. She just hoped her cousin would listen to reason.

Loraine stood on the porch a few minutes as she asked God for wisdom in knowing what to say. Drawing in a deep breath, she stepped into the stamp shop. She found Katie bent over a piece of pegboard where some scissors and paper punches hung.

"I hear you'll be leaving us tomorrow," she said, stepping up to Katie.

"That's right," Katie said. "Clarence and Mae are planning to leave sooner than they expected."

Loraine touched Katie's shoulder. "Do you really have to go?"

Katie nodded, and tears gathered in her eyes. "It's the best thing for me right now."

"How come?"

Katie sank into a chair at her mother's desk. "Eunice has spread so many rumors about me, and with her and Freeman planning to get married next spring, it wouldn't be right for me and Freeman to remain close friends."

Loraine's eyebrows shot up. "Wayne and Freeman are pretty good friends, and as far as I know, Freeman hasn't mentioned anything to Wayne about marrying Eunice."

Katie shrugged. "They probably won't let too many people know until the time gets closer, but Eunice told me herself that she and Freeman would be getting married."

"Speaking of Freeman," Loraine said, "did you hear that he got hurt while he was pruning some trees in their yard?"

Katie bolted out of her chair. "When did that happen?"

"Yesterday morning. Eunice's daed came by the taxidermy shop with a fish he wanted stuffed, and he told Wayne that Freeman had been pruning some trees in their yard and fell off the ladder." Loraine's brows puckered. "I guess Freeman ended up in the emergency room with some broken ribs and a collapsed lung."

Katie covered her mouth with the palm of her hand. "That's baremlich!"

"You're right, it's terrible," Loraine agreed. "Eunice's daed said that Eunice told him that Freeman was in a lot of pain the day that it happened."

"Is he still in the hospital?"

"I don't think so. From what Wayne was told, Freeman was supposed to be released some time today."

Katie moved quickly toward the door. "When my mamm comes out of the bathroom, would you tell her I had an errand to run?" She scooted out the door before Loraine could respond.

CHAPTER 44

A s Katie headed out with her horse and buggy, she reminded herself to relax, breathe deeply, and stay focused on the road. She hadn't had a panic attack in several weeks, and she sure didn't need one now.

A flock of geese honked overhead and landed in a nearby field. At the same time, a car whipped past Katie, going much too fast, and she gripped the reins tightly, fearing that her horse might spook. Dixie, however, did okay, and so did Katie. She was more relaxed than she'd expected.

Katie hoped Freeman was home from the hospital and that she was doing the right thing in going to see him. She just couldn't leave Indiana without saying good-bye, and she needed to know that he was all right.

When Katie turned up the Bontragers' driveway, she saw a horse and buggy at the hitching rail near the barn. Apparently, Freeman must be home, and he already had some company. Katie didn't want to say good-bye to Freeman in front of anyone else, and she considered leaving a note, along with the banana nut cake she'd brought for him on the porch. But she wanted to say good-bye to Freeman in person, so she quickly dismissed that idea.

She pulled up to the other side of the rail, climbed down from the buggy, and secured her horse. Then she retrieved the container of cake and sprinted for the house.

Stepping onto the back porch, she rapped on the door. A few seconds later, she was greeted by Fern.

"I heard about Freeman's accident," Katie said. "I wanted to come by and see how he's doing."

"His ribs are very sore, but he's getting along okay." Fern glanced over her shoulder. "Knowing my energetic bruder, he'll be back on his feet in no time at all."

"Can I see him for a few minutes? I want to see how he's doing."

"Eunice is visiting with him right now. They're talking about some personal things, so I don't want to interrupt."

"Oh, I see." Katie heard muffled voices through the screen door and figured it was Freeman talking to Eunice. She cringed when she heard the words *love* and *marriage*. Eunice had obviously been telling the truth about getting married next spring. For all Katie knew, they might get married even sooner—maybe right after Freeman joined the church.

She stared at the toes of her sneakers, trying to decide what to do. It had taken courage to come over here, and she couldn't leave without at least letting Freeman know she'd been here.

Katie handed Fern the container with the cake inside. "Would you give this to Freeman and tell him that I'll be leaving for Florida tomorrow and wanted to say good-bye?"

Fern tipped her head as she took the cake. "Are you moving back to Florida?"

Katie nodded. "I'll be living with my daed's cousin and his wife until I'm able to get a job and a place of my own."

"Oh, I see. Well, that's probably for the best." Fern's mouth turned up at the corners. "You were happier there, right?"

"Jah, I was." Katie could barely speak around the lump in her throat. She really didn't want to leave Indiana, but hearing Freeman and Eunice talking about love and marriage made her even more certain that she was doing the right thing by moving back to Florida. "Will you tell Freeman I was here and give him the cake?" she asked in a voice barely above a whisper.

573

Fern gave a quick nod. "I wish you the best in Florida, Katie."

"Danki." Katie dashed down the steps and raced across the lawn. She quickly untied her horse and scrambled into the buggy. As soon as she took her seat, the dam broke and tears flowed freely down her cheeks.

As she guided Dixie down the lane and onto the road, she could barely see because of her tears, and her throat felt so clogged she could hardly swallow.

❦

"I'm sorry, Eunice," Freeman said, "but there's no point in us going out, because we can never have a permanent relationship."

"Why not?"

Freeman searched for truthful words that wouldn't hurt Eunice too much. "I, um, think we both know that our relationship isn't based on anything more than physical attraction."

Eunice's nose twitched. "Are you saying that the only thing you like about me is my pretty face?"

"It's not that. It's just that—" He blotted his sweaty forehead with the back of his hand and cleared his throat a couple of times.

"You're in love with Katie, aren't you?"

He nodded slowly. "But I don't know if—"

"How can you love her?" Eunice scowled at him. "Katie has emotional problems, and she's so immature."

Freeman's fingers clenched as irritation welled in his chest. He was trying to be nice to Eunice, but he was getting tired of hearing her put Katie down all the time. "Katie's panic attacks are getting better, and she's not immature!"

"Well, if you want my opinion, anyone who'd keep a baby when she should have notified the sheriff is immature," Eunice huffed.

"I'll admit that wasn't a good decision on Katie's part, but she's trying to make good decisions now, and she's able to cope with things a lot better."

Eunice left the sofa and dropped to the floor on her knees in front of Freeman. "Katie doesn't love you, Freeman."

A Cousin's PRAYER

"Maybe not now, but in time, she might. We've become good friends, and—"

"If she loved you, she wouldn't be moving back to Florida."

"What?" Heat shot up his neck and cascaded onto his cheeks.

"I talked to Katie's mamm the other day when I dropped off some candles at Ada's. She mentioned that Katie plans to move back to Sarasota. She wouldn't be doing that if she loved you, now would she?" Eunice looked up at him with questioning eyes and a hopeful smile. "Won't you please give us another chance? I'm sure if we spend more time together—"

"Did JoAnn say when Katie plans to move?"

"Uh—I think she said in a few days, but I'm not really sure."

He breathed a sigh of relief. That would give him time to heal enough so he could go over to Katie's and talk to her. Maybe if he came right out and told her that he loved her, she'd reconsider. Then again, a declaration of love might scare her off.

Just then Fern stepped into the room holding a plastic container with a cake inside. "Katie came by a few minutes ago, and she wanted me to give you this." She set the container on the coffee table.

"Did she say anything else?"

Fern glanced over at Eunice then back at Freeman. "She said she was leaving for Florida tomorrow morning and asked me to tell you good-bye."

Freeman groaned as he closed his eyes and pushed against the pillow. He couldn't believe Katie was leaving so soon. Never in all his twenty-two years had he felt like this. The physical pain in his ribs was nothing compared to the emotional pain in his heart.

❧ ❧

Eunice smiled to herself. Katie was leaving even sooner than she'd expected, which meant she'd no longer be a threat. Given a little more time, Eunice was sure that Freeman would forget about Katie, and then he'd see Eunice in a different light.

"I think I'd better go and let you get some rest," Eunice said, rising to her feet. "I'll be back tomorrow to see how you're doing."

Freeman opened his eyes and slowly shook his head. "Don't bother, Eunice. It's over between us."

Her mouth dropped open, and her eyelids drooped. "You— you can't mean that."

"Jah, I do. It's your fault Katie's leaving."

Indignation rose in Eunice's chest. "How can it be my fault?"

He shifted on the sofa and moaned. "If you hadn't started so many rumors about Katie, I don't think she'd ever have decided to go back to Florida."

Eunice thrust out her chin and was going to defend herself when Fern stepped up to her and said, "Maybe it'd be best if you went home now. Freeman looks tired, and he needs to rest."

Eunice gave a quick nod and rushed out the door. She hurried to her buggy, untied the horse, and was soon on her way.

"Well," she mumbled, gripping the reins, "I may never have Freeman, but Katie won't, either."

Eunice drew in a couple of deep breaths, trying to calm herself as she pulled out of the driveway. The trees lining the road swayed in the breeze, and the twittering of birds could be heard all around, but she barely took notice. "At the rate I'm going, I'll never find a husband," she mumbled. "Why have all my boyfriends pushed me away?"

Eunice had gone only a short ways when she spotted a dead possum in the road. She guided her horse and buggy around it but had just moved back into her lane when the sunlight caught a piece of metal lying on the shoulder of the road. The flash of light from the reflection temporarily blinded her and apparently startled her horse. He whinnied, stopped dead in the road, and then backed straight into the ditch.

Eunice snapped the reins, but the horse wouldn't budge. She reached for the buggy whip and cracked it over the horse's head. He lunged forward, but the buggy didn't move. The wheels were stuck.

She cracked the whip again, and the horse reared up. Clutching the reins, she tried to get him under control, but he only tossed his head from side to side and stomped his feet.

Suddenly, the buggy lunged forward, rocked back and forth,

and jerked to the right. The next thing Eunice knew, it had flipped on its side, spilling her out.

She felt groggy from hitting the hard ground, but she didn't think she'd been seriously hurt. Her first impulse was to jump up and run after her horse, which had managed to break free from the buggy and was galloping down the road. Before Eunice could make a move, she heard the rumble of buggy wheels coming down the road from the opposite direction. A few seconds later, the horse and buggy pulled in behind her rig. Andrew got out and secured his horse to a low-hanging branch.

"Are you all right?" he asked, rushing over to Eunice.

Inhaling slowly, she nodded and said, "I think so."

He reached out his hand to her. "How'd your buggy end up in the ditch?"

She stood and brushed a clump of dirt from her dress; then she quickly explained how her horse had reacted to the reflection and had backed into the ditch.

"Don't think I can do much about your horse," Andrew said. "He took off down the road like a flash of lightning and is probably halfway to your place by now. I'd be happy to give you a ride home, and then I can come back for your buggy later on."

"Danki." Eunice hoped her smile would convey the feelings of gratitude she felt. This was the second time Andrew had offered his help when she was in need. *Hmm. . .maybe he would make a good husband.*

❧ ❧

As Freeman lay on the sofa, he decided he had to see Katie, and it had to be now. Gritting his teeth, he winced as he rose from the sofa. He was almost to the back door when Fern stepped out of the kitchen and snapped her fingers. "Just where do you think you're going?"

"To the barn to get my horse."

"What for?"

"I need to see Katie."

"Oh no, you don't." She positioned herself between him and

577

the door. "You're not up to going anywhere right now, much less hitching the horse to the buggy."

He leaned around her and reached for the doorknob, but a searing pain shot through his ribs, and he braced himself against the wall for support.

Fern snapped her fingers again and pointed to the living room. "You ought to be lying down, and there's no need for you to see Katie today."

"Jah, there is. She's leaving tomorrow morning; you said so yourself." He grunted and held his hands against his sore ribs. "I wish you'd have invited her in so I could've talked to her."

"Would you like me to go out to the phone shed and leave a message for Katie on their answering machine?"

He shook his head. "She might not get the message before she leaves in the morning. I need to talk to her now."

Fern folded her arms and stared at Freeman as if he didn't have a lick of sense. Several seconds went by; then she puckered her lips and said, "You're in love with Katie, aren't you?"

"Jah. I don't know if she could ever love me, but I can't stand the thought of her leaving without me telling her the way that I feel."

Fern moved away from the door. "If you're determined to go, then let's wait until after supper, because it's almost done."

"Us? Are you suggesting that you'll go with me?"

She nodded.

"Huh-uh. I need to speak with Katie alone."

"That's fine; I'll wait in the buggy while you talk to her, but I can't stay here and worry while you go there alone."

Freeman took a few minutes to think things through; then he finally nodded. It would be a lot easier if Fern drove the buggy. He turned toward the living room. "I'm going back to the sofa to rest. Call me when supper's ready."

❧ ❧

When Katie entered the barn after supper that evening, she was greeted by the gentle nicker of the horses in their stalls and the sweet smell of hay.

She seated herself on a bale of straw and listened to the soft cooing of the pigeons in the rafters overhead. She'd come to say good-bye to Dixie and the other animals, but now that she was here, all she wanted to do was sit and cry. She would miss this place—her family, friends, and even the critters who lived in the barn. Most of all, she would miss Freeman. In the months since she'd come home from Florida, she had allowed herself to get closer to him than anyone else. She hadn't even felt that close to Timothy. It had been as if she and Freeman were soul mates. The only problem was that she loved him and he loved Eunice.

Katie moved across the room, reached over the gate in Dixie's stall, and stroked the horse's soft nose. Dixie whinnied and nuzzled Katie's hand.

Maybe it's best that I didn't get to say good-bye to Freeman, she decided. *It would have been too painful. At least this time I'm not running away from the memory of the accident that took Timothy's life. This time I'm going because I can't stand the idea of seeing Freeman with Eunice, which to me is just as painful as losing someone in death.*

Katie backed away from the stall, doubled over, and gave in to her tears. She would never let herself fall in love again. She would be an old maid for the rest of her life.

CHAPTER 45

Freeman woke up with a start. The room was dark, and at first, he didn't know where he was. Then he remembered that right after supper he'd gone back to the living room to rest one more time while Fern cleaned up the kitchen. They were supposed to head over to Katie's as soon as Fern got done with the dishes. Apparently, he'd fallen asleep. What he couldn't figure out was why Fern hadn't awakened him. It made him wonder if she'd let him sleep so he couldn't see Katie. From some of the things Fern had said in the past, Freeman knew that she liked Eunice a lot and hoped Eunice and Freeman would become a couple. He also knew that Fern saw Katie as an immature girl who had too many emotional problems, so it wouldn't surprise him if Fern purposely had let him sleep.

Freeman pulled himself to a sitting position, turned on the gas lamp on the table near the sofa, and groaned when he looked at the clock above the fireplace mantel. It was almost midnight! It was too late to go over to Katie's now. He wished he knew exactly what time she planned to leave in the morning. Now he'd have to set his alarm clock to go off early and hope he would make it over to the Millers' place before Katie left. If he didn't get there on time, he might be making an unplanned trip to Florida.

❧ ❧

"I wish you'd change your mind and stay here with us," Mom said tearfully as Katie set her suitcase by the front door.

"I wish I could, but going back to Pinecraft is the best thing for me right now. Maybe someday I'll come home again, but that might be a long time off."

Mom pulled Katie into her arms and gave her a hug. "I want you to know something before you go."

"What's that?"

"I'm sorry if I've seemed pushy or controlling. Since you're the youngest of my kinner, it's been hard for me to let go and allow you to make your own decisions." She gently patted Katie's back. "I hope you know how much I love you and only want what's best for you."

Katie nearly choked on the sob rising in her throat. "I know that, Mom, and I love you, too."

"Your mamm and I will come down to Florida to visit you this winter," Dad said, joining them in the hall. "It'll be good to get out of the cold, snowy weather we'll no doubt have here."

"I'd like that," Katie said as she hugged him. "Maybe I'll even have a place of my own by then."

Beep! Beep!

"That must be Clarence and Mae's driver," Dad said. He picked up Katie's suitcase and opened the door.

She followed him outside, and Mom walked beside her to the van. Clarence and Mae were in the back, but when Dad put Katie's suitcase inside, they both got out to say their good-byes to Mom and Dad.

"Take care of our girl," Mom said, hugging Mae.

"We will," Clarence and Mae both said.

Katie wanted to remind Mom once more that she wasn't a little girl but figured there was nothing to be gained by that. In her parents' eyes, she would always be their little girl.

Katie grimaced at the sinking feeling in the pit of her stomach. *If I never get married, I'll never know the joy of being a mother.* That thought hurt more than she cared to admit. Ever since Katie had been a little girl playing with her dolls, she'd wanted to be a mother. But some things weren't meant to be, and she'd have to learn to accept them and make a life for herself without a husband or children.

"We'd better get into the van now," Clarence said. "Our driver, Bill, is anxious to get going."

Katie gave Mom and Dad one last hug good-bye. She was just getting ready to climb into the van when a horse and buggy rumbled up the driveway. She waited to see who it was, and her breath caught when Freeman climbed down from the buggy.

"Thank the Lord I'm not too late," he said, walking slowly toward her.

"Too late for what?" Dad asked, looking at Freeman.

"Too late to speak to Katie." Freeman stood at her side. "Could we talk in private for a few minutes?"

The rhythm of Katie's heartbeat picked up speed. "Well, uh, we were just about to leave."

"I don't want you to go until you've heard what I have to say."

Katie looked at Dad, hoping for his approval. He stuck his head into the van and said something to their English driver. Then he turned to Freeman and gave a nod. "Bill said he'd wait another five minutes."

Freeman took Katie's arm and led her over to the porch. "Can we sit down? My ribs are really hurting."

She felt immediate concern. "You probably shouldn't be out of bed. What were you thinking, driving your buggy over here like that when you just came home from the hospital?"

"I didn't drive myself. Fern's waiting for me in the buggy."

"Even so, it's not good for you to—"

Freeman put his finger against Katie's lips. "I need you to listen to what I have to say."

Katie nodded and motioned for him to take a seat in one of the wicker chairs on the porch. Once he was seated, she sat in the chair next to him. "What'd you want to say?"

Freeman grimaced, as though in pain.

"Are you hurting really bad?" she asked.

"Jah, right here." Freeman placed his hand against his chest. "Why are you going back to Florida, Katie?"

She swallowed a couple of times, hoping she wouldn't break down in tears. "I. . .uh. . .think I'll be happier there."

He crinkled his nose. "I don't want you to go, Katie, and well, I wanted to say that if you ever decide to love again, I. . .I'd like to be the one."

Katie's heart began to pound, and her mouth felt so dry she could barely speak. She'd never expected to hear Freeman say such a thing to her. "What about Eunice? I thought you were going to marry her."

Freeman shook his head vigorously. "I never planned to marry Eunice. She may have wanted it, but I can't make a lifetime commitment to someone I don't love. Truthfully, I don't think Eunice really loves me, either. I think she's just looking for a husband, and in due time she'll find someone else—hopefully someone she really loves." He reached for Katie's hand and gave her fingers a gentle squeeze. "It's you I love, and after I've joined the church this fall, I'd like us to be married." His face sobered. "That is, if you'll have me."

A wide smile spread across Katie's face. "I love you, too, and I'd be honored to be your wife." The words came out in a wondering tone as the meaning of his words sank in. Freeman loved her, not Eunice.

Freeman stroked Katie's cheek as he gazed into her eyes. "You're the girl—I mean, the woman for me. I've known it ever since we were kinner." He leaned closer until their lips were almost touching.

Beep! Beep!

Katie's eyes snapped open, and her gaze went to the van waiting to take her away. "I'll be right back!" she hollered over her shoulder as she tore across the yard. When she reached the van, she leaned inside, grabbed her suitcase, and shut the door. "I'm not moving to Florida," she said, smiling at Mom and Dad. "I'm staying right here, and when the time is right, I'm going to marry Freeman."

Mom looked at Dad, and Dad looked at Mom. Both of their faces broke into wide smiles.

Katie handed her suitcase to Dad then hurried back to the

WANDA E. BRUNSTETTER

porch and took a seat beside Freeman.

"Were your folks happy to hear that you're staying?" he asked.

Katie nodded and smiled. "I used to think that God never answered any of my prayers, but I've come to realize that He answered every one—just not always the way I wanted Him to." She reached over and boldly took Freeman's hand. " 'God hath not given me the spirit of fear, but of power, and of love, and of a sound mind.' He's answered my prayers and helped me deal with my panic attacks. Best of all, He's given you to me."

Freeman leaned close to Katie, and this time there was no horn honking to stop his tender kiss.

Being careful not to cause further injury to Freeman's ribs, Katie gave him a gentle hug. "I pray that all of my cousins will be there on our wedding day," she whispered in his ear. "And I pray that God will give us many years together as husband and wife."

Katie's Banana Nut Cake

2 cups flour
1⅔ cups sugar
1 teaspoon salt
¾ teaspoon baking powder
1½ teaspoons baking soda
⅔ cup shortening
⅔ cup sour milk or buttermilk
3 eggs
1 teaspoon vanilla
1½ cups mashed bananas
⅔ cup chopped nuts

Mix all ingredients thoroughly and pour into a greased and floured 9 x 13 x 2 inch pan. Bake at 350 degrees for 35–40 minutes.

DISCUSSION QUESTIONS

1. Katie Miller had a difficult time accepting her boyfriend's death, and afterward, she went through a period of depression. Has someone you know gone through something similar? If so, how did you try to help them work through their depression?

2. List some ways you can help someone going through depression. What should you not do when someone's dealing with depression?

3. Did Katie's folks do the right thing by sending her to live with her grandparents after Timothy died? Do you think Katie's parents were supportive of her, or were they too controlling?

4. When Katie returned to Indiana her depression turned into anxiety attacks. At first, Katie tried to hide the attacks, feeling embarrassed and confused by her unexplained symptoms. Have you or someone you know ever suffered from anxiety attacks? If so, were you embarrassed by the symptoms? Did you tell someone about the feelings or try to hide them?

5. Why it is important to share your feelings with someone when you're going through depression or some kind of an emotional problem?

6. What are some ways you can help someone dealing with anxiety attacks? Do you think there's ever a time when a person can deal with these kinds of attacks alone, or do they always need the guidance of a trained professional?

7. When Loraine miscarried, she was deeply saddened, although she accepted it as God's will. What are some ways you can help someone who has lost a baby?

8. When Katie found a baby on her porch and decided not to notify the sheriff right away, she told Freeman about it. Did Freeman do the right thing when he agreed to keep Katie's secret? What would have been a better way for Freeman to have helped Katie?

9. Is there ever a time when it's all right to gossip or talk about someone's problems?

10. Eunice was jealous of the attention Freeman gave Katie, so she gossiped about Katie and tried to make her look bad. What should a person do when they know someone is gossiping about them?

11. What life's lessons did you learn from reading *A Cousin's Prayer*?

12. Were there any verses of scripture that spoke to your heart? If so, in what way might you use that scripture to deal with some situation in your own life?

13. What did you learn about the Amish way of life that you didn't know before?

A Cousin's
CHALLENGE

INDIANA COUSINS | BOOK 3

DEDICATION/ACKNOWLEDGMENTS

To Ada Nancy Smoker, who has taught many deaf children over the years and provided me with much information about the hearing impaired. To Sandy Rose for the information on hearing loss she shared with me. To Deborah Trevett for sharing with me some things about her own loss of hearing. To the following Indiana friends who answered many of my questions during the making of this series: Irene and Melvin Miller and family; Betty and Richard Miller and family; Orley Lambright and family; Karen and Dave Lehman, Katie and Mary Yoder; Marilyn Hostetler; Mary Alice and Harley Yoder and family; Doretta and Mark Yoder; Orley and Dianna Yoder and family; Harley Miller; Bob Kurth; and Arlene and Wayne Randolph. I also wish to thank my editors, Rebecca Germany and Becky Durost Fish, for their help with the editing process. Thanks also to the following people who shared some of their humorous stories with me: Jake Smucker, Betty Miller, and Lorine VanCorbach.

I will instruct thee and teach thee in the way which thou shalt go:
I will guide thee with mine eye.

PSALM 32:8

CHAPTER 1

Quiet darkness met Jolene Yoder as she stepped into Aunt Dorcas's kitchen. After losing her hearing two years ago in a van accident, she'd become used to the quiet. There were even times when she saw it as a blessing rather than a hindrance. Oh, she missed some things—twittering birds, rain splattering on the roof, the soft *mew* of a kitten, and her mother's gentle voice. What she didn't miss were blaring car horns, squeaking doors, roaring thunder, and the shrill voices of people shouting.

She flipped on the light switch and glanced around. Aunt Dorcas was obviously not at home. If she were, she'd be in the kitchen, starting supper. Maybe she was still at the sewing circle, where she and several women from her Mennonite church were making quilts and other items for the Mennonite Relief Sale that would take place later this fall.

Someone touched Jolene's shoulder, and she whirled around. *"Sorry if I startled you,"* Uncle Charlie signed.

"It's okay," Jolene spoke as she signed. She understood that tapping her shoulder was sometimes the best way to get her attention. "I thought Aunt Dorcas would be home by now. Do you know why she's so late?"

"When she left this morning, she said she planned to make a few stops on her way home from church this afternoon." Uncle Charlie spoke rather than signed, and Jolene interpreted by reading his lips.

"Guess I'd better start supper so we can eat as soon as she gets home."

"Would you consider making chicken potpie?"

She nodded and grinned. Uncle Charlie might not have a Pennsylvania Dutch background, but he sure liked Pennsylvania Dutch food.

"If you don't need me for anything, I think I'll go back to the living room and finish reading the newspaper," Uncle Charlie said.

"I can manage, so go right ahead."

"We've sure enjoyed having you here." He patted her arm and ambled from the room.

She quirked an eyebrow. What had Uncle Charlie meant when he'd said "enjoyed"? It sounded as if he thought she had plans to leave.

Jolene shrugged and turned toward the stove. He probably hadn't meant anything.

She had just started the broth for the potpie when Aunt Dorcas got home. "Sorry I'm late," she both said and signed. "It took me much longer to do my errands than I expected, and traffic was terrible between here and Lancaster."

"No problem. I've already started supper." Jolene motioned to the bubbling broth on the stove, filling the room with a savory fragrance. "It shouldn't take too long."

Aunt Dorcas pulled out two chairs at the table. "Would you sit a minute? I'd like to talk to you about something." Her expression was solemn.

"Is something wrong?"

"While you were at the dentist's this morning, I talked to your mother on the phone."

"How is she? Are things going well at home?"

Aunt Dorcas nodded. "She had a message for you."

"What was it?"

"The school board met yesterday, and they asked if you'd come home."

Jolene's eyebrows rose. "How come? They know I can't teach anymore."

"Two deaf children have moved with their family from Millersburg, Ohio, to your hometown of Topeka, Indiana. Their parents have the Rh factor, and the children haven't been able to hear since they were born. They've each had a year of schooling, but they need someone who can sign and read lips to continue their education."

Jolene shook her head. "Huh-uh; I'm not ready for that."

"You've been with us two years now and have become proficient at signing and reading lips," Aunt Dorcas said. "I think you're more than ready to go home and teach those special children."

"Why don't their parents send them somewhere else to learn? There are lots of good schools for the deaf, like the one here in Pennsylvania where you've taught."

"They did take the children somewhere to learn how to sign, but they want the family to be together at home now." Aunt Dorcas placed her hand gently on Jolene's arm. "They want you to provide their basic schooling and teach them how to read lips."

A gentle breeze floated through the open window and fluttered the curtains. Jolene shivered. She felt comfortable and confident here in Pennsylvania. She'd made friends with some of the deaf students Aunt Dorcas taught. The thought of going home sent a ripple of apprehension up her spine.

"You've missed teaching school; you've mentioned it so many times," Aunt Dorcas said.

"I know, but this would be different. I'd be teaching children who can't hear."

"That's right. And since *you* can't hear, who better to teach them?"

Aunt Dorcas's innocent question pried through Jolene's numbness, and she turned to stare out the window. She tried to envision what each person in her family was doing right now, for she truly did miss them. She tried to picture herself back home again, teaching two deaf children how to read and write. She thought about her cousins and how nice it would be to spend time with them again. She even thought about her buggy horse, Belle, and wondered if the easygoing mare missed her.

After several minutes of contemplation, Jolene turned to Aunt Dorcas and said, "Call Mom, and tell her to let the school board know that I'll be home by the end of the week."

CHAPTER 2

The clean scent of freshly laundered sheets on Jolene's bed brought a smile to her lips. She'd arrived home last night and had been greeted enthusiastically by her family. Her brother Andrew had even given Jolene one of his balloon creations made to look like a flower. She was grateful that she knew how to read lips, since no one in her immediate family knew how to sign. She wanted to begin working on that right away and hoped that once Mom, Dad, and Andrew learned, one of them might be willing to sign during their church services.

Jolene slipped out of bed and stretched her arms over her head. She padded across the cold hardwood floor in her bare feet and stared out the window. The morning sun cast a golden haze over their cornfield. Her nose twitched as the smell of burning leaves, a sure sign of fall, drifted through the open window. Dad must be working in the yard already. He'd always gotten up early to do his chores so he could be in his buggy shop by eight o'clock.

Jolene turned away from the window, and her gaze came to rest on the hope chest sitting at the foot of her bed. She'd received it as a birthday present when she'd turned sixteen and had started filling it right away with a variety of things she might need when she got married. *I guess that may never happen, since I don't have a boyfriend,* she thought. *Even if I did have one, would any man want to marry a woman who can't hear?*

Knowing she couldn't give in to self-pity and needed to get

downstairs to help with breakfast, Jolene moved over to her dresser. She picked up her hairbrush and began brushing her long hair, which hung below her waist.

Sometime this morning, she wanted to see her cousins Loraine, Ella, and Katie. Then this evening, she planned to meet with the school board and talk about teaching the two deaf children who'd moved to the area.

Uneasiness tightened her chest. Was she really ready to begin teaching again? What if the children were difficult to teach? What if she didn't have all the skills she needed? Maybe she'd made a mistake in agreeing to take this position.

A vibration she felt told Jolene someone must be knocking on her door, so she turned from the window and yelled, "Come in!" At least she thought she'd yelled the words. Since Jolene could no longer hear her own voice, she couldn't be sure how loud she'd spoken.

When the door opened, her brother Andrew stepped into the room. "Mom said to tell you that breakfast is almost ready."

Jolene was glad Andrew had spoken slowly while looking directly at her. Otherwise, she couldn't have read his lips. She smiled and said, "Tell her I'll be down as soon as I get dressed and have my hair put up in place."

Andrew hesitated a minute as though he might want to say something more, but then he gave a quick nod and hurried out the door.

Jolene sighed. Did Andrew feel uncomfortable talking to her? Would he be willing to learn sign language so they could communicate better? She certainly hoped so.

❧ ❧

"Is Jolene up?" Mom asked when Andrew entered the kitchen.

"*Jah.* Said she'd be right down." Andrew poured himself a cup of coffee and took a seat at the table. "It's hard to think of her being *daab.* I mean, she seemed to understand every word I said to her. It made me feel like she's not really deaf."

"Remember what she told us last night? She was reading your

lips, the way your *daed*'s sister taught her to do while she was living in Pennsylvania." Mom set a plate of toast on the table.

"It just seems strange to me, that's all." Andrew blew on his coffee and took a tentative sip. "Do you think she'll be able to teach those daab *kinner*?"

Mom's forehead wrinkled. "Of course she can teach the deaf children. Jolene was a good teacher before she lost her hearing, and I'm sure she'll be a good teacher to the daab kinner, too."

He drummed his fingers along the edge of the table. "You think she'll expect us to learn how to talk with our hands?"

"Uh-huh. Before Jolene went to bed last night, she told me and your daed that she hoped we would all be willing to learn signing." Mom took a jug of Dad's homemade apple cider from their propane-operated refrigerator. "Jolene's right, Andrew. If we're going to communicate with her and tell her what others are saying, we need to learn sign language."

"But if she can read our lips, why do we have to learn how to sign?"

Mom set the cider on the table and took a seat across from him. "We need to understand the signs Jolene uses when she talks, and we need to learn to sign. It will help us all if we can communicate that way. And when others are speaking, like the ministers during church, hopefully one of us will be able to sign so Jolene will know what they're saying."

"Maybe those two daab kinner, too?"

"Jah. It would help them as well."

"Sorry I'm late," Jolene said when she entered the room. "It felt so good to sleep in my own bed that I slept longer than I thought I would."

Mom smiled. "That's okay. Your daed's still outside, so we won't be ready to eat until he comes in."

"Dad went back to bed?" Jolene asked with a look of surprise.

Mom's eyebrows shot up. "I think you *missverschtch* what I said."

"Didn't you say that Dad's in bed?"

Mom shook her head and then glanced over at Andrew with

a strange expression. He was beginning to realize that just because Jolene could read lips it didn't mean she understood every word they said.

Jolene moved closer to Mom. "Would you please repeat yourself? It would help, too, if you spoke a little slower this time."

"Your daed is still outside doing his chores," Mom said slowly. "We'll eat when he comes in."

Holding her right hand in front of her body, Jolene then brought it up and rested her thumb on her chest. "I. . ." She flicked her index finger off her thumb in front of her forehead. "Understand. I understand."

Mom looked over at Andrew. "We should both try that."

He grunted. "It looks too hard."

"Would you show us again?" Mom asked Jolene.

Jolene repeated the sentence, as well as the action with her hand, while Mom and Andrew tried to follow along.

"Don't think I'll ever catch on," Andrew mumbled as he tried to flick his thumb the way Jolene had done.

"Sure you will. It just takes practice," Jolene said. "There's a lot I can teach you if you're willing to learn."

"We'll all learn." Mom smiled. "You can start by giving us a lesson this evening after supper."

~≈ ≈~

As Lonnie Hershberger stepped into the barn, he was greeted by the unmistakable sound of grunting pigs awaiting their breakfast.

He groaned. Slopping hogs was not his favorite thing to do. But as much as he disliked it, he'd follow through on the promise he'd made to Pop to help out whenever he could.

Lonnie and his family had moved from Arthur, Illinois, to Middlebury, Indiana, a few months ago. Soon after their arrival, Lonnie had begun working for Rueben Yoder, tuning wind chimes. Lonnie had been playing the harmonica since he was a boy, and he had a good ear for music. Learning to tune the chimes had come easily to him, and he enjoyed his new job more than any other he'd held. Certainly more than working with pigs.

When Lonnie and his folks had first moved to Indiana, he'd thought he would miss Illinois. But the only thing he missed was his girlfriend, Carolyn, whom he'd been writing to at least once a week. In Lonnie's last letter, he'd invited Carolyn to visit Indiana. He hoped he'd receive a letter from her soon and that she'd be willing to come.

He dumped the food into the trough and watched as the mother hogs rustled their snouts into the slop, while their babies nudged the sows' udders for milk. The greedy little piglets bit each other and carried on as though they were starving to death.

"Knock it off!" Lonnie reached over the stall and nudged one of the piglets with a stick, hoping to break up the fight. The mother pig let out a high-pitched squeal, jerked her head around, and bit Lonnie's hand.

"Ow!" Fiery pain shot up his arm. "Let go, you stupid *sau!*"

The sow hung on, tearing into Lonnie's flesh. He ground his teeth together as sweat beaded up on his forehead and trickled onto his cheeks. "Let go!"

He swatted the sow's rump with the stick. When she finally let go, he breathed a sigh of relief but winced when he saw blood oozing from the wound in his hand.

A wave of anger swept over him. "Oh, great! Now I'll probably need stitches!" He kicked the stall door as another burst of pain shot up his arm.

CHAPTER 3

When breakfast was over and the dishes were done, Jolene slipped on a sweater. "I'm going over to see Ella," she said to Mom, who sat in front of her quilting frame on the sunporch. "Then I plan to stop and see Loraine and Katie."

"That's a good idea. I'm sure they'll be real glad to see you again." Mom had turned her head toward Jolene, and when she spoke, her lips moved slowly, making it easier for Jolene to know what she'd said.

"I'll be back in time to help with supper," Jolene signed as she spoke. Even though Mom didn't know how to talk with her hands yet, Jolene thought it was good for her to see the hand positions. This evening when the family gathered for their first lesson, she would show them some specific words and letters.

Mom smiled as her fingers moved deftly, creating an intricate pattern on the quilt that was taking shape on her quilting frame. "Could you hand me those *schpelle*?" she asked, pointing to the container of pins on the sewing machine.

Jolene picked up the pins and gave them to Mom. "Guess I'd better get going."

"*Danki*, and have a *gut* day."

Jolene nodded and scooted out the door. Her nose twitched as the distinctive odor of wood smoke drifted across the pasture from their neighbor's chimney. There had been a day when she probably wouldn't have noticed the smoke, but her sense of smell

602

had gotten keener since she'd lost her hearing.

As Jolene walked toward the barn to get her horse, a blustery breeze hit her full in the face. She looked up and saw the branches in the trees way up high hitting each other. Then she glanced at the dead leaves on the ground and noticed the wet, earthy smell they gave off. They were well into fall, and soon winter would be ushered in by cold snow and harsh winds. Maybe by then, her family would be able to communicate through signing, and she'd feel more at ease. She'd been gone so long that she almost felt as if she didn't belong here anymore. She'd been comfortable living with Aunt Dorcas and Uncle Charlie. Even though she'd missed her family in Indiana, Pennsylvania had begun to feel like her home. Maybe after a few more days, she'd feel like she was part of the family again.

Something soft and fuzzy brushing Jolene's leg brought her thoughts to a halt. She looked down and smiled at the silver-gray kitten staring up at her. It couldn't have been more than a few weeks old.

She bent over and picked up the kitten. Its nose felt soft, like a swatch of velvet, and Jolene felt the vibration of the kitten's purrs against her chest. "Where's your *mamm*, little one? Should we see if she's in the barn?"

The kitten opened its tiny mouth in a silent *meow*. Jolene patted its soft, furry head. "We'll find your mother, don't worry."

When Jolene opened the barn door and stepped inside, she was greeted by the aroma of sweaty horse flesh mixed with sweet-smelling hay. She smiled. Some things never changed.

She spotted Fluffy, the mother cat, sleeping in a pile of straw, and placed the kitten beside her. As Jolene was getting ready to open the gate to her horse's stall, Andrew showed up.

Jolene saw his lips move as he turned his head toward the stall, but she had no idea what he'd said. She tapped his shoulder. "I didn't understand you. Please, look at me when you speak."

He turned toward her with a sheepish expression. "Sorry. I was just saying that I heard you were going over to see Ella, so I thought I'd get your horse hitched to the buggy for you."

Even though it had been some time since Jolene had hitched a horse or driven a buggy, she was sure she could do it. But she didn't want to appear ungrateful, so she smiled and said, "Danki, I appreciate that."

Andrew touched Jolene's arm. "I'm sorry for the way I acted this morning. I'm just not sure I can learn to talk with my hands."

She thumped his arm. "I learned how to do it. I'm sure you can, too."

"Guess we'll have to see how it goes." Andrew took Jolene's horse, Belle, from her stall. As he led Belle out of the barn, Jolene followed.

She marveled at the agility of Andrew's sun-bronzed hands as he worked easily to hitch Belle to the buggy. He'd done it much faster than she ever could.

When Andrew finished the job, he held the horse while Jolene climbed into the buggy. "Guess I'd better get my own horse and buggy ready to go now," he said, poking his head into the buggy and looking directly at Jolene. "I need to get to the harness shop or I'll be late for work."

"All right then. Have a good day." Jolene picked up the reins and got the horse moving. When she reached the end of the lane, she was relieved to see that no cars were coming in either direction. Getting the feel for driving the buggy again would be easier with less traffic on the road.

As Jolene traveled along, she felt the rhythmic vibrations of the horse's hooves pounding against the pavement. This was another sense that had increased since she'd become deaf. Even though she couldn't hear any cars that came up behind her, she could sense their presence by the vibration of the wheels on the road and see them by looking in her buggy's side mirrors.

Jolene relaxed against the seat, enjoying the fall foliage and gazing at the many Amish farms scattered along this stretch of road. Despite the comfort she'd come to know in Pennsylvania, she had missed Indiana and its wide-open spaces. Even though this area was often visited by tourists, it wasn't nearly as congested or commercialized as what she'd seen in Lancaster County, Pennsylvania.

After a short drive, Jolene guided Belle up the driveway to Uncle Rueben and Aunt Verna's place and pulled up to the hitching rail near the barn. Just as she was climbing down from the buggy, Ella came out the front door and sprinted across the lawn.

"*Ach*, it's so good to see you!" Ella said, rushing up to Jolene. Her pale blue eyes filled with tears, and she gave Jolene a welcoming hug. "Are you able to read my lips?" she asked after she'd pulled away.

"Jah, but it would be easier for me to know what you're saying if you could talk with your hands."

"I'm not sure I could learn to do that. I think it would be too hard."

"It's not that difficult. I'm going to teach my family, and I'd be happy to teach you if you'd like to learn."

"I'm willing to try." Ella motioned to the house and then turned her head in that direction.

Even though Jolene could see Ella's lips move, she had no idea what she'd said. She stepped in front of Ella. "In order for me to read your lips, I need to see your face."

A blotch of red erupted on Ella's cheeks. "Sorry about that. What I said was, 'Let's get your horse put in the corral; then we can go inside for a cup of tea while we get caught up on one another's lives.'"

"That sounds good, but I can't stay too long. I want to stop and see how Loraine and Katie are doing."

"If you stay awhile, you won't have to stop and see them, because they're both coming over here soon."

"They are?"

"Jah. We knew you were supposed to get home last night, so we made plans to meet here and then go by your place and take you out for lunch."

"That sounds nice, but it'll be harder for us to visit at a restaurant with so many people around."

"What if we stay here and have lunch?"

Jolene smiled. "That's fine with me. I'd be more comfortable eating here than at a restaurant, anyway."

They'd just gotten Belle put in the corral when a horse and buggy came up the drive. Thinking it must be Katie or Loraine, Jolene turned and waved. After the buggy had pulled up to the hitching rail and the driver got out, she was surprised to see that it wasn't either one of her cousins. It was a young Amish man with wavy blond hair. She was sure she'd never seen him before.

Ella must have known him, though, for she rushed right over. They talked a few minutes, but with their backs to Jolene, she had no idea what they were saying.

Finally, they turned, and the young man followed Ella as she headed back toward Jolene. His chiseled cheeks and prominent jaw dwarfed his narrow nose, and his eyes were the rich brown color of spring soil. Jolene couldn't help but feel his curious gaze, and her face heated.

"I'd like you to meet Lonnie Hershberger," Ella said, looking at Jolene. "He and his family moved here a few months ago, and Lonnie's been working for my daed, tuning and cutting the pieces of pipe that make up our wind chimes." She looked over at Lonnie and smiled, and then she motioned to Jolene and looked back at her. "This is my cousin Jolene. She's the one I told you had been living in Pennsylvania, where she learned to sign and read lips."

"It's nice to meet you." Lonnie shook Jolene's hand. That's when she noticed a large bandage wrapped around his other hand.

"One of my daed's ornery pigs bit me this morning," Lonnie explained. "The wound was so bad that I had to get stitches and a tetanus shot."

Jolene grimaced. "Does it hurt much?"

"Not so much at the moment, but it sure did when the *dumm sau* bit me." Lonnie's thick eyebrows almost met his nose when he frowned.

"Will you be able to work today?" Ella asked. Her question was directed at Lonnie, but she was turned toward Jolene enough so that she could read her lips.

Lonnie's frown deepened. "Afraid not. With only one good hand, I won't be able to cut any pipes."

"That's too bad. I'm sure Papa will be sorry to hear about your hand," Ella said.

"Guess I'd better go tell him right now. Is he up at the shop?" Lonnie asked.

"Jah."

Lonnie gave Jolene a brief nod. "Nice meeting you."

"It was nice meeting you, too."

As Lonnie headed up the driveway toward the shop, Ella turned to Jolene and smiled. "He's nice, and he's sure got an ear for music. Before Lonnie came along, Papa couldn't find anyone besides himself to tune the chimes. We're fortunate to have Lonnie working for us."

Jolene didn't voice her thoughts, but seeing the way Ella's face lit up when she talked about Lonnie made her wonder if there might be something going on between them. As they reached the porch steps, Jolene said, "Lonnie's nice looking, don't you think?"

Ella's eyebrows shot up. "After only one meeting, are you interested in him?"

Jolene shook her head vigorously. "Ach, no! I just meant. . ."

Ella touched Jolene's arm. "I hope you don't have any ideas about Lonnie, because he's got a girlfriend back in Illinois, and I believe she might be coming here for a visit soon. I suspect from what Lonnie's said that he hopes to marry her."

Jolene's mouth dropped open. Before she could explain her question, a cloud of dust swirled across the yard as another horse and buggy rolled in. The lathered-up horse, flipping its head from side to side, headed straight for the barn.

CHAPTER 4

I'm sorry to hear that," Rueben said after Lonnie told him about the sow biting his hand. "Guess you won't be able to work today."

"Probably not for a few days. Hopefully by Monday I'll be able to use my injured hand." Lonnie grimaced as frustration boiled in his soul. He wished he didn't have to miss any work. He'd been trying to save up enough money so he could ask Carolyn to marry him, but the more work he missed, the longer it would be before he felt free to ask. Of course, Pop thought Lonnie ought to work for him full-time, slopping and butchering pigs. What was the fun in that? Making wind chimes was a lot more enjoyable.

Besides, Rueben appreciated Lonnie's work; he'd said so many times. And he didn't criticize everything Lonnie did the way Pop often did. Nothing seemed to be good enough for Pop: not the way Lonnie groomed the horses, not the way he butchered hogs, not even the way he fed the stupid swine. In Pop's mind, there was always a better way of doing things. His way; that's what he thought was best.

"You're lookin' mighty glum," Rueben said, nudging Lonnie's arm. "Are you that upset about missing a day's work?"

"Guess maybe I am. Can't afford to miss too many days, that's for sure." Lonnie glanced around Rueben's shop. Pieces of pipe that he'd cut yesterday lay on a table where Charlene, Rueben's seventeen-year-old daughter, was busy stringing the chimes. On another table lay several more pieces of pipe still needing to be cut and tuned. Lonnie figured Rueben would probably take over his job until he returned to work, which meant he wouldn't be free to make deliveries and pick up supplies, like he normally did.

"I know what you mean about not wanting to miss too many days of work," Rueben said. "In this day and age, we all need some kind of steady employment." His deeply set blue eyes darkened as he pulled his fingers through the ends of his full, red beard. "So many businesses are going under. I'll admit that I'm a little worried about whether folks will keep buying wind chimes with the economic distress we're facing right now."

"I'm sure everything will be okay," Lonnie said. "Many businesses outside of our area buy your chimes. If you were only relying on local businesses, it might be a concern, but jobs aren't as scarce in some other places as they are right here."

Rueben's face relaxed a bit. "You've got a good point. Guess I need to let go of my worries and leave my business in God's hands."

"That's the best way, all right. Think I'd better head for home and put some ice on my hand. Since there's no church in our district this Sunday, I probably won't see you until Monday."

"See you then," Rueben said with a nod.

Lonnie went out the door, but he'd only taken a few steps when he spotted a horse and buggy coming up the driveway at a very fast pace. The horse was lathered up, and no one was driving the buggy. He raced down the driveway, waving his hands, hoping to detour the horse. Ella, who'd been standing near the corral next to her cousin, started after the horse at the same time.

The horse was almost to the barn when it screeched to a stop and stood pawing the ground.

Ella grabbed the horse's bridle. "Whew. . .that's a relief! I thought for sure that crazy animal was going to run into the side of our barn."

"I wonder whose rig this is and how come there's no driver," Lonnie said.

"I have no idea where the driver is, but this is the horse Papa sold my cousin Katie's daed a week ago. He's always been a bit of a challenge."

609

"Your cousin's daed or the horse?" Lonnie asked with a chuckle.

Ella grinned. "There might be times when Aunt JoAnn thinks Uncle Jeremy's a bit of a challenge, but I was referring to the horse."

Lonnie studied Ella for a minute. Her reddish blond hair and pale blue eyes stood in sharp contrast to Jolene's dark brown hair and vivid blue eyes. It was hard to believe they were cousins. In the few minutes he'd visited with them before going to Rueben's shop, Lonnie had determined that the young women's personalities were very different, too. Ella could be quite outspoken and was a take-charge kind of person. Jolene, on the other hand, seemed a bit more reserved. Maybe that was because she couldn't hear.

Lonnie was grateful for his two good ears. He didn't know what he'd do if he couldn't hear the beautiful melody of the wind chimes he helped create. The melodious sounds made him think about David in the Bible and the harp he used to play.

Ella's eyebrows drew together as she frowned. "Since this is the horse my daed sold Uncle Jeremy, I'm wondering if Katie should have been driving the buggy."

"What do you mean, 'should have been'?" Lonnie questioned.

"Katie's supposed to come over here this morning, and so is my cousin Loraine. Maybe the horse got away from Katie before she could get into the buggy." Ella stroked the horse's mane. "Is that what happened, big fellow? Did you get in a hurry to go and then decide to head over here because it's the place you know best?"

The horse nuzzled Ella's hand in response.

"Would you like me to look for Katie on my way home?" Lonnie asked. "If she's out searching for the horse, I might see her walking alongside the road."

Before Ella could respond, another horse and buggy rolled into the yard. When it pulled up to the hitching rail, Ella's cousins Loraine and Katie stepped down. Katie looked relieved when she saw her horse, but Loraine didn't seem to notice. She was too busy greeting Jolene.

"I was trying to get in my buggy to come over here when the

horse took off without me. I'm glad to see he came here and isn't out on the road running for who knows where," Katie said.

"That's what I thought might have happened," Ella said. "Guess it'll take some time for the horse to get used to its new home and owners."

"I would have used my horse, Dixie, but I thought I'd give Dad's new horse a try." Katie smiled. "There was a day when something like this would have put my nerves on edge, but I'm dealing better with everything now." She turned to Jolene and gave her a hug. When she pulled back, she smiled and said, "It's so good to see you again. Welcome home."

Jolene smiled. "It's good to see you, too."

Lonnie turned to Ella. "Would you like me to help you put the horses in the corral?"

"I appreciate the offer," Ella said, "but it might be hard for you to do with only one good hand."

"Ach, my! What happened to your hand?" Loraine asked.

Lonnie explained his accident and then grimaced. "My hand's starting to throb again, so I think I ought to head for home."

"That's probably a good idea," Ella said. "It might help if you put some ice on it."

"That's just what I was planning to do." Lonnie gave Ella a nod and sprinted to his buggy.

❧ ❧

After the horses had been put away, Ella led the way to the house, where Jolene and her cousins took seats around the kitchen table. Ella's mother, Aunt Verna, set a pot of tea and five cups on the table and then joined them.

"Jolene and I decided we'd like to have lunch here today instead of at a restaurant," Ella said. "It will be easier for us to visit without so many interruptions."

"That's fine with me," Loraine said. "Sometimes it can be awfully noisy at a restaurant."

"And since we won't have to travel anywhere, it'll give us more time to visit. Oh, and it'll be easier for me to read your lips if you all look at me when you talk," Jolene quickly added.

"There's some leftover chicken noodle soup in the refrigerator," Aunt Verna said. "I'll heat that up and make sandwiches to go with it." She got up from the table. "I'll get it started right now while you young women visit."

The sunlight streaming through the kitchen window spread a warm glow across the table. When Jolene took a sip of tea, she felt its warming comfort flow through her. It was nice to be with her cousins again. This was the first time they'd all been together since the horrible accident that had changed each of their lives in some way.

"How does it feel to be home?" Loraine asked, touching Jolene's arm.

"It feels good, but I'm a little *naerfich* about teaching again."

"I don't think there's any reason for you to feel nervous. You were a good teacher before, so I'm sure you'll do fine," Katie said.

"This will be different, though. The children I've come home to teach are deaf like me, which could be a challenge."

"What kind of challenge?" Loraine asked.

"What if I can't communicate well enough with the children? What if they don't understand what I'm saying?"

"You'll do fine," Ella said. "Just believe in yourself and ask God to help you."

Jolene sighed. "Since I lost my hearing from the accident, I've lost some of the confidence. I—I'm not sure I'll fit in."

Aunt Verna turned from the stove and stood in front of Jolene. "You're still the same person, so you'll fit in just fine." She patted Jolene's shoulder and then hurried back to the stove.

Feeling the need to change the subject, Jolene turned to Loraine and asked, "How are Wayne and Crist doing with their taxidermy business?"

"Pretty well, but with jobs being scarce and money so tight, they're concerned that folks might stop bringing things in to be stuffed. If that should happen, they'll need to find some other way to make a living." Loraine smiled. "I do have some good news to share with you."

"What's that?" Katie asked.

"Wayne and I are expecting a *boppli*. We're hoping and praying that this baby will be healthy and I'll be able to carry it to full term."

"That is good news," Ella said. "I'll be praying with you about the baby."

Jolene nodded, and so did Katie, although Jolene couldn't help but feel a bit envious. She longed to be a wife and mother.

"I'm so pleased that you'll be here when Freeman and I get married in the spring," Katie said to Jolene.

Jolene smiled. "At least I won't miss this wedding." She turned to Loraine. "Sorry I had to miss yours, but Aunt Dorcas needed my help after her carpal tunnel surgery."

"I know, and I understand. We're just glad you're home now."

Aunt Verna peered out the kitchen window. Frowning, she turned to face them again.

"What's wrong?" Ella asked.

"Not what, but who. Eunice Byler's buggy is in the yard, and she's heading for the house. She probably came by to deliver the soap I ordered from her awhile back."

"Don't you want the soap, Mama?" Ella asked.

"Of course I do."

"Then why are you frowning?"

A rosy color flooded Aunt Verna's cheeks. "Eunice tends to be quite the gossip. Once she gets going, it's hard to make her stop." She glanced at the stove then back again. "I hope she doesn't expect an invitation to join us for lunch."

"Who's Eunice?" Jolene asked.

"She and her family moved here after you went to Pennsylvania," Ella said.

Katie grimaced. "Eunice used to have her *kapp* set for Freeman. I think she was very disappointed when he chose me instead of her."

When the back door opened, Jolene leaned forward, anxious to meet Eunice. All this talk made her curious about just what kind of person Eunice was.

CHAPTER 5

When Eunice stepped into the Yoders' cozy kitchen, a tantalizing aroma wafted up to her nose. Her stomach rumbled, and she licked her lips. Maybe she would be invited to stay for lunch.

"*Guder mariye*," Eunice said, smiling at Ella, who sat at the table with Loraine, Katie, and a young woman Eunice had never met.

"Our morning's almost over, so I guess I'll say good afternoon." Ella glanced at the dark-haired woman who sat beside her. "This is my cousin Jolene. She's been living in Pennsylvania for the last two years and has returned to Indiana to teach the two daab kinner who moved here a few weeks ago."

"Oh, you're Andrew's sister, aren't you?" Eunice asked without looking at Jolene.

Jolene gave no response.

Eunice frowned and repeated her question.

Still no reply.

"Humph! Well, don't answer me then," Eunice muttered.

"Jolene's deaf. You have to look directly at her when you speak so she's able to read your lips."

Eunice's face heated. How could she have been so stupid? She remembered now that Andrew had told her about his sister losing her hearing in the accident they'd been in two years ago.

Eunice knew that if she was going to get Andrew to be interested in her, she needed to get to know his sister.

"Your *bruder* Andrew did mention that you've been living in Pennsylvania." Eunice spoke slowly, emphasizing each word as she looked at Jolene. "I should have remembered that you'd lost your hearing."

"Did he tell you that I've come home to teach Sylvia and Irvin Troyer?"

"I didn't know that until Ella mentioned it just now." Eunice shifted uneasily. It felt strange to speak to someone who couldn't hear. It was hard to believe that Jolene could know what she was saying by reading her lips. "I hope that the Troyer children are well mannered and easy to teach. Fern and I are good friends, and she's told me some stories about some of the more stubborn scholars she teaches." She wrinkled her nose. "Makes me glad I'm not a teacher."

"I'm sure there are a lot of rewards in being a teacher." Ella looked at Jolene. "Isn't that right?"

"Were you speaking to me?" Jolene asked.

"Jah. I said that I'm sure there are lots of rewards in being a teacher."

Jolene smiled and nodded. "I've always enjoyed teaching."

Eunice looked over at Katie. She hadn't said a word since she'd entered the room. She knew Katie didn't like her, but did she have to be so rude? After all, Katie was the one who'd ended up with Freeman, even though he'd been Eunice's boyfriend first. If anyone had a reason to hold a grudge, it was Eunice. Everything had been going just fine between her and Freeman until Katie came between them. She guessed it didn't matter anymore, because Katie and Freeman would be getting married in the spring. Besides, Eunice had her eye on Andrew now.

Eunice's gaze went to Verna, who stood in front of the stove, stirring what smelled like delicious soup. The fragrant aroma beckoned her to sit awhile and enjoy the warmth of Verna's kitchen. "What are you cooking?" she asked, moving closer to the stove. "It sure smells good."

"It's chicken noodle soup," Verna replied rather stiffly. "We'll be having it for lunch."

Eunice hesitated, still hoping she might be invited to join

WANDA E. BRUNSTETTER

them. When Verna said nothing, Eunice handed her the paper sack she held. "I brought the soap you ordered."

"Just put it on the table," Verna said over her shoulder. "I'll get my purse and pay you in a minute."

"Would you like me to get your purse, Mama?" Ella offered.

Verna shook her head. "That's okay; I'll get it. Just stay where you are and visit with your cousins."

Ella took a sip of tea and blotted her lips with a napkin.

Loraine leaned closer to Katie. "Have you gotten any new stamps in the stamp shop lately?"

Katie smiled. "As a matter of fact, we have. Last week's shipment had. . ."

Eunice rested her hip against the cupboard as she tuned out the conversation going on at the table. She felt like an intruder and wished Ella or one of the cousins would at least invite her to sit and visit.

Eunice turned and glanced out the kitchen window, allowing her thoughts to wander. *Sure wish I knew if Andrew was interested in me. I wonder if he'll ever ask me to go out with him. If he doesn't, I'll need to look for someone else, because I sure don't want to end up an old maid like Freeman's sister, Fern.*

Tired of feeling left out, Eunice moved over to the table, pulled out the empty chair next to Jolene, and plunked down. When Jolene turned to look at her, Eunice smiled and said, "I don't know if anyone's told you or not, but I sell soaps and scented candles. Maybe you'd like to host a party sometime."

Jolene's eyebrows drew together. "Could you repeat that, please?"

"I sell candles and scented soaps. Would you like to host a party sometime?"

"I—I don't know. Starting Monday I'll be busy teaching, so—"

"You won't be teaching all the time. You could host the party some evening or on a Saturday."

"I'll have to see how it goes."

Eunice was about to say something more when Verna handed her the money she owed. "Here you go. Danki for bringing my order by."

616

"You're welcome." Eunice waited to see if anyone would say anything else to her. When they didn't, she looked at Loraine and said, "Before I came here, I delivered some candles to Lydia Beechy. She said she'd gotten a letter from her son, Jake, who lives in Montana."

Loraine smiled. "That's nice. I'm sure she was glad to hear from him."

"Didn't you used to go out with Jake?"

"Jah, but that was a long time ago."

"From what I've heard, Jake's always been kind of wild."

Loraine shook her head. "He's not wild, just free spirited."

"Maybe so, but I heard—"

Ella cleared her throat loudly. "How many more deliveries do you have to make today, Eunice?"

"Four, and then I need to go to Shipshe to pick up a prescription for my mamm."

"Is your mother sick?" Verna asked, turning away from the stove.

"Not really, but she needs medicine for her high blood pressure."

Verna's forehead wrinkled. "I didn't realize she had high blood pressure."

"She just found out a few days ago, but the doctor said she should be fine as long as she eats right and takes her medicine." Eunice drummed her fingers along the edge of the table. "Speaking of eating right, have any of you noticed how much weight our bishop has put on lately? Why, I'll bet he weighs nearly—"

"Oh my, look at the time." Ella motioned to the clock. "It's almost noon, so maybe we should get lunch on the table and see if Papa and Charlene are planning to join us today."

"I'm sure they will," Verna said. "Neither one asked me to pack a lunch for them this morning, so I don't think they're planning to eat at the shop."

"What can we do to help?" Katie asked, pushing away from the table.

"Why don't you and Jolene set the table? Then Loraine

can fill the glasses with apple cider, while Ella and I make the sandwiches."

Eunice clamped her teeth together. It was obvious that she wasn't going to be asked to stay for lunch. They were clearly hoping she'd leave.

With an audible sigh, Eunice pushed her chair aside and stood. "Guess I'd better get going." She cast a quick glance in Jolene's direction. "It was nice meeting you. I hope we'll get the chance to get to know each other better."

Jolene gave a quick nod. Eunice figured she might not have understood what she'd said. Either that, or she was just plain rude.

"Well, then, I'll be on my way." Eunice hurried out the door. It didn't take a genius to know that her presence wasn't wanted.

❧ ❧

Jolene shifted uneasily in her chair. Even though she hadn't liked some of the things Eunice had said, she wasn't comfortable with the way the others had treated her. It was as though they were anxious for Eunice to leave and weren't interested in anything she had to say. Of course, much of what Eunice had said did seem like gossip.

Ella looked over at Jolene and quirked an eyebrow. "What'd you think of Eunice?"

"She seems nice enough, but she's quite the talker," Jolene replied.

"Oh, she's a talker, all right—either yammering away about nothing at all or spreading rumors and gossip." Ella stuck her finger in her mouth, as though she were gagging.

Katie nudged Jolene's arm. "You'd better forewarn your bruder, because I have a hunch that Eunice has her kapp set for him."

"What makes you think that?" Jolene asked.

"Didn't you see the sappy look on her face when she mentioned his name?"

"No, not really. I was concentrating more on trying to read her lips."

Loraine poked Katie's arm and said something to her, but Jolene didn't get what she'd said because she wasn't looking directly at her.

"Was Loraine saying something to me?" she asked, turning to Katie.

Katie shook her head. "She was reminding me of how Andrew rescued Eunice when her buggy flipped over in a ditch several weeks ago. Ever since then, she's been hanging around Andrew every chance she gets."

Ella touched Jolene's arm. "I'd warn him if I were you. . .just in case he has any ideas about going out with Eunice."

"Would that really be so bad?" Jolene asked.

All three heads bobbed.

"I don't think Eunice would make a good sister-in-law—or a good wife, for that matter." Ella's serious expression caused Jolene to worry. If Eunice was as bad as her cousins seemed to think, then maybe she should say something to Andrew. Or would it be better to let him find out for himself what kind of person Eunice was?

※ ※

Lonnie whistled as he headed up the driveway with the mail in his hands. He'd received a letter from Carolyn and could hardly wait to read it. If she agreed to marry him, they'd be living in Indiana, since this was where Lonnie's job was now. Carolyn made friends easily; he was sure she'd fit in and make new friends here.

The tune Lonnie whistled became louder. It was amazing how finding the letter had improved his mood. It was enough to make him forget about the pain in his hand.

The trees lining their driveway creaked as the wind picked up. Lonnie clung to the mail. *Sure wouldn't want Carolyn's letter to blow away.*

He was almost to the house when his twelve-year-old sister Sharon rushed out the door with a panicked expression. "I'm in big trouble, Lonnie. Really big trouble!" She grabbed the sleeve of his jacket.

"What'd you do now?" Sharon was the youngest in his family,

and she always seemed to be in some kind of a fix. It had been that way ever since she was old enough to walk and talk.

Her hazel-colored eyes filled with tears. "I—I spilled beet juice on my bed quilt."

"How'd you do that? Your quilt's supposed to be on your bed, not in the kitchen."

"I wasn't in the kitchen. I was cleaning my room and got hungry for a snack." She blinked a couple of times. "I came down to the kitchen and fixed myself a bowl of pickled beets."

Lonnie's forehead wrinkled. "Please don't tell me you took the beets upstairs to your room."

"I know it was a dumm thing to do, but I set the bowl on my nightstand, and then I took a seat on my bed. When I reached for the bowl, I bumped the lamp beside my bed. It jostled the bowl, and the next thing I knew there was a trail of beet juice on the edge of my quilt." Sharon's chin trembled. "Mom's gonna pitch a fit when she and Pop come home from town and find out what I did. I'll probably get a *bletsching* and be given extra chores to do."

Lonnie chuckled in response to her fears about getting a spanking. Although Sharon was a bit accident-prone, she rarely disobeyed. He couldn't remember the last time she'd been disciplined harshly by either one of their parents. "I doubt you'll get a bletsching, but you might be right about having to do extra chores." Lonnie reached for the handle on the screen door. "Why don't you try washing the part of the quilt that has beet juice on it?"

"I tried that already, but the red's still there." Sharon's nose began to run, mixing with her tears. She sniffed a couple of times. "You got any ideas what I should do, Lonnie?"

He shrugged. "If it were me, I'd try putting some bleach or peroxide on the stain, and then I'd wash it really good."

She swiped at her tears with the back of her hand. "You think that might work?"

"It's worth a try. Maybe by the time the folks get home, you'll have the beet juice out and your quilt will be good as new."

"But how am I supposed to get it dry in time? There's not much sun today, and Mom and Dad will probably be here in a couple of hours. That might not give the wet spot on the quilt enough time to dry."

"Why don't you drape it over the clothes rack and set it in front of the stove?"

"I guess that might work." Her lips turned up. "Danki, Lonnie; I appreciate your suggestion."

"No problem. That's what big brothers are for." Lonnie slipped Carolyn's letter in his jacket pocket and handed Sharon the rest of the mail. "Put this on the table, would you? I'm going out to the barn to read my letter."

"Sure." Sharon gave him another smile and scurried into the house.

Whistling all the way, Lonnie hurried to the barn.

As soon as he stepped inside, he lit a kerosene lantern and found a seat on a bale of straw. Tearing Carolyn's letter open, he read it silently to himself:

Dear Lonnie,

I received your letter yesterday, inviting me to come to Topeka for a visit. I'd love to see where you live and spend time with you and your family. Mom said I can have some time off from our general store, so my plan is to get a bus ticket and arrive in Elkhart two weeks from today. If you could hire a driver to pick me up, it would be appreciated.

Lonnie smiled as he folded the letter and returned it to his pocket. Then he leaned his head against the wooden beam behind him, feeling fully relaxed. Carolyn was coming for a visit. In just a couple of weeks, he could ask her to marry him. Except for the throbbing in his hand and the fact that he'd lost out on some pay, this day wasn't going so bad after all.

Lonnie closed his eyes and let his mind wander as he pictured himself and Carolyn on their wedding day. He saw the two of them standing before the bishop, answering his questions and agreeing to stay married until they were separated by death.

He continued to daydream, thinking about how his life would

be once they were married and raising a family of their own. How many children would they have? If they had girls, would they have hair the color of golden wheat and sparkling blue eyes like Carolyn? Would the girls enjoy quilting and working with flowers the way she did? Would their boys take after him, with wavy blond hair and closely set brown eyes? Would they have an ear for music, like their father had?

Bam! The barn door opened and shut with a bang, and Lonnie's eyes snapped open. Sharon, wide-eyed and red-faced, rushed into the barn. "Lonnie, come, *schnell!*"

Lonnie groaned, feeling irritated by the interruption. "Where is it you want me to go quickly, Sharon?"

Tears coursed down her cheeks. "My quilt's on fire!"

CHAPTER 6

Lonnie's heart pounded as he raced for the house. When he stepped inside, he saw smoke and flames coming from the kitchen.

He grabbed a towel from a wall peg, wet it at the utility sink, and draped it over his head. Then he grabbed a bucket, filled it with water, and dashed into the kitchen. The quilt, which had been hung over a wooden rack near the stove, was in flames. Lonnie threw the bucket of water over it, filled the bucket once more, and doused it again. When the fire was out, he grabbed the soggy quilt and hauled it outside.

"It's ruined!" Sharon sobbed as she dropped to the ground beside the remains of her quilt. "I—I didn't put the rack too close to the stove, so I don't know how it caught on fire."

"What'd you clean it with—bleach or peroxide?" Lonnie asked.

"Peroxide. I found a big bottle of it in the utility room and poured some on the spot where the beet juice was."

"Did you mix it with water or use it full strength?" Lonnie questioned.

"I poured some into a smaller container, and then I put it on the quilt full strength." She hiccuped on a sob. "That stuff smelled horrible; it made me cough and gag."

Lonnie groaned. The peroxide that had been sitting in the utility room had been the 30 percent industrial kind and should

623

have been diluted with water before use. He'd read several articles in *The Budget* about fires that had been started because people had used 30 percent peroxide full strength and exposed whatever they'd been cleaning to the sun or some other heat source. Of course, Lonnie wasn't sure if it was the peroxide that had caused Sharon's quilt to catch on fire or if it had been placed too close to the stove. He'd been in such a hurry to get the fire out he hadn't noticed how close the drying rack had been set. Either way, the quilt was ruined, and his sister would be in trouble with their mother.

"Guess it's my fault this happened," he mumbled. "I should have never suggested that you put peroxide on the quilt." He rapped the side of his head. "Just never dreamed you'd use Dad's 30 percent peroxide at full strength."

"What am I gonna do, Lonnie?" Sharon wailed. "When Mom and Pop get back from town, I'll get a bletsching for sure."

"You won't get a bletsching. I'll explain what happened, and everything will be fine." Lonnie turned toward the house. "I need to get back inside and clear out the smoke and ashes. While I'm doing that, you can get the wheelbarrow."

"What for?"

"So we can haul the quilt out to the garbage."

"Oh, okay." Sharon hurried off toward the barn to get the wheelbarrow, and Lonnie went into the house.

He'd just gotten some windows open and had begun to clean up the mess when he heard the sound of buggy wheels rumbling into the yard. *Oh, great, the folks must be home.*

By the time Lonnie stepped outside, Mom was already out of the buggy and standing beside Sharon, staring at the ruined quilt while shaking her head. The wheelbarrow was parked nearby.

Tearfully, Sharon explained what had happened.

Mom moaned. "How could you have been so foolish, Sharon?"

"It's not entirely her fault," Lonnie said, stepping between them. "I'm the one who suggested she use peroxide to get out the beet juice. I just didn't think she'd use the bottle of peroxide on the utility porch or that she'd put it on full strength."

"What in the world were you thinking, boy?" Pop asked when he joined them. "You oughta know better than to tell your sister to use that stuff." He grunted, and his pale, bushy eyebrows pulled tightly together. "What a *dummkopp*."

"I'm not a dunce, and I didn't think she'd—"

Pop glared at Lonnie. "Your mamm worked real hard making that quilt, and I think you oughta pay her what it'll cost to buy material to make a new one."

Mom shook her head. "He doesn't have to do that, Ezra. I've got plenty of material on hand. Enough so that Sharon can make a new quilt for her bed."

Sharon puckered her lips. "But Mom, I don't know how to sew a quilt."

"Then it's time you learned." Mom nudged Sharon's arm. "And for taking those beets up to your room, you'll have extra chores to do for the next two weeks." She grimaced. "The fire never would have happened if you'd eaten the beets in the kitchen like you know you're supposed to do."

Lonnie bent down, scooped up the quilt, and dropped it into the wheelbarrow. He was on his way to the garbage can when Pop, walking briskly beside him, grabbed hold of his arm. "What are you doing home? Didn't Rueben have any work for you today?"

Lonnie held up his bandaged hand. "Couldn't do much with this hurting the way it does."

"You managed to put out a fire and haul Sharon's quilt outside. How do you account for that?"

Lonnie gritted his teeth. Was Pop trying to provoke him into an argument? "Seemed like putting out the fire was an emergency, so I ignored the pain in my hand." Lonnie hurried off before Pop could say anything more.

❧ ❦ ❧

As Jolene headed down the road toward the Troyers' place, her stomach twisted with nervousness. What if Sylvia and Irvin didn't like her? Worse yet, what if the children's parents didn't like her? She remembered Aunt Dorcas telling her that it was very important for a teacher of deaf students to get acquainted with the students' parents. This, she'd said, would help the teacher understand the things the children might tell her that had happened at home. Getting to know the parents also helped the teacher see how the parents were dealing with the children and their loss of hearing.

Jolene tightened her grip on the reins. It wasn't in her nature to worry so much or get worked up over things. She knew she needed to relax and commit this to God.

She whispered a prayer, took a few deep breaths, and relaxed her grip on the reins. By the time she'd pulled off the road and was heading up the Troyers' driveway, she felt calmer and a bit more confident.

Jolene pulled up to the hitching rail and stepped down from the buggy. She'd just finished securing the horse when a tall, freckle-faced man with red hair stepped out of the barn. Figuring he must be the children's father and having been told that he could sign, Jolene used signing as she spoke the words.

"I'm Jolene Yoder. I've been hired by the school board to teach your children."

He gave an enthusiastic nod and signed as he spoke. "I'm Harvey Troyer, Sylvia and Irvin's daed. It's good you have come. We know that the teacher at the Amish schoolhouse can't teach them, and we don't relish the idea of sending them away to school."

"I understand."

Jolene spent the next several minutes talking with Harvey about how she'd lost her own hearing and had received training from her aunt in Pennsylvania, who'd been teaching deaf students a good many years. Then they talked about Jolene's previous years as a teacher and how she wanted to be a good teacher to his children as well.

"I hope to not only teach the children their lessons, but also how to formulate words and read lips," she said.

"That would be a good thing." He smiled. "Now let's go in the house so you can meet my wife, Mary, and the children. Sylvia and Irvin both know how to sign and have had one year of schooling, so I don't think teaching them will be a problem."

"I'm looking forward to meeting them," Jolene said.

Harvey led the way, and when they entered the house, Jolene was met by the enticing sweet smell of gingerbread. She followed Harvey into the kitchen, where a woman with light brown hair and pale blue eyes stood near the stove. A little boy who looked to be about three years old played with some pots and pans on the floor near her feet. A wooden cradle sat nearby with a baby inside.

"Mary, this is Jolene Yoder." Harvey motioned to Jolene. "She's the one who'll be teaching Irvin and Sylvia."

Mary smiled as she spoke to Jolene and signed, "I'm happy to meet you." She turned to her husband then and said something. He nodded and left the room. When he returned, two young children were with him.

"This is Sylvia." Harvey patted the brown-haired, blue-eyed girl on the head, and then he did the same to the boy with red hair and freckles. "This is our oldest child, Irvin."

Jolene signed to the children that she was happy to meet them and was anxious to begin teaching on Monday.

The seconds ticked by as the children stared at her, making no effort to sign anything in return.

"I think my kinner are kind of shy right now. I'm sure they'll warm up to you once you begin teaching them," Mary said.

Jolene decided to try again. She got down on her knees, so she was eye-level with Sylvia. *"How old are you?"* she signed.

Sylvia dropped her gaze and scuffed the toe of her sneaker on the floor. After a few seconds, she looked up and signed, *"I'm seven."*

Jolene looked over at Irvin. *"How old are you?"*

The boy shrugged.

Harvey nudged Irvin's arm. *"Your teacher asked you a question."*

The boy gave no response.

"Don't be stubborn now," Harvey signed. *"Tell Jolene how old you are."*

Irvin shook his head.

Jolene had a hunch that the boy might be the defiant type.

She'd seen it in a few of the older scholars when she'd taught school before the accident. If that was the case, he'd probably be difficult to teach.

Oh, Lord, she silently prayed. *What have I gotten myself into?*

CHAPTER 7

J olene glanced around the small classroom she'd been given to teach her two students. It was upstairs in the small schoolhouse, set apart from the rest of the scholars, but it had been equipped with the supplies she would need—a blackboard, chalk, paper, pencils, and plenty of books. Being in the schoolhouse brought back a flood of memories from the days when she'd been downstairs sitting at the desk Fern Bontrager now occupied. It made Jolene realize how much she'd missed teaching.

She took a seat at the desk that had been provided for her as she waited for Irvin and Sylvia to arrive. *If the scholars in Fern's class knew how to sign, I'd be able to teach them, not just the deaf children.* She sighed. *Guess I should be grateful for this opportunity to teach and stop wishing for the impossible.*

Jolene felt the floor vibrate, and she turned toward the door. Sylvia entered the room, wearing an eager expression. Irvin trailed behind her, head down and shoulders slumped.

"Good morning," Jolene signed. She pointed to the low-hung shelf across the room. *"You can put your lunch pails over there."*

Sylvia smiled and placed her lunch pail on the shelf, but Irvin scuffed the toe of his boot on the floor and stared up at Jolene like he had no idea what she'd signed.

Twice more Jolene told the boy to put his lunch pail on the shelf, but he didn't budge. It made no sense, because Irvin's father had assured her that both of his children understood signing.

She was sure the boy was just being stubborn and testing her patience.

Finally, in exasperation, Jolene signed to Irvin, *"If you don't put your lunch pail on the shelf right now, you'll have to stand in the corner."*

No response.

Jolene took hold of Irvin's arm and led him to the corner. He stood like that while she showed Sylvia to her desk.

It gave Jolene no pleasure to begin the day like this, but after having taught hearing students, she knew she must be firm without being mean. After ten minutes went by, she turned Irvin toward her and signed, *"Please put your lunch pail on the shelf."*

She was relieved when he shuffled across the room and did as she'd asked. *"Now, please take a seat,"* she signed, and then she pointed to the desk next to Sylvia's.

Irvin glanced over at his sister, back at Jolene, and then ambled over to his desk and sat down.

Jolene sent up a silent prayer. *Thank You, Lord.*

Before starting their lessons, Jolene had the children stand and sign the Lord's Prayer. Then she opened her Bible and signed as she read Proverbs 16:24 out loud:

" 'Pleasant words are as an honeycomb, sweet to the soul, and health to the bones.' " She decided that the verse was a timely reminder for her as well as the children.

As they began their arithmetic lesson, Sylvia gave Jolene her full attention, but Irvin appeared disinterested, looking away whenever Jolene signed anything to him, and drawing silly pictures on his tablet instead of the numbers she'd written on the blackboard. Jolene knew she'd need to come up with some way to get through to the boy. She wished she could talk to Aunt Dorcas about this. With all the experience her aunt had teaching deaf children, she was sure to have some idea what Jolene could do. When she got home from school today she would ask Mom to call Aunt Dorcas and relay her concerns.

~⁂~

Ella and her brother Larry had just taken a seat in the waiting room at the dentist's office when Loraine entered the room.

"*Wie geht's?*" Loraine asked, taking a seat on the other side of Ella.

"I'm doing fine." Ella motioned to Larry. "He's had a toothache for the last few days, so he's missing a few hours of school this morning to get it taken care of."

Larry grunted. "Rather be in school any old day than here right now."

Loraine offered him a sympathetic smile. "You'll do fine. Dr. Hopkins is a good dentist."

"What are you here for?" Larry asked.

"I'm just here for a cleaning and checkup." Loraine turned to Ella. "I'm surprised your mamm didn't bring Larry to the dentist. I figured you'd be working in your daed's shop this morning. We heard about Lonnie's injured hand."

Ella grimaced. "Mama's not feeling well, so she asked me to bring Larry in. Besides, Papa can get along without me for a few hours. I'm just doing the books and helping string some of the chimes. He assured me that he and Charlene could manage fine while I'm gone."

"I'm sorry to hear your mamm's not feeling well," Loraine said. "She seems to be sick a lot, doesn't she?"

Ella nodded and glanced over at Larry. She didn't want to express her concerns in front of the boy, but she was worried about her mother—had been ever since the van accident two years ago, when her brother Raymond had been killed. Ella figured it would be hard for any parent to lose a child, but she thought it was taking Mama much longer to come to grips with Raymond's death than it should have. Unless Mama's fatigue and shakiness were caused by something else. Maybe it wasn't just grief over losing Raymond. Maybe there was something physically wrong with Mama. If she'd only agree to see the doctor and let him run a few tests. But no, Mama thought everything could be cured by taking a dose of castor oil or some concoction made with apple cider vinegar and honey. Not that those things would do her any harm, but they hadn't kept Mama from feeling so tired, and they weren't a substitute for seeing the doctor.

"We're ready for you now," the dental assistant said when she stepped up to Larry.

He looked over at Ella, as if seeking her approval. When she nodded, he rose from his chair and followed the young woman into the other room, walking slowly with his head down.

"He wasn't happy about coming here," Ella said to Loraine. "In fact, he griped about it all the way from our house into town."

"I'm sure he'll be fine once he's numbed up and his tooth stops hurting."

"Jah."

Loraine reached over and touched Ella's arm. "You look like something's bothering you. Are you worried about your mamm?"

"Uh-huh. You know, she hasn't been the same since Raymond died, and I don't think it's just emotional." Ella's forehead wrinkled. "I don't want Larry or my sisters to know that I'm worried about Mama, though. No point in upsetting them, too."

"Have you talked to your daed about this?"

"I've tried, but he's either too busy to listen or makes light of it." Ella groaned. "I wonder just how sick Mama will have to get before she's willing to see the *dokder*."

"Would you like me to see if my mamm will speak to your mamm about seeing the doctor?" Loraine asked.

Ella shrugged. "I doubt she'll make any headway, but if she's willing, then I guess it's worth a try."

"When I'm done here I'll swing by my folks' place and ask her."

"Danki." Ella reached for a magazine and thumbed through a couple of pages. Aunt Priscilla and Mama had always been close. If anyone could get through to Mama, it might be Aunt Priscilla.

"I have a few worries of my own this morning," Loraine said with a lingering sigh.

Ella, feeling immediate concern, snapped the magazine closed. "What kind of worries? It's nothing about the boppli, I hope."

"No, everything's going fine with my pregnancy. Wayne told me this morning that he's worried because the taxidermy business has slowed down all of a sudden. He's afraid if things get any worse he won't be able to support us." Deep wrinkles formed in Loraine's forehead. "With a boppli on the way, it's even more frightening to think of Wayne being without a job."

Ella's fingernails dug into the armrests on her chair. "So many of our people are out of work and struggling financially. I'm beginning to wonder if things will ever turn around for us."

"It's very frightening," Loraine said, "but we've got to keep the faith and do whatever we can to make extra money. Wayne's good at woodworking, and he's made a few nice pieces of furniture for our house. He's also made some things for his folks' new home. I suggested to him this morning that he start making more things. Maybe he can sell them to one of the local furniture stores." She smiled, despite her obvious concerns.

"In the meantime, we just need to keep praying and trusting that God will provide for our needs."

~≈ ~

"Guder mariye," Andrew said when he entered Tiffany's Restaurant in Topeka and found Wayne waiting for him at a table near the back. They'd decided to meet for breakfast before they began work for the day. Freeman would also be joining them.

Wayne looked up at Andrew and smiled. "Mornin'. Is this table okay with you?"

"Suits me just fine." Andrew pulled out a chair and took a seat. "No sign of Freeman yet, huh?"

"Nope. I'm sure he'll be along soon, though. He'd never pass up the opportunity to be in such good company as ours."

Andrew chuckled. "I doubt he's coming here for our company. More than likely it's to fill his belly with ham and eggs."

"You're probably right about that." Wayne thumped his stomach a couple of times. "I hope he gets here soon, 'cause my belly's startin' to rumble."

A young English waitress came to their table. "Would you like to place your orders?" she asked, smiling at Andrew.

"Just some coffee for now," he replied. "We're waiting on a friend."

The waitress left the table and returned a few minutes later with two cups and a pot of coffee.

Andrew had just poured some coffee into the cups when Freeman walked in. "Sorry for making you wait, but I had a bike that needed fixing right away this morning and it took me longer than I expected." Freeman took a seat. "Have you two ordered your meals yet?"

Wayne shook his head. "Figured we'd wait for you."

Freeman thumped Wayne's back a couple of times. "It's sure nice to have such good friends."

The waitress showed up again and took their orders. While they waited for their food, they visited about the weather and caught up on each other's lives.

It wasn't long until the waitress returned with their orders: scrambled eggs and ham for Wayne; pancakes with maple syrup for Andrew; and a ham-and-cheese omelet for Freeman.

About halfway through their meal, Eunice showed up at their table. "This is a nice surprise," she said, smiling down at Andrew.

He nodded and reached for his cup of coffee to wash down the hunk of pancake he'd just put in his mouth. "I'm surprised to see you out so early this morning."

"I needed a few things at the Shoe and Boot store and decided to stop here for some breakfast first."

"Oh, I see."

Eunice leaned on the edge of the table. "I met your sister on Saturday, over at Ella's. She seems like a nice person."

Andrew nodded. "Jolene's one of the nicest people I know—even if she is my *schweschder*."

Wayne needled Andrew in the ribs. "You probably wouldn't say that if Jolene was sitting here, would you?"

Andrew shrugged. "I'll bet I would. I say nice things about everyone in my family."

"My sister's pretty nice, too," Freeman put in. "And I'm not ashamed to say it."

Eunice bobbed her head. "Fern and I have become good friends. She's one of the nicest people I know." She gave Andrew another heart-melting smile. "I hope Jolene and I can become friends, too."

"If you want to be her friend, then it might be a good idea for you to learn how to sign so you can communicate with her better," Andrew said. "Sometimes it's hard for her to read lips, so signing's the better way to go." He grunted. "Of course, I've only had one lesson in signing, and I've got a long way to go. I do plan to learn, though, and so do my folks. Jolene's going to have regular signing sessions at our house once or twice a week, so you're welcome to join us."

Eunice moved closer to Andrew. "That sounds interesting, but I'm not sure I'd have time for signing lessons right now. I'm keeping very busy selling soaps and scented candles."

"Well, if you ever find the time, I'm sure Jolene would be willing to teach you."

"I'll keep that in mind, but I'd better get going now." Eunice gave Andrew one last smile then hurried across the room, glancing over her shoulder before she went out the door.

Wayne poked Andrew's arm. "I think it's safe to say that Eunice is definitely interested in you."

Andrew shrugged. "Maybe so; I don't know."

"*Kumme* now," Wayne said. "Are you blind?"

"What do you mean?"

"Couldn't you see the look of longing on her face when she was talking to you?" Wayne bumped Andrew's elbow. "What about you? Are you interested in Eunice?"

Andrew reached for his coffee and took a sip. "She's a friend, nothing more."

"Better make sure you keep it that way," Freeman spoke up. "Eunice might look good in the face, but she's a gossip and has been known to cause trouble with that unruly tongue of hers." He grunted. "I've had firsthand experience with her, so I know what I'm talking about."

"You've got nothing to worry about, because I'm not getting involved with Eunice." Andrew set his cup down and leaned his elbows on the table. "Besides, some people change, and there are some good things about Eunice."

"Name me one thing, besides the fact that she has a pretty face."

"Let's see now. . . ." Andrew drummed his fingers along the edge of the table. "She's *schmaert* enough to have started her own business, and from what I've heard, she's doing pretty well with it, too."

"That's fine as feathers," Freeman said, "but it doesn't make her a nice person."

"She wants to become Jolene's friend," Andrew said. "That seems nice to me. Besides, she's interesting to talk to."

"Oh, jah, she always has a lot to say." Freeman reached for a piece of toast and slathered it with apple butter. "Unfortunately, much of what Eunice says is nothing but gossip."

"You can think whatever you like," Andrew said, "but the Bible says we aren't to judge others, so I'm giving Eunice the benefit of the doubt."

CHAPTER 8

As Jolene pedaled her bike toward the schoolhouse, she reflected on some of the things that had been going on with her two students. It had been a busy week since she'd started teaching the children, and she'd made some headway with Sylvia, but as far as she could tell, she'd made none at all with Irvin. He just didn't seem to want to learn.

Last night after Mom had spoken with Aunt Dorcas on the phone, Jolene and Mom had discussed the situation. Mom said that Aunt Dorcas had talked about her days of teaching and said that she'd had a few students who'd been stubborn and didn't want to learn. It took patience, perseverance, and a willingness to keep trying new things. Aunt Dorcas felt certain that eventually Jolene would find something that would spark an interest in Irvin.

I hope Aunt Dorcas is right, Jolene thought as she turned her bike up the lane leading to the school. *I'll feel like a failure if I can't get through to Irvin.*

Jolene parked her bike beside several others and had just stepped into the schoolyard, when she saw some of the boys from Fern's class pointing at a smaller figure huddled on the ground near a clump of bushes. As she drew closer, she realized it was Irvin.

"What's going on?" she asked Kyle Beechy.

He pointed at Irvin. "I asked him a question, and he wouldn't answer, so I poked him a couple of times. What's the matter with that fellow? Is he dumm?"

"No, he's not dumb. He can't hear what you're saying because he's deaf." Jolene was glad Irvin hadn't learned to read lips yet. The quiver of his jaw and the tears glistening in his eyes let her know that he was quite upset. He didn't need to know that he'd been called dumb.

She reached for Irvin's hand, but he just sat there, shaking his head. *"Come with me into the schoolhouse,"* she signed.

"I don't want to go to school. I want to go home."

"What'd he say?" Kyle asked.

"He said he doesn't want to go to school."

Kyle wrinkled his freckled nose. "He'll be even dumber if he don't go to school." He nudged his younger brother, Elmer. "Ain't that right?"

Elmer bobbed his head. "Jah, that's right. He'll be dumber than dirt."

The boys who stood nearby laughed. Jolene couldn't hear their laughter, of course, but seeing their open mouths and the way they were holding their sides let her know that they were laughing. It made her angry to see Irvin being treated this way.

"It's not right to make fun of anyone—especially someone with a disability." She pointed to herself. "I can't hear, either. Does that make me dumm?"

Kyle blinked a couple of times. "You don't have to yell. I'm standin' right here."

"Sorry." Jolene hoped her words came out a little quieter this time.

"How come you can talk, but that boy don't say a word?" Kyle asked, pointing at Irvin.

"As you know, I lost my hearing two years ago, but Irvin and his sister were born deaf. If a person is born deaf, it's difficult for them to learn how to speak clearly because they can't hear what they're saying." Jolene glanced across the schoolyard and spotted Sylvia playing with Arie Smucker by the swings. It appeared that she'd been accepted—at least by one of the scholars. "I'll be teaching Irvin and his sister phonetics, as well as how to read lips," Jolene said. "Hopefully, they'll be able to talk some, too."

"He won't learn." Kyle shook his head. "He's too dumm to learn."

Jolene clapped her hands in front of Kyle's face. "Stop saying that! Irvin is not dumb!"

Just then Fern rushed up to Jolene, wearing a look of concern. "What's going on here? I could hear you shouting from inside the schoolhouse."

Hoping her voice didn't sound as shaky as she felt, Jolene explained what had happened. She motioned to Kyle and Elmer. "I'll never get through to Irvin if these boys keep making fun of him. Nobody likes to be teased, and I'm afraid if it continues, Irvin will refuse to come to school."

Fern shook her finger at the boys. "You ought to know better than to tease. I want you both to apologize to Irvin."

Kyle turned his hands upward. "What for? He won't hear a word I say."

Jolene compressed her lips to keep from shouting at the insolent boy.

"Jolene can let Irvin know what you say by signing to him," Fern said.

"What's signing?" Kyle asked.

"It's a way of talking with your hands," Fern replied.

"Oh, that." Kyle raised his chin a notch and shook his head. "I still ain't sorry for sayin' he's dumm, and I won't apologize."

Jolene was stunned. She'd never seen a student so defiant before. Irvin had definitely met his match. "He was teasing Irvin by laughing and poking him, too," she told Fern.

Fern tapped Kyle's shoulder and squinted her eyes. "You need to apologize to Irvin, and you'd better do it now."

The seconds ticked by as the boy stared at the ground, making no move to apologize for his behavior.

Jolene ground her teeth together. It was disrespectful for any student to speak to his teacher that way. Seeing the way Irvin had been treated by Kyle made Jolene even more determined to get through to him and see that he received a good education.

Fern took hold of Kyle's arm. "If you won't apologize to Irvin, then you can stay after school for the rest of the week."

He kicked at a clump of grass with the toe of his boot. "I can't stay after school. I've got chores to do at home."

"Then apologize to Irvin."

"Tell him I'm sorry," Kyle said to Jolene.

Fern nudged Elmer.

"Me, too," the younger boy said.

Jolene gave a nod then squatted down beside Irvin and signed, *"Kyle and Elmer said to tell you that they're sorry for teasing you."*

"They'll do it again; you'll see!" Irvin scrambled to his feet and raced into the schoolhouse.

Kyle and Elmer ran across the lawn and joined some of the other boys who sat on the fence.

Fern turned to Jolene. "I'll make sure every one of my scholars knows that they'll be in trouble with me if they tease your students."

"If they could only communicate with Irvin and Sylvia, things might be better," Jolene said.

"I think I have an idea."

"What's that?"

"How would you like to come into my class a few times a week and teach the scholars to sign?" Fern smiled. "I think it would be good if I learned how to sign, too."

"I'd like that." As Jolene headed for the schoolhouse, she felt a little better about things.

❧ ❧

There was a spring in Lonnie's step as he headed for the pigpen with a bucket of slop. He was in good spirits, and it had nothing to do with feeding and watering smelly pigs.

His injured hand felt much better, and as soon as he was done with his chores, he'd head over to the Yoders' to work for Rueben.

In just one week, Carolyn would be coming. It would be great to see her again, and he had figured out exactly how and when he'd propose. He didn't know what he'd do if she turned him down. He loved her so much, and while she'd never actually said the words, he felt sure that she loved him, too.

By the time Lonnie reached the pigpen, the wind had picked up, scattering fallen leaves all over the yard. If the wind kept blowing, maybe the leaves would blow out of the yard and no one would have to rake them.

Lonnie poured the slop into the trough and watched with disgust as the gluttonous hogs raced for it, grunting noisily while pushing and shoving each other with their snouts.

"Dirty, greedy pigs," he mumbled. "I'm glad I don't have to smell you all day."

Lonnie turned on the water and filled the watering trough before he headed back toward the house. As he approached the place where their propane tank sat, he halted and sniffed the air. The pungent rotten-egg aroma of propane gas drifted up to his nose. Could there be a leak in the line, or had the nozzle on the tank not been closed tight enough?

He was tempted to move closer to investigate but decided that it would be best to call the company that delivered their propane and ask them to come and check things out.

Lonnie hurried down the driveway toward their phone shed, but he'd only made it halfway there when an earth-shattering explosion shook the ground beneath his feet. When he turned his head, he saw flames shooting into the air and a fence post coming straight at him!

CHAPTER 9

Jolene handed Sylvia and Irvin their pieces of paper and asked them to copy the words she'd written on the blackboard. She'd tried talking to Irvin about what had happened outside before school started, but he wouldn't respond to her at all.

Maybe I should have a talk with Irvin's parents. Jolene tapped her pencil on the edge of her desk. *But if they find out that Irvin was teased by those boys, they might take him out of this school and send him elsewhere for his education. I'd really like the chance to prove that I can teach these children, so maybe I should speak with Kyle and Elmer's parents instead, and let them know that their boys were antagonizing Irvin.* She continued to tap her pencil. *No, that might make things worse. If Lydia or Joe Beechy punishes Kyle and Elmer for teasing, then the boys might try to get even with Irvin and torment him even more.*

She leaned back in her chair and tried to relax, deciding that it was best not to say anything to either set of parents right now. She'd wait and see if the boys could work things out on their own. In the meantime, she needed to concentrate on teaching.

While the children did their assignment, Jolene made a list of projects she planned for them to do—making posters to hang in their class and cutting out pictures to color during recess when the weather turned cold and they couldn't play outside. She hoped that doing some fun projects might draw Irvin out of his shell. She knew it must be hard for the children to have moved from

642

their home in Ohio and come here where nearly everyone was a stranger.

If only Irvin could make some friends, she thought. *Everyone needs a good friend.*

Jolene didn't know what she'd do without the friendship she'd established with her cousins. Even when she'd been living several hundred miles away, she'd kept in touch with Loraine, Ella, and Katie through letters. And even when they'd each gone through trials of their own, she'd felt their love and support.

Pulling her thoughts aside, Jolene glanced at the battery-operated clock on the far wall. It was time to collect the children's papers.

She rose from her chair and stepped up to Sylvia's desk. *"Are you finished?"* she signed.

Sylvia nodded and handed Jolene her paper.

"Thank you." Jolene moved over to Irvin's desk. When she looked down at his paper she was stunned. He hadn't written one single word!

She groaned inwardly and made a decision. As much as it pained her to do it, she would stop by his house after school and speak to his parents about this.

~❧ ❧~

"I thought Lonnie would be returning to work today," Ella said when she entered her father's shop and didn't see Lonnie in front of his workbench.

"I don't know what's up. Last time I saw him he said he'd be comin' in this morning." Papa shrugged. "He's not usually late, so I guess it's fair to say that his hand must still be hurting." He frowned. "But then, he should've at least come by and told me if he didn't feel up to workin' today."

Ella couldn't argue with that, but it wasn't like Lonnie to be so inconsiderate. He'd always come to work early and sometimes stayed late to finish a job. He often whistled while he worked and usually wore a smile, so she knew he must enjoy working here. His hand was either still hurting, or else something had come up at home to keep him from being here today. She hoped it was nothing serious.

For the next hour, Ella worked quietly, inserting some recent purchases and customer invoices into the ledger. While she did that, Papa cut some pipe for new chimes, and Charlene kept busy stringing the pieces of pipe together.

At ten o'clock, the shop door opened and Jolene's father, Uncle Alvin, stepped in.

"Guder mariye," Ella said, smiling up at him. "Did you come to buy a new set of wind chimes or just to visit with Papa awhile?"

Uncle Alvin removed his hat and fanned his face with it, although Ella didn't know why, because it was a chilly fall day. "Came to see if you'd heard about the explosion that took place over at the Hershbergers' early this morning," he said.

"Which Hershberger?" Papa asked. "The bishop or his nephew Ezra?"

"It happened over at Ezra Hershberger's place," Uncle Alvin replied.

A sense of alarm shot through Ella as she slowly shook her head. "We haven't heard anything."

Papa hurried over to his brother. "What kind of explosion?"

"From what I was told, the Hershbergers' propane tank blew up."

"Ach, that's *baremlich*! Was anyone hurt?" Charlene asked, joining the group.

Uncle Alvin nodded soberly. "You're right. It is quite terrible. Lonnie got hit in the head by a flying fence post and was knocked out cold. Heard he was taken to the hospital, but that's all I know for sure."

Ella felt like her heart had leaped into her throat. She hoped Lonnie wasn't seriously hurt. They'd had enough tragedies in their community over the last few years.

❦ ❧

A sharp pain shot through Lonnie's head as he slowly opened his eyes. He blinked at the blurred image of a middle-aged woman looking down at him. She wore some kind of a uniform, like that of a nurse.

He tried to sit up, but his head hurt too much. It was all he could do to keep his eyes open.

The woman shook her head and her lips moved, but Lonnie couldn't make out what she'd said. It must be because his head felt like it had been stuffed with cotton.

"Wh–where am I?" He winced. That was strange. He couldn't hear his own voice, either.

The woman picked up a notepad by his bed and wrote something on it. Then she held it in front of his face. The words were blurred, but he could make a few of them out. *Parents. Waiting room. I'll get them.*

Lonnie grimaced as the truth set in. He was in the hospital, and his folks were waiting to see him. He must have been given some pills that had made his brain feel fuzzy and clogged his ears. But why was he in the hospital?

When the nurse set the tablet down and hurried from the room, Lonnie closed his eyes, struggling for some memory that would let him know how he'd gotten here.

He remembered getting up, eating breakfast, doing a few chores in the barn, and going to feed the smelly hogs. Then, as he'd headed back to the house, he'd smelled something funny.

Another jolt of pain shot through Lonnie's head as the memory of everything that had happened flashed into his mind. He'd been heading to the phone shed to report a propane leak. Then he'd heard a terrible explosion, turned, and saw a fence post coming straight at him. It had hit him in the head with such force that he'd been knocked to the ground. That was the last thing he remembered.

Lonnie felt the pressure of someone's hand on his arm, and his eyes popped open. Mom stared down at him with tears in her eyes. Pop stood beside her, wearing a grim expression.

"Wh–what happened to me? H–how bad am I hurt?" Again, Lonnie couldn't hear his own voice, and that scared him a lot.

Mom picked up the notepad from the table by his bed and

wrote something on it. Her lips were pinched, like she was holding back tears, as she held the notepad in front of Lonnie's face.

Our propane tank exploded. Apparently you were hit in the head by one of our fence posts. Your daed found you lying near the phone shed.

Pop's lips moved as he leaned over Lonnie, shaking his head.

Lonnie put both hands against his ears. "I—I can't hear you! Why can't I hear what you're saying?" His throat hurt, and he knew he must be shouting.

Pop stepped away from the bed, and Mom wrote something else on the tablet and showed it to Lonnie.

When the post hit your head, it caused a concussion, and the doctor just told us that there was severe damage to the auditory nerves in both your ears.

"Is—is that why I can't hear?"

She nodded.

"How long until I can hear again?"

Mom slowly shook her head as tears pooled in her eyes and dripped onto her cheeks. *The doctor isn't sure, but you may never get your hearing back,* she wrote on the tablet. *We'll have to wait and see how it goes.*

Lonnie swallowed around the lump in his throat. If he couldn't hear, he couldn't tune chimes. If he couldn't tune chimes, he didn't have a job. If he didn't have a job, he couldn't get married.

CHAPTER 10

Jolene's heart pounded as she stood on the Troyers' back porch, prepared to knock on their door. As soon as school was over for the day, she'd pedaled her bike over here, hoping to arrive before Irvin and Sylvia, who had walked to school. She wanted to speak to the children's parents without the children knowing she'd been here.

Mary, the children's mother, opened the door before Jolene was able to knock.

"I was looking out the kitchen window and saw you coming up the driveway," Mary signed as she spoke. "If you came to see Irvin and Sylvia, they aren't home from school yet."

"I'm glad they're not here, because I wanted to speak to you alone. Is your husband here? I think he should know what I have to say, too."

Mary shook her head. "He's out in the fields, gathering hay. Come inside and tell me what's on your mind." She held the door open for Jolene.

Jolene stepped inside and breathed deeply as the sweet smell of apples and cinnamon wafted up to her nose. "Are you making applesauce?" she asked, hoping to stall for time. She really didn't want to say what was on her mind.

"Jah, I've been working on it a good portion of the day. Just put the last batch in the pressure cooker a few minutes ago." She motioned to the kitchen table. "Have a seat, and I'll pour us some coffee."

647

Jolene pulled out a chair and sat down. She really didn't have time for coffee but didn't want to be rude.

"Would you like to try some of my applesauce bread?" Mary set a cup of coffee in front of Jolene, along with a plate that held several slices of deliciously moist-looking bread.

"No, thank you. I can't stay that long, but I wanted to talk to you about your children."

"Are they doing well in school?"

Jolene took a sip of coffee as she thought about the best way to say what was on her mind. "Sylvia's doing well and seems eager to learn." She paused and clasped her hands together. The expectant look on Mary's face made this even more difficult. She drew in a quick breath. "I wish I could say the same for Irvin."

Mary's forehead wrinkled. "What do you mean?"

"He's not responsive in class and won't do his lessons. I asked the children to copy some words I'd written on the blackboard, but Irvin left his paper blank."

"He didn't write down any of the words?"

Jolene shook her head.

"Maybe they were too difficult for him."

"They were simple words, and Sylvia was able to write them all."

The corners of Mary's mouth turned down. "I don't understand it. Irvin's not dumb."

"I don't think Irvin's dumb, either, but I do think either he's not happy with me as his teacher, or he's upset because he's new here and hasn't made any friends."

"But there are lots of other boys his age at school."

"That's true, but Irvin keeps to himself, and. . ." Jolene stopped speaking and let her hands fall into her lap. She'd almost told Mary about the teasing that had gone on this morning.

Just then a blast of cool air floated into the kitchen, and Irvin and Sylvia raced into the room.

Sylvia went to the sink for a drink of water, but Irvin halted as soon as he saw Jolene. *"It wasn't my fault,"* he signed to his mother. *"Kyle Beechy's the one who started it."*

Her eyebrows furrowed. *"Started what?"*

Irvin looked at Jolene, as though expecting her to say something.

"I didn't tell your mother anything about what happened this morning," she signed to him.

"Tell me what?" Mary asked her son.

He squinted his eyes and stared at her. Jolene could almost see the gears shifting in his head. *"It was nothin', Mama."*

Mary, obviously not willing to give up on the subject, signed in return, *"Tell me what happened, Irvin."*

He dropped his gaze to the floor.

Mary looked at Jolene. "Do you know anything about this?"

As much as Jolene didn't want to tell Mary about Kyle and his brother teasing Irvin, she knew it was time to explain what had happened.

※ ※

"Are you feeling sick again?" Ella asked when she entered the living room and found her mother lying on the sofa.

Mama yawned and pulled herself to a sitting position. "I'm not sick, just a bit tired and shaky this afternoon."

Ella was tempted to suggest that Mama make an appointment to see the doctor, but that subject had been discussed too many times, and Mama wouldn't budge. Loraine's mother had come by a few days ago and almost insisted that Mama see the doctor, but it was to no avail. Ella wondered what it would take for Mama to realize that she needed to have some tests run in order to find out why she was tired and shaky so much of the time. Mama had also begun to put on some weight, and she seemed to be thirsty a lot.

"Should I start supper now, or do you want me to wait awhile?" Ella asked, turning her focus to their immediate need.

"Guess you'd better wait until Charlene and your daed are ready to quit work for the day. When your daed came in for lunch, he said they'd probably be working late since they're getting behind and didn't have Lonnie's help again today."

Ella's eyebrows squeezed together. "I wish we'd get some word on how Lonnie's doing."

"Have you been out to the phone shed lately to check the

answering machine?" Mama asked. "Maybe someone from his family has called and left a message."

Ella nodded. "I checked for messages before I came into the house, and there was no word from the Hershbergers."

The back door opened and banged shut. A few seconds later, Larry raced into the room.

"Did ya hear the news?"

"What news?" Ella and Mama asked at the same time.

Larry's eyes were wide, and his face was flushed. "Joe Beechy fell off the roof of his house and was rushed to the hospital this afternoon!"

"Oh, dear Lord," Mama moaned. "Not another tragedy in our community."

⋘ ⋙

"Jake, there's a phone call for you!"

Jake turned toward his boss's wife, wondering who'd be calling him in the middle of the day. "Can you take a message for me, Peggy?" he called in return.

She leaned over the porch railing and waved the dishrag in her hand. "I think you'd better take the call!"

Jake grunted as he wiped the sweat from his forehead. He'd been working in the corral with a difficult horse and didn't want to let up until he'd made some progress. But he figured if he didn't take the phone call, Peggy would keep hollering and waving that piece of cloth.

Maybe it's someone from home, Jake thought as he made his way up to the house. When he'd left Indiana and returned to Montana after Wayne and Loraine had told him they were in love and wanted to get married, he'd given his boss's phone number to Mom and Dad so they could keep in touch.

"Who is it, do you know?" Jake asked, stepping onto the porch.

Peggy nodded. "It's your mother. She said it was important and that she needs to speak to you right away." Peggy opened the back door and motioned to the kitchen. "You can take the call in there."

Jake hurried into the kitchen and picked up the phone. "Hi, Mom, it's Jake."

"Oh, Jake, I–I'm so glad you're there." Mom's voice trembled when she spoke. "There's been an accident. You need to come home!"

CHAPTER 11

$\mathbf{A}$s Jake's truck approached Middlebury, anxious thoughts filled his mind. When he'd talked to Mom on the phone, she'd said Dad's injuries weren't critical, but that he had two broken legs, some broken ribs, and lots of bumps and bruises. Dad would be laid up for several months, unable to work. As much as Jake hated the idea of taking over Dad's horseshoeing business, he felt obligated to do it. He didn't really mind shoeing horses; he just didn't want to do it full-time. Someday when the time was right, he hoped to have his own business—raising and training horses. He knew he wouldn't make the kind of money shoeing horses for Dad that he made back on the ranch in Montana, but he'd only be here a few months, and then he could head back to Montana, where he was accepted for the person he was and there were no painful memories from the past.

Jake's thoughts went to Loraine and Wayne. He hadn't seen them since he'd returned to Montana over a year ago, but he'd kept in touch by phone a few times. At least no one could say he'd run off to do his own thing and forgotten about his family and friends, the way he'd done the first time he'd left Indiana. He could still see the look of sadness on Loraine's face when he'd told her was leaving for Montana that first time, and his mind took him back to the past. . . .

❦ ❧

"Loraine, there's something I need to tell you."
"What is it, Jake? Why are you looking at me so seriously?"

Jake directed his horse and buggy to the side of the road and reached for Loraine's hand. "I—I'm planning to go away for a while."

"Go away?"

He nodded. "My cousin Sam, who used to live in Illinois, moved to Montana a few months ago, and. . .uh. . .I thought I'd spend the summer with him."

"Which Amish community in Montana did Sam move to?"

"None of them. Sam's working on a ranch in Montana for an English man who raises horses." Jake swallowed so hard that his Adam's apple bobbed up and down. "I want to try out the English way of life for a while—before I make a decision about joining the church." He paused and swiped his tongue across his lower lip. "The wages the man is offering per week are more than I can make working for my daed in a month, so I really can't pass on this opportunity."

Loraine's mouth hung slightly open. "What?"

"I said—"

"I heard what you said. I just can't believe you said it."

"It's not like I'll be gone forever. Probably just for the summer, that's all." He squeezed her fingers and smiled. "You'll wait for me, won't you?"

Loraine sat, staring at him.

"Say something, Loraine. Will you wait for me or not?"

Tears welled in her eyes. "For how long, Jake?"

"Until I come back to Indiana." Jake pulled her into his arms and kissed her on the mouth. "Just a few months, that's all," he whispered.

Loraine drew in a shaky breath and nodded slowly. "Jah, Jake. I'll wait for you."

⸺⁂⸺

As Jake's mind snapped back to the present, he shook his head. He'd really blown it with Loraine by not coming back soon enough or staying in contact with her while he was in Montana. Truth was, he probably wouldn't have returned to Indiana the first time if he hadn't heard about the terrible accident Loraine and her cousins had been involved in.

After he'd returned home, he'd tried to reestablish his

relationship with Loraine, but when he finally realized she was in love with Wayne, he'd given them his blessing and returned to Montana. It hadn't been easy for Jake to leave home the second time, but in his heart, he felt it was the right thing to do.

After Jake had returned to Montana, it had taken several months for him to come to grips with the fact that Loraine would never be his. He'd told himself that he'd done the right thing by giving Loraine and Wayne his blessing, and in time, Jake's broken heart had begun to heal. Any romantic feelings he'd had for Loraine were now just a pleasant memory. While Jake had no interest in anyone at the moment, he was prepared to follow his heart should the right woman come along.

Jake's thoughts shifted as his folks' place came into view. He grimaced. *I hope Dad's going to be okay, and I hope he appreciates my coming home to help out and doesn't criticize everything I do.*

He pulled his truck up near the barn, turned off the engine, and stepped out.

When Jake entered the house, he found Mom in the kitchen, stirring a pot of something on the stove. She turned to face him, a grim expression on her face. *What, no "It's good to see you, Jake; I'm so glad you're home"?* This wasn't like Mom at all. She usually gave Jake a hug and said how much she'd missed him.

He stepped forward and slipped his arms around her waist. "It's good to see you, Mom. How's Dad doing?"

"He's hurting real bad and not one bit happy about being laid up." Her voice cracked, and she cleared her throat. "It could be some time before he's able to work again."

"I'll take over for him until he's better. You know I will."

Mom's bottom lip quivered. "Then you'll leave again." Her words were crisp and to the point.

Jake only shrugged and turned toward the door. "I'd better go see Dad. Is he in his room?"

"Jah, but he's asleep right now. I'd rather you didn't wake him."

"Oh, okay." Jake turned back around. "Where are my brothers and sisters? Are they still at school?"

"Jah. They should be here soon, I expect." Mom motioned to the table. "Why don't you take a seat and we can visit while I finish making my stew. I'd like to hear what you've been up to lately."

Jake pulled out a chair and sat down. "Pretty much the same old thing. . .breaking horses. . .and doing lots of chores around my boss's ranch. Oh, and I've starting training some horses to pull buggies and wagons."

Her eyebrows lifted as she handed him a cup of coffee. "Are there Amish in Montana?"

"There are a few small Amish communities, but the horses we've been training are to pull carriages and wagons at a dude ranch not far from my boss's spread."

"What's a dude ranch?"

"It's a place where folks go to relax, hike the trails, and have some good clean fun. At this dude ranch, a person can take horseback riding lessons, and they also offer hayrides and buggy rides."

"Do you like it better in Montana than here?"

Jake took a sip of coffee as he contemplated her question.

"Did you hear what I said, Jake?"

"I heard. Just wasn't quite sure how to answer."

She grunted. "It's a simple enough question. Do you like it better in Montana than you do here?"

"I like some things about it, but I miss some things about Indiana, too."

"Since you haven't come back and joined the church, I assume that means you're planning to stay English." Mom's comment was more of a statement rather than a question.

Jake gnawed on his lower lip as he watched her slice carrots and drop them into the pot of boiling stew. Part of him had wanted to return to Indiana and join the Amish church, but the longer he'd stayed away, the harder it had been to come back. He'd originally wanted to open his own business right here, but that was when he thought he'd marry Loraine. If he stayed in Indiana now and tried to open his own business, he wondered if Dad would give him a hard time and pressure him to give up the idea and shoe horses instead.

Lifting his elbows and flexing his shoulders, Jake stretched and yawned. He'd think about this some other time. Right now, he needed to concentrate on doing what was right by filling in for Dad and taking care of his family.

"Are you tired, son?" Mom asked.

"A little. It was a long drive."

"If you want to go lie down, I'll call you when supper's ready."

Jake shook his head. "If I lie down, I'll fall asleep and might not wake up until morning." He pushed away from the table. "Think I'll go outside and get my stuff out of the truck."

"You can put everything in your room," Mom said. "Kyle wanted to move in there when you left for Montana, but I told him no, that you might be back."

"Thanks, I appreciate that." Jake smiled at Mom then went out the door.

❦

Jolene trudged wearily up the stairs to her classroom. She'd just taught her first lesson in signing to Fern's class, and it hadn't gone well. The children who'd originally shown an interest in learning to sign hadn't acted interested at all. Jolene wondered if it had something to do with Kyle Beechy. She'd seen the way he looked at Irvin and Sylvia today—like they had two heads or something. Kyle had made it clear that he wanted no part in learning how to sign. Even when Fern asked the class to be attentive as Jolene taught them to sign some simple words, Kyle had remained aloof and disagreeable.

When Fern tried to coax him to take part, the fire in Kyle's eyes and the firm set of his jaw had said it all. He would not even try to sign. And his constant interruptions with silly questions that had nothing to do with signing made it obvious that he was determined to see that the other scholars didn't learn signing, either.

Someone tapped Jolene's shoulder, and she whirled around. Fern stood on the step below her. "The children have gone outside for recess, and I was wondering if you'd like to join us in a game of ball." She spoke slowly while looking directly at Jolene.

Jolene shook her head. "I'm not in the mood to play ball right now."

Fern followed Jolene upstairs to her classroom and leaned on the front of the desk when Jolene took a seat. "You look upset. Is it because the scholars didn't catch on to what you were trying to show them?"

Jolene gave a slow nod.

"I think you just need to give it some time. Signing is new to the children." Fern shrugged. "I had trouble following along with what you were trying to teach us, too, but I'm sure with some practice I'll be able to learn."

"Anyone can learn to sign if they want to," Jolene said. "I'm just afraid that some—especially Kyle Beechy—don't want to learn."

Fern traced an ink stain on the desk with her finger then looked up at Jolene and frowned. "Kyle's my most challenging student, but these last few days, he's been more difficult than usual. I think he's probably upset about his daed falling off the roof."

Jolene suspected there was more going on with Kyle than just his dad's accident. He'd been mean to Irvin before that had happened. The boy obviously had a chip on his shoulder, and he seemed to enjoy causing trouble. Well, Jolene couldn't worry about that right now. She had her own students to teach, and that's where she needed to keep her focus. Irvin, while cooperating a little better the past few days, still wasn't staying focused on his lessons the way she felt he should be. If Kyle kept tormenting Irvin, Jolene planned to speak with Kyle's parents. Today, however, she wanted to stop by the stamp shop and pick up a few things on her way home. She planned to make some get-well cards—one for Jake's dad, and one for Lonnie Hershberger.

❦ ❧

Lonnie lay in his hospital bed, staring at the ceiling. He'd just been told by the doctor that the damage to his auditory nerves was severe and had caused complete hearing loss. It was a shocking blow, and Lonnie felt as if his whole world had caved in. He couldn't imagine spending the rest of his life in total silence. It would be like being trapped in a cave with no way out. He couldn't imagine not being able to hear his own voice. . .the warble of birds. . .a cat's meow. . .or the tinkle of wind chimes. There were so many things he would miss.

Pop tapped Lonnie on the shoulder, and he turned his head, barely able to swallow around the lump stuck in his throat. Pop picked up the notepad lying on the table beside Lonnie's bed and wrote something on it. His lips moved silently as he handed the notepad to Lonnie.

Lonnie's eyes had trouble focusing due to the tears he felt. He tried to blink them away as he read Pop's message: *There is one positive thing in all this. Jolene Yoder's here, and she'll be able to teach you how to read lips and talk with your hands.*

Lonnie said nothing; he just stared at the food on his meal tray that he hadn't touched.

Then Mom took the tablet and wrote something. *I know you're disappointed, and so are we.*

Angry words rolled around in Lonnie's head, and he gripped the edge of his sheet until his fingers turned numb. "You got that right," he mumbled. At least he thought his words had come out mumbled. Since he couldn't hear his own voice, he couldn't be sure how he'd sounded.

Disappointments are like weeds in the garden, Mom continued to write. *You can let them grow and take over your life, or you can rout them out and let the flowers sprout.*

Another wave of anger swept over Lonnie, and he slammed his fist on his meal tray so hard that the glass of milk toppled over and the silverware tumbled to the floor. "I don't want to talk with my hands or think about flowers and weeds! I want to hear with my ears!"

CHAPTER 12

W hat's this?" Lonnie asked when his mother handed him an envelope shortly after he'd returned home from the hospital several days after his accident.

Mom's lips moved, but he had no idea what she'd said.

Lonnie gripped the edge of the sofa where he lay with his head propped on two pillows. "What? You know I can't hear you!" Irritation welled in his soul. Oh, how he wished he could change what had happened to him. If he could just turn back the hands of time, he'd never have gone anywhere near that propane tank. But then, if he hadn't checked on it and discovered the leak, someone else, maybe Mom, might have been hit by something from the explosion.

Mom pointed to the return address on the envelope, and Lonnie's heart gave a lurch. It was from Carolyn. The last few days had been a blur—more like a terrible nightmare, really. In the confusion and frustration of learning that he'd lost his hearing, he'd forgotten that Carolyn was supposed to be here in a few days. As anxious as he was to be with her again, he wasn't sure he wanted her to see him like this.

With an unsteady hand, Lonnie tore open the envelope and read Carolyn's note.

Dear Lonnie,
I would have called and spoken to you on the phone, but
I knew you wouldn't be able to hear me. When your mamm

*called to let us know that you'd been in an accident and had
lost your hearing, I was shocked. I can't imagine what it must
be like not to be able to hear. I hope you're not in a lot of pain.*

*Speaking of pain. . . .Mama came down with a bad
case of shingles, and she's really miserable. She has so much
itching and nerve pain that she can hardly function. Under
the circumstances, I think it's best if I don't come to see you
right now. It'll give you a chance to rest up and heal without
feeling that you have to entertain me. As soon as my mamm's
feeling better, I'll come there. In the meantime, get plenty of
rest and write me back when you feel up to it.*

*As always,
Carolyn*

Lonnie let the letter fall to the floor. A mixture of relief and
disappointment flooded his soul. He wasn't ready to face Carolyn
right now, so in some ways he was glad she wasn't coming. He
didn't know how she'd react to him being deaf, and he wasn't
prepared to ask her to marry someone who couldn't hear a word
she said. Even so, he wondered if her decision not to come meant
she didn't want to see him. Maybe she couldn't deal with the idea
of having a boyfriend who was deaf.

Mom wrote something on the tablet and handed it to Lonnie.
What did Carolyn have to say?

Lonnie handed the letter to Mom and waited until she'd had
a chance to read it. When she finished, he said, "I can't help but
wonder if Carolyn's not using her mamm's shingles as an excuse
not to come."

Mom's eyebrows furrowed as she scrawled a reply. *Why would
she do that?*

"Because I can no longer hear."

*I'm sure that's not the reason. Carolyn's a good daughter and
obviously feels that her mamm needs her right now. I'm sure she'll be
out to see you as soon as she can.*

Lonnie tossed the tablet aside and closed his eyes. "I'm tired.
Wake me when it's time for supper."

The last thing Lonnie remembered before drifting off to sleep was Mom gently stroking his cheek, the way she'd done when he was a boy and didn't feel well.

⁓ ⁓

As Jolene and her family gathered on the front porch to sing and visit after their signing lesson, Jolene felt suddenly out of place. Everyone but her could hear the words to the songs. Everyone on the porch knew exactly what the others were saying without having to read their lips.

Now don't start with the self-pity, she berated herself. At least her family had taken an interest in learning to sign, and they hadn't acted disinterested or belligerent about it like Kyle and some of the other scholars at school. Andrew had surprised her by saying that if he learned to sign well enough he might be able to use sign language at church when the sermons were preached. Jolene was pleased about that. Not only would the signing benefit her, but it would help her two deaf students as well.

Andrew bumped Jolene's arm, interrupting her thoughts. To her surprise, he signed some of the words to "Amazing Grace."

Jolene smiled and signed along with him, showing him and the others the way to sign for each of the words. Soon everyone joined in, and they were all signing and singing "Amazing Grace."

Jolene found herself beginning to relax, and for the first time since she'd come home, she felt like part of the family again.

Just as they were finishing up the song, a horse and buggy entered the yard. It pulled up to the hitching rail, and Ezra Hershberger climbed out of the buggy.

When he joined them on the porch, he said a few words to Dad then moved over to where Jolene sat and stopped in front of her.

"As you may have heard, our son Lonnie has lost his hearing. My *fraa* and I were wondering if you'd be willing to teach him how to sign and read lips."

Jolene gave a nod. "If Lonnie's willing, I'd be happy to teach him."

Ezra grimaced. "I'm not sure my son's willing to do much of

anything right now, but he's gotta be able to communicate, so like it or not, he'll learn."

❧ ❧

After supper that evening, Lonnie felt the need to be alone. It had been awkward watching his folks carry on a conversation with his sister, Sharon, and having no idea what any of them had said. Well, at least none of his married sisters had come to supper this evening. They'd have probably hovered over Lonnie and tried to baby him, the way Mom had done since he'd come home from the hospital.

No one seemed to notice when Lonnie grabbed the walking stick he'd been using to help with his temporary loss of balance and headed out the back door. Mom and Sharon were in the kitchen doing dishes, and Pop had gone to the living room to read the newspaper.

Lonnie took a seat in one of the wicker chairs on the porch. He closed his eyes and leaned his head back. A vision of Carolyn popped into his head, and he swallowed around the familiar lump in his throat. Would it be fair to ask Carolyn to marry a man who couldn't hear? What kind of husband would he be? Could he provide for a wife and family?

Sure won't be able to tune wind chimes anymore, he thought with regret. *Fact is I need my hearing for most any kind of work I might want to do.*

Someone tapped Lonnie's shoulder, and his eyes popped open. Wayne Lambright stared down at him. Of course, Lonnie hadn't heard Wayne's horse and buggy come into the yard, and that only fueled his irritation.

Wayne's mouth moved, but Lonnie had no idea what he was saying.

"Can't hear you. Can't hear a thing anymore!" Lonnie reached for the tablet and pen sitting on the small table on the porch and handed it to Wayne.

Wayne wrote something and handed it back to Lonnie. *I heard you were home from the hospital and I wanted to see how you were doing.*

662

"I've been better."

Wayne took the tablet and wrote something else: *I was sorry to hear about your accident. After losing my leg, I think I know a little of how you must be feeling right now.*

Lonnie grunted. At least he thought it was a grunt.

Wayne seated himself in the chair beside Lonnie. *Is there anything I can do to help?* he wrote.

Lonnie shook his head. "Not unless you can give me back my hearing."

I can't do that, but I can help by offering my support and listening when you need to talk about your feelings.

"My feelings?" Lonnie popped a couple of knuckles. "I'll tell you how I feel. I feel like my life's over. All the plans I'd made are shot to ribbons."

What plans have you made?

"I'd planned to propose to Carolyn, but I don't see how I can expect her to marry me now that I can't hear."

You shouldn't let your disability stand in the way of your happiness, Wayne wrote.

"That's easy enough for you to say. You've still got two good ears."

That's true, but I've only got one good leg, and when I first lost it I was angry, bitter, and full of self-pity. Because of my foolish pride, I almost lost Loraine to her old boyfriend, Jake Beechy.

"I'm not worried about anything like that," Lonnie said. "There is no one like Jake in Carolyn's life. I just don't see how I can expect her to marry a man who can't hear or provide a decent living to support a wife and family."

You may not be able to tune wind chimes anymore, but I'm sure there's something you can do without being able to hear. You can still help your daed raise hogs, you know.

"Puh!" White-hot anger boiled in Lonnie's chest. If the only job he could do was raise smelly pigs, then he didn't care if he ever worked again!

CHAPTER 13

Jolene's heart pounded as she directed her horse and buggy down the road after school the following afternoon. She had two stops to make before going home, and she dreaded them both. When she'd tried to give Fern's class another signing lesson today, she'd had problems with Kyle again. Not only had he been unwilling to learn, but he'd convinced two of the other boys to ignore her as well. If that hadn't been enough, during recess Jolene had caught Kyle poking at Irvin with a stick, and he'd written Irvin a note saying he was a dummkopp who had no ears.

Jolene's first response had been to want to tell Kyle to stop tormenting Irvin, but after taking a few minutes to think things through, she'd decided it was best if she said nothing to Kyle. If he'd been one of her students, she would have punished him on the spot. Instead she'd spoken to Fern about the problem and had left it up to her to discipline the boy. But after thinking about it the rest of the day and seeing how Irvin had pulled further into his shell, she'd made a decision. Before going over to see Lonnie, she would stop at the Beechys' place and talk to Kyle's folks. Jolene hoped they would do something about their son's antagonistic attitude. If not, she didn't know what she would do.

Jolene's thoughts shifted to Lonnie. She hoped he'd be open to the idea of her teaching him total communication, but after the comment Lonnie's dad had made the other evening about Lonnie not being willing to do much of anything, she figured he might offer some resistance.

Guess I'd better wait and see how it goes and just deal with things as they come, she told herself as she turned up the Beechys' driveway. She'd just pulled her horse up to the hitching rail when Jake stepped out of the barn. He seemed surprised to see her, and the crimson color that spread across his cheeks let her know that he was either embarrassed or a bit uncomfortable in her presence. Maybe he'd never been around a deaf person before. Or maybe he was uncomfortable about the fact that he'd obviously chosen not to join the Amish church and had become part of the English world.

Hoping to put Jake's mind at ease, Jolene smiled and said, "How's your daed doing, Jake? I understand you came home to help out while his legs are healing."

Jake nodded and shifted from one foot to the other, as though he was nervous.

"I'm sure your help is appreciated."

"I have nothing to write on. Can you read my lips?" he asked.

"As long as you look directly at me when you're talking, I'm able to read your lips."

Jake seemed to relax a little as he leaned on the hitching rail.

Jolene glanced toward the house then back at Jake. "Is your mamm at home? I'd like to speak to her about something."

He shook his head. "Dad's sleeping and Mom went over to see the bishop's wife today. I think her and some of the women are having a *Gluckin*, because Mom took some of her sewing along to join the others as they spend the day visiting and doing whatever handwork they brought along. Is there something I can help you with, Jolene?"

She quickly related how Kyle had been acting toward Irvin and ended it by saying that Kyle didn't want to learn how to sign and had convinced some of the other children not to participate, either.

Jake's lips compressed as he squinted. "No point in bothering my folks about this; I'll take care of the situation."

"I know we can't force Kyle to learn how to sign, but I do want him to stop picking on Irvin."

"Maybe if I were to learn how to sign, Kyle would take an interest."

"I'd be glad to teach you."

"Would you have time for that?"

"I'll make the time. You can come by the schoolhouse some afternoon, whenever you're ready to begin."

～❧～

Lonnie had just taken a seat on the sofa when his mother entered the living room with Jolene Yoder.

Mom wrote a message on the notebook she carried then handed it to Lonnie.

Lonnie grimaced as he read: *Jolene's here to talk with you about learning to read lips and talk with your hands.*

"Not interested," he said, handing the notebook back to Mom.

With a look of frustration, Mom handed Jolene the notebook and left the room.

Jolene took a seat on the other end of the sofa, wrote something on the notebook, and handed it to Lonnie. *As I'm sure you know, I've been hired to teach Irvin and Sylvia Troyer. Besides their regular studies, one of the things they'll be learning from me is total communication, which includes signing and lip reading. I was wondering if you'd like to learn as well.*

He shrugged. "What for?"

Jolene wrote something else: *So you can communicate with others. Lip reading's especially important when you're with people who can hear, and signing's important when you communicate with those who are deaf. On the job, out shopping, and doing business...those are all things we do, and we need to be able to interact with people.*

Lonnie shook his head. "I have no job, so I won't be interacting that much. I can't tune wind chimes now that I can't hear!"

Our deafness doesn't have to be a disability, she wrote.

He slouched against the sofa and folded his arms. "It's a

disability when I can't do the kind of work I enjoy." Lonnie thought about Job 2:10, which Pop had showed him after breakfast that morning: *"Shall we receive good at the hand of God, and shall we not receive evil?"* He knew there were others, like Job, who'd suffered and faced trials worse than him, but his deafness was still a bitter pill to swallow.

There are other jobs that don't require you to hear, Jolene wrote.

He shook his head stubbornly. "I don't want any other job!"

Jolene scrawled something else on the notebook, handed it to Lonnie, and left the room.

Lonnie stared at what she'd written and the words blurred on the page: *Believe it or not, I understand how you feel. If you change your mind, please let me know.*

CHAPTER 14

A s Jolene pedaled her bike to school the next day, she thought about her visit with Lonnie. Didn't he realize that he'd never be able to live a normal life unless he could communicate with others? He was bitter and angry right now, but then she'd felt that way, too, after she'd lost her hearing. She'd come to accept her disability, and learning total communication from her aunt had not only changed her way of thinking, but it had also opened up a whole new world for her.

I think I'll stop by the Hershbergers' after school again today, Jolene decided. *Maybe I can get Lonnie to change his mind about letting me tutor him.*

Jolene's thoughts turned to other things. Fern had reminded her class at the close of school yesterday that today would be pet day where anyone could bring a pet to share with the class. Irvin and Sylvia were invited to bring their pets, too, and Jolene hoped it might spark an interest in Irvin. She'd seen several cats at the Troyers' place, as well as a dog, so she figured the children might bring one of those.

As Jolene entered the schoolyard, she spotted Kyle and his brother Elmer trudging across the yard, each holding one end of a birdcage. A colorful parrot flapped its wings against the cage and hopped up and down. It seemed like an unusual pet for boys as rambunctious as Kyle and Elmer. Jolene pictured them having a big shaggy dog that liked to bark and make a nuisance of itself.

Several children had gathered around Kyle and Elmer and were pointing at the parrot. Both boys beamed, obviously enjoying the attention.

Maybe that's all those two need, Jolene thought as she parked her bike and headed across the yard. *With their daed laid up and their mamm extra busy right now, Kyle and Elmer might not be getting much attention at home. When I see Jake again, I'll mention it to him.*

Jolene was almost to the schoolhouse when she saw Irvin and Sylvia sitting on the porch. Sylvia had a kitten in her lap. Irvin had just removed a turtle from the cardboard box sitting near his feet.

"Good morning," Jolene signed. *"I'm glad to see that you brought your pets."*

Sylvia nodded enthusiastically and signed, *"My kitten's name is Mittens. She has four white paws."*

Jolene smiled. *"Mittens is a cute kitten."* She looked at Irvin. *"What's your turtle's name?"*

He tipped his head and stared at her like he didn't have a clue what she'd signed.

Jolene signed again. *"What's your turtle's name?"*

Irvin stared straight ahead.

Sylvia nudged Irvin's arm, but he ignored her. She looked up at Jolene and signed, *"The turtle's name is Tommy."*

Jolene was sure Irvin was just being stubborn by refusing to respond to her question. She was tempted to tell Sylvia to let her brother speak for himself, but she decided not to make an issue of it. She pointed to the schoolhouse and signed, *"Let's go inside. You can put your pets in their carriers and bring them upstairs. When the other class is ready for show and tell, we'll go downstairs and join them."*

Sylvia put the kitten inside its carrier, and Irvin put the turtle back in the box. Then Jolene followed the children up the stairs to their classroom.

As the children approached their desks, Sylvia stood in front of Irvin with her back to Jolene. She stayed like that a few seconds before she finally turned and faced Jolene. *"I told my brother that he'd better pay attention and do his lessons today."* Her forehead

669

wrinkled as she pursed her lips. *"Said I'd tell Papa if he didn't."*

Jolene bit back a chuckle, and then she told the children that it was time for them to sign the Lord's Prayer.

Sometime later as Jolene was about to give the children their arithmetic lesson, Fern entered the room, looking quite distraught. Jolene moved closer so she could read Fern's lips.

"My helper, Becky, isn't feeling well, and I need to take her home," Fern said. "Would you mind taking over my class while I'm gone?"

Jolene's mouth went dry. "You—you want me to teach the scholars?"

"You won't have to teach—just have them show their pets while I'm gone." Fern touched Jolene's arm. "It won't take me long to drive Becky home, and I'm sure you'll do fine while I'm gone."

Jolene gave a slow nod. If all she had to do was oversee the children as they showed their pets, it shouldn't be too hard.

"Get your pets; we're going downstairs," Jolene signed to the children. Sylvia jumped right up and got her kitten, and Irvin, though moving slowly, picked up the box with his turtle inside. They both tromped down the stairs ahead of Jolene.

As soon as Fern left with Becky, Jolene went to the blackboard and wrote: *Those of you who brought small indoor pets can show them now. Afterward, we'll go outside to see the bigger pets.*

Before Jolene had the chance to explain that they would take turns showing their pets, Elmer Beechy raced across the room where his parrot's cage sat on a shelf. He fumbled with the latch but was unable to open it.

Kyle leaped out of his chair, pushed his brother aside, and pulled the latch open. The parrot hopped out, flapped its wings, and swooped over the children's desks.

Pandemonium broke out as most of the girls ducked down on the floor, while several boys leaped out of their seats and chased after the bird. Jolene clapped her hands, trying to get the scholars' attention, but she was completely ignored. While the parrot continued to fly around the room, Kyle, wearing a smug expression, took a seat at his desk and stared straight ahead as though nothing out of the ordinary had happened.

Jolene stood in front of Kyle's desk. "Please catch the parrot and put him away!"

He cupped his hands around his ears. "What was that? I can't hear you."

Jolene gritted her teeth. In her previous years of teaching, she'd never encountered such a difficult child. Even though Kyle had been in her class two years ago, he'd been much younger then and had never given her any problems. The way he acted now made no sense, but it had to stop!

Suddenly, Irvin jumped out of his seat, raced to the back of the room, and jerked the door open. The parrot made another circle of the room and flew out the door. Kyle leaped out of his seat and chased after it.

Jolene was tempted to go after Kyle but decided it was best to let the boy go and try to get the rest of the class under control. She motioned to Sylvia and signed, *"Why don't you show us your kitten?"*

Sylvia left her seat and was about to open her pet carrier when Kyle burst into the room, riding his pony. He stopped in front of the blackboard, leaned down, scooped up a piece of chalk and wrote in big letters: *MY PONY'S NAME IS SHADOW.*

Jolene's hand shook as she pointed to the door. "Take that animal outside! The schoolhouse is no place for a horse!"

"It's not a horse; it's a pony," Kyle said, looking at her defiantly.

Jolene groaned; her patience was gone. Why did this young boy have to be such a challenge? Determined not to let Kyle know how upset she was, Jolene grabbed the pony's bridle and led him out the door. When she returned to the classroom, she found a stool and told Kyle he had to sit in the corner until Fern returned. She'd be glad when school was over for the day and she could go home and collapse on the sofa. Then she remembered her decision to see Lonnie. She hoped that visit would go better than the rest of her day.

❧ ❧

When Eunice pulled up to the hitching rail at the Yoders' place, she spotted Andrew talking to a young, dark-haired man she'd never seen before.

Andrew smiled when Eunice stepped down from her buggy, and her heart skipped a beat.

"Have you met Jake Beechy?" Andrew asked.

Eunice shook her head. She knew Jake's parents and siblings, but she'd never met him.

"Jake was in Montana when you moved to Indiana, but he's back now, taking care of his daed's business." Andrew motioned to Jake. "He came over to shoe a couple of our horses."

"I see." Eunice smiled at Jake. "It's nice to meet you."

"Nice to meet you, too," Jake said as he pulled some tools from the back of his pickup.

Eunice couldn't help but notice the dimple in Jake's chin. His dark hair and deeply set blue green eyes were in sharp contrast to Andrew's light brown hair and hazel-colored eyes. While both men were nice looking, Jake was far more handsome. But then, good looks weren't everything. Eunice was attracted to Andrew's easygoing, soft-spoken ways.

"I came by to deliver the candles your mamm ordered at the party she hosted awhile back," she told Andrew.

"Want me to get them out of the buggy for you?" he asked.

"I'd appreciate that." Eunice went around to the back of her buggy and motioned to the box full of candles.

Andrew whistled. "Mom sure ordered a lot!"

"Oh, they're not all hers. Most of them are what the other women who came to her party ordered."

"Sounds like you had a successful party."

Eunice smiled. "I did."

Andrew reached into the buggy and lifted the box with ease, and then he headed across the yard with Eunice following on his heels. When he reached the house, he set the box on the porch and turned to face her. "My mamm's not here right now, but I'll make sure she knows these are here as soon as she gets home."

"What about your sister? Is she at home?"

"Nope. She's still at the schoolhouse."

"Oh." Eunice hesitated, wondering if she should invite Andrew to her house for supper one night next week, but she changed her mind. When she'd been trying to win Freeman Bontrager's heart last year, she'd become too pushy and had sent him straight into the arms of Katie Miller. She wouldn't make that mistake again.

"Tell your mamm and schweschder that I'm sorry I missed them," she said.

"I will."

Eunice hurried across the yard. When she reached the place where Jake had begun shoeing one of the horses, she paused. "I'll probably see you again soon because my daed has a couple of horses he needs to have shoed."

"No problem," Jake said as she untied her horse. "Tell him to give me a call."

"I will." Eunice stepped into her buggy and gathered up the reins. When she reached the end of the driveway, she glanced over her shoulder and saw Andrew waving at her. She smiled. *If I don't chase after him, maybe he'll chase after me.*

※ ※

Lonnie gripped the stick he was using to steady himself and kicked a pebble, sending it flying up the driveway. He'd been sitting on the front porch and had seen the mailman go by, so, despite his equilibrium being off some due to his loss of hearing, he'd walked down to pick up the mail. He'd hoped that there would be another letter from Carolyn, but there'd been nothing but a stack of bills. On the one hand, he was disappointed that there was no letter from her. On the other hand, he felt a sense of relief. If Carolyn didn't write, he wouldn't have to write back. What was there to say? She already knew he'd lost his hearing, as well as his job. Without a job, he couldn't offer her a future. Without a job he enjoyed, he'd never be truly happy.

Wayne had suggested that he didn't need his hearing for every kind of job. But what job could he do that wouldn't require him to hear? Jobs were scarce here in Indiana, and even if he could find something he was able to do with his hearing loss, he didn't want just any old job. He wanted a job he enjoyed, like the one he'd had making wind chimes.

When Lonnie stepped onto the porch, he dropped the mail on a little table and flopped into one of the wicker chairs with a groan. He was surprised when he glanced toward the road and saw Jolene pedaling her bike up the driveway. She pushed it near the house, climbed off, and pulled a notebook from her backpack. Then she stepped onto the porch and handed the notebook to Lonnie.

He squinted at the words she'd written: *I've been thinking about you and wondering if you'd reconsider and let me to teach you how to sign and read lips.*

He surprised himself when he gave a slow nod. "When can we begin?"

I can't do it today, she wrote, *but if you can come by the schoolhouse after school lets out tomorrow, I can start teaching you then.*

"I'll be there." *But I don't have to like it,* he told himself.

❧ ❧

Jake had just finished cleaning the barn when he spotted Kyle riding up the driveway on his pony.

"How'd it go at school today?" Jake asked after Kyle halted his pony near the barn and climbed down.

The boy frowned. "It was baremlich."

"What was so terrible about it?"

"I got in trouble for somethin' I didn't do—least not on purpose, anyway."

"What was that?"

"I was tryin' to get the parrot's cage open so Elmer could show the dumm bird, and the crazy critter hopped out and scared the scholars when it flew around the room. Then that daab buwe, Irvin, opened the door, and the bird flew outside. Jolene blamed me for the whole thing." Kyle's forehead wrinkled as he squeezed his eyebrows together. "I always get in trouble for things that ain't my fault."

"Did you tell Jolene that you didn't let the parrot out on purpose?"

"Jah, but she didn't believe me. Made me sit in the corner

674

facing the wall while the other kids showed their pets." Kyle grunted. "Had to sit that way for half an hour."

Jake frowned. "That doesn't seem fair to me. Would you like me to have a talk with Jolene about this?"

Kyle shook his head vigorously. "I'd be in more trouble if you did that."

Jake leaned against the barn door and thought. "How come Jolene was the one who punished you? I thought she was hired to teach the deaf children, not your class."

"Becky got sick, so Fern took her home." Kyle shuffled his feet a few times. "Jolene took over until Fern got back, but instead of teachin', she asked us to show our pets."

"So didn't you get to show yours?"

"Huh-uh. Sat in the corner the whole time."

"That doesn't seem right to me. You took your pony to school to show it to the scholars, and you should have had the right to do so. Think I'll go over to the schoolhouse right now and have a talk with her about this." Jake moved toward the back of the barn where his truck was parked. He'd get there quicker if he didn't take the time to hitch his horse to a buggy.

Kyle grabbed the sleeve of Jake's jacket. "She ain't there. Left as soon as school was out."

"Then I'll head over to her house and talk to her."

"She ain't there, neither. Heard her tell Fern that she was goin' over to see Lonnie Hershberger after school."

Jake was tempted to head over to Lonnie's and have a talk with Jolene but figured it'd be best if he spoke to her privately. He'd wait an hour and then go over to Jolene's house. He needed to get to the bottom of this before the day was out.

CHAPTER 15

Jolene eased herself onto the sofa and closed her eyes. She'd been fighting a headache most of the day, and by the time she'd left Lonnie's, the headache had gotten worse. She hadn't argued when Mom suggested that she rest awhile before it was time to start supper. Maybe a short nap would soothe her jangled nerves and relieve the headache. She'd been planning to stop by the Beechys' place and talk to Jake about his brother's antics with the pony but had decided it could wait until after supper. Maybe by then, she'd have a better idea of what to say.

Jolene was on the verge of drifting off when Mom entered the room.

"Sorry if I startled you." Mom's lips moved slowly. "Jake Beechy is on the porch. He says he needs to speak to you right away."

"That's good, because I need to speak with him, too. Please tell him to come in." Jolene swung her legs over the side of the sofa and sat up. A few seconds later, Jake entered the room. The frown on his face made Jolene wonder if Kyle had already told him about the pony episode.

"My brother Kyle came home from school pretty upset today," Jake said before Jolene could open her mouth. "I'd like to know why you assumed he'd intentionally let Elmer's parrot out of its cage."

Jolene squinted as she rubbed her forehead. "I didn't assume that at all."

Jake's brows drew together. "Then why'd you punish him for it?"

"I didn't. I—"

"I don't think it was fair that you made him sit in the corner while the others showed their pets."

Jolene shook her head. "Letting the parrot out of its cage is not why I punished Kyle. I made him sit in the corner after he rode his pony into the schoolhouse."

Jake's eyes widened. "What?"

"It's true. Kyle went outside, and when he came back in, he was riding his pony."

A muscle in Jake's face quivered as he lowered himself into the nearest chair. "Kyle never said a word about riding his pony into the schoolhouse. No wonder you made him sit in the corner. Now that I know the truth, I'll make sure he's punished."

Jolene thought a minute as she formulated her words. "I wonder if Kyle might be taking his frustrations out at school because he's not getting enough attention at home."

"What makes you think that?"

"The boy seems so angry all the time, and it's gotten worse since your daed's accident."

Jake thumped the dimple in his chin a few times. "Guess you could be right. Now that Dad can't do any of his chores, Kyle's expected to do more than he normally did. He doesn't have much time for play these days, and whenever anyone says something to Kyle, they're usually asking him to do another chore."

Jolene was about to comment when Ella stepped into the room. She took one look at Jake and halted. Then she quickly looked at Jolene. "Sorry, I didn't realize you had company."

"Didn't you see my buggy outside?" Jake asked.

"I did see a buggy, but I didn't know it was yours." Ella said something else to Jake, but since her head was turned, Jolene couldn't make out what it was. Jake said something then, but his head was turned now, too. Even without hearing what Jake and Ella were saying, Jolene knew by their body language that something unpleasant was going on.

Jake rose from his seat and stood in front of Jolene. "I'll be heading for home now, but you can rest easy—my brother won't be riding his pony into the schoolhouse ever again." He glanced at Ella and hurried from the room.

"What was going on between you and Jake?" Jolene asked Ella after the door had closed behind Jake.

Ella's face flamed. "That man makes me so mad!"

"Did he say something to upset you?"

Ella flopped onto the sofa beside Jolene and said something, but her head was turned toward the window.

Jolene tapped Ella's arm. "I can't understand what you're saying unless you look at me."

Ella turned toward Jolene. "Sorry. You speak so well that I keep forgetting you can't hear what I'm saying."

Jolene smiled, appreciating the compliment. "Since I can't hear, I never know if I'm speaking clear enough or at the correct volume. Sometimes I find it hard to concentrate on reading lips, too."

"I imagine it would be hard."

"It's really a lot easier for me if someone signs."

"I suppose it would be, but signing seems difficult to me."

"It's not that hard to learn. There are four of us in this community now who can't hear, so for the benefit of us all, I'm hoping more people will learn how to sign."

"I'd like to learn." Ella smiled. "Can I be one of your first adult students?"

"Actually, I've already begun teaching Mom, Dad, and Andrew. And starting tomorrow, I'll be giving Lonnie lessons after school's out for the day. If you'd like to come to the schoolhouse, you can have your first lesson with him."

"Won't that make it harder, having two of us to teach at the same time?"

"Not really. Lonnie seemed a little nervous about learning to sign, so maybe having someone else in the room who wants to learn will help put his mind at ease."

"I guess we could give it a try. If Lonnie seems uneasy with me being there, maybe we can figure out some other time for you to teach me."

"That'll be fine." Jolene touched Ella's arm. "Getting back to Jake—did he say something to upset you?"

Ella frowned. "Said he was surprised I wasn't married and raising a family by now."

"Why would that upset you?"

"I think he was trying to rub it in that I'm still an old maid."

"You're not an old maid."

"Jah, I am. I'm twenty-four years old and don't even have a boyfriend."

"I don't have one either, and I'm more of an old maid than you are because I'll probably never get married."

"Why do you say that?"

"Think about it, Ella. What man would want to marry a woman who can't hear what he says to her?" Jolene massaged her forehead. "Even if I were to marry, I'm afraid of becoming a *mudder*."

"How come?"

"What if one of my kinner were to hurt himself and cry for help? Unless I was in the same room and saw it happen, I'd never know that he'd been injured."

"Lots of deaf people marry and have kinner," Ella said. "I'm sure they have ways of learning to cope."

"Maybe so, but it wouldn't be the same as if I could hear." The throbbing in Jolene's head increased. "It doesn't really matter, because I'm happy teaching my students. I don't need to get married and have kinner of my own."

"Me neither. I've learned to accept the fact that I'm destined to be an old maid."

"Wouldn't you like to meet a man and fall in love?"

Ella shrugged. "Maybe, but I don't know who it'd be."

"What about Lonnie or Jake? They're both single and nice looking."

"In case you've forgotten what I told you the other day, Lonnie has a girlfriend in Illinois." Ella wrinkled her nose. "And I'd never consider Jake as a boyfriend."

"Why not?"

"Besides the fact that Jake will no doubt head back to Montana as soon as his daed's on his feet, he can't be trusted to keep his word about anything!"

"Are you referring to something in particular?"

"Sure am. When he and Loraine were going out, he made all kinds of promises about them having a future together, but then he ran off to Montana and didn't bother to keep in touch."

"That's in the past, Ella. Loraine's been over Jake for a long time, and she's happily married to Wayne."

"But Jake lied to Loraine. He let her believe that he loved her and was coming back."

"Jake wasn't much more than a teenager when he went to Montana the first time, and what he did then doesn't mean he can't be trusted now."

"It's not the only time Jake has lied. He lied to—" Ella's cheeks turned pink and she abruptly stopped talking.

"What were you going to say?" Jolene asked. "Who'd Jake lie to?"

Ella shrugged. "It doesn't matter. The point is, Jake's not the right man for me."

"I'm sure the right man will come along when the time is right." Jolene yawned, struggling to keep her eyes open.

"I'd better go and let you rest. When I first arrived, your mamm said you had a headache and had come in here to lie down." Ella patted Jolene's arm in a motherly fashion.

Jolene smiled with gratitude. She really did need to rest, as the throbbing in her head had gotten worse. "I'll see you tomorrow afternoon."

Ella nodded and hurried out the door.

❧ ❧

By the time Jake got home from Jolene's, he'd worked himself up pretty good. He had half a notion to find Kyle, haul him out to the woodshed, and give him a spanking for saying that Jolene had punished him for letting the parrot out. "He should have told me the truth about riding the pony into the schoolhouse," Jake mumbled as he led his horse to the barn.

Even after Jake had put the horse in its stall and brushed him down thoroughly, he was still fuming. He didn't want to deal with Kyle but knew someone had to. Dad wasn't up to it, and Mom had enough on her plate, trying to keep up with household chores and caring for Dad and the children.

Jake fed his horse some oats, left the barn, and walked slowly to the house, knowing he needed to calm down before he spoke to Kyle. He found Mom in the kitchen, peeling potatoes in front of the sink.

"Where's Kyle?" he asked. "I need to speak to that boy!"

"He's in the living room, doing his homework."

Jake started in that direction but halted when Mom called, "What's going on? You look *umgerennt*. Has Kyle done something wrong?"

Jake turned to face his mother. "I *am* upset, and I'll tell you why as soon as I've spoken to Kyle." He hurried from the room.

Jake discovered Kyle sprawled out on the sofa, reading a book. "I thought you were supposed to be doing your homework. At least that's what Mom thinks you're doing."

Kyle rolled over on his side and glared at Jake. "For your information, I'm finished with it."

"Then you ought to be outside doing your chores."

"I'll do 'em after supper."

Jake marched across the room and halted in front of the sofa. "Sit up. I want to talk to you."

Kyle made no move to get up.

Jake nudged Kyle's leg. "Sit up and move over so I can sit down."

Kyle grunted and pulled himself to a sitting position.

Jake took a seat beside him and cleared his throat.

"What's wrong? Have ya got somethin' stuck in your throat?"

Jake squinted at Kyle. "I just talked to Jolene, and I want to know why you lied to me about the reason you were punished at school today."

Kyle's cheeks flamed, and he dropped his gaze to the floor.

"Answer me, Kyle. Why didn't you tell me that you'd ridden your pony into the schoolhouse?"

Kyle shrugged. "Figured you'd blab it to Mom, and then I'd be in trouble with her."

"I can't speak for our mamm, but you're in big trouble with me! Not only for pulling such a crazy stunt with the pony, but for lying about the reason you were punished." Jake grimaced. "Not to mention making me look like a fool for accusing Jolene of wrongly punishing you." He rose to his feet. "Come with me to the barn. I've got some extra chores for you to do."

"I don't have to do what you say!" Kyle's face darkened. "You ain't my daed!"

"That's true, but Dad's not in any shape to be doling out punishment right now, so I'm filling in for him until he's back on his feet." Jake motioned to the door. "Now get on out to the barn and be quick about it!"

Kyle sat with his arms folded.

Jake was out of patience. If this was what it was like to be a father, then he was in no hurry to settle down and get married. "You'd better do as I say, little brother!"

"You ain't my boss."

"I am until Dad's better, so get off that sofa and get out to the barn!" Jake's hand shook as he pointed to the door. No wonder Jolene had put Kyle in the corner. She should have kept him after school and given him a bunch of chores to do at the schoolhouse.

Just then, Dad rolled into the room in his wheelchair. The top of his nearly gray hair stood on end, and his clothes were wrinkled, like he'd just woken up. "What's all the yelling about?" Dad's eyes narrowed as he stared at Jake.

Jake debated whether he should tell Dad about Kyle's antics at school. He didn't want to upset him, but he guessed Dad had the right to know what had gone on. He quickly related the whole thing and ended it by saying, "I think Kyle needs to be punished, so I'm sending him out to the barn to do some extra chores."

"It's your mamm's and my place to punish our kinner, not yours," Dad said gruffly. "You need to stay out of things that are none of your business."

Jake's fingers curled into the palms of his hands until his nails dug into his flesh. "Everything around here's my business these days."

Dad leveled him with a look that could have stopped a runaway horse. "What's that supposed to mean?"

Jake sighed deeply. "As soon as I heard that you'd been hurt, I left my job in Montana to come back here and take over shoeing horses for you, not to mention doing all the chores you used to do around here." He pointed to Kyle, who still sat slumped on the sofa. "I think that gives me the right to dole out punishment to my contrary little brother whenever it's needed, don't you?"

"No, I don't! And as far as you leavin' Montana to come here, I'm sure that you're only here out of obligation." Dad glanced down at the casts on his legs. "If I was a bettin' man, I'd bet that as soon as I'm able to work again, you'll trot right on back to Montana to play cowboy with a bunch of wild horses!"

"What's going on in here?" Mom asked as she entered the room. She looked first at Jake and then at Dad.

"I'm settin' our oldest son straight on a few things," Dad mumbled. "He seems to think him coming home to help out gives him the right to punish our kinner."

"Just Kyle right now." Jake repeated the story of the day's events to Mom. "A few extra chores won't kill the boy, and I figured I was doing you and Dad a favor by taking over."

Mom slowly shook her head. "You should have told me about this sooner and let me handle the discipline of Kyle."

"That's right," Dad interjected. "If you knew so much about discipline, you would have disciplined yourself and not run off to Montana like you did!" Sweat beaded on his forehead. "Ever since you turned sixteen, you've been nothing but rebellious."

"I'm not rebellious. I'm just trying to—"

Dad clapped his hands. "Don't interrupt me when I'm speaking, boy! You need to think things through, set your priorities straight, and decide what's the right thing to do."

Jake had listened to about as much as he could take. "Do

what you will with my spoiled brother, but I'd appreciate it if you stopped trying to make me feel guilty for all my decisions!" He whirled around and stalked out of the room. He could hardly wait for Dad's legs to heal so he could head back to Montana!

CHAPTER 16

J olene dismissed her class of two to go home and smiled when Irvin gave her a nod and signed, *"See you tomorrow, Teacher."* Things had gone better today, and for that she was grateful.

She glanced at the rules she'd written on the blackboard that morning:

1. *Pay attention.*
2. *Don't bother others.*
3. *Behave in class.*
4. *Use total communication (signing, finger spelling, speech, and lip reading).*
5. *Remember to do your homework and bring it to school.*
6. *Cooperate and share with others.*

Consequences for Not Obeying:
1. *Name on the board—warning.*
2. *One check—stand against the wall.*
3. *Two checks—parents will be told.*

Jolene had made it clear to both Irvin and Sylvia that she expected them to follow those rules. She figured the children's folks had made a few rules, too, for Sylvia, who'd cooperated from the beginning, had been even more attentive today, and Irvin had actually done most of his work. She had a hunch that Sylvia had

685

told on Irvin, and he'd probably been punished at home for not paying attention in class and refusing to do what Jolene asked.

Jolene had just taken a notebook and pen from her desk when she felt a swish of air. She looked up and saw Lonnie step into the room. When the door swung shut, he said, "I'm here for my lesson."

Knowing that the school desks were too small for Lonnie's tall frame, Jolene pulled out the chair at her desk and motioned for him to sit down.

He hesitated then asked, "Where are you going to sit?"

Jolene moved over to the blackboard and wrote: *I'll stand for now.* Then she wrote the letter *A* and turned to face Lonnie. She made the hand gesture for *A*, with her fingers balled into the palm of her hand and her thumb facing up. Next she wrote the letter *B* and made the hand gesture, with all four fingers facing up and the thumb pulled inward across the palm of the hand. She continued writing the letters of the alphabet and making the proper hand signs until she'd done each one.

Lonnie looked at her with an eyebrow quirked and a perplexed expression. Was it really that hard to understand, or didn't he want to learn?

Maybe I'm going too fast, Jolene decided. She pointed to the letter *A* and made the hand sign for it again. Then she wrote on the blackboard and asked Lonnie to make the same hand sign she'd just made.

He did as she requested but without much enthusiasm. Then she showed him again how to make the hand signs for the letters *B* and *C*. They practiced each of those several times then moved on to the letters *D*, *E*, and *F*. Jolene was about to start with the letter *G* when Ella stepped into the room.

"Sorry I'm late," she said, looking at Jolene. "I went with my daed to run some errands, and it took longer than we expected. He dropped me off here and suggested I go home with you after my lesson. He has a few more errands to run here in Topeka, so he'll pick me up at your place later this afternoon."

"That's fine," Jolene said, "but we'll have to walk to my house because that's how I came to school today."

Ella smiled. "That's okay. It's a nice day, and I'll enjoy the walk."

Jolene motioned to the blackboard and explained to Ella what she'd taught Lonnie so far. "Why don't you have a seat at one of the scholars' desks and follow along?"

Ella pulled out a chair and took a seat. The desk was a bit small for her, but she was short and fit in the chair a lot better than Lonnie would have.

Ella smiled at Lonnie, but he sat stony faced with his arms folded.

Jolene went to the blackboard and wrote: *Ella wants to learn how to sign, so I invited her to join us today.* She pointed to the letter *A.* When she made the hand sign for it, Ella did the same.

"I wish I hadn't come," Lonnie said.

"What was that?" she wrote on the board.

"Nothing."

Jolene thought Lonnie had said he wished he hadn't come, but she couldn't be sure because toward the end of his sentence, he'd lowered his head. She continued to show Ella how to make the letters *B, C, D,* and *E;* then she pointed to the letter *F* and made the sign for that, but Lonnie didn't respond.

A few seconds later, he jumped to his feet. "I'm going home."

Before Jolene had a chance to respond, Lonnie raced out the door. She groaned and flopped into the chair where he'd been sitting. *"Es is mir verleed."*

"Why are you discouraged?" Ella asked.

"I'm not a good teacher. I feel like a failure."

Ella left her seat and stood in front of Jolene. "You need to stop questioning everything you do and quit blaming yourself for things that aren't your fault. It's obvious that Lonnie doesn't want to learn."

Jolene blinked back the tears stinging her eyes. "I think Lonnie's discouraged and probably a bit overwhelmed because there's so much to learn."

"Maybe I should bake him a loaf of friendship bread and attach a verse of scripture like I've done for several others in our community when they've gone through trying times."

"That's a thought. I don't know if he'll appreciate it, though." Jolene motioned to the blackboard then looked back at Ella. "Do you want to continue with the lesson, or are you ready to head for home?"

"You look tired and stressed," Ella said. "Maybe we should put the lesson on hold and start walking to your house."

Jolene nodded and pushed away from her desk. She was beginning to feel another headache coming on.

⁓※⁓

As Ella and Jolene walked along the shoulder of the road, the afternoon sun shone in a crystal blue sky. Despite the chilly fall weather they'd been having, the sun had shone nearly every day that week.

A slight breeze lifted the ribbon ties on Ella's head covering, while it whispered through the nearly bare trees that were close to the road.

Ella glanced at Jolene as she walked by her side. What a shame she couldn't hear the wind or any of nature's other sweet sounds. Ella couldn't imagine what it must be like for her cousin. It would be horrible to lose one's ability to hear. Yet Jolene seemed to be coping fairly well. *Better than I would be if I'd lost my hearing,* Ella thought.

They hadn't gone far when a hefty white goose waddled down the driveway of an English farmer's house, honking as it went.

Ella nudged Jolene's arm and pointed to the goose. "Looks like there's trouble heading our way."

"What was that? I can't tell what you're saying unless you look at me."

The goose gave a loud *honk* and started running toward them.

"It's a goose! Probably a mean goose!" Ella shouted, making sure that Jolene could see her face.

As the goose grew closer, it headed for Jolene. She gasped and started running in circles.

Suddenly the goose stopped, turned, and ran after Ella. She gave it a nudge with her foot. The goose stood still a few moments, but then it started after her again. Her heart pounding, Ella nudged the goose again, with a little more force. It turned and waddled a few steps toward home, but then it did a sudden U-turn and came after Jolene again.

Jolene and Ella started running down the road, but the goose was much faster than Ella anticipated and soon overtook them. She screeched to a halt and gave the goose a sterner nudge with her foot, which sent the goose rolling in the tall grass along the shoulder of the road. But it quickly got back up and came after her again, honking and raising a ruckus.

Jolene took hold of Ella's arm. "Have you noticed that the goose hasn't actually bitten either one of us?"

Ella drew in a shaky breath and shook her head. "The only thing I've noticed is that it won't quit running after us."

"Hold still, Ella. I think this silly old goose just wants to walk with us."

Ella froze. Sure enough, the dumb goose came right up, leaned into her leg, and looked up at her like she was a long-lost friend.

Ella leaned over so she was eye to eye with the goose. "I'm sorry for rolling you with my foot and anything else I did that might have traumatized you."

Like an obedient dog, the silly goose proceeded to waddle alongside Ella. Finally, at Jolene's suggestion, they turned back toward the farmhouse the goose had come from. When they got there, Ella walked the goose back to its yard, where it honked a farewell and waddled off like nothing had ever happened.

Ella joined Jolene at the end of the driveway, and they both started laughing. Jolene laughed so hard that tears rolled down her cheeks. Ella smiled as they headed back down the road. Jolene had seemed so down after Lonnie left the schoolhouse in a huff. It was good to see her relax and find some humor in what had started out to be a very stressful event. Maybe that's what they all needed these days—to look for the humorous side of things.

≈ ≈

As Lonnie drew close to home, a feeling of guilt washed over him. He'd acted like a spoiled brat and knew he should have stayed and finished his lesson. For some reason, though, having Ella there had made him feel nervous. Maybe it was because she seemed so capable. Maybe it was because he didn't want her to see how stupid he was. He'd had a hard enough time concentrating on what Jolene had shown him, and remembering the finger positions had been no easy task. At the rate he was going, he'd never learn to sign the entire alphabet, much less be able to sign any words.

Lonnie guided his horse up the driveway and halted near the barn. After he unhitched the horse, he spent some time brushing the animal down. This gave him the opportunity to think things through a bit more. By the time he was done, he'd made a decision. After supper, he'd go over to Jolene's and apologize for his childish behavior.

When Lonnie headed for the house, he saw Mom sitting in a chair on the back porch, peeling potatoes. When he stepped onto the porch, she wrote something on the tablet that had been lying beside her and handed it to him. It read: *You're home sooner than I expected. How'd your first lesson with Jolene go?*

"Not good. There's too much to learn." Lonnie chose not to elaborate.

It'll get easier with time and practice. Mom smiled and continued to write. *As soon as you learn how to sign, your daed and I will ask Jolene to teach us.*

Lonnie shrugged.

Mom wrote something else on the tablet. *I think I know something that will lift your spirits.*

"What's that?"

There's a letter for you on the table. It's from Carolyn.

He hurried into the house and tore open the envelope, but he'd only read a few words when his heart started to pound:

Dear Lonnie,

This is hard for me to say, but I won't be coming to see you after all. I've met someone, and. . .

The words blurred on the page, and Lonnie blinked against the unexpected tears behind his eyes. He sank into a nearby chair. Carolyn wasn't coming; she'd found someone else. Was it because she didn't want to be stuck with a man who couldn't hear?

What was the use in learning to sign or read lips if he couldn't have Carolyn? Without her, his life had no meaning. So much for that time when she'd told him she thought God had brought them together!

Lonnie lifted his gaze toward the ceiling and railed at God for the injustices He allowed. "It's not fair! Nothing in my life is fair anymore!" He sprang from the chair, knocking it to the floor. He was glad he couldn't hear the *crash*.

Lonnie dashed across the room and jerked open the back door with such force that he felt the vibration when it hit the wall.

When he stepped onto the porch, he drew in a couple of shaky breaths. Then, taking the stairs two at a time, he headed straight for the barn. This day couldn't be over soon enough to suit him!

CHAPTER 17

"How are things going at school?" Loraine asked Jolene when they met at the hardware store in Shipshewana the following afternoon.

Jolene shrugged. "Things are a little better with Irvin and Sylvia, but Lonnie doesn't seem to want to learn."

"Oh that's right, you had. . ." Loraine turned her head as she reached for a stack of baby blankets.

Jolene tapped Loraine's arm. "What did you say? I couldn't see your lips."

Loraine's cheeks colored as she faced Jolene. "Sorry."

"Reading lips is the only way I can know what others are saying, unless they know how to sign."

"Speaking of signing," Loraine said. "I understand that you're going to be teaching Ella."

"That's right. She had her first lesson yesterday and another one this afternoon. Lonnie was supposed to have another lesson with us today, too, but he didn't show up."

"Maybe he got busy with something at home."

"I hope that's all it was. He seemed upset when he left the schoolhouse yesterday, and I was concerned that he might not come back today."

"I'm sure he'll be back for more lessons. He won't be able to communicate without learning to sign and read lips."

"You're probably right. I'll give him a few more days, and if he

692

doesn't show up, I'll go over to his house and talk to him about it." Jolene motioned to the blanket Loraine held. "Are you getting ready for the big day?"

Loraine smiled. "I can hardly wait until the boppli's born this spring."

"I'm happy for you."

"I've been concerned about our finances, but Wayne's begun making wooden items, and he's already sold a few things to some of the furniture stores in the area, so I think we'll be okay."

"What about Ada and Crist? Are they getting by on what Crist makes in his taxidermy shop?"

"So far, but Wayne will be taking less money from the business now that he's found a way to supplement our income, so Crist will earn most of the profits."

"I guess Ada could always look for a job if she needed to."

Loraine shrugged. "Maybe, but she likes being at home."

"She might find something she could make and sell from her home like some folks in our community have done."

"I'm sure she'll help out if she needs to, so I'm trying not to worry about it."

Jolene swallowed hard. It was a challenge not to worry about a lot of things these days.

～❧ ❧～

As Ella approached the Hershbergers' place, her breath caught. The sun peeked out between fluffy white clouds, casting a golden light on the pastures surrounding their farm. The fields of drying corn rustled, and birds chirped a happy chorus in the trees overhead. Fall was a beautiful time of year.

Ella secured her horse to the hitching rail and reached inside the buggy to get the friendship bread she'd made for Lonnie. Then she sprinted to the house and knocked on the door. A few moments later, Lonnie's mother, Irene, answered her knock.

"I came to see how Lonnie's doing and to give him a loaf of friendship bread." Ella handed the bread to Irene. "There's a verse of scripture attached to the wrapping."

"That's nice of you. I'm sure Lonnie will appreciate the gesture." Irene opened the door wider. "Come inside, and we can chat awhile."

Ella followed Irene into the kitchen, and Irene placed the loaf of bread on the counter. "Please, have a seat," she said, motioning to the table.

When Ella sat down, she noticed the late-afternoon shadows bouncing off the walls. The days were getting shorter, and soon it would be dark by late afternoon—a sure sign that winter was coming.

"Would you like a cup of coffee or some tea?" Irene asked.

"No, thanks."

"How are things at your place? Is your daed keeping busy in his shop?"

"Since he hasn't found anyone to take Lonnie's place, he's busy enough, but it's mostly with out-of-state orders right now."

"Lonnie misses his job tuning wind chimes. He's been miserable ever since he lost his hearing." Irene sighed deeply. "Now, with Carolyn breaking up with him, he feels worse than ever."

"When did that happen?"

"He got a letter from her yesterday, saying she'd met someone else. He's convinced that she broke up with him because of his disability. Now he's despondent and doesn't want to learn how to sign or read lips."

"Is Lonnie at home now?" Ella asked. "I'd like to speak to him."

"He's out in the barn." Irene took a tablet and pen from the desk in the kitchen and handed it to Ella. "You'll need this so you can communicate with him."

"Okay." Ella left her seat, plucked the scripture verse off the loaf of friendship bread, and scurried out the door.

She found Lonnie in the barn, sitting on a bale of straw, staring at the rafters. When she touched his shoulder, he jumped.

"Sorry if I startled you."

"Huh?"

Using the tablet and pen Irene had given her Ella scrawled a note and handed it to Lonnie. He read her words with a look of

694

disinterest. *I went to the schoolhouse this afternoon for another signing lesson and was disappointed that you weren't there.*

"I changed my mind about learning to sign."

How come? Ella wrote in reply.

"Carolyn broke up with me. Nothing matters anymore now."

Ella saw the anger and pain on Lonnie's face, even heard it in his voice. She wished there was something she could say to make him feel better. It was never fun to be jilted.

Ella wrote again on the tablet: *I brought you a loaf of friendship bread with a verse of scripture attached. I think the verse might help you understand that God has a plan for your life.*

"Some plan! There's no way you could understand what I'm going through. You still have two good ears."

That's true, but I've suffered losses. Ella squeezed onto the bale of straw beside him. *You're not the only one who's lost your hearing. Jolene lost hers in the accident we were in, and she's learned to cope with her handicap. She doesn't sit around feeling sorry for herself because she can't hear, either.*

"It's not just my loss of hearing that's got me down. It's the fact that Carolyn broke up with me because of it." He slowly shook his head. "I can't understand why God allows people to do such hurtful things."

People aren't puppets, and I don't think anyone really understands why bad things happen to good people. Ella lifted her pen as she thought about what more she should say. *God has a plan for your life, and I think you should let Jolene teach you to communicate through signing and lip reading so that others don't have to write everything down.* She handed Lonnie the verse of scripture that had been attached to the bread: *"I will instruct thee and teach thee in the way which thou shalt go: I will guide thee with mine eye. Psalm 32:8."*

He read the verse but gave no response.

If Jolene's willing to give up her time to teach you, don't you think you ought to quit feeling sorry for yourself because life's handed you a harsh blow and learn from her?

His face blanched then quickly turned pink. "I guess both Jolene and I share a great loss."

Ella nodded.

"My miserable situation isn't her fault, and I guess she only wants to help me."

Does that mean you'll come back for more lessons? Ella wrote.

"I guess so."

That's great. I'll see you at the schoolhouse tomorrow afternoon.

꙯

For the last fifteen minutes, Jake had been sitting at the kitchen table, drinking a cup of coffee and visiting with his mother while she prepared supper.

He enjoyed this quiet time, watching her slice carrots and potatoes into the pot of vegetable soup. While he was living in Montana and sleeping in the bunkhouse, he'd missed times like this. There'd always been such an easy camaraderie between him and Mom.

Not like me and Dad, Jake thought ruefully. *We've never seen eye to eye on much of anything.* Jake still hadn't gotten over Dad hollering at him for trying to discipline Kyle.

Stretching his arms over his head, Jake yawned.

"If you're tired, why don't you go lie down?" Mom suggested. "I'll call you when supper's ready."

Before Jake could reply, Dad wheeled into the kitchen. "Thought I heard voices in here." He looked over at Jake. "How come you're not outside doin' the afternoon chores?"

"They're done already."

"Oh." Dad maneuvered his wheelchair up to the table and reached for the coffeepot. "So, Jake, how's business been going this week?" he asked as he poured coffee into the cup Mom handed him. "Are you managing to keep up?"

"I'm doing fine."

"Are you making sure to get the horses' hooves cleaned and trimmed real good before you put on their shoes?"

Irritation welled in Jake's chest. "I know how to shoe a horse, Dad."

"Jah, well, you haven't been helping me for some time."

"I did plenty of shoeing at the ranch in Montana, along with lots of other things that involved horses."

"Humph!" Dad folded his arms and glared at Jake. "All you ever seem to talk about is Montana."

A muscle in Jake's jaw quivered. Wouldn't Dad ever let up?

"If you had a lick of sense, you'd forget about Montana, stay here, and join the church."

Jake didn't like the way this conversation was going, and he was afraid if he stayed much longer, he and Dad would end up in a full-blown argument. He pushed his chair away from the table, dumped his coffee into the sink, and strode across the room.

"Where are you going?" Mom called.

"I've got a few more chores to do in the barn."

"I thought you said you'd done all the chores," Dad said.

Jake just hurried out the door.

Once outside, he leaned against the porch railing and watched the horses grazing in the pasture. He probably had enough money saved up to put a down payment on a place of his own if he had a mind to, but he wasn't sure whether he wanted to settle in Indiana or Montana. If he stayed here, there might be more conflict with Dad than there already was. If he went back to Montana, Mom would be hurt.

At one time, Jake had thought he was ready to join the Amish church, but now he wasn't sure it would be the right thing for him to do. He didn't want to make a lifelong commitment to something just because it's what his folks wanted. The decision to be Amish or not was between him and God, not him and Dad.

A spark of anger and a flare of determination settled over Jake. He'd made up his mind a long time ago that he would make his own decisions. Dad would just have to deal with whatever he decided. Jake knew he couldn't do anything until Dad's legs healed sufficiently. In the meantime, he would keep out of Dad's way as much as possible and try to stay busy.

CHAPTER 18

The following day, Ella finished her work in Dad's shop early and headed to the schoolhouse for another signing lesson. The scholars were just leaving when she arrived, and she greeted Fern, who stood on the porch. "Is Jolene in her classroom? I came for my signing lesson."

"She's still here. She gave the children in my class another lesson today, too."

"I didn't realize they were learning to sign. Was that your idea or Jolene's?" Ella asked.

"Both. We thought it would help Irvin and Sylvia if they could communicate with the other children." Fern motioned to Kyle Beechy, who was about to climb onto his bike. "He's given Irvin a hard time about not being able to hear, so I think learning to speak with his hands will be a good thing for him. It'll give him a better idea of what it's like for people who are deaf."

"I hope it helps." Ella moved toward the stairs. "Guess I'd better get up there before Jolene thinks I'm not coming." When she reached the first step, she turned back around. "Will you be at the young people's volleyball game on Friday night at the 850 Center?"

"I don't know," Fern replied. "I hadn't really thought about going. I'm really not much of a volleyball player."

"You should go. I'm sure it'll be a lot of fun, even if you just sit and watch."

Fern smiled. "If I do go, then I'll go by myself. Freeman and Katie will probably go, and I'm sure they'd like some time alone as they travel to and from the game. It'll be difficult enough for them after they're married and living in the same house with me."

"They do want you to continue living there, right?"

"I believe so, but even though Grandma left the house to both Freeman and me, I offered to move out so he and Katie can have the house to themselves after they're married." A stiff breeze blew under the eaves of the porch, and Fern pulled the collar of her jacket tighter. "Freeman insists that the house is half mine and says he wants me to stay on."

"What does Katie say about it?"

"She agrees with Freeman—even said she enjoyed my company."

"Then I'm sure everything will be fine."

"Thanks. I'll see you later," Fern added as she stepped out the doorway. "I need to get home and start supper before Freeman closes his bike shop. He's usually hungry as a mule by the end of the day."

Ella chuckled as she hurried up the stairs. When she entered Jolene's classroom and saw no sign of Lonnie, she was disappointed.

She stepped up to Jolene's desk. "I'm sorry to see that Lonnie's not here. I stopped by to see him yesterday, and he said he'd be coming today."

"Did he say why he missed the last lesson?" Jolene asked.

Ella was on the verge of telling Jolene that Lonnie's girlfriend had broken up with him, when the door swung open and Lonnie stepped into the room.

"I'm sorry for missing yesterday's lesson," he said.

Jolene wrote a message for him on the blackboard: *You're here now; that's all that matters. Since you and Ella want to learn how to sign, I think it would be good if you both come here a few days a week for signing, and then since Lonnie will also need to learn lip reading, maybe he can come on a different day just for that.*

"That's fine," Lonnie said.

Ella agreed, too. She was glad Lonnie had come, but his

somber expression told her that it would be awhile before he got over being jilted by Carolyn.

Jolene erased the board and had just written the first five letters of the alphabet, when the door opened and Jake stepped in.

He walked up to Jolene and said, "I heard you were giving a lesson on signing here today, and I wondered if I could join you."

She smiled. "You're more than welcome to join us."

"Oh, great," Ella muttered.

Jolene glanced over at Ella, and she must have noticed the scowl on her face, for she quickly added, "Of course, if you'd rather come by my house for lessons on the evenings I'll be teaching my family how to sign, you're welcome to do that."

"I just might," Jake said, "but I'm here now, so I may as well get in on this lesson."

~§ §~

Ella felt relieved when the lesson was over and Lonnie and Jake had gone. It was hard for her to be in the same room with Jake. Watching the way he'd kept flirting with Jolene made her sick to her stomach. At least it had seemed like flirting.

"What's wrong with you today?" Jolene asked. "For someone who said they wanted to learn how to sign, you didn't show much interest. Every time I looked your way, you were scowling."

"Jake isn't to be trusted."

Jolene's brows puckered. "What's Jake got to do with it?"

"Nothing. I mean, it irritated me that he was here, and I had trouble concentrating."

"Why would you feel irritated because Jake wants to learn how to sign?"

"I don't care whether he learns to sign or not. What riles me is the way he always manages to worm his way into people's lives. Then he jerks the rug out from under them as soon as they start to have feelings for him."

"Are you referring to the fact that Jake hurt Loraine when he took off for Montana and didn't keep in touch with her, or do you have feelings for Jake?"

Ella's face heated. "Of course not! The only feelings I have for Jake are feelings of irritation."

"Did you ever think that maybe Jake going to Montana and leaving Loraine in the lurch was a blessing?"

"How could it be a blessing?"

"Loraine and Wayne wouldn't be happily married right now if Jake hadn't left."

Ella grunted. "No, Loraine and Jake would be happily married."

"You don't know that. They might not have gotten married even if Jake had stayed in Indiana. And if they had gotten married, it doesn't mean they would have been as happy together as Loraine and Wayne seem to be."

"You could be right." Ella pursed her lips. "But since Jake left Indiana twice, then I'm sure he's bound to leave again."

"Maybe he will go back to Montana when his daed's doing better, but that's Jake's decision. It's no reason for you to sit here with a long face and ignore everything I was trying to teach today."

"You're right. I shouldn't have let my feelings about Jake affect my desire to learn signing." Ella touched Jolene's arm. "Can I offer you a bit of advice?"

"What's that?"

"Don't let Jake get too close to you, and don't listen to any promises he makes."

"What are you talking about?"

"Couldn't you see the way he was flirting with you this afternoon?" Ella asked. "If you're not careful, he'll break your heart, the way he did Loraine's."

Jolene's mouth hung slightly open. "Did you just say what I thought you said—that Jake was flirting with me today, and that he might break my heart?"

Ella nodded. "That's exactly what I said."

"You're kidding, right?"

"No, I'm not. The whole time you were showing us what finger positions to use for certain letters and words, Jake sat there grinning like a lovesick *hund*. He even winked at you."

Jolene shook her head. "I think he was just being friendly. And hopefully he enjoyed the lesson."

"People don't wink at the teacher because they're enjoying the lesson. You didn't see Lonnie winking, did you?"

"Well, no, but—"

"You'd do well to heed my advice and stay as far away from Jake as possible."

"You're serious, aren't you?" Jolene's cheeks had turned a deep rosy pink, matching the color of her dress.

"I am serious. You need to watch out for Jake and keep hold of your heart so he doesn't break it."

"Yes, Mother."

"I mean it, Jolene. Jake's not to be trusted."

"I'm glad Lonnie came back today," Jolene said, abruptly changing the subject. "I was worried that I'd said something to upset him the other day."

"It wasn't you that kept Lonnie from coming yesterday; it was his girlfriend, Carolyn."

"What do you mean?"

"When I stopped by his place yesterday, I found out that he'd gotten a letter from Carolyn saying she'd found someone else and was breaking up with Lonnie."

Deep wrinkles formed across Jolene's forehead. "No wonder he seemed so sullen today. I'm surprised he came here at all."

"He wasn't going to, but I gave him a little pep talk and shared a verse of scripture with him."

"I'm sorry to hear he was jilted like that, but maybe in the long run it'll work out for the best."

"What do you mean?"

"Maybe God has someone else in mind for Lonnie—someone who'll make him happier and be a better wife than Carolyn."

"That could be, I suppose."

"Maybe that someone will be you."

Ella's eyes widened. "I have no more interest in Lonnie than I do Jake. Besides, it's too soon for Lonnie to show an interest in anyone." She twirled the ends of her head-covering ties around her fingers. "If and when Lonnie does take an interest in someone, I'm sure it won't be me."

"How do you know?"

"Because we have nothing in common."

"Jah, you do. You both like wind chimes, and you and Lonnie used to work together in your daed's shop."

"That's true, but Lonnie can't work there anymore, and the fact that we both like wind chimes isn't reason enough for him to be interested in me."

"One never knows how things will go."

"Changing the subject," Ella quickly said, "are you planning to go to the volleyball game on Friday evening?"

"I don't think so."

"It'll be like old times."

Jolene nibbled on her lower lip. "I wouldn't be comfortable there."

"Why not?"

"I'd feel out of place, like I didn't fit in."

"You can sit on the sidelines with me, and we'll be out of place together. How will that be?"

"Well, maybe I'll go if Andrew does." Jolene rose from her chair. "In the meantime, I need to get home and help Mom start supper. Our lesson went longer than I'd planned."

"Then I took up more of your time by talking about Jake and Lonnie."

Jolene glanced at the clock. "It's okay. I'll still be home in plenty of time to help with supper."

❧ ❧

Andrew had just pulled his horse and buggy up to their hitching rail when he saw Jolene's buggy pull in behind him.

"How come you're so late?" he asked when she stepped down from her buggy.

"I had another lesson to teach; only this time Ella wasn't the only one there. Lonnie and Jake came, too."

"It makes sense that Lonnie would come, but why was Jake there?"

"He thinks if he learns to sign, his brother Kyle might take more of an interest in what I'm trying to teach Fern's class."

"Guess that makes sense."

"Do you really think Jake will go back to Montana once his daed's doing better?"

Andrew shrugged. "With Jake, who knows?"

"Ella doesn't trust Jake. She thinks he'll break someone's heart and then leave for Montana again."

"Who's heart does she think he'll break?"

"Mine."

Andrew's eyebrows lifted high. "How's he gonna break your heart? You're not in love with him, are you?"

"Of course not! I haven't been back from Pennsylvania very long, so when would I have had the chance to fall in love with anyone?"

"Good point."

Jolene clutched the folds in her dress. "Ella seems to think that Jake was flirting with me today. After the lesson she warned me about him and said I shouldn't be alone with him."

Andrew unhitched Jolene's horse then turned to face her. "I think Ella's right about Jake leaving again, but I doubt he'll be around long enough to make a move on you or anyone else. But I do think it would be best if you don't have any of your lessons alone with him."

"Surely you don't think I have anything to worry about where Jake's concerned."

"Probably not, but I'd feel better if you didn't put yourself in a compromising position."

"I won't. He'll either have his lessons with Lonnie and Ella, or he'll come over here and learn with our family." She smiled. "I invited him to join us some evening."

"I guess that'd be okay. At least that way I can keep an eye on him."

She nudged his arm. "Changing the subject, I was wondering

if you're planning to attend the volleyball game on Friday night."

"Definitely. Wouldn't miss it for the world."

Jolene quirked an eyebrow. "I've never seen you so excited about a social before. What's up?"

"Nothing. I've been working hard lately, and it'll be nice to let down and have some fun."

"There wouldn't be someone special you're looking forward to seeing, would there?"

Andrew was relieved when Jake pulled up in his buggy just then. He wasn't ready to talk about his interest in Eunice. Besides, some things about Eunice bothered him, and unless she changed, he wouldn't begin a serious relationship with her.

"I've been thinking about what you said at the schoolhouse," Jake said to Jolene when he joined them.

"What was that?" she asked.

"About coming over here for lessons." Jake shook his head. "I don't think I ought to go to the schoolhouse for lessons if Ella's going to be there."

"How come?" Andrew asked before Jolene could respond.

"I fooled around a lot this afternoon during our lesson, thinking it might put Ella at ease, but she seemed irritated and edgy the whole time. I know Ella doesn't like me, although I don't know why." Jake kicked a pebble with the toe of his boot then looked back at Jolene. "Can I come over here for lessons instead?"

She nodded. "That's fine with me. Everyone in the family is busy with other things for the rest of this week, but on Monday evening we'll have another lesson. Could you come over then?"

"Sure." Jake smiled at Jolene. "Will I see you at the game on Friday night?"

"We'll both be there," Andrew was quick to say. *And I'll be watching out for my sister.*

CHAPTER 19

Jolene sat on the sidelines, watching the game of volleyball that had begun a short time after she and Andrew had arrived. Andrew, who enjoyed any kind of ball, had joined the game right away. Jolene, already feeling out of place, had opted to sit and watch. It would be hard to play volleyball, knowing she wouldn't be able to hear what her teammates were shouting to each other. Reading lips would be nearly impossible with everyone running and jumping after the ball.

Jolene glanced around the building to see if Lonnie had come, but there was no sign of him. He'd probably decided not to come, knowing he wouldn't be able to communicate with anyone without the use of a tablet and pen. It would probably be some time before Lonnie felt ready to attend a social event such as this. Jolene looked forward to teaching him how to sign and read lips and hoped he'd catch on quickly now that they'd begun regular lessons.

She glanced back at the volleyball players and was surprised to see Ella and Jake playing on the same team. As much as Ella disliked Jake, it made no sense that she'd be on his team. Maybe she'd had no choice as to which side she played on.

Someone touched Jolene's shoulder, and her head jerked to the right. Fern smiled down at her. "Mind if I join you?"

"Of course not; have a seat." Jolene motioned to the folding chair beside her then turned to face Fern when she sat down. "It sure is a nice evening," she said. "Not cold and windy like it's been the last few days."

Fern smiled. "Sometimes when the fall weather turns warm we get a surprise cold snap with snow." She rubbed the bridge of her nose as her smile was replaced with a frown. "I hope winter doesn't come early this year, because I'm in no hurry for snow."

"Your scholars will probably like it, though," Jolene said. "Most kinner love playing in the snow."

"That's true. I enjoyed making snowmen and sledding down the hill behind the schoolhouse when I was a girl." Fern touched Jolene's arm. "How are things going with the lessons you've been giving after school? Are your adult students catching on to signing as easily as some of the kinner in my class seem to be?"

Jolene shook her head. "Children learn new things easier than most adults, but I'm sure that, given a little time, Lonnie and Ella will catch on."

"What about Jake? I hear that he came over to the schoolhouse to sit in on a lesson on signing from you, too."

"He came once, but he's decided to take part in the lessons I'm giving my family." Jolene debated about telling Fern that Ella felt uncomfortable around Jake but decided it'd be best not to say anything.

"I guess Jake's keeping busy shoeing horses and doing his daed's chores. Taking evening lessons will probably be easier for him."

Jolene nodded and was about to say something more when she spotted Eunice heading their way, holding a bag of ice against her left hand.

❧ ❧

Eunice flopped down on the chair beside Fern and groaned. "I'm never playing volleyball again!"

"How come?" Fern asked.

Eunice held up her hand and grimaced. "I was trying to hit the ball over the net, when Matthew Stoltzfus got in my way and knocked me down. When I landed, my left hand took the brunt of the fall, and I think I may have sprained my wrist."

"Are you sure it's not broken?" Fern asked with a look of concern. "Maybe you should go to the hospital and have it x-rayed."

"If it was broken, I don't think I could do this." Eunice lifted the bag of ice and wiggled her fingers, and then she turned her hand palm up. "It does hurt, though."

"That's exactly why I decided not to play. Volleyball can be a dangerous sport." Fern nudged Jolene's arm, and Jolene turned to look at her. "Have you ever gotten hurt playing volleyball?"

"A few times. But I haven't played since I lost my hearing."

"There must be lots of things deaf people can't do," Eunice said.

Jolene pulled back like she'd been stung by a bee. "There are lots of things deaf people *can* do."

Eunice's face heated. "I didn't mean you couldn't play. I just meant. . ."

Jolene stood, smoothing the wrinkles in her dress. "I think I'll go see if there's any more hot apple cider." She hurried away.

So much for trying to befriend Andrew's sister. Eunice turned to Fern. "It was sure rude of Jolene to walk off like that. She didn't even let me finish my sentence."

"She probably couldn't see your lips and didn't realize you were speaking. Whenever you speak to Jolene, you need to look directly at her."

"I forgot."

"Maybe you should learn how to sign. Jolene's been giving lessons after school."

"I really don't have time for that right now. I've been busy hosting candle parties in the evenings and making soap deliveries during the day, and there's not much time for anything else." Eunice flicked a piece of lint from her dress. Truth was, signing seemed difficult to her. She'd never been good at learning new things and was afraid that she wouldn't be able to learn how to sign. If she messed up, she didn't want to embarrass herself in front of anyone.

"I know you're busy," Fern said, "but tell me who isn't busy these days?"

Eunice was relieved when Katie showed up and started a conversation with Fern. If Fern had kept pressuring her about learning to sign, she might have ended up telling her that she was afraid to try. It wasn't easy for Eunice to admit that she felt like a failure. With the exception of Fern, Eunice had never been able to keep a friend. She knew that because of her shiny blond hair and vivid blue eyes, some men thought she was pretty. Yet even though she'd had several boyfriends, she hadn't been able to keep one. Maybe she wasn't smart enough. Eunice had struggled with reading and math when she was in school, and she had no artistic skills whatsoever. About the only thing she had ever succeeded at was her new soap and candle business.

"Are you okay?"

Eunice jumped at the sound of a man's voice. She looked up and saw Andrew staring down at her, his dark eyes revealing the depth of his concern. "When I saw you fall, I was worried that you may have broken a bone or something."

Eunice smiled, despite the pain in her wrist. "I think I just sprained my wrist, so I'm not going to play ball anymore tonight."

"Are you sure? Maybe you should have it x-rayed."

"I'm fine, really. What I would like, though, is something to drink."

"I'll get you a glass of apple cider." Andrew started to walk away, but Eunice, feeling left out of the conversation between Fern and Katie, decided to join him. As they headed to the refreshment table, loud voices erupted from the players. The game had stopped. Jake and Ella were standing nose to nose.

∼⋇∼

"Would you please stay out of my way?"

Ella planted both hands on her hips and stared up at Jake, wishing she wasn't so short so she could look him directly in the eye. "I was not in your way; you were in my way!"

"No, I wasn't."

"Jah, you were. Seems like every time I reach for the ball you step in front of me."

"That's because you've been reaching into my playing space."

Ella gritted her teeth. It wasn't her choice to play on the same team with Jake, but they'd both been chosen to play on this side of the net, so she'd decided to make the best of it. She'd figured as long as he stayed out of her way, everything would be fine.

"Are we playing or what?" someone hollered.

Ella took her position as Jake picked up the ball and served it over the net. Things went okay until the ball came her way again. She leaped for it just as Jake rushed forward, ducking his head. *Smack!*—their foreheads collided with a sickening thud.

"You did that on purpose!" Ella winced and rubbed her forehead.

"Did not."

"Jah, you did!"

"No, I didn't, Ella." Although looking a bit perturbed as he rubbed his forehead, Jake kept his voice calm.

Ella's hand shook as she pointed at him. "You—you—oh, never mind!" She whirled around and marched off the court.

"Are you okay?" Jolene asked when Ella joined her at the refreshment table and quickly poured herself a glass of apple cider. "Looks like you've got a good-sized bump on your forehead."

Ella touched the bump and winced. "Jah, and it sure does hurt."

"Want me to get some ice for you?"

Before Ella could reply, Jake sauntered up. "You okay, Ella? Need me to get you some ice?"

"I'll live." Ella figured that, as much as her head hurt, Jake's must hurt, too, but she was so irritated with him that she didn't bother to ask.

"You sure?"

"Sure that I'll live or sure that I don't need any ice?"

Jake chuckled. "I was talking about the ice."

"I'm fine. If I need any ice, I'll get it."

"Suit yourself." Jake turned to Jolene, wearing that same goofy grin he'd had at the schoolhouse the other day. He said something, but his voice was so low, Ella couldn't make out what he'd said.

Ella edged a bit closer to Jolene, hoping she could pick up on their conversation. If Jake even suggested that he give Jolene a ride home tonight, she was prepared to intervene.

"I'm looking forward to next Monday night," Jake said to Jolene, his smile widening. "I think it'll be easier for me to learn signing with your family than it would if I came over to the schoolhouse."

Ella was glad to hear that Jake wouldn't be joining her and Lonnie at the schoolhouse, but she wished he wouldn't spend any time with Jolene. At least they wouldn't be alone.

Jake and Jolene continued to visit, and Ella continued to fume. Once, Jake glanced over at Ella with a strange expression, but then he looked quickly away. Was he deliberately trying to irritate her by talking to Jolene?

Ella was about to interrupt their conversation when someone called her name. She turned. Cara Cummings, one of her English neighbors, was racing across the room.

"Your dad collapsed in your living room, and your mom asked me to come get you right away!"

CHAPTER 20

"I hope whatever happened to my uncle Rueben isn't serious," Andrew said to Eunice as he watched Cara Cummings's car pull away. "Ella's neighbor sounded desperate to take her home, and from the look I saw on Ella's face, I think she feared the worst."

"Maybe it's nothing serious. Maybe Ella's neighbor is just overly alarmed. Some people get that way when someone passes out, you know." Eunice was trying to show Andrew that she was concerned, but he gave her a blank stare and shook his head.

"I don't think Cara was overly alarmed. She wouldn't have driven clear out here to get Ella if she didn't think the situation was serious." He glanced over to where Jolene sat with Katie and Fern. "I'm going to see if Jolene wants to go over to Ella's with me. If something terrible has happened to her daed, then she'll need our support." Before Eunice could respond, Andrew hurried away. She wished she could have visited with him longer but appreciated the fact that he was so concerned about his family. Andrew would probably make a good husband someday.

❧ ❧

"I'm glad you suggested that we go over to Ella's," Jolene said to Andrew as their horse and buggy left Topeka and headed down Highway 5. "When I saw Ella leave with Cara in such a hurry I was worried."

Andrew turned in his seat so he was facing her. "I have a hunch

Ella's going to need our support."

"Are you saying you think Uncle Rueben might die?"

"Let's just hope for the best." There were deep wrinkles etched in his forehead.

"Instead of hoping, I'd rather pray."

"Jah, we need to do that, too."

Jolene closed her eyes and prayed, *Heavenly Father, please be with Uncle Rueben and the rest of his family.*

~≪ ≫~

When Cara Cummings's car pulled into the yard, Ella's heart leaped into her throat. A beam of light from the ambulance parked near her house flashed crimson against the barn. Whatever had happened to Papa must be serious, or an ambulance wouldn't have been called.

Ella leaped from the car and raced to the house with her heart hammering so hard she could hear it echo in her head.

When she stepped into the living room, a scream tore from her throat. Papa lay on the floor, pale and unmoving. Two paramedics stood nearby, talking to Charlene, while Mama knelt beside Papa, sobbing as if her heart would break. Ella looked at Larry, who stood beside their younger sisters as though in a daze. "Wh–what happened?" she rasped.

"Papa came into the house after doin' some chores and said he felt kinda funny. Then all of a sudden he clutched at his chest and. . .and he fell on the floor." Larry motioned to the paramedics. "They think Papa had a heart attack." He swiped at the tears running down his flushed cheeks and sniffed. "They told Mama that Papa is dead."

Ella felt the blood drain from her face. She tried to speak but couldn't make her lips move. A jumble of thoughts tumbled around in her head like a windmill going at full speed. This couldn't be happening. Papa couldn't be dead. There must be some mistake!

CHAPTER 21

Despite Ella's resolve not to break down during Papa's graveside service, salty tears mixed with tepid raindrops and rolled down her cheeks. She sniffed deeply and glanced at Mama, who stood between her and Charlene. Poor Mama's body shook as she leaned on Ella and sobbed. Ella knew that when Papa died, a part of Mama had gone with him. They'd been together over twenty-five years. In all the years Ella had been alive, she'd never heard either of her parents say an unkind word about each other, and only a few times had she heard them disagree on anything.

Ella thought about how Lonnie's uncle, Bishop James Hershberger, and his wife, Sadie, had stopped by their house the other day to offer condolences. *"One generation comes, another passes away,"* the bishop had said. *"Many people miss out on great blessings because they don't understand why God allows certain things. They question Him rather than accepting His will."*

While Papa's casket was being lowered into the ground, Ella prayed. *Lord, I don't know why You took my daed, but please be with us in the days ahead, and help me to accept this as Your will.*

As the seriousness of the situation settled fully into Ella's mind, troubled thoughts tumbled around in her head. Larry wasn't old enough to take over Papa's business, and she didn't know anything about running it except how to do the books. She couldn't expect Charlene to take over everything Papa had done. Mama knew nothing about making wind chimes. Besides, it was

714

all she could do to keep up with household chores and care for the younger children. None of them could take over Papa's wind chime business, so how in the world were they going to support themselves?

Even though many folks from their community had rallied around these past few days, bringing in food and offering to do whatever was needed, it wouldn't be right to expect help from others indefinitely. Not when she was able-bodied and ought to take responsibility for her family's welfare. Charlene was old enough to work outside the home. Maybe if they both got jobs, they could earn enough money to take care of Mama and their siblings. Trouble was, someone really needed to be at home helping Mama and making sure she didn't overdo. Maybe it would be best if Charlene stayed home and Ella found a job.

Ella glanced over at Jolene and Andrew, who stood nearby with their family. She'd been ever so grateful when they'd shown up at her house the night Papa died. Mama had needed her support, and with Andrew and Jolene taking over the responsibility of the children, Ella had been able to concentrate on helping Mama make the necessary arrangements for Papa's body to be taken to the funeral home.

Ella blinked as the crowd of mourners moved away from the gravesite. She'd been so caught up in her thoughts that she hadn't even realized the service was over.

Mama's chin quivered and her eyes glistened with tears as she looked at Ella. "I. . .I know that death is a part of living, but it–it's such a terrible thing."

Ella squeezed Mama's hand. First Raymond had been taken from them, and now Papa. She wondered how much more her family could bear.

Bishop Hershberger, holding a large black umbrella, stepped up to them. *"Da Herr sei mit du."*

The bishop's wife, Sadie, nodded in agreement. "Jah, may the Lord be with you."

He's going to have to be, Ella thought as they moved away from the gravesite. *Because I sure can't take care of my family alone.*

As Ella and her family approached their buggy, she saw Jake, whose rig was parked nearby, glance her way. She wondered if his look of sympathy was genuine or the result of doing what he thought was expected of him.

Turning away, Ella grabbed the reins and backed up her horse. As she led the procession of black buggies toward their house, where the funeral dinner would be served, she made a decision. Tomorrow morning she would look for a job.

❧ ❧

Jake flicked the reins to get his horse and buggy moving and watched the Yoders' rig up ahead. His heart went out to Ella and her family. It couldn't be easy losing someone so close to you. Even with the disagreements that often took place between him and Dad, Jake couldn't imagine not having Dad around.

As he clucked to his horse to make him go faster, Jake made a decision. Even though he and Ella were not on the best of terms, he would find some way to help her family.

CHAPTER 22

The following night, Ella sat on the front porch steps, watching the stars come out. The rain had stopped several hours ago, and dusk had settled over the land like a soft pink blanket.

She drew in a deep breath and released it with a shuddering sigh. With Papa gone, nothing would ever be the same. It didn't look like they'd be able to support themselves. She'd spent most of the day going from store to store in Topeka, looking for a job. She'd been told by each of the store managers that there were no openings. Then she'd gone to Middlebury but found no work there, either. Should she put a notice in places like *The Budget* or *The Connection* and hope to sell off Papa's wind chime supplies? If she did, it could be awhile before she had any response. Since she'd had no luck finding a job in the places she'd been to today, tomorrow she would go to Shipshewana and try her luck there.

She swallowed hard as she stared up at the night sky. "What am I going to do, Lord? If I can't find a job, how am I going to take care of my family?"

She heard only the whistle of the wind under the eaves of the house and the singsong *ribbet, ribbet* of the frogs living near the pond out behind their place.

The screen door creaked, and when Ella glanced over her shoulder, she saw Charlene.

"What are you doing out here by yourself?" Charlene asked, taking a seat beside Ella on the step.

"Just sitting. . .thinking. . .trying to figure out some way to support this *familye*."

"God will take care of our family; you'll see."

Ella choked back a sob and reached up to touch her head covering. She was sure it was still held firmly in place and needed no adjusting, but it gave her something to do with her hands.

"It's okay to cry, you know. God gave us tear ducts for a reason."

Ella nodded. Her freckle-faced teenage sister with her big blue eyes and innocent smile suddenly seemed more mature than she was.

Ella's gaze went to Papa's shop at the end of the driveway. "It's hard to understand why God takes some and leaves others." She swallowed hard and drew in a shaky breath. "I mean, Papa always seemed so healthy. For some time now, Mama's been the sickly one. It makes no sense why God took Papa."

"Are you saying you think God should have taken Mama instead?"

"*Nee*, of course not! I just meant that it doesn't make sense the way Papa's heart gave out on him when he seemed so healthy."

"Guess only God knew Papa's heart was weak." Charlene touched Ella's arm. "Do you think Papa's in heaven with Jesus?"

"Jah, I do. Papa was a God-fearing man. He believed in Jesus and tried to live a good Christian life. I'm sure he's in heaven right now, walking the streets of gold and listening to the angels sing."

"I miss him so much. I know Mama does, too." Tears welled in Charlene's eyes, and she sniffed a couple of times. "What'll we do if we can't find jobs, Ella?"

"We'll find something. At least one of us needs to, and I think it ought to be me."

"How come?"

"Because I'm the oldest, and it's my job to take care of our family. Mama needs your help here, doing chores and taking care of the kinner."

Charlene stood, smoothing the wrinkles in her dress. "Can we talk about this later? Right now I think we should go inside and see if Mama needs us for anything."

"You go ahead," Ella said. "I'll be in shortly."

"Okay, but don't sit out here too long. It's getting colder by the minute."

"I'll be fine. Tell Mama I'll be in soon."

The door clicked shut behind Charlene, and Ella went back to brooding. She needed to trust God to take care of them, but she couldn't sit around idly and wait for an answer.

❧ ❧

Lonnie paced between his horse's stall and the wall behind him, where he and Pop had placed a stack of hay earlier in the week. It was hard to believe that Rueben Yoder was dead. Lonnie had just seen Rueben a few days ago, when he'd stopped by the hardware store in Shipshewana. Rueben had looked and acted just fine.

It must be hard for Ella and her family to have lost Rueben. He'd been a good man, kind and fair in his business dealings, and he'd never said a harsh word to Lonnie during the time he'd worked for him. *Not like Pop, who's always criticized me.* Lonnie grimaced. *Guess I shouldn't be thinking that way about my own daed. But for the grace of God, it could have been Pop who'd died of a heart attack. Besides, since my accident, Pop has been nicer to me. Maybe it's because he feels sorry for me because I'm deaf.*

Lonnie wondered why it often took a tragedy to make people show kindness and compassion to one another. *Doesn't the Bible teach in John 13 that we are to love one another as Christ loved us? Maybe I haven't been kind enough to Pop. Maybe I should force myself to take more interest in his smelly pigs.* He slowly shook his head. *That doesn't mean I want to help raise and butcher hogs for the rest of my life, though.*

I wish I could find some kind of work that I'd enjoy as much as I did making wind chimes. I wonder what will become of Rueben's business now that he's gone? Lonnie knew that Ella did the books and Charlene worked on assembling the wind chimes, but someone needed to run the operation and tune the chimes.

If I still had my hearing, I could help Ella run the business. Lonnie sank to a bale of hay and slumped against the wall, questioning God yet again as to why he'd lost his hearing.

Suddenly an idea popped into Lonnie's head. Was it a whisper from God or his own wishful thinking? *Maybe I could assemble the chimes, and then Charlene could learn how to tune and cut pieces of pipe. Ella could keep doing the books, and if she needed help ordering parts and supplies, I could help with that, too.*

Lonnie hoped Ella would be open to the idea. He knew how stubborn and independent she could be.

Think I'll stop by and see Ella tomorrow morning, he decided. *Hopefully she'll like my idea.*

CHAPTER 23

After a restless night, Ella decided that the first thing she needed to do after breakfast was to go over Papa's books to get an accurate estimate of where they were financially. Before Papa died, she'd kept the receipt book from their customers' orders up to date, as well as the lists of supplies they had in the shop and supplies they needed to order. Trouble was, only Papa had known exactly how much he actually made and how much was in the bank. Ella needed to be sure they had enough money to live on until she was able to find a job.

"I'll be out in Papa's shop if you need me for anything," Ella said to Charlene.

"Okay," Charlene called as she hurried down the hall, carrying a breakfast tray for Mama.

Ella glanced out the kitchen window. Seeing that it was still raining, she slipped into her jacket and grabbed an umbrella. As she opened the back door, a blast of cold wind hit her in the face. She shivered and decided against opening the umbrella, which would no doubt have turned inside out.

Pulling the collar of her jacket tightly around her neck, Ella dashed across the yard. She entered the shop and had just turned on the gas lights and propane stove, when a deep sense of loss flooded her soul. This was Papa's place. It didn't seem right that he wasn't here, sitting at his workbench with a smile on his face. He'd loved making wind chimes and had taken great care crafting each one.

Tears clouded Ella's vision, and she covered her mouth to stifle a sob. If she missed Papa this much, how must Mama feel?

"I need to get myself under control," she murmured. "It'll do no good to sit here feeling sorry for myself." Taking a seat at her desk, she opened the bottom drawer and retrieved the ledger, which she hadn't seen since the day before Papa died.

Ella's eyebrows furrowed as she scanned the places of business that carried their wind chimes. "Order Canceled" had been written next to half of the names.

Ella scratched her head. How could that be? She hadn't seen any cancellations when she'd last gotten the mail.

She squinted at the ledger and realized that "order canceled" had been written in Papa's handwriting. Sometime before Papa's death, maybe that same day, he'd picked up the mail and discovered the canceled orders.

Ella's gaze traveled around the room, and she spotted the wind chimes that had already been finished. Maybe it was a good thing some places had canceled their orders, because they didn't have nearly enough chimes to fill all the orders she'd thought they had.

She grimaced. It wouldn't matter if they had one hundred orders; they couldn't fill them—not just her and Charlene. Besides, even if Papa hadn't died, sooner or later he'd have probably lost his business. In these hard economic times it seemed that not so many people wanted wind chimes. Papa had mentioned that their business was slacking off, and he'd been concerned about having enough money to pay all his bills.

Ella let her head fall forward, resting it on the wooden desk. *Dear Lord, please show me what to do.* She stayed like that for several minutes, thinking, praying, and fighting back tears of frustration. She hated being in a situation that seemingly had no answers. She hated feeling so helpless.

Ding! Ding!

Ella jerked her head up and turned. Lonnie stood by the door.

"I hope you weren't busy," he said, speaking louder than usual, she assumed, because he couldn't hear his own voice.

He handed Ella the tablet he'd pulled from inside his jacket, and she quickly wrote him a note: *I came in here to go over the books.* She wished they knew how to sign well enough so that she wouldn't have to write everything down.

"I didn't get to talk to you much at the funeral the other day," Lonnie said. "You were busy with others, and I didn't want to intrude." He paused a few seconds. "With your daed gone, I know things will be difficult for you financially, and I have an idea I wanted to share with you."

Ella swallowed hard. Their financial situation was even worse than he could imagine. *What's your idea?* she wrote.

"I thought maybe I could take over Charlene's job and she could tune the chimes."

That's a nice thought, but it won't work.

"Is it because I can't hear? Because if that's the reason—"

She shook her head and scrawled another note. *Papa's business is in trouble. There are more bills than we have money for, and several places of business have canceled their orders. I'm afraid Papa's business will have to be sold.*

Lonnie's eyebrows drew together. "I'm sorry to hear that. Aren't there some other places you could contact about selling your daed's chimes?"

I don't know of any others, Ella wrote. *Even if there were any who'd be willing to place an order, the three of us could never keep the business going.*

"How can you be sure?"

For one thing, Charlene's tone deaf. She can't even carry a tune when she sings, so she'd never be able to tune the chimes.

"Maybe she could do the books and you could tune the chimes."

That wouldn't work, either. Charlene's not good at math. She'd mess up the books for sure.

He scratched his head. "There has to be someone you could hire who has a good ear for tuning chimes."

We don't have enough money to pay anyone. We've been struggling financially for some time, and now that we've lost several orders, we're in worse shape than ever. Ella stopped writing and squeezed her eyes shut, hoping the action would keep her persistent tears at bay. When she opened them again, Lonnie was staring at her in a curious way. Was it compassion she saw on his face, or something else?

I appreciate your offer, she wrote, *but there's only one thing for me to do.*

"What's that?"

I'm going to send out the wind chimes to the people who have already placed orders, and then I'll have to close the shop and sell everything.

"Then what'll you do? How will your family survive?"

I'll be heading into Shipshe as soon as I'm done here to look for a job.

"Jobs are hard to come by these days."

Ella grimaced. She didn't need that reminder. *I'll find something. I have to.*

❦

"Where are you off to in this nasty weather?" Jake's mother asked when he slipped into his jacket and started for the back door.

"I've got a horse to shoe over at Crist Lambright's. Then I'm planning to stop by and see Ella on my way home."

Mom's eyebrows furrowed. "Why would you need to see her?"

"I didn't get to speak with her at the funeral the other day, and I want to offer my condolences." Jake pulled his stocking cap on his head. "Thought I'd ask if they have any chores that need to be done while I'm there."

"I'm sure Ella's family is taking care of their chores. She does have several siblings, you know."

Jake couldn't believe his mother's clipped tone. "Ella only has five siblings who are living, and they're all younger than her. The little ones can't do heavy chores. Besides, with the exception of Charlene, the kinner will be in school all day."

"I realize that," Mom said with a huff, "but there are others in the community who will help out. With your daed laid up, you've got enough to do right here."

Jake stared hard at his mother. "What's wrong, Mom? You act as though you don't want me to help Ella's family. Doesn't the *Biwel* teach that we're to help our neighbors?"

Mom pursed her lips. "Don't quote scriptures to me, young man. If you had any interest in what the Bible says, you would have joined the church by now!"

Jake jerked his head, feeling as though he'd been slapped. "Now you're talking like Dad. I thought you understood why I haven't made up my mind about becoming Amish yet."

She shook her head. "I've never said I understood it. I've just chosen not to say too much, hoping that if I didn't push you too hard you'd make the right decision."

"The right decision being that I join the church, you mean?"

She shrugged.

"At one time I thought moving home and joining the church was what I wanted, but when Loraine married Wayne—"

"We've been over this before. You can't base your decisions about getting baptized and joining the church on whether someone agrees to marry you." Mom's voice raised a notch, and her cheeks colored to a deep crimson. "It's a commitment to God and to the ways of the church you've grown up in—the church our ancestors of old gave their lives for in martyrdom."

"I know all that, and someday, when I feel the time's right, I'll make my decision about whether to join the church or not." Jake put his hand on the doorknob. "In the meantime, I'm going over to shoe Crist's horse. After that, I'll be heading to the Yoders', and if they need any chores done, I'll do 'em."

"What if Ella won't let you?"

Jake turned to face his mother. "Why wouldn't she let me?"

"Do I need to remind you that every time you and Ella are anywhere near each other, you end up in an argument?" She took a step toward Jake. "Think about it, son. Ella doesn't like you, and I don't think it's a good idea for you to put yourself in a position that could lead to another argument with her—especially when she and her family are grieving for Rueben."

"I won't say anything to upset Ella or anyone else in her family. I just want to let them know that I'm available to help out."

Mom turned her hands palm up, clinging to a dishcloth. "Do as you like, but don't be surprised if Ella says no."

CHAPTER 24

W hen Ella entered the hardware store in Shipshewana, she spotted her friend Esther behind the counter. Forcing a smile, she stepped up to Esther and said, "I need a job. Is there anything available here right now?"

"I'm afraid not," Esther said with a shake of her head. "I doubt we'll be hiring until spring, and that's only if the economic situation takes a turn for the better."

"Oh, I see." Ella swallowed around the lump in her throat. She was beginning to think she'd never find a job.

"Have you checked at any of the restaurants in town to see about working in the kitchen or waiting tables?" Esther asked.

"I've checked just about everywhere, for every kind of job." Ella turned away from the counter. "I'd better go." She hurried off before Esther could respond.

She'd just entered the corridor between the hardware store and the fabric store, when she saw Katie heading her way.

"I'm surprised to see you out shopping today," Katie said. "I know your mamm took your daed's death pretty hard, and I figured you'd be home with her."

"Charlene's staying with Mama so I can look for a job."

"But you have a job selling wind chimes."

Ella shook her head. "Even if Papa were still here, we'd soon have to close the shop."

"How come?"

727

Ella explained about the canceled orders and Lonnie's offer to trade jobs with Charlene. "But you see," she said, "even if Charlene could tune the chimes, we can't continue to operate if we can't find places to buy and sell our chimes." She rubbed the bridge of her nose and blinked. She would not give in to her tears.

Katie slipped her arm around Ella's waist. "Are you okay?"

"I'm afraid I won't be able to find work and that I'll let my family down."

"Whenever I get frightened and think I might have another panic attack, I remind myself that these are just feelings and that they'll soon pass. I know that the sooner I focus on God and His power, the faster I'll see relief from my fears." Katie gently patted Ella's back. "God will give you the strength for each new day. Remember, you don't have to bear your burdens alone. Your family and friends are here to help in any way we can. One of the reasons we Amish survive is because we rely on God and one another."

Ella sniffed and dabbed at her eyes. "I appreciate that reminder."

"I thought I'd go to the Blue Gate for lunch today. Would you like to join me?" Katie asked. "It might lift your spirits a little."

"Danki for the offer, but I've been gone quite awhile and need to get home and check on Mama. When I left home this morning, she was still in bed and hadn't eaten any breakfast."

"I'm sure it'll take some time for her to come to grips with your daed's death." A look of sadness passed over Katie's face, but it was quickly replaced with a smile. "When Timothy died, I thought my life was over, but now I have Freeman, and we're very happy."

"Are you suggesting that my mamm will fall in love and get married again?" Just the thought of Mama being with some other man made Ella's skin prickle.

Katie shook her head. "I'm not saying that at all. I just meant that in time the pain won't be so intense and your mamm will be able to laugh again."

Ella sighed. "It's not just Mama grieving over Papa that worries me. She's struggled with health issues ever since Raymond died, and stress seems to make it worse."

"I know what you mean about that. One thing you need to remember is that God doesn't want you to worry. He wants you to trust Him in all things."

"Sometimes that's easier said than done."

"One of the scriptures that helped me the most when I was having panic attacks is Isaiah 41:10: 'Fear thou not; for I am with thee: be not dismayed; for I am thy God: I will strengthen thee; yea, I will help thee; yea, I will uphold thee with the right hand of my righteousness.'"

Tears sprang to Ella's eyes despite her resolve to remain in control. "Danki for those words. I'll try to remember."

❧ ❧

As Jake neared the Yoders' place, he rehearsed what he was going to say to Ella. He hoped she'd be cordial when he offered his help. After their encounter during the volleyball game, he wasn't sure what to expect.

Maybe I won't have to talk to Ella, Jake thought. *Maybe she'll be busy with something and her mamm will answer the door.*

As Jake turned his horse and buggy up the Yoders' driveway, a giant puddle came into view. When the water splashed up, his horse whinnied and tossed its head.

"Aw, quit acting like a boppli," Jake hollered. "You've been through plenty of mud puddles before."

The horse whinnied again and plodded up the driveway as if he was in no hurry to get where they were going.

"I'd have been better off if I'd left you at home and driven my truck today," Jake mumbled. To keep the peace at home he'd parked his truck behind the barn and had been driving the horse and buggy most places. If he had to travel any farther than fifteen miles, he used the truck, regardless of how Dad felt about the vehicle. He also used it whenever he had to go anywhere to shoe a horse. It was easier and cheaper than hiring a driver to haul him and his shoeing tools around.

Jake didn't understand the way Dad carried on over him owning a truck. Many young people in their community who hadn't joined the church owned cars and trucks. Jake figured Dad's irritation had more to do with his having moved to Montana than it did with him driving a motorized vehicle.

When Jake entered the Yoders' yard, he spotted Charlene hanging clothes on the line. He stopped the horse, tied it to the hitching rail, and sprinted across the yard to join her. "Is your mamm at home?" he asked.

Charlene nodded and motioned to the house. "She's in bed, though, and I don't want to disturb her."

Jake figured after the ordeal Verna and her family had just been through she was probably exhausted, but it did surprise him to hear that she was still in bed this late in the day. "Is Ella here?" he asked.

"Huh-uh. She went to Shipshe to look for a job."

"Won't she continue to work in the wind chime shop?"

Charlene shook her head. "Not with Papa gone. We could never keep the place going on our own. Is there something I can help you with?"

"Actually, I'm here to help you." Jake cleared his throat a couple of times. "I mean, I was wondering if you need my help with anything."

Charlene gave a slow nod and pointed to the barn. "The horses have been fed already, but their stalls need to be mucked out."

"No problem. I'll take care of that right now. When I'm done, if there's anything else you need me to do, just say the word."

"That's so nice of you, Jake. There's a lot we could use help with around here." Charlene smiled sweetly. "I think my sister's wrong about you."

Jake was on the verge of asking Charlene to be specific about what she'd meant but changed his mind. He already knew what Ella thought of him, so he didn't need to hear whatever Charlene might say that would confirm the fact. Instead of asking any questions about Ella, Jake headed determinedly for the barn.

As soon as Ella pulled into her yard, she spotted a horse tied to their hitching rail with an open buggy parked nearby. *Who'd be using an open buggy in this chilly weather?* she wondered.

She glanced around the yard but saw no sign of anyone. A line full of clothes flapped in the breeze, so Charlene had done what she'd been asked and gotten the laundry done. She must be inside, visiting with whoever had come to pay them a call.

Ella unhitched her horse, Pet, from the buggy and led her to the barn. When she drew near the horse's stall, she halted. Jake was inside, spreading fresh straw on the floor.

"What are you doing here?" Ella's voice came out in a squeak.

"Came to help out." Jake reached for Pet's bridle and led her into the stall before Ella could respond.

She flopped onto a bale of hay inside the stall and stared at the floor. "Who said we needed your help with anything?"

"Charlene did. When I told her I came to help, she said the stalls needed to be mucked out."

"We can manage the chores on our own, Jake."

His boots stopped in front of her, and she was forced to look up. "Not to worry; I'll help whether you want me to or not because I know things have to be really hard for you right now." He stepped forward as if to comfort her, but she leaned away.

Jake grunted and took a step back. "What's your problem, Ella?"

She lifted her hand in exasperation. "Don't you understand? We don't need your help!"

"Sure you do." He moved close to the stall door and made a sweeping gesture of the barn. "Lots of chores need be done here, not to mention other areas around your place."

"We'll get them done without your help." Ella's cheeks burned like fire. No one had ever been able to get under her skin the way Jake did.

"Look, Ella, I just want to be your friend."

"Jah, right. False friends are like dandelions—they're found everywhere."

Jake held his palms down, as if trying to calm a nervous horse. "I'm not a false friend."

Ella tapped her foot as her impatience mounted. "Just leave, Jake. I'm getting tired of saying this. We don't need your help! We can manage on our own!"

Jake didn't budge. As he stared at her, the silence between them grew thick like a heavy blanket of fog.

After several moments of deafening quiet, Ella spoke again. "If you won't leave, then I will." She stood up so quickly that she lost her balance. *Thunk*—she bumped her head on Jake's chin.

"Yeow!" they both hollered.

Ella grimaced and rubbed the top of her head. "The last bump you gave me is barely healed, and now I've got another one!"

Jake stuck out his tongue and swished it from side to side. "Why don't you watch what you're doin', Ella? You made me bite my tongue!"

"Sorry," they said in unison.

Jake reached out as if he might touch her, but then he quickly jumped back. "Are—are you okay?"

"I'm fine. You'd better go now, before any more damage is done."

He shook his head and folded his arms. "I'm not leaving. I started a job, and I aim to finish it."

Ella exhaled a puff of frustration. "Fine then, do whatever you like!" With her back straight and her head held high, she left the stall and walked out of the barn.

❦

Jolene glanced at the clock on her classroom wall. The school day would be over soon, and she felt frustrated because there was so much more she wished to teach. Both Sylvia and Irvin had been quite attentive today. She was pleased at how well they were learning to read lips. As she'd prepared her lesson for the children, she remembered what her aunt had taught her about a deaf person being very alert to the expression of people. Jolene knew she'd have to remember to make her facial expressions be one of the ways she communicated with the children. When she said, "Sit down" or "Pay attention," it had to show on her face.

Today she had worked on voiceless consonants: *h*; *wh*; *p*; *t*; *k*; *ca*; *co*; *cu*; *ck*, which to her surprise, the children had seemed to understand quite well. A few minutes ago, she'd given them each an easy-reading fiction book. They seemed quite content, and Sylvia even giggled when she read something humorous.

When Jolene saw Irvin chuckle, she was even more surprised. She left her desk and went to see what he thought was so funny.

Wearing a big grin, Irvin looked up at her then pointed to a page in his book and said, "There are many black cows, but they all give white milk."

"Good job, Irvin." Jolene signed as she spoke. She smiled and patted the top of his head. It was so good to see that he was not only learning, but actually seemed to enjoy being in school. Now if she could just get through to Jake's brother Kyle. When she'd given Fern's class another lesson on signing this morning, Kyle still hadn't participated. But at least he hadn't made any trouble. She guessed that was something to be grateful for.

When Jolene dismissed Irvin and Sylvia to go home a short time later, she reached into her desk and pulled out a hand mirror. Lonnie would be coming by for another lesson today, and since she was sure Ella wouldn't be here, she decided to work with Lonnie on lip reading.

Jolene had just placed the mirror on her desk when Eunice entered the room.

"Hello, Jolene. I was wondering if you could do something for me."

"What's that?"

Eunice's cheeks colored. She leaned on Jolene's desk, as if needing it for support. "Well, you see..." She paused and moistened her lips with the tip of her tongue. "I'd like to learn how to sign, but I don't want anyone to know about it—especially Andrew."

"How come?"

The crimson color that had splashed over Eunice's cheeks deepened. "I...uh...want it to be a surprise. Would you be willing to teach me to sign and not tell anyone?"

Jolene didn't understand Eunice's reason for wanting to keep it a secret, but she nodded and said, "If you'd like to come by here on Friday afternoon, we can begin then."

"And you won't tell anyone?"

"It'll be our little secret."

A look of relief flooded Eunice's face. "Danki, Jolene."

Eunice turned and was almost to the door when Lonnie stepped in. Jolene didn't know whether Eunice had said anything to him or not, because Eunice's back was to her now.

When Eunice left the room, Jolene moved aside so Lonnie could sit at her desk. Then she smiled and pointed to the blackboard, where she'd written him a message: *Today, we're going to begin learning how to read lips, since you'll need that in order to communicate with others who can hear.*

Apprehension flickered in Lonnie's eyes. "Not sure I'm ready for that."

Yes, you are, she wrote. *If you're going to communicate with hearing people, then you need to be able to read lips.* How many times had she told him this already? Was he just being stubborn, or didn't he get it?

"I stopped by to see Ella today and suggested that I do Charlene's job of putting the wind chimes together so Charlene could tune and cut the pipe," Lonnie said, suddenly changing the subject. "Ella said that won't work because Charlene's tone deaf and can't tune chimes. She also said her daed's business is in trouble and will have to close, so she's going out to look for a job today."

Jolene grimaced. In these hard times, things were bad enough, but now with Uncle Rueben gone, Ella had a lot of responsibility on her shoulders. What she really needed was a job that would keep her at home where she could look out for her mother. But what kind of a job could it be?

CHAPTER 25

When Lonnie entered Freeman's bike shop to see about getting a new tube for the flat tire on his bike, Jake was talking to Freeman. Not wishing to interrupt, Lonnie dropped to his knees and began to pet Freeman's dog, Penny. Every time Lonnie visited the bike shop, the cocker spaniel was either sleeping on the braided rug near the door or making a pest of herself with the ball she kept dropping at the customers' feet.

Lonnie glanced over at Freeman and Jake and wondered what they were saying. Since Jake was turned toward him, he tried to read his lips. It was good practice to do so. Jolene had told him that during one of their lessons. Lonnie was no expert on lip reading yet, but he was pretty sure Jake had said something about Jolene. He kept watching Jake's lips. Had he said something about asking Jolene out?

Lonnie wondered if he should try to discourage Jolene from seeing Jake. While Jake seemed like a nice enough fellow, Lonnie had heard that Jake had trouble staying in one place. Lonnie was just beginning to get to know Jolene, and she seemed like a nice young woman. If she was interested in Jake, then she'd be hurt if he left Indiana.

A few more customers entered the shop, and Lonnie began to feel uncomfortable about watching Jake's lips. *Guess it's really none of my business what Jake says or does,* he decided. *I have enough of my own problems to deal with.*

735

Penny's tail swished against Lonnie's arm, so he turned his attention to her again. The dog's mouth opened, and as she pressed her body against him, Lonnie actually felt the vibration of her bark. This surprised him, because until he'd lost his hearing, he'd taken for granted the things he could feel, taste, smell, and see. When he'd first found out he was deaf, one of his nurses had told him that his other senses would become stronger. He guessed she'd been right.

The dog swished her tail again, snatched Lonnie's stocking cap, and tore across the room. Lonnie couldn't let the mutt have his hat; it had been a Christmas gift from Mom. He took off after the dog, waving his hands. "Give me back my cap!"

Penny zipped to the left, and then to the right, with Lonnie right on her heels. Freeman stopped talking to Jake and got in on the chase. Round and round the room they went, until the dog darted in between a row of bikes. Lonnie made a lunge for his cap, which was still hanging from the dog's mouth. He missed, and the bikes toppled over, landing on the floor.

Lonnie's face heated. "I'm so sorry, Freeman. I hope nothing broke."

Freeman said something, but Lonnie couldn't tell what. All eyes seemed to be on him, which made him feel even more embarrassed than he already was. He leaned in between the bikes, grabbed his cap, and raced out the door.

~ ❧ ~

For the last several days Ella had kept so busy doing chores and trying to help Mama cope that she hadn't had time to continue looking for a job. She'd gone to the bank the other day and now knew that it wouldn't be long until they were out of money. They might have to start selling off things like she'd seen some other people do because of a job loss.

Ella removed the tea kettle from the stove and took a seat between Mama and Charlene at the table. As much as she dreaded it, they needed to discuss a few things.

"I need to tell you something, Mama," Ella said as she handed her mother a cup of tea.

Mama looked at Ella with a pained expression. "Not more bad news, I hope."

Ella swallowed around the lump in her throat. She wished she didn't have to tell Mama the truth about their financial situation. "I'm afraid it is bad news. After looking through Papa's books the other day, I discovered that several wind chime orders had been canceled. Since then, I've been to the bank and discovered that we have very little money left in our account." Ella blinked hard to keep her tears from flowing. "Between that and the fact that Charlene and I can't run the shop by ourselves, I've come to the conclusion that after we send out the few orders we have, we'll need to close the shop."

Mama sat staring at her cup. Ella wondered if she'd even heard.

Charlene's face turned crimson, and she slammed her hand on the table so hard that it jiggled their cups. "It's not fair that we lost Papa so unexpectedly! Do we have to lose his business, too?"

"Lots of things in life aren't fair, but. . ." Mama paused and blew her nose on her napkin. *"Mer muss ausbeharre bis ans end."*

"Why must we bear it until the end, Mama?" Charlene's eyes flashed angrily, no longer the calm young woman she'd been the other evening. "Why doesn't God bring only good things to the people who follow Him?"

Lines of strain etched Mama's face as she reached over and touched Charlene's arm. "God didn't promise that His people would never suffer. Tribulations are part of living in this sinful world."

Ella marveled at her mother's wise remark. Despite the grief Mama had been dealing with, she was ministering to her hurting daughter. Mama truly was a remarkable woman, and that made Ella even more determined to take care of her and the rest of the family. Until she found a job, Ella would find it difficult to be hopeful, but she knew for her family's sake that she must remain positive.

She pushed away from the table. "I think I ought to get the dishes done. We can talk about our financial situation some other time."

"I believe you're right. If we all think about this for a while, maybe one of us will come up with a plan." Mama stood. "It's a chilly evening. I think I'll take my tea and go to the living room so I can sit by the fire." She walked out, leaving Ella and Charlene alone.

Ella moved over to the sink and pulled a dirty kettle into the water where she'd placed some other dishes to soak. As she scrubbed the pot vigorously, soapy water cascaded over her hands and dripped back into the sink. It felt good to keep busy. It was the only thing that kept her from breaking down in a puddle of tears.

"You want me to dry, or are you gonna let the dishes drain?" Charlene asked.

Ella shrugged. "It doesn't really matter. If you'd like to join Mama in the living room, that's fine with me. Just be sure you don't say anything that might upset her."

Charlene thrust out her lower lip as she frowned. "I'm not gonna do or say anything to upset Mama, and you need to quit bein' so bossy."

"Someone has to be in charge now that Papa's gone. As the oldest, it's my job to look out for Mama and see that our family is taken care of."

Charlene opened her mouth like she might say more, but then she closed it and left the room.

Ella grabbed another kettle and sloshed the sponge around as she blinked back tears of anger and frustration. *Oh, Papa,* she silently cried. *I miss you so much.*

The back door banged, causing Ella to jump. Either Charlene had gone outside, or someone had come into the house.

~≈ ≈~

When Jolene entered her aunt's kitchen with Loraine and Katie, she wasn't surprised to find Ella in front of the sink with a sponge in her hand. Ever since Jolene could remember, Ella had always kept busy. Even when they were young girls, Ella thought she needed to be working when she should have been playing. She was the kind of person who always seemed to put other people's needs ahead of her own.

"We came to see how you're doing," Jolene said, stepping up to Ella so she could see her face. Loraine and Katie moved close to the sink, too.

"I'm doing as well as can be expected." Ella's smile appeared to be forced; there was no laughter behind her eyes. "If you'd like to have a seat at the table, I'll pour us some tea."

Everyone took seats, and Ella served the tea, along with a loaf of freshly baked friendship bread.

Jolene's fingers curled around the handle of the warm cup. It felt like old times, the four cousins sitting together. Only they weren't innocent young girls anymore. One of them was married and expecting a baby; one was on the brink of marriage; and the other two had a lot of responsibility on their shoulders.

Loraine transferred her cup from one hand to the other, while Katie blotted her lips with a napkin. "This bread is really good, Ella. You're better at baking than anyone I know."

"Danki." Ella smiled, although again, it appeared to be forced. She was obviously putting up a brave front, but Jolene knew her cousin was hurting.

"Is there anything we can do to help you?" Loraine asked. Jolene was glad everyone faced her, even when they spoke to Ella.

Ella's eyes filled with tears. She blinked rapidly, as though trying to keep herself from crying. "Guess the thing we need most is a lot of prayer, because short of a miracle, we'll soon be out of money."

"What do you mean?" Katie asked.

Ella told them about her dad's business and how there was no way she and Charlene could keep it going. "So I need to find a job," she said. "Unfortunately, none of the places I've been to so far are hiring right now."

Everyone agreed that they would pray for Ella's family, and then they sat quietly together, drinking their tea and eating the friendship bread.

Soon after Jolene had taken a second piece of bread and

covered it with butter, an idea popped into her head. "I think I know a way you can make some money," she said, smiling at Ella.

"What's that?" Ella asked, slouching in her chair.

"Why don't open a home-based bakery? You could sell fresh baked goods to others in our community and to the tourists."

Ella blinked a couple of times and sat up straight. "You really think I could do that?"

"I don't see why not."

"I agree with Jolene," Loraine said. "With your baking skills, I'll bet in no time you'd have all kinds of business."

"Oh, I don't know. There are so many things I'd have to do first, and there's really no place for a bakeshop in the house."

"Maybe you could use your daed's shop," Katie suggested. "It'll be empty after you sell off your daed's things."

Ella tapped her fingers along the edge of the table. "The building would need a lot of work to turn it into a bakeshop. We'd have to buy an oven, a refrigerator, a bakery cabinet, and so many other things."

"You'd also need to have the place inspected by the health department and get the proper license," Loraine put in. "It would take some doing, but if it's God will, then I'm sure it'll all work out."

Ella tugged her earlobe. "I'm not sure it would work, but I'll give it some thought."

"And don't forget to pray," Jolene said with a smile. "Remember now, we'll all be praying with you."

CHAPTER 26

Ella filled the sink with hot water and added some detergent. A glint of light shone through the kitchen window from the full moon outside. She was relieved that the day was almost over. She was eager to get the dishes done and head upstairs to her room. She would need to rise with the call of the rooster tomorrow morning, for there'd be plenty of chores waiting for her to do before breakfast. She and Charlene would keep busy the rest of the day, painting the barn.

"I don't know about you, but I'm all done in," Charlene said as she pulled a clean dish towel from the drawer.

Ella nodded. "I've always enjoyed baking before, but since I opened the bakeshop two weeks ago, it seems like all I do is bake and wait on customers."

"But your business is doing well, and it's already making us some money. Isn't that so?"

"Jah, and I'm grateful for the money that some in our community donated so I could buy everything I needed to get the business going. The only problem is, I'm kept so busy with the bakeshop that I can't keep up with all the chores that need to be done around here, which is why I'll be closing the shop tomorrow in order to paint the barn." Ella smiled at Charlene. "I appreciate the way you've taken over so many of the household chores, waited on customers, and have even helped with some of the baking. If Mama felt better, I'm sure she'd do more, too."

Charlene's nose crinkled. "Do you think there's something seriously wrong with Mama? Should we insist that she see the doctor?"

Ella dipped her hands into the soapy water and picked up another dish. "I don't think we can insist that Mama do anything. But we do need to keep praying about the matter, and I may ask Aunt Priscilla to speak with Mama again, too."

"Good idea. Let's hope she'll listen this time."

❦ ❧

Several buckets of white paint sat in the driveway along with a bucket of water for cleaning brushes and rollers. Ella had put Larry and Amelia in charge of the younger siblings so Mama could rest. Charlene would paint the lower half of the barn, while Ella climbed the ladder and did the upper half, since Charlene was afraid of heights.

"It's too cold to be doing this," Charlene complained. "I'd rather be inside where it's warm and toasty."

"You'll warm up once you start working." Ella motioned to the bucket of paint near Charlene. "Now get busy and stop complaining."

Charlene frowned. "You're bossing me around again, and I don't like it!"

"I wouldn't boss you at all if you did what you're supposed to do." Ella grabbed her paint bucket and a brush and then scurried up the ladder. Truthfully, she didn't like the idea of painting the barn any more than Charlene, but it needed to be done. Complaining wouldn't help. If Papa hadn't died, he'd have had the barn painted already. Just a few days before his death, he'd told Ella that he wanted to get the painting done before winter set in.

Ella swallowed around the lump that seemed to be clogging her throat a good deal of the time these days and forced herself to concentrate on what she was doing. With each stroke of the brush, she reminded herself that she was doing this for Papa.

Ella had just started painting around the opening of the loft when she heard the familiar rumble of buggy wheels. She looked down and saw Jake climb out of his buggy. He tied his horse to the hitching rail, walked toward the barn, and looked up at her. "What are you doing up there?" he hollered.

"What's it look like?" she called in return.

"Looks like you're tryin' to paint the barn."

"I'm not trying; I *am* painting the barn."

"You should have asked for help."

"Charlene's helping me."

Jake looked around. "She's not here now."

"She probably went to the house for a few minutes."

"If you'll come down off that ladder, I'll take your place."

Ella stiffened. Jake had no right to tell her what to do. She clamped her teeth tightly together and kept painting.

"If you won't come down, then I guess I'll do some painting down here, 'cause it looks to me like Charlene didn't finish what she started."

Ella clenched the paintbrush so tightly that her fingers turned numb. Did Jake really want to help, or was he just trying to irritate her? She slapped another blob of paint on the barn and didn't look down.

"You've got a lot on your shoulders these days," Jake called. "I know it can't be easy, and you shouldn't be expected to do everything alone."

Ella ignored him and kept painting until Charlene showed up and hollered, "Mama's up from her nap, and she set some doughnuts and hot coffee on the table. Why don't you take a break and come inside for a while?"

"In a minute. I want to finish what I started up here before I take a break."

"Does that invitation for doughnuts and coffee include me?" Jake asked.

"Jah, sure," Charlene said sweetly. "You're more than welcome to join us, and I appreciate you taking over my job of painting."

Ella almost gagged. Why was Charlene being so nice to Jake? Didn't she realize he couldn't be trusted? More than likely, he'd come over here to make himself look good in his folks' eyes. He probably thought his dad would be nicer to him if he knew Jake had come here to help. Well, if Jake was going in the house, then Ella was going there, too. She couldn't take the chance that he'd say or do something to upset Mama—or that he'd flirt with Charlene. It seemed as if Jake liked to flirt with every young woman he knew—everyone but Ella. Well, that was fine with her! If Jake ever tried to flirt with her, she'd be quick to put him in his place.

When Ella finished painting around the opening of the loft, she shifted her paintbrush to the other hand and slowly descended the ladder. She'd only gone down a few rungs when her foot slipped. She lost her grip on the bucket, and it fell. When she tried to catch hold of it, the ladder wobbled. Ella shouted for Charlene to hold it steady, but it was too late—Ella and the ladder tumbled to the ground.

CHAPTER 27

Sprawled on the ground, with one foot wedged against the ladder and wet paint running down one arm, Ella stared up at Jake with a bewildered expression. "Wh–what happened?"

"The ladder toppled, and you fell. I tried to catch you, but your foot hit me in the head, and I lost my balance." Jake dropped to his knees beside her. "Are you hurt? Do you think anything's broken?"

She gave a noncommittal grunt and winced as she tried to sit up. "My. . .my head's throbbing, and so's my arm."

Jake held his hand gently against her shoulder. "Don't move. You might have a broken bone."

"Jake's right; your arm—especially your wrist—is beginning to swell, and I'll bet it's broken." Charlene bent close to Ella, her eyes huge.

"It can't be broken." Tears glistened in Ella's eyes. "How am I supposed to bake if my arm is broken?"

"Let's not put the buggy before the horse," Jake said. "We need to get you to the doctor so we know if it's broken. Then you can worry about how you're going to do any baking." He reached up to rub his forehead.

"Are you okay?" Charlene asked, bending close to Jake.

"It's nothing; just a little bump is all." He looked at Ella and said, "I'm starting to get used to bumps on the head."

Just then, Verna, Ella's mother, came running out of the house.

"Ach! What happened to you, Ella? I looked out the kitchen window and saw you lying on the ground."

"She fell off the ladder," Jake explained. "Her wrist is really swollen, and I think her arm might be broken."

The look Ella shot Jake was as chilling as the crisp fall air. "I can speak for myself, Jake Beechy."

Verna looked up at the barn then back at Ella. "I knew this painting job was too much for my girls. I should have insisted that we ask some of the men we know to paint the barn for us."

"I'll take Ella into the house, and we'll get some ice to put on her arm," Jake said, looking at Verna. "If you or Charlene will go out to your phone shed and call one of your drivers to take us to the hospital, Ella can have her arm looked at."

Verna bobbed her head. "That's a good idea. I'm glad you're here, Jake. You're thinking more clearly than the rest of us right now." She patted Ella's shoulder. "I'll call Marge Nelson and see if she's free to take us to the hospital."

Without hesitation, Jake bent down, scooped Ella into his arms, and started across the yard.

"What do you think you're doing?" she screeched.

"I'm taking you to the house."

"Put me down! It's not my leg that's broken. I'm perfectly capable of walking to the house by myself."

"You're full of *hochmut*, you know that?"

"I am not full of pride. Now put me down!"

"No, I'm going to carry you."

"No, you're not!"

Ella's lips may have told Jake no, but he could tell she was in no shape to walk on her own, so he kept hold of her as he continued walking toward the house.

"Did you hear what I said?"

"I heard you, but I'm not putting you down." Jake quickened his steps. "You had a nasty bump on the head, and you might get dizzy and pass out if you try to walk."

"Jake's right," Charlene agreed as she hurried along beside them. "You hit your head pretty hard, and you could have a concussion like the one you had when you were in that horrible van accident."

Ella opened her mouth like she might say something more, but then she quickly clamped it shut. When Jake felt her body begin to relax, he smiled and stepped onto the porch.

❦ ❧

Jolene hauled several braided throw rugs out to the porch and draped them over the railing. She'd just picked up the broom to beat the dust from the rugs when a pickup truck barreled up the driveway. It stopped near the house, and Jake got out. Why was he driving his truck instead of his horse and buggy?

"Hello, Jake," Jolene said when he stepped onto the porch. "I'm surprised to see you this afternoon."

"I came by to tell you about Ella."

"What about her?"

He leaned against the porch railing, but when his hip touched one of the rugs, he pulled quickly away. "Ella fell off the ladder when she was trying to paint her daed's barn."

Jolene gasped. "That's baremlich! Is she hurt badly?"

"Not as bad as she could have been, but the terrible thing is she did break her arm." Jake's eyebrows pulled together. "When Verna couldn't get ahold of their driver, I went home and got my truck so I could drive Ella to the hospital. Then I waited there with Verna until Ella had her arm set in a cast." He thumped his chin a couple of times. "Ella's really worried about how she'll keep up with that bakeshop of hers now that she only has the use of one hand."

"Maybe I can help out after I'm done teaching in the afternoons," Jolene said.

Jolene's mother came out the door just then and stepped up to Jolene. "I heard what you said, and I think helping Ella would be too much for you."

"How come?"

"Because you're already overextending yourself with the signing lessons you're teaching after school." Mom touched Jolene's arm. "I've got more time on my hands than you do, so I'll go over to

Ella's and help out with the baking a few times a week. I'm sure that once the word gets out, others will help, too."

"I hope Ella's more receptive to their help than she was with mine today. If she'd gotten off that ladder when I asked her to and let me paint the upper part of the barn, she wouldn't have fallen." Jake grimaced. "She's the most stubborn, determined woman I know." He motioned to Jolene. "Nothing at all like you."

"I don't know about that," Jolene replied. "I can be pretty determined and stubborn, too—just in a different way than my cousin."

≈⁂≈

Ella struggled to keep her eyes open as she reclined on the sofa. The prescription pain medication made her drowsy. It was hard to focus on Mama, Charlene, and the younger children who were gathered around her, wearing anxious expressions.

"Does your arm hurt a lot?" Sue Ann asked.

Ella forced a smile, not wishing to frighten her six-year-old sister. "Not so much." But her whole arm had throbbed until the medication had taken effect.

Mama took a seat on the sofa beside Ella and motioned to her cast. "I'm awfully sorry that you fell and broke your arm, but I'm grateful you weren't seriously hurt. Don't think I could deal with another tragedy in this family."

"Me, neither," Charlene put in. "Our family needs some happy times."

Ella blinked back stinging tears. Because of her carelessness in coming down the ladder, she'd almost brought more grief to her family. She thanked the Lord that she hadn't been seriously injured. "I'm sorry. I should have been more careful."

"You shouldn't have been paintin' the barn at all," Larry chimed in. "I'll bet Jake would've helped sooner if you'd asked, and so would some of the other men in our community."

Ella grimaced. She didn't want to rely on others for help, and she didn't want Jake hanging around. The next time they needed help, if she couldn't do it, she'd ask someone else.

CHAPTER 28

The days sped by with the delicate shifting of fall into winter. Ella had finally resigned herself to the fact that, she needed to accept help from her family and friends. Everyone but Jake, that is. Her irritation mounted every time he came over and offered his help. Charlene said Ella ought to be willing to accept anyone's help no matter how she felt about them personally. Ella knew her sister was right, but it was hard to accept help from Jake when she knew he'd be going back to Montana soon and would leave his family in the lurch.

Ella was also afraid that Jolene might have fallen into Jake's trap. Due to the signing lessons, Jolene had seen a lot of him lately and had told Ella that she was excited about the possibility of Jake and Andrew taking turns signing the message for the deaf people at church. Obviously, Jolene didn't realize that Jake wouldn't be sticking around. He'd probably fed her a bunch of lies, the way he had Loraine. The sparkle in Jolene's eyes whenever she talked about Jake was enough to make Ella sick. He had her believing he was a nice person, but she didn't really know him. Not the way Ella did.

"I wish he'd leave Indiana right now," Ella fumed as she opened the oven to check the bread she had baking. The intense heat from the oven hit her in the face and made her feel dizzy. Seeing that the bread wasn't done, she quickly shut the door. She was glad that she had the cast off her arm now and could at least

749

do more things on her own.

Tap. Tap. Tap.

"Someone's at the door!" Charlene hollered from the living room, where she'd gone to dust and clean windows.

Ella dropped her potholders to the counter and went to answer the door. When she opened it, she was surprised to find Jake standing on the porch, holding a purple and white African violet with lacy edges.

"Guder mariye. Figured I'd catch you here before you opened your bakeshop for the day." Jake grinned and handed Ella the plant.

"Morning." She stared at the African violet. "Who's this for?"

"I bought it for you. Charlene said you liked African violets, so I figured you might like this one."

Ella's brows puckered. Was Jake trying to butter her up? Did he think she might put in a good word for him where Jolene was concerned?

"That frown you're wearing makes me think you don't like African violets," he said.

"It's not that. I just wondered why you'd buy me a plant."

"Just told you—Charlene said you liked African violets. You've been so down lately, and I figured it might put a smile on your face."

"Okay, well—danki." Ella took the plant and started to close the door, but Jake stuck the toe of his boot inside, which kept the door from closing. "It's cold out here. Aren't you going to invite me in for a cup of hot coffee?"

Ella contemplated his request. She wanted to tell him to head for home, but that would be rude. Besides, she'd have to answer to Mama if she sent Jake off in this chilly weather without something warm to drink.

She brushed some flour from her apron and opened the door wider. "Follow me."

When they entered the kitchen, Ella set the plant on the counter and took two cups down from the cupboard. By the time she'd placed a pot of coffee on the table, Jake had removed his jacket and stocking cap and taken a seat.

He sniffed the air. "Something sure smells good in here. Have you got something baking in the oven?"

"It's friendship bread. I sell more of that than anything else in my bakeshop." She motioned to some loaves cooling on the counter. "Would you like some to go with your coffee?"

"Sure, that sounds good, but let me cut it for you." Jake jumped up, cut several slices, placed them on a plate, and set it on the table.

"Danki," Ella mumbled, and then she took a seat two chairs away from him.

❧ ❧

Jake picked up a piece of the bread, and his mouth watered when he took the first bite. "Umm. . .this tastes *wunderbaar.*"

"I'm glad you like it," Ella mumbled, staring at the table. Why did she always avoid looking at him?

They sat silently as the minutes ticked by. If Jake had known what to say, he would have offered more conversation.

Finally, Ella pushed back her chair and hurried over to the stove. "I need to check on my bread."

"Need any help with that?"

"No, thanks. I can manage." Ella grabbed a potholder and opened the oven door. She removed some nicely browned loaves and placed them on the cooling racks she'd set on the counter.

"How come you're baking in here and not in your bakeshop?"

"I sometimes do my baking here in the mornings before going out to the shop. Having the oven on for a while helps warm the kitchen without having to light the stove we normally use for heat."

"Guess that makes sense. Is there anything you'd like me to do while I'm here?" Jake asked. "I've got a few hours before I have to be back home."

She shook her head. "I can't think of a thing that needs to be done."

Jake had a hard time believing that, but he decided not to push it. He glanced at the counter across the room. "I'd like to buy

751

a loaf of that bread, and also some doughnuts if you have some to sell."

"I have some doughnuts in the shop," she said, "but there'll be no charge."

"How come?"

"With all the chores you've done around here in the last few weeks, I should pay you."

"No way! You need to make a living."

"We're getting along okay, and I won't take any money from you today."

Jake took a drink of coffee as he pondered things. Ella's fierce independence both amused and irritated him. He wondered what was behind her unwillingness to accept his help or his money. Was she like that with everyone or just him? Whenever he said anything to her, she acted so defensive, and he was getting tired of it. *"Ferwas bischt allfat so schtarkeppich?"* he asked.

Her lips puckered as she glared at him. "Why am *I* always so stubborn? You're the one who's stubborn. Stubborn and. . ."

"Jah, well, I'm stubborn because my daed taught me to be that way. He's the most stubborn man I know."

She smiled, but he suspected she was gritting her teeth and wishing he would go.

"I'll tell you what," he said, carefully choosing his words. "I'll accept the bread, but I insist on paying for the doughnuts."

To his relief, Ella gave a quick nod then quickly launched into telling him about the success of her bakeshop.

Jake was happy to talk about the bakeshop. It seemed to put her at ease. She seemed almost like the old Ella he'd known when they were children.

They talked about the bakeshop a few more minutes, and then Jake made a huge mistake. He mentioned Ella's dad, and what a nice man he'd been.

Unexpected tears spilled over and dribbled down Ella's cheeks. She quickly grabbed a napkin and blotted them away.

Oh, great, now I've made her cry. Jake left his seat and sat in the chair beside Ella. "I'm sorry. I shouldn't have mentioned your daed. I wasn't thinking about how it'd make you feel."

She blinked a couple of times, and the heavy sadness in her face finally lifted. "It's okay. I can't allow myself to fall apart every time my daed's name is mentioned. He's gone and he's not coming back, so I may as well get used to the idea."

"It still has to hurt," Jake said. "I know I'd feel awful if something happened to either one of my folks."

She nodded slowly. "It does hurt, but I can't waste time feeling sorry for myself when there's so much work to be done. I need to focus on taking care of my family."

"You're right, family's important, but you have to think of yourself, too."

She didn't reply.

"My daed's legs have taken much longer to heal than the doctor had hoped, but he'll finally be getting his casts off tomorrow," Jake said, moving their conversation in another direction. "Then he'll begin physical therapy."

"How long will it be before he's able to shoe horses again?"

Jake shrugged. "Can't really say. Guess it all depends on how well he responds to the therapy."

She opened her mouth like she might say something more, but then she closed it again. It seemed like she'd been doing a lot of that lately—at least whenever Jake was around.

After several more minutes of silence, Jake pushed back his chair and stood. "Guess I'll head out now, so if you'll get the bread and doughnuts for me, I'll be on my way."

The look of relief that came over Ella's face told Jake all he needed to know. She still didn't like him and probably never would.

He followed Ella out to her shop, and as soon as she'd put the bread and doughnuts in a paper sack, Jake paid her. He'd just opened the door to leave when Lonnie stepped into the bakeshop. He seemed to be coming around here a lot lately. At least he'd come by nearly every time Jake had been here. It made Jake wonder if something was going on between Lonnie and Ella. Well, if there was, it was none of his business.

CHAPTER 29

Ella had just begun mixing the batter for some gingerbread when the bell on the door of her bakeshop jingled. She hurried into the front room just in time to see Jake step through the doorway.

"Wie geht's?" he asked.

"I'm fine; just busy is all."

"Guess that's nothing new for you, is it?" Jake smiled and moved over to the glass-topped display case where the baked goods were kept. "I came here to buy a few things, and I insist on paying for everything this time."

"What do you need?"

He touched his chin dimple as he eyed the baked goods. "Let's see now. . . . I'll take three loaves of bread, a dozen glazed doughnuts, and two packages of dinner rolls."

"Anything else?"

"Think that'll be all for this time."

Jake had been making a habit of coming by for baked goods at least twice a week, and Ella wondered if his family really needed that much or if he just bought things in order to help them out financially. Since she hadn't let him do too many chores for them, she had a hunch he was trying to make up for that by buying bread, cookies, and pies. It didn't make sense why he insisted on helping, though. Especially when the two of them didn't get along that well.

She hurriedly packaged up the items he'd requested, and then after he'd paid her, she moved toward the back room. "If you'll excuse me, I have some gingerbread I need to finish mixing."

"Mind if I tag along? Maybe we can visit for a few minutes."

With a brief nod, she said, "You're welcome to come along, but I don't know how much talking I'll be able to do. If another customer comes in, I'll have to drop what I'm doing and wait on them."

"Where's Charlene? Doesn't she usually wait on customers when you're baking?"

"Charlene's not here right now. She went with Mama to a doctor's appointment."

"Is your mamm feelin' poorly?" Jake asked as he followed Ella into the kitchen.

"Mama hasn't felt well for a long time, and it's taken us this long to finally convince her to see the doctor. I hope he'll run some tests and that we'll find out what's wrong with her soon." Ella frowned. "She's really tired most of the time, and she's put on quite a bit of weight even though she doesn't eat very much."

"Hopefully it's nothing serious," Jake said. "Maybe she just needs more rest."

"It seems like all Mama does is rest." Ella sighed. "It's hard not to worry about her."

Jake leaned against the counter and watched as Ella started mixing the gingerbread dough. "Maybe you'll have some answers soon."

"I hope so." She stifled a yawn.

Jake moved closer to where she stood. "You talk about your mamm being tired, and yet every time I see you, there are dark circles under your eyes. Right now, you look like you're about to fall asleep." He nudged her arm. "As my mamm often says to me, *'Ich iwwerduh mich net.'*"

"I am not overextending myself, and I'm not going to fall asleep." Was Jake trying to start another argument? Was that the reason he'd come over here today—so he could needle her some more?

"Would you like me to give you some examples of how you overextend yourself?"

She tapped her foot out of frustration and shook her head.

Jake held up one finger. "You're working in the bakeshop six days a week." Another finger shot up. "You clean the house—"

"Charlene helps with that."

"Okay, Charlene helps, but I've seen you cleaning several times when I've come by to see if you needed my help with anything."

Ella clenched her teeth. *Then why don't you quit coming by?*

Jake held up a third finger. "You do outside chores that are meant for a man." A fourth finger joined the other three. "You're taking signing lessons from Jolene." He held up his thumb. "And I've seen you in town running errands and grocery shopping. If all that's not overextending yourself, then I don't know what is."

"I'll say it again," Ella spoke through tight lips. "I am not overextending myself. I do what I do because it needs to be done, and it's really none of your business how hard I work or how much I choose to do."

"Okay, okay, don't get so riled."

"I'm not riled."

"Jah, you are, and you seem so uptight. Maybe you ought to ask someone to give you a foot massage. My mamm used to give me foot massages when I was a buwe, and that always helped me relax."

Ella nearly laughed out loud, thinking how Jake must have looked getting a foot massage from his mother when he was a boy. "I don't need a foot massage," she mumbled.

Jake motioned to the table. "Well, then, I think you ought to sit down and take a deep breath or have something warm to drink. That can be relaxing, too."

The thought of taking a break did sound appealing, but Ella didn't want Jake to think she was taking his advice, so she shook her head and muttered, "I can't sit down; I've got more baking to do."

"Suit yourself, but if you're not going to take a break, then would you mind if I sit for a few minutes? It's mighty cold out this afternoon, and I'd like the chance to thaw out before I have to hit the road again."

"Feel free to have a seat. As soon as I get my gingerbread in the oven, I'll bag up your order."

"You did that already, remember?" Jake motioned to the sack on the counter.

Ella's face heated. "Oh, that's right."

Jake flopped into a chair.

Ella turned back to her job.

Jake popped his knuckles a few times and hummed a familiar tune.

Ella fanned her hot face with the corner of her apron and tried to ignore him. She really did wish he'd go home.

By the time Ella had put the gingerbread in the oven, she realized she needed a break.

"Would you like a cup of hot chocolate or some coffee?" she asked Jake.

He grinned like a little boy. "Hot chocolate sounds good."

She poured hot water into two cups and added some powdered cocoa mix. Then she placed the cups on the table along with some friendship bread, fresh butter, and a jar of homemade elderberry jelly.

"I'm glad to see you took my advice about taking a break," Jake said when she seated herself in the chair opposite him.

She picked up her cup and lifted it to her lips. One sip of the hot chocolate sent a ripple of warmth surging through her. She really had needed a break.

"Say, what's that on your nose?" Jake asked, leaning forward and squinting at Ella.

She lifted her hand. "Where?"

"Right there." Jake stood and moved quickly to the other side of the table.

As he started toward her, Ella shooed him away with her hands and then swiped at her nose. "Don't bother; I'm sure I can get it."

"Oh, great, now you made it worse." Jake bent down and reached his hand toward her face. Without thinking, she grabbed his hand, and in so doing, a strange prickly sensation zinged up her arm. She let go of his hand as quickly as she'd grabbed it.

A hint of a smile flitted across Jake's face, revealing the deep dimples in his cheeks. Was he laughing at her? Did he know about the strange sensation she'd felt? Had he felt it, too?

"I was just going to rub off that speck of flour on your nose, because you look really funny like that." Jake's eyes sparkled with laughter. "Now the whole side of your nose is white with flour."

Feeling rather foolish, Ella reached up to wipe her nose. "There, is that better?"

Jake stared at her, his placid expression unreadable. Several seconds went by, and then his face broke into a wide smile. "Jah, that's much better."

Ella was relieved when he returned to his side of the table and sat down. She drank her hot chocolate and pushed her chair aside. "I think I'd better get back to work now."

"Okay. I'll leave you to it, then." Jake grabbed his sack of baked goods and moved toward the door. "Thanks for the goodies," he called over his shoulder before the door banged shut.

Ella breathed a sigh of relief. Every time Jake came around, she felt flustered. She wished she could make him stay home, but knowing Jake's pattern, he'd probably be back in a few days to buy more doughnuts or bread.

Ella had just started to clean up the mess she'd made from the gingerbread when the back door swung open and Mama stepped into the room. "Was that Jake Beechy's buggy I saw leaving our place as we were coming in?" she asked.

Ella gave a quick nod. "He came by for some baked goods."

"Again? Seems like he was just here a few days ago." Mama gave Ella a knowing look. "He's been coming around a lot lately. Is there something going on between you two?"

Ella shook her head. "The only thing going on between me and Jake is a lot of tension."

"Maybe you feel irritated whenever he comes around because you're attracted to him."

"That's *lecherich*, Mama. There's nothing about Jake that I'm attracted to."

Mama gave Ella's arm a little squeeze. "It may not be as ridiculous as you think. I didn't like your daed all that well when we first met, either."

"I didn't just meet Jake. I've known him since we were kinner." Ella plopped her hands against her hips and frowned. *"Der Jake is en lidderlicher kall."*

"Despicable is a very harsh word to be calling Jake. You need to think about the way you speak of others, Ella. I doubt that Jake's as bad as you make him out to be." Suddenly Mama's eyes filled with tears. "Before your daed and I started going out, there were times when he irritated me to no end with his teasing."

"What'd he do?"

"Well, when we were young and still in school, he used to poke me in the ribs to make me giggle, and it hurt. And whenever he came over to visit my bruder, he used to sneak upstairs to my room and put straw in my bed." Mama chuckled. "I didn't realize it back then, but he only did those things to get my attention. It wasn't until we were teenagers that I began to realize your daed wanted to take me out."

"And you still wanted to go out with him after all the mean things he'd done to you when you were a kinner?"

"Oh, jah. I had a big crush on him, even though I didn't like most of the things he'd done. I knew he'd grow up someday, and I hoped when he did that he'd see me as a woman he could love and not just as someone to tease." Mama reached for a paper towel and blotted the tears clinging to her lashes. "I miss your daed so much and would give anything to have him here teasing me right now."

As Ella reflected on her mother's words, she felt a prickly sensation creep up her spine. She'd had a crush on Jake when they were children, but she'd never admitted it to anyone, not even her cousins. She'd never told a soul about the promise Jake had made when he'd walked her to school, carrying her books, either. She'd thought he liked her as much as she liked him. She'd thought he had really meant it when he'd promised to take her for a ride in his buggy when he turned sixteen. But no, the first time Jake took a girl for a ride, it had been Loraine, not Ella.

She shivered despite the warmth in the bakeshop. Jake was a liar; he wasn't to be trusted.

"Are you all right, Ella?" Mama asked. "You look umgerennt."

Ella blinked. "I'm not upset. I was just thinking."

"About what?"

"It was nothing important." No way could she tell Mama what she'd been thinking. Ella touched Mama's arm. "I should have asked right away. How'd it go at the doctor's?"

Mama shrugged. "Okay."

"Did he run any tests? Does he know why you're so tired and shaky?"

"Calm down, Ella. You sound like a screech owl."

Ella hadn't realized her voice had risen. "I'm sorry, Mama. I'm just worried about you. You've been feeling poorly far too long."

"The doctor thinks I either have hypoglycemia or diabetes. He's scheduled me for some blood tests on Friday."

Ella hoped Mama had hypoglycemia rather than diabetes, because she knew it could be controlled by a change in her diet. If Mama started eating regularly instead of picking at her food, and if she made sure she ate the right kinds of food, then hopefully, she'd feel better in no time.

❧ ❧

When Lonnie pulled his horse and buggy into the schoolyard, several children were heading for home, including Sylvia and Irvin. Irvin waved, and Lonnie waved back then signed to Irvin, *"Have a good afternoon."* He was pleased that he knew how to sign enough words to make sentences now. As his lessons with Jolene had continued, he'd begun to feel more confident that he'd soon be talking easily with his hands without feeling self-conscious or unsure of himself.

Lonnie's folks were taking signing lessons from Jolene as well, which made it easier for Lonnie to communicate at home. Mama had caught on so well that she and Lonnie could carry on a conversation without her having to write everything down.

Lonnie started across the yard and saw Eunice heading that way on her bike. She halted when she saw him, turned the bike around, and took off down the road. Lonnie shrugged. He could never figure out why Eunice did any of the things she did. She was nothing like Jolene, that was for sure.

When Lonnie entered the schoolhouse, he nearly bumped into Fern, who was coming out the door. Her face colored, and she signed, *"Sorry."*

"Me, too," Lonnie signed back. He was glad Jolene had been teaching Fern and some of the children in her class how to sign. It made it easier than trying to read people's lips. Even so, he knew the day was coming when he'd have to rely on lip reading more than signing in order to get a job that took him outside his home.

Sure wish there was something I could do besides work with Pop's hogs. Lonnie grunted as he tromped up the steps to Jolene's classroom. *I wonder how hard it's going to be to find a job once I start seriously looking.*

Lonnie knew he could continue helping Pop with the hogs for as long as he wanted, and even though things seemed to be better between him and Pop, raising hogs wasn't the kind of work he cared to do. He needed something that was more of a challenge— not that pigs couldn't be challenging at times. What he wanted was something fun, something he'd really enjoy.

When Lonnie entered Jolene's classroom, he found her sitting at her desk, looking over some paperwork. She didn't look up, so he assumed she hadn't realized he'd come in. If she'd been able to hear, he would have cleared his throat loudly. Under the circumstances, he figured the best thing to do was to tap her on the shoulder.

He walked slowly up the desk, and when his hand connected with Jolene's shoulder, she jumped. He jumped, too, because for some unknown reason, a jolt of electricity had shot up his arm. He shrugged it off, attributing it to the fact that there must be static electricity in the air from the cold weather they'd been having.

Jolene patted her flushed cheeks and signed, *"Are you ready for another lesson on lip reading?"*

Lonnie bobbed his head, feeling suddenly nervous and shy in her presence. It made no sense; he'd been alone with Jolene several times and had never felt like this.

"Before we begin our lesson," Jolene signed, *"I'd like your opinion on something."*

"What do you need my opinion on?" Lonnie asked, hoping he'd understood what she'd said and had signed the right words.

"This is kind of lengthy, so I'm going to write it out." Jolene picked up the tablet on her desk and wrote: *I know you and Andrew have become friends, so I hope you won't repeat what I'm about to tell you.*

Lonnie shook his head and signed, *"I won't repeat."*

Jolene smiled and continued to write. *As you might know, Andrew has recently begun going out with Eunice Byler.*

Lonnie shrugged in reply. Who Andrew went out with was none of his business.

From some of the things Andrew has said to me, I know he has more than a passing interest in her.

"Maybe so," Lonnie signed.

I'm afraid Eunice might not be right for Andrew.

"How come?"

Because she likes to gossip. I spoke with her yesterday, and she told me some things that were none of my business—things that, in my opinion, didn't bear repeating.

Lonnie frowned, and he spoke out loud. "I'm not much of an expert on love, but I think Andrew's smart enough to know whether Eunice is right for him or not. Of course, I misjudged Carolyn and thought she was the one for me." He groaned. "One thing's for certain. I'll never fall in love again."

"How do you know?"

"It'd be hard for me to trust another woman not to hurt me the way Carolyn did. Besides, what kind of husband and father would I make when I can't hear?"

Before Jolene could comment, Kyle Beechy rushed into the room. His lips moved fast as he waved his hands. Lonnie had no idea what the boy was saying.

≈ ⁂ ≈

Seeing the urgent look on Kyle's face sent a wave of panic through Jolene. She put her fingers to her lips to shush the boy. "Slow down,

Kyle. I'm not able to read your lips when you're talking so fast."

The color in the boy's blue eyes darkened like the night sky. "Irvin's been hit by a car. He couldn't hear it coming. I tried to warn him, but he couldn't hear me, either." Tears gathered in the corners of Kyle's eyes, and he blinked several times. "You've gotta come with me, Teacher. I think Irvin might be dead!"

Jolene jumped out of her chair, grabbed her coat, and raced down the steps behind Kyle. When she opened the schoolhouse door, a blast of frosty air stung her nose.

As she ran along the shoulder of the road behind Kyle, the frigid air caused her throat to ache from breathing too deeply. She turned once and saw Lonnie sprinting behind them. He caught up to her in a few long strides.

When they came upon the scene of the accident, Jolene's breath caught in her throat. A car was parked along the shoulder of the road, and a young woman stood beside it, tears streaming down her face. Several children, including Sylvia, were gathered around the small form lying on the ground near the car. Irvin was still breathing, but blood seeped from a gash in his head, and he wasn't moving.

In the whirlwind of confusion, one thing was clear: The boy was hurt and needed immediate medical attention.

CHAPTER 30

"Stop crying, and tell me what's wrong," Jake said when he arrived home from Ella's and found his little brother sitting on the back porch, bawling like a wounded heifer.

Kyle looked up at Jake and choked on a sob. "Ir–Irvin's in the hospital. He might even be dead, and—and it's all my fault!"

Jake's forehead wrinkled. "What are you talking about?"

"If I knew how to sign, I could've warned him."

Jake set the sack full of bakery items on the porch and took a seat beside Kyle. "Tell me what happened."

Kyle gulped and sniffed a few times as he poured out the story of how Irvin had been hit by a car, and how he'd run to the schoolhouse to get help.

"Did you push Irvin in front of the car?" Jake asked.

Kyle shook his head.

"Then why do you think the accident was your fault?"

Kyle swiped at his tear-stained face. "I. . .I was teasin' him about not bein' able to hear, and he started runnin' real fast. He must not have been watchin' where he was goin', 'cause he ran in front of the car. I called out to him, but of course, he couldn't hear my warning."

"That's terrible, and I'm real sorry to hear it, but there's one thing I don't understand."

"What's that?"

"Since Irvin can't hear, and you haven't learned how to sign, how'd he know you were teasing him?"

Kyle's shoulders shook as he hung his head. "I. . .I poked him a couple of times. Then I guess he read my lips when I said he was a dummkopp who can't talk right and acts like a boppli."

Jake clenched his fists. "How many times have you been told not to tease?"

"A lot."

"And yet you keep doing it?" Jake glared at his brother. "What makes you keep teasing Irvin when you know it's wrong?"

Kyle leaned forward, letting his head drop into his hands. "I–I'm mad at you, and since I can't say what I want. . ." His voice trailed off as sniffling and hiccups took over.

Jake placed his hand on Kyle's head. "How come you're mad at me?"

Kyle mumbled something about Jake leaving, but Jake could only make out a few words because the boy was crying so hard.

"Sit up, dry your eyes, and tell me what's on your mind," Jake said, gently patting Kyle's back.

Several seconds went by before Kyle finally lifted his head. "I'm mad 'cause you moved to Montana. And—and then you keep comin' back."

"You don't like it when I come home?"

"It's not that—it's just that when you're gone, Dad's real cranky and moody. Mom cries a lot, too." Kyle gulped in a quick breath. "Then whenever you come back, Dad's crankier than ever, and Mom makes over you like you're her favorite son. I wish you'd make up your mind 'bout where you're gonna live and then stay put once and for all. Maybe if you decided to stay in Montana, Mom and Dad would accept the idea and stop frettin' over you all the time. Or better yet, if you stayed here, we'd all be happy."

Kyle's words jolted Jake to the core. He knew Mom and Dad weren't happy about him living in Montana, but until this moment, he'd had no idea it had affected his little brother so, or that Kyle had been carrying all this pent-up anger toward him.

Jake knew he'd have to work on improving his relationship with Kyle. He also needed to make a definite decision about whether he should stay in Indiana or return to Montana. Right now, though, they needed to find out how Irvin was doing.

～ ⁓

"Why are you getting home so late?" Mom asked when Jolene entered the kitchen. "It's way past time for supper, and I was beginning to worry."

Jolene slipped off her heavy woolen shawl and hung it over the back of a chair. "Irvin was hit by a car after school, and I stayed with him at the hospital until his folks got there."

"What happened? Is Irvin badly hurt? Is he. . ."

Mom's lips were moving so fast that Jolene couldn't keep up. She held up her hand. "Please, one question at a time."

"Sorry. Sometimes I still forget that you're reading my lips."

Jolene motioned to the table. "Let's have a seat, and I'll tell you about it."

They both found chairs, and Jolene explained how she'd ridden in the ambulance with Irvin while Lonnie went to notify his folks. Then when Irvin's folks arrived at the hospital, Jolene had stayed with them until they'd gotten some word on Irvin's condition. Jolene drew in a deep breath. "We were so relieved when the doctor came out and said Irvin hadn't been critically injured, although he did require several stitches in his forehead, and his collarbone is broken."

Mom shook her head slowly. "It's a miracle that boy wasn't killed. What was he doing in the street, anyway?"

"I'm not sure. Kyle Beechy's the one who came and got me, and he was so upset, I couldn't get many details from him." Jolene paused and licked her dry lips. "With Irvin being deaf, I'm sure he didn't realize the car was coming."

"Is it any wonder that I worry when you take the horse and buggy out?" Mom touched Jolene's arm. "If a car honked its horn to warn you that it was passing, you'd never know it."

"I'm very cautious whenever I go out on the road. I watch my side mirrors and look over my shoulder often when I'm in the buggy. The rest I leave in God's hands."

"You're right, of course; we need to put every part of our lives in God's capable hands." Mom gave Jolene's arm a gentle squeeze. "But I'm a mudder, and I guess it's just my nature to worry about my kinner, no matter how old they are or how cautious they might be." She glanced toward the door then looked back at Jolene. "Someone's knocking, so I'd better see who it is."

Mom hurried from the room, while Jolene remained at the table. A few minutes later, Mom was back with Jake at her side.

"Do you have any word on Irvin?" he asked, taking a seat beside Jolene. "My little bruder's really worried about him."

Jolene explained everything that had transpired at the hospital.

"Kyle blames himself for the accident," Jake said, "because he was teasing Irvin, and then Irvin ran into the road in order to get away from him."

"I don't know how many times I've asked Kyle to stop tormenting Irvin," Jolene said, shaking her head. "Will he never learn?"

Jake's solemn expression lightened a bit. "I think he's finally learned his lesson. Right before I came here, he told me that if Irvin lives, he'll apologize for all the teasing he's done. He even said that he wants to get to know Irvin better, and believe it or not, he's now willing to learn how to sign."

"That's good news, and you can let Kyle know that Irvin will live, because his injuries are not life threatening." Jolene's shoulders lifted and then fell as she released a deep sigh. "Maybe God will take this near tragedy and bring something good from it."

CHAPTER 31

It had been two weeks since Irvin's accident. Due to the broken collarbone, when he returned to school he wore a sling to keep from lifting his arm, and there was still a red mark on his forehead where he'd been cut, but otherwise he looked pretty chipper. Even more amazing, it appeared as though Irvin and Kyle might actually become friends. When Jolene went downstairs to give Fern's class another signing lesson, Kyle had surprised her by participating. He'd even invited Irvin to sit beside him. By the time class was over, Kyle had learned how to sign a few words, including the word *friend*.

"*Guess what, Teacher,*" Sylvia signed when she and Irvin entered Jolene's classroom after their lesson downstairs.

"*What?*"

"*It's snowing!*"

"*Is that so?*" Jolene went to the window and peered out. Sure enough, the ground was covered with a thin layer of white.

"*Can we make a snowman during recess?*" Irvin asked.

Jolene patted the top of his head. "*You're not supposed to use your right arm yet, and I don't think you can roll a snowball too easily with just one hand.*"

"*Irvin can watch while you and me make the snowman.*" Sylvia then turned to Irvin and signed, "*Would that be all right with you?*"

He tipped his head as though mulling things over. Finally, he gave a quick nod.

"*Since that is all settled, are you two ready to begin your lessons?*" Jolene asked.

Both children nodded and then hurried to the chairs at their desks. Jolene smiled. It was good to see her young students so well adjusted and eager to learn. Her adult students were catching on to signing, too. Last Sunday in church, Andrew had signed part of the bishop's sermon. Having him do that had given the worship service a lot more meaning for Jolene. After church, Jake had told her that he might like to try signing at the next service. Things were definitely looking up.

~❦~

Jake smiled as he listened to his horse's hooves crunch in the snow and watched the steam escaping his horse's nostrils. It had begun snowing earlier today, and the snowflakes were so big they looked like spun sugar. He'd always liked snowy weather and had enjoyed playing in the snow when he was a boy.

Wish I had time to play in it right now, Jake thought as he guided his horse up the Yoders' driveway. *Maybe when Kyle and Elmer get home from school, we can make a snow fort.*

When Jake hopped down from his buggy, the stiffening breeze ruffled the hair peeking out from under his stocking cap. Winter was definitely here, for it was getting colder every day.

Jake put the horse in the barn, and once he had the animal settled in one of the stalls, he hurried toward the bakeshop. As Jake stepped onto the porch, wet snow fell from his boots in slushy clumps. He entered the shop, and the sweet smell of cinnamon and apples assaulted his senses.

He'd only been standing by the bakery counter a few seconds when Ella stepped out of the back room, carrying two pies. She blinked a couple of times and jumped back when she saw him. "Ach, I didn't hear you come in!"

"Guess the bell above your door isn't working," he said. "At least I didn't hear it ring when I opened the door."

Ella glanced up at the bell and frowned. "It's not there. Someone must have taken it down."

"Who'd do that?"

She shrugged. "I have no idea. It might have been Larry. He likes to fool with things, so he probably took the bell thinking he could make it louder or something."

"Speaking of Larry, is he still at school?"

"Jah."

Jake leaned on the counter and stared at Ella. She had a good heart and cared deeply for her family. He wished she liked him better, though. The wall she'd built between them was thicker than dense fog, and at this close range he could see the fine lines on her forehead. She might be prettier if she didn't frown so much. Jake didn't know why, but he found himself strangely attracted to her. He just wished he could figure out some way to break through that barrier she'd built. He also wished he knew what she had against him. He was tempted to ask but didn't want to start an argument. They'd had too many of those already.

"What can I do for you?" Ella asked. "Are you after more baked goods?"

"Not this time." He rubbed the glass countertop with the sleeve of his jacket in an effort to dispel the fingerprints that were there. "I. . .uh. . .wondered if you needed my help with anything."

"Huh-uh. We're fine."

"I thought you might need some wood chopped or something."

"I'm planning to do that after I close the bakeshop for the day."

"Why don't you let me do it for you? I'm sure you've got better things to do than try to chop wood."

"*Try* to chop wood?" Her forehead wrinkled deeply. "Are you saying that I'm not capable of chopping wood?"

"I'm not sayin' that at all. I just meant. . ."

She pushed past him, slipped into her jacket, and rushed out the door.

Jake quickly followed. *I'm here to help out,* he reminded himself. *And it's not because I have an interest in a sharp-tongued woman who clearly doesn't want me around. It's because I care about her family and want to do the right thing, so despite Ella's protests, I'll continue to offer my help.*

Ella sloshed her way through the snow out to the woodpile behind the barn. She picked up a hunk of wood and was about to reach for the ax when Jake stepped in front of her. She gulped. With him standing only inches away, it was hard to think. . .hard to breathe. She was about to ask him to move back when he spoke first.

"I have a few hours free this afternoon, and I'd really like to give you a hand. Isn't there something you'd like me to do?" Jake's tone was soft, his face sincere.

Ella hesitated. Since Papa's death, she'd come to realize that as much as she wanted to be independent, she couldn't do everything in her own strength. Then last night, she'd read Galatians 6:2: *"Bear ye one another's burdens, and so fulfil the law of Christ."* It was a gentle reminder that she needed to let others help out during their time of need. She guessed that even meant Jake.

Jake touched Ella's arm. "Did you hear my question?"

She nodded and lifted her lips in a slow smile. "How much experience have you had at baking?"

His eyebrows lifted. "Huh?"

"When I'm done chopping wood I'll be doing some more baking. Since you're so anxious to help out, I thought maybe. . ."

Jake held up his hand. "I can do a lot of chores, but there's one thing I can't do, and that's bake." He crinkled his nose and winked at her. "Unless, of course, you like things burned."

Ella's cheeks grew warm. Was Jake flirting with her? Oh, surely not; he was just trying to be funny. She shivered and picked up the axe, but Jake grabbed hold of her arm before she could take a swing.

"Why don't you head back inside where it's warm? I'll have this wood chopped in no time at all."

Jake's self-assured attitude only refueled Ella's anger. Didn't he ever give up? Did he enjoy making her mad?

He moved closer, so close she could feel the tension between them. "I'm not leaving here until I chop some wood, so you may as well hand me that ax."

"From what I remember, you're kind of accident-prone. How do I know you won't cut yourself?"

"If I do, then you'll have to doctor me up." He wiggled his eyebrows playfully. "You'd better get inside now and make sure you have some bandages ready for me."

She grunted and started for the bakeshop. Jake Beechy was impossible! She didn't know what Loraine had ever seen in him—for that matter, what Jolene saw in him now.

Ella cringed. She hoped Jolene didn't end up marrying Jake. The thought of him being her cousin-in-law didn't set well with her.

She stopped walking, turned, and cupped her hands over her mouth. "Make sure you don't leave any of that wood unchopped! Things done by halves are never done right."

"You think you know everything, Ella!"

Her jaw clenched against the cold, and she fired back, "Jah, well, you think everyone should do as you say!"

"You're kind of cute when you're riled like that! Your nose twitches, and your cheeks turn red!" His voice carried in the crisp, cold air.

Ella glared at him, sensing that he was making fun of her. How did Jake always manage to make her feel so stupid? "The only reason my nose is red is because it's so cold out here!" She leaned down, grabbed a wad of snow, and formed it into a ball. Then she pulled her arm way back and chucked the snowball at Jake.

"Hey!" He brushed the snow off the sleeve of his jacket, bent down, and grabbed some snow of his own.

Ella knew what was coming, so she hurried for the bakeshop as fast as she could. She'd just stepped onto the porch, when—*splat!*—a chunk of icy snow hit the back of her neck. She was tempted to retaliate, but it was cold out here, and she had baking to do. She'd get even with Jake some other time.

Ella stepped into the bakeshop and headed straight for the stove to thaw out.

Maybe what I need is something to warm my insides. After she'd poured herself a cup of coffee, she glanced out the window and watched as Jake swung the axe. He made it look so easy. She'd never have admitted it to him, but she hated chopping wood and knew it would have taken her twice as long as it would Jake.

Ella noticed Jake glancing toward the bakeshop, so she moved quickly away from the window. No point in letting him think she'd been watching. He might get the wrong idea.

She took a seat at the table near the stove and continued to fume. Why hadn't Jake ever seen her as a capable woman? Why did he think he was so much better at doing things than her? Why couldn't Jake. . .

Ella halted her thoughts and pushed away from the table. She had to quit thinking about Jake and get some baking done.

~≈ ≈~

Sometime later, Jake entered the bakeshop. His face was red and glistened with sweat. "Whew! It's gettin' colder out there by the minute." He rubbed his hands briskly together. "Sure feels good to be inside where it's warm."

"Danki for cutting the wood," Ella said.

"No problem. What else would you like me to do?"

Go home. She forced a smile. "I don't need anything else done right now."

"Sure you do. There's always chores that need to be done. Would you like me to muck out the stalls in the barn?" Jake pointed to the sink. "Or I could wash those dishes you've got piled up from your baking."

She shook her head. "I can do them." *That's one thing I'm sure I can do better than you.*

"If you won't let me help with anything else, then at least let me give you some money."

"Money for what?"

"To help with a few bills, which I'm sure you must have." Jake pulled some money from his pocket and placed it on the table. "When I was at Jolene's the other day, she mentioned that things have been kind of slow for you here in the bakery. She said you're worried about not having enough money to get through the winter."

Ella avoided his steady gaze as an eerie silence moved in around them. It irritated her that Jolene had told Jake about things that were none of his business. She pushed the money toward him. "I've told you before; we're getting by fine on our own!"

"Then I'll buy some bread."

"What?"

"I said, 'I'll buy some bread.'"

"Fine. How many loaves do you need?"

"Ten."

Her eyebrows shot up. "What in the world are you going to do with ten loaves of bread?"

"I'll find a use for 'em."

"What are you planning to do. . .feed bread to your horses?"

"Maybe." He pointed to the wad of bills. "How much do I owe you?"

"Why do you think you need to help us, Jake?"

"My mamm always says, 'If you give a little, you get back much more.'"

"Just what is it you expect to get back?"

"I don't expect anything." Jake pushed the money toward her. "I'm going to give you this no matter what you say, so you may as well take it agreeably."

"And I say you're not!" she challenged. "Why don't you forget about helping us and stay home with your horses?"

"I can't do that. It'd be like trying to walk around with only one shoe."

"Then I guess you'd better get used to walking that way."

He jammed his hands into his jacket pockets, looking dejected. Ella couldn't be sure if he was actually hurt by her comment or just putting on an act.

A lump formed in Ella's throat as she stared at the money. They really did need it. Tears pricked the backs of her eyes, and she feared they'd soon be rolling down her cheeks. Jake had reduced her to tears again, yet deep down inside, she appreciated his help.

Ella rose from her chair and glanced out the window. "It's snowing harder now, so I'll get your ten loaves of bread, and then you can be on your way. You wouldn't want to get caught in a snowstorm." She hurried to the other room before Jake could see the tears that had started dribbling down her cheeks. She hoped he wouldn't come over here again anytime soon.

CHAPTER 32

Ella dropped into a chair at the kitchen table and fanned her face with the corner of a cotton dish towel. "Whew, it's so hot in here!"

Mama, who sat across from Ella, dropping lettuce leaves into a bowl, nodded. "I'm wondering if we should hire someone to put a second oven in your bakeshop so you don't have to use this one when you have a lot of baking to do. All the baking you've done this morning has heated up the house like nobody's business. Come summer, it'll only be worse."

Ella nodded. "I try to do most of my baking in the morning, but it doesn't seem to make much difference. A hot oven makes for a hot house, that's for sure." She sighed. "Don't see how we can afford to buy a second oven for the bakeshop right now, much less hire someone to put it in. What I'm making from the bakery is barely enough to put food on the table."

Mama dropped a few more pieces of lettuce into the bowl and yawned. "Sure wish there was more I could do to help out, but I'm so tired much of the time." She groaned. "I still can't believe the results of my blood test showed that I have diabetes."

"The dokder said it might take awhile to get your blood sugar regulated, and you've only been on the diet he gave you a few weeks. I'm sure between changing your diet and taking the medication he prescribed, you'll feel better soon."

Tears gathered in the corners of Mama's eyes. "When your

daed and I were first married, I had the energy and strength of two women my age. I feel so worthless now."

Ella swallowed hard. She hated to see Mama looking so sad. She left her seat and bent to give Mama a hug. "You're not worthless. You might not be able to do as much as you once did, but you do what you can, and that's what counts. So please don't worry about it."

" 'I can do all things through Christ which strengtheneth me,'" Mama quoted from the book of Philippians. "Without His help I couldn't do anything. We just need to keep joy in our souls and praise on our lips as we trust God to provide for our needs." She patted Ella's arm. "We'll be okay; you'll see."

Mama's words made Ella aware that she still tried to do too much in her own strength. She motioned to the packages of cakes and cookies on the counter. "I'll be glad when spring's here and the tourists come to the area. If I do a little advertising, hopefully some of them will come out here to our bakeshop."

"*Your* bakeshop, Ella." Mama's light tone contrasted with the serious expression on her face. "It's *your* bakery that's supporting us right now."

"I've never thought of it as being mine. You and Charlene help out, and even the younger ones do whatever they can."

"That's true. We all chip in whenever it's necessary, and we'll continue to do our best."

"I know you will." Ella glanced out the window and sighed. *"Ich bin bereit fer friehyaahr."*

Mama laughed. "Winter's barely started and you're ready for spring?"

"Jah. In the spring I'm planning to take some of my baked goods to the farmer's market in Elkhart, and when the Shipshewana flea market opens in May, I might sell some things there, too."

"That's a good idea," Mama said, "but you can't be in three places at once. With the exception of Charlene, and maybe Larry, the kinner can't run a stand by themselves at either one of the markets."

"Maybe by then we'll be making enough money so I can hire someone to work the stands. Guess we'll have to wait and see how it goes."

"Give me that piece of puzzle!" Amelia shouted from the living room.

"No! You took the one I was gonna choose!" Helen hollered.

Mama's eyebrows furrowed. "Sounds like two of my girls are arguing again. Seems like all Amelia and Helen have done since they got out of bed is argue and fuss." She rubbed her forehead with the back of her hand. "I'll be glad when Monday comes and they're back in school."

"It's not your turn! If you don't let go of that, I'll tell Mama!" Helen's shrill voice carried into the kitchen.

"All that chitter chatter is hurting my ears," Mama said, dropping the lettuce and placing both hands against her ears.

Ella pushed her chair aside. She didn't care how loud the children hollered when they were outside, but not in the house. There was no excuse for them to be arguing that way and upsetting Mama. "I'll take care of their childish prattle," she said as she hurried from the room.

❦

Lonnie drew in a deep breath and smiled as he watched the cows in the stall closest to him crunch away on the sweet-smelling hay he'd given them earlier that morning. For the last hour, he'd been out in the barn, sanding the legs of the small end table he'd made to give Mom for Christmas. He rather liked being out here. It gave him a sense of peace to be alone with the animals. It was a good time to think. Unfortunately, all he'd been able to think about so far today was Jolene, and that bothered him. Whenever he was with her, his insides felt warm and comforted, but he didn't know if he could trust those feelings. Jolene had an inner beauty about her that went much deeper than her pretty face and sparkling blue eyes. He was sure Jolene's beauty started in her heart and shone through her eyes and smile. If being too sweet could be considered a flaw, then maybe Jolene wasn't as perfect as she seemed. There had to be something about her that Lonnie didn't like, but for the life of him, he couldn't think of what it was. He'd have to be careful not to let himself get any closer to her than he already had. He couldn't allow himself to fall in love again.

Forcing his thoughts aside, Lonnie stood and moved the stool he'd been sitting on closer to the stove. If it weren't for the warmth from the fire, his hands would have numbed quickly in the biting cold.

Someone touched Lonnie's shoulder, and he jerked around. He was relieved to see Wayne standing there and not Pop wanting him to do some chore that involved smelly pigs.

Wayne smiled and withdrew a notebook and pen from his jacket pocket. He wrote something on it and handed it to Lonnie. Lonnie was glad Wayne had written his thoughts, as he still wasn't able to read lips very well.

I have a few things I need to pick up in Shipshe and wondered if you'd like to go along. Thought maybe we could stop someplace for coffee and doughnuts.

"That sounds nice, but I'm in the middle of something right now." Lonnie motioned to the legs he'd been sanding.

Did you make that? Wayne wrote.

Lonnie nodded. "It's a surprise for Mom. I'm planning to give it to her for Christmas."

Wayne's lips puckered like he had whistled. Lonnie missed not being able to hear the melody of a whistle.

Wayne picked up the tablet again and wrote something else: *I'm impressed. I had no idea you had a talent for woodworking.*

"I've fooled around with it off and on ever since I was a boy but never figured anything I made was very good."

Well, this sure is. Wayne ran his fingers over one of the table legs. *You've done a fine job with it.*

Lonnie's face heated. He wasn't used to receiving such compliments, especially not for his woodworking skills.

Would you be interested in coming to work for me? Wayne wrote.

"In your taxidermy shop?"

No, in my new woodworking shop. I'm only helping my daed

part-time with taxidermy right now because there's not really enough work for both of us. But I've been able to sell several things that I've made in my woodshop to some of the furniture stores in the area. I think that might turn into a profitable business for me.

Lonnie wasn't convinced that the table he'd made was really that good, but feeling a sense of nervous excitement, he said that he'd be willing to try working for Wayne.

Wayne smiled and wrote, *Let's head for Shipshe, and we can talk about this some more.*

<hr>

The landscape was barely visible under the blanket of white that had fallen the night before, and Jake was on his way home after shoeing an unruly horse. To make matters worse, he'd had to fight slippery roads and blustery snow, both coming and going.

Good thing my truck has four-wheel drive, Jake thought as he peered through the front windshield. He wondered how things would be if he sold his truck and joined the church. He'd have to drive his horse and buggy everywhere except for when he went places that would require him to hire an English driver. *Guess it would take some getting used to for me to let someone else haul me around, but if I were to get my own business going here, I wouldn't have to shoe horses anymore.*

Jake thought about some of the fellows he'd grown up with and how many of them were married and raising families. He wondered if it had been hard for any of them who'd owned vehicles to give them up when they joined the church. He knew it hadn't been an issue for Wayne, because he'd never owned a car. Even if he had, Wayne loved Loraine so much that he'd probably have given up most anything in order to marry her.

Jake wondered if he'd ever feel that much love for a woman. Even when he'd thought he was in love with Loraine, he'd run off to Montana and done his own thing. Soon after he'd moved to Montana, he'd become interested in his boss's daughter, Roxanne, but that hadn't lasted long and had never been really serious. Maybe he was incapable of the kind of love Wayne had for Loraine. Maybe he really was selfish and self-centered, like Dad had accused him of being on several occasions. *Guess I need to pray more and ask God to take away any selfish desires that aren't pleasing to Him.*

Jake's musings halted when he turned up his folks' driveway. He parked his truck behind the barn so Dad didn't have to see it every time he looked out the window.

As Jake started walking toward the house, a bird flew from a nearby tree, sending a shower of snowflakes onto his head. He brushed it off and hurried on.

As soon as Jake stepped onto the back porch, he heard his folks' voices coming from the kitchen window, which was open a crack.

"*Er hot scheins sei verschtand verlore,*" Dad said.

Who seems to have lost his reason? Jake wondered. He stood there a few minutes, listening; then, when he realized it was him they were talking about, he decided to wait a few minutes before going in so he could hear more of what they were saying.

"I blame you for nagging Jake to join the church and for trying to make him do things your way. Truth is, I think it's your fault Jake left home in the first place."

"Stop badgering me. We've been through all this before."

"But if you hadn't pressured Jake so much and worked him so hard when he was a buwe, I'm sure he'd have stayed in Indiana and would have joined the church by now."

There was a long pause, and then Mom started up again. "I'm just heartsick that Jake will be going back to Montana soon. I've gotten used to him being here, and I'll miss him so much."

Jake leaned against the wall and drew in a couple of deep breaths. First he'd had to deal with slippery driving conditions; then a contrary horse that didn't want to be shoed; and now this? The day couldn't get much worse!

"You baby Jake too much; that's what I've gotta say."

"I do not baby him. I just—"

Jake opened the door and stepped into the kitchen. Mom and Dad looked up. Dead silence fell on the room.

Jake turned to Mom and said, "Where'd you get the idea that I'd be leaving for Montana soon?"

Mom blinked a couple of times. "I. . .uh. . .ran into Eunice at the grocery store the other day. She said you told her that you'd be leaving soon."

Jake shook his head. "I never said any such thing. All I told Eunice when I met up with her at Jolene's the other day was that I needed to make up my mind soon about whether to return to Montana or not."

"Have you made up your mind?" Dad asked, leveling Jake with a piercing look.

Jake dug his nails into the palms of his hands. He hated being put on the spot.

"Have you made up your mind or not?"

"You don't have to shout," Mom said. "Is it any wonder Jake doesn't want to live near his family?"

Dad grunted. "That's not the reason, and you know it. Our son thinks he's too good for us. He's never been happy doing what he does best. Wants to own a bunch of wild horses like he's been tryin' to train out west."

Irritation welled in Jake's soul. It took all his willpower not to dash out the door and take off down the road in his truck. "I wasn't *trying* to train horses, Dad. That was my job. I'm not bragging, but I think I did it rather well." He glanced out the window at the barn. "Besides, the kind of horses I want to train aren't wild—they need to learn how to pull a buggy. And I don't just want to train horses," he added. "I'm also hoping to raise a certain breed of horses that I can sell for profit. That's what I've been working and saving my money for."

Dad folded his arms. "Makin' lots of money. That's all you're interested in, isn't it, Jake?"

"No, it's not! I want to raise and train horses because that's what I enjoy doing. And while I might be good at shoeing horses, I've never enjoyed it all that much."

"Maybe you could train horses to pull our buggies here," Mom said. "That would bring in even more money than you're making now filling in for your daed in his business."

"I'll give it some thought," Jake said.

"What is there to think about?" Dad hollered. "Do you have to think about it 'cause you don't know if you're staying here or not?"

"I wish you would lower your voice, Joe." Mom's chin trembled. "This isn't the way God intended for family members to speak to each other."

Dad frowned. "Jah, well, if he'd listen to what I have to say and quit walkin' through life with one foot in the world, there'd be no dispute here or any raised voices."

Jake tapped his foot as his patience waned further. He'd been on the verge of telling his folks that he'd decided not to return to Montana, but now he was having second thoughts. With the snowy weather making it hard to travel, he figured the best thing to do was to wait until spring to make his decision. In the meantime, he needed to put as much space between himself and Dad as possible, so he whirled around and started for the door.

"Where are you going?" Mom called. "It's almost time for lunch."

"I'm not hungry. I'm going outside to the barn so I can have some time alone to think." Jake jerked open the door and let it close behind him a little harder than usual. If things didn't improve around here by spring, he would definitely return to Montana.

CHAPTER 33

Jolene had just entered the bath and body store in Shipshewana to do some Christmas shopping, when she spotted Katie at the cash register. She waited until Katie finished paying for her purchases, and then she stepped up to her and said, "I'm surprised to see you in town this afternoon. I figured you'd be at the stamp shop waiting on desperate customers buying last-minute Christmas presents."

"I was there earlier, but I had a dental appointment this afternoon and decided to come here afterward to do some Christmas shopping of my own." Katie grinned. "I want to get something nice for Freeman."

Jolene smiled. "It won't be long before spring is upon us. Are you getting excited about your wedding in April?"

"Oh, jah, I can hardly wait."

A pang of jealousy stabbed Jolene's heart. She didn't even have a boyfriend, and even if she had one, there were no guarantees that she'd ever get a marriage proposal.

A vision of Lonnie popped into Jolene's head. She'd never admit it, but she was beginning to have strong feelings for him. Of course, it didn't matter how she felt, because he'd told her that he would never look for love again.

To complicate matters, Jolene suspected that Lonnie might be interested in Ella, for he talked about her a lot. But given his reservations about marriage, it was unlikely that he'd ever act upon those feelings.

"Are you all right?" Katie asked, nudging Jolene's arm. "Your eyes are misting up like you're on the verge of tears."

Jolene gave Katie a hug. "I'm just happy for you and Freeman."

Tears welled in Katie's eyes. "I never thought I could be this happy. After all the depression and anxiety I went through after Timothy died, I never thought I'd live a normal life again." Her eyes brightened, and a smile stretched across her face. "God is so good. Every day, I praise and thank Him for helping me to overcome my panic attacks."

"We all have much to be thankful for," Jolene agreed.

～๑ ๑～

You look like you're enjoying your work, Wayne wrote on the tablet he then handed to Lonnie.

"Next to tuning wind chimes, I've never had a job I enjoy so much." Lonnie signed as he spoke, since Wayne had sat in on a few lessons while Jolene was teaching her family and Jake. Lonnie figured it might help his new boss learn quicker if he signed whenever he spoke.

I'm glad to hear you like the work. Don't forget what I told you earlier. I want you to feel free to use my tools to work on your own projects during your lunch hour and breaks, Wayne wrote.

"I'll remember that." Lonnie had plans to not only make his mother and sisters something for Christmas, but Jolene as well. He wanted it to be a thank-you gift for her teaching him to sign and read lips. Although he still wasn't comfortable with lip reading, he hoped he'd eventually get better at it and could use that skill in public rather than relying on the tablet and pen he kept in his pocket.

Lonnie worked quietly for the next few hours. When it was time for lunch, he ate quickly and started working on a bird feeder for Jolene. As he cut the pieces of wood, he thought about how kind and patient she'd been with him. Even when he'd been irritable and negative, she'd remained optimistic and helpful, always encouraging him to keep trying and not to give up. There was something about Jolene's gentle, sweet spirit that drew him to her. There'd been times when he'd been tempted to ask her out, but fear of her rejection had always held him back. Besides, what did he have to offer a woman? He couldn't make any kind of commitment. The thought of becoming a husband and maybe a father scared him to death.

Lonnie wanted to believe that God would provide for his needs and help him through any situation, but being deaf limited him in so many ways. Sometimes the fear he felt was almost paralyzing. Other times, especially when he was with Jolene, he felt as if he could accomplish most anything. But did he trust his feelings enough that he could open his heart to her?

Pulling his thoughts aside, Lonnie picked up the hammer and a nail. He needed to get busy on the bird feeder or he'd never get it done.

"Yeow!" The hammer missed the nail and hit his thumb instead.

He grimaced and stuck his thumb between his teeth. *Guess that's what I get for thinking more about Jolene than what I'm doing.*

When the throbbing subsided, Lonnie went back to work. A short time later, Freeman showed up with his dog.

Penny leaped into Lonnie's lap, and he dropped his hammer. "Ouch!" It landed on his toe.

Freeman picked the dog up and said something, but Lonnie couldn't make out the words. Oh, how he wished he could hear.

Wayne came to his rescue, handing Freeman a tablet and pen.

Sorry my excitable mutt jumped on you, Freeman wrote. *She got nervous on the way over because she's scared of the wind. Sometimes she gets so scared that her whole body vibrates.*

"It's okay. No harm was done." Lonnie went back to work on the bird feeder, and Freeman moved over to Wayne's desk. A few minutes later, the dog jumped into Lonnie's lap again. This time she knocked the birdhouse to the floor, and a piece of the roof chipped off.

Lonnie groaned. At this rate, he'd never get Jolene's gift done in time for Christmas.

For the last week Jake had been planning to do some Christmas shopping, but between the horses he had to shoe and the horses he'd begun training recently, he hadn't made it to town. He was glad he'd taken Mom's suggestion and run an ad in the paper, because he'd already gotten some business from folks who needed their buggy horses trained. He'd also bought a few horses that he planned to train and then sell to folks who were in need of a good buggy horse. He enjoyed the training process a lot more than shoeing, but until Dad was working full-time again, Jake knew he'd have to keep shoeing horses.

Jake had just finished shoeing two of their bishop's buggy horses and had a few hours free until it was time to head for home, so he was on his way to Shipshewana to buy a few gifts. He wanted to get Mom a new set of dishes, as she'd mentioned the other day that her old ones had several chips. Buying presents for his younger siblings should be easy enough, since they were usually happy with most any toy. What to get Dad was the question. Whatever Jake decided on, he was sure Dad wouldn't like it. He never liked much of anything Jake said or did. Jake knew it wouldn't be right to leave Dad out, however, so he figured he'd better come up with something.

Jake parked his truck in front of the Red Barn and went inside to look around the various shops. He bought a couple of toys for his younger siblings then decided to head over to the furniture store outside of Shipshewana. Maybe he'd buy Dad a new reclining chair. The one he had now was falling apart, and Dad did like to put his feet up at night and recline while he read the newspaper. Jake hoped if he bought something Dad actually needed, it might improve his attitude toward him. It might make him realize that Jake could do a few things right.

Jake was about to get into his truck when Eunice Byler walked by. She smiled sweetly and said, "It's nice to see you, Jake. What brings you to Shipshe on such a cold, snowy day?"

"I might ask you the same question," he said.

"I've been delivering some of my candles and soaps to a few of the stores in the area. The ones I brought in before to sell on consignment have all sold." Her smile widened. "I think it must be because everyone's buying them for Christmas presents."

"Guess that makes sense." Jake started to walk away but changed his mind. He'd been wanting to confront Eunice about telling Mom that he planned to leave Indiana, and since there was no one around to hear their conversation, this was the perfect opportunity.

"I've been meaning to ask you something," Jake said.

"What's that?"

"I'm wondering why you told my mamm that I planned to leave Indiana soon."

"I never said that."

"Mom said you did. Said you told her that the last time you spoke with her."

Eunice's cheeks flushed a bright pink. "I. . .uh. . .did talk to her, but I didn't really say you'd be leaving soon. I just mentioned that I figured you might be leaving soon since your daed's legs have healed and he's back at work. Besides," she quickly added, "you did say you might be going back to Montana, remember?"

"That's true, but I only said 'might.' I think you jumped to conclusions. And about my daed—the doctor said he should wait until he's fully recovered to start shoeing horses again." Truth was, with the way Dad limped around, Jake wasn't sure he'd ever be able to shoe horses again. Jake didn't want to keep shoeing horses permanently. It would mean he'd have less time for training horses. Besides, Dad needed something to do. If he kept busy, he wouldn't have so much time to think of things he didn't like about Jake.

"I'm sorry to hear your daed's still not able to work. I didn't realize. . ." Eunice stopped talking, leaned closer to Jake, and touched his arm. "I hope what I said about you leaving didn't create a problem between you and your mamm."

Jake shrugged. "It's no big deal. I just told her I'd be sticking around—through the winter at least."

"Does that mean you might not go back to Montana?"

"It all depends."

"On what?"

Jake grimaced. Eunice was sure the nosy one. He'd never met a woman so full of questions—or so irritating. Except for Ella, that is. Nobody, other than Dad, could get under his skin the way Ella did. He still couldn't figure out what she had against him, and that bothered him nearly as much as his strained relationship with Dad. He'd tried to be nice and help Ella's family, but she didn't seem to appreciate it. If he could only do something to convince her that he wasn't as bad as she thought. *Maybe I should buy her a Christmas present. Maybe then she'd realize—*

"Did you hear what I said?" Eunice gave the sleeve of Jake's jacket a tug.

Jake's mind snapped back to the present. "Wh–what was that?"

"I was wondering if you're going to the Christmas program at the schoolhouse next week."

"Guess I'll have to, since some of my brothers and sisters have parts in it."

Eunice smiled. "I'll be there, too, because my brother Richard will be playing the part of Joseph." She shifted her purse to her other arm. "I'd better get into the store now and see how many bars of soap they need. It was nice seeing you, Jake."

"Same here," Jake said as he climbed into his truck.

❦

As Andrew stood beside his horse and buggy watching Eunice and Jake, disappointment flooded his soul. He'd thought Eunice was interested in him, but he guessed he'd been mistaken. From the way Eunice kept touching Jake's arm and leaning so close to him, Andrew was sure she must be interested in Jake. *He'll probably end up breaking her heart the way he did Loraine's. Maybe I should warn her.* Andrew shook his head. *No, she might not appreciate that, and I don't want her to know that I'm jealous. Guess the best thing for me to do is to wait and see what happens. If Eunice and Jake are seeing each other, there's probably nothing I can do about it.*

Andrew had been planning to buy Eunice something for Christmas, but after seeing her and Jake together, he decided against it. He didn't want her to think he was being pushy or trying to buy her love. No, the best thing for him to do was to stay clear of Eunice for a while and keep his focus on more important things. The only trouble was, he couldn't think of anything or anyone more important than Eunice.

Andrew's shoulders slumped as he crossed his arms over his chest. He felt totally defeated.

CHAPTER 34

I can't believe Christmas is only two days away," Jolene said to Andrew as she made his lunch on a Saturday morning toward the end of December.

"I know. I hope Mom's over the flu by then. None of us will enjoy the holiday if she's sick." He signed the words as he spoke.

Jolene was pleased that Andrew had caught on so quickly to signing. He was the only one in the family who had, although Mom and Dad were still trying. She would continue to teach them until they could sign well enough to communicate easily with her. Even Eunice was able to sign fairly well now. Jolene wondered what Andrew would think when he found out.

Andrew glanced out the kitchen window and groaned. "It's snowing again, and I'm sure the roads will be slippery. Sure wish I didn't have to go to work today."

Jolene nodded, feeling empathy for him. "Since it's Saturday, I won't have to teach, but I do have some work to do around here." She sighed. "I'll be glad when spring comes and we don't have to worry so much about the roads. At least not the kind of worry that winter weather causes."

"You know what Mom always says: 'In the winter our blood runs more slowly and we can let go of last year's worries.'" Andrew grinned at Jolene and signed, *"So I'm with you. Let's look forward to spring."*

"I certainly am. In the meantime, though, I need to get your lunch finished so you can be off to work."

"Is there anything I can do to help?"

"Guess you can get out whatever you want to drink."

"Sure, I can do that." Andrew went to the refrigerator and took out a bottle of apple juice, which he placed on the counter beside his lunch pail. "Can I ask you something, Jolene?"

"Of course."

"If someone's beginning to have strong feelings for someone, but they think that person has strong feelings for someone else, should they say anything?" Andrew hesitated and pursed his lips. "I mean should the person who has strong feelings for someone tell them and risk rejection, or would it be better if they kept it to themselves?"

Jolene tipped her head and stared at Andrew. "Would this 'someone' who has strong feelings for someone happen to be you?"

His face reddened, and he gave her a sheepish grin as he nodded.

"Is the other someone Eunice Byler?"

"Jah."

"Are you in love with her?"

"I haven't gone out with Eunice enough to know if what I'm feeling for her is love, but I do have strong feelings for her." Andrew frowned. "But I'm worried that she might have feelings for Jake."

"What makes you think that?"

"I've seen them together a few times. The other day I saw them with their heads real close, and Eunice was touching Jake's arm."

Jolene bit back a chuckle. The hound dog look on Andrew's face was humorous enough, but the thought that Jake might be interested in Eunice was ridiculous.

"Jake will be going back to Montana in the spring," Jolene said. "So I don't think he's much of a threat."

"How do you know he's going back?"

"Eunice told me, when she came for a. . ." Jolene stopped talking. She'd almost blurted out Eunice's secret.

"What were you going to say? You really don't think there's anything going on with them?"

"I. . .uh. . .think the only person Eunice is interested in is you."

Andrew shrugged. "Guess I'll have to wait and see how it goes."

She smiled. "I guess you will."

❧ ❧

Eunice watched the swirl of snow out the front window of her buggy and knew she'd better concentrate on the road. She didn't want to end up in the ditch like so many other buggies had during frigid weather like this.

I hope Andrew's working today, she thought. She'd been disappointed that she hadn't been able to speak to him at the school Christmas program last week. He'd left before she'd had the chance. She glanced at the small package on the seat beside her. She hoped he'd like the leather wallet she'd bought for him as a Christmas present. She also hoped he wouldn't think she was too forward by giving him a gift, but he had come to her place for supper a few times, and he'd brought her home from more than one young people's gathering. Still, that didn't mean he cared for her as much as she cared for him. Maybe it was only a strong attraction she felt for Andrew, but when she was with him, she found herself wanting to be a better person. . .someone he could trust. . .someone he might even come to love.

Eunice's buggy jerked to one side, halting her thoughts. She gripped the reins as the horse picked up speed, but despite her best efforts, her buggy slid off the road. "Easy, Dolly. Easy, girl," she clucked. "We'd better take it easy or we'll end up stuck in some ditch."

Eunice was relieved when she was able to guide the horse and buggy back onto the road. She knew she'd better stop thinking about Andrew and pay attention to the road.

A short time later, Eunice pulled her horse and buggy up to the hitching rail outside the harness shop in Topeka. Her excitement mounted, but when she entered the shop, her palms grew sweaty as nervous tension took over. Drawing in a deep breath to help steady her nerves, she moved toward the back of the shop. She found Andrew in front of his workbench, punching holes in a bulky leather strap. Not wishing to disturb his concentration, she stood off to one side.

When he finished the strap and reached for another one, he looked up. That's when he noticed her.

"Wie geht's, Eunice? What brings you out on such a cold, snowy morning?"

She moistened her lips with the tip of her tongue. "I've been delivering some soap and candle orders, and I stopped by to. . ."

"Maybe you should have asked your daed to make the deliveries. The roads are really nasty this morning, and a horse can be hard to handle on snow and ice."

"You sound like Jake. I heard him mention to my daed that. . ."

Andrew's face reddened. *"Duh mich net mit ihm vergleiche!"*

Eunice slapped one hand against her hip. "Don't get so testy, Andrew. I was not comparing you to Jake. I only meant that you and Jake. . ."

"I'd rather not talk about Jake."

"How come?"

"Because I think my cousin Ella's right about Jake. He can't be trusted." Andrew pulled another hunk of leather toward him.

Eunice had begun to realize, here of late, that she never listened carefully enough to what was being said, but she was sure Andrew had just said that Jake couldn't be trusted. What that had to do with Jake telling her dad that horses could be hard to control in the snow, she couldn't imagine.

"I didn't come over here to talk about Jake or start an argument with you, Andrew." Eunice hoped her voice sounded calmer than she felt right now.

"What did you come for?"

"To deliver your Christmas present," she signed.

Andrew set the hunk of leather aside and stared at her with a blank expression. He must not have understood what she'd signed. She'd probably messed it up, but good.

His blank expression faded, and his face broke into a wide smile. "When'd you learn how to sign?"

"Did—did you understand what I said to you?"

"Sure did. You said you came to deliver my Christmas present."

Eunice felt the tension in her shoulders and neck dissipate. "That's what I said, all right."

Andrew's mouth hung slightly open as he continued to stare at her. "But how? I mean, you said you were too busy to take signing lessons."

"I have been busy, but I used it as an excuse not to take lessons with you and your family."

"How come?"

Eunice's face heated as she dropped her gaze to the floor. "Because I thought it would be hard to learn, and I. . .I didn't want to make a fool of myself in front of you."

"You thought if you couldn't learn signing I'd think you were foolish?"

She lifted her gaze and nodded. "I was never very bright in school, and there are so many things I can't do well. I've felt like a failure most of my life, and I didn't want you to be disappointed in me, too."

"If you were trying to learn to sign, I sure wouldn't have been disappointed." Andrew moved away from his workbench and took a step toward Eunice. "How did you learn, anyway?"

Eunice explained how she'd been secretly taking lessons from Jolene at the schoolhouse on the days Jolene wasn't teaching Lonnie or Ella. She ended by saying, "I wanted it to be a surprise."

"It's a surprise, all right. A very pleasant surprise."

She smiled. "I don't know how to sign a lot yet, but I plan to keep learning from Jolene and practicing at home. Hopefully I'll get better with time, but it may take me longer than most because I'm not very good at catching on to new things. As I said, I've always felt like a failure, and—"

Andrew held up his hand. "I've never considered you to be a failure, and you're not dumb, either. You created a good business for yourself, and that had to have taken some doing. Not only that, but you're a real good cook." He moved a bit closer. "I've enjoyed myself whenever you've had me over for supper."

"Really?"

"Said so, didn't I?"

She smiled and handed him the gift she had tucked under one arm. "I hope you like what I got you."

Andrew gave his left earlobe a quick tug and made a funny little grunting sound. "Uh. . .how come you bought me something for Christmas?"

"I bought you a gift because you're my friend, and I—"

"Did you buy Jake something for Christmas, too?"

"What? No! Besides what I got for my family, you're the only one I've bought a gift for."

He scratched the side of his head. "But I thought you and Jake. . ."

"What did you think about me and Jake?"

"I thought you liked him and that the two of you might be going out."

"What in the world gave you that idea?"

"I've seen you talking to him a few times, and the other day in Shipshe, I saw the two of you standing real close." Andrew leaned on his workbench, as though he needed it for support. "For a minute there, I was afraid Jake was gonna kiss you."

Eunice almost laughed out loud as she shook her head. "The only man I care about is you, Andrew Yoder."

"Really?"

"Really."

Andrew stepped close to her side, so that his left arm was brushing her right arm.

She trembled from the wave of warmth she felt whenever he was near.

He glanced around, as though worried they might be seen, but there was no one else in the room. Then slowly, he lowered his head until his mouth was almost against her ear. "I've come to care for you, Eunice, and I hope you'll consider what I'm about to say."

"Wh–what's that?" she asked breathlessly.

"I'd like you to be my steady girlfriend and go out only with me, but there's one little problem."

"What problem?"

Andrew raked his fingers through the back of his hair.

Confusion, mingled with fear, converged on Eunice. "Andrew, what's the matter? What problem is there between us?"

He cleared his throat a couple of times. "It's a problem with your mouth."

Instinctively, she reached up and touched her mouth. "You—you don't like my mouth?"

Andrew took a step back. "Actually, it's not your mouth I have the problem with, it's what comes out of your mouth, in the form of gossip."

She moaned. "Oh, that."

"The Bible says in Proverbs 11:13 that a talebearer reveals secrets. And in Proverbs 10:19 we're told that 'in the multitude of words there wanteth not sin: but he that refraineth his lips is wise.'"

"Jah, Andrew, I know that. I read those same passages in the Biwel the other night, and it made me realize that I have a weakness. But God spoke to my heart." Tears welled in Eunice's eyes. "And with His help I'll try to do better because I know that gossiping is wrong."

He nodded. "It can hurt others when we talk about them."

"You're right, and I don't do it to be mean. Sometimes I'm just not listening close enough to what's being said and I get mixed up about things." She grimaced. "Of course, I guess the best thing is for me not to repeat what I've heard."

Andrew nodded and looked like he was going to reach for her hand, but just then, the door of the harness shop opened and an English man stepped in with a saddle.

"I'd better go," Eunice said. "I'll see you at church tomorrow, Andrew."

"I'll look forward to that." He lifted the gift she'd given him. "Danki for this. I'll bring you a gift on Christmas morning."

Feeling as though she were floating on a cloud, Eunice stepped out the door. When she was a safe distance from the shop, she laughed and spun around in the cascade of heavy snowflakes falling from the sky. They clumped her lashes together and melted on her nose and lips. She licked them and giggled. Her starched head covering absorbed the heavy wetness of the snow, but she didn't care. Andrew cared for her and wanted her to be his steady girlfriend, and he didn't think she was stupid.

Eunice lifted her gaze to the sky. *Please help me, Lord. Help me to remember to bridle my tongue.*

❧ ❦

As Lonnie trudged up the road toward Jolene's house, he shivered. The long walk through the snow had dampened his back with sweat, and a chill had set in. His horse had thrown a shoe last night, so he'd decided it would be best not to make him pull the buggy until Jake could put on new shoes. Besides, a walk in the brisk air wouldn't hurt him any. It would give him time to think about some of the things that had been weighing heavily on his mind.

In an effort to keep his thoughts off the cold, Lonnie quickened his steps and focused on the scenery and peacefulness of this silent winter day. He recalled that days like this were often silent, even to those who could hear. Every branch and twig was covered under a thick blanket of white. Ice crystals clung to the fence posts surrounding some of the farms he passed. He was tempted to stop and pull one off the way he had as a boy, but he figured he needed to keep going.

Lonnie glanced across the road, where two German shepherd pups frolicked in the snow. Winter was a beautiful time of the year. He just wished it wasn't so cold.

By the time Lonnie reached Jolene's house, he was sweating profusely and had begun to shiver. He was both excited and apprehensive about giving her the gift he'd made. He didn't know exactly when it had happened, but sometime during these last few months, he'd come to care deeply for Jolene. That scared him—a lot. He wasn't sure if she cared for him, and even if she did, he knew they had no future together. Maybe he'd made a mistake in making her a gift. Maybe he should turn around and head for home.

I'm here now, so guess I may as well give her the gift, Lonnie decided. Besides, it would feel good to get out of the cold for a few minutes. With a sense of determination he didn't really feel, he tucked the package for her under one arm and rapped on the door.

A few seconds later, Jolene's mother, Leah, answered his knock. "Guder mariye," he signed as he spoke the words. "Is Jolene at home?"

"She's in the kitchen," Leah signed in reply. Lonnie felt good about being able to communicate with her this way.

He brushed the snow off his jacket and followed as Leah led the way to the kitchen. He was relieved when she left the room and padded down the hall. It would be easier if he spoke to Jolene alone.

He found Jolene sitting at the table, reading her Bible. When he touched her shoulder, she looked up and offered him a friendly smile. "Good morning. You look really wet," she said, signing and speaking at the same time. "Is it snowing again?"

"Not at the moment. I walked over, so I've been sweating."

She motioned to the stove. "You should stand over there and get warm."

He set the gift on the table and moved across the room, enjoying the heat radiating from the stove. *"The gift is for you,"* he signed.

Her eyes lit up. *"Do I have to wait until Christmas to open it?"* she asked, signing the question.

He shook his head. "It's not really a Christmas present. It's just something I made to say thanks for teaching me total communication."

"I've been glad to do it, so no thanks is—"

"What was that?" Lonnie hadn't understood all the words she'd said.

"I appreciate the gesture." Jolene picked up the gift and tore the wrapping from it. When she removed the bird feeder, she smiled. *"This is nice. I'll enjoy using it to feed the birds the rest of this winter."*

Lonnie was on the verge of saying something else when Jake stepped into the room. He grinned at Jolene and handed her a gift.

"What's this for?" she asked, tipping her head.

"It's a Christmas present, and it's my way of saying thanks for teaching me to sign. You can open it now if you like."

Jolene tore the wrapping aside and withdrew a box full of scented candles in various sizes. There was also a beautiful leather journal inside.

Jolene sniffed the candles and smiled at Jake. "Thank you. That was very thoughtful of you."

"I bought the candles from Eunice. Figured you might like the journal to write down your thoughts about teaching."

"I appreciate them both."

Lonnie cringed. He'd been able to read their lips, and even if he hadn't, it didn't take a genius to see how much Jolene liked Jake's gift. The homemade bird feeder Lonnie had given her didn't look nearly as good as Jake's store-bought gift. He was sure she liked Jake's gift better.

"I should be going," Lonnie said, and he moved quickly toward the door.

Jolene touched his arm and he turned around. *"I offered Jake a cup of coffee. Would you like one, too?"*

"I'd better go." Lonnie hurried out the door. Keeping the way he felt about Jolene to himself was a difficult task. Seeing the way she'd looked at Jake was unbearable.

�֍ ֍

Exhausted after arising early to get her baking done, Ella took a seat by the fireplace in the living room and draped one of Mama's old quilts around her. Hopefully she'd have a few minutes of quiet to herself before it was time to open the bakeshop.

She pulled the quilt tighter around her shoulders and moved her chair closer to the fire. Flames leaped from the glowing embers, sending a wave of warmth into the room.

Ella leaned her head against the back of the chair and closed her eyes. Christmas was only a few days away, and there was still so much to do.

Tears burned the backs of Ella's eyes as she reflected on last Christmas. *Oh, Papa, I still miss you so much. This will be our first Christmas without you.*

She mentally shook herself. *I can't let the pain of losing Papa ruin our Christmas. I need to put on a happy face for the rest of the family.*

Ella rose from her chair and headed for the kitchen, where she removed the tea kettle from the stove. She'd just poured herself a cup of tea, when she heard the whinny of a horse. She glanced out the window and saw a horse and buggy parked in the yard. Figuring it must be an early customer, she hurried to the back door. As soon as she opened it, a swirl of cold air entered the house. She was surprised to see Jake plodding through the snow toward the bakeshop.

"I'm not open yet!" she hollered.

Jake turned and tromped up to the house. "Thought I'd see if you were there before I came here," he said, stepping onto the porch.

"You just visited my bakeshop two days ago, so please, don't tell me you need more bread," Ella said.

Jake shook his head. "Came to bring you this." He withdrew an envelope from his pocket and held it out to her.

"What is it?"

"Something I thought you might need during the holidays. Call it an early Christmas present." He handed her the envelope. "Go ahead, open it."

Feeling a bit awkward because she had no gift for him, Ella opened the envelope and gasped. There was five hundred dollars inside! Irritation welled in her soul. "What's all this money for, Jake?"

"I thought you could use it to buy your family some gifts."

She dropped the money into the envelope and handed it back to him. "I don't need your money. I've already bought gifts for my family."

"I just thought. . ." Jake stopped talking and dropped his gaze to the porch.

Ella could see the hurt look on his face. She squeezed her eyes shut, knowing she should take back her unkind words but was somehow unable to do so. She was tired of Jake coming over here all the time, buying baked goods she was sure he didn't need and volunteering to do chores she didn't want him to do. Now he wanted to give her money again! Why did dealing with Jake have to be such a challenge? This had to stop!

She opened her mouth to spew angry words, but before she could say anything, Jake dropped the envelope to the little table near the door, turned, and sloshed his way through the snow to his buggy.

Ella's legs trembled as she stepped into the house. Then she dashed into the living room, flopped onto the sofa, and gave in to her threatening tears.

CHAPTER 35

*W*ould you please pass the potatoes?" Jolene's mother signed. She then pointed to the bowl of potatoes sitting in front of Jolene.

Jolene smiled and handed the potatoes to Andrew, who sat beside her, and then he passed them to Mom. It was good to see Mom doing more signing. She was getting so much better at it, too.

Dad looked over at Jolene and signed, *"It's real good to have you back with us."*

Andrew nodded. *"We've missed not having you here for Christmas the last couple of years."*

"I've missed being here, and I'm glad to be home," Jolene said as she signed.

"Do you enjoy teaching Sylvia and Irvin?" one of Jolene's married sisters, Barbara, who was visiting from Wisconsin, asked.

"I sure do."

"I heard you got some nice gifts from your two older students." Barbara grinned and nudged Jolene's arm. "It appears that you might have two men interested in you."

Jolene shook her head. "Lonnie and Jake are just my friends." *Although I wish Lonnie could be more than that,* she mentally added.

Jolene's other married sister, Anna Rose, needled Jolene in the ribs. "Friends who like to give you Christmas presents. I wouldn't be surprised if you don't end up marrying one of them."

"That's not going to happen," Jolene said with a shake of her head.

803

"How do you know?" Dad asked.

"Because I'm quite sure that Jake will be leaving for Montana in the spring."

Mom pursed her lips. "That's too bad. I'm sure Jake's folks will be very disappointed when he goes."

"I'm sure they will." Jolene forked a piece of ham onto her plate. "Even if Jake should decide to stay in Indiana, I'd still have no interest in him—at least not in a romantic sort of way."

"What about Lonnie?" Anna Rose asked. "From what you've said about him in your letters, I think he'd make a good husband."

"Lonnie told me once that he has no plans to marry," Jolene said around a mouthful of mashed potatoes.

"How come?"

"He was deeply hurt when his girlfriend broke up with him. Besides, he thinks his deafness would hamper him from being a good husband and father." Jolene blotted her lips with a napkin. "I can relate to that kind of thinking because I'm not sure I'd make a good mother, either."

"That's *lecherich*," Andrew said. "A lot of deaf people get married."

Figuring they needed a new topic of conversation, Jolene quickly changed the subject. "Are you planning to go over to see Eunice today?" she asked Andrew.

Andrew's face turned crimson. "Uh-huh. Thought I might head over there after we've finished our dinner."

"Is Eunice your *aldi*?" Anna Rose asked.

Andrew ate a piece of ham then washed it down with a drink of water. "I believe she *is* my girlfriend."

"Are you sure getting involved with Eunice is a good idea?" Mom asked with a look of concern. "She has been known to spread quite a bit of gossip."

"Eunice is trying to change," Andrew said. "She has a lot of good qualities others don't see, and she told me the other day that she knows it's wrong to gossip, and I believe she's mending her ways."

"If Andrew's interested in Eunice, then I think we should give her a chance," Jolene put in.

Mom reached over and patted Andrew's hand. "We'll support your decision to court whomever you want."

"I appreciate that." He looked over at Jolene and smiled. "You did good at keeping Eunice's secret. She surprised me when she came by the harness shop the other day and signed a few words."

Jolene grinned back at him. "I'm pleased with her progress."

They continued to visit as they ate their meal, and when everyone was finished, all heads bowed for a second silent prayer.

Heavenly Father, Jolene prayed, *Thank You for the opportunity for us all to be together this Christmas. Thank You for my teaching job and for my students. Please guide and direct each of us in the days ahead.*

❧ ❧

"I have presents for all of you," Jake said to his family after they'd eaten their Christmas dinner. "I'll get the ones that are in my room, but I'll need help with the one I have for Dad that's hidden in the barn."

Dad's eyebrows shot up. "You hid something there without me knowing it?"

"Uh-huh, that was the purpose—to keep you from knowing about it. It's behind a stack of hay in one of the empty stalls." Jake smiled, feeling in a cheerful mood. "I'll get the gifts that are in my room first, though." He hurried out of the dining room and returned a few minutes later with a sack full of presents.

Dad sat stony-faced as Jake handed out the gifts, but everyone else seemed happy enough.

"This is great!" Kyle said after he'd opened the fishing pole Jake had given him. "Maybe you and me can do some fishin' when spring comes around."

Deciding it might be best not to discuss his plans for the spring, Jake thumped his brother's arm. "We'll have to see how it goes."

Next, Jake gave his teenage sister, Marilyn, a gift. Her face fairly glowed when she opened a box full of rubber stamps. "Danki, Jake."

He smiled. "I thought you might enjoy them since I know you like to keep all the postcards and letters you received from friends in your scrapbook."

"What'd ya get for me, Jake?" his younger brother Vern asked with an expectant look.

Jake handed the boy a box. "See if you like this."

Vern tore the wrapping aside and lifted the lid on the box. When he reached inside and pulled out a baseball bat and a glove, his eyes lit up. "Danki, Jake! This is just what I've been wantin'!"

Jake looked over at Elmer then. "Your gift's out on the porch."

Elmer jumped up and raced out the door. A few minutes later he returned, pushing a shiny new bike into the room. "Danki, Jake. I really needed a new bike!"

Dad, who'd sat quietly as the children opened their gifts, grunted and frowned at Jake. "Looks to me like you spent a lot of money on those presents."

"From the way my sister and brothers are grinning, I'd say it was money well spent." Jake placed a large box on the table in front of his mother. "Now it's your turn, Mom. I hope you like what's inside."

Mom fumbled with the box, and when she saw finally got it open, a wide smile stretched across her face. "A new set of dishes is exactly what I need. Danki, Jake."

"You're welcome." Jake looked over at Kyle and Elmer. "You two look like you're pretty strong today. How'd you like to help me bring in Dad's gift?"

The boys nodded agreeably and raced to get their jackets, as did Jake. "We'll be back soon," Jake called over his shoulder as they hurried to the door. "Meet us in the living room!"

When Jake and his brothers returned to the house with a large box, he found the rest of his family seated on chairs in the living room.

Dad, who'd taken a seat in his old easy chair, looked up at Jake and said, "What in the world's in that big box?"

"It's your Christmas present." Jake took out his pocket knife and cut the sides of the box open, revealing a beautiful new recliner, upholstered in blue. He stood off to one side, awaiting Dad's response.

"Now why'd you waste your money on something I don't even need when we've got bills that have to be paid?" Dad mumbled.

Jake opened his mouth to reply, but Dad cut him off when he thumped the arm of his old chair and said, "There's nothin' wrong with this old chair. I sure don't need a new one."

"Now, Joe," Mom was quick to say, "Jake must have wanted you to have a new chair, so I think—"

"I don't care what you think," Dad bellowed. "I'm gettin' tired of you always takin' Jake's side!" Before Mom could say anything in her own defense, Dad turned to Jake with a scowl. "As far as I'm concerned, you buying this expensive chair is just your way of showing off."

Jake's mouth dropped open like a broken window hinge. "How is me buying you a nice Christmas present showing off?"

"You're trying to remind us of how much money you made workin' in Montana." Dad snorted. "If you want to throw your money around why don't you buy something sensible like a horse and buggy?"

"I have a horse and buggy," Jake retorted.

"Jah, well, when you left Indiana the first time I laid claim to that horse and buggy. I've just been lettin' you borrow it since you came home."

White-hot anger surged in Jake's soul. He wished he'd never bought Dad the new chair! He shouldn't have bought him anything at all! He wondered why he'd bothered to come home and help out. Dad didn't appreciate it; that was for sure.

"You gonna try out that chair, Dad?" Kyle asked.

Dad shook his head and grunted. "Nope."

"So what do you want me to do?" Jake asked, his irritation mounting. "Am I supposed to take the chair back to the furniture store?"

"The chair's here's now," Mom was quick to say. "If your stubborn daed won't sit in it then I sure will." She flopped into the chair and reclined it back as far as it would go. "Now this is a very comfortable chair, and it looks much nicer than our old one does."

"I like it, too," Kyle spoke up.

"Nobody asked you, boy!" Dad's eyes narrowed as he glared at Kyle. "So just keep your opinions to yourself."

Mom looked at Dad and shook her head. "You don't have to be so harsh. Jake bought you a nice gift for Christmas, and you should appreciate it."

Dad rose from his chair with an undignified grunt and limped across the room.

"Where are you going?" Mom called to his retreating form.

"Out to the barn, where I won't have to look at that expensive chair!"

When the door slammed shut behind Dad, Jake sank to the sofa. He felt like a heel. "I'm sorry for ruining everyone's Christmas," he mumbled.

Mom shook her head. "It's not your fault, Jake. You were only trying to make everyone happy by buying those gifts. Your daed... well, he's just so frustrated right now that he can't accept anything from you."

"Frustrated because I won't do everything he says, you mean?"

She shrugged.

"Dad will cool down soon; you'll see," Kyle said, touching Jake's arm. "I'll bet in a few days he'll be sittin' in that new chair with a big ol' smile on his face."

Jake wasn't so sure about that, but he didn't voice his thoughts. Instead, he turned in his chair and stared into the glowing fireplace embers.

After a few minutes, he closed his eyes and tried to relax, but suddenly, Ella came to mind. He thought about the encounter he'd had with her the other day. She hadn't been any happier about the money he'd given her than Dad had been with his new chair. Jake had to wonder if she would keep the money he'd left there or if she'd end up throwing it in his face.

He grimaced and opened his eyes. *Guess I probably ruined Ella's Christmas, too.*

⊰ ⊱

It had been difficult for Ella to look happy when she'd gotten up Christmas morning, but for the benefit of her family, she knew she had to. While she was sure that her younger siblings still missed Papa, they were full of excitement. Everyone had seemed pleased with the small gifts she'd given them, and although Mama's face looked strained, she'd put up a brave front.

As they sat at the table, eating their Christmas dinner, all the earlier chatting had ceased, and everyone seemed intent on finishing their meal.

"What's for dessert?" Larry asked after he'd cleaned his plate.

"I made apple and pumpkin pies," Ella said. "They're in the kitchen."

Larry licked his lips. "Umm. Think I'll have some of both."

"None for me," Mama said with a shake of her head. "My blood sugar was higher than it should have been when I tested it this morning, and I don't want to send it any higher by eating a piece of sugary pie."

"I made one sugar-free pie, just for you." Ella reached over and patted her mother's hand.

"That was considerate of you, but I think I'll wait awhile to have dessert." Mama sighed. "I hope you get more bakery business soon, because with the cost of my diabetes medicine, I'm worried that we won't have enough money to pay for that as well as all the other things we need."

Ella forced a smile. "We'll get by somehow, Mama. We just need to hang on until spring, and then I'm sure things will pick up."

"I hope so."

Ella pushed her chair away from the table and stood. "Guess I'll go get those pies now."

"Want me to help?" Charlene called as Ella started across the room.

"Thanks anyway, but I can manage."

809

When Ella stepped into the kitchen, lit only by the propane light above the table, she headed over to the counter where she'd set the pies. She was about to pick up one of the pumpkin pies when she spotted an envelope on one end of the counter.

She grimaced. The money Jake had given her the other day was inside that envelope. In her haste to get everything done before Christmas, she'd forgotten that she'd laid the envelope there after he'd left it on the porch. She planned to take it back to him one day this week.

Ella removed the money from the envelope and stared at it a few seconds. *We really could use this right now. What's more important: preserving my pride or seeing that my family's needs are met?* With Mama in need of regular medication, the answer came through to Ella rather quickly. She would take the money into Mama and tell her it was a gift from Jake. Then, when she saw the look of gratitude and relief on Mama's face, she'd remember to be thankful.

CHAPTER 36

When spring arrived, the snow left in a rush, and the air was soon scented with budding flowers and trees. Ella's bakery business had picked up a bit, and for that she was thankful. Mama had been managing her diabetes better, too, which meant she was able to help out more. Charlene, though still busy helping Mama with household chores, had more time to spend in the bakeshop with Ella.

When Ella stepped outside one Monday morning in the middle of March, the shrill cry of a crow drew her attention upward. Soon the birds would be building nests, and babies would be born not long after that.

Ella smiled. Katie and Freeman would be getting married in a few weeks, and Loraine was due to have her baby soon.

She shook the dust mop she held and sighed. *I wonder if I'll ever have the privilege of becoming a mother. Probably not, since I don't have a boyfriend. No, there's not much prospect of marriage for me.*

She glanced up the driveway, where Larry, Amelia, and Helen were heading to school. *Guess I'll have to be content helping Mama raise my little brother and sisters.*

She squeezed her eyes tightly shut. *I hope Mama never marries again. I don't think I could bear it if some other man moved in here and tried to take Papa's place.*

"Are you sleeping or just holding that dust mop in your hand?"

At the sound of Charlene's voice, Ella whirled around. "I was just thinking, that's all."

"Thinking about some fellow, I'll bet."

"Of course not." Ella gave the dust mop a couple of good shakes. "There is no fellow in my life."

"What about Jake?"

"What about him?"

"He comes around here often enough. I figured the two of you might be going steady by now."

Ella swatted her sister's arm. "You're such a kidder."

Charlene shook her head. "I'm not kidding. I've seen the way Jake stares at you when he thinks you're not looking."

"More than likely Jake's glaring, not staring at me. As I'm sure you've noticed, Jake and I don't see eye to eye on much of anything." Ella turned toward the door. "We need to finish cleaning up the kitchen before it's time to go out to the bakeshop. Are you coming?"

"Work. . .work. . .work. That's all we ever do," Charlene mumbled as they stepped into the house. "Why don't we close the bakeshop for a few hours this afternoon and go over to Katie's stamp shop? We could buy a few stamps and make some cards or do some scrapbooking this evening."

"We don't have extra money to buy stamps right now. Even if we did, I don't have time to make cards." Ella motioned to the bakeshop. "In case you've forgotten, we have a lot of baking that needs to be done today."

Charlene groaned and leaned against the kitchen counter.

Feeling a little guilty for making her sister work so hard, Ella said, "If you'd like to visit the stamp shop this afternoon, go right ahead, but you'll have to go alone."

Charlene's brows puckered, and she shook her head. "If you're not going to the stamp shop, then neither am I."

❧ ❧

Jake stuck his pitchfork into a pile of manure and quickly mounted the cart in front of the spreader. Giving his horse the signal to go, he guided the rig down the lane toward the field. He'd promised Dad he'd help him get the field ready for planting corn, and they needed to get it done quickly because the shadowy sky overhead signaled that rain might be forthcoming.

Unexpectedly, Jake's thoughts went to Ella. He hadn't seen her since their last church service nearly two weeks ago. He'd decided to quit going over to her place to offer his help so often, since he knew it wasn't appreciated. Despite the desire he had to help Ella's family, he was trying hard to stay away, knowing he couldn't let himself get involved with her.

"Not that she'd ever let me be involved," Jake mumbled. He smacked the side of his head. "Why would I want to be involved with someone who clearly can't stand me, and why do I think about Ella so much? All we ever do is argue and get on each other's nerves."

Jake remembered when he and Ella were children that he'd seen a different side of her—a softer, pleasanter side. She'd been cute and spunky back then, and still was, really. Ella hadn't been so defensive and edgy when she was a girl, and even though he'd never told anyone, for a while he'd had a bit of a crush on her. He'd even carried her books a few times as they'd walked to school. Ella had been full of smiles and acted like she was his friend.

I wonder what happened to change her attitude toward me. Was it because I took off for Montana to work on the horse ranch and left her cousin in the lurch? Should I bring that up and see what her reaction is, or would it be better to leave it alone?

Jake grew more confused about his feelings for Ella all the time. Something about her fascinated him. Maybe it was her spunky spirit, or it could be her pretty, reddish blond hair and pale blue eyes.

He shook his head. *No, I just think I'm attracted to her because she's a challenge. She's like a wild, untamed horse that needs to be broken.* Not that he wanted to break Ella's spirit. He just wished he could get her to lower her defenses.

Determinedly, Jake pushed Ella to the back of his mind. He needed to think about something else.

His thoughts went to Kyle, who had asked Jake if the two of them could go fishing after school. Knowing he needed to give Kyle more of his attention, Jake had agreed. As soon as Kyle got home from school, if it wasn't raining, they'd head out.

❧ ❦

"Sure can't wait to show Larry the fish we caught in his pond," Kyle said as he and Jake walked across the field behind the Yoders' place that afternoon.

"You should have invited Larry to fish with us; then you wouldn't have had to compete with me." Jake thumped his brother lightly on the head. "I did catch the biggest fish, after all."

Kyle snorted. "That's only 'cause you got lucky when that big old fish snagged your line."

Jake chuckled. "What can I say? He must have liked my bait."

When Jake and Kyle entered the Yoders' yard, he spotted Ella taking clothes down from the line. Before he had the chance to say anything, Kyle bounded up to her and announced, "Guess what? My bruder caught the biggest fish I've ever seen, and he took it outa your pond!"

Ella quirked an eyebrow. "Is that so?"

Kyle bobbed his head and grinned. "Show it to her, Jake. Show Ella that big old fish you caught!"

Jake reached into the plastic sack he'd brought along and withdrew the fish. "What do you think?"

Ella gasped, and her cheeks flushed a deep crimson. "Th–that fish was never meant to be caught!"

Jake's forehead wrinkled as he stared at the fish. "What do you mean?"

"It's a plecostomus. My daed put it there last spring to keep the pond clean."

"What's a pleco—whatever you called it?" Kyle asked.

"It eats algae and can grow up to two feet long." Ella motioned to the fish. "It's also known as a suckermouth catfish."

Jake groaned. He felt like a dunce. "I thought I'd caught a

plain old catfish. If I'd had any idea it was a suckermouth, I'd have thrown it right back."

"You should have asked before you decided to fish in our pond."

"Guess maybe I should have, but I've seen other people fish there, so I figured you wouldn't care."

She dropped the towel she held into the clothes basket and slapped her hand against her hip. "Well, you figured wrong!"

Kyle, who stood at Jake's side with a worried expression, gave Jake's shirtsleeve a tug. "I think we oughta go, don't you?"

Jake didn't want to go. He wanted to make Ella see that she was making too much out of him fishing without her permission. And she ought to realize that he hadn't caught the suckermouth on purpose.

Kyle gave Jake's shirtsleeve another tug. "Are we goin' or not?"

"In a minute." Jake moved closer to Ella. "How much did you pay for the plecostomus? I'll pay you whatever it's worth."

"I have no idea what Papa paid for the fish. Even if I did, I don't want your money."

"How come?" Kyle asked before Jake could respond.

"Because your bruder has given us enough already." Ella bent down, lifted the clothes basket into her arms, and stomped off toward the house.

"Guess you're in big trouble with Ella, huh, Jake?" Kyle asked.

Jake nodded. "Jah, but then that's nothin' new."

❧ ❧

By the time Ella entered the house, she'd worked herself up so much that she could barely breathe. Jake had a lot of nerve fishing in their pond without asking! As much time as he'd spent fishing over the years, he ought to know the difference between a regular catfish and a suckermouth!

"What's that long face all about?" Mama asked when Ella entered the kitchen and placed the basket of clothes on the table.

Ella told Mama how Jake had caught the plecostomus and mentioned how angry she'd been when he'd told her about it.

"It doesn't sound to me as if Jake caught the fish on purpose, and I don't think you should have made such an issue of it." Mama shook her head. "I'm not sure how much good that fish did for the pond anyway. The last time I looked, there was quite a bit of algae in it."

Ella frowned. "Well, it was a waste of a perfectly good fish. I don't think it's edible, so Jake's getting just what he deserves. . .a worthless suckerfish!"

Mama blew out her breath and rolled her eyes, looking thoroughly disgusted. "I don't know what's happened to my carefree girl, but ever since your daed died, you've been negative and edgy." She shook her finger at Ella, the way she'd done when Ella was a girl. "Jake's been nothing but helpful to us. I think you ought to apologize for getting so upset about the fish."

"Me, apologize to him? Oh, Mama, you don't know how many irritating things Jake's said to me since he came back from Montana. He's never said he was sorry, either. Not even once."

"Jake might not be aware that he's said or done things that have irritated you."

"I'm sure he's aware of it, all right. I think he does certain things just to irritate me."

"Whether that's true or not, the Bible tells us in Matthew 7:12 that we are to do to others as we would have done to us." Mama motioned to the Bible she'd left on the table after they'd had their devotions that morning. "Matthew 6:14 reminds us that if we don't forgive others, our Father will not forgive us."

Ella nodded slowly. "I know that Mama, but with Jake. . ."

Mama held up her hand. "In God's eyes, Jake's no different than anyone else. It's God's will that you forgive him."

Ella's face heated with shame. She knew Mama was right. She also knew she was being petty and overly sensitive about the plecostomus. "I'll apologize to Jake the next time I see him," she said.

～≈～

Jake dropped his brother off at home, and then he got his horse and buggy and headed over to Crist's taxidermy shop with the fish. He figured since he'd caught the dumb thing and couldn't eat it, he may as well have it stuffed.

When Jake stepped into the taxidermy shop, he was surprised to see Wayne working there instead of Crist.

"Where's your daed, and how come you're here and not in your woodshop?" Jake asked as he stepped up to Wayne.

"Pop took Mom to see the chiropractor. Her back kinked up last night when she was getting ready for bed." Wayne motioned to the deer hide on the workbench in front of him. "So I told Pop I'd work here while he's gone, and I put Lonnie in charge of my shop."

"Oh, I see." Jake removed the plecostomus from the plastic bag and told Wayne how he'd accidentally caught it, including the part about how mad Ella had become when he'd told her about it.

"You know Ella," Wayne said as he rubbed the side of his nose. "She's always gotten upset easily. It's just in her nature."

"Tell me about it. But I think she gets more upset with me than anyone else." Jake pointed to the fish. "So can I leave this with you to have it stuffed? Thought it'd make a nice little trophy to hang on the wall."

Wayne shrugged. "Suit yourself."

Jake leaned against one end of the workbench, and after they'd visited about a few others things, he picked up a stuffed squirrel sitting on the shelf behind him and tossed it into the air like it was a baseball.

Wayne snickered and shook his head. "Are you ever gonna grow up and quit fooling around?"

"Beats me."

"You'll never find a woman if you keep acting like a *bensel*."

Jake frowned. "I'm not a silly child, and I'm not lookin' for a woman, so I should be able to act any way I want."

Wayne lifted his gaze to the ceiling. "I think we'd better change the subject."

"Good idea." Jake placed the squirrel back on the shelf. "What's new with you these days?"

WANDA E. BRUNSTETTER

"Not a whole lot. Loraine and I are just waiting patiently for the boppli to make its appearance." Wayne pulled his fingers through the ends of his beard. "Speaking of babies, Tripod, that pet ewe of mine with only three legs, gave birth to twin lambs this morning. Would you like to go out to the barn and take a look?"

Jake nodded, but before they could make a move to leave the shop, Loraine rushed into the room with a worried expression. "I've been in labor for the last few hours." She touched her bulging stomach. "I think it's time to go to the New Eden Care Center, because I'll soon have this boppli."

CHAPTER 37

When Lonnie pedaled his bike up the driveway leading to the schoolhouse, he noticed some of the scholars were taking advantage of the nice weather to play an after-school baseball game. What took him by surprise was seeing Jolene standing near second base. Had she forgotten about their lesson, or had she just gotten caught up in the game?

Lonnie had kept an emotional distance from Jolene ever since he'd given her the bird feeder for Christmas. He'd been on the verge of asking her out that day, but after Jake had shown up with his gift for Jolene and Lonnie had seen her response to it, he'd chickened out and changed his mind. It was probably better that way, since he really had nothing to offer her.

Lonnie moved closer to the baseball field and watched as Kyle Beechy stepped up to home plate, wearing a determined look on his face.

Fifteen-year-old Daniel Stoltzfus was the pitcher, and he threw the ball right over the plate.

Kyle swung the bat hard but missed. He gritted his teeth and took his stance again.

Daniel took aim and threw the ball once more. This time Kyle hit the ball with such force that it sailed over the pitcher's head and landed clear out in center field. Several boys scrambled for the ball, but by the time James Smucker had picked it up, Kyle was halfway around the bases. Unless someone acted fast, he was sure to make a home run.

James quickly threw the ball toward second base. Jolene, however, wasn't looking his way and didn't see the ball coming.

Lonnie cupped his hands around his mouth and hollered, "Look out, Jolene!"

Of course, she couldn't hear him, and he was too far away for her to read his lips.

The ball smacked Jolene's knee with such force that she crumpled to the ground.

Lonnie raced onto the field and dropped down beside her. *"Hold still. Your leg might be broken,"* he signed.

"I'm sure it's not broken; I think it's just bruised." Jolene grasped Lonnie's arm and slowly rose to her feet.

Everyone clambered around. Lonnie felt frustrated because they all seemed to be talking at once, and he couldn't make out what anyone was saying.

Finally, Jolene held up her hand to quiet them. Then with a brave smile she said, "I'm fine. Lonnie will help me into the schoolhouse. Go on with your game."

As Lonnie walked beside Jolene, letting her lean on his arm, he thought this was just another example of why he could never consider asking her to marry him. It would be difficult enough for a deaf person to be married to someone who could hear, but if two deaf people got married, it was just asking for trouble. How could either of them be good parents? What if they had children and one of them called for help? Beyond that, what if Jolene betrayed him the way Carolyn had done? So many unanswered questions all led to one thing: He'd stupidly allowed himself to fall in love with Jolene.

❧ ❧

When they entered the schoolhouse, Jolene gasped at the stark emotion she saw in Lonnie's eyes. Her heart pounded with sudden hope. Maybe he cared about her as much she cared for him. If he did, he'd sure been keeping it to himself. Ever since Christmas, he'd only come around when he needed a lesson, and he never said much to her of a personal nature. The day he'd given her the bird feeder as a Christmas present, she'd hoped he might ask her out. Instead, soon after Jake had shown up, Lonnie had rushed out the door.

Maybe it's a good thing I'm not going out with anyone, she told herself. *Men are hard to figure out, and I've got enough to deal with just teaching school.*

"*If your leg's hurting too much, maybe we should forget about my lesson today,*" Lonnie signed, pulling Jolene's thoughts back to the present.

She shook her head. "*I'll be fine. I don't think I should try to tackle the stairs, though. If you don't mind, we'll have our lesson down here in Fern's classroom.*"

"*I don't mind.*" Lonnie pulled out the chair at Fern's desk, and Jolene took a seat. "*Should I go upstairs and get the hand mirror?*"

"*Yes, please.*"

"*How about some ice to put on your knee?*"

"*That'd be good. There's an ice pack in my lunch box.*"

Lonnie hesitated a few seconds; then when she waved him on, he hurried from the room. He returned a few minutes later with the mirror and Jolene's lunch box. When he handed it to her, the gentle, caring expression on his face was almost her undoing.

She fought the urge to tell him how much she'd come to care for him, but that would be too bold. Unless he made the first move, she would keep the feelings she felt for him locked away in her heart.

⚜ ⚜

When Jake stepped into the taxidermy shop, Crist turned from the job he was working on and offered him a friendly smile. "Afternoon, Jake. If you came to check on your fish, I'm afraid it's not ready yet."

"No, I didn't think it would be done this soon. Came to see Wayne and find out whether Loraine had her *boppli.*"

Crist nodded enthusiastically. "She had a baby boy two days ago. She and the little guy are doin' real well." He glanced out the window. "Wayne's probably working in his shop, but Loraine, Ada, Priscilla, and the boppli are up at the house if you'd like to stop in and say hello."

"Maybe some other time. I just stopped by to find out if she'd given birth, and I wanted to know if everything went okay. I'm sure my mamm will expect a full report when I get home."

Crist chuckled. "Most women are like that, all right. I know my Ada sure is. Nothing much goes on in this community without her knowing it."

"Speaking of Ada," Jake said, "when I was here the other day Wayne said she was having trouble with her back. Is she feeling better?"

"Jah, the chiropractor fixed her right up."

"That's good. Well, guess I'd best be on my way. I have one more stop to make before I head for home." Jake turned toward the door. "Tell Wayne I said congratulations on becoming a daed."

"I will."

─❦─

Ella had just put the CLOSED sign in her bakeshop window when the door swung open, nearly knocking her off her feet. Her heart pounded when she saw that it was Jake.

"I'm just closing. But if you really need something, I can stay open a few more minutes and get it for you."

"I don't need anything this time." Jake shifted his weight from one foot to the other then leaned against the display counter as he stared inside.

"Are you sure you don't want something? Chocolate chip cookies are on sale this week."

"Sounds good, but I'd better not." Jake patted his stomach. "Can't afford to get fat if I'm gonna have the energy to keep training horses." He cleared his throat a couple of times. "Actually, the reason I stopped by is to say—"

"I'm sorry," Ella blurted out.

Jake tipped his head. "What was that?"

"I said, 'I'm sorry.'"

A funny little grin spread over Jake's face. "That's exactly what I was going to say." He stepped closer to Ella. So close that she could feel his warm breath on her face. "What is it that you're sorry for?"

The gentleness in Jake's voice surprised Ella. She swallowed a couple of times and wiped her damp hands on the sides of her apron. "I'm. . .uh. . .sorry for the way I acted when you told me you'd caught our plecostomus."

His grin grew wider. "You were pretty mad about that."

She clenched her fingers against her sides. Was he trying to goad her into another argument? "What are *you* sorry for, Jake?"

"I'm not sorry for catching the fish because it wasn't my fault that the critter took hold of my bait." He took another step toward Ella. "But I am sorry that I didn't take the fish off my line and put him back in the pond."

She shrugged. "What's done is done. Let's just forget about it, shall we?"

"I can't really forget about it because I took that old sucker catfish over to the taxidermy shop to have it stuffed. When it's done, I thought I'd bring it over here so you can hang it on your wall." Jake looked quite pleased with himself. Did he really think he'd done a good thing?

"What are you trying to do, Jake, rub salt in my wounds?"

" 'Course not. I just thought. . ."

"Oh, I know, you expect me to put in on my wall so that every time I look at it I'll remember how you killed our fish!"

Jake's eyebrows furrowed. "Are you saying you don't want the fish?"

"That's exactly what I'm saying!"

He took two steps closer. . .so close, they were almost touching noses. "Fine then, I'll take the fish and hang it on *my* bedroom wall!"

"That's a good idea; you do that, Jake!"

"I will!"

Jake continued to stare at Ella; then, in a surprise gesture, he reached out and tipped her chin up with his thumb.

Ella was surprised by the wild flutter of her pulse when he touched her. She stood motionless, caught up in the moment. Her heart thumped so hard she could barely breathe.

Slowly, Jake lowered his head and captured her lips in a kiss so tender and sweet that it stole her breath away. As the kiss continued, Ella wrapped her arms around Jake's neck.

Suddenly Ella pulled away, heat flooding her face.

"S–sorry about that," Jake stammered. "I–I'd better go." He stared at her a moment longer, as though trying to memorize her face, then turned and rushed out the door.

Ella flopped onto the stool behind the counter and closed her eyes. *Dear Lord, please make me strong. Help me not to lose my heart to Jake all over again.*

CHAPTER 38

Ella tied her horse to a post on the back porch, prepared to give it a bath. She was planning to visit Loraine today, because she hadn't seen the baby yet. But her silly horse had decided to roll in the mud in the corral.

For some reason, the horse acted more fidgety than usual, and it made her think about Jake and how easily he handled horses. She found herself wishing that Jake was here right now. Two days had passed since their unexpected kiss, and Ella still hadn't shaken off the feelings it had brought on. For the life of her, she couldn't figure out why she'd allowed Jake to kiss her. Or for that matter, what had possessed him to do it. It wasn't like they were a courting couple. Since they mostly argued when they were together, it made no sense that he'd want to kiss her.

Ella let her mind wander back to the past. . .back to when she'd had a schoolgirl crush on Jake and had waited anxiously at the end of their driveway for him to show up and walk her to school every day. She knew now that what she'd felt for Jake back then wasn't love, but she sure had liked him a lot. Ella had often wondered how things might have gone if Jake had taken her for a ride in his buggy when he'd turned sixteen. Would they have started going out? Would she have become his steady girl? Even if they had started dating, Jake might have left for Montana. It could have been her instead of Loraine left pining for Jake and hoping for a letter.

I'm not that little girl with a crush on Jake anymore, Ella told herself. *I'm a grown woman who should know better than to let herself fall for Jake again.*

A horsefly buzzed nearby, and Ella's horse whinnied and jerked its head. "Hold still, Pet," Ella mumbled. "You know you're only making things worse!"

Pet continued to thrash her head and snap at the fly, while Ella tried to steady the animal with one hand and hold onto the hose with the other hand.

Whoosh!—Pet jerked again, flicking the hose with her tail. That, in turn, caused the water to squirt Ella right in the face.

"Thanks a lot," Ella mumbled. "You're the one who needs a bath, not me." She grasped the hose and sprayed some water on Pet's legs.

The fly buzzed again, and Pet tossed her head and stamped her front hooves. Ella shot a spray of water at the fly but hit the horse's head instead. Pet reared up, knocking the hose out of Ella's hand and breaking the rope that had secured her to the post. The hose flipped this way and that, shooting water in all directions. By the time Ella was able to grasp it, her clothes were soaking wet. She looked around and spotted the horse's hind end as it disappeared into the barn.

"I don't need this today," Ella grumbled.

She was about to turn off the hose, when a horse and buggy pulled into the yard. It stopped in front of the hitching rail, and Jake got out. "Are we having a bit of trouble?" he asked when he joined her. "You look like a cat caught in a rainstorm."

Ella wrinkled her nose. "Very funny."

Jake chuckled. "If you're trying to give yourself a shower with the hose, then maybe you'd better go inside and get a bar of soap."

"For your information, I was trying to give my horse a bath, but she got upset when a horsefly kept buzzing her. Then she broke free from the porch post where she was tied, and the hose got knocked out of my hand and shot water all over me."

"What made you tie the horse to the post on the porch?"

"Well, I . . ."

"Probably would have been better if you'd tied her to the corral fence or the hitching rail."

"I wanted to be close to the hose, so I thought—"

"Horses are very powerful animals, Ella. You never know what they're going to do."

"I realize that, but—"

"You've got to let the horse know who's boss right away, or it'll take advantage of you."

"Are you saying I know nothing about my horse?"

"No, I'm just saying that you need to be in control."

Ella's temper flared, and she opened her mouth to defend herself but stopped when she felt a nudge at her heart. Angry words didn't solve a thing. Like Mama had mentioned the other day, the Bible taught that she should treat others the way she would want them to treat her.

"I'd like to continue this discussion," Ella said, "but I need to get inside and change into some dry clothes so I can go see Loraine and Wayne's new boppli."

"Would you like me to get your horse and hitch it to the buggy while you change clothes?" Jake offered.

Ella almost said she could do it herself but changed her mind. "Jah, sure, I'd appreciate that." She started up the stairs but turned back around. "Pet's in the barn."

"I kinda figured that, since I didn't see her out here." Jake sprinted for the barn, and Ella entered the house.

When she stepped outside a short time later, carrying the gift she'd bought for Loraine's baby, she saw Jake standing beside her horse, shaking his head.

"What's wrong? How come Pet's not hitched to my buggy?" Ella asked.

He pointed to the horse's right front foot. "She's missing a shoe."

Ella grimaced. "That's just great! Guess I won't be going over to see Loraine's boppli after all, because Charlene and Mama had some errands to run in town, and they took our other driving horse."

"I'd shoe the horse for you right now," Jake said, "but I don't have any of my tools with me."

"That's okay. I can go over to Loraine's some other time." She flopped onto the porch step with a weary sigh.

Jake put Pet in the corral then joined Ella on the porch. "Why don't I drive you over to Loraine's and we can both see the baby? After that, I'll stop by my place, pick up my tools, and shoe your horse when I bring you home."

Ella hesitated but finally nodded.

They headed for Jake's buggy, and when Jake reached for Ella's hand to help her up, she felt an unexpected tingle. *It must be my imagination.*

As they turned onto the road, tension wound around them. Ella figured she needed to say something to help herself relax, so she pointed across the road and said, "Looks like there are plenty of trees being tapped for maple syrup this spring."

"Yep. Sure looks that way."

Ella searched for something else to talk about. Anything to keep from thinking about the kiss that she and Jake had shared the last time they were together. "Do you enjoy working with horses and training them to pull buggies more than you do shoeing them?"

"I definitely prefer to train 'em." Jake looked over at her and smiled. "Once I get my own business going, I probably won't do any shoeing."

His own business? Did that mean Jake was planning to stay in Indiana? Did Ella dare to ask?

"Of course, training horses isn't all fun and games," Jake continued. "Some horses can be real stubborn, and some are just plain high strung. I once had a horse that kept throwing his head back, so I had to come up with a way to make him stop."

"What'd you do?"

"I took a plastic bag and filled it with warm water. Then I got a split piece of leather, and whenever the horse threw his head back, I smacked the leather strap in the air so it made a loud *crack*. At the same time, I broke the bag of water between the horse's ears."

Ella's interest was piqued. "What did that accomplish?"

"The noise and the warm water made the horse think he must have been hurt and was bleeding. Believe it or not, it settled him right down."

"Hmm. . .that's interesting. Are there some specific things that might make a horse spook or act up?"

"Yep. When a horse is going down the road pulling a buggy it can get spooked by several things. Mailboxes; flower beds; people walking; cows or horses running in an open field. Oh, and a horse can get pretty upset when a loud semitruck roars past." Jake's nose crinkled. "Some horses like to rear up and take off, and I have to be ready for that. Of course, some horses are so temperamental that they can never be trained to pull a buggy."

"Where do you buy the horses you train?" Ella questioned.

"From horse dealers, who get them from the race track. When I get the horses, they're already harness trained but not trained to pull a buggy. So that's my job. I always start by getting them to pull a cart, and then we progress to the buggy."

"I know how important it is to have a dependable horse," Ella said. "We have enough buggy accidents caused by other vehicles on the road. We don't need unruly horses causing more accidents."

"That's for sure. Buggies aren't cheap, and when one's destroyed because of an accident, the Amish man who owns the rig is out a lot of money." Jake let go of the reins, lifted one hand, and turned it palm up. "Since an Amish man doesn't have insurance to replace the buggy, the way most Englishers have with their cars, it's not always easy to get a new rig right away."

"That's true."

They rode in silence awhile; then to Ella's surprise, Jake draped his arm over the back of the seat, so his hand touched her shoulder. "Would you like to go out to supper with me one night next week?"

Ella's spine tingled and she sat up straight. "I. . .uh. . .don't think that's a good idea, Jake."

"Why not?"

"Because we'd probably end up arguing the whole evening."

"That's what we do, Ella." Jake's eyes sparkled with laughter, and Ella found herself smiling in response.

"I'm not sure why we argue so much," she said in a near whisper.

"Maybe it's because we're so much alike."

She shook her head. "I don't think so. We're about as different as the sun and the moon."

"So are you saying that you won't go out with me because I'm not like you?"

"That's not what I meant." Ella thought about the kiss they'd shared the other day. She had a feeling Jake had been as shocked by it as she'd been. She also thought about the promise she'd made to herself, not to let herself get involved with Jake.

What happened between us was nothing more than a fleeting attraction, she decided. *Jake and I have nothing in common, and I'm sure that I'd never be able to trust him again.*

Jake bumped Ella's arm. "Answer me, Ella. Is the reason you won't go out to supper with me because I'm not like you?"

"No, not really. It's just that I don't think we should start something we can't finish." Ella steeled her heart against Jake's lopsided grin and looked away.

Jake reached over and tucked a wayward strand of hair under Ella's head covering, and then he let his fingers glide down the length of her face. His gentle touch was almost her undoing.

∼≈ ≈∼

Jake moistened his lips and fought the urge to kiss Ella. Ever since he'd tasted her lips the other day, he'd wanted to kiss her again. *What's wrong with me?* he wondered. *Why would I want to kiss someone who clearly doesn't like me? It just has to be because I see Ella as a spirited challenge—like one of my unruly horses.*

Jake forced himself to keep his eyes on the road. It was ridiculous to think such thoughts.

When they pulled into the driveway leading to Wayne and Loraine's place, Jake halted his horse and buggy.

"What are we stopping here for?" Ella questioned.

"I. . .uh. . .had an urge to. . ." Jake never finished his sentence. Instead, he pulled Ella into his arms. When his lips touched hers, it seemed as if the whole world had receded into nothingness. The kiss was exhilarating and had been worth the wait.

Ella was the first to pull away again, and he couldn't help but notice that her fair complexion had become mottled with red.

"I probably should apologize for that," he murmured, "but I'm not going to. You know why?"

"Wh–why?"

"Because I enjoyed it, and I think you did, too."

Ella looked down at her hands clasped in her lap.

As Jake continued to stare at her, the truth slammed into him with such force that he almost fell out of the buggy. He was in love with Ella!

Clearing his throat, he was prepared to declare his love and take his chances on her reaction, but before he could get a word out, Ella spoke first.

"I. . .uh. . .hope you didn't get the wrong impression when I let you kiss me."

"What do you mean?"

"I'm not sure what's been happening between us lately, but I think we both realize that we can never be more than friends."

Disappointment flooded Jake's soul. It made no sense, given the way she'd responded to his kiss. For some reason, Ella seemed to be holding back. He'd been hoping for more than friendship, but if that was all Ella wanted, then he'd have to accept her decision no matter how much it hurt. Her friendship was better than nothing—and it'd be better than them arguing all the time.

CHAPTER 39

"For someone's who's going to a wedding, you sure look glum today," Charlene said to Ella as they met each other in the hall outside their bedrooms.

"I'm not glum, just tired." Ella yawned. "I worked hard yesterday getting Katie's cake done, and after I delivered the cake, I spent the rest of the day helping Katie and several others set things up for the wedding meal." She smiled at Charlene and gave her shoulder a gentle squeeze. "I appreciate your taking over in the bakeshop for me so I could help Katie."

"No problem; I was glad to do it."

Ella sniffed the air as she descended the stairs behind her sister. "Smells like Mama has the coffee going already."

"Jah, she's been feeling better lately and seems to be getting a lot more done." Charlene halted when she got to the bottom of the stairs and turned to face Ella. "Are you looking forward to being one of Katie's witnesses today?"

"I am, and I'm sure Jolene is, too."

"Who'd you say Freeman asked to be his witnesses?"

"Andrew and Lonnie."

"Do you wish he'd asked Jake so you could be with him all day?"

Ella's mouth went dry. Why did Charlene have to bring up Jake? She'd been trying so hard not to think about him.

Charlene poked Ella's arm. "Well, do you wish you could be with Jake today?"

"Of course not."

"Are you sure? I mean, every time Jake comes around, I see a look of longing on your face."

Ella shook her head. "You're wrong. The only look you see on my face when Jake's around is a look of frustration." Even as Ella spoke the words, she couldn't deny her own feelings to herself. The fascination she'd had for Jake as a child had resurfaced soon after he'd started coming around offering to help out. She'd never have admitted it to Charlene, but she'd begun to see a side of Jake she hadn't seen before. He could be kind, helpful, and interesting to talk to. Every time Jake came over, Ella found herself wishing Jake would see her as more than someone who needed his help. Maybe he did. He'd kissed her, not once, but twice. And he'd invited her to have supper with him. Was Jake just toying with her affections, or did he have feelings for her? The question that haunted Ella the most was whether Jake could be trusted not to hurt her again.

"Guess we'd better get into the kitchen and help with breakfast," Charlene said, bumping Ella's arm. "It wouldn't be good for one of the bride's attendants to be late for the wedding."

Still half asleep from getting to bed too late the night before, Jake stumbled across the room and stubbed his toe on the end of the bedpost. A burst of pain shot up his leg, and he groaned. Limping over to the dresser, he jerked the bottom drawer open to retrieve a pair of clean socks. He'd slept longer than he'd planned to and needed to get dressed and down to breakfast soon, or he'd be late for Freeman and Katie's wedding.

Jake reached inside the drawer for a pair of dark-colored socks but only found one. The rest were all white. "There's gotta be another black sock in here somewhere. They can't all be in the wash," he muttered. He fumbled around for the matching sock but found none. In exasperation, he pulled the drawer out and set it on the floor. After a bit more fumbling, he finally located another black sock near the back of the drawer. When he lifted the drawer to put it back in place he caught a glimpse of something wedged between the bottom drawer and the wood that separated it from the drawer above. It looked like a piece of paper.

Jake reached inside and pulled it out. The paper had been folded in half, and one end was torn clean off. He unfolded it and squinted at the words written there.

I can't believe you lied to me, Jake. You promised when you turned sixteen and got your own buggy that I'd be the first one you took for a ride. I'll never trust you again!

Jake stared at the note for several minutes. The rest of the page—probably where the person who'd written the note had signed their name—was gone.

Jake scratched the side of his head. *I wonder who wrote this note and how it got in my drawer.*

He sat there a few minutes, letting his mind take him back to the past. The first girl he'd taken out after he'd turned sixteen was Loraine, so the note couldn't have been from her. *Who'd I make such a promise to?* he asked himself. *Who wrote me this note, and how come I don't remember anyone giving me the note?*

Tap! Tap! Tap! Someone knocked on Jake's door. "Who is it?" he hollered.

"It's me, Kyle. Mom said to tell you that breakfast is almost ready, so you'd better get a move on, 'cause it'll be time to leave for the wedding soon."

"Okay. Tell her I'm coming."

Jake put the drawer back in place and stuck the note inside his coat pocket, which he'd laid out the night before to wear to the wedding. He'd think more about this later.

━━◈◈━━

When Jolene and her family pulled into the Bontragers' yard to attend Katie and Freeman's wedding, she was surprised to see Lonnie, dressed in a dark-colored frock coat and matching trousers, pacing in front of the buggy shed, where the wedding would take place. She'd known him long enough to tell when he was nervous, and the fact that he was pacing was a good indication that he must be quite anxious this morning.

As soon as Dad stopped the buggy, Jolene climbed down and hurried over to Lonnie. *"How come you're pacing?"* she signed.

He grimaced. *"I'm nervous about being one of Freeman's witnesses."*

"There's no need to be nervous. You won't have to do a lot—just sit with Freeman during the wedding service and also the meal afterward."

Lonnie nodded, although he didn't look convinced. He'd come a long way these last few months, but it was obvious he still had some doubts.

"I mean it. Everything will be okay."

"I'm not so sure about that. There will be a lot of people here today. I'm still having trouble reading lips."

"Don't worry; we'll have Jake and Andrew to interpret for us through signing."

"I think it would have been better if Freeman had picked Jake as one of his witnesses, instead of me," Lonnie signed.

"What makes you say that?"

"Jake has more confidence than I do. If he'd been asked to be one of Freeman's attendants, the two of you could have been together today."

"I'd rather be with you than Jake."

Lonnie tipped his head. *"What was that?"*

"I'd rather be with you than Jake," Jolene repeated, speaking as she signed.

"You don't have to say that just to make me feel better. I've accepted the fact that you and Jake are going out."

Jolene's mouth dropped open. *"Where'd you get that idea?"*

"I've seen you two together a lot, and you liked his Christmas gift more than—"

"Jake and I are not going out."

Lonnie didn't seem to grasp what she'd said, so she repeated it, signing as she spoke.

"You're not interested in Jake?"

835

"Only as a friend."

Was that a look of relief she saw on Lonnie's face? Could it possibly mean that he might have feelings for her? Had he been holding back all this time because he thought she and Jake were going out, or was his deafness the reason he'd been keeping his distance? Jolene wanted to say more, but she spotted Katie on the other side of the building, motioning for her to come. *"The bride is waiting for me, so I'd better go."*

"Guess I'd better find Freeman, too," Lonnie signed.

A sense of sadness crept over Jolene as she joined Katie and saw the happiness glowing on her face. Lonnie had given no definite indication that he saw her as anything more than a friend. And with Lonnie being set against marriage, the chance of him asking her out was slim. She'd have to accept that fact and focus on being happy for Katie and Freeman today.

As Jake sat on a backless wooden bench on the men's side of the buggy shed, he couldn't keep his eyes off Ella. She sat in a straight-back chair between Katie and Jolene, facing Freeman and his two witnesses, Andrew and Lonnie. Ella looked prettier than ever today. She wore a dark blue dress that brought out the color of her pale blue eyes, and a white cape with matching apron. On her head, she wore the black head covering that was typically worn to their church by young women before they were married.

Ella glanced over at Jake then quickly looked away, turning her attention to the message Bishop Hershberger was preaching from the book of Ruth. Toward the end of his message, he quoted from 1 Corinthians and Ephesians. Jake paid special attention when the bishop read Ephesians 5:31: " 'For this cause shall a man leave his father and mother, and shall be joined unto his wife, and they two shall be one flesh.' "

Katie seemed to radiate a blissful glow as she and Freeman left their chairs and stood before the bishop to say their vows, but Jake could only concentrate on Ella. He wondered how she would look on her wedding day. He knew Ella would be a pretty bride, and he found himself wondering what kind of wife and mother she'd make.

A vision of Ella sitting in a rocking chair, holding a baby with reddish blond hair, popped into Jake's head. He knew Ella could bake, because he'd tasted many of her baked goods. He'd also seen how well she managed a home and had witnessed the love and gentleness she showed, not only to her mother, but to her younger siblings as well. He felt sure Ella would make a good wife and mother.

Ella looked his way again then quickly averted her gaze. *Sure wish I knew when Ella started disliking me so much. When we were kinner, I thought we were friends.*

As Jake continued to ponder this question, he realized that Ella had cooled off toward him around the time he'd started courting Loraine. He just wasn't sure why. Until recently, after she'd let him kiss her, Ella had shown no interest in him at all. At least not in a positive way. It made no sense. . .unless. . . Jake's spine stiffened, and he nearly fell off his bench. Unless Ella had written that note.

As Katie and Freeman spoke their vows before the bishop, Jake made a decision. The first chance he had to speak with Ella alone, he'd come right out and ask if she'd written the note.

⊱ ⊰

As Ella sat on one side of Katie during the wedding meal, she had a hard time concentrating on anything other than Jake. He sat at a table directly across from her, looking more handsome than usual in a white shirt, dark trousers, and matching jacket. He kept looking at her, and she wondered what was going through his mind. Was he thinking about the day they'd gone to see Loraine's baby, and the kiss they'd shared in his buggy? Ella still couldn't believe she'd let her guard down like that—not once, but twice she'd been foolish enough to let him kiss her. The mixture of feelings she had for Jake made no sense at all. One minute she felt irritated by everything he said. The next minute she was melting in his arms like butter left out on a hot summer day.

Ella's mouth went dry as a sudden realization hit her full in the face. She was in love with Jake and wished she could be his wife!

That's crazy thinking, she told herself. *Jake doesn't love me. Besides, he's given me no reason to trust him. He probably only kissed me just to prove he could do it. He probably thinks he's such a good catch that any woman would throw herself at his feet.*

Ella reached for her glass of water and was about to take a drink, when Jake left his seat and headed toward the bride and groom's corner table.

"I have a couple of horses to shoe this afternoon, so I have to leave soon," he said, looking first at Katie and then Freeman. "Just wanted to say congratulations and wish you all the best."

"Danki, Jake." Freeman's smile stretched ear to ear, and Katie fairly beamed. Ella couldn't help feeling a bit envious. If only she and Jake could be that happy. If only it was their wedding day.

Jake glanced her way, but she quickly looked away, and as he talked more with Katie and Freeman, she began a conversation with Jolene. "Did you ever see so much food?" she asked, signing as she spoke.

Jolene smiled and patted her stomach. "After today, I probably won't have to eat for the rest of the week."

"Me neither," Andrew spoke up. He nudged Lonnie and signed, *"How about you? Are you getting enough to eat today?"*

"I've already had more than my share," Lonnie said with a grin.

Ella was about to ask Jolene another question when someone tapped her on the shoulder. She turned and gulped. Jake stood behind her wearing a serious expression. "I wonder if I could speak to you for a minute," he whispered, bending close to her ear.

"Uh. . .sure. What did you want to say?"

"Not here." Jake motioned toward the door with his head. "Can you meet me outside?" His voice was so low, she could barely hear him.

Ella shook her head. "In case you hadn't noticed, I'm busy eating."

"I don't see anything on your plate right now." Before Ella could respond, Jake leaned over her shoulder and reached for her plate. In the process, he bumped her glass of water, knocking it over and soaking the front of Ella's dress.

Jake grabbed the glass and set it upright. "Oops, sorry about that. You'd better go outside and let the sun dry your dress."

Ella gritted her teeth, but before she could formulate a response, Jake disappeared outside.

Ella waited a few minutes then excused herself. When she stepped outside, she found Jake leaning on the corral fence, as though waiting for her.

"What's so important that you had to drag me away from the wedding meal?" she asked, stepping up to him.

He chuckled. "I didn't drag you anywhere. Looks to me as if you came out here of your own free will."

"Jah, well, that's because I needed to let my dress dry out." She frowned. "Do you enjoy humiliating me, Jake?"

"No, of course not. Why do you always assume the worst where I'm concerned?" He touched her arm, and she shivered.

"Are you cold?"

"No, I'm fine."

"I don't think so, Ella. I don't think you're ever really fine when you're with me."

"What's that supposed to mean?"

He reached into his pocket, pulled out a piece of paper that had been folded in half, and handed it to her. "Is this *your* handwriting?"

Ella opened it and gasped as she stared at the words. "Wh– where'd you get this?"

"Found it this morning. It was stuck in the back of my sock drawer."

"Oh, I see." Ella's voice quavered, and her hands shook so badly that she had to hold them tightly against her sides.

"I vaguely remember finding the note in our mailbox soon after I turned sixteen, but I'm not sure how it got in my sock drawer." Jake leveled Ella with a look that could have stopped a wild horse in its tracks. "Did you write that note?"

Tears welled in her eyes, and she blinked several times to keep them from spilling over. "You do enjoy humiliating me, don't you, Jake?"

He shook his head. " 'Course not. I just want to know if—"

"I wrote the note, okay? In case you've forgotten, you used to walk me to school every day, and you even carried my books. Then one day you promised that I'd be the first person you took for a ride when you got your own horse and buggy. You lied to me, Jake." Ella's voice rose higher, but she didn't care. Jake had forced her to admit she'd written the note, and she wasn't going to stop until she'd told him everything she'd been keeping bottled up inside her these last ten years. "There was a day when I would have fallen at your feet just to be near you, but did you care about that? No! You just made promises you never planned to keep!"

"Ella, I'm sorry. I never meant to hurt you." Jake took a step toward her and reached out his hand.

She jumped back, afraid that if he touched her she'd dissolve in a puddle of tears. "To you, I was probably just a little girl with a big crush, but you shouldn't have made me a promise that you didn't plan to keep."

Jake's face turned red. "I wasn't intentionally trying to break a promise. I—"

Ella's hand shook as she pointed her finger at Jake. "It wasn't bad enough that you lied to me; you had to go and break my cousin's heart by lying to her, too."

"If you're referring to the fact that I went to Montana, I did plan to come back and marry Loraine, but things happened, and I—" Jake broke off his words and took a deep breath. "I know what I did was wrong, but I've apologized to Loraine. She's forgiven me, so why can't you?"

Ella knew she was being childish, holding a grudge for something that had happened ten years ago. Even so, it was hard to believe that Jake wouldn't lie to her again. If she only knew for sure that Jake would be staying in Indiana. If she just knew how Jake felt about her now.

"I think my dress is dry enough, and I need to get back in

there," she said. "Besides, you've got a horse to shoe."

"That's true, but I'd rather talk to you."

"No, Jake, there's really nothing else for us to talk about." Ella turned and fled.

Ella dropped the silverware they'd used at breakfast into the sink's soapy water and glanced out the kitchen window. It was the third week of April, and the grass had turned a deep emerald green. She smiled when she spotted several white butterflies hovering over the field near their barn. New life: That's what spring always brought. New life and a new hope.

Ella's thoughts went to her cousins. Katie and Freeman were happily married and settling into a routine in the home they shared with Fern. Loraine and Wayne were enjoying little Jonas, the precious baby boy Loraine had given birth to several weeks ago. Ella had gone over there a couple of times since she and Jake had first paid the baby a visit. It was always a joy to hold little Jonas, and it made the longing she felt to be a mother even stronger.

"Jake," Ella murmured. He'd seemed so interested in the baby and had even asked if he could hold him. Ella wondered what kind of father Jake would make—if he ever married and had children, that is. He'd probably fool around and tease quite a bit, the way he'd done when he was a boy and still did now, for that matter. But he'd probably make his children behave, the way she'd seen him do with his siblings. A healthy balance of love and discipline is what all children needed.

Ella's face heated as she thought about the discussion she'd had with Jake at Katie and Freeman's wedding. She'd had trouble thinking of much else. Jake had come over a few times to buy baked goods since the wedding, but there'd been no mention of the discussion they'd had. He had, however, mentioned that he planned to stay in Indiana and buy some land so he could start his own business. Ella wondered if Jake's decision to stay had anything to do with her. She wouldn't ask, but did she dare hope?

No, I can't be the reason Jake's decided to stay. He doesn't even know I'm interested in him. Ella's face grew hotter. *Maybe he does know how I feel, since I allowed him to kiss me. Not once, but twice, no less! I wish I knew how Jake felt about me. I wish I knew if. . .*

She sloshed the sponge in the warm water as more confusing thoughts swirled in her head. The day she and Jake had gone over to Loraine's, he'd asked her to have supper with him, but she'd turned him down. Had that been the right thing to do, or should she have said yes? He might have taken her answer to mean that she wasn't interested in him.

If I'd have said yes, he'd have known I was interested, Ella reasoned. *Can I trust my feelings for Jake, or should I keep a safe distance from him?*

A prayer came to mind, and she closed her eyes. *What am I supposed to do, Lord? Tell me what to do, and I'll do it.*

～❦～

Jake had spent the last two weeks trying to figure out what to do about Ella. He'd read Proverbs 17:25: "A foolish son is a grief to his father, and bitterness to her that bare him." It had caused him to realize that one of the reasons he'd left home in the first place was to get away from Dad and his constant accusations. But that had been a foolish thing to do, because he'd managed to hurt his folks, Loraine, and Ella, too. Even though he and Dad didn't see eye to eye on many things, Jake's place was at home. He'd never be truly happy if he stayed in Montana and remained English. Oh, he'd be returning to Montana, and soon, but it was only to pick up his things and buy a few horses.

He didn't want to go, however, until he'd spoken to Ella first. Now that he knew why she didn't trust him, he hoped to put her mind at ease. He also hoped that once she realized he was going to stay in Indiana and join the Amish church, she'd be more receptive to the idea of going out with him. Maybe, if she went out with him a few times, she'd realize that they weren't so bad together and could actually have a good time. Maybe she would forgive him for not keeping his promise to her when she was a girl. Maybe, if she'd let him, Jake could start over and do things right.

I wonder if I should talk to someone about Ella, Jake thought as he headed out to the barn to check on the new horse he'd bought. *It should be someone who knows her well and might have some influence with her.*

He was almost to the barn when an idea popped into his head. He could speak to Jolene about Ella when he had his next signing lesson. Better yet, he could stop by the schoolhouse that afternoon.

❧ ❧

"How come your scholars look so sad?" Jolene asked Fern as the children filed out of the school.

"Allen Stutzman's daed was here a few minutes ago and gave us the news that Allen's been diagnosed with leukemia." Fern's face revealed her sorrow as she slowly shook her head. "Things don't look good for Allen. Ella's brother Larry took it the hardest, and I'm worried about him because it hasn't been that long since he lost his daed. I'm afraid if he loses his best friend, too, he might sink into depression."

Jolene's heart went out to Larry, but she felt especially sad for Allen and his family. She hoped the boy's folks would be able to get him the kind of treatment he needed, and she prayed that he would live.

"One of the scholars told me that, on the way out, Larry said something about not wanting to go home," Fern reported.

"I'm sure he was just talking. From what I know of my cousin, he always goes straight home from school so he can have a treat from Ella's bakery."

"I hope he went straight home today, because he's going to

need a bit of consoling." Fern stepped out the door. "See you tomorrow, Jolene."

Jolene watched as Fern climbed onto her bicycle and pedaled down the driveway. She was almost to the end when a horse and buggy rolled in. Jolene was surprised when she recognized the driver as Jake, because he wasn't supposed to have a lesson until Monday evening at her home.

❦

When Jake strolled up to the schoolhouse, he greeted Jolene with a smile, but she didn't smile in return.

"What's wrong? You look like you've lost your best friend."

Jolene motioned for Jake to take a seat on the porch step, and she did the same. Then she told him about Allen Stutzman and about Larry's reaction to his friend's illness.

"That's a shame." Jake rubbed his chin. "I was planning to stop by Ella's bakeshop today. While I'm there, I'll ask how Larry's doing. In the meantime, there's something I'd like to talk to you about."

"What's that?"

"Umm. . .it's about Ella." Jake ran his hand across his sweaty forehead. It wasn't going to be easy to admit how he felt about Jolene's cousin, but if she had any influence on Ella, it might be worth the embarrassment.

"What about Ella?"

"I'm. . .uh. . .well, I think I'm in love with her." There, it was out. Jake sat back and waited for Jolene's response.

She stared at him for several seconds, and then her face broke into a wide smile. "I suspected as much."

His eyebrows lifted. "You knew?"

She nodded. "Does Ella feel the same way about you?"

"I'm not sure, but I think she used to."

"What do you mean?"

Jake explained about the promise he'd made to Ella when she was a girl and said he'd never thought much about it before. He went on to explain that he now realized that Ella'd had a crush on him back then. He blew out his breath in one long sigh. "Some time ago, I asked her to go out to supper with me, but she said no."

"That doesn't mean she doesn't like you. She could have been too busy."

"I wish that were true, but the real reason Ella won't go out with me is because she doesn't trust me, and besides, she says we argue all the time." Jake touched Jolene's arm. "Would you be willing to put in a good word for me with Ella?"

"I suppose I could do that," Jolene said, "but I think it would be better if you did some things that might help win Ella's heart."

"Got any suggestions?"

"You might buy her a gift; say some nice things about her when she's around; stop over to see her more often; maybe volunteer to do some chores around their place."

"I've already done plenty of chores, and that hasn't helped me win her favor. I've also bought lots of baked goods and given her some money at Christmas." Jake grimaced. "I've stopped over there more often than I probably should, and I think I've worn out my welcome. The only thing I haven't done is to say some nice things about Ella to her face."

"I don't suppose you've told her that you're in love with her?"

"No. I was afraid she wouldn't believe me, and I'm even more afraid of her rejection."

"You won't know until you try." Jolene gave Jake's arm a gentle squeeze. "My advice is to go see Ella and say something nice, then wait and see what her reaction is."

"Okay! I'll do that right now." Jake grinned as hope rose in his chest. "And while I'm there, I'll have a talk with Larry and see if I can cheer him up a bit." He raced across the yard to his buggy, more anxious than ever to see Ella.

CHAPTER 41

Ella glanced out her bakeshop window. Amelia and Helen had come home from school over an hour ago and said that Larry had walked home by himself, a different way. Ella was getting worried and felt tempted to go look for him but didn't want to leave the shop unattended. Charlene had taken Mama to a doctor's appointment, and Amelia and Helen couldn't watch Sue Ann and also wait on any customers who might come into the bakeshop.

Why would Larry walk home by himself? Ella fumed. *He knows he's supposed to walk with the girls.* She sighed. *Guess if he's not home by the time Mama and Charlene get here, I'll have to look for him.*

Ella ushered her three young sisters into the back room of her bakeshop and gave them some cut-up apples and milk to snack on. When she heard her shop door open, she headed that way to see who'd come in. She was both pleased and surprised to see that it was Jake.

He offered her a dimpled, kind of shy-looking grin. "Afternoon, Ella."

"Hello, Jake," Ella said, feeling suddenly shy herself in his presence. She wondered if whenever he looked at her, he thought about the kisses they'd shared. "What can I do for you today?"

He cleared his throat a couple of times. "I. . .uh. . .wanted to tell you how much I enjoyed those sweet rolls you sold my mamm the other day. They were sure good."

"I'm glad you liked them." Ella swallowed hard. Jake was

looking at her in a peculiar way that made her toes curl inside her sneakers.

"With your baking skills, you'll make a good wife for some lucky fellow someday."

A wave of heat flooded Ella's face. "I doubt that I'll ever get married."

"What makes you say that?"

Ella leaned on the counter for added support. The intense look on Jake's face made her squirm. "For one thing, I need to help my mamm raise my bruder and schweschdere. Then there's the fact that I don't have a—"

"Speaking of your brother—I stopped at the schoolhouse before I came here, and Jolene mentioned how upset Larry had been when he'd heard about Allen Stutzman."

"What about Allen?"

"He has leukemia. Figured you knew."

She shook her head. "I knew he hadn't been feeling well, but I had no idea he'd been diagnosed with leukemia."

"Guess all the scholars took it pretty hard, Larry most of all. Jolene said she overheard him telling one of the scholars that he didn't want to go home."

Alarm rose in Ella's soul. "Larry's over an hour late. You don't suppose. . ."

"He's probably off by himself somewhere, thinking about his friend and trying to come to grips with it."

"Larry took Papa's death pretty hard. If he loses Allen, I don't know what he'll do." She glanced at the battery-operated clock on the far wall. "I'd like to go look for him, but Mama and Charlene are still at the doctor's, and I don't want to leave my younger sisters unattended."

Before Jake could respond, an idea popped into Ella's head. "If you wouldn't mind staying with them for a short time, I'll hop on my bike and go search for Larry."

"I've got a better idea," Jake said. "I'll look for Larry, and you can stay here with your sisters."

"You wouldn't mind?"

" 'Course not. What are friends for if not to help each other?"

Friends. At least Jake considered her a friend. She managed a weak smile. "I appreciate that, Jake."

He leaned across the counter and gave her shoulder a quick squeeze. "Not to worry; I'll find Larry and bring him home."

～✖ ✗～

Jolene's arms swung at her sides as she hurried toward the variety store in Topeka. She needed to buy a baby gift and get over to Loraine's before it was time to start supper. Jolene had visited Loraine and her baby a few times, but she still hadn't bought him a gift.

She'd no sooner entered the store when she saw something that made her blood run cold. A man wearing a ski mask that covered his eyes and nose stood near the counter, holding a gun in his hand. Sadie Smucker, the store owner, along with Eunice Byler and an English woman Jolene didn't recognize, stood next to the counter with their hands raised over their heads.

Jolene halted her footsteps, not sure what she should do. Gathering her wits about her, she decided that the only thing she could do was to run back outside and get some help. She was about to do that when Eunice turned and looked at her. So did the gunman.

He pivoted the gun toward Jolene. "Come over here!"

With her heart pounding and her legs shaking so badly she could barely walk, Jolene made her way across the room. When she reached the counter, the gunman grabbed her arm and pulled her roughly to his side. She winced but made no move to protest for fear that he might shoot her or one of the other women.

The man said something to Sadie then, but his head was turned away from Jolene and she couldn't make out what he'd said. Then he said something to Eunice and the other woman. They nodded, cast a quick glance at Jolene, and followed Sadie out the door.

Jolene looked up at the gunman and said, "Please, let me go."

"Not a chance! You're my ticket to freedom."

CHAPTER 42

Lonnie had just tied his horse to the hitching rail near the grocery store in Topeka when he spotted Jolene going into one of the stores down the street. He was tempted to follow but wasn't sure what he'd say to her if he did. He wanted to believe things could work out for them, despite their inability to hear, but he was still full of doubts and fears. He needed to trust God to help him not be afraid, but ever since his accident, he'd struggled with a lack of faith.

Lonnie was about to head for the grocery store when he saw Sadie Smucker, the owner of the store where Jolene had gone, rush out the front door with Eunice Byler and a middle-aged English woman. They stood in a huddle for a few minutes, and then Sadie scurried next door to the pharmacy.

Lonnie glanced at the store again, wondering what was going on. Why had the others come out but not Jolene? Maybe one of Sadie's clerks was inside waiting on Jolene, but if that was the case, then why were the English woman and Eunice wearing panicked expressions while clinging to each other? And why had Sadie appeared to be in such a hurry to go to the drugstore?

Lonnie hurried down the sidewalk and stepped up to Eunice. "I saw Jolene go in there a few minutes ago," he said, pointing to the store. "Is she still there?"

Eunice nodded, her eyes wide with fear. Her mouth moved quickly as she spoke, making it difficult for Lonnie to read her lips.

"I can only understand what you're saying if you speak slowly enough so I can read your lips. Would you please repeat what you said?"

Eunice spoke again, slowing her speech, and she signed a few of the words. "There's a man with a gun in the store. He's holding Jolene hostage. He told Sadie to phone the police and to say that he'd be waiting for them when they got here."

Lonnie's heart gave a lurch. "Doesn't the man know that when the police get here he'll be arrested?"

The English woman spoke this time. "He told Sadie that he wanted money. When she said that she only had a few hundred dollars in the store, he said he needed a lot more." She paused and moistened her lips. "I believe he's holding the Amish woman, hoping he can make a deal with the police."

Lonnie's stomach twisted. Jolene was alone with a crazed man who held a gun. If the man didn't get what he wanted, he might kill her. The thought that he might lose the woman he loved chilled Lonnie to the bone.

As he stared at the store, emotion tightened in his chest. The sense of longing to share his life with Jolene suddenly filled him with purpose. He'd do anything to protect her, even lay down his own life if necessary.

Lonnie drew in a deep breath, sent up a quick prayer, and dashed down the street.

❧ ❦

Jake had driven up and down the road between Ella's place and the schoolhouse several times without finding a single sign of Larry. He figured the boy had probably taken a shortcut through the woods, but it would only be a shortcut if he'd come straight home. *Or maybe,* Jake thought as he came to a dirt road leading to one of the neighboring ponds, *Larry hiked in there to do some thinking.*

Jake guided his horse and buggy up the dirt road and followed it until he came to the pond. He breathed a sigh of relief when he spotted Larry sitting on a log near the water.

Not wishing to startle the boy, Jake tied his horse to a tree and headed for the pond, whistling loudly as he walked.

Larry turned and looked, but as soon as he saw Jake, he jumped up and started for the other side of the pond. Jake hurried after him. "Hold up, Larry! I need to talk to you!"

"What about?" Larry called over his shoulder as he kept walking.

"Just want to share a couple of things with you."

"What kind of things?"

"Let's have a seat, and I'll tell you."

Larry took a few more steps then halted and turned to face Jake. "Is it about Ella? Are you wantin' me to put in a good word for you with her?"

"Huh?"

" 'Cause if you are wantin' me to put in a good word, you can forget it. I heard Ella tell Mama that she don't trust you; and neither do I." Larry's chin quivered. "I think you came here to try and make me go home."

Jake caught up to Larry and put both hands on the boy's shoulder. "You're late getting home from school, and Ella's worried about you."

"I ain't goin' home."

"Why not?"

"Just ain't, that's all."

"Is it because you're upset about Allen being so sick?"

Tears welled in Larry's eyes. "How'd you hear about that?"

"Jolene told me. She said you were pretty upset when you left school today."

Larry blinked a couple of times. "You'd be upset, too, if your best friend was gonna die."

Jake shook his head. "You don't know that Allen's going to die. You need to pray and trust God where Allen's concerned. I'm sure his folks will see that he gets the best possible care."

"Maybe so, but that don't mean Allen won't die."

"There are no guarantees in life," Jake said. "The only guarantee we have is that God loved us so much that He sent His Son to die for us." He waited a few minutes, to let Larry think about what he'd said. "There are many people with leukemia who've been helped. Allen has a good chance of surviving if he gets proper treatment."

"You really think so?"

"Sure do." Jake squeezed Larry's shoulders. "Your family needs you. Since your daed died, you're the man in the family. Don't you think your place is at home with your mamm and schweschdere?"

Larry stared at the pond, his shoulders shaking. With tears streaming down his cheeks, he finally nodded. "I really do care about Mama and my sisters."

"Then let's go." Jake led the way to his horse and buggy, but they'd only gone a short ways when the toe of his boot clipped a rock, and he stumbled. The ground spiraled up toward him, and then everything went black.

CHAPTER 43

Ella had just stepped onto the porch of her bakeshop to shake some flour from her apron, when Larry came running up the driveway. Relief flooded her soul.

Red-faced and sweating profusely, Larry dashed across the grass and leaped onto the porch. "Jake f–fell and hit his h–head on a rock! I th–think he might be dead!" Larry's eyes were wide with fear, and his chin trembled so bad that he stuttered.

Ella sucked in her breath. "What happened? Where's Jake?"

Larry quickly told Ella how Jake had talked him into going home. He sniffed a couple of times, struggling to hold back his tears. "If Jake hadn't come lookin' for me, he wouldn't have stumbled. If he dies, it'll be my fault."

Ella didn't have time to argue; she needed to get to Jake and see how badly he'd been hurt. She took hold of Larry's shoulders and bent down so she could look him in the eye. "Where's Jake now?"

"He's lyin' on the path leadin' to the Lehmans' pond. I can take you there right now."

Larry turned toward the driveway, but Ella stepped in front of him. "I need you to stay here and keep an eye on the girls."

"Can't Mama do that?"

"She's not here. Charlene took her to the doctor's this afternoon and they aren't back yet."

"But I can't stay here. I need to see how Jake's doin'." Tears rolled down Larry's cheeks. "Need to know if he's dead or not."

Ella swallowed around the lump in her throat. Jake couldn't be dead. She needed him to know how much she cared, needed him to know that she wanted to be more than his friend and that she'd forgiven him.

With a firm hand, Ella turned Larry toward the bakeshop. "Go inside now and watch your sisters. I'll be back as soon as I can."

Larry nodded and hurried inside. Ella raced to the barn and grabbed her bike. *Dear God,* she prayed as she pedaled quickly down the driveway, *please don't let Jake die.*

⋟ ⋞

Jolene's face broke out in a cold sweat as she sat in a chair, watching the gunman pace from the window to the counter and back. As the minutes ticked by, he seemed to become more agitated. Surely Sadie had phoned the sheriff by now. Would he and his deputies be here soon? Would they barge into the store and maybe shoot the gunman, or would they stay outside and try to talk him into giving himself up?

Jolene closed her eyes. *Dear Lord,* she prayed, *please give me the wisdom to know what I should do or say.*

When she opened her eyes, she was surprised to see the front door open, and even more surprised when Lonnie dashed into the store.

When the gunman rushed forward, pointing the gun at Lonnie, Jolene covered her mouth to stifle a scream. Gathering her wits about her, she leaped off the chair and hollered, "Don't shoot! He's my friend!"

Jolene had no idea whether the man had given a reply, for his back was to her. He did, however, lower the gun a bit and motion Lonnie to move away from the door.

As Lonnie's gaze connected with Jolene's, she saw the look of concern on his face. Had he come in here to save her, or was he just an unsuspecting customer like she had been?

The gunman said something to Lonnie, and then he quickly locked the door. Jolene was surprised he hadn't done that sooner. Maybe this was his first criminal act and he hadn't known what

855

to do. Maybe the man behind the ski mask was as frightened as she was right now. Was it possible that she could talk him into giving himself up? It was worth a try, and it was better than doing nothing.

She moved forward and positioned herself so the man could see her face. "I don't know why you're keeping us here, but what you're doing is wrong, and I—"

"Shut up and sit down!" Although Jolene couldn't hear the intensity of the man's voice, she knew from the way his lips had formed the words that he'd yelled at her.

He kept pacing, waving the gun, and saying something Jolene couldn't make out. Every once in a while he stopped and looked at his watch, and then he started pacing again.

"We've got to do something," Lonnie signed to Jolene.

"I know, but what?"

"I'm not sure, but I need to get you out of here." He glanced toward the back of the store. *"Ask if you can use the restroom."*

"I don't need to use the restroom."

"Ask anyway. If he says you can use it, maybe you can sneak out the back door."

Jolene nodded. That made good sense. She didn't know why she hadn't thought of it herself.

She left her chair and approached the man cautiously. "I need to use the restroom."

"Sit down!"

"I really need to use it right away."

His lips compressed as he tilted his head. "You'd better not try anything funny."

Jolene's heart began to race. If she were able to sneak out the back door, the man would soon realize she was missing. She was sure that would make him angrier than he already was, and if he got any angrier, he might hurt Lonnie.

"I guess I don't need the restroom that bad," she said. "I can wait."

"Suit yourself." He motioned to the chair beside Lonnie. "Now go sit with your friend and stop bothering me; I need to think."

Jolene complied.

"What happened? Did you ask about using the restroom?" Lonnie signed.

"I did ask, and he said I could, but I changed my mind."

Lonnie's forehead puckered. *"How come?"*

"Because I was worried that if I escaped, he might—"

The man stepped up to Lonnie and held the gun near his head. "What are you two doing, waving your hands around like that?"

"We're both deaf." Jolene signed as she spoke. "This is how we communicate."

"But you've been talking to me. How'd you know what I was saying if you can't hear?"

"We were reading your lips," Lonnie said before Jolene could respond.

"So you can only know what I'm saying if I'm looking right at you?"

Lonnie and Jolene both nodded.

He waved the gun over their heads. "Well, understand this: If someone doesn't show up soon with the money I asked for, neither one of you will make it outa here alive!"

CHAPTER 44

J ake! Can you hear me, Jake?"

Jake's eyelids fluttered, and he slowly opened his eyes. He saw Ella looking down at him with a worried expression. "Wh– what happened? Where'd you come from?"

"Larry came to get me. He said you'd fallen and hit your head on a rock." Ella dropped to her knees and cradled Jake's head in her lap. Then she gently probed his head with her fingertips. "I don't see any blood, but there's a lump on your forehead. I think you'd better see a doctor to be sure that you don't have a concussion."

"At least it's not you with a bump on your head this time."

Ella apparently didn't see the humor in what Jake had said, for she didn't even smile.

Jake reached up and touched his forehead. "Aw, it's just a little bump. I don't think there's any need for me to see a doctor." He made no move to sit up, however, enjoying the warmth of her hands as they cradled his head.

"Well, I think there is." Ella's expression turned to genuine concern.

Jake wondered if this might be a good time to tell her how he felt. Would she be receptive to what he had to say? He sat up and reached for Ella's hand. He was relieved when she didn't pull it away. "I. . .uh. . .know we've had our share of disagreements in the past. . . ."

"And still have," she said, a slight smile playing on her lips.

"Guess that's how it'll always be between us, but I hope we've come to the point where we can be friends again." He held his breath, waiting for her response. He didn't want to say too much until he knew how she felt about him. No point in making a fool of himself. Not that he hadn't done plenty of that in the past.

Ella nibbled on her bottom lip as he rubbed his thumb across her knuckles. "I'm not sure how it happened, but even though we don't agree on everything, I do think we can be friends—maybe even good friends."

"Friends don't always have to agree." He grinned. "They can agree to disagree."

"I guess you're right."

Jake rolled his tongue around in his mouth as he tried to figure out what to say next. He was on the verge of blurting out that Ella was more than a friend to him—that he'd fallen in love with her—but he decided this probably wasn't the best time or place to make such an admission. He needed to do a few things yet—things that would hopefully secure his future.

"I need to get home," Jake said, rising to his feet.

"What about seeing the doctor?"

"If I start feeling dizzy or have any other weird symptoms, I'll call the doctor," he promised.

"Jake, I really think. . ."

He leaned down and kissed her and was pleased when she responded. When they pulled apart, he motioned to his horse and buggy, still tied to a tree. "I'll put your bike in the back of my rig and give you a lift home. Then I'll be on my way home, too."

"Do you promise to see the doctor if you start having any problems?"

"Said so, didn't I?"

"Guess I'll have to take you at your word." Ella smiled as he helped her into his buggy. "Larry will be relieved to know that you're not dead."

Jake's eyes widened. "He thought I was dead?"

Ella nodded. "He was very worried about you, and so was I."

"Really?"

She gave his arm a little squeeze. "Said so, didn't I?"

Jake chuckled and continued to do so as he climbed into the driver's side of the buggy.

"I'm glad you think what I said was so funny." Ella needled him in the ribs. "I really was worried about you."

"I'm glad you were." He clucked to the horse to get him moving, and then he reached over and clasped Ella's hand. "Does that mean you've forgiven me for not keeping my promise to take you out when I turned sixteen?"

"Jah." Tears welled in her eyes as she nodded.

"Should we go out to supper this evening and celebrate?"

"That offer's really tempting, but I think you ought to take it easy for the rest of the evening," Ella said, gently squeezing his fingers. "Your daed's doing better now, so maybe he can do your chores."

Jake winked. "Yes, Mother."

Tiny wrinkles formed across her forehead as she frowned. "I'm serious, Jake. You fell hard enough to knock yourself out, and you could have a concussion."

"You worry too much. I'll be fine, really."

When she leaned her head on his shoulder, a ripple of warmth shot through him. He thought he could spend the rest of his life sitting beside her like this.

"Were you able to talk to Larry about Allen?" Ella asked.

"Uh. . .yes. I think I gave him some hope when I said that Allen's folks would see that he got good care. I also told him that there's been many people with leukemia who've been helped."

"I hope and pray that Allen's one of those who makes it."

"Me, too."

They rode silently the rest of the way, but Jake didn't mind. He enjoyed this time alone with Ella, and words didn't seem necessary.

When Jake turned his buggy up Ella's driveway, she smiled at him and said, "I'll come over to your place to check on you in the morning."

Jake tipped her chin up so he could look into her eyes. "Would you mind giving me a couple of days?"

Her brows furrowed as confusion registered on her face.

"There's something I need to do before we talk again." Jake leaned over and kissed her cheek. "Why don't you come by next Monday?"

Her mouth formed an *O*. "Next week? But Jake, I—"

He held up his hand. "Please, Ella, for once, just do what I say, okay?"

She pursed her lips and lifted her shoulders. "Okay, but just this once."

❧ ❧

Lonnie watched as the gunman looked out the window then suddenly pivoted and waved the gun in the air. He marched over to Lonnie and Jolene and said, "The sheriff's out there with a bunch of his deputies. They're calling for me to give myself up." He shook his head determinedly. "But that's not gonna happen."

Lonnie turned to Jolene and signed, *I'm going to try talking to him.*

Fear shone clearly in Jolene's eyes as she nodded slowly.

Lonnie rose to his feet, praying for the right words. He could see that the gunman was getting more agitated all the time. If something didn't happen soon, he and Jolene could end up dead.

"Why are you doing this?" Lonnie asked the man.

"You really want to know?"

"Yes, I do."

"I've been out of work for nearly a year. If I don't get some money soon, I'll lose everything—my house, my car, and probably my family." He rubbed the side of his face, almost pulling the ski mask off in the process. "All me and my wife do anymore is argue. She said she's thinking about leaving me, and if things don't turn around for us soon, I'm sure she will."

"I think I understand a bit of how you must feel," Lonnie said. "I was out of work for a while after the accident that caused me to go deaf. I became bitter and feared that I'd never find a job.

But I prayed and asked God to help me, and after a while, the right job came along." Lonnie smiled, although his hands were sweaty, and he figured his voice was probably shaky. "My new job is something I can do without being able to hear, and I'm happier now than I ever thought possible." As Lonnie continued to share with the man, he found that his own faith was being strengthened and a sense of peace had crept over him. For the first time since he'd lost his hearing, Lonnie realized that he wasn't a weak or incapable man. Despite his handicap, Lonnie could still be used by God if he was willing to listen and obey the Lord's gentle nudging.

In a surprise gesture, the gunman pulled off his ski mask. He was much younger than Lonnie had thought, and his face was pale and gaunt.

The man lowered his head into his hands and sobbed. "I can't pray and ask God for anything, because I'm a worthless, no-good bum."

Lonnie touched the man's arm. "What's your name?"

The man lifted his head. "Fred. Fred Hastings."

Lonnie prayed again, asking God to give him the right words. "I have good news for you, Fred."

"What's that?"

"God loved the world so much that He sent His Son to die for your sins. He doesn't care who you are or what you've done. He wants you to believe on His name. He wants you to confess your sins and ask Him to come into your heart. When you do that, He'll forgive you and cleanse your heart. You'll become a new creature in Christ."

Fred stared at him blankly. He might not be completely convinced, but at least he was listening.

"Here's something else to consider," Lonnie went on to say. "If the demands you gave the sheriff aren't met, which they probably won't be, you'll go to jail for a time. But if you kill us, you'll be faced with a murder charge."

Fred blinked a couple of times. "I hadn't thought about that. I was so desperate to get some money that I wasn't thinking at all."

"If you give yourself up right now, you'll probably go to jail if the state presses charges. But it'll go better for you if you don't carry this any further."

"You really think so?"

"Yes, and the Amish community will help you and your family. I can let some people know, and I'm sure they'll see that your family's cared for while you're in jail."

"The Amish would really do that?"

Lonnie nodded. "I think any Christian would want to help."

Fred stared at Lonnie then handed him the gun. "I'm giving myself up. You and your lady friend are free to go."

"All right, but we'll all go out together." Lonnie laid the gun on the counter, unlocked and opened the door, and then hollered to the sheriff, "Don't shoot! We're coming out!"

The minute they stepped out the door, the sheriff waved his hands and said something Lonnie couldn't understand. As they moved closer to the sheriff, Lonnie was able to read his lips and realized that he'd told the gunman to drop to the ground.

Fred did as he was told. A few seconds later, Lonnie grabbed Jolene's hand and hurried toward the sheriff.

After that, everything happened so fast. Fred was handcuffed, put in one of the patrol cars, and whisked away. Lonnie, Jolene, Sadie, Eunice, and the English woman spent some time explaining to the sheriff what had happened inside the store. Then Lonnie asked the sheriff if he could get the gunman's address so they could do something to help his family. The sheriff agreed, and by the time he'd finished taking their statements, Lonnie was exhausted. Noticing that Jolene had begun to tremble, he knew she must be exhausted, too.

Lonnie was about to suggest that he and Jolene go over to where he'd tied his horse and buggy, when Andrew dashed down the sidewalk, waving his hands.

"Someone came into the harness shop and said you were being held hostage in one of the stores," Andrew said, running up to Eunice.

"Ach, it was horrible," she said with tears streaming down her face. "We're all lucky to be alive."

While Andrew consoled Eunice, Lonnie took Jolene's hand and led her away. When they reached his buggy, he pulled her into his arms and propped his chin on her head. He felt her sobs against his chest and gently patted her back. He loved this sweet woman more than life itself and knew he could never be truly happy unless they were together. He was no longer afraid to let her know how he felt. With God's guidance, he was no longer a helpless, fearful man.

※ ※

Jolene felt the vibration of Lonnie's heart beating under her ears. Had he been as frightened as she'd been while they were in the store? He certainly hadn't acted scared. The way he'd talked the gunman into giving himself up had amazed her. It made her love him all the more.

Jolene pulled slowly away from Lonnie and took a deep breath to ease the tightening in her throat. *"I know you think we can't be together,"* she signed, *"but don't you think you should let me decide what's best for me?"*

"What makes you think I think we can't be together?"

"You've said many times that—"

Lonnie lifted his hand and signed, *"I love you. You're my best friend."*

She made a circle with her right index finger. *"Always."*

His fingers curved under her chin, and his look went straight to her heart. At that moment, Jolene knew that Lonnie loved her as much as she loved him.

"I do believe we can be together, so when the time's right, do you think you might consider marrying me?" he signed.

She nodded affirmatively as she moved her right hand up and down, forming the word *yes*.

Lonnie helped her into his buggy, and when they were both seated, he lowered his head and kissed her tenderly on the mouth.

Jolene knew that she and Lonnie would face challenges, but if they kept their faith in God and sought His help every day, she was sure they could face anything together.

CHAPTER 45

Ella knew that Jake wanted her to wait until next Monday to see him, but by Friday, she couldn't wait any longer. She needed to know if he was all right; she needed to let him know how much she cared.

So she packaged up a loaf of friendship bread, climbed into her buggy, and guided her horse down the driveway. She'd left Charlene in charge of the bakeshop; Amelia, Helen, and Larry were still in school; and Mama and Sue Ann were both taking a nap, so this was a good time for her to go.

It was a beautiful spring afternoon, and Ella enjoyed the ride, absorbing the sweet smell of someone's newly mown grass, the beauty of budding trees and flowers in bloom. It was a perfect day to take a ride with Jake, and if he felt up to it, maybe they could.

Ella smiled as she thought about the way Jake had looked at her the other day—as though he only had eyes for her.

Is that the way he used to look at Loraine? Ella had cared so much for Jake, even back then, that she'd tried not to notice how he'd looked at Loraine.

Ella was sure that Jake was over Loraine and that he had no interest in Jolene. But one question remained: Was Jake ready to make a commitment to her?

A short time later, with a sense of anticipation, Ella pulled her horse and buggy up to the hitching rail by the Beechys' barn. After she'd climbed down and secured her horse, she reached into the buggy for the friendship bread and sprinted to the house.

Jake's mother answered soon after Ella knocked on the back door. "I came over to see how Jake's doing." Ella held out the bread. "And I brought this for him."

Lydia pursed her lips. "Didn't Jake tell you?"

"Tell me what?"

"He's not here."

"Where is he?"

"He left for Montana four days ago. Went by plane, despite his daed's protests."

Ella felt as if her heart had stopped beating. Despite what Jake had said about staying in Indiana, he'd left again.

"What a fool I was for trusting him," Ella mumbled.

Lydia tipped her head. "What was that?"

"Jake told me he was staying in Indiana, and I was foolish enough to believe him."

Lydia opened the door wider and motioned Ella inside. "I think we need to talk."

Ella reluctantly followed Lydia into the kitchen. She didn't see that they had much to talk about, unless Lydia planned to make excuses for her son's bad behavior.

"Are you sure Jake didn't tell you he was making a trip to Montana?" Lydia asked after they'd taken seats at the table.

Ella shook her head. "He never said a word."

"Maybe he wanted to surprise you."

"Oh, I'm surprised all right."

"Do you think Jake plans to stay in Montana? Is that why you're wearing such a long face?"

"Well, isn't he planning to stay there?"

"Nee. Jake has every intention of coming back here as soon as he—"

The back door flew open. Jake's dad stumbled into the room. His face was white, and his eyes were rimmed with tears.

"Joe, what's wrong?" Lydia hurried over to him.

He opened his mouth, but the only sound that came out was a strangled sob.

Lydia grabbed hold of his arm and gave it a shake. "Tell me what's wrong!"

"I was in the phone shed checkin' messages, and there—there was one from Jake's boss in Montana."

"What'd it say?"

Joe drew in a couple of shaky breaths and then dropped to his knees. "Jake's dead!"

CHAPTER 46

Ella stared at Jake's dad, trying to let his words register. As their meaning sunk in, a shaft of pain stabbed her heart. Jake was dead. But how? When? Where? A dozen questions filled Ella's head.

Lydia dropped to her knees beside her husband. "What happened? Tell me exactly what the message on our answering machine said."

Joe lifted his ravaged face and drew in a shuddering breath. "Jake borrowed his boss's truck to pick up some horses, but he never made it back to the ranch because he—he was in an accident." Joe sniffed deeply and swiped at the tears running down his cheeks. "Our son's body was burned beyond recognition."

Lydia gasped, and Ella grabbed the back of the nearest chair for support.

"This is all my fault," Joe lamented as he rose to his feet. He began to pace. "If I'd only been nicer to Jake, he'd never have left home in the first place."

Lydia ambled across the room as though in a daze and dropped into a chair at the table. Her whole body trembled as she clutched the folds in her dress. "Ach, my son, Jake!"

Ella sat beside Lydia and held the other woman's hands as she fought for control. She couldn't be sure whether the tears that splashed onto their hands were hers or Lydia's. She just knew they both loved Jake and would miss him terribly.

Ella could certainly relate to Joe's cries, for she, too, felt as if

869

she were to blame for Jake's death. *If I hadn't been so mean to him after Papa died, he might have joined the church by now and never left Indiana. Why did Jake leave again?* she wondered. *Was he really planning to come back here, or had he changed his mind and decided that he liked Montana better?*

If there was only some way to undo the past. If Ella could just see Jake's face again and say that she loved him. If there'd ever been any doubt about that, it had been erased the day Jake had fallen and hit his head. Seeing him passed out on the ground had almost been Ella's undoing. Hearing that he was dead had broken her heart. Ella felt like she'd waited her whole life to find a man she could love, and just when she'd found him, he'd been snatched away.

Ella knew Jake's parents needed time alone to grieve for their son, and she needed to be alone as well. So as Joe reached for Lydia and they clung to one another, Ella slipped silently out the back door.

She stood on the porch, gazing at the Beechys' yard and losing herself in the memory of the way Jake had looked at her the last time she'd seen him. She knew now that Jake could be trusted, but he wouldn't be coming home.

When Jake's horse stuck his head over the corral fence and whinnied, she blinked hard and couldn't stop the flow of tears. Jake was dead. It was too late for them. Collapsing onto the porch step, she sobbed.

Ella heard the roar of an engine drawing closer, so she quickly dried her eyes with her apron, trying to pull herself together. An oversized truck was coming up the driveway, pulling an equally large horse trailer. Someone was probably bringing Joe some horses to shoe.

I don't think Joe's in any shape to speak with anyone right now. Maybe I should tell the customer what happened and ask him to come back some other time. Ella grimaced. *I hope I can explain things without breaking down.*

Ella stepped off the porch and started walking across the lawn. She'd only made it halfway there when the truck door opened.

Jake stepped out. Her heart stopped midbeat. It couldn't be Jake. Jake was dead.

Ella blinked a couple of times, thinking she must be imagining things. But she wasn't, for Jake was strolling across the lawn with a huge grin on his face. As he drew closer, he opened his arms to Ella, and she ran into his embrace.

"Have you missed me as much as I've missed you?" Jake murmured, nuzzling the top of her head.

"Oh, Jake, we thought you were dead."

Jake pulled back and looked at her strangely. "As you can see, I'm very much alive. What gave you the idea I was dead?"

Ella quickly explained.

Jake's eyes widened, and he shook his head. "Oh, no! That wasn't me in my boss's truck. Andy, one of the fellows who works at the ranch, said he needed the truck, so I caught a ride with one of the other guys into town so I could pick up the truck and trailer I needed to rent in order to come back here." Jake paused and reached for Ella's hand. "That was three days ago. I've been on the road ever since."

Ella was so overcome with joy that all she could do was stare up at Jake and squeeze his hand.

Finally, as if coming out of a daze, she motioned to the house and said, "You've got to go inside and see your folks. They're in shock and grieving for you."

Jake bounded up the porch steps, pulling Ella along. When they stepped into the kitchen, Lydia looked at Jake as if she were seeing a ghost. Ella heard the poor woman's breath catch in quick, ragged gasps. "Jake! Is. . .is it really you?"

"Jah, Mom, it's me."

Jake's dad, who'd been standing in front of the sink, whirled around quickly, dropping a glass. "Jake! I. . .I can't believe it's you! We were told you'd been killed—that you'd been burned up in your boss's truck."

"It wasn't me, Dad." Jake moaned. "Andy must be the person who died. He borrowed our boss's rig, not me."

Lydia leaped out of her chair and threw her arms around Jake.

"I'm sorry to hear about your friend, but I thank the Lord that you're alive!"

Joe joined Jake and his mother in a three-way hug. "Same goes for me, son. I can't tell you how glad I am."

Ella was so overcome with emotion that she could hardly speak, when Jake pulled her to his side and whispered, "Can I talk to you outside for a minute?"

"I guess so. If your folks don't mind."

Lydia grabbed a napkin from the center of the table and dabbed at her eyes. "Go right ahead."

Jake looked at his dad.

Joe gave Jake another hug. "It's fine with me, but I'd like to say something first."

"What's that?" Jake asked.

"I'm sorry for the way I've treated you. I've griped and complained and badgered you about joining the church." Joe reached for a napkin and blew his nose. "Will you forgive me, Jake? Can we start over? I'll see if I can make it better between us."

Jake nodded as tears coursed down his cheeks. "If you forgive me. I know I haven't been the ideal son."

"But you're *my* son, and that's what counts." Joe sniffed deeply. "I love you very much."

"I love you, too, Dad." Jake looked around. "Where are my little brothers and sisters?"

"They're not home right now," Lydia answered. "Fern and Jolene were taking their scholars on a field trip to celebrate the last day of school."

"So they don't think I'm dead?"

Joe shook his head. "They know nothing about the message."

"Hopefully, by now, my boss knows it wasn't me in his truck, but I'll need to give him a call, just the same." Jake glanced down at Ella and smiled. "As soon as I'm done talking to my aldi, that is."

Ella basked in the warmth of Jake's smile. It felt wonderful to hear him call her his girlfriend.

When they stepped onto the porch, Jake motioned to the truck and horse trailer parked in the driveway. "See that rig?"

Ella nodded.

"I've got some horses in there, and that's going to be the beginning of our future together."

"What are you saying, Jake?"

He slipped his arm around her waist and pulled her to his side. "I'm saying that I love you, and as soon as I join the church, I want you to become my wife."

She opened her mouth to respond, but he spoke again. "And I want you to know that even if you say you won't marry me, I'll love you until the day I die."

"Oh, Jake, don't even speak of it."

"You don't want me to speak of marrying you?"

"No, not that. I don't want to hear anything about you dying."

"The Bible says that it's appointed that everyone must die." He bent his head and nuzzled her ear. "Will you marry me and grow old with me until death takes one of us away?"

Ella's vision clouded as tears squeezed between her lashes. She cleared her throat so she could speak clearly. "Jah, Jake, I'll marry you—until death do we part."

Jake took Ella in his arms and kissed her tenderly. All the challenges she'd faced in the last several months faded. She could think only about her future as Mrs. Jake Beechy.

EPILOGUE

Five years later

As Jolene watched her husband and two little girls ride the carousel at Hershey Park, her heart swelled with love. Lonnie smiled at her, and she basked in its glow. Today, she and Lonnie had come here with their extended family, including Jolene's cousins Ella, Katie, and Loraine along with their husbands and children. Jolene's brother Andrew and his wife, Eunice, had been invited, too, but they'd stayed home because Eunice was due to have their second baby soon and wasn't feeling up to the trip.

Jolene thought about Fern. Last year, the schoolteacher had married Devon Bontrager, a widower. Fern, who'd been so sure she would never marry and have children, was now happily caring for Devon's six rambunctious boys.

Jolene chuckled as she looked at Ella and Jake's little boy, Joe. A chunk of cotton candy hung off his chin. He swiped it away with the back of his hand and grinned up at his mother. Wayne and Loraine stood watching their three children, two boys and a girl, as they scrambled onto a ride. Then there were Katie and Freeman, happily watching their two little towheaded boys holding stuffed tigers in their arms.

When Lonnie and the girls got off their ride, Lonnie signed, *"Hasn't this been a fun day?"*

Jolene nodded. *"Making a trip to Hershey Park was worth the wait."*

"Marrying you, now that was worth the wait." He reached for

her hand and gave her fingers a gentle squeeze.

She smiled and closed her eyes as she sent up a prayer. *Heavenly Father, I'm thankful that the van accident, which nearly destroyed our lives, has somehow brought us all closer to each other— and to You. You used the tragic accident for Your good, and each of us cousins has learned that, despite the challenges we've had to face, trusting in You is the only way.*

RECIPE FOR ELLA'S FRIENDSHIP BREAD

1 cup starter (see recipe below)
⅔ cup vegetable oil
2 cups unbleached white flour
1 cup sugar
3 eggs
1½ teaspoons baking powder
1 teaspoon cinnamon
½ teaspoon vanilla
½ teaspoon salt
½ teaspoon baking soda
1 cup raisins, chocolate chips, chopped nuts, dates,
    and/or apples

Combine all ingredients in a nonmetal bowl and mix well. Place batter into two well-greased, lightly floured 9½ x 5½ x 3½ baking pans. Bake at 350 degrees for 45 to 50 minutes or until an inserted toothpick comes out clean. Place on a rack and cool for 10 minutes before removing from pans. Cool bread thoroughly on racks before cutting into slices and serving.

STARTER

1 cup sugar
1 cup milk
1 cup unbleached white flour

Combine all ingredients in a large, nonmetal bowl. Stir with a nonmetal spoon. Cover the bowl lightly with plastic wrap. Do not refrigerate. Store at room temperature. Stir the mixture every day for 17 days. On day 18, do nothing. On days 19, 20, and 21, stir the mixture again. On day 22, stir and add the following ingredients:

1 cup sugar
1 cup milk
1 cup unbleached white flour

Stir again. On days 23, 24, 25, and 26, stir the mixture. On day 27, add the following ingredients:

1 cup sugar
1 cup milk
1 cup unbleached white flour

Stir well. You should now have about 4 cups of starter. Give 1 cup of the starter to each of two friends and keep the remaining 2 cups for yourself. Use one cup of the starter to make a loaf of friendship bread. Keep the other cup for your own starter.

TO KEEP THE STARTER GOING

Do not refrigerate the starter, and do not use a metal bowl or spoon. On day 1 (the day you receive the starter), do nothing. On days 2, 3, and 4, stir the mixture. On day 5, stir in:

1 cup sugar
1 cup milk
1 cup unbleached white flour

Pour the mixture into a large, nonmetal mixing bowl; cover lightly with plastic wrap. This mixture will rise. On days 6, 7, 8, and 9, stir. On day 10, stir in the following ingredients:

1 cup sugar
1 cup milk
1 cup unbleached white flour

Give 1 cup of the starter to each of two friends to make their own bread, keep one cup for your own bread, and keep one cup as your own starter for future breads. Be sure to give the recipe for the starter, as well as the directions for making the bread, to each of your friends, too.

DISCUSSION QUESTIONS

1. Some people in Jolene's family saw her deafness as a handicap. What are some ways we can help others who have physical limitations to see that they can live a useful life?

2. When Lonnie lost his hearing he became bitter and angry at God. Why do people often blame God for the bad things that happen to them? If God can prevent bad things from happening, why doesn't He?

3. Everyone deals with death and other tragic losses in different ways. When Ella's father died, Ella dealt with her grief by staying busy and looking out for others' needs instead of her own. Is there ever a time when it's okay to hide our true feelings when going through grief? Is it healthy to overlook one's own needs in order to minister to others?

4. When Jake returned home after his father was injured he did his best to help out, even though he didn't enjoy shoeing horses. Why then, didn't Jake's father seem to appreciate the sacrifice Jake made? Have you ever felt that a sacrifice you made went unappreciated? How did it make you feel?

5. When Jolene's family realized that they needed to learn how to communicate with Jolene, everyone in the family made an effort to learn how to sign. Has there ever been a time in your life when you've had to learn something new in order to help someone with a disability? Did it make you feel closer to that person?

6. A lot of misunderstandings occurred in this story. Misunderstandings are the biggest cause of dissension among family members and friends. What are some ways we can deal with misunderstandings that occur between us and our friends or family?

7. Lonnie was afraid of making a commitment to Jolene because he thought their hearing loss would be a determent to marriage. Have you ever been afraid of doing something

because you felt as if you were hindered by something else? Did you shy away from it, or did you decide that with God's help you could overcome any obstacle?

8. Too often children tease others with a disability. What are some ways we can teach our children and grandchildren to have more understanding toward someone who is physically or mentally challenged?

9. Were there any verses of scripture in this book that spoke to you personally? Did any of the verses help you see things in a different light? Without being preachy or pushy, how can we use scriptures to help someone who's going through a difficult situation?

10. While reading A Cousin's Challenge did you learn anything new about the Amish way of life? How might we want to incorporate some of the things the Amish do into our own lives?

ABOUT THE AUTHOR

WANDA E. BRUNSTETTER enjoys writing about the Amish because they live a peaceful, simple life. Wanda's interest in the Amish and other Plain communities began when she married her husband, Richard, who grew up in a Mennonite church in Pennsylvania. Learning about her Anabaptist great-great-grandparents increased Wanda's interest in the Plain People. Wanda has made numerous trips to Lancaster County and has several friends and family members living near that area. She and her husband have also traveled to other parts of the country, meeting various Amish families and getting to know them personally. She hopes her readers will learn to love the wonderful Amish people as much as she does.

Wanda and her husband have been married over forty years. They have two grown children and six grandchildren. In her spare time, Wanda enjoys photography, ventriloquism, gardening, reading, stamping, and having fun with her family.

In addition to her novels, Wanda has written two Amish cookbooks, an Amish devotional, nine Amish children's books, several novellas, stories, articles, poems, and puppet scripts.

Visit Wanda's Web site at www.wandabrunstetter.com and feel free to e-mail her at wanda@wandabrunstetter.com.

Other Books by Wanda E. Brunstetter:

Lydia's Charm

Brides of Lehigh Canal Series

Kelly's Chance
Betsy's Return
Sarah's Choice

Daughters of Lancaster County Series

The Storekeeper's Daughter
The Quilter's Daughter
The Bishop's Daughter

Brides of Lancaster County Series

A Merry Heart
Looking for a Miracle
Plain and Fancy
The Hope Chest

Sisters of Holmes County Series

A Sister's Secret
A Sister's Test
A Sister's Hope

Brides of Webster County Series

Going Home
On Her Own
Dear to Me
Allison's Journey

White Christmas Pie

Nonfiction

The Simple Life
A Celebration of the Simple Life
Wanda E. Brunstetter's Amish Friends Cookbook
Wanda E. Brunstetter's Amish Friends Cookbook, Vol. 2

Children's Books

Rachel Yoder—Always Trouble Somewhere Series (8 books)
The Wisdom of Solomon

BRIDES *of* LANCASTER COUNTY

Nestled along the country roads of Lancaster Valley, Pennsylvania, the Amish still cherish and cultivate the virtues realized by living a plain and simple life. In this collection of four complete novels, bestselling author Wanda E. Brunstetter transports the reader to this secluded corner of rural America and provides a refreshing glimpse into a culture noted for its hard-working, family-oriented people of strong religious faith. Despite their horse-and-buggy pace in a high-speed world, when it comes to romance, the Amish find their hearts racing at top speed. The Brides of Lancaster County tells the stories of four Amish young adults as they explore their place in the world—while finding true love in the process.

Daughters
of Lancaster
County

The riveting story of a kidnapped Amish child is told through three bestselling novels set in Lancaster, Pennsylvania's Amish country. From the beginning, Naomi Fisher blames herself for the family's tragedy and journeys away from home to find a purpose for living. Abby Miller leaves her successful Ohio quilt shop to help the Fisher family, but how long can she continue to put her dreams on hold? Leona Weaver is dedicated to her family and community, but when she falls in love with an outsider, could this friendship bring the haunting tale of a kidnapped boy full circle?

BRIDES *of* WEBSTER COUNTY

Tucked along the back roads of
Missouri is a peaceful Amish community, home to four women who are
struggling with their faith. Barbara
has been widowed with four children
to raise and no one to run the family
business. Faith has a career among
the world but wants her daughter
to be raised with her Amish family. Melinda wants to be a vet and
an Amish, but she can't have both.
Allison's upbringing as a tomboy
hasn't prepared her to become a proper Amish wife. Will each
woman meet a man who can help them along the path to content-
ment within their community and to trust in God?